NORA ROBERTS

BLUE DAHLIA

JOVE
New York

A JOVE BOOK
Published by Berkley
An imprint of Penguin Random House LLC
375 Hudson Street, New York, New York 10014

ISBN: 9780515138559

First Edition: November 2004

Printed in the United States of America
27 29 31 30 28 26

Cover illustration by Yuan Lee
Cover design by Steven Ferlauto

Against the backdrop of a house steeped in history and a thriving new gardening business, three women unearth the memories of the past in the first novel of #1 *New York Times* bestselling author Nora Roberts's In the Garden Trilogy.

A Harper has always lived at Harper House, the centuries-old mansion just outside of Memphis. And for as long as anyone alive remembers, the ghostly Harper Bride has walked the halls, singing lullabies at night . . .

Trying to escape the ghosts of the past, young widow Stella Rothchild, along with her two energetic little boys, has moved back to her roots in southern Tennessee—and into her new life at Harper House and the In the Garden nursery. She isn't intimidated by the house—nor its mistress, local legend Roz Harper. Despite a reputation for being difficult, Roz has been nothing but kind to Stella, offering her a comfortable new place to live and a challenging new job as manager of the flourishing nursery. As Stella settles comfortably into her new life, she finds a nurturing friendship with Roz and with expectant mother Hayley. And she discovers a fierce attraction to ruggedly handsome landscaper Logan Kitridge.

But someone isn't happy about the budding romance . . . the Harper Bride. As the women dig into the history of Harper House, they discover that grief and rage have kept the Bride's spirit alive long past her death. And now, she will do anything to destroy the passion that Logan and Stella share . . .

Turn the page for a complete list of titles by Nora Roberts and J. D. Robb from Berkley . . .

Nora Roberts

HOT ICE
SACRED SINS
BRAZEN VIRTUE
SWEET REVENGE
PUBLIC SECRETS
GENUINE LIES
CARNAL INNOCENCE
HONEST ILLUSIONS
DIVINE EVIL
PRIVATE SCANDALS
HIDDEN RICHES
TRUE BETRAYALS
MONTANA SKY
SANCTUARY
HOMEPORT
THE REEF
RIVER'S END
CAROLINA MOON
THE VILLA
MIDNIGHT BAYOU
THREE FATES
BIRTHRIGHT
NORTHERN LIGHTS
BLUE SMOKE
ANGELS FALL
HIGH NOON
TRIBUTE
BLACK HILLS
THE SEARCH
CHASING FIRE
THE WITNESS
WHISKEY BEACH
THE COLLECTOR
TONIGHT AND ALWAYS
THE LIAR
THE OBSESSION

Series

Irish Born Trilogy
BORN IN FIRE
BORN IN ICE
BORN IN SHAME

Dream Trilogy
DARING TO DREAM
HOLDING THE DREAM
FINDING THE DREAM

Chesapeake Bay Saga
SEA SWEPT
RISING TIDES
INNER HARBOR
CHESAPEAKE BLUE

Gallaghers of Ardmore Trilogy
JEWELS OF THE SUN
TEARS OF THE MOON
HEART OF THE SEA

Three Sisters Island Trilogy
DANCE UPON THE AIR
HEAVEN AND EARTH
FACE THE FIRE

Key Trilogy
KEY OF LIGHT
KEY OF KNOWLEDGE
KEY OF VALOR

In the Garden Trilogy
BLUE DAHLIA
BLACK ROSE
RED LILY

Circle Trilogy
MORRIGAN'S CROSS
DANCE OF THE GODS
VALLEY OF SILENCE

Sign of Seven Trilogy
BLOOD BROTHERS
THE HOLLOW
THE PAGAN STONE

Bride Quartet
VISION IN WHITE
BED OF ROSES
SAVOR THE MOMENT
HAPPY EVER AFTER

The Inn BoonsBoro Trilogy
THE NEXT ALWAYS
THE LAST BOYFRIEND
THE PERFECT HOPE

The Cousins O'Dwyer Trilogy
DARK WITCH
SHADOW SPELL
BLOOD MAGICK

The Guardians Trilogy
STARS OF FORTUNE
BAY OF SIGHS
ISLAND OF GLASS

Ebooks by Nora Roberts

Cordina's Royal Family
AFFAIRE ROYALE
COMMAND PERFORMANCE
THE PLAYBOY PRINCE
CORDINA'S CROWN JEWEL

The Donovan Legacy
CAPTIVATED
ENTRANCED
CHARMED
ENCHANTED

The O'Hurleys
THE LAST HONEST WOMAN
DANCE TO THE PIPER
SKIN DEEP
WITHOUT A TRACE

Night Tales
NIGHT SHIFT
NIGHT SHADOW
NIGHTSHADE
NIGHT SMOKE
NIGHT SHIELD

The MacGregors
PLAYING THE ODDS
TEMPTING FATE
ALL THE POSSIBILITIES
ONE MAN'S ART
FOR NOW, FOREVER
REBELLION/IN FROM THE COLD
THE MACGREGOR BRIDES
THE WINNING HAND
THE MACGREGOR GROOMS
THE PERFECT NEIGHBOR

The Calhouns
COURTING CATHERINE
A MAN FOR AMANDA
FOR THE LOVE OF LILAH
SUZANNA'S SURRENDER
MEGAN'S MATE

Irish Legacy
IRISH THOROUGHBRED
IRISH ROSE
IRISH REBEL

LOVING JACK
BEST LAID PLANS
LAWLESS

BLITHE IMAGES
SONG OF THE WEST
SEARCH FOR LOVE
ISLAND OF FLOWERS
THE HEART'S VICTORY
FROM THIS DAY
HER MOTHER'S KEEPER
ONCE MORE WITH FEELING
REFLECTIONS
DANCE OF DREAMS
UNTAMED
THIS MAGIC MOMENT
ENDINGS AND BEGINNINGS
STORM WARNING
SULLIVAN'S WOMAN
FIRST IMPRESSIONS
A MATTER OF CHOICE

LESS OF A STRANGER
THE LAW IS A LADY
RULES OF THE GAME
OPPOSITES ATTRACT
THE RIGHT PATH
PARTNERS
BOUNDARY LINES
DUAL IMAGE
TEMPTATION
LOCAL HERO
THE NAME OF THE GAME
GABRIEL'S ANGEL
THE WELCOMING
TIME WAS
TIMES CHANGE
SUMMER LOVE
HOLIDAY WISHES

Nora Roberts & J. D. Robb

REMEMBER WHEN

J. D. Robb

NAKED IN DEATH
GLORY IN DEATH
IMMORTAL IN DEATH
RAPTURE IN DEATH
CEREMONY IN DEATH
VENGEANCE IN DEATH
HOLIDAY IN DEATH
CONSPIRACY IN DEATH
LOYALTY IN DEATH
WITNESS IN DEATH
JUDGMENT IN DEATH
BETRAYAL IN DEATH
SEDUCTION IN DEATH
REUNION IN DEATH
PURITY IN DEATH
PORTRAIT IN DEATH
IMITATION IN DEATH
DIVIDED IN DEATH
VISIONS IN DEATH
SURVIVOR IN DEATH
ORIGIN IN DEATH
MEMORY IN DEATH
BORN IN DEATH
INNOCENT IN DEATH
CREATION IN DEATH
STRANGERS IN DEATH
SALVATION IN DEATH
PROMISES IN DEATH
KINDRED IN DEATH
FANTASY IN DEATH
INDULGENCE IN DEATH
TREACHERY IN DEATH
NEW YORK TO DALLAS
CELEBRITY IN DEATH
DELUSION IN DEATH
CALCULATED IN DEATH
THANKLESS IN DEATH
CONCEALED IN DEATH
FESTIVE IN DEATH
OBSESSION IN DEATH
DEVOTED IN DEATH
BROTHERHOOD IN DEATH
APPRENTICE IN DEATH

Anthologies

FROM THE HEART
A LITTLE MAGIC
A LITTLE FATE

MOON SHADOWS
(with Jill Gregory, Ruth Ryan Langan, and Marianne Willman)

The Once Upon Series
(with Jill Gregory, Ruth Ryan Langan, and Marianne Willman)

ONCE UPON A CASTLE
ONCE UPON A STAR
ONCE UPON A DREAM
ONCE UPON A ROSE
ONCE UPON A KISS
ONCE UPON A MIDNIGHT

SILENT NIGHT
(with Susan Plunkett, Dee Holmes, and Claire Cross)

OUT OF THIS WORLD
(with Laurell K. Hamilton, Susan Krinard, and Maggie Shayne)

BUMP IN THE NIGHT
(with Mary Blayney, Ruth Ryan Langan, and Mary Kay McComas)

DEAD OF NIGHT
(with Mary Blayney, Ruth Ryan Langan, and Mary Kay McComas)

THREE IN DEATH

SUITE 606
(with Mary Blayney, Ruth Ryan Langan, and Mary Kay McComas)

IN DEATH

THE LOST
(with Patricia Gaffney, Mary Blayney, and Ruth Ryan Langan)

THE OTHER SIDE
(with Mary Blayney, Patricia Gaffney, Ruth Ryan Langan, and Mary Kay McComas)

TIME OF DEATH

THE UNQUIET
(with Mary Blayney, Patricia Gaffney, Ruth Ryan Langan, and Mary Kay McComas)

MIRROR, MIRROR
(with Mary Blayney, Elaine Fox, Mary Kay McComas, and R. C. Ryan)

DOWN THE RABBIT HOLE
(with Mary Blayney, Elaine Fox, Mary Kay McComas, and R. C. Ryan)

Also available . . .

THE OFFICIAL NORA ROBERTS COMPANION
(edited by Denise Little and Laura Hayden)

For Dan and Jason.
You may be men, but you'll always be my boys.

If the plant root ball is tightly packed with roots,
these should be gently loosened.
They need to spread out after planting,
rather than continue to grow in a tight mass.

—FROM THE *TREASURY OF GARDENING*,
ON TRANSPLANTING POTTED PLANTS

And 'tis my faith that every flower
Enjoys the air it breathes.

—WORDSWORTH

PROLOGUE

Memphis, Tennessee
August 1892

BIRTHING A BASTARD WASN'T IN THE PLANS. WHEN she'd learned she was carrying her lover's child, the shock and panic turned quickly to anger.

There were ways of dealing with it, of course. A woman in her position had contacts, had avenues. But she was afraid of them, nearly as afraid of the abortionists as she was of what was growing, unwanted, inside her.

The mistress of a man like Reginald Harper couldn't afford pregnancy.

He'd kept her for nearly two years now, and kept her well. Oh, she knew he kept others—including his wife—but they didn't concern her.

She was still young, and she was beautiful. Youth and beauty were products that could be marketed. She'd done so, for nearly a decade, with steely mind and heart. And she'd profited by them, polished them with the grace and charm she'd learned by watching and emulating the fine ladies who'd visited the grand house on the river where her mother had worked.

She'd been educated—a bit. But more than books and music, she'd learned the arts of flirtation.

She'd sold herself for the first time at fifteen and had pocketed knowledge along with the coin. But prostitution wasn't her goal, any more than domestic work or trudging off to the factory day after day. She knew the difference between whore and mistress. A whore traded quick and cold sex for pennies and was forgotten before the man's fly was buttoned again.

But a mistress—a clever and successful mistress—offered romance, sophistication, conversation, gaiety along with the commodity between her legs. She was a companion, a wailing wall, a sexual fantasy. An ambitious mistress knew to demand nothing and gain much.

Amelia Ellen Conner had ambitions.

And she'd achieved them. Or most of them.

She'd selected Reginald quite carefully. He wasn't handsome or brilliant of mind. But he was, as her research had assured her, very rich and very unfaithful to the thin and proper wife who presided over Harper House.

He had a woman in Natchez, and it was said he kept another in New Orleans. He could afford another, so Amelia set her sights on him. Wooed and won him.

At twenty-four, she lived in a pretty house on South Main and had three servants of her own. Her wardrobe was full of beautiful clothes, and her jewelry case sparkled.

It was true she wasn't received by the fine ladies she'd once envied, but there was a fashionable half world where a woman of her station was welcome. Where *she* was envied.

She threw lavish parties. She traveled. She *lived.*

Then, hardly more than a year after Reginald had tucked her into that pretty house, her clever, craftily designed world crashed.

She would have hidden it from him until she'd gathered the courage to visit the red-light district and end the thing. But he'd caught her when she was violently ill, and he'd studied her face with those dark, shrewd eyes.

And he'd known.

He'd not only been pleased but had forbidden her to end

the pregnancy. To her shock, he'd bought her a sapphire bracelet to celebrate her situation.

She hadn't wanted the child, but he had.

So she began to see how the child could work for her. As the mother of Reginald Harper's child—bastard or no—she would be cared for in perpetuity. He might lose interest in coming to her bed as she lost the bloom of youth, as beauty faded, but he would support her, and the child.

His wife hadn't given him a son. But she might. She *would.*

Through the last chills of winter and into the spring, she carried the child and planned for her future.

Then something strange happened. It moved inside her. Flutters and stretches, playful kicks. The child she hadn't wanted became her child.

It grew inside her like a flower that only she could see, could feel, could know. And so did a strong and terrible love.

Through the sweltering, sticky heat of the summer she bloomed, and for the first time in her life she knew a passion for something other than herself and her own comfort.

The child, her son, needed her. She would protect it with all she had.

With her hands resting on her great belly, she supervised the decorating of the nursery. Pale green walls and white lace curtains. A rocking horse imported from Paris, a crib handmade in Italy.

She tucked tiny clothes into the miniature wardrobe. Irish and Breton lace, French silks. All were monogrammed with exquisite embroidery with the baby's initials. He would be James Reginald Conner.

She would have a son. Something at last of her own. Someone, at last, to love. They would travel together, she and her beautiful boy. She would show him the world. He would go to the best schools. He was her pride, her joy, and her heart. And if through that steamy summer, Reginald came to the house on South Main less and less, it was just as well.

He was only a man. What grew inside her was a son.

She would never be alone again.

When she felt the pangs of labor, she had no fear. Through the sweaty hours of pain, she held one thing in the front of her mind. Her James. Her son. Her child.

Her eyes blurred with exhaustion, and the heat, a living, breathing monster, was somehow worse than the pain.

She could see the doctor and the midwife exchange looks. Grim, frowning looks. But she was young, she was healthy, and she *would* do this thing.

There was no time; hour bled into hour with gaslight shooting flickering shadows around the room. She heard, through the waves of exhaustion, a thin cry.

"My son." Tears slid down her cheeks. "My son."

The midwife held her down, murmuring, murmuring, "Lie still now. Drink a bit. Rest now."

She sipped to soothe her fiery throat, tasted laudanum. Before she could object, she was drifting off, deep down. Far away.

When she woke, the room was dim, the draperies pulled tight over the windows. When she stirred, the doctor rose from his chair, came close to lift her hand, to check her pulse.

"My son. My baby. I want to see my baby."

"I'll send for some broth. You slept a long time."

"My son. He'll be hungry. Have him brought to me."

"Madam." The doctor sat on the side of the bed. His eyes seemed very pale, very troubled. "I'm sorry. The child was stillborn."

What clutched her heart was monstrous, vicious, rending her with burning talons of grief and fear. "I heard him cry. This is a lie! Why are you saying such an awful thing to me?"

"She never cried." Gently, he took her hands. "Your labor was long and difficult. You were delirious at the end of it. Madam, I'm sorry. You delivered a girl, stillborn."

She wouldn't believe it. She screamed and raged and

wept, and was sedated only to wake to scream and rage and weep again.

She hadn't wanted the child. And then she'd wanted nothing else.

Her grief was beyond name, beyond reason.

Grief drove her mad.

one

Southfield, Michigan

September 2001

She burned the cream sauce. Stella would always remember that small, irritating detail, as she would remember the roll and boom of thunder from the late-summer storm and the sound of her children squabbling in the living room.

She would remember the harsh smell, the sudden scream of the smoke alarms, and the way she'd mechanically taken the pan off the burner and dumped it in the sink.

She wasn't much of a cook, but she was—in general—a *precise* cook. For this welcome-home meal, she'd planned to prepare the chicken Alfredo, one of Kevin's favorites, from scratch and match it with a nice field greens salad and some fresh, crusty bread with pesto dipping sauce.

In her tidy kitchen in her pretty suburban house she had all the ingredients lined up, her cookbook propped on its stand with the plastic protector over the pages.

She wore a navy-blue bib apron over her fresh pants and shirt and had her mass of curling red hair bundled up on top of her head, out of her way.

She was getting started later than she'd hoped, but work had been a madhouse all day. All the fall flowers at the garden center were on sale, and the warm weather brought customers out in droves.

Not that she minded. She loved the work, absolutely loved her job as manager of the nursery. It felt good to be back in the thick of it, full-time now that Gavin was in school and Luke old enough for a play group. How in the world had her baby grown up enough for first grade?

And before she knew it, Luke would be ready for kindergarten.

She and Kevin should start getting a little more proactive about making that third child. Maybe tonight, she thought with a smile. When she got into *that* final and very personal stage of her welcome-home plans.

As she measured ingredients, she heard the crash and wail from the next room. Glutton for punishment, she thought as she dropped what she was doing to rush in. Thinking about having another baby when the two she had were driving her crazy.

She stepped into the room, and there they were. Her little angels. Gavin, sunny blond with the devil in his eyes, sat innocently bumping two Matchbox cars into each other while Luke, his bright red hair a dead ringer for hers, screamed over his scattered wooden blocks.

She didn't have to witness the event to *know.* Luke had built; Gavin had destroyed.

In their house it was the law of the land.

"Gavin. Why?" She scooped up Luke, patted his back. "It's okay, baby. You can build another."

"My house! My house!"

"It was an accident," Gavin claimed, and that wicked twinkle that made a bubble of laughter rise to her throat remained. "The car wrecked it."

"I bet the car did—after you aimed it at his house. Why can't you play nice? He wasn't bothering you."

"I was playing. He's just a baby."

"That's right." And it was the look that came into her eyes that had Gavin dropping his. "And if you're going to be a baby, too, you can be a baby in your room. Alone."

"It was a stupid house."

"Nuh-uh! Mom." Luke took Stella's face in both his hands, looked at her with those avid, swimming eyes. "It was good."

"You can build an even better one. Okay? Gavin, leave him alone. I'm not kidding. I'm busy in the kitchen, and Daddy's going to be home soon. Do you want to be punished for his welcome home?"

"No. I can't do *anything*."

"That's too bad. It's really a shame you don't have any toys." She set Luke down. "Build your house, Luke. Leave his blocks alone, Gavin. If I have to come in here again, you're not going to like it."

"I want to go *outside*!" Gavin mourned at her retreating back.

"Well, it's raining, so you can't. We're all stuck in here, so behave."

Flustered, she went back to the cookbook, tried to clear her head. In an irritated move, she snapped on the kitchen TV. God, she missed Kevin. The boys had been cranky all afternoon, and she felt rushed and harried and overwhelmed. With Kevin out of town these last four days she'd been scrambling around like a maniac. Dealing with the house, the boys, her job, all the errands alone.

Why was it that the household appliances waited, just waited, to go on strike when Kevin left town? Yesterday the washer had gone buns up, and just that morning the toaster oven had fried itself.

They had such a nice rhythm when they were together, dividing up the chores, sharing the discipline and the pleasure in their sons. If he'd been home, he could have sat down to play with—and referee—the boys while she cooked.

Or better, he'd have cooked and she'd have played with the boys.

She missed the smell of him when he came up behind her to lean down and rub his cheek over hers. She missed curling up to him in bed at night, and the way they'd talk in the dark about their plans, or laugh at something the boys had done that day.

For God's sake, you'd think the man had been gone four months instead of four days, she told herself.

She listened with half an ear to Gavin trying to talk Luke into building a skyscraper that they could both wreck as she stirred her cream sauce and watched the wind swirl leaves outside the window.

He wouldn't be traveling so much after he got his promotion. Soon, she reminded herself. He'd been working so hard, and he was right on the verge of it. The extra money would be handy, too, especially when they had another child—maybe a girl this time.

With the promotion, and her working full-time again, they could afford to take the kids somewhere next summer. Disney World, maybe. They'd love that. Even if she were pregnant, they could manage it. She'd been squirreling away some money in the vacation fund—and the new-car fund.

Having to buy a new washing machine was going to seriously damage the emergency fund, but they'd be all right.

When she heard the boys laugh, her shoulders relaxed again. Really, life was good. It was perfect, just the way she'd always imagined it. She was married to a wonderful man, one she'd fallen for the minute she'd set eyes on him. Kevin Rothchild, with his slow, sweet smile.

They had two beautiful sons, a pretty house in a good neighborhood, jobs they both loved, and plans for the future they both agreed on. And when they made love, bells still rang.

Thinking of that, she imagined his reaction when, with the kids tucked in for the night, she slipped into the sexy new lingerie she'd splurged on in his absence.

A little wine, a few candles, and . . .

The next, bigger crash had her eyes rolling toward the ceiling. At least this time there were cheers instead of wails.

"Mom! Mom!" Face alive with glee, Luke rushed in. "We wrecked the *whole* building. Can we have a cookie?"

"Not this close to dinner."

"Please, please, please, *please*!"

He was pulling on her pants now, doing his best to climb up her leg. Stella set the spoon down, nudged him away from the stove. "No cookies before dinner, Luke."

"We're starving." Gavin piled in, slamming his cars together. "How come we can't eat something when we're hungry? Why do we have to eat the stupid fredo anyway?"

"Because." She'd always hated that answer as a child, but it seemed all-purpose to her now.

"We're all eating together when your father gets home." But she glanced out the window and worried that his plane would be delayed. "Here, you can split an apple."

She took one out of the bowl on the counter and grabbed a knife.

"I don't like the peel," Gavin complained.

"I don't have time to peel it." She gave the sauce a couple of quick stirs. "The peel's good for you." Wasn't it?

"Can I have a drink? Can I have a drink, too?" Luke tugged and tugged. "I'm thirsty."

"God. Give me five minutes, will you? Five minutes. Go, go *build* something. Then you can have some apple slices and juice."

Thunder boomed, and Gavin responded to it by jumping up and down and shouting, "Earthquake!"

"It's not an earthquake."

But his face was bright with excitement as he spun in circles, then ran from the room. "Earthquake! Earthquake!"

Getting into the spirit, Luke ran after him, screaming.

Stella pressed a hand to her pounding head. The noise was insane, but maybe it would keep them busy until she got the meal under control.

She turned back to the stove, and heard, without much interest, the announcement for a news bulletin.

It filtered through the headache, and she turned toward the set like an automaton.

Commuter plane crash. En route to Detroit Metro from Lansing. Ten passengers on board.

The spoon dropped out of her hand. The heart dropped out of her body.

Kevin. Kevin.

Her children screamed in delighted fear, and thunder rolled and burst overhead. In the kitchen, Stella slid to the floor as her world fractured.

THEY CAME TO TELL HER KEVIN WAS DEAD. STRANGERS at her door with solemn faces. She couldn't take it in, couldn't believe it. Though she'd known. She'd known the minute she heard the reporter's voice on her little kitchen television.

Kevin couldn't be dead. He was young and healthy. He was coming home, and they were having chicken Alfredo for dinner.

But she'd burned the sauce. The smoke had set off the alarms, and there was nothing but madness in her pretty house.

She had to send her children to her neighbor's so it could be explained to her.

But how could the impossible, the unthinkable ever be explained?

A mistake. The storm, a strike of lightning, and everything changed forever. One instant of time, and the man she loved, the father of her children, no longer lived.

Is there anyone you'd like to call?

Who would she call but Kevin? He was her family, her friend, her life.

They spoke of details that were like a buzz in her brain, of arrangements, of counseling. They were sorry for her loss.

They were gone, and she was alone in the house she and Kevin had bought when she'd been pregnant with Luke. The house they'd saved for, and painted, and decorated together. The house with the gardens she'd designed herself.

The storm was over, and it was quiet. Had it ever been so quiet? She could hear her own heartbeat, the hum of the heater as it kicked on, the drip of rain from the gutters.

Then she could hear her own keening as she collapsed on the floor by her front door. Lying on her side, she gathered herself into a ball in defense, in denial. There weren't tears, not yet. They were massed into some kind of hard, hot knot inside her. The grief was so deep, tears couldn't reach it. She could only lie curled up there, with those wounded-animal sounds pouring out of her throat.

It was dark when she pushed herself to her feet, swaying, light-headed and ill. Kevin. Somewhere in her brain his name still, over and over and over.

She had to get her children, she had to bring her children home. She had to tell her babies.

Oh, God. Oh, God, how could she tell them?

She groped for the door, stepped out into the chilly dark, her mind blessedly blank. She left the door open at her back, walked down between the heavy-headed mums and asters, past the glossy green leaves of the azaleas she and Kevin had planted one blue spring day.

She crossed the street like a blind woman, walking through puddles that soaked her shoes, over damp grass, toward her neighbor's porch light.

What was her neighbor's name? Funny, she'd known her for four years. They carpooled, and sometimes shopped together. But she couldn't quite remember. . . .

Oh, yes, of course. Diane. Diane and Adam Perkins, and their children, Jessie and Wyatt. Nice family, she thought dully. Nice, normal family. They'd had a barbecue together just a couple weeks ago. Kevin had grilled chicken.

He loved to grill. They'd had some good wine, some good laughs, and the kids had played. Wyatt had fallen and scraped his knee.

Of course she remembered.

But she stood in front of the door not quite sure what she was doing there.

Her children. Of course. She'd come for her children. She had to tell them. . . .

Don't think. She held herself hard, rocked, held in. Don't think yet. If you think, you'll break apart. A million pieces you can never put together again.

Her babies needed her. Needed her now. Only had her now.

She bore down on that hot, hard knot and rang the bell.

She saw Diane as if she were looking at her through a thin sheen of water. Rippling, and not quite there. She heard her dimly. Felt the arms that came around her in support and sympathy.

But your husband's alive, you see, Stella thought. Your life isn't over. Your world's the same as it was five minutes ago. So you can't know. You can't.

When she felt herself begin to shake, she pulled back. "Not now, please. I can't now. I have to take the boys home."

"I can come with you." There were tears on Diane's cheeks as she reached out, touched Stella's hair. "Would you like me to come, to stay with you?"

"No. Not now. I need . . . the boys."

"I'll get them. Come inside, Stella."

But she only shook her head.

"All right. They're in the family room. I'll bring them. Stella, if there's anything, anything at all. You've only to call. I'm sorry. I'm so sorry."

She stood in the dark, looking in at the light, and waited.

She heard the protests, the complaints, then the scrambling of feet. And there were her boys—Gavin with his father's sunny hair, Luke with his father's mouth.

"We don't want to go yet," Gavin told her. "We're playing a game. Can't we finish?"

"Not now. We have to go home now."

"But I'm winning. It's not fair, and—"

"Gavin. We have to go."

"Is Daddy home?"

She looked down at Luke, his happy, innocent face, and nearly broke. "No." Reaching down, she picked him up, touched her lips to the mouth that was so like Kevin's. "Let's go home."

She took Gavin's hand and began the walk back to her empty house.

"If Daddy was home, he'd let me finish." Cranky tears smeared Gavin's voice. "I want Daddy."

"I know. I do too."

"Can we have a dog?" Luke wanted to know, and turned her face to his with his hands. "Can we ask Daddy? Can we have a dog like Jessie and Wyatt?"

"We'll talk about it later."

"I want Daddy," Gavin said again, with a rising pitch in his voice.

He knows, Stella thought. He knows something is wrong, something's terribly wrong. I have to do this. I have to do it now.

"We need to sit down." Carefully, very carefully, she closed the door behind her, carried Luke to the couch. She sat with him in her lap and laid her arm over Gavin's shoulder.

"If I had a dog," Luke told her soberly, "I'd take care of him. When's Daddy coming?"

"He can't come."

"'Cause of the busy trip?"

"He . . ." Help me. God, help me do this. "There was an accident. Daddy was in an accident."

"Like when the cars smash?" Luke asked, and Gavin said nothing, nothing at all as his eyes burned into her face.

"It was a very bad accident. Daddy had to go to heaven."

"But he has to come home after."

"He can't. He can't come home anymore. He has to stay in heaven now."

"I don't want him there." Gavin tried to wrench away, but she held him tightly. "I want him to come home *now*."

"I don't want him there either, baby. But he can't come back anymore, no matter how much we want it."

Luke's lips trembled. "Is he mad at us?"

"No. No, no, no, baby. No." She pressed her face to his hair as her stomach pitched and what was left of her heart throbbed like a wound. "He's not mad at us. He loves us. He'll always love us."

"He's dead." There was fury in Gavin's voice, rage on his face. Then it crumpled, and he was just a little boy, weeping in his mother's arms.

She held them until they slept, then carried them to her bed so none of them would wake alone. As she had countless times before, she slipped off their shoes, tucked blankets around them.

She left a light burning while she walked—it felt like floating—through the house, locking doors, checking windows. When she knew everything was safe, she closed herself into the bathroom. She ran a bath so hot the steam rose off the water and misted the room.

Only when she slipped into the tub, submerged herself in the steaming water, did she allow that knot to snap. With her boys sleeping, and her body shivering in the hot water, she wept and wept and wept.

SHE GOT THROUGH IT. A FEW FRIENDS SUGGESTED SHE might take a tranquilizer, but she didn't want to block the feelings. Nor did she want to have a muzzy head when she had her children to think of.

She kept it simple. Kevin would have wanted simple. She chose every detail—the music, the flowers, the photographs—of his memorial service. She selected a silver box for his ashes and planned to scatter them on the lake. He'd proposed to her on the lake, in a rented boat on a summer afternoon.

She wore black for the service, a widow of thirty-one, with two young boys and a mortgage, and a heart so broken she wondered if she would feel pieces of it piercing her soul for the rest of her life.

She kept her children close, and made appointments with a grief counselor for all of them.

Details. She could handle the details. As long as there was something to do, something definite, she could hold on. She could be strong.

Friends came, with their sympathy and covered dishes and teary eyes. She was grateful to them more for the distraction than the condolences. There was no condolence for her.

Her father and his wife flew up from Memphis, and them she leaned on. She let Jolene, her father's wife, fuss over her, and soothe and cuddle the children, while her own mother complained about having to be in the same room as *that woman*.

When the service was over, after the friends drifted away, after she clung to her father and Jolene before their flight home, she made herself take off the black dress.

She shoved it into a bag to send to a shelter. She never wanted to see it again.

Her mother stayed. Stella had asked her to stay a few days. Surely under such circumstances she was entitled to her mother. Whatever friction was, and always had been, between them was nothing compared with death.

When she went into the kitchen, her mother was brewing coffee. Stella was so grateful not to have to think of such a minor task, she crossed over and kissed Carla's cheek.

"Thanks. I'm so sick of tea."

"Every time I turned around that woman was making more damn tea."

"She was trying to help, and I'm not sure I could've handled coffee until now."

Carla turned. She was a slim woman with short blond hair. Over the years, she'd battled time with regular trips to the surgeon. Nips, tucks, lifts, injections had wiped away some of the years. And left her looking whittled and hard, Stella thought.

She might pass for forty, but she'd never look happy about it.

"You always take up for her."

"I'm not taking up for Jolene, Mom." Wearily, Stella sat. No more details, she realized. No more something that has to be done.

How would she get through the night?

"I don't see why I had to tolerate her."

"I'm sorry you were uncomfortable. But she was very kind. She and Dad have been married for, what, twenty-five years or so now. You ought to be used to it."

"I don't like having her in my face, her and that twangy voice. Trailer trash."

Stella opened her mouth, closed it again. Jolene hadn't come from a trailer park and was certainly not trash. But what good would it do to say so? Or to remind her mother that she'd been the one who'd wanted a divorce, the one to leave the marriage. Just as it wouldn't do any good to point out that Carla had been married twice since.

"Well, she's gone now."

"Good riddance."

Stella took a deep breath. No arguments, she thought, as her stomach clenched and unclenched like a fist. Too tired to argue.

"The kids are sleeping. They're just worn out. Tomorrow . . . we'll just deal with tomorrow. I guess that's the way it's going to be." She let her head fall back, closed her eyes. "I keep thinking this is a horrible dream, and I'll wake up any second. Kevin will be here. I don't . . . I can't imagine life without him. I can't stand to imagine it."

The tears started again. "Mom, I don't know what I'm going to do."

"Had insurance, didn't he?"

Stella blinked, stared as Carla set a cup of coffee in front of her. "What?"

"Life insurance. He was covered?"

"Yes, but—"

"You ought to talk to a lawyer about suing the airline. Better start thinking of practicalities." She sat with her own coffee. "It's what you're best at, anyway."

"Mom"—she spoke slowly as if translating a strange foreign language—"Kevin's dead."

"I know that, Stella, and I'm sorry." Reaching over, Carla gave Stella's hand a pat. "I dropped everything to come here and give you a hand, didn't I?"

"Yes." She had to remember that. Appreciate that.

"It's a damn fucked-up world when a man of his age dies for no good reason. Useless waste. I'll never understand it."

"No." Pulling a tissue out of her pocket, Stella rubbed the tears away. "Neither will I."

"I liked him. But the fact is, you're in a fix now. Bills, kids to support. Widowed with two growing boys. Not many men want to take on ready-made families, let me tell you."

"I don't want a man to take us on. God, Mom."

"You will," Carla said with a nod. "Take my advice and make sure the next one's got money. Don't make my mistakes. You lost your husband, and that's hard. It's really hard. But women lose husbands every day. It's better to lose one this way than to go through a divorce."

The pain in Stella's stomach was too sharp for grief, too cold for rage. "Mom. We had Kevin's memorial service today. I have his ashes in a goddamn box in my bedroom."

"You want my help." She waggled the spoon. "I'm trying to give it to you. You sue the pants off the airline, get yourself a solid nest egg. And don't hook yourself up with some loser like I always do. You don't think divorce is a hard knock, too? Haven't been through one, have you? Well, I have. Twice. And I might as well tell you it's coming up on three. I'm done with that stupid son of a bitch.

You've got no idea what he's put me through. Not only is he an inconsiderate, loudmouthed asshole, but I think he's been cheating on me."

She pushed away from the table, rummaged around, then cut herself a piece of cake. "He thinks I'm going to tolerate that, he's mistaken. I'd just love to see his face when he gets served with the papers. Today."

"I'm sorry your third marriage isn't working out," Stella said stiffly. "But it's a little hard for me to be sympathetic, since both the third marriage and the third divorce were your choice. Kevin's dead. My husband is dead, and that sure as hell wasn't my choice."

"You think I want to go through this again? You think I want to come here to help you out, then have your father's bimbo shoved in my face?"

"She's his wife, who has never been anything but decent to you and who has always treated me kindly."

"To your face." Carla stuffed a bite of cake into her mouth. "You think you're the only one with problems? With heartache? You won't be so quick to shrug it off when you're pushing fifty and facing life alone."

"You're pushing fifty from the back end, Mom, and being alone is, again, your choice."

Temper turned Carla's eyes dark and sharp. "I don't appreciate that tone, Stella. I don't have to put up with it."

"No, you don't. You certainly don't. In fact, it would probably be best for both of us if you left. Right now. This was a bad idea. I don't know what I was thinking."

"You want me gone, fine." Carla shoved up from the table. "I'd just as soon get back to my own life. You never had any gratitude in you, and if you couldn't be on my back about something you weren't happy. Next time you want to cry on somebody's shoulder, call your country bumpkin stepmother."

"Oh, I will," Stella murmured as Carla sailed out of the room. "Believe me."

She rose to carry her cup to the sink, then gave in to the petty urge and smashed it. She wanted to break everything as she'd been broken. She wanted to wreak havoc on the world as it had been on her.

Instead she stood gripping the edge of the sink and praying that her mother would pack and leave quickly. She wanted her out. Why had she ever thought she wanted her to stay? It was always the same between them. Abrasive, combative. No connection, no common ground.

But God, she'd wanted that shoulder. Needed it so much, just for one night. Tomorrow she would do whatever came next. But she'd wanted to be held and stroked and comforted tonight.

With trembling fingers she cleaned the broken shards out of the sink, wept over them a little as she poured them into the trash. Then she walked to the phone and called a cab for her mother.

They didn't speak again, and Stella decided that was for the best. She closed the door, listened to the cab drive away.

Alone now, she checked on her sons, tucked blankets over them, laid her lips gently on their heads.

They were all she had now. And she was all they had.

She would be a better mother. She swore it. More patient. She would never, never let them down. She would never walk away when they needed her.

And when they needed her shoulder, by God, she would give it. No matter what. No matter when.

"You're first for me," she whispered. "You'll always be first for me."

In her own room, she undressed again, then took Kevin's old flannel robe out of the closet. She wrapped herself in it, in the familiar, heartbreaking smell of him.

Curling up on the bed, she hugged the robe close, shut her eyes, and prayed for morning. For what happened next.

two

Harper House

January 2004

SHE COULDN'T AFFORD TO BE INTIMIDATED BY THE house, or by its mistress. They both had reputations.

The house was said to be elegant and old,with gardens that rivaled Eden. She'd just confirmed that for herself.

The woman was said to be interesting, somewhat solitary, and perhaps a bit "difficult." A word, Stella knew, that could mean anything from strong-willed to stone bitch.

Either way, she could handle it, she reminded herself as she fought the need to get up and pace. She'd handled worse.

She needed this job. Not just for the salary—and it was generous—but for the structure, for the challenge, for the doing. Doing more, she knew, than circling the wheel she'd fallen into back home.

She needed a life, something more than clocking time, drawing a paycheck that would be soaked up by bills. She needed, however self-help-book it sounded, something that fulfilled and challenged her.

Rosalind Harper was fulfilled, Stella was sure. A beautiful ancestral home, a thriving business. What was it like, she wondered, to wake up every morning knowing exactly where you belonged and where you were going?

If she could earn one thing for herself, and give that gift to her children, it would be the sense of knowing. She was afraid she'd lost any clear sight of that with Kevin's death. The sense of doing, no problem. Give her a task or a challenge and the room to accomplish or solve it, she was your girl.

But the sense of knowing who she was, in the heart of herself, had been mangled that day in September of 2001 and had never fully healed.

This was her start, this move back to Tennessee. This final and face-to-face interview with Rosalind Harper. If she didn't get the job—well, she'd get another. No one could accuse her of not knowing how to work or how to provide a living for herself and her kids.

But, God, she wanted *this* job.

She straightened her shoulders and tried to ignore all the whispers of doubt muttering inside her head. She'd *get* this one.

She'd dressed carefully for this meeting. Businesslike but not fussy, in a navy suit and starched white blouse. Good shoes, good bag, she thought. Simple jewelry. Nothing flashy. Subtle makeup, to bring out the blue of her eyes. She'd fought her hair into a clip at the nape of her neck. If she was lucky, the curling mass of it wouldn't spring out until the interview was over.

Rosalind was keeping her waiting. It was probably a mind game, Stella decided as her fingers twisted, untwisted her watchband. Letting her sit and stew in the gorgeous parlor, letting her take in the lovely antiques and paintings, the sumptuous view from the front windows.

All in that dreamy and gracious southern style that reminded her she was a Yankee fish out of water.

Things moved slower down here, she reminded herself. She would have to remember that this was a different pace from the one she was used to, and a different culture.

The fireplace was probably an Adams, she decided. That lamp was certainly an original Tiffany. Would they call those drapes portieres down here, or was that too Scarlett O'Hara? Were the lace panels under the drapes heirlooms?

God, had she ever been more out of her element? What was a middle-class widow from Michigan doing in all this southern splendor?

She steadied herself, fixed a neutral expression on her face, when she heard footsteps coming down the hall.

"Brought coffee." It wasn't Rosalind, but the cheerful man who'd answered the door and escorted Stella to the parlor.

He was about thirty, she judged, average height, very slim. He wore his glossy brown hair waved around a movie-poster face set off by sparkling blue eyes. Though he wore black, Stella found nothing butlerlike about it. Much too artsy, too stylish. He'd said his name was David.

He set the tray with its china pot and cups, the little linen napkins, the sugar and cream, and the tiny vase with its clutch of violets on the coffee table.

"Roz got a bit hung up, but she'll be right along, so you just relax and enjoy your coffee. You comfortable in here?"

"Yes, very."

"Anything else I can get you while you're waiting on her?"

"No. Thanks."

"You just settle on in, then," he ordered, and poured coffee into a cup. "Nothing like a fire in January, is there? Makes you forget that a few months ago it was hot enough to melt the skin off your bones. What do you take in your coffee, honey?"

She wasn't used to being called "honey" by strange men who served her coffee in magnificent parlors. Especially since she suspected he was a few years her junior.

"Just a little cream." She had to order herself not to stare at his face—it was, well, delicious, with that full mouth, those sapphire eyes, the strong cheekbones, the sexy little dent in the chin. "Have you worked for Ms. Harper long?"

"Forever." He smiled charmingly and handed her the coffee. "Or it seems like it, in the best of all possible ways. Give her a straight answer to a straight question, and don't take any bullshit." His grin widened. "She *hates* it when people kowtow. You know, honey, I love your hair."

"Oh." Automatically, she lifted a hand to it. "Thanks."

"Titian knew what he was doing when he painted that color. Good luck with Roz," he said as he started out. "Great shoes, by the way."

She sighed into her coffee. He'd noticed her hair *and* her shoes, complimented her on both. Gay. Too bad for her side.

It was good coffee, and David was right. It was nice having a fire in January. Outside, the air was moist and raw, with a broody sky overhead. A woman could get used to a winter hour by the fire drinking good coffee out of—what was it? Meissen, Wedgwood? Curious, she held the cup up to read the maker's mark.

"It's Staffordshire, brought over by one of the Harper brides from England in the mid-nineteenth century."

No point in cursing herself, Stella thought. No point in cringing about the fact that her redhead's complexion would be flushed with embarrassment. She simply lowered the cup and looked Rosalind Harper straight in the eye.

"It's beautiful."

"I've always thought so." She came in, plopped down in the chair beside Stella's, and poured herself a cup.

One of them, Stella realized, had miscalculated the dress code for the interview.

Rosalind had dressed her tall, willowy form in a baggy olive sweater and mud-colored work pants that were frayed at the cuffs. She was shoeless, with a pair of thick brown socks covering long, narrow feet. Which accounted, Stella supposed, for her silent entry into the room.

Her hair was short, straight, and black.

Though to date all their communications had been via phone, fax, or e-mail, Stella had Googled her. She'd wanted background on her potential employer—and a look at the woman.

Newspaper and magazine clippings had been plentiful. She'd studied Rosalind as a child, through her youth. She'd marveled over the file photos of the stunning and delicate bride of eighteen and sympathized with the pale, stoic-looking widow of twenty-five.

There had been more, of course. Society-page stuff, gossipy speculation on when and if the widow would marry again. Then quite a bit of press surrounding the forging of the nursery business, her gardens, her love life. Her brief second marriage and divorce.

Stella's image had been of a strong-minded, shrewd woman. But she'd attributed those stunning looks to camera angles, lighting, makeup.

She'd been wrong.

At forty-six, Rosalind Harper was a rose in full bloom. Not the hothouse sort, Stella mused, but one that weathered the elements, season after season, and came back, year after year, stronger and more beautiful.

She had a narrow face angled with strong bones and deep, long eyes the color of single-malt scotch. Her mouth, full, strongly sculpted lips, was unpainted—as, to Stella's expert eye, was the rest of that lovely face.

There were lines, those thin grooves that the god of time reveled in stamping, fanning out from the corners of the dark eyes, but they didn't detract.

All Stella could think was, Could I be you, please, when I grow up? Only I'd like to dress better, if you don't mind.

"Kept you waiting, didn't I?"

Straight answers, Stella reminded herself. "A little, but it's not much of a hardship to sit in this room and drink good coffee out of Staffordshire."

"David likes to fuss. I was in the propagation house, got caught up."

Her voice, Stella thought, was brisk. Not clipped—you

just couldn't clip Tennessee—but it was to the point and full of energy. "You look younger than I expected. You're what, thirty-three?"

"Yes."

"And your sons are . . . six and eight?"

"That's right."

"You didn't bring them with you?"

"No. They're with my father and his wife right now."

"I'm very fond of Will and Jolene. How are they?"

"They're good. They're enjoying having their grandchildren around."

"I imagine so. Your daddy shows off pictures of them from time to time and just about bursts with pride."

"One of my reasons for relocating here is so they can have more time together."

"It's a good reason. I like young boys myself. Miss having them around. The fact that you come with two played in your favor. Your résumé, your father's recommendation, the letter from your former employer—well, none of that hurt."

She picked up a cookie from the tray, bit in, without her eyes ever leaving Stella's face. "I need an organizer, someone creative and hardworking, personable and basically tireless. I like people who work for me to keep up with me, and I set a strong pace."

"So I've been told." Okay, Stella thought, brisk and to the point in return. "I have a degree in nursery management. With the exception of three years when I stayed home to have my children—and during which time I landscaped my own yard and two neighbors'—I've worked in that capacity. For more than two years now, since my husband's death, I've raised my sons and worked outside the home in my field. I've done a good job with both. I can keep up with you, Ms. Harper. I can keep up with anyone."

Maybe, Roz thought. Just maybe. "Let me see your hands."

A little irked, Stella held them out. Roz set down her

coffee, took them in hers. She turned them palms up, ran her thumbs over them. "You know how to work."

"Yes, I do."

"Banker suit threw me off. Not that it isn't a lovely suit." Roz smiled, then polished off the cookie. "It's been damp the last couple of days. Let's see if we can put you in some boots so you don't ruin those very pretty shoes. I'll show you around."

THE BOOTS WERE TOO BIG, AND THE ARMY-GREEN rubber hardly flattering, but the damp ground and crushed gravel would have been cruel to her new shoes.

Her own appearance hardly mattered when compared with the operation Rosalind Harper had built.

In the Garden spread over the west side of the estate. The garden center faced the road, and the grounds at its entrance and running along the sides of its parking area were beautifully landscaped. Even in January, Stella could see the care and creativity put into the presentation with the selection and placement of evergreens and ornamental trees, the mulched rises where she assumed there would be color from bulbs and perennials, from splashy annuals through the spring and summer and into fall.

After one look she didn't want the job. She was desperate for it. The lust tied knots of nerves and desire in her belly, the kinds that were usually reserved for a lover.

"I didn't want the retail end of this near the house," Roz said as she parked the truck. "I didn't want to see commerce out my parlor window. Harpers are, and always have been, business-minded. Even back when some of the land around here was planted with cotton instead of houses."

Because Stella's mouth was too dry to speak, she only nodded. The main house wasn't visible from here. A wedge of natural woods shielded it from view and kept the long, low outbuildings, the center itself, and, she imagined, most of the greenhouses from intruding on any view from Harper House.

And just look at that gorgeous old ruby horse chestnut!

"This section's open to the public twelve months a year," Roz continued. "We carry all the sidelines you'd expect, along with houseplants and a selection of gardening books. My oldest son's helping me manage this section, though he's happier in the greenhouses or out in the field. We've got two part-time clerks right now. We'll need more in a few weeks."

Get your head in the game, Stella ordered herself. "Your busy season would start in March in this zone."

"That's right." Roz led the way to the low-slung white building, up an asphalt ramp, across a spotlessly clean porch, and inside.

Two long, wide counters on either side of the door, Stella noted. Plenty of light to keep it cheerful. There were shelves stocked with soil additives, plant foods, pesticides, spin racks of seeds. More shelves held books or colorful pots suitable for herbs or windowsill plants. There were displays of wind chimes, garden plaques, and other accessories.

A woman with snowy white hair dusted a display of sun catchers. She wore a pale blue cardigan with roses embroidered down the front over a white shirt that looked to have been starched stiff as iron.

"Ruby, this is Stella Rothchild. I'm showing her around."

"Pleased to meet you."

The calculating look told Stella the woman knew she was in about the job opening, but the smile was perfectly cordial. "You're Will Dooley's daughter, aren't you?"

"Yes, that's right."

"From . . . up north."

She said it, to Stella's amusement, as if it were a Third World country of dubious repute. "From Michigan, yes. But I was born in Memphis."

"Is that so?" The smile warmed, fractionally. "Well,

that's something, isn't it? Moved away when you were a little girl, didn't you?"

"Yes, with my mother."

"Thinking about moving back now, are you?"

"I have moved back," Stella corrected.

"Well." The one word said they'd see what they'd see. "It's a raw one out there today," Ruby continued. "Good day to be inside. You just look around all you want."

"Thanks. There's hardly anywhere I'd rather be than inside a nursery."

"You picked a winner here. Roz, Marilee Booker was in and bought the dendrobium. I just couldn't talk her out of it."

"Well, *shit*. It'll be dead in a week."

"Dendrobiums are fairly easy care," Stella pointed out.

"Not for Marilee. She doesn't have a black thumb. Her whole arm's black to the elbow. That woman should be barred by law from having anything living within ten feet of her."

"I'm sorry, Roz. But I did make her promise to bring it back if it starts to look sickly."

"Not your fault." Roz waved it away, then moved through a wide opening. Here were the houseplants, from the exotic to the classic, and pots from thimble size to those with a girth as wide as a manhole cover. There were more accessories, too, like stepping-stones, trellises, arbor kits, garden fountains, and benches.

"I expect my staff to know a little bit about everything," Roz said as they walked through. "And if they don't know the answer, they need to know how to find it. We're not big, not compared to some of the wholesale nurseries or the landscaping outfits. We're not priced like the garden centers at the discount stores. So we concentrate on offering the unusual plants along with the basic, and customer service. We make house calls."

"Do you have someone specific on staff who'll go do an on-site consult?"

"Either Harper or I might go if you're talking about a

customer who's having trouble with something bought here. Or if they just want some casual, personal advice."

She slid her hands into her pockets, rocked back and forth on the heels of her muddy boots. "Other than that, I've got a landscape designer. Had to pay him a fortune to steal him away from a competitor. Had to give him damn near free rein, too. But he's the best. I want to expand that end of the business."

"What's your mission statement?"

Roz turned, her eyebrows lifted high. There was a quick twinkle of amusement in those shrewd eyes. "Now, there you are—that's just why I need someone like you. Someone who can say 'mission statement' with a straight face. Let me think."

With her hands on her hips now, she looked around the stocked area, then opened wide glass doors into the adjoining greenhouse. "I guess it's two-pronged—this is where we stock most of our annuals and hanging baskets starting in March, by the way. First prong would be to serve the home gardener. From the fledgling who's just dipping a toe in to the more experienced who knows what he or she wants and is willing to try something new or unusual. To give that customer base good stock, good service, good advice. Second would be to serve the customer who's got the money but not the time or the inclination to dig in the dirt. The one who wants to beautify but either doesn't know where to start or doesn't want the job. We'll go in, and for a fee we'll work up a design, get the plants, hire the laborers. We'll guarantee satisfaction."

"All right." Stella studied the long, rolling tables, the sprinkler heads of the irrigation system, the drains in the sloping concrete floor.

"When the season starts we have tables of annuals and perennials along the side of this building. They'll show from the front as people drive by, or in. We've got a shaded area for ones that need shade," she continued as she walked through, boots slapping on concrete. "Over here we keep our herbs, and through there's a storeroom for extra pots and plastic flats, tags. Now, out back here's greenhouses for stock plants, seedlings, preparation areas. Those two will open to the public, more annuals sold by the flat."

She crunched along gravel, over more asphalt. Shrubs and ornamental trees. She gestured toward an area on the side where the stock wintering over was screened. "Behind that, closed to the public, are the propagation and grafting areas. We do mostly container planting, but I've culled out an acre or so for field stock. Water's no problem with the pond back there."

They continued to walk, with Stella calculating, dissecting. And the lust in her belly had gone from tangled knot to rock-hard ball.

She could *do* something here. Make her mark over the excellent foundation another woman had built. She could help improve, expand, refine.

Fulfilled? she thought. Challenged? Hell, she'd be so busy, she'd be fulfilled and challenged every minute of every day.

It was perfect.

There were the white scoop-shaped greenhouses, worktables, display tables, awnings, screens, sprinklers. Stella saw it brimming with plants, thronged with customers. Smelling of growth and possibilities.

Then Roz opened the door to the propagation house, and Stella let out a sound, just a quiet one she couldn't hold back. And it was pleasure.

The smell of earth and growing things, the damp heat. The air was close, and she knew her hair would frizz out insanely, but she stepped inside.

Seedlings sprouted in their containers, delicate new growth spearing out of the enriched soil. Baskets already planted were hung on hooks where they'd be urged into early bloom. Where the house teed off there were the stock plants, the parents of these fledglings. Aprons hung on pegs, tools were scattered on tables or nested in buckets.

Silently she walked down the aisles, noting that the containers were marked clearly. She could identify some of the plants without reading the tags. Cosmos and columbine, petunias and penstemon. This far south, in a few short weeks they'd be ready to be laid in beds, arranged in patio pots, tucked into sunny spaces or shady nooks.

Would she? Would she be ready to plant herself here, to root here? To bloom here? Would her sons?

Gardening was a risk, she thought. Life was just a bigger one. The smart calculated those risks, minimized them, and worked toward the goal.

"I'd like to see the grafting area, the stockrooms, the offices."

"All right. Better get you out of here. Your suit's going to wilt."

Stella looked down at herself, spied the green boots. Laughed. "So much for looking professional."

The laugh had Roz angling her head in approval. "You're a pretty woman, and you've got good taste in clothes. That kind of image doesn't hurt. You took the time to put yourself together well for this meeting, which I neglected to do. I appreciate that."

"You hold the cards, Ms. Harper. You can put yourself together any way you like."

"You're right about that." She walked back to the door, gestured, and they stepped outside into a light, chilly drizzle. "Let's go into the office. No point hauling you around in the wet. What are your other reasons for moving back here?"

"I couldn't find any reason to stay in Michigan. We moved there after Kevin and I were married—his work. I think, I suppose, I've stayed there since he died out of a kind of loyalty to him, or just because I was used to it. I'm not sure. I liked my work, but I never felt—it never felt like my place. More like I was just getting from one day to the next."

"Family?"

"No. No, not in Michigan. Just me and the boys.

Kevin's parents are gone, were before we married. My mother lives in New York. I'm not interested in living in the city or raising my children there. Besides that, my mother and I have . . . tangled issues. The way mothers and daughters often do."

"Thank God I had sons."

"Oh, yeah." She laughed again, comfortably now. "My parents divorced when I was very young. I suppose you know that."

"Some of it. As I said, I like your father, and Jolene."

"So do I. So rather than stick a pin in a map, I decided to come here. I was born here. I don't really remember, but I thought, hoped, there might be a connection. That it might be the place."

They walked back through the retail center and into a tiny, cluttered office that made Stella's organized soul wince. "I don't use this much," Roz began. "I've got stuff scattered between here and the house. When I'm over here, I end up spending my time in the greenhouses or the field."

She dumped gardening books off a chair, pointed to it, then sat on the edge of the crowded desk when Stella took the seat.

"I know my strengths, and I know how to do good business. I've built this place from the ground up, in less than five years. When it was smaller, when it was almost entirely just me, I could afford to make mistakes. Now I have up to eighteen employees during the season. People depending on me for a paycheck. So I can't afford to make mistakes. I know how to plant, what to plant, how to price, how to design, how to stock, how to handle employees, and how to deal with customers. I know how to organize."

"I'd say you're absolutely right. Why do you need me—or someone like me?"

"Because of all those things I can—and have done—there are some I don't like. I don't like to organize. And we've gotten too big for it to fall only to me how and what to stock. I want a fresh eye, fresh ideas, and a good head."

"Understood. One of your requests was that your nursery manager live in your house, at least for the first several months. I—"

"It wasn't a request. It was a requirement." In the firm tone, Stella recognized the *difficult* attributed to Rosalind Harper. "We start early, we work late. I want someone on hand, right on hand, at least until I know if we're going to find the rhythm. Memphis is too far away, and unless you're ready to buy a house within ten miles of mine pretty much immediately, there's no other choice."

"I have two active young boys, and a dog."

"I like active young boys, and I won't mind the dog unless he's a digger. He digs in my gardens, we'll have a problem. It's a big house. You'll have considerable room for yourself and your sons. I'd offer you the guest cottage, but I couldn't pry Harper out of it with dynamite. My oldest," she explained. "Do you want the job, Stella?"

She opened her mouth, then took a testing breath. Hadn't she already calculated the risks in coming here? It was time to work toward the goal. The risk of the single condition couldn't possibly outweigh the benefits.

"I do. Yes, Ms. Harper, I very much want the job."

"Then you've got it." Roz held out a hand to shake. "You can bring your things over tomorrow—morning's best—and we'll get y'all settled in. You can take a couple of days, make sure your boys are acclimated."

"I appreciate that. They're excited, but a little scared too." And so am I, she thought. "I have to be frank with you, Ms. Harper. If my boys aren't happy—after a reasonable amount of time to adjust—I'll have to make other arrangements."

"If I thought differently, I wouldn't be hiring you. And call me Roz."

SHE CELEBRATED BY BUYING A BOTTLE OF CHAMPAGNE and a bottle of sparkling cider on the way back to her father's home. The rain, and the detour, put her in a nasty knot of mid-afternoon traffic. It occurred to her that however awkward it might be initially, there were advantages to living essentially where she worked.

She got the job! A dream job, to her point of view. Maybe she didn't know how Rosalind—call me Roz—Harper would be to work for, and she still had a lot of boning up to do about the nursery process in this zone—and she couldn't be sure how the other employees would handle taking orders from a stranger. A Yankee stranger at that.

But she couldn't wait to start.

And her boys would have more room to run around at the Harper . . . estate, she supposed she'd call it. She wasn't ready to buy a house yet—not before she was sure they'd stay, not before she had time to scout out neighborhoods and communities. The fact was, they were crowded in her father's house. Both he and Jolene were more than accommodating, more than welcoming, but they couldn't stay indefinitely jammed into a two-bedroom house.

This was the practical solution, at least for the short term.

She pulled her aging SUV beside her stepmother's snappy little roadster and, grabbing the bag, dashed through the rain to the door.

She knocked. They'd given her a key, but she wasn't comfortable just letting herself in.

Jolene, svelte in black yoga pants and a snug black top, looking entirely too young to be chasing sixty, opened the door.

"I interrupted your workout."

"Just finished. Thank God!" She dabbed at her face with a little white towel, shook back her cloud of honey-blond hair. "Misplace your key, honey?"

"Sorry. I can't get used to using it." She stepped in, listened. "It's much too quiet. Are the boys chained in the basement?"

"Your dad took them into the Peabody to see the afternoon duck walk. I thought it'd be nice for just the three of them, so I stayed here with my yoga tape." She cocked her head to the side. "Dog's snoozing out on the screened porch. You look smug."

"I should. I'm hired."

"I knew it, I knew it! Congratulations!" Jolene threw out her arms for a hug. "There was never any question in my mind. Roz Harper's a smart woman. She knows gold when she sees it."

"My stomach's jumpy, and my nerves are just plain shot. I should wait for Dad and the boys, but . . ." She pulled out the champagne. "How about an early glass of champagne to toast my new job?"

"Oh, twist my arm. I'm so excited for you I could just pop!" Jolene slung an arm around Stella's shoulders as they turned into the great room. "Tell me what you thought of Roz."

"Not as scary in person." Stella set the bottle on the counter to open while Jolene got champagne flutes out of her glass-front display cabinet. "Sort of earthy and direct, confident. And that house!"

"It's a beaut." Jolene laughed when the cork popped. "My, my, what a decadent sound in the middle of the afternoon. Harper House has been in her family for generations. She's actually an Ashby by marriage—the first one. She went back to Harper after her second marriage fizzled."

"Give me the dish, will you, Jolene? Dad won't."

"Plying me with champagne to get me to gossip? Why, thank you, honey." She slid onto a stool, raised her glass. "First, to our Stella and brave new beginnings."

Stella clinked glasses, drank. "Mmmmm. Wonderful. Now, dish."

"She married young. Just eighteen. What you'd call a good match—good families, same social circle. More important, it was a love match. You could see it all over them. It was about the time I fell for your father, and a woman recognizes someone in the same state she's in. She was a late baby—I think her mama was near forty and her daddy heading to fifty when she came along. Her mama was never well after, or she enjoyed playing the frail wife—depending on who you talk to. But in any case, Roz lost them both within two years. She must've been pregnant with her second son. That'd be . . . shoot. Austin, I think. She and John took over Harper House. She had the three boys, and the youngest barely a toddler, when John was killed. You know how hard that must've been for her."

"I do."

"Hardly saw her outside that house for two, three years, I guess. When she did start getting out again, socializing, giving parties and such, there was the expected speculation. Who she'd marry, when. You've seen her. She's a beautiful woman."

"Striking, yes."

"And down here, a lineage like hers is worth its weight and then some. Her looks, her bloodline, she could've had any man she wanted. Younger, older, or in between, single, married, rich, or poor. But she stayed on her own. Raised her boys."

Alone, Stella thought, sipping champagne. She understood the choice very well.

"Kept her private life private," Jolene went on, "much to Memphis society's consternation. Biggest to-do I recall was when she fired the gardener—well, both of them. Went after them with a Weedwacker, according to some reports, and ran them right off the property."

"Really?" Stella's eyes widened in shocked admiration. "Really?"

"That's what I heard, and that's the story that stuck, truth or lie. Down here, we often prefer the entertaining lie to the plain truth. Apparently they'd dug up some of her plants or something. She wouldn't have anybody else after that. Took the whole thing over herself. Next thing you know—though I guess it was about five years later—she's building that garden place over on her west end. She got married about three years ago, and divorced—well, all you had to do was blink. Honey, why don't we make that two early glasses of champagne?"

"Why don't we?" Stella poured. "So, what was the deal with the second husband?"

"Hmmm. Very slick character. Handsome as sin and twice as charming. Bryce Clerk, and he *says* his people are from Savannah, but I don't know as I'd believe a word coming out of his mouth if it was plated with gold. Anyway, they looked stunning together, but it happened he enjoyed looking stunning with a variety of women, and a wedding ring didn't restrict his habits. She booted him out on his ear."

"Good for her."

"She's no pushover."

"That came through loud and clear."

"I'd say she's proud, but not vain, tough-minded but not hard—or not too hard, though there are some who would disagree with that. A good friend, and a formidable enemy. You can handle her, Stella. You can handle anything."

She liked people to think so, but either the champagne or fresh nerves was making her stomach a little queasy. "Well, we're going to find out."

THREE

SHE HAD A CAR FULL OF LUGGAGE, A BRIEFCASE stuffed with notes and sketches, a very unhappy dog who'd already expressed his opinion of the move by vomiting on the passenger seat, and two boys bickering bitterly in the back.

She'd already pulled over to deal with the dog and the seat, and despite the January chill had the windows wide open. Parker, their Boston terrier, sprawled on the floor looking pathetic.

She didn't know what the boys were arguing about, and since it hadn't come to blows yet, let them go at it. They were, she knew, as nervous as Parker about yet another move.

She'd uprooted them. No matter how carefully you dug, it was still a shock to the system. Now all of them were about to be transplanted. She believed they would thrive. She had to believe it or she'd be as sick as the family dog.

"I hate your slimy, stinky guts," eight-year-old Gavin declared.

"I hate your big, stupid butt," six-year-old Luke retorted.

"I hate your ugly elephant ears."

"I hate your whole ugly *face*!"

Stella sighed and turned up the radio.

She waited until she'd reached the brick pillars that flanked the drive to the Harper estate. She nosed in, out of the road, then stopped the car. For a moment, she simply sat there while the insults raged in the backseat. Parker sent her a cautious look, then hopped up to sniff at the air through the window.

She turned the radio off, sat. The voices behind her began to trail off, and after a last, harshly whispered, "And I hate your entire body," there was silence.

"So, here's what I'm thinking," she said in a normal, conversational tone. "We ought to pull a trick on Ms. Harper."

Gavin strained forward against his seat belt. "What kind of trick?"

"A tricky trick. I'm not sure we can pull it off. She's pretty smart; I could tell. So we'd have to be really sneaky."

"I can be sneaky," Luke assured her. And her glance in the rearview mirror told her the battle blood was already fading from his cheeks.

"Okay, then, here's the plan." She swiveled around so she could face both her boys. It struck her, as it often did, what an interesting meld of herself and Kevin they were. Her blue eyes in Luke's face, Kevin's gray-green ones in Gavin's. Her mouth to Gavin, Kevin's to Luke. Her coloring—poor baby—to Luke, and Kevin's sunny blond to Gavin.

She paused, dramatically, noted that both her sons were eagerly focused.

"No, I don't know." She shook her head regretfully. "It's probably not a good idea."

There was a chorus of pleas, protests, and a great deal of seat bouncing that sent Parker into a spate of enthusiastic barking.

"Okay, okay." She held up her hands. "What we do is,

we drive up to the house, and we go up to the door. And when we're inside and you meet Ms. Harper—this is going to have to be really sneaky, really clever."

"We can do it!" Gavin shouted.

"Well, when that happens, you have to pretend to be . . . this is tough, but I think you can do it. You have to pretend to be polite, well-behaved, well-mannered boys."

"We can do it! We . . ." Luke's face scrunched up. "Hey!"

"And I have to pretend not to be a bit surprised by finding myself with two well-behaved, well-mannered boys. Think we can pull it off?"

"Maybe we won't like it there," Gavin muttered.

Guilt roiled up to churn with nerves. "Maybe we won't. Maybe we will. We'll have to see."

"I'd rather live with Granddad and Nana Jo in their house." Luke's little mouth trembled, and wrenched at Stella's heart. "Can't we?"

"We really can't. We can visit, lots. And they can visit us, too. Now that we're going to live down here, we can see them all the time. This is supposed to be an adventure, remember? If we try it, really try it, and we're not happy, we'll try something else."

"People talk funny here," Gavin complained.

"No, just different."

"And there's no snow. How are we supposed to build snowmen and go sledding if it's too stupid to snow?"

"You've got me there, but there'll be other things to do." Had she seen her last white Christmas? Why hadn't she considered that before?

He jutted his chin out. "If she's mean, I'm not staying."

"That's a deal." Stella started the car, took a steadying breath, and continued down the drive.

Moments later she heard Luke's wondering: "It's big!"

No question about that, Stella mused, and wondered how her children saw it. Was it the sheer size of the three-storied structure that overwhelmed them? Or would they notice the details? The pale, pale yellow stone, the majestic columns, the charm of the entrance that was covered by the double stairway leading to the second floor and its pretty wraparound terrace?

Or would they just see the bulk of it—triple the size of their sweet house in Southfield?

"It's really old," she told them. "Over a hundred and fifty years old. And Ms. Harper's family's lived here always."

"Is she a hundred and fifty?" Luke wanted to know and earned a snort and an elbow jab from his brother.

"Dummy. Then she'd be *dead.* And there'd be worms crawling all over her—"

"I have to remind you, polite, well-mannered, well-behaved boys don't call their brothers dummy. See all the lawn? Won't Parker love being taken for walks out here? And there's so much room for you to play. But you have to stay out of the gardens and flower beds, just like at home. Back in Michigan," she corrected herself. "And we'll have to ask Ms. Harper where you're allowed to go."

"There's really big trees," Luke murmured. "Really big."

"That one there? That's a sycamore, and I bet it's even older than the house."

She pulled around the parking circle, admiring the use of Japanese red maple and golden mop cedar along with azaleas in the island.

She clipped on Parker's leash with hands that were a lot more steady than her heart rate. "Gavin, you take Parker. We'll come out for our things after we go in and see Ms. Harper."

"Does she get to boss us?" he demanded.

"Yes. The sad and horrible fate of children is to be bossed by adults. And as she's paying my salary, she gets to boss me, too. We're all in the same boat."

Gavin took Parker's leash when they got out. "I don't like her."

"That's what I love about you, Gavin." Stella ruffled his wavy blond hair. "Always thinking positive. Okay, here we go." She took his hand, and Luke's, gave each a gentle squeeze. The four of them started toward the covered entry.

The doors, a double set painted the same pure and glossy white as the trim, burst open.

"At last!" David flung out his arms. "Men! I'm no longer outnumbered around here."

"Gavin, Luke, this is Mr.—I'm sorry, David, I don't know your last name."

"Wentworth. But let's keep it David." He crouched down, looked the rapidly barking Parker in the eye. "What's your problem, buddy?"

In response, Parker planted his front paws on David's knee and lapped, with great excitement, at his face.

"That's more like it. Come on in. Roz'll be right along. She's upstairs on the phone, skinning some supplier over a delivery."

They stepped into the wide foyer, where the boys simply stood and goggled.

"Pretty ritzy, huh?"

"Is it like a church?"

"Nah." David grinned at Luke. "It's got fancy parts, but it's just a house. We'll get a tour in, but maybe you need some hot chocolate to revive you after your long journey."

"David makes wonderful hot chocolate." Roz started down the graceful stairs that divided the foyer. She was dressed in work clothes, as she'd been the day before. "With lots of whipped cream."

"Ms. Harper, my boys. Gavin and Luke."

"I'm very pleased to meet you. Gavin." She offered a hand to him.

"This is Parker. He's our dog. He's one and a half."

"And very handsome. Parker." She gave the dog a friendly pat.

"I'm Luke. I'm six, and I'm in first grade. I can write my name."

"He cannot either." Gavin sneered in brotherly disgust. "He can only print it."

"Have to start somewhere, don't you? It's very nice to

meet you, Luke. I hope you're all going to be comfortable here."

"You don't look really old," Luke commented, and had David snorting out a laugh.

"Why, thank you. I don't feel really old either, most of the time."

Feeling slightly ill, Stella forced a smile. "I told the boys how old the house was, and that your family's always lived here. He's a little confused."

"I haven't been here as long as the house. Why don't we have that hot chocolate, David? We'll sit in the kitchen, get acquainted."

"Is he your husband?" Gavin asked. "How come you have different last names?"

"She won't marry me," David told him, as he herded them down the hall. "She just breaks my poor, weeping heart."

"He's teasing you. David takes care of the house, and most everything else. He lives here."

"Is she the boss of you, too?" Luke tugged David's hand. "Mom says she's the boss of all of us."

"I let her think so." He led the way into the kitchen with its granite counters and warm cherry wood. A banquette with sapphire leather cushions ranged under a wide window.

Herbs thrived in blue pots along the work counter. Copper pots gleamed.

"This is my domain," David told them. "I'm boss here, just so you know the pecking order. You like to cook, Stella?"

"I don't know if 'like's' the word, but I do know I can't manage anything that would earn a kitchen like this."

Two Sub-Zero refrigerators, what looked to be a restaurant-style stove, double ovens, acres of counter.

And the little details that made a serious work space homey, she noted with relief. The brick hearth with a pretty fire simmering, the old china cupboard filled with antique glassware, forced bulbs of tulips and hyacinths blooming on a butcher block table.

"I live to cook. I can tell you it's pretty frustrating to waste my considerable talents on Roz. She'd just as soon eat cold cereal. And Harper rarely makes an appearance."

"Harper's my oldest son. He lives in the guest house. You'll see him sometimes."

"He's the mad scientist." David got out a pot and chunks of chocolate.

"Does he make monsters? Like Frankenstein?" As he asked, Luke snuck his hand into his mother's again.

"Frankenstein's just pretend," Stella reminded him. "Ms. Harper's son works with plants."

"Maybe one day he'll make a giant one that talks."

Delighted, Gavin sidled over toward David. "Nuh-uh."

" 'There are more things in heaven and earth, Horatio.' Bring that stool over, my fine young friend, and you can watch the master make the world's best hot chocolate."

"I know you probably want to get to work shortly," Stella said to Roz. "I have some notes and sketches I worked on last night I'd like to show you at some point."

"Busy."

"Eager." She glanced over as Luke let go of her hand and went over to join his brother on the stool. "I have an appointment this morning with the principal at the school. The boys should be able to start tomorrow. I thought I could ask at the school office for recommendations for before- and after-school care, then—"

"Hey!" David whipped chocolate and milk in the pot. "These are my men now. I figured they'd hang out with me, providing me with companionship as well as slave labor, when they're not in school."

"I couldn't ask you to—"

"We could stay with David," Gavin piped up. "That'd be okay."

"I don't—"

"Of course, it all depends." David spoke easily as he

added sugar to the pot. "If they don't like PlayStation, the deal's off. I have my standards."

"I like PlayStation," Luke said.

"Actually, they have to *love* PlayStation."

"I do! I do!" They bounced in unison on the stool. "I *love* PlayStation."

"Stella, while they're finishing up here, why don't we get some of your things out of the car?"

"All right. We'll just be a minute. Parker—"

"Dog's fine," David said.

"Well. Be right back, then."

Roz waited until they were at the front door. "David's wonderful with kids."

"Anyone could see." She caught herself twisting the band of her watch, made herself stop. "It just feels like an imposition. I'd pay him, of course, but—"

"You'll work that out between you. I just wanted to say—from one mother to another—that you can trust him to look after them, to entertain them, and to keep them—well, no, you can't trust him to keep them out of trouble. I'll say serious trouble, yes, but not the ordinary sort."

"He'd have to have superpowers for that."

"He practically grew up in this house. He's like my fourth son."

"It would be tremendously easy this way. I wouldn't have to haul them to a sitter." Yet another stranger, she thought.

"And you're not used to things being easy."

"No, I'm not." She heard squeals of laughter rolling out from the kitchen. "But I want my boys to be happy, and I guess that's the deciding vote right there."

"Wonderful sound, isn't it? I've missed it. Let's get your things."

"You have to give me the boundaries," Stella said as they went outside. "Where the boys can go, where they can't. They need chores and rules. They're used to having them at home. Back in Michigan."

"I'll give that some thought. Though David—despite

the fact that I'm the boss of all of you—probably has ideas on all that already. Cute dog, too, by the way." She hauled two suitcases out of the back of the SUV. "My dog died last year, and I haven't had the heart to get another. It's nice having a dog around. Clever name."

"Parker—for Peter Parker. That's—"

"Spider-Man. I did raise three boys of my own."

"Right." Stella grabbed another suitcase and a cardboard carton. She felt her muscles strain even as Roz carried her load with apparent ease.

"I meant to ask who else lives here, or what other staff you have."

"It's just David."

"Oh? He said something about being outnumbered by women before we got here."

"That's right. It would be David, and me, and the Harper Bride."

Roz carried the luggage inside and started up the steps with it. "She's our ghost."

"Your . . ."

"A house this old isn't haunted, it would be a damn shame, I'd think."

"I guess that's one way to look at it."

She decided Roz was amusing herself with a little local color for the new kid on the block. Ghosts would add to the family lore. So she dismissed it.

"You can have your run of the west wing. I think the rooms we've earmarked will suit best. I'm in the east wing, and David's rooms are off the kitchen. Everyone has plenty of privacy, which I've always felt is vital to good relations."

"This is the most beautiful house I've ever seen."

"It is, isn't it?" Roz stopped a moment, looking out the windows that faced one of her gardens. "It can be damp in the winter, and we're forever calling the plumber, the electrician, someone. But I love every inch of it. Some might think it's a waste for a woman on her own."

"It's yours. Your family home."

"Exactly. And it'll stay that way, whatever it takes. You're just down here. Each room opens to the terrace. I'll leave it to you to judge if you need to lock the one in the boys' room. I assumed they'd want to share at this age, especially in a new place."

"Bull's-eye." Stella walked into the room behind Roz. "Oh, they'll love this. Lots of room, lots of light." She laid the carton and the suitcase on one of the twin beds. But antiques." She ran her fingers over the child-size chest of drawers. "I'm terrified."

"Furniture's meant to be used. And good pieces respected."

"Believe me, they'll get the word." Please, God, don't let them break anything.

"You're next door. The bath connects." Roz gestured, angled her head. "I thought, at least initially, you'd want to be close."

"Perfect." She walked into the bath. The generous claw-foot tub stood on a marble platform in front of the terrace doors. Roman shades could be pulled down for privacy. The toilet sat in a tall cabinet built from yellow pine and had a chain pull—wouldn't the boys get a kick out of that!

Beside the pedestal sink was a brass towel warmer already draped with fluffy sea-green towels.

Through the connecting door, her room was washed with winter light. Rhizomes patterned the oak floor.

A cozy sitting area faced the small white-marble fireplace, with a painting of a garden in full summer bloom above it.

Draped in gauzy white and shell pink, the canopy bed was accented with a generous mountain of silk pillows in dreamy pastels. The bureau with its long oval mirror was gleaming mahogany, as was the charmingly feminine dressing table and the carved armoire.

"I'm starting to feel like Cinderella at the ball."

"If the shoe fits." Roz set down the suitcases. "I want you to be comfortable, and your boys to be happy because I'm going to work you very hard. It's a big house, and

David will show you through at some point. We won't bump into each other, unless we want to."

She shoved up the sleeves of her shirt as she looked around. "I'm not a sociable woman, though I do enjoy the company of people I like. I think I'm going to like you. I already like your children."

She glanced at her watch. "I'm going to grab that hot chocolate—I can't ever resist it—then get to work."

"I'd like to come in, show you some of my ideas, later today."

"Fine. Hunt me up."

SHE DID JUST THAT. THOUGH SHE'D INTENDED TO bring the kids with her after the school meeting, she hadn't had the heart to take them away from David.

So much for her worries about their adjustment to living in a new house with strangers. It appeared that most of the adjustments were going to be on her end.

She dressed more appropriately this time, in sturdy walking shoes that had already seen their share of mud, jeans with considerable wear, and a black sweater. With her briefcase in hand, she headed into the main entrance of the garden center.

The same woman was at the counter, but this time she was waiting on a customer. Stella noted a small dieffenbachia in a cherry-red pot and a quartet of lucky bamboo, tied with decorative hemp, already in a shallow cardboard box.

A bag of stones and a square glass vase were waiting to be rung up.

Good.

"Is Roz around?" Stella asked.

"Oh . . ." Ruby gestured vaguely. "Somewhere or the other."

She nodded to the two-ways behind the counter. "Would she have one of those with her?"

The idea seemed to amuse Ruby. "I don't think so."

"Okay, I'll find her. That's so much fun," she said to the

customer, with a gesture toward the bamboo. "Carefree and interesting. It's going to look great in that bowl."

"I was thinking about putting it on my bathroom counter. Something fun and pretty."

"Perfect. Terrific hostess gifts, too. More imaginative than the usual flowers."

"I hadn't thought of that. You know, maybe I'll get another set."

"You couldn't go wrong." She beamed a smile, then started out toward the greenhouses, congratulating herself as she went. She wasn't in any hurry to find Roz. This gave her a chance to poke around on her own, to check supplies, stock, displays, traffic patterns. And to make more notes.

She lingered in the propagation area, studying the progress of seedlings and cuttings, the type of stock plants, and their health.

It was nearly an hour before she made her way to the grafting area. She could hear music—the Corrs, she thought—seeping out the door.

She peeked in. There were long tables lining both sides of the greenhouse, and two more shoved together to run down the center. It smelled of heat, vermiculite, and peat moss.

There were pots, some holding plants that had been or were being grafted. Clipboards hung from the edges of tables, much like hospital charts. A computer was shoved into a corner, its screen a pulse of colors that seemed to beat to the music.

Scalpels, knives, snippers, grafting tape and wax, and other tools of this part of the trade lay in trays.

She spotted Roz at the far end, standing behind a man on a stool. His shoulders were hunched as he worked. Roz's hands were on her hips.

"It can't take more than an hour, Harper. This place is as much yours as mine, and you need to meet her, hear what she has to say."

"I will, I will, but damn it, I'm in the middle of things here. You're the one who wants her to manage, so let her manage. I don't care."

"There's such a thing as manners." Exasperation rolled into the overheated air. "I'm just asking you to pretend, for an hour, to have a few."

The comment brought Stella's own words to her sons back to her mind. She couldn't stop the laugh, but did her best to conceal it with a cough as she walked down the narrow aisle.

"Sorry to interrupt. I was just . . ." She stopped by a pot, studying the grafted stem and the new leaves. "I can't quite make this one."

"Daphne." Roz's son spared her the briefest glance.

"Evergreen variety. And you've used a splice side-veneer graft."

He stopped, swiveled on his stool. His mother had stamped herself on his face—the same strong bones, rich eyes. His dark hair was considerably longer than hers, long enough that he tied it back with what looked to be a hunk of raffia. Like her, he was slim and seemed to have at least a yard of leg, and like her he dressed carelessly in jeans pocked with rips and a soil-stained Memphis University sweatshirt.

"You know something about grafting?"

"Just the basics. I cleft-grafted a camellia once. It did very well. Generally I stick with cuttings. I'm Stella. It's nice to meet you, Harper."

He rubbed his hand over his jeans before shaking hers. "Mom says you're going to organize us."

"That's the plan, and I hope it's not going to be too painful for any of us. What are you working on here?" She stepped over to a line of pots covered with clean plastic bags held clear of the grafted plant by four split stakes.

"Gypsophilia—baby's breath. I'm shooting for blue, as well as pink and white."

"Blue. My favorite color. I don't want to hold you up. I

was hoping," she said to Roz, "we could find somewhere to go over some of my ideas."

"Back in the annual house. The office is hopeless. Harper?"

"All right, okay. Go ahead. I'll be there in five minutes."

"Harper."

"Okay, ten. But that's my final offer."

With a laugh, Roz gave him a light cuff on the back of the head. "Don't make me come back in here and get you."

"Nag, nag, nag," he muttered, but with a grin.

Outside, Roz let out a sigh. "He plants himself in there, you have to jab a pitchfork in his ass to budge him. He's the only one of my boys who has an interest in the place. Austin's a reporter, works in Atlanta. Mason's a doctor, or will be. He's doing his internship in Nashville."

"You must be proud."

"I am, but I don't see nearly enough of either of them. And here's Harper, practically under my feet, and I have to hunt him like a dog to have a conversation."

Roz boosted herself onto one of the tables. "Well, what've you got?"

"He looks just like you."

"People say. I just see Harper. Your boys with David?"

"Couldn't pry them away with a crowbar." Stella opened her briefcase. "I typed up some notes."

Roz looked at the stack of papers and tried not to wince. "I'll say."

"And I've made some rough sketches of how we might change the layout to improve sales and highlight non-plant purchases. You have a prime location, excellent landscaping and signage, and a very appealing entrance."

"I hear a 'but' coming on."

"But . . ." Stella moistened her lips. "Your first-level retail area is somewhat disorganized. With some changes it would flow better into the secondary area and on through to your main plant facilities. Now, a functional organizational plan—"

"A functional organizational plan. Oh, my God."

"Take it easy, this really won't hurt. What you need is a chain of responsibility for your functional area. That's sales, production, and propagation. Obviously you're a skilled propagator, but at this point you need me to head production and sales. If we increase the volume of sales as I've proposed here—"

"You did charts." There was a touch of wonder in Roz's voice. "And graphs. I'm . . . suddenly afraid."

"You are not," Stella said with a laugh, then looked at Roz's face. "Okay, maybe a little. But if you look at this chart, you see the nursery manager—that's me—and you as you're in charge of everything. Forked out from that is your propagator—you and, I assume, Harper; production manager, me; and sales manager—still me. For now, anyway. You need to delegate and/or hire someone to be in charge of container and/or field production. This section here deals with staff, job descriptions and responsibilities."

"All right." On a little breath, Roz rubbed the back of her neck. "Before I give myself eyestrain reading all that, let me say that while I may consider hiring on more staff, Logan, my landscape designer, has a good handle on the field production at this point. I can continue to head up the container production. I didn't start this place to sit back and have others do all the work."

"Great. Then at some point I'd like to meet with Logan so we can coordinate our visions."

Roz's smile was thin, and just a little wicked. "That ought to be interesting."

"Meanwhile, since we're both here, why don't we take my notes and sketches of the first-level sales section and go through it on the spot? You can see better what I have in mind, and it'll be simpler to explain."

Simpler? Roz thought as she hopped down. She didn't think anything was going to be simpler now.

But it sure as holy hell wasn't going to be boring.

four

Everything was perfect. She worked long hours, but much of it was planning at this stage. There was little Stella loved more than planning. Unless it was *arranging*. She had a vision of things, in her head, of how things could and should be.

Some might see it as a flaw, this tendency to organize and project, to nudge those visions of things into place even when—maybe particularly when—others didn't quite get the picture.

But she didn't see it that way.

Life ran smoother when everything was where it was meant to be.

Her life had—she'd made certain of it—until Kevin's death. Her childhood had been a maze of contradictions, of confusions and irritations. In a very real way she'd lost her father at the age of three when divorce had divided her family.

The only thing she clearly remembered about the move from Memphis was crying for her daddy.

From that point on, it seemed she and her mother had butted heads over everything, from the color of paint on the walls to finances to how to spend holidays and vacations. Everything.

Those same *some people* might say that's what happened with two headstrong women living in the same house. But Stella knew different. While she was practical and organized, her mother was scattered and spontaneous. Which accounted for the four marriages and three broken engagements.

Her mother liked flash and noise and wild romance. Stella preferred quiet and settled and committed.

Not that she wasn't romantic. She was just sensible about it.

It had been both sensible and romantic to fall in love with Kevin. He'd been warm and sweet and steady. They'd wanted the same things. Home, family, future. He'd made her happy, made her feel safe and cherished. And God, she missed him.

She wondered what he'd think about her coming here, starting over this way. He'd have trusted her. He'd always believed in her. They'd believed in each other.

He'd been her rock, in a very real way. The rock that had given her a solid base to build on after a childhood of upheaval and discontent.

Then fate had kicked that rock out from under her. She'd lost her base, her love, her most cherished friend, and the only person in the world who could treasure her children as much as she did.

There had been times, many times, during the first months after Kevin's death when she'd despaired of ever finding her balance again.

Now she was the rock for her sons, and she would do whatever she had to do to give them a good life.

With her boys settled down for the night, and a low fire burning—she was *definitely* having a bedroom fireplace in her next house—she sat on the bed with her laptop.

It wasn't the most businesslike way to work, but she didn't feel right asking Roz to let her convert one of the bedrooms into a home office.

Yet.

She could make do this way for now. In fact, it was cozy and for her, relaxing, to go over the order of business for the next day while tucked into the gorgeous old bed.

She had the list of phone calls she intended to make to suppliers, the reorganization of garden accessories and the houseplants. Her new color-coordinated pricing system to implement. The new invoicing program to install.

She had to speak with Roz about the seasonal employees. Who, how many, individual and group responsibilities.

And she'd yet to corner the landscape designer. You'd think the man could find time in a damn week to return a phone call. She typed in "Logan Kitridge," bolding and underlining the name.

She glanced at the clock, reminded herself that she would put in a better day's work with a good night's sleep.

She powered down the laptop, then carried it over to the dressing table to set it to charge. She really was going to need that home office.

She went through her habitual bedtime routine, meticulously creaming off her makeup, studying her naked face in the mirror to see if the Time Bitch had snuck any new lines on it that day. She dabbed on her eye cream, her lip cream, her nighttime moisturizer—all of which were lined, according to point of use, on the counter. After slathering more cream on her hands, she spent a few minutes searching for gray hairs. The Time Bitch could be sneaky.

She wished she was prettier. Wished her features were more even, her hair straight and a reasonable color. She'd dyed it brown once, and *that* had been a disaster. So, she'd just have to live with . . .

She caught herself humming, and frowned at herself in the mirror. What song was that? How strange to have it stuck in her head when she didn't even know what it was.

Then she realized it wasn't stuck in her head. She *heard* it. Soft, dreamy singing. From the boys' room.

Wondering what in the world Roz would be doing

singing to the boys at eleven at night, Stella reached for the connecting door.

When she opened it, the singing stopped. In the subtle glow of the Harry Potter night-light, she could see her sons in their beds.

"Roz?" she whispered, stepping in.

She shivered once. Why was it so cold in there? She moved, quickly and quietly to the terrace doors, checked and found them securely closed, as were the windows. And the hall door, she thought with another frown.

She could have sworn she'd heard something. *Felt* something. But the chill had already faded, and there was no sound in the room but her sons' steady breathing.

She tucked up their blankets as she did every night, brushed kisses on both their heads.

And left the connecting doors open.

BY MORNING SHE'D BRUSHED IT OFF. LUKE COULDN'T find his lucky shirt, and Gavin got into a wrestling match with Parker on their before-school walk and had to change his. As a result, she barely had time for morning coffee and the muffin David pressed on her.

"Will you tell Roz I went in early? I want to have the lobby area done before we open at ten."

"She left an hour ago."

"An hour ago?" Stella looked at her watch. Keeping up with Roz had become Stella's personal mission—and so far she was failing. "Does she *sleep*?"

"With her, the early bird doesn't just catch the worm, but has time to sauté it with a nice plum sauce for breakfast."

"Excuse me, but *eeuw*. Gotta run." She dashed for the doorway, then stopped. "David, everything's going okay with the kids? You'd tell me otherwise, right?"

"Absolutely. We're having nothing but fun. Today, after school, we're going to practice running with scissors, then find how many things we can roughhouse with that can poke our eyes out. After that, we've moving on to flammables."

"Thanks. I feel very reassured." She bent down to give Parker a last pat. "Keep an eye on this guy," she told him.

LOGAN KITRIDGE WAS PRESSED FOR TIME. RAIN HAD delayed his personal project to the point where he was going to have to postpone some of the fine points—again—to meet professional commitments.

He didn't mind so much. He considered landscaping a perpetual work in progress. It was never finished. It *should* never be finished. And when you worked with Nature, Nature was the boss. She was fickle and tricky, and endlessly fascinating.

A man had to be continually on his toes, be ready to flex, be willing to compromise and swing with her moods. Planning in absolutes was an exercise in frustration, and to his mind there were enough other things to be frustrated about.

Since Nature had deigned to give him a good, clear day, he was taking it to deal with his personal project. It meant he had to work alone—he liked that better in any case—and carve out time to swing by the job site and check on his two-man crew.

It meant he had to get over to Roz's place, pick up the trees he'd earmarked for his own use, haul them back to his place, and get them in the ground before noon.

Or one. Two at the latest.

Well, he'd see how it went.

The one thing he couldn't afford to carve out time for was this new manager Roz had taken on. He couldn't figure out why Roz had hired a manager in the first place, and for God's sake a Yankee. It seemed to him that Rosalind Harper knew how to run her business just fine and didn't need some fast-talking stranger screwing with the system.

He liked working with Roz. She was a woman who got things done, and who didn't poke her nose into his end of things any more than was reasonable. She loved the work, just as he did, had an instinct for it. So when she did make a suggestion, you tended to listen and weigh it in.

She paid well and didn't hassle a man over every detail.

He could tell, just *tell*, that this manager was going to be nothing but bumps and ruts in his road.

Wasn't she already leaving messages for him in that cool Yankee voice about time management, invoice systems, and equipment inventory?

He didn't give a shit about that sort of thing, and he wasn't going to start giving one now.

He and Roz had a system, damn it. One that got the job done and made the client happy.

Why mess with success?

He drove his full-size pickup through the parking area, wove through the piles of mulch and sand, the landscape timbers, and around the side loading area.

He'd already eyeballed and tagged what he wanted—but before he loaded them up, he'd take one more look around. Plus there were some young evergreens in the field and a couple of hemlocks in the balled and burlapped area that he thought he could use.

Harper had grafted him a couple of willows and a hedgerow of peonies. They'd be ready to dig in this spring, along with the various pots of cuttings and layered plants Roz had helped him with.

He moved through the rows of trees, then turned around and backtracked.

This wasn't right, he thought. Everything was out of place, changed around. Where were his dogwoods? Where the hell were the rhododendrons, the mountain laurels he'd tagged? Where was his goddamn frigging magnolia?

He scowled at a pussy willow, then began a careful, step-by-step search through the section.

It was all different. Trees and shrubs were no longer in

what he'd considered an interesting, eclectic mix of type and species, but lined up like army recruits, he decided. Alphabetized, for Christ's sweet sake. In frigging Latin.

Shrubs were segregated, and organized in the same anal fashion.

He found his trees and, stewing, carted them to his truck. Muttering to himself, he decided to head into the field, dig up the trees he wanted there. They'd be safer at his place. Obviously.

Bur first he was going to hunt up Roz and get this mess straightened out.

STANDING ON A STEPLADDER, ARMED WITH A BUCKET of soapy water and a rag, Stella attacked the top of the shelf she'd cleared off. A good cleaning, she decided, and it would be ready for her newly planned display. She envisioned it filled with color-coordinated decorative pots, some mixed plantings scattered among them. Add other accessories, like raffia twine, decorative watering spikes, florist stones and marbles, and so on, and you'd have something.

At point of purchase, it would generate impulse sales.

She was moving the soil additives, fertilizers, and animal repellents to the side wall. Those were basics, not impulse. Customers would walk back there for items of that nature, and pass the wind chimes she was going to hang, the bench and concrete planter she intended to haul in. With the other changes, it would all tie together, and with the flow, draw customers into the houseplant section, across to the patio pots, the garden furniture, all before they moved through to the bedding plants.

With an hour and a half until they opened, and if she could shanghai Harper into helping her with the heavy stuff, she'd have it done.

She heard footsteps coming through from the back, blew her hair out of her eyes. "Making progress," she began. "I know it doesn't look like it yet, but . . ."

She broke off when she saw him.

Even standing on the ladder, she felt dwarfed. He had to be six-five. All tough and rangy and fit in faded jeans with bleach stains splattered over one thigh. He wore a flannel shirt jacket-style over a white T-shirt and a pair of boots so dinged and scored she wondered he didn't take pity and give them a decent burial.

His long, wavy, unkempt hair was the color she'd been shooting for the one time she'd dyed her own.

She wouldn't have called him handsome—everything about him seemed rough and rugged. The hard mouth, the hollowed cheeks, the sharp nose, the expression in his eyes. They were green, but not like Kevin's had been. These were moody and deep, and seemed somehow *hot* under the strong line of brows.

No, she wouldn't have said handsome, but arresting, in a big and tough sort of way. The sort of tough that looked like a bunched fist would bounce right off him, doing a lot more damage to the puncher than the punchee.

She smiled, though she wondered where Roz was, or Harper. Or somebody.

"I'm sorry. We're not open yet this morning. Is there something I can do for you?"

Oh, he knew that voice. That crisp, cool voice that had left him annoying messages about functional organizational plans and production goals.

He'd expected her to look like she'd sounded—a usual mistake, he supposed. There wasn't much cool and crisp about that wild red hair she was trying to control with that stupid-looking kerchief, or the wariness in those big blue eyes.

"You moved my damn trees."

"I'm sorry?"

"Well, you ought to be. Don't do it again."

"I don't know what you're talking about." She kept a grip on the bucket—just in case—and stepped down the ladder. "Did you order some trees? If I could have your name, I'll see if I can find your order. We're implementing a new system, so—"

"I don't have to order anything, and I don't like your new system. And what the hell are you doing in here? Where *is* everything?"

His voice sounded local to her, with a definite edge of nasty impatience. "I think it would be best if you came back when we're open. Winter hours start at ten A.M. If you'd leave me your name . . ." She edged toward the counter and the phone.

"It's Kitridge, and you ought to know since you've been nagging me brainless for damn near a week."

"I don't know . . . oh. Kitridge." She relaxed, fractionally. "The landscape designer. And I haven't been nagging," she said with more heat when her brain caught up. "I've been trying to contact you so we could schedule a meeting. You haven't had the courtesy to return my calls. I certainly hope you're not as rude with clients as you are with coworkers."

"Rude? Sister, you haven't seen rude."

"I have two sons," she snapped back. "I've seen plenty of rude. Roz hired me to put some order into her business, to take some of the systemic load off her shoulders, to—"

"Systemic?" His gaze rose to the ceiling like a man sending out a prayer. "Jesus, are you always going to talk like that?"

She took a calming breath. "Mr. Kitridge, I have a job to do. Part of that job is dealing with the landscaping arm of this business. It happens to be a very important and profitable arm."

"Damn right. And it's my frigging arm."

"It also happens to be ridiculously disorganized and apparently run like a circus. I've been finding little scraps of paper and hand-scribbled orders and invoices—if you can call them that—all week."

"So?"

"So, if you'd bothered to return my calls and arrange for

a meeting, I could have explained to you how this arm of the business will now function."

"Oh, is that right?" That west Tennessee tone took on a soft and dangerous hue. "You're going to explain it to me."

"That's exactly right. The system I'm implementing will, in the end, save you considerable time and effort with computerized invoices and inventory, client lists and designs, with—"

He was sizing her up. He figured he had about a foot on her in height, probably a good hundred pounds in bulk. But the woman had a mouth on her. It was what his mother would have called bee stung—pretty—and apparently it never stopped flapping.

"How the hell is having to spend half my time on a computer going to save me anything?"

"Once the data is inputted, it will. At this point, you seem to be carrying most of this information in some pocket, or inside your head."

"So? If it's in a pocket, I can find it. If it's in my head, I can find it there, too. Nothing wrong with my memory."

"Maybe not. But tomorrow you may be run over by a truck and spend the next five years in a coma." That pretty mouth smiled, icily. "Then where will we be?"

"Being as I'd be in a coma, I wouldn't be worried about it. Come out here."

He grabbed her hand, pulled her toward the door. "Hey!" she managed. Then, *"Hey!"*

"This is business." He yanked open the door and kept pulling her along. "I'm not dragging you off to a cave."

"Then let go." His hands were hard as rock, and just as rough. And his legs, she realized, as he strode away from the building, ate up ground in long, hurried bites and forced her into an undignified trot.

"Just a minute. Look at that."

He gestured toward the tree and shrub area while she struggled to get her breath back. "What about it?"

"It's messed up."

"It certainly isn't. I spent nearly an entire day on this area." And had the aching muscles to prove it. "It's cohesively arranged so if a customer is looking for an ornamental tree, he—or a member of the staff—can find the one that suits. If the customer is looking for a spring-blooming shrub or—"

"They're all lined up. What did you use, a carpenter's level? People come in here now, how can they get a picture of how different specimens might work together?"

"That's your job and the staff's. We're here to help and direct the customer to possibilities as well as their more definite wants. If they're wandering around trying to find a damn hydrangea—"

"They might just spot a spirea or camellia they'd like to have, too."

He had a point, and she'd considered it. She wasn't an idiot. "Or they may leave empty-handed because they couldn't easily find what they'd come for in the first place. Attentive and well-trained staff should be able to direct and explore with the customer. Either way has its pros and cons, but I happen to like this way better. And it's my call.

"Now." She stepped back. "If you have the time, we need to—"

"I don't." He stalked off toward his truck.

"Just wait." She jogged after him. "We need to talk about the new purchase orders and invoicing system."

"Send me a frigging memo. Sounds like your speed."

"I don't want to send you a frigging memo, and what are you doing with those trees?"

"Taking them home." He pulled open the truck door, climbed in.

"What do you mean you're taking them home? I don't have any paperwork on these."

"Hey, me neither." After slamming the door, he rolled the window down a stingy inch. "Step back, Red. Wouldn't want to run over your toes."

"Look. You can't just take off with stock whenever you feel like it."

"Take it up with Roz. If she's still the boss. Otherwise, better call the cops." He gunned the engine, and when she stumbled back, zipped into reverse. And left her staring after him.

Cheeks pink with temper, Stella marched back toward the building. Serve him right, she thought, just serve him right if she did call the police. She snapped her head up, eyes hot, as Roz opened the door.

"Was that Logan's truck?"

"Does he work with clients?"

"Sure. Why?"

"You're lucky you haven't been sued. He storms in, nothing but complaints. Bitch, bitch, bitch," Stella muttered as she swung past Roz and inside. "He doesn't like this, doesn't like that, doesn't like any damn thing as far as I can tell. Then he drives off with a truckload of trees and shrubs."

Roz rubbed her earlobe thoughtfully. "He does have his moods."

"Moods? I only saw one, and I didn't like it." She yanked off the kerchief, tossed it on the counter.

"Pissed you off, did he?"

"In spades. I'm trying to do what you hired me to do, Roz."

"I know. And so far I don't believe I've made any comments or complaints that could qualify as bitch, bitch, bitch."

Stella sent her a horrified look. "No! Of course not. I didn't mean—God."

"We're in what I'd call an adjustment period. Some don't adjust as smoothly as others. I like most of your ideas, and others I'm willing to give a chance. Logan's used to doing things his own way, and that's been fine with me. It works for us."

"He took stock. How can I maintain inventory if I don't know what he took, or what it's for? I need paperwork, Roz."

"I imagine he took the specimens he'd tagged for his

personal use. If he took others, he'll let me know. Which is not the way you do things," she continued before Stella could speak. "I'll talk to him, Stella, but you might have to do some adjusting yourself. You're not in Michigan anymore. I'm going to let you get back to work here."

And she was going back to her plants. They generally gave her less trouble than people.

"Roz? I know I can be an awful pain in the ass, but I really do want to help you grow your business."

"I figured out both those things already."

Alone, Stella sulked for a minute. Then she got her bucket and climbed up the ladder again. The unscheduled meeting had thrown her off schedule.

"I DON'T LIKE HER." LOGAN SAT IN ROZ'S PARLOR with a beer in one hand and a boatload of resentment in the other. "She's bossy, rigid, smug, and shrill." At Roz's raised brows, he shrugged. "Okay, not shrill—so far—but I stand by the rest."

"I do like her. I like her energy and her enthusiasm. And I need someone to handle the details, Logan. I've outgrown myself. I'm just asking that the two of you try to meet somewhere in the middle of things."

"I don't think she has any middle. She's extreme. I don't trust extreme women."

"You trust me."

He brooded into his beer. That was true enough. If he hadn't trusted Roz, he wouldn't have come to work for her, no matter what salary and perks she'd dangled under his nose. "She's going to have us filling out forms in triplicate and documenting how many inches we prune off a damn bush."

"I don't think it'll come to that." Roz propped her feet comfortably on the coffee table and sipped her own beer.

"If you had to go and hire some sort of manager, Roz, why the hell didn't you hire local? Get somebody in who understands how things work around here."

"Because I didn't want a local. I wanted her. When she comes down, we're going to have a nice civilized drink followed by a nice civilized meal. I don't care if the two of you don't like each other, but you will learn how to get along."

"You're the boss."

"That's a fact." She gave him a companionable pat on the thigh. "Harper's coming over, too. I browbeat him into it."

Logan brooded a minute longer. "You really like her?"

"I really do. And I've missed the company of women. Women who aren't silly and annoying, anyway. She's neither. She had a tough break, Logan, losing her man at such a young age. I know what that's like. She hasn't broken under it, or gone brittle. So yes, I like her."

"Then I'll tolerate her, but only for you."

"Sweet talker." With a laugh, Roz leaned over to kiss his cheek.

"Only because I'm crazy about you."

Stella came to the door in time to see Logan take Roz's hand in his, and thought, Oh, shit.

She'd gone head-to-head, argued with, insulted, and complained about her boss's lover.

With a sick dread in her stomach, she nudged her boys forward. She stepped inside, plastered on a smile. "Hope we're not late," she said cheerily. "There was a small homework crisis. Hello, Mr. Kitridge. I'd like you to meet my sons. This is Gavin, and this is Luke."

"How's it going?" They looked like normal kids to him rather than the pod-children he'd expected someone like Stella to produce.

"I have a loose tooth," Luke told him.

"Yeah? Let's have a look, then." Logan set down his beer to take a serious study of the tooth Luke wiggled with his tongue. "Cool. You know, I've got me some pliers in my toolbox. One yank and we'd have that out of there."

At the small horrified sound from behind him, Logan turned to smile thinly at Stella.

"Mr. Kitridge is just joking," Stella told a fascinated Luke. "Your tooth will come out when it's ready."

"When it does, the Tooth Fairy comes, and I get a *buck*."

Logan pursed his lips. "A buck, huh? Good deal."

"It makes blood when it comes out, but I'm not scared."

"Miss Roz? Can we go see David in the kitchen?" Gavin shot a look at his mother. "Mom said we had to ask you."

"Sure. You go right on."

"No sweets," Stella called out as they dashed out.

"Logan, why don't you pour Stella a glass of wine?"

"I'll get it. Don't get up," Stella told him.

He didn't look quite as much like an overbearing jerk, she decided. He cleaned up well enough, and she could see why Roz was attracted. If you went for the *über*virile sort.

"Did you say Harper was coming?" Stella asked her.

"He'll be along." Roz gestured with her beer. "Let's see if we can all play nice. Let's get this business out of the way so we can have an enjoyable meal without ruining our digestion. Stella's in charge of sales and production, of managing the day-to-day business. She and I will, for now anyway, share personnel management while Harper and I head up propagation."

She sipped her beer, waited, though she knew her own power and didn't expect an interruption. "Logan leads the landscaping design, both on- and off-site. As such, he has first choice of stock and is authorized to put in for special orders, or arrange trades or purchases or rentals of necessary equipment, material or specimens for outside designs. The changes Stella has already implemented or proposed—and which have been approved by me—will stay or be put in place. Until such time as I decide they don't work. Or if I just don't like them. Clear so far?"

"Perfectly," Stella said coolly.

Logan shrugged.

"Which means you'll cooperate with each other, do what's necessary to work together in such a way for both of you to function in the areas you oversee. I built In the

Garden from the ground up, and I can run it myself if I have to. But I don't choose to. I choose to have the two of you, and Harper, shoulder the responsibilities you've been given. Squabble all you want. I don't mind squabbles. But get the job done."

She finished off her beer. "Questions? Comments?" After a beat of silence, she rose. "Well, then, let's eat."

five

It was, all things considered, a pleasant evening. Neither of her kids threw any food or made audible gagging noises. Always a plus, in Stella's book. Conversation was polite, even lively—particularly when the boys learned Logan's first name—the same name used by the X-Men's Wolverine.

It was instant hero status, given polish when it was discovered that Logan shared Gavin's obsession with comic books.

The fact that Logan seemed more interested in talking to her sons than her was probably another plus.

"If, you know, the Hulk and Spider-Man ever got into a fight, I think Spider-Man would win."

Logan nodded as he cut into rare roast beef. "Because Spider-Man's quicker, and more agile. But if the Hulk ever caught him, Spidey'd be toast."

Gavin speared a tiny new potato, then held it aloft on his fork like a severed head on a pike. "If he was under the influence of some evil guy, like . . ."

"Maybe Mr. Hyde."

"Yeah! Mr. Hyde, then the Hulk could be *forced* to go after Spider-Man. But I still think Spidey would win."

"That's why he's amazing," Logan agreed, "and the Hulk's incredible. It takes more than muscle to battle evil."

"Yeah, you gotta be smart and brave and stuff."

"Peter Parker's the smartest." Luke emulated his brother with the potato head.

"Bruce Banner's pretty smart, too." Since it made the kids laugh, Harper hoisted a potato, wagged it. "He always manages to get new clothes after he reverts from Hulk form."

"If he was really smart," Harper commented, "he'd figure out a way to make his clothes stretch and expand."

"You scientists," Logan said with a grin for Harper. "Never thinking about the mundane."

"Is the Mundane a supervillain?" Luke wanted to know.

"It means the ordinary," Stella told him. "As in, it's more mundane to eat your potatoes than to play with them, but that's the polite thing to do at the table."

"Oh." Luke smiled at her, an expression somewhere between sweet and wicked, and chomped the potato off the fork. "Okay." After the meal, she used the excuse of the boys' bedtime to retreat upstairs. There were baths to deal with, the usual thousand questions to answer, and all that end-of-day energy to burn off, which included one or both of them running around mostly naked.

Then came her favorite time, when she drew a chair between their beds and read to them while Parker began to snore at her feet. The current pick was *Mystic Horse*, and when she closed the book, she got the expected moans and pleas for just a little more.

"Tomorrow, because now I'm afraid it's time for sloppy kisses."

"Not sloppy kisses." Gavin rolled onto his belly to bury his face in the pillow. "Not that!"

"Yes, and you must succumb." She covered the back of his head, the base of his neck with kisses while he giggled.

"And now, for my second victim." She turned to Luke and rubbed her hands together.

"Wait, wait!" He threw out his hand to ward off the attack. "Do you think my tooth will fall out tomorrow?"

"Let's have another look." She sat on the side of his bed, studying soberly as he wiggled the tooth with his tongue. "I think it just might."

"Can I have a horse?"

"It won't fit under your pillow." When he laughed, she kissed his forehead, his cheeks, and his sweet, sweet mouth.

Rising, she switched off the lamp, leaving them in the glow of the night-light. "Only fun dreams allowed."

"I'm gonna dream I get a horse, because dreams come true sometimes."

"Yes, they do. 'Night now."

She walked back to her room, heard the whispers from bed to bed that were also part of the bedtime ritual.

It had become their ritual, over the last two years. Just the three of them at nighttime, where they had once been four. But it was solid now, and good, she thought, as a few giggles punctuated the whispers.

Somewhere along the line she'd stopped aching every night, every morning, for what had been. And she'd come to treasure what was.

She glanced at her laptop, thought about the work she'd earmarked for the evening. Instead, she went to the terrace doors.

It was still too cool to sit out, but she wanted the air, and the quiet, and the night.

Imagine, just imagine, she was standing outside at night in January. And not freezing. Though the forecasters were calling for more rain, the sky was star-studded and graced with a sliver of moon. In that dim light she could see a camellia in bloom. Flowers in winter—now that was something to add to the plus pile about moving south.

She hugged her elbows and thought of spring, when the air would be warm and garden-scented.

She wanted to be here in the spring, to see it, to be part of the awakening. She wanted to keep her job. She hadn't realized how much she wanted to keep it until Roz's firm, no-nonsense sit-down before dinner.

Less than two weeks, and she was already caught up. Maybe too much caught, she admitted. That was always a problem. Whatever she began, she needed to finish. Stella's religion, her mother called it.

But this was more. She was emotional about the place. A mistake, she knew. She was half in love with the nursery, and with her own vision of how it could be. She wanted to see tables alive with color and green, cascading flowers spilling from hanging baskets that would drop down along the aisles to make arbors. She wanted to see customers browsing and buying, filling the wagons and flatbeds with containers.

And, of course, there was that part of her that wanted to go along with each one of them and show them exactly how everything should be planted. But she could control that.

She could admit she also wanted to see the filing system in place, and the spreadsheets, the weekly inventory logs.

And whether he liked it or not, she intended to visit some of Logan's jobs. To get a feel for that end of the business.

That was supposing he didn't talk Roz into firing her.

He'd gotten slapped back, too, Stella admitted. But he had home-field advantage.

In any case, she wasn't going to be able to work, or relax, or think about anything else until she'd straightened things out.

She would go downstairs, on the pretext of making a cup of tea. If his truck was gone, she'd try to have a minute with Roz.

It was quiet, and she had a sudden sinking feeling that they'd gone up to bed. She didn't want that picture in her head. Tiptoeing into the front parlor, she peeked out the window. Though she didn't see his truck, it occurred to her she didn't know where he'd parked, or what he'd driven in the first place.

She'd leave it for morning. That was best. In the morning, she would ask for a short meeting with Roz and get everything back in place. Better to sleep on it, to plan exactly what to say and how to say it.

Since she was already downstairs, she decided to go ahead and make that tea. Then she would take it upstairs and focus on work. Things would be better when she was focused.

She walked quietly back into the kitchen, and let out a yelp when she saw the dim figure in the shaded light. The figure yelped back, then slapped at the switch beside the stove.

"Just draw and shoot next time," Roz said, slapping a hand to her heart.

"I'm sorry. God, you scared me. I knew David was going into the city tonight and I didn't think anyone was back here."

"Just me. Making some coffee."

"In the dark?"

"Stove light was on. I know my way around. You come down to raid the refrigerator?"

"What? No. No!" She was hardly that comfortable here, in another woman's home. "I was just going to make some tea to take up while I do a little work."

"Go ahead. Unless you want some of this coffee."

"If I drink coffee after dinner, I'm awake all night."

It was awkward, standing here in the quiet house, just the two of them. It wasn't her house, Stella thought, her kitchen, even her quiet. She wasn't a guest, but an employee.

However gracious Roz might be, everything around them belonged to her.

"Did Mr. Kitridge leave?"

"You can call him Logan, Stella. You only sound pissy otherwise."

"Sorry. I don't mean to be." Maybe a little. "We got off

on the wrong foot, that's all, and I . . . oh, thanks," she said when Roz handed her the teakettle. "I realize I shouldn't have complained about him."

She filled the kettle, wishing she'd thought through what she wanted to say. Practiced it a few times.

"Because?" Roz prompted.

"Well, it's hardly constructive for your manager and your landscape designer to start in on each other after one run-in, and less so to whine to you about it."

"Sensible. Mature." Roz leaned back on the counter, waiting for her coffee to brew. Young, she thought. She had to remember that despite some shared experiences, the girl was more than a decade younger than she. And a bit tender yet.

"I try to be both," Stella said, and put the kettle on to boil.

"So did I, once upon a time. Then I decided, screw that. I'm going to start my own business."

Stella pushed back her hair. Who was this woman who was elegant to look at even in the hard lights? Who spoke frank words in that debutante-of-the-southern-aristocracy voice and wore ancient wool socks in lieu of slippers? "I can't get a handle on you. I can't figure you out."

"That's what you do, isn't it? Get handles on things." She shifted to reach up and behind into a cupboard for a coffee mug. "That's a good quality to have in a manager. Might be irritating on a personal level."

"You wouldn't be the first." Stella let out a breath. "And on that personal level, I'd like to add a separate apology. I shouldn't have said those things about Logan to you. First off, because it's bad form to fly off about another employee. And second, I didn't realize you were involved."

"Didn't you?" The moment, Roz decided, called for a cookie. She reached into the jar David kept stocked, pulled out a snickerdoodle. "And you realized it when . . ."

"When we came downstairs—before dinner. I didn't mean to eavesdrop, but I happened to notice . . ."

"Have a cookie."

"I don't really eat sweets after—"

"Have a cookie," Roz insisted and handed one over. "Logan and I are involved. He works for me, though he doesn't quite see it that way." An amused smile brushed over her lips. "It's more a *with me* from his point of view, and I don't mind that. Not as long as the work gets done, the money comes in, and the customers are satisfied. We're also friends. I like him very much. But we don't sleep together. We're not, in any way, romantically involved."

"Oh." This time she huffed out a breath. "Oh. Well, I've used up my own, so I'll have to borrow someone else's foot to stuff in my mouth."

"I'm not insulted, I'm flattered. He's an excellent, specimen. I can't say I've ever thought about him in that way."

"Why?"

Roz poured her coffee while Stella took the sputtering kettle off the burner. "I've got ten years on him."

"And your point would be?"

Roz glanced back, a little flicker of surprise running over her face, just ahead of humor. "You're right. That doesn't, or shouldn't, apply. However, I've been married twice. One was good, very good. One was bad, very bad. I'm not looking for a man right now. Too damn much trouble. Even when it's good, they take a lot of time, effort, and energy. I'm enjoying using all that time, effort, and energy on myself."

"Do you get lonely?"

"Yes. Yes, I do. There was a time I didn't think I'd have the luxury of being lonely. Raising my boys, all the running around, the mayhem, the responsibilities."

She glanced around the kitchen, as if surprised to find it quiet, without the noise and debris generated by young boys. "When I'd raised them—not that you're ever really done, but there's a point where you have to step back—I thought I wanted to share my life, my home, myself with someone. That was a mistake." Though her expression stayed easy and pleasant, her tone went hard as granite. "I corrected it."

"I can't imagine being married again. Even a good marriage is a balancing act, isn't it? Especially when you toss in careers, family."

"I never had all of them at once to juggle. When John was alive, it was home, kids, him. I wrapped my life around them. Only wrapped it tighter when it was just me and the boys. I'm not sorry for doing that," she said after a sip of coffee. "It was the way I wanted things. The business, the career, that started late for me. I admire women who can handle all those balls."

"I think I was good at it." There was a pang at remembering, a sweet little slice in the heart. "It's exhausting work, but I hope I was good at it. Now? I don't think I have the skill for it anymore. Being with someone every day, at the end of it." She shook her head. "I can't see it. I could always picture Kevin and me, all the steps and stages. I can't picture anyone else."

"Maybe he just hasn't come into the viewfinder yet."

Stella lifted a shoulder in a little shrug. "Maybe. But I could picture you and Logan together."

"Really?"

There was such humor, with a bawdy edge to it, that Stella forgot any sense of awkwardness and just laughed. "Not that way. Or I started to, then engaged the impenetrable mind block. I meant you looked good together. So attractive and easy. I thought it was nice. It's nice to have someone you can be easy with."

"And you and Kevin were easy together."

"We were. Sort of flowed on the same current."

"I wondered. You don't wear a wedding ring."

"No." Stella looked at her bare finger. "I took it off about a year ago, when I started dating again. It didn't seem right to wear it when I was with another man. I don't feel married anymore. It was gradual, I guess."

At the half question, Roz nodded. "Yes, I know."

"Somewhere along the line I stopped thinking, What would Kevin say about this. Or, What would Kevin do, or think, or want. So I took off my ring. It was hard. Almost as hard as losing him."

"I took mine off on my fortieth birthday," Roz murmured. "I realized I'd stopped wearing it as a tribute. It had become more of a shield against relationships. So I took it off on that black-letter day," she said with a half smile. "Because we move on, or we fade away."

"I'm too busy to worry about all of this most of the time, and I didn't mean to get into it now. I only wanted to apologize."

"Accepted. I'm going to take my coffee up. I'll see you in the morning."

"All right. Good night."

Feeling better, Stella finished making her tea. She would get a good start in the morning, she decided as she carried it upstairs. She'd get a good chunk of the reorganizing done, she'd talk with Harper and Roz about which cuttings should be added to inventory, *and* she'd find a way to get along with Logan.

She heard the singing, quiet and sad, as she started down the hall. Her heart began to trip, and china rattled on the tray as she picked up her pace. She was all but running by the time she got to the door of her sons' room.

There was no one there, just that same little chill to the air. Even when she set her tea down, searched the closet, under the bed, she found nothing.

She sat on the floor between the beds, waiting for her pulse to level. The dog stirred, then climbed up in her lap to lick her hand.

Stroking him, she stayed there, sitting between her boys while they slept.

ON SUNDAY, SHE WENT TO HER FATHER'S FOR brunch. She was more than happy to be handed a mimosa and ordered out of the kitchen by Jolene.

It was her first full day off since she'd started at In the Garden, and she was scheduled to relax.

With the boys running around the little backyard with Parker, she was free to sit down with her father.

"Tell me everything," he ordered.

"Everything will go straight through brunch, into dinner, and right into breakfast tomorrow."

"Give me the highlights. How do you like Rosalind?"

"I like her a lot. She manages to be straightforward and slippery. I'm never quite sure where I stand with her, but I do like her."

"She's lucky to have you. And being a smart woman, she knows it."

"You might be just a tiny bit biased."

"Just a bit."

He'd always loved her, Stella knew. Even when there had been months between visits. There'd always been phone calls or notes, or surprise presents in the mail.

He'd aged comfortably, she thought now. Whereas her mother waged a bitter and protracted war with the years, Will Dooley had made his truce with them. His red hair was overpowered by the gray now, and his bony frame carried a soft pouch in the middle. There were laugh lines around his eyes and mouth, glasses perched on his nose.

His face was ruddy from the sun. The man loved his gardening and his golf.

"The boys seem happy," he commented.

"They love it there. I can't believe how much I worried about it, then they just slide in like they've lived there all their lives."

"Sweetheart, if you weren't worrying about some such thing, you wouldn't be breathing."

"I hate that you're right about that. Anyway, there are still a few bumps regarding school. It's so hard being the new kids, but they like the house, and all that room. And they're crazy about David. You know David Wentworth?"

"Yeah. You could say he's been part of Roz's household since he was a kid, and now he runs it."

"He's great with the kids. It's a weight off knowing they're with someone they like after school. And I like Harper, though I don't see much of him."

"Boy's always been a loner. Happier with his plants. Good looking," he added.

"He is, Dad, but we'll just stick with discussing leaf-bud cuttings and cleft grafting, okay?"

"Can't blame a father for wanting to see his daughter settled."

"I am settled, for the moment." More, she realized, than she would have believed possible. "At some point, though, I'm going to want my own place. I'm not ready to look yet—too much to do, and I don't want to rock the boat with Roz. But it's on my list. Something in the same school district when the time comes. I don't want the boys to have to change again."

"You'll find what you're after. You always do."

"No point in finding what you're not after. But I've got time. Right now I'm up to my ears in reorganizing. That's probably an exaggeration. I'm up to my ears in organizing. Stock, paperwork, display areas."

"And having the time of your life."

She laughed, stretched out her arms and legs. "I really am. Oh, Dad, it's a terrific place, and there's so much untapped potential yet. I'd like to find somebody who has a real head for sales and customer relations, put him or her in charge of that area while I concentrate on rotating stock, keep ahead of the paperwork, and juggle in some of my ideas. I haven't even touched on the landscape area. Except for a head butt with the guy who runs that."

"Kitridge?" Will smiled. "Met him once or twice, I think. Hear he's a prickly sort."

"I'll say."

"Does good work. Roz wouldn't tolerate less, I can promise you. He did a property for a friend of mine about two years ago. Bought this old house, wanted to concentrate on rehabbing it. Grounds were a holy mess. He hired Kitridge for that. Showplace now. Got written up in a magazine."

"What's his story? Logan's?"

"Local boy. Born and bred. Though it seems to me he moved up north for a while. Got married."

"I didn't realize he's married."

"Was," Will corrected. "Didn't take. Don't know the details. Jo might. She's better at ferreting out and remembering that sort of thing. He's been back here six, eight years. Worked for a big firm out of the city until Roz scooped him up. Jo! What do you know about the Kitridge boy who works for Roz?"

"Logan?" Jolene peeked around the corner. She was wearing an apron that said, JO'S KITCHEN. There was a string of pearls around her neck and fuzzy pink slippers on her feet. "He's sexy."

"I don't think that's what Stella wanted to know."

"Well, she could see that for herself. Got eyes in her head and blood in her veins, doesn't she? His folks moved out to Montana, of all places, two, three years ago."

She cocked a hip, tapped a finger on her cheek as she lined up her data. "Got an older sister lives in Charlotte now. He went out with Marge Peters's girl, Terri, a couple times. You remember Terri, don't you, Will?"

"Can't say as I do."

"'Course you do. She was homecoming and prom queen in her day, then Miss Shelby County. First runner-up for Miss Tennessee. Most agree she missed the crown because her talent wasn't as strong as it could've been. Her voice is a little bit, what you'd call slight, I guess."

As Jo talked, Stella just sat back and enjoyed. Imagine knowing all this, or caring. She doubted she could remember who the homecoming or prom queens were from her own high school days. And here was Jo, casually pumping out the information on events that were surely a decade old.

Had to be a southern thing.

"And Terri? She said Logan was too serious-minded for

her," Jo continued, "but then a turnip would be too serious-minded for that girl."

She turned back into the kitchen, lifting her voice. "He married a Yankee and moved up to Philadelphia or Boston or some place with her. Moved back a couple years later without her. No kids."

She came back with a fresh mimosa for Stella and one for herself. "I heard she liked big-city life and he didn't, so they split up. Probably more to it than that. Always is, but Logan's not one to talk, so information is sketchy. He worked for Fosterly Landscaping for a while. You know, Will, they do mostly commercial stuff. Beautifying office buildings and shopping centers and so on. Word is Roz offered him the moon, most of the stars, and a couple of solar systems to bring him into her operation."

Will winked at his daughter. "Told you she'd have the details."

"And then some."

Jo chuckled, waved a hand. "He bought the old Morris place on the river a couple of years ago. Been fixing it up, or having it fixed up. *And* I heard he was doing a job for Tully Scopes. You don't know Tully, Will, but I'm on the garden committee with his wife, Mary. She'll complain the sky's too blue or the rain's too wet. Never satisfied with anything. You want another Bloody Mary, honey?" she asked Will.

"Can't say as I'd mind."

"So I heard Tully wanted Logan to design some shrubbery, and a garden and so on for this property he wanted to turn over."

Jolene kept on talking as she walked back to the kitchen counter to mix the drink. Stella exchanged a mile-wide grin with her father.

"And every blessed day, Tully was down there complaining, or asking for changes, or saying this, that, or the other. Until Logan told him to screw himself sideways, or words to that effect."

"So much for customer relations," Stella declared.

"Walked off the job, too," Jolene continued. "Wouldn't set foot on the property again or have any of his crew plant a daisy until Tully agreed to stay away. That what you wanted to know?"

"That pretty much covers it," Stella said and toasted Jolene with her mimosa.

"Good. Just about ready here. Why don't you go on and call the boys?"

WITH THE INFORMATION FROM JOLENE ENTERED INTO her mental files, Stella formulated a plan. Bright and early Monday morning, armed with her map and a set of MapQuest directions, she set out for the job site Logan had scheduled.

Or, she corrected, the job Roz thought he had earmarked for that morning.

She was going to be insanely pleasant, cooperative, and flexible. Until he saw things her way.

She cruised the neighborhood that skirted the city proper. Charming old houses, closer to each other than to the road. Lovely sloping lawns. Gorgeous old trees. Oak and maple that would leaf and shade, dogwood and Bradford pear that would celebrate spring with blooms. Of course, it wouldn't be the south without plenty of magnolias along with enormous azaleas and rhododendrons.

She tried to picture herself there, with her boys, living in one of those gracious homes, with her lovely yard to tend. Yes, she could see that, could see them happy in such a place, cozy with the neighbors, organizing dinner parties, play dates, cookouts.

Out of her price range, though. Even with the money she'd saved, the capital from the sale of the house in Michigan, she doubted she could afford real estate here. Besides, it would mean changing schools again for the boys, and she would have to spend time commuting to work.

Still, it made a sweet, if brief, fantasy.

She spotted Logan's truck and a second pickup outside a two-story brick house.

She could see immediately it wasn't as well kept as most of its neighbors. The front lawn was patchy. The foundation plantings desperately needed shaping, and what had been flower beds looked either overgrown or stone dead.

She heard the buzz of chain saws and country music playing too loud as she walked around the side of the house. Ivy was growing madly here, crawling its way up the brick. Should be stripped off, she thought. That maple needs to come down, before it falls down, and that fence line's covered with brambles, overrun with honeysuckle.

In the back, she spotted Logan, harnessed halfway up a dead oak. Wielding the chain saw, he speared through branches. It was cool, but the sun and the labor had a dew of sweat on his face, and a line of it darkening the back of his shirt.

Okay, so he was sexy. Any well-built man doing manual labor looked sexy. Add some sort of dangerous tool to the mix, and the image went straight to the lust bars and played a primal tune.

But sexy, she reminded herself, wasn't the point.

His work and their working dynamics were the point. She stood well out of the way while he worked, and scanned the rest of the backyard.

The space might have been lovely once, but now it was neglected, weedy, overgrown with trash trees and dying shrubs. A sagging garden shed tilted in the far corner of a fence smothered in vines.

Nearly a quarter of an acre, she estimated as she watched a huge black man drag lopped branches toward a short, skinny white man working a splitter. Nearby a burly-looking mulcher waited its turn to chew up the rest.

The beauty here wasn't lost, Stella decided. It was just buried.

It needed vision to bring it to life again.

Since the black man caught her eye, Stella wandered over to the ground crew.

"Help you, Miss?"

She extended her hand and a smile. "I'm Stella Rothchild, Ms. Harper's manager."

"'Meetcha. I'm Sam, this here is Dick."

The little guy had the fresh, freckled face of a twelve-year-old, with a scraggly goatee that looked as if it might have grown there by mistake. "Heard about you." He sent an eyebrow-wiggling grin toward his coworker.

"Really?" She kept her tone friendly, though her teeth came together tight in the smile. "I thought it would be helpful if I dropped by a couple of the jobs, looked at the work." She scanned the yard again, deliberately keeping her gaze below Logan's perch in the tree. "You've certainly got yours cut out for you with this."

"Got a mess of clearing to do," Sam agreed. Covered with work gloves, his enormous hands settled on his hips. "Seen worse, though."

"Is there a projection on man-hours?"

"Pro*jec*tion." Dick sniggered and elbowed Sam.

From his great height, Sam sent down a pitying look.

"You want to know about the plans and, uh, projections," he said, "you need to talk to the boss. He's got all that worked up."

"All right, then. Thanks. I'll let you get back to work."

Walking away, Stella took the little camera out of her bag and began to take what she thought of as "before" pictures.

HE KNEW SHE WAS THERE. STANDING DOWN THERE all pressed and tidy with her wild hair pulled back and shaded glasses hiding her big blue eyes.

He'd wondered when she would come nag him on a job, as it appeared to him she was a woman born to nag. At least she had the sense not to interrupt.

Then again, she seemed to be nothing *but* sense.

Maybe she'd surprise him. He liked surprises, and he'd gotten one when he met her kids. He'd expected to see a couple of polite little robots. The sort that looked to their domineering mother before saying a word. Instead he'd found them normal, interesting, funny kids. Surely it took some imagination to manage two active boys.

Maybe she was only a pain in the ass when it came to work.

Well, he grinned a little as he cut through a branch. So was he.

He let her wait while he finished. It took him another thirty minutes, during which he largely ignored her. Though he did see her take a camera—Jesus—then a notebook out of her purse.

He also noticed she'd gone over to speak to his men and that Dick sent occasional glances in Stella's direction.

Dick was a social moron, Logan thought, particularly when it came to women. But he was a tireless worker, and he would take on the filthiest job with a blissful and idiotic grin. Sam, who had more common sense in his big toe than Dick had in his entire skinny body, was, thank God, a tolerant and patient man.

They went back to high school, and that was the sort of thing that set well with Logan. The continuity of it, and the fact that because they'd known each other around twenty years, they didn't have to gab all the damn time to make themselves understood.

Explaining things half a dozen times just tried his patience. Which he had no problem admitting he had in short supply to begin with.

Between the three of them, they did good work, often exceptional work. And with Sam's brawn and Dick's energy, he rarely had to take on any more laborers.

Which suited him. He preferred small crews to large. It was more personal that way, at least from his point of view. And in Logan's point of view, every job he took was personal.

It was his vision, his sweat, his blood that went into the land. And his name that stood for what he created with it.

The Yankee could harp about forms and systemic bullshit all she wanted. The land didn't give a rat's ass about that. And neither did he.

He called out a warning to his men, then topped the old, dead oak. When he shimmied down, he unhooked his harness and grabbed a bottle of water. He drank half of it down without taking a breath.

"Mr. . . ." No, friendly, Stella remembered. She boosted up her smile, and started over. "Nice job. I didn't realize you did the tree work yourself."

"Depends. Nothing tricky to this one. Out for a drive?"

"No, though I did enjoy looking at the neighborhood. It's beautiful." She looked around the yard, gestured to encompass it. "This must have been, too, once. What happened?"

"Couple lived here fifty years. He died a while back. She couldn't handle the place on her own, and none of their kids still live close by. She got sick, place got rundown. She got sicker. Kids finally got her out and into a nursing home."

"That's hard. It's sad."

"Yeah, a lot of life is. They sold the place. New owners got a bargain and want the grounds done up. We're doing them up."

"What've you got in mind?"

He took another slug from the water bottle. She noticed the mulcher had stopped grinding, and after Logan sent a long, narrowed look over her shoulder, it got going again.

"I've got a lot of things in mind."

"Dealing with this job, specifically?"

"Why?"

"Because it'll help me do my job if I know more about yours. Obviously you're taking out the oak and I assume the maple out front."

"Yeah. Okay, here's the deal. We clear everything out that can't or shouldn't be saved. New sod, new fencing. We knock down the old shed, replace it. New owners want lots of color. So we shape up the azaleas, put a weeping cherry out front, replacing the maple. Lilac over there, and a magnolia on that side. Plot of peonies on that side, rambling roses along the back fence. See they got that rough little hill toward the back there, on the right? Instead of leveling it, we'll plant it."

He outlined the rest of it quickly, rolling out Latin terms and common names, taking long slugs from his water bottle, gesturing.

He could see it, he always could—the finished land. The small details, the big ones, fit together into one attractive whole.

Just as he could see the work that would go into each and every step, as he could look forward to the process nearly as much as the finished job.

He liked having his hands in the dirt. How else could you respect the landscape or the changes you made in it? And as he spoke he glanced down at her hands. Smirked a little at her tidy fingernails with their coat of glossy pink polish.

Paper pusher, he thought. Probably didn't know crabgrass from sumac.

Because he wanted to give her and her clipboard the full treatment and get her off his ass, he switched to the house and talked about the patio they intended to build and the plantings he'd use to accent it.

When he figured he'd done more talking than he normally did in a week, he finished off the water. Shrugged. He didn't expect her to follow everything he'd said, but she couldn't complain that he hadn't cooperated.

"It's wonderful. What about the bed running on the south side out front?"

He frowned a little. "We'll rip out the ivy, then the clients want to try their hand at that themselves."

"Even better. You've got more of an investment if you dig some yourself."

Because he agreed, he said nothing and only jingled some change in his pocket.

"Except I'd rather see winter creeper than yews around the shed. The variegated leaves would show off well, as would the less uniform shape."

"Maybe."

"Do you work from a landscape blueprint or out of your head?"

"Depends."

Should I pull all his teeth at once, or one at a time, she thought, but maintained the smile. "It's just that I'd like to see one of your designs, on paper, at some point. Which leads me to a thought I'd had."

"Bet you got lots of them."

"My boss told me to play nice," she said, coolly now. "How about you?"

He moved his shoulder again. "Just saying."

"My thought was, with some of the reorganizing and transferring I'm doing, I could cull out some office space for you at the center."

He gave her the same look he'd sent his men over her shoulder. A lesser woman, Stella told herself, would wither under it. "I don't work in a frigging office."

"I'm not suggesting that you spend all your time there, just that you'd have a place to deal with your paperwork, make your phone calls, keep your files."

"That's what my truck's for."

"Are you trying to be difficult?"

"Nope. I can do it without any effort at all. How about you?"

"You don't want the office, fine. Forget the office."

"I already have."

"Dandy. But *I* need an office. *I* need to know exactly what stock and equipment, what materials you'll need for this job." She yanked out her notebook again. "One red maple, one magnolia. Which variety of magnolia?"

"Southern. *Grandiflora gloriosa*."

"Good choice for the location. One weeping cherry," she continued, and to his surprise and reluctant admiration, she ran down the entire plan he'd tossed out at her.

Okay, Red, he thought. Maybe you know a thing or two about the horticulture end of things after all.

"Yews or winter creeper?"

He glanced back at the shed, tried both out in his head. Damn if he didn't think she was right, but he didn't see why he had to say so right off. "I'll let you know."

"Do, and I'll want the exact number and specimen type of other stock as you take them."

"I'd be able to find you . . . in your office?"

"Just find me." She turned around, started to march off.

"Hey, Stella."

When she glanced back, he grinned. "Always wanted to say that."

Her eyes lit, and she snapped her head around again and kept going.

"Okay, okay. Jesus. Just a little humor." He strode after her. "Don't go away mad."

"Just go away?"

"Yeah, but there's no point in us being pissed at each other. I don't mind being pissed as a rule."

"I never would've guessed."

"But there's no point, right at the moment." As if he'd just remembered he had them on, he tugged off his work gloves, stuck them finger-first in his back pocket. "I'm doing my job, you're doing yours. Roz thinks she needs you, and I set a lot of store by Roz."

"So do I."

"I get that. Let's try to stay out from under each other's skin, otherwise we're just going to give each other a rash."

She inclined her head, lifted her eyebrows. "Is this you being agreeable?"

"Pretty much, yeah. I'm being agreeable so we can both do what Roz pays us to do. And because your kid has a copy of *Spider-Man* Number 121. If you're mad, you won't let him show it to me."

Now she tipped down her sunglasses, peered at him over the tops. "This isn't you being charming, is it?"

"No, this is me being sincere. I really want to see that issue, firsthand. If I was being charming, I guarantee you'd be in a puddle at my feet. It's a terrible power I have over women, and I try to use it sparingly."

"I just bet."

But she was smiling as she got into her car.

SIX

HAYLEY PHILLIPS WAS RIDING ON FUMES AND A DYING transmission. The radio still worked, thank God, and she had it cranked up with the Dixie Chicks blasting out. It kept her energy flowing.

Everything she owned was jammed into the Pontiac Grandville, which was older than she was and a lot more temperamental. Not that she had much at this point. She'd sold everything that could be sold. No point in being sentimental. Money took you a lot more miles than sentiment.

She wasn't destitute. What she'd banked would get her through the rough spots, and if there were more rough spots than she anticipated, she'd earn more. She wasn't aimless. She knew just where she was going. She just didn't know what would happen when she got there.

But that was fine. If you knew everything, you'd never be surprised.

Maybe she was tired, and maybe she'd pushed the rattling old car farther than it wanted to go that day. But if she and it could just hang on a few more miles, they'd get a break.

She didn't expect to get tossed out on her ear. But, well, if she was, she'd just do what needed to be done next.

She liked the look of the area, especially since she'd skirted around the tangle of highways that surrounded Memphis. On this north edge beyond the city, the land rolled a bit, and she'd seen snatches of the river and the steep bluffs that fell toward it. There were pretty houses—the neat spread of the suburbs that fanned out from the city limits, and now the bigger, richer ones. There were plenty of big old trees, and despite some walls of stone or brick, it *felt* friendly.

She sure could use a friend.

When she saw the sign for In the Garden, she slowed. She was afraid to stop, afraid the old Pontiac would just heave up and die if she did. But she slowed enough to get a look at the main buildings, the space in the security lights.

Then she took a lot of slow breaths as she kept driving. Nearly there. She'd planned out what she would say, but she kept changing her mind. Every new approach gave her a dozen different scenes to play out in her head. It had passed the time, but it hadn't gelled for her.

Maybe some could say that changing her mind was part of her problem. But she didn't think so. If you never changed your mind, what was the point of having one? It seemed to Hayley she'd known too many people who were stuck with one way of thinking, and how could that be using the brain God gave you?

As she headed toward the drive, the car began to buck and sputter.

"Come on, come on. Just a little more. If I'd been paying attention I'd've got you gas at the last place."

Then it conked on her, half in, half out of the entrance between the brick pillars.

She gave the wheel a testy little slap, but it was half-hearted. Nobody's fault but her own, after all. And maybe it was a good thing. Tougher to kick her out if her car was out of gas, and blocking the way.

She opened her purse, took out a brush to tidy her hair. After considerable experimentation, she'd settled back on her own oak-bark brown. At least for now. She was glad she'd gotten it cut and styled before she'd headed out. She liked the longish sweep of side bangs and the careless look of the straight bob with its varying lengths.

It made her look easy, breezy. Confident.

She put on lipstick, powdered off the shine.

"Okay. Let's get going."

She climbed out, hooked her purse over her shoulder, then started the walk up the long drive. It took money—old or new—to plant a house so far from the road. The one she'd grown up in had been so close, people driving by could practically reach out and shake her hand.

But she didn't mind that. It had been a nice house. A good house, and part of her had been sorry to sell it. But that little house outside Little Rock was the past. She was heading toward the future.

Halfway up the drive, she stopped. Blinked. This wasn't just a house, she decided as her jaw dropped. It was a mansion. The sheer size of it was one thing—she'd seen big-ass houses before, but nothing like this. This was the most beautiful house she'd ever laid eyes on outside of a magazine. It was Tara and Manderley all in one. Graceful and *female*, and strong.

Lights gleamed against windows, others flooded the lawn. As if it were welcoming her. Wouldn't that be nice?

Even if it wasn't, even if they booted her out again, she'd had the chance to see it. That alone was worth the trip.

She walked on, smelling the evening, the pine and woodsmoke.

She crossed her fingers on the strap of her purse for luck and walked straight up to the ground-level doors.

Lifting one of the brass knockers, she gave three firm raps.

Inside, Stella came down the steps with Parker. It was her turn to walk him. She called out, "I'll get it."

Parker was already barking as she opened the door.

She saw a girl with straight, fashionably ragged brown hair, a sharply angled face dominated by huge eyes the color of a robin's egg. She smiled, showing a bit of an overbite, and bent down to pet Parker when he sniffed at her shoes.

She said, "Hi."

"Hi." Where the hell had she come from? Stella wondered. There was no car parked outside.

The girl looked to be about twelve. And very pregnant.

"I'm looking for Rosalind Ashby. Rosalind Harper Ashby," she corrected. "Is she home?"

"Yes. She's upstairs. Come in."

"Thanks. I'm Hayley." She held out a hand. "Hayley Phillips. Mrs. Ashby and I are cousins, in a complicated southern sort of way."

"Stella Rothchild. Why don't you come in, sit down. I'll go find Roz."

"That'd be great." Swiveling her head back and forth, Hayley tried to see everything as Stella led her into the parlor. "Wow. You've just got to say wow."

"I did the first time I saw it. Do you want anything? Something to drink?"

"I'm okay. I should probably wait until . . ." She stayed on her feet, wandered to the fireplace. It was like something on a television show, or the movies. "Do you work in the house? Are you, like, the housekeeper?"

"No. I work at Roz's nursery. I'm the manager. I'll just go get Roz. You should sit down."

"It's okay." Hayley rubbed her pregnant belly. "We've been sitting."

"Be right back." With Parker in tow, Stella dashed off.

She hurried up the stairs, turned into Roz's wing. She'd only been in there once, when David had taken her on the grand tour, but she followed the sounds of the television and found Roz in her sitting room.

There was an old black-and-white movie on TV. Not that Roz was watching. She sat at an antique secretary, wearing baggy jeans and a sweatshirt as she sketched on a pad. Her feet were bare, and to Stella's surprise, her toenails were painted a bright candy pink.

She knocked on the doorjamb.

"Hmm? Oh, Stella, good. I was just sketching out an idea I had for a cutting garden along the northwest side of the nursery. Thought it might inspire customers. Come take a look."

"I'd love to, but there's someone downstairs to see you. Hayley Phillips. She says she's your cousin."

"Hayley?" Roz frowned. "I don't have a cousin Hayley. Do I?"

"She's young. Looks like a teenager. Pretty. Brown hair, blue eyes, taller than me. She's pregnant."

"Well, for God's sake." Roz rubbed the back of her neck. "Phillips. Phillips. My first husband's grandmother's sister—or maybe it was cousin—married a Phillips. I think."

"Well, she did say you were cousins in a complicated southern sort of way."

"Phillips." She closed her eyes, tapped a finger in the center of her forehead as if to wake up memory. "She must be Wayne Phillips's girl. He died last year. Well, I'd better go see what this is about."

She got up. "Your boys settled down for the night?"

"Yes, just."

"Then come on with me."

"Don't you think you should—"

"You've got a good level head. So come on, bring it with you."

Stella scooped Parker up and, hoping his bladder would hold, went downstairs with Roz.

Hayley turned as they came in. "I think this is the most completely awesome room. It makes you feel cozy and special just to be in it. I'm Hayley. I'm Wayne Phillips's daughter. My daddy was a connection of your first husband's, on his mother's side. You sent me a very nice note of condolence when he passed last year."

"I remember. I met him once. I liked him."

"So did I. I'm sorry to come this way, without calling or asking, and I didn't mean to get here so late. I had some car trouble earlier."

"That's all right. Sit down, Hayley. How far along are you?"

"Heading toward six months. The baby's due end of May. I should apologize, too, because my car ran out of gas right at the front of your driveway."

"We can take care of that. Are you hungry, Hayley? Would you like a little something to eat?"

"No, ma'am, I'm fine. I stopped to eat earlier. Forgot to feed the car. I have money. I don't want you to think I'm broke or here for a handout."

"Good to know. We should have tea, then. It's a cool night. Hot tea would be good."

"If it's not too much trouble. And if you've got decaffeinated." She stroked her belly. "Hardest thing about being pregnant's been giving up caffeine."

"I'll take care of it. Won't be long."

"Thanks, Stella." Roz turned back to Hayley as Stella went out. "So, did you drive all the way from . . . Little Rock, isn't it?"

"I did. I like to drive. Like to better when the car's not acting up, but you have to do what you have to do." She cleared her throat. "I hope you've been well, Cousin Rosalind."

"I have been, very well. And you? Are you and the baby doing well?"

"We're doing great. Healthy as horses, so the doctor said. And I feel just fine. Feel like I'm getting big as a house, but I don't mind that, or not so much. It's kind of interesting. Um, your children, your sons? They're doing fine?"

"Yes, they are. Grown now. Harper, that's my oldest, lives here in the guest house. He works with me at the nursery."

"I saw it—the nursery—when I was driving in." Hayley

caught herself rubbing her hands on the thighs of her jeans and made herself stop. "It looks so big, bigger than I expected. You must be proud."

"I am. What do you do back in Little Rock?"

"I worked in a bookstore, was helping manage it by the time I left. A small independent bookstore and coffee shop."

"Managed? At your age?"

"I'm twenty-four. I know I don't look it," she said with a hint of a smile. "I don't mind that, either. But I can show you my driver's license. I went to college, on partial scholarship. I've got a good brain. I worked summers there through high school and college. I got the job initially because my daddy was friends with the owner. But I earned it after."

"You said managed. You don't work there now."

"No." She was listening, Hayley thought. She was asking the right questions. That was something. "I resigned a couple of weeks ago. But I have a letter of recommendation from the owner. I'd decided to leave Little Rock."

"It seems a difficult time to leave home, and a job you're secure in."

"It seemed like the right time to me." She looked over as Stella wheeled in a tea cart. "Now *that* is just like the movies. I know saying that makes me sound like a hick or something, but I can't help it."

Stella laughed. "I was thinking exactly the same as I loaded it up. I made chamomile."

"Thanks. Stella, Hayley was just telling me she's left her home and her job. I'm hoping she's going to tell us why she thinks this was the right time to make a couple of drastic moves."

"Not drastic," Hayley corrected. "Just big. And I made them because of the baby. Well, because of both of us. You've probably figured out I'm not married."

"Your family isn't supportive?" Stella asked.

"My mother took off when I was about five. You may not remember that," she said to Roz. "Or you were too polite to mention it. My daddy died last year. I've got aunts and uncles, a pair of grandmothers left, and cousins. Some are still in the Little Rock area. Opinion is . . . mixed about my current situation. Thanks," she added after Roz had poured out and offered her a cup.

"Well, the thing is, I was awfully sad when Daddy passed. He got hit by a car, crossing the street. Just one of those accidents that you can never understand and that, well, just don't seem right. I didn't have time to prepare for it. I guess you never do. But he was just gone, in a minute."

She drank tea and felt it soothe her right down to the bones she hadn't realized were so tired. "I was sad, and mad and lonely. And there was this guy. It wasn't a one-night stand or anything like that. We liked each other. He used to come in the bookstore, flirt with me. I used to flirt back. When I was alone, he was comforting. He was sweet. Anyway, one thing led to another. He's a law student. Then he went back to school, and a few weeks later, I found out I was pregnant. I didn't know what I was going to do. How I was going to tell him. Or anybody. I put it off for a few more weeks. I didn't know what I was going to do."

"And when you did?"

"I thought I should tell him face-to-face. He hadn't been coming into the store like he used to. So I went by the college to look him up. Turned out he'd fallen in love with this girl. He was a little embarrassed to tell me, seeing as we'd been sleeping together. But it wasn't like we'd made each other any promises, or been in love or anything. We'd just liked each other, that's all. And when he talked about this other girl, he got all lit up. You could just see how crazy he was about her. So I didn't tell him about the baby."

She hesitated, then took one of the cookies Stella had arranged on a plate. "I can't resist sweets. After I'd thought about it, I didn't see how telling him would do any of us any good."

"That was a very hard decision," Roz told her.

"I don't know that it was. I don't know what I expected

him to do when I went to tell him, except I thought he had a right to know. I didn't want to marry him or anything. I wasn't even sure, back that far, that I was going to keep the baby."

She nibbled on the cookie while she rubbed a hand gently over the mound of her belly. "I guess that's one of the reasons I went out there, to talk to him. Not just to tell him about it, but to see what he thought we should do. But sitting with him, listening to him go on about this girl—"

She stopped, shook her head. "I needed to decide what to do about it. All telling him would've done was made him feel bad, or resentful or scared. Mess up his life when all he'd really tried to do was help me through a bad time."

"And that left you alone," Stella pointed out.

"If I'd told him, I still would've been alone. The thing is, when I decided I'd keep the baby, I thought about telling him again, and asked some people how he was doing. He was still with that girl, and they were talking about getting married, so I think I did the right thing. Still, once I started to show, there was a lot of gossip and questions, a lot of looks and whispers. And I thought, What we need is a fresh start. So I sold the house and just about everything in it. And here I am."

"Looking for that fresh start," Roz concluded.

"I'm looking for a job." She paused, moistened her lips. "I know how to work. I also know a lot of people would step back from hiring a woman nearly six months along. Family, even distant, through-marriage sort of family, might be a little more obliging."

She cleared her throat when Roz said nothing. "I studied literature and business in college. I graduated with honors. I've got a solid employment record. I've got money—not a lot. My partial scholarship didn't cover everything, and my daddy was a teacher, so he didn't make much. But I've got enough to take care of myself, to pay rent, buy food, pay for this baby. I need a job, any kind of a job for now. You've got your business, you've got this house. It takes a lot of people to help run those. I'm asking for a chance to be one of them."

"Know anything about plants, about gardening?"

"We put in flower beds every year. Daddy and I split the yard work. And what I don't know, I can learn. I learn quick."

"Wouldn't you rather work in a bookstore? Hayley managed an independent bookstore back home," Roz told Stella.

"You don't own a bookstore," Hayley pointed out. "I'll work without pay for two weeks."

"Someone works for me, she gets paid. I'll be hiring the seasonal help in a few weeks. In the meantime . . . Stella, can you use her?"

"Ah . . ." Was she supposed to look at that young face and bulging belly and say no? "What were your responsibilities as manager?"

"I wasn't, like, officially the manager. But that's what I did, when you come down to it. It was a small operation, so I did some of everything. Inventory, buying, customer relations, scheduling, sales, advertising. Just the bookstore end of it. There was a separate staff for the coffee shop."

"What would you say were your strengths?"

She had to take a breath, calm her nerves. She knew it was vital to be clear and concise. And just as vital to her pride not to beg. "Customer relations, which keyed into sales. I'm good with people, and I don't mind taking the extra time you need to take to make sure they get what they want. If your customers are happy, they come back, and they buy. You take the extra steps, personalize service, you get customer loyalty."

Stella nodded. "And your weaknesses?"

"The buying," she said without hesitation. "I'd just want to buy everything if it was up to me. I had to keep reminding myself whose money I was spending. But sometimes I didn't hear myself."

"We're in the process of reorganizing, and some

expanding. I could use some help getting the new system in place. There's still a lot of computer inputting—some of it very tedious—to deal with."

"I can handle a keyboard. PC and Mac."

"We'll go for the two weeks," Roz decided. "You'll get paid, but we'll consider the two weeks a trial balloon for all of us. If it doesn't work out, I'll do what I can to help you find another job."

"Can't say fairer than that. Thanks, Cousin Rosalind."

"Just Roz. We've got some gas out in the shed. I'll go get it, and we'll get your car up here so you can get your things in."

"In? In here?" Shaking her head, Hayley set her cup aside. "I said I wasn't after a handout. I appreciate the job, the chance at the job. I don't expect you to put me up."

"Family, even distant-through-marriage family, is welcome here. And it'll give us all a chance to get to know each other, to see if we're going to suit."

"You live here?" Hayley asked Stella.

"Yes. And my boys—eight and six. They're upstairs asleep."

"Are we cousins?"

"No."

"I'll get the gas." Roz got to her feet and started out.

"I'll pay rent." Hayley rose as well, instinctively laying a hand on her belly. "I pay my way."

"We'll adjust your salary to compensate for it."

When she was alone with Stella, Hayley let out a long, slow breath. "I thought she'd be older. And scarier. Though I bet she can be plenty scary when she needs to. You can't have what she has, and keep it, grow it, without knowing how to be scary."

"You're right. I can be scary, too, when it comes to work."

"I'll remember. Ah, you're from up north?"

"Yes. Michigan."

"That's a long way. Is it just you and your boys?"

"My husband died about two and a half years ago."

"That's hard. It's hard to lose somebody you love. I guess all three of us know about that. I think it can make *you* hard if you don't have something, someone else to love. I've got the baby."

"Do you know if it's a boy or a girl?"

"No. Baby had its back turned during the sonogram." She started to chew on her thumbnail, then tucked the thumb in her fist and lowered it. "I guess I should go out, take the gas Roz is getting."

"I'll go with you. We'll take care of it together."

IN AN HOUR THEY HAD HAYLEY SETTLED IN ONE OF the guest rooms in the west wing. She knew she gawked. She knew she babbled. But she'd never seen a more beautiful room, had never expected to be in one. Much less to be able to call it her own, even temporarily.

She put away her things, running her fingers over the gleaming wood of the bureau, the armoire, the etched-glass lampshades, the carving of the headboard.

She would earn this. That was a promise she made to herself, and her child, as she indulged in a long, warm bath. She would earn the chance she'd been given and would pay Roz back in labor and in loyalty.

She was good at both.

She dried off, then rubbed oil over her belly, her breasts. She wasn't afraid of childbirth—she knew how to work hard toward a goal. But she was really hoping she could avoid stretch marks.

She felt a little chill and slipped hurriedly into her nightshirt. Just at the edge of the mirror, just at the corner of her vision, she caught a shadow, a movement.

Rubbing her arms warm, she stepped through to the bedroom. There was nothing, and the door was closed, as she'd left it.

Dog-tired, she told herself and rubbed her eyes. It had been a long trip from the past to the verge of the future.

She took one of the books she'd had in her suitcase—the

rest, ones she hadn't been able to bring herself to sell, were still packed in the trunk of her car—and slipped into bed.

She opened it to where she'd left it bookmarked, prepared to settle herself down, as she did most nights, with an hour of reading.

And was asleep with the light burning before she'd finished the first page.

AT ROZ'S REQUEST, STELLA ONCE AGAIN WENT INTO her sitting room and sat. Roz poured them each a glass of wine.

"Honest impression?" she asked.

"Young, bright, proud. Honest. She could have spun us a sob story about being betrayed by the baby's father, begged for a place to stay, used her pregnancy as an excuse for all manner of things. Instead she took responsibility and asked to work. I'll still check her references."

"Of course. She seemed fearless about the baby."

"It's after you have them you learn to be afraid of everything."

"Isn't that the truth?" Roz scooped her fingers through her hair twice. "I'll make a few calls, find out a little more about that part of the Ashby family. I honestly don't remember very well. We never had much contact, even when he was alive. I do remember the scandal when the wife took off, left him with the baby. From the impression she made on me, and you, apparently he managed very well."

"Her managerial experience could be a real asset."

"Another manager." Roz, in a gesture Stella took as only half mocking, cast her eyes to heaven. "Pray for me."

seven

It didn't take two weeks. After two days, Stella decided Hayley was going to be the answer to her personal prayer. Here was someone with youth, energy, and enthusiasm who understood and appreciated efficiency in the workplace.

She knew how to read and generate spreadsheets, understood instructions after one telling, and respected color codes. If she was half as good relating to customers as she was with filing systems, she would be a jewel.

When it came to plants, she didn't know much more than the basic this is a geranium, and this is a pansy. But she could be taught.

Stella was already prepared to beg Roz to offer Hayley part-time work when May got closer.

"Hayley?" Stella poked her head in the now efficient and tidy office. "Why don't you come out with me? We've got nearly an hour before we open. We'll have a lesson on shade plants in Greenhouse Number Three."

"Cool. We're input through the H's in perennials. I don't know what half of them are, but I'm doing some reading up at night. I didn't know sunflowers were called Helia . . . wait. Helianthus."

"It's more that Helianthus are called sunflowers. The perennial ones can be divided in spring, or propagated by seeds—in the spring—or cuttings in late spring. Seeds from annual Helianthus can be harvested—from that big brown eye—in late summer or early fall. Though the cultivars hybridize freely, they may not come true from the seeds collected. And I'm lecturing."

"That's okay. I grew up with a teacher. I like to learn."

As they passed through the counter area, Hayley glanced out the window. "Truck just pulled in over by the . . . what do y'all call them? Pavers," she said before Stella could answer. "And, mmmm, just *look* at what's getting out of that truck. Mister tall, dark, and totally *built.* Who's the hunk?"

Struggling not to frown, Stella lifted a shoulder in a shrug. "That would be Logan Kitridge, Roz's landscape designer. I suppose he does score fairly high on the hunk-o-meter."

"Rings my bell." At Stella's expression, Hayley pressed a hand to her belly and laughed. "I'm pregnant. Still have all working parts, though. And just because I'm not looking for a man doesn't mean I don't want to look at one. Especially when he's yummy. He really is all tough and broody-looking, isn't he? What is it about tough, broody-looking men that gives you that tickle down in the belly?"

"I couldn't say. What's he doing over there?"

"Looks like he's loading pavers. If it wasn't so cool, he'd pull off that jacket. Bet we'd get a real muscle show. God, I do love my eye candy."

"That sort'll give you cavities," Stella mumbled. "He's not scheduled for pavers. He hasn't put in the order for pavers. Damn it!"

Hayley's eyebrows shot up as Stella stomped to the door and slammed out. Then she pressed her nose to the window, prepared to watch the show.

"Excuse me?"

"Uh-huh?" Hayley's answer was absent as she tried to get a better look outside. Then she popped back from the window, remembering spying was one thing, getting caught at it another. She turned, put on an innocent smile. And decided she'd gotten a double serving of eye candy.

This one wasn't big and broody, but sort of lanky and dreamy. And hot damn. It took an extra beat for her brain to engage, but she was quick.

"Hey! You must be Harper. You look just like your mama. I didn't get a chance to meet you yet, 'cause you never seemed to be around wherever I was around. Or whenever. I'm Hayley. Cousin Hayley from Little Rock? Maybe your mama told you I was working here now."

"Yeah. Yeah." He couldn't think of anything else. Could barely think at all. He felt lightning-struck and stupid.

"Do you just *love* working here? I do already. There's so much of everything, and the customers are so friendly. And Stella, she's just amazing, that's all. Your mama's like, I don't know, a goddess, for giving me a chance this way."

"Yeah." He winced. Could he *be* any more lame? "They're great. It's great." Apparently he could. And damn it, he was good with women. Usually. But one look at this one had given him some sort of concussion. "You, ah, do you need anything?"

"No." She gave him a puzzled smile. "I thought you did."

"I need something? What?"

"I don't know." She laid a hand on the fascinating mound of her belly and laughed, all throaty and free. "You're the one who came in."

"Right. Right. No, nothing. Now. Later. I've got to get back." Outside, in the air, where he should be able to breathe again.

"It was nice meeting you, Harper."

"You, too." He glanced back as he retreated and saw she was already back at the window.

* * *

OUTSIDE, STELLA SPED ACROSS THE PARKING AREA. She called out twice, and the second time got a quick glance and an absent wave. Building up steam as she went, she pumped it out the minute she reached the stacks of pavers.

"What do you think you're doing?"

"Playing tennis. What does it look like I'm doing?"

"It looks like you're taking material you haven't ordered, that you haven't been authorized to take."

"Really?" He hauled up another stack. "No wonder my backhand is rusty." The truck shuddered as he loaded. "Hey."

Much to her amazement, he leaned toward her, sniffed. "Different shampoo. Nice."

"Stop smelling me." She waved him away by flapping a hand at his chin as she stepped back.

"I can't help it. You're standing right there. I have a nose."

"I need the paperwork on this material."

"Yeah, yeah, yeah. Fine, fine, fine. I'll come in and take care of it after I'm loaded."

"You're supposed to take care of it *before* you load."

He turned, aimed a hot look with those mossy green eyes. "Red, you're a pain in the ass."

"I'm supposed to be. I'm the manager."

He had to smile at that, and he tipped down his sunglasses to look over them at her. "You're real good at it, too. Think of it this way. The pavers are stored on the way to the building. By loading first, then coming in, I'm actually being more efficient."

The smile morphed into a smirk. "That'd be important, I'd think, if we were doing, say, a projection of man-hours."

He took a moment to lean against the truck and study her. Then he loaded another stack of pavers. "You standing here watching me means you're wasting time, and likely adding to your own man-hours."

"You don't come in to handle the paperwork, Kitridge, I'll hunt you down."

"Don't tempt me."

He took his time, but he came in.

He was calculating how best to annoy Stella again. Her eyes went the color of Texas bluebonnets when she was pissed off. But when he stepped in, he saw Hayley.

"Hey."

"Hey," she said back and smiled. "I'm Hayley Phillips. A family connection to Roz's first husband? I'm working here now."

"Logan. Nice to meet you. Don't let this Yankee scare you." He nodded toward Stella. "Where are the sacred forms, and the ritual knife so I can slice open a vein and sign them in blood?"

"My office."

"Uh-huh." But he lingered rather than following her. "When's the baby due?" he asked Hayley.

"May."

"Feeling okay?"

"Never better."

"Good. This here's a nice outfit, a good place to work *most* of the time. Welcome aboard." He sauntered into Stella's office, where she was already at her computer, with the form on the screen.

"I'll type this one up to save time. There's a whole stack of them in that folder. Take it. All you have to do is fill them in as needed, date, sign or initial. Drop them off."

"Uh-huh." He looked around the room. The desk was cleared off. There were no cartons, no books sitting on the floor or stacked on chairs.

That was too bad, he thought. He'd liked the workaday chaos of it.

"Where's all the stuff in here?"

"Where it belongs. Those pavers were the eighteen-inch round, number A-23?"

"They were eighteen-inch rounds." He picked up the framed photo on her desk and studied the picture of her boys and their dog. "Cute."

"Yes, they are. Are the pavers for personal use or for a scheduled job?"

"Red, you ever loosen up?"

"No. We Yankees never do."

He ran his tongue over his teeth. "Um-hmm."

"Do you know how *sick* I am of being referred to as 'the Yankee,' as though it were a foreign species, or a disease? Half the customers who come in here look me over like I'm from another planet and may not be coming in peace. Then I have to tell them I was born here, answer all sorts of questions about why I left, why I'm back, who my *people* are, for Christ's sake, before I can get down to any sort of business. I'm from Michigan, not the moon, and the Civil damn War's been over for quite some time."

Yep, just like Texas bluebonnets. "That would be the War Between the damn States this side of the Mason-Dixon, honey. And looks to me like you loosen up just fine when you get riled enough."

"Don't 'honey' me in that southern-fried twang."

"You know, Red, I like you better this way."

"Oh, shut up. Pavers. Personal or professional use?"

"Well, that depends on your point of view." Since there was room now, he edged a hip onto the corner of the desk. "They're for a friend. I'm putting in a walkway for her—my own time, no labor charge. I told her I'd pick up the materials and give her a bill from the center."

"We'll consider that personal use and apply your employee discount." She began tapping keys. "How many pavers?"

"Twenty-two."

She tapped again and gave him the price per paver, before discount, after discount.

Impressed despite himself, he tapped the monitor. "You got a math nerd trapped in there?"

"Just the wonders of the twenty-first century. You'd find it quicker than counting on your fingers."

"I don't know. I've got pretty fast fingers." Drumming them on his thigh, he kept his gaze on her face. "I need three white pine."

"For this same *friend*?"

"No." His grin flashed, fast and crooked. If she wanted to interpret "friend" as "lover," he couldn't see any point in saying the pavers were for Mrs. Kingsley, his tenth-grade English teacher. "Pine's for a client. Roland Guppy. Yes, like the fish. You've probably got him somewhere in your vast and mysterious files. We did a job for him last fall."

Since there was a coffeemaker on the table against the wall, and the pot was half full, he got up, took a mug, and helped himself.

"Make yourself at home," Stella said dryly.

"Thanks. As it happens, I recommended white pine for a windbreak. He hemmed and hawed. Took him this long to decide to go for it. He called me at home yesterday. I said I'd pick them up and work him in."

"We need a different form."

He sampled the coffee. Not bad. "Somehow I knew that."

"Are the pavers all you're taking for personal use?"

"Probably. For today."

She hit Print, then brought up another form. "That's three white pine. What size?"

"We got some nice eight-foot ones."

"Balled and burlapped?"

"Yeah."

Tap, tap, tap, he thought, with wonder, and there you go. Woman had pretty fingers, he noted. Long and tapered, with that glossy polish on them, the delicate pink of the inside of a rose petal.

She wore no rings.

"Anything else?"

He patted his pockets, eventually came up with a scrap of paper. "That's what I told him I could put them in for."

She added the labor, totaled, then printed out three copies while he drank her coffee. "Sign or initial," she told him. "One copy for my files, one for yours, one for the client."

"Gotcha."

When he picked up the pen, Stella waved a hand. "Oh, wait, let me get that knife. Which vein did you plan to open?"

"Cute." He lifted his chin toward the door. "So's she."

"Hayley? Yeah, she is. And entirely too young for you."

"I wouldn't say entirely. Though I do prefer women with a little more . . ." He stopped, smiled again. "We'll just say more, and stay alive."

"Wise."

"Your boys getting a hard time in school?"

"Excuse me?"

"Just considering what you said before. Yankee."

"Oh. A little, maybe, but for the most part the other kids find it interesting that they're from up north, lived near one of the Great Lakes. Both their teachers pulled up a map to show where they came from."

Her face softened as she spoke of it. "Thanks for asking."

"I like your kids."

He signed the forms and found himself amused when she groaned—actually groaned—watching him carelessly fold his and stuff them in his pocket.

"Next time could you wait until you're out of the office to do that? It hurts me."

"No problem." Maybe it was the different tone they were ending on, or maybe it was the way she'd softened up and smiled when she spoke of her children. Later, he might wonder what possessed him, but for now, he went with impulse. "Ever been to Graceland?"

"No. I'm not a big Elvis fan."

"Ssh!" Widening his eyes, he looked toward the door. "Legally, you can't say that around here. You could face fine and imprisonment, or depending on the jury, public flogging."

"I didn't read that in the Memphian handbook."

"Fine print. So, I'll take you. When's your day off?"

"I . . . It depends. You'll take me to Graceland?"

"You can't settle in down here until you've experienced Graceland. Pick a day, I'll work around it."

"I'm trying to understand here. Are you asking me for a date?"

"I wasn't heading into the date arena. I'm thinking of it more as an outing, between associates." He set the empty mug on her desk. "Think about it, let me know."

SHE HAD TOO MUCH TO DO TO THINK ABOUT IT. SHE couldn't just pop off to Graceland. And if she could, and had some strange desire to do so, she certainly wouldn't pop off to Graceland with Logan.

The fact that she'd admired his work—and all right, his build—didn't mean she liked him. It didn't mean she wanted to spend her very valuable off-time in his company.

But she couldn't help thinking about it, or more, wondering why he'd asked her. Maybe it was some sort of a trick, a strange initiation for the Yankee. You take her to Graceland, then abandon her in a forest of Elvis paraphernalia and see if she can find her way out.

Or maybe, in his weird Logan way, he'd decided that hitting on her was an easier away around her new system than arguing with her.

Except he hadn't seemed to be hitting on her. Exactly. It had seemed more friendly, off the cuff, or impulsive. And he'd asked about her children. There was no quicker way to cut through her annoyance, any shield, any defense than a sincere interest in her boys.

And if he was just being friendly, it seemed only polite, and sensible, to be friendly back.

What did people wear to Graceland, anyway?

Not that she was going. She probably wasn't. But it was smart to prepare. Just in case.

In Greenhouse Three, supervising while Hayley watered propagated annuals, Stella pondered on the situation.

"Ever been to Graceland?"

"Oh, sure. These are impatiens, right?"

Stella looked down at the flat. "Yeah. Those are Busy Lizzies. They're doing really well."

"And these are impatiens too. The New Guinea ones."

"Right. You do learn fast."

"Well, I recognize these easier because I've planted them before. Anyway, I went to Graceland with some pals when I was in college. It's pretty cool. I bought this Elvis bookmark. Wonder what ever happened to that? Elvis is a form of Elvin. It means 'elf-wise friend.' Isn't that strange?"

"Stranger to me that you'd know that."

"Just one of those things you pick up somewhere."

"Okay. So, what's the dress code?"

"Hmm?" She was trying to identify another flat by the leaves on the seedlings. And struggling not to peek at the name on the spike. "I don't guess there is one. People just wear whatever. Jeans and stuff."

"Casual, then."

"Right. I like the way it smells in here. All earthy and damp."

"Then you made the right career choice."

"It could be a career, couldn't it?" Those clear blue eyes shifted to Stella. "Something I could learn to be good at. I always thought I'd run my own place one day. Always figured on a bookstore, but this is sort of the same."

"How's that?"

"Well, like you've got your new stuff, and your classics. You've got genres, when it comes down to it. Annuals, biennials, perennials, shrubs and trees and grasses. Water plants and shade plants. That sort of thing."

"You know, you're right. I hadn't thought of it that way."

Encouraged, Hayley walked down the rows. "And

you're learning and exploring, the way you do with books. And we—you know, the staff—we're trying to help people find what suits them, makes them happy or at least satisfied. Planting a flower's like opening a book, because either way you're starting something. And your garden's your library. I could get good at this."

"I don't doubt it."

She turned to see Stella smiling at her. "When I am good at it, it won't just be a job anymore. A job's okay. It's cool for now, but I want more than a paycheck at the end of the week. I don't just mean money—though, okay, I want the money too."

"No, I know what you mean. You want what Roz has here. A place, and the satisfaction of being part of that place. Roots," Stella said, touching the leaves of a seedling. "And bloom. I know, because I want it too."

"But you have it. You're so totally smart, and you know where you're going. You've got two great kids, and a . . . a position here. You worked toward this, this place, this position. I feel like I'm just starting."

"And you're impatient to get on with it. So was I at your age."

Hayley's face beamed good humor. "And, yeah, you're so old and creaky now."

Laughing, Stella pushed back her hair. "I've got about ten years on you. A lot can happen, a lot can change—yourself included—in a decade. In some ways I'm just starting, too—a decade after you. Transplanting myself, and my two precious shoots here."

"Do you get scared?"

"Every day." She laid a hand on Hayley's belly. "It comes with the territory."

"It helps, having you to talk to. I mean, you were married when you went through this, but you—well, both you and Roz had to deal with being a single parent. It helps that you know stuff. Helps having other women around who know stuff I need to know."

With the job complete, Hayley walked over to turn off

the water. "So," she asked, "are you going to Graceland?"

"I don't know. I might."

WITH HIS CREW SPLIT BETWEEN THE WHITE PINES AND the landscape prep on the Guppy job, Logan set to work on the walkway for his old teacher. It wouldn't take him long, and he could hit both the other work sites that afternoon. He liked juggling jobs. He always had.

Going directly start to finish on one too quickly cut out the room for brainstorms or sudden inspiration. There was little he liked better than that *pop*, when he just saw something in his head that he knew he could make with his hands.

He could take what was and make it better, maybe blend some of what was with the new and create a different whole.

He'd grown up respecting the land, and the whims of Nature, but more from a farmer's point of view. When you grew up on a small farm, worked it, fought with it, he thought, you understood what the land meant. Or could mean.

His father had loved the land, too, but in a different way, Logan supposed. It had provided for his family, cost them, and in the end had gifted them with a nice bonanza when his father had opted to sell out.

He couldn't say he missed the farm. He'd wanted more than row crops and worries about market prices. But he'd wanted, needed, to work the land.

Maybe he'd lost some of the magic of it when he'd moved north. Too many buildings, too much concrete, too many limitations for him. He hadn't been able to acclimate to the climate or culture any more than Rae had been able to acclimate here.

It hadn't worked. No matter how much both of them had tried to nurture things along, the marriage had just withered on them.

So he'd come home, and ultimately, with Roz's offer,

he'd found his place—personally, professionally, creatively. And was content.

He ran his lines, then picked up his shovel.

And jabbed the blade into the earth again.

What had he been thinking? He'd asked the woman out. He could call it whatever he liked, but when a guy asked a woman out, it was a frigging date.

He had no intention of dating toe-the-line Stella Rothchild. She wasn't his type.

Okay, sure she was. He set to work turning the soil between his lines to prep for leveling and laying the black plastic. He'd never met a woman, really, who wasn't his type.

He just liked the breed, that's all. Young ones and old ones, country girls and city-slicked. Whip smart or bulb dim, women just appealed to him on most every level.

He'd ended up married to one, hadn't he? And though that had been a mistake, you had to make them along the way.

Maybe he'd never been particularly drawn to the structured, my-way-or-the-highway type before. But there was always a first time. And he liked first times. It was the second times and the third times that could wear on a man.

But he wasn't attracted to Stella.

Okay, shit. Yes, he was. Mildly. She was a good-looking woman, nicely shaped, too. And there was the hair. He was really gone on the hair. Wouldn't mind getting his hands on that hair, just to see if it felt as sexy as it looked.

But it didn't mean he wanted to date her. It was hard enough to deal with her professionally. The woman had a rule or a form or a damn system for everything.

Probably had them in bed, too. Probably had a typed list of bullet points, dos and don'ts, all with a mission statement overview.

What the woman needed was some spontaneity, a little shake of the order of things. Not that he was interested in being the one to provide it.

It was just that she'd looked so pretty that morning, and

her hair had smelled good. Plus she'd had that sexy little smile going for her. Before he knew it, he'd been talking about taking her to Graceland.

Nothing to worry about, he assured himself. She wouldn't go. It wasn't the sort of thing a woman like her did, just for the hell of it. As far as he could tell, she didn't do *anything* for the hell of it.

They'd both forget he'd even brought it up.

BECAUSE SHE FELT IT WAS IMPERATIVE, AT LEAST FOR the first six months of her management, Stella insisted on a weekly progress meeting with Roz.

She'd have preferred a specific time for these meetings, and a specific location. But Roz was hard to pin down.

She'd already held them in the propagation house and in the field. This time she cornered Roz in her own sitting room, where she'd be unlikely to escape.

"I wanted to give you your weekly update."

"Oh. Well, all right." Roz set aside a book on hybridizing that was thick as a railroad tie, and took off her frameless reading glasses. "Time's zipping by. Ground's warming up."

"I know. Daffodils are ready to pop. So much earlier than I'm used to. We've been selling a lot of bulbs. Back north, we'd sell most of those late summer or fall."

"Homesick?"

"Now and then, but less and less already. I can't say I'm sorry to be out of Michigan as we slog through February. They got six inches of snow yesterday, and I'm watching daffodils spearing up."

Roz leaned back in the chair, crossed her sock-covered feet at the ankles. "Is there a problem?"

"So much for the illusion that I conceal my emotions under a composed façade. No, no problem. I did the duty call home to my mother a little while ago. I'm still recovering."

"Ah."

It was a noncommittal sound, and Stella decided she could interpret it as complete non-interest or a tacit invitation to unload. Because she was brimming, she chose to unload.

"I spent the almost fifteen minutes she spared me out of her busy schedule listening to her talk about her current boyfriend. She actually calls these men she sees boyfriends. She's fifty-eight years old, and she just had her fourth divorce two months ago. When she wasn't complaining that Rocky—and he's actually named Rocky—isn't attentive enough and won't take her to the Bahamas for a midwinter getaway, she was talking about her next chemical peel and whining about how her last Botox injection hurt. She never asked about the boys, and the only reference she made to the fact that I was living and working down here was to ask if I was tired of being around the jerk and his bimbo—her usual terms for my father and Jolene."

When she'd run out of steam, Stella rubbed her hands over her face. "Goddamn it."

"That's a lot of bitching, whining, and venom to pack into a quarter of an hour. She sounds like a very talented woman."

It took Stella a minute—a minute where she let her hands slide into her lap so she could stare into Roz's face. Then she let her own head fall back with a peal of laughter.

"Oh, yeah. Oh, yeah, she's loaded with talent. Thanks."

"No problem. My mama spent most of her time—at least the time we were on earth together—sighing wistfully over her health. Not that she meant to complain, so she said. I very nearly put that on her tombstone. 'Not That I Mean to Complain.' "

"I could put 'I Don't Ask for Much' on my mother's."

"There you go. Mine made such an impression on me that I went hell-bent in the opposite direction. I could probably cut off a limb, and you wouldn't hear a whimper out of me."

"God, I guess I've done the same with mine. I'll have to think about that later. Okay, on to business. We're sold out of the mixed-bulb planters we forced. I don't know if you want to do others this late in the season."

"Maybe a few. Some people like to pick them up, already done, for Easter presents and so on."

"All right. How about if I show Hayley how it's done? I know you usually do them yourself, but—"

"No, it's a good job for her. I've been watching her." At Stella's expression, she inclined her head. "I don't like to look like I'm watching, but generally I am. I know what's going on in my place, Stella, even if I do occasionally miss crossing a T."

"And I'm there to cross them, so that's all right."

"Exactly. Still, I've left her primarily to you. She working out for you?"

"More than. You don't have to tell her something twice, and when she claimed she learned fast she wasn't kidding. She's thirsty."

"We've got plenty to drink around here."

"She's personable with customers—friendly, never rushed. And she's not afraid to say she doesn't know, but she'll find out. She's outside right now, poking around your beds and shrubs. She wants to know what she's selling."

She moved to the window as she spoke, to look out. It was nearly twilight, but there was Hayley walking the dog and studying the perennials. "At her age, I was planning my wedding. It seems like a million years ago."

"At her age, I was raising two toddlers and was pregnant with Mason. Now *that* was a million years ago. And five minutes ago."

"It's off topic, again, of the update, but I wanted to ask if you'd thought about what you'll do when we get to May."

"That's still high season for us, and people like to freshen up the summer garden. We sell—"

"No, I meant about Hayley. About the baby."

"Oh. Well, she'll have to decide that, but I expect if she

decides to stay on at the nursery, we'll find her sit-down work."

"She'll need to find child care, when she's ready to go back to work. And speaking of nurseries . . ."

"Hmm. That's thinking ahead."

"Time zips by," Stella repeated.

"We'll figure it out."

Because she was curious, Roz rose to go to the window herself. Standing beside Stella she looked out.

It was a lovely thing, she decided, watching a young woman, blooming with child, wandering a winter garden.

She'd once been that young woman, dreaming in the twilight and waiting for spring to bring life.

Time didn't just zip by, she thought. It damn near evaporated on you.

"She seems happy now, and sure of what she's going to do. But could be after she has the baby, she'll change her mind about having the father involved." Roz watched Hayley lay a hand on her belly and look west, to where the sun was sinking behind the trees and into the river beyond them. "Having a live baby in your arms and the prospect of caring for it single-handed's one hell of a reality check. We'll see when the time comes."

"You're right. And I don't suppose either of us knows her well enough to know what's best. Speaking of babies, it's nearly time to get mine in the tub. I'm going to leave the weekly report with you."

"All right. I'll get to it. I should tell you, Stella, I like what you've done. What shows, like in the customer areas, and what doesn't, in the office management. I see spring coming, and for the first time in years, I'm not frazzled and overworked. I can't say I minded being overworked, but I can't say I mind not being, either."

"Even when I bug you with details?"

"Even when. I haven't heard any complaints about Logan in the past few days. Or from him. Am I living in a fool's paradise, or have you two found your rhythm?"

"There are still a few hitches in it, and I suspect there'll be others, but nothing for you to worry about. In fact, he made a very friendly gesture and offered to take me to Graceland."

"He did?" Roz's eyebrows drew together. "Logan?"

"Would that be out of the ordinary for him?"

"I couldn't say, except I don't know that he's dated anyone from work before."

"It's not a date, it's an outing."

Intrigued, Roz sat again. You never knew what you'd learn from a younger woman, she decided. "What's the difference?"

"Well, a date's dinner and a movie with potential, even probable, romantic overtones. Taking your kids to the zoo is an outing."

Roz leaned back, stretched out her legs. "Things do change, don't they? Still, in my book, when a man and a woman go on an outing, it's a date."

"See, that's my quandary." Since conversation seemed welcomed, Stella walked over again, sat on the arm of the chair facing Roz. "Because that's my first thought. But it seemed like just a friendly gesture, and the 'outing' term was his. Like a kind of olive branch. And if I take it, maybe we'd find that common ground, or that rhythm, whatever it is we need to smooth out the rough spots in our working relationship."

"So, if I'm following this, you'd go to Graceland with Logan for the good of In the Garden."

"Sort of."

"And not because he's a very attractive, dynamic, and downright sexy single man."

"No, those would be bonus points." She waited until Roz stopped laughing. "And I'm not thinking of wading in that pool. Dating's a minefield."

"Tell me about it. I've got more years in that war zone than you."

"I like men." She reached back to tug the band ponytailing her hair a little higher. "I like the company of men. But dating's so complicated and stressful."

"Better complicated and stressful than downright boring, which too many of my experiences in the field have been."

"Complicated, stressful, or downright boring, I like the sound of 'outing' much better. Listen, I know Logan's a friend of yours. But I'd just like to ask if you think, if I went with him, I'd be making a mistake, or giving the wrong impression. The wrong signal. Or maybe crossing that line between coworkers. Or—"

"That's an awful lot of complication and stress you're working up over an outing."

"It is. I irritate myself." Shaking her head, she pushed off the chair. "I'd better get bath time started. Oh, and I'll get Hayley going on those bulbs tomorrow."

"That's fine. Stella—are you going on this outing?"

She paused at the doorway. "Maybe. I'll sleep on it."

eight

SHE WAS DREAMING OF FLOWERS. AN ENCHANTING garden, full of young, vital blooms, flowed around her. It was perfect, tidied and ordered, its edges ruler-straight to form a keen verge against the well-trimmed grass.

Color swept into color, whites and pinks, yellows and silvery greens, all soft and delicate pastels that shimmered in subtle elegance in the golden beams of the sun.

Their fragrance was calming and drew a pretty bevy of busy butterflies, the curiosity of a single shimmery hummingbird. No weed intruded on its flawlessness, and every blossom was full and ripe, with dozens upon dozens of buds waiting their turn to open.

She'd done this. As she circled the bed it was with a sense of pride and satisfaction. She'd turned the earth and fed it, she'd planned and selected and set each plant in exactly the right place. The garden so precisely matched her vision, it was like a photograph.

It had taken her years to plan and toil and create. But now everything she'd wanted to accomplish was here, blooming at her feet.

Yet even as she watched, a stem grew up, sharp and

green, crowding the others, spoiling the symmetry. Out of place, she thought, more annoyed than surprised to see it breaking out of the ground, growing up, unfurling its leaves.

A dahlia? She'd planted no dahlias there. They belonged in the back. She'd specifically planted a trio of tall pink dahlias at the back of the bed, exactly one foot apart.

Puzzled, she tilted her head, studied it as the stems grew and thickened, as buds formed fat and healthy. Fascinating, so fascinating and unexpected.

Even as she started to smile, she heard—felt?—a whisper over the skin, a murmur through her brain.

It's wrong there. Wrong. It has to be removed. *It will take and take until there's nothing left.*

She shivered. The air around her was suddenly cool, with a hint of raw dampness, with bleak clouds creeping in toward that lovely golden sun.

In the pit of her belly was a kind of dread.

Don't let it grow. It will strangle the life out of everything you've done.

That was right. Of course, that was right. It had no business growing there, muscling the others aside, changing the order.

She'd have to dig it out, find another place for it. Reorganize everything, just when she'd thought she was finished. And look at that, she thought, as the buds formed, as they broke open to spread their deep blue petals. It was entirely the wrong color. Too bold, too dark, too bright.

It was beautiful; she couldn't deny it. In fact, she'd never seen a more beautiful specimen. It looked so strong, so vivid. It was already nearly as tall as she, with flowers as wide as dinner plates.

It lies. It lies.

That whisper, somehow female, somehow raging, slithered into her sleeping brain. She whimpered a little, tossed restlessly in her chilly bed.

Kill it! Kill it. Hurry before it's too late.

No, she couldn't kill something so beautiful, so alive, so vivid. But that didn't mean she could just leave it there, out of its place, upsetting the rest of the bed.

All that work, the preparation, the *planning*, and now this. She'd just have to plan another bed and work it in. With a sigh, she reached out, feathered her fingers over those bold blue petals. It would be a lot of work, she thought, a lot of trouble, but—

"Mom."

"Isn't it pretty?" she murmured. "It's so *blue*."

"Mom, wake up."

"What?" She tumbled out of the dream, shaking off sleep as she saw Luke kneeling in the bed beside her.

God, the room was freezing.

"Luke?" Instinctively she dragged the spread over him. "What's the matter?"

"I don't feel good in my tummy."

"Aw." She sat up, automatically laying a hand on his brow to check for fever. A little warm, she thought. "Does it hurt?"

He shook his head. She could see the gleam of his eyes, the sheen of tears. "It feels sick. Can I sleep in your bed?"

"Okay." She drew the sheets back. "Lie down and bundle up, baby. I don't know why it's so cold in here. I'm going to take your temperature, just to see." She pressed her lips to his forehead as he snuggled onto her pillow. Definitely a little warm.

Switching on the bedside lamp, she rolled out to get the thermometer from the bathroom.

"Let's find out if I can see through your brain." She stroked his hair as she set the gauge to his ear. "Did you feel sick when you went to bed?"

"Nuh-uh, it was . . ." His body tightened, and he made a little groan.

She knew he was going to retch before he did. With a mother's speed, she scooped him up, dashed into the bathroom. They made it, barely, and she murmured and stroked and fretted while he was sick.

Then he turned his pale little face up to hers. "I frew up."

"I know, baby. I'm sorry. We're going to make it all better soon."

She gave him a little water, cooled his face with a cloth, then carried him back to her bed. Strange, she thought, the room felt fine now.

"It doesn't feel as sick in my tummy anymore."

"That's good." Still, she took his temperature—99.1, not too bad—and brought the wastebasket over beside the bed. "Does it hurt anywhere?"

"Nuh-uh, but I don't like to frow up. It makes it taste bad in my throat. And my other tooth is loose, and maybe if I frow up again, it'll come out and I won't have it to put under my pillow."

"Don't you worry about that. You'll absolutely have your tooth for under your pillow, just like the other one. Now, I'll go down and get you some ginger ale. You stay right here, and I'll be back in just a minute. Okay?"

"Okay."

"If you have to be sick again, try to use this." She set the wastebasket beside him on the bed. "I'll be right back, baby."

She hurried out, jogging down the stairs in her nightshirt. One of the disadvantages of a really big house, she realized, was that the kitchen was a mile away from the bedrooms.

She'd see about buying a little fridge, like the one she'd had in her dorm room at college, for the upstairs sitting room.

Low-grade fever, she thought as she rushed into the kitchen. He'd probably be better by tomorrow. If he wasn't, she'd call the doctor.

She hunted up ginger ale, filled a tall glass with ice, grabbed a bottle of water, and dashed back upstairs.

"I get ginger ale," she heard Luke say as she walked back down the hall to her room. "Because I was sick. Even though I feel better, I can still have it. You can have some, too, if you want."

"Thanks, honey, but—" When she swung into the room, she saw Luke was turned away from the door, sitting back against the pillows. And the room was cold again, so cold that she saw the vapor of her own breath.

"She went away," Luke said.

Something that was more than the cold danced up her spine. "Who went away?"

"The lady." His sleepy eyes brightened a bit when he saw the ginger ale. "She stayed with me when you went downstairs."

"What lady, Luke? Miss Roz? Hayley?"

"Nuh-uh. The lady who comes and sings. She's nice. Can I have *all* the ginger ale?"

"You can have some." Her hands shook lightly as she poured. "Where did you see her?"

"Right here." He pointed to the bed, then took the glass in both hands and drank. "This tastes good."

"You've seen her before?"

"Uh-huh. Sometimes I wake up and she's there. She sings the dilly-dilly song."

Lavender's blue, dilly dilly. Lavender's green. That's the song she'd heard, Stella realized with a numb fear. The song she'd caught herself humming.

"Did she—" No, don't frighten him, she warned herself. "What does she look like?"

"She's pretty, I guess. She has yellow hair. I think she's an angel, a lady angel? 'Member the story about the guard angel?"

"Guardian angel."

"But she doesn't have wings. Gavin says she's maybe a witch, but a good one like in *Harry Potter*."

Her throat went desert dry. "Gavin's seen her too?"

"Yeah, when she comes to sing." He handed the glass back to Stella, rubbed his eyes. "My tummy feels better now, but I'm sleepy. Can I still sleep in your bed?"

"Absolutely." But before she got into bed with him, Stella turned on the bathroom light.

She looked in on Gavin, struggled against the urge to pluck him out of his bed and carry him into hers.

Leaving the connecting doors wide open, she walked back into her room.

She turned off the bedside lamp, then slid into bed with her son.

And gathering him close, she held him as he slept.

HE SEEMED FINE THE NEXT MORNING. BRIGHT AND bouncy, and cheerfully told David over breakfast that he'd thrown up and had ginger ale.

She considered keeping him home from school, but there was no fever and, judging by his appetite, no stomach problems.

"No ill effects there," David commented when the boys ran up to get their books. "You, on the other hand, look like you put in a rough one." He poured her another cup of coffee.

"I did. And not all of it because Luke was sick. After he 'frew up,' he settled down and slept like a baby. But before he settled down, he told me something that kept me awake most of the night."

David rested his elbows on the island counter, leaned forward. "Tell Daddy all."

"He says . . ." She glanced around, cocking an ear so she'd hear the boys when they came back down. "There's a lady with yellow hair who comes into his room at night and sings to him."

"Oh." He picked up his dishcloth and began to mop the counter.

"Don't say 'oh' with that silly little smile."

"Hey, I'll have you know this is my amused smirk. Nothing silly about it."

"David."

"Stella," he said with the same stern scowl. "Roz told you we have a ghost, didn't she?"

"She mentioned it. But there's just one little problem with that. There are no such things as ghosts."

"So, what, some blonde sneaks into the house every night, heads to the boys' room, and breaks out in song? *That's* more plausible?"

"I don't know what's going on. I've heard someone singing, and I've felt . . ." Edgy, she twisted the band of her watch. "Regardless, the idea of a ghost is ridiculous. But something's going on with my boys."

"Is he afraid of her?"

"No. I probably just imagined the singing. And Luke, he's six. He can imagine anything."

"Have you asked Gavin?"

"No. Luke said they'd both seen her, but . . ."

"So have I."

"Oh, please."

David rinsed the dishcloth, squeezed out the excess water, then laid it over the lip of the sink to dry. "Not since I was a kid, but I saw her a few times when I'd sleep over. Freaked me out at first, but she'd just sort of *be* there. You can ask Harper. He saw her plenty."

"Okay. Just who is this fictional ghost supposed to be?" She threw up a hand as she heard the thunder of feet on the stairs. "Later."

SHE TRIED TO PUT IT OUT OF HER MIND, AND SUCceeded from time to time when the work took over. But it snuck back into her brain, and played there, like the ghostly lullaby.

By midday, she left Hayley working on bulb planters and Ruby at the counter, and grabbing a clipboard, headed toward the grafting house.

Two birds, she thought, one stone.

The music today was Rachmaninoff. Or was it Mozart? Either way, it was a lot of passionate strings and flutes. She passed the staging areas, the tools, the soils and additives and rooting mediums.

She found Harper down at the far end at a worktable with a pile of five-inch pots, several cacti as stock plants, and a tray of rooting medium. She noted the clothespins, the rubber bands, the raffia, the jar of denatured alcohol.

"What do you use on the Christmas cactus?"

He continued to work, using his knife to cut a shoot from the joint of a scion plant. He had beautiful hands, she noted. Long, artistic fingers. "Apical-wedge, then? Tricky, but probably best with that specimen because of the flat stems. Are you creating a standard, or hybridizing?"

He made his vertical slit into the vascular bundle and still didn't answer.

"I'm just wondering because—" She set her hand on his shoulder, and when he jumped and let out a muffled shout, she stumbled back and rammed into the table behind her.

"Shit!" He dropped the knife and stuck the thumb it had nicked in his mouth. "Shit!" he said again, around his thumb, and tugged headphones off with his free hand.

"I'm sorry. I'm so sorry! How bad are you cut? Let me see."

"It's just a scratch." He took it out of his mouth, rubbed it absently on his grimy jeans. "Not nearly as fatal as the *heart attack* you just brought on."

"Let me see the thumb." She grabbed his hand. "You've got dirt in it now."

He saw her gaze slide over toward the alcohol and ripped his hand out of hers. "Don't even think about it."

"Well, it should at least be cleaned. And I really am sorry. I didn't see the headphones. I thought you heard me."

"It's okay. No big. The classical's for the plants. If I listen to it for too long, my eyes get glassy."

"Oh?" She picked up the headphones, held one side to one ear. "Metallica?"

"Yeah. My kind of classical." Now he looked warily at her clipboard. "What's up?"

"I'm hoping to get an idea of what you'll have ready in here to put out for our big spring opening next month. And what you have at the stage you'd want it moved out to the stock greenhouse."

"Oh, well . . ." He looked around. "A lot of stuff. Probably. I keep the staging records on computer."

"Even better. Maybe you could just make me a copy. Floppy disk would be perfect."

"Yeah, okay. Okay, wait." He shifted his stool toward the computer.

"You don't have to do it this minute, when you're in the middle of something else."

"If I don't, I'll probably forget."

With a skill she admired, he tapped keys with somewhat grungy fingers, found what he was after. He dug out a floppy, slid it into the data slot. "Look, I'd rather you didn't take anything out when I'm not here."

"No problem."

"How's, um, Hayley working out?"

"An answer to a prayer."

"Yeah?" He reached for a can of Coke, took a quick drink. "She's not doing anything heavy or working around toxics. Right?"

"Absolutely not. I've got her doing bulb planters right now."

"Here you go." He handed her the floppy.

"Thanks, Harper. This makes my life easier. I've never done a Christmas cactus graft." She clipped the floppy to her board. "Can I watch?"

"Sure. Want to do one? I'll talk you through."

"I'd really like to."

"I'll finish this one up. See, I cut a two-, maybe two-and-a-half-inch shoot, straight through the joint. I've cut the top couple inches from the stem of the stock plant. And on the way to slicing my finger—"

"Sorry."

"Wouldn't be the first time. I made this fine, vertical cut into the vascular bundle."

"I got that far."

"From here, we pare slivers of skin from both sides of the base of the scion, tapering the end, and exposing the central core." Those long, artistic fingers worked cleverly and patiently. "See?"

"Mmm. You've got good hands for this."

"Came by them naturally. Mom showed me how to graft. We did an ornamental cherry when I was about Luke's age. Now we're going to insert the scion into the slit on the stock stem. We want the exposed tissues of both in contact, and match the cut surfaces as close as you can. I like to use a long cactus spine. . . ." He took one from a tray and pushed it straight into the grafted area.

"Neat and organic."

"Uh-huh. I don't like binding with raffia on these. Weakened clothespins are better. Right across the joint, see, so it's held firm but not too tight. The rooting medium's two parts cactus soil mix to one part fine grit. I've already got the mix. We get our new baby in the pot, cover the mix with a little fine gravel."

"So it stays moist but not wet."

"You got it. Then you want to label it and put it in an airy position, out of full sun. The two plants should unite in a couple of days. Want to give it a shot?"

"Yeah." She took the stool when he vacated it, and began, following his directions carefully. "Ah, David was telling me about the house legend this morning."

"That's good." His gaze stayed focused on her hands, and the plant. "Keep the slice really thin. Legend?"

"You know, woo-woo, ghost."

"Oh, yeah, the sad-eyed blonde. Used to sing to me when I was a kid."

"Come on, Harper."

He shrugged, took another sip of Coke. "You want?" He tipped the can from side to side. "I've got more in the cooler under here."

"No, but thanks. You're saying a ghost used to come in your room and sing to you."

"Up until I was about twelve, thirteen. Same with my brothers. You hit puberty, she stops coming around. You need to taper the scion now."

She paused in her work only long enough to slide a glance up at his face. "Harper, don't you consider yourself a scientist?"

He smiled at her with those somewhat dreamy brown eyes. "Not so much. Some of what I do is science, and some of what I do requires knowing some science. But down at it, I'm a gardener."

He two-pointed the Coke can into his waste bin, then bent down to get another out of his cooler. "But if you're asking if I find ghosts at odds with science, not so much either. Science is an exploration, it's experimentation, it's discovery."

"I can't argue with your definition." She went back to the work. "But—"

He popped the top. "Gonna Scully me?"

She had to laugh. "It's one thing for a young boy to believe in ghosts, and Santa Claus, and—"

"You're trying to say there's no Santa Claus?" He looked horrified. "That's just sick."

"But," she continued, ignoring him, "it's entirely another when it's a grown man."

"Who are you calling a grown man? I think I'm going to have to order you out of my house. Stella." He patted her shoulder, transferred soil, then casually brushed it off her shirt. "I saw what I saw, I know what I know. It's just part of growing up in the house. She was always . . . a benign presence, at least to me and my brothers. She gave Mom grief now and then."

"What do you mean, grief?"

"Ask Mom. But I don't know why you'd bother, since you don't believe in ghosts anyway." He smiled. "That's a good graft. According to family lore, she's supposed to be one of the Harper brides, but she's not in any of the paintings or pictures we have." He lifted a shoulder. "Maybe she was a servant who died there. She sure knows her way around the place."

"Luke told me he saw her."

"Yeah?" His gaze sharpened as Stella labeled the pot. "If you're worried that she might hurt him, or Gavin, don't. She's, I don't know, maternal."

"Perfect, then—an unidentified yet maternal ghost who haunts my sons' room at night."

"It's a Harper family tradition."

AFTER A CONVERSATION LIKE THAT, STELLA NEEDED something sensible to occupy her mind. She grabbed a flat of pansies and some trailing vinca from a greenhouse, found a couple of nice free-form concrete planters in storage, loaded them and potting soil onto a flatbed cart. She gathered tools, gloves, mixed up some starter solution, and hauled everything out front.

Pansies didn't mind a bit of chill, she thought, so if they got a few more frosts, they wouldn't be bothered. And their happy faces, their rich colors would splash spring right at the entryway.

Once she'd positioned the planters, she got her clipboard and noted down everything she'd taken from stock. She'd enter it in her computer when she was finished.

Then she knelt down to do something she loved, something that never failed to comfort her. Something that always made sense.

She planted.

When the first was done, the purple and yellow flowers cheerful against the dull gray of the planter, she stepped back to study it. She wanted its mate to be as close to a mirror image as she could manage.

She was half done when she heard the rumble of tires on gravel. Logan, she thought, as she glanced around and identified his truck. She saw him start to turn toward the material area, then swing back and drive toward the building.

He stepped out, worn boots, worn jeans, bad-boy black-lensed sunglasses.

She felt a little itch right between her shoulder blades.

"Hey," he said.

"Hello, Logan."

He stood there, his thumbs hooked in the front pockets of his work pants and a trio of fresh scratches on his forearms just below the rolled-up sleeves of his shirt.

"Picking up some landscape timbers and some more black plastic for the Dawson job."

"You're moving right along there."

"It's cooking." He stepped closer, studied her work. "Those look good. I could use them."

"These are for display."

"You can make more. I take those over to Miz Dawson, the woman's going to snap them up. Sale's a sale, Red."

"Oh, all right." She'd hardly had a *minute* to think of them as her own. "Let me at least finish them. You tell her she'll need to replace these pansies when it gets hot. They won't handle summer. And if she puts perennials in them, she should cover the planters over for winter."

"It happens I know something about plants myself."

"Just want to make sure the customer's satisfied."

He'd been polite, she thought. Even cooperative. Hadn't he come to give her a materials list? The least she could do was reciprocate. "If Graceland's still on, I can take off some time next Thursday." She kept her eyes on the plants, her tone casual as a fistful of daisies. "If that works for you."

"Thursday?" He'd been all prepared with excuses if she happened to bring it up. Work was jamming him up, they'd do it some other time.

But there she was, kneeling on the ground, with that damn hair curling all over the place and the sun hitting it. Those blue eyes, that cool Yankee voice.

"Sure, Thursday's good. You want me to pick you up here or at the house?"

"Here, if that's okay. What time works best for you?"

"Maybe around one. That way I can put the morning in."

"That'll be perfect." She rose, brushed off her gloves and set them neatly on the cart. "Just let me put together a price for these planters, make you up an order form. If she decides against them, just bring them back."

"She won't. Go ahead and do the paperwork." He dug a many folded note out of his pocket. "On these and the materials I've got down here. I'll load up."

"Good. Fine." She started inside. The itch had moved from her shoulder blades to just under her belly button.

It wasn't a date, it wasn't a date, she reminded herself. It wasn't even an outing, really. It was a gesture. A goodwill gesture on both sides.

And now, she thought as she walked into her office, they were both stuck with it.

NINE

"I DON'T KNOW HOW IT GOT TO BE THURSDAY."

"It has something to do with Thor, the Norse god." Hayley hunched her shoulders sheepishly. "I know a lot of stupid things. I don't know why."

"I wasn't looking for the origin of the word, more how it got here so fast. Thor?" Stella repeated, turning from the mirror in the employee bathroom.

"Pretty sure."

"I'll just take your word on that one. Okay." She spread out her arms. "How do I look?"

"You look really nice."

"Too nice? You know, too formal or prepared?"

"No, just right nice." The fact was, she envied the way Stella looked in simple gray pants and black sweater. Sort of tailored, and curvy under it. When she wasn't pregnant, she herself tended to be on the bony side and flat-chested.

"The sweater makes you look really built," she added.

"Oh, God!" Horrified, Stella crossed her arms, pressing them against her breasts. "Too built? Like, hey, look at my boobs?"

"No." Laughing, Hayley tugged Stella's arms down. "Cut it out. You've got really excellent boobs."

"I'm nervous. It's ridiculous, but I'm nervous. I *hate* being nervous, which is why I hardly ever am." She tugged at the sleeve of her sweater, brushed at it. "Why do something you hate?"

"It's just a casual afternoon outing." Hayley avoided the D word. They'd been over that. "Just go and have fun."

"Right. Of course. Stupid." She shook herself off before walking out of the room. "You've got my cell number."

"Everybody has your cell number, Stella." She cast a look at Ruby, who answered it with chuckle. "I think the mayor probably has it on speed dial."

"If there are any problems at all, don't hesitate to use it. And if you're not sure about anything, and can't find Roz or Harper, just call me."

"Yes, Mama. And don't worry, the keg's not coming until three." She slapped a hand over her mouth. "Did I say keg? Peg's what I meant. Yeah, I meant Peg."

"Ha ha."

"And the male strippers aren't a definite." She got a hoot of laughter out of Ruby at that and grinned madly. "So you can chill."

"I don't think chilling's on today's schedule."

"Can I ask how long it's been since you've been on a date—I mean, an outing?"

"Not that long. A few months." When Hayley rolled her eyes, Stella rolled hers right back. "I was busy. There was a lot to do with selling the house, packing up, arranging for storage, researching schools and pediatricians down here. I didn't have time."

"And didn't have anyone who made you want to make time. You're making it today."

"It's not like that. Why is he late?" she demanded, glancing at her watch. "I knew he'd be late. He has 'I'm chronically late for mostly everything' written all over him."

When a customer came in, Hayley patted Stella's shoulder. "That's my cue. Have a good time. May I help you?" she asked, strolling over to the customer.

Stella waited another couple of minutes, assuring herself that Hayley had the new customer in hand. Ruby rang up two more. Work was being done where work needed to be done, and she had nothing to do but wait.

Deciding to do her waiting outside, she grabbed her jacket.

Her planters looked good, and she figured her display of them was directly responsible for the flats of pansies they'd moved in the past few days. That being the case, they could add a few more planters, do a couple of half whiskey barrels, add some hanging pots.

Scribbling, she wandered around, picking out the best spots to place displays, to add other touches that would inspire customers to buy.

When Logan pulled up at quarter after one, she was sitting on the steps, listing the proposed displays and arrangements and dividing up the labor of creating them.

She got up even as he climbed out of the truck. "I got hung up."

"No problem. I kept busy."

"You okay riding in the truck?"

"Wouldn't be the first time." She got in, and as she buckled her seat belt, studied the forest of notes and reminders, sketches and math calculations stuck to his dashboard.

"Your filing system?"

"Most of it." He turned on the CD player, and Elvis rocked out with "Heartbreak Hotel." "Seems only right."

"Are you a big fan?"

"You've got to respect the King."

"How many times have you been to Graceland?"

"Couldn't say. People come in from out of town, they want to see it. You visit Memphis, you want Graceland, Beale Street, ribs, the Peabody's duck walk."

Maybe she could chill, Stella decided. They were just talking, after all. Like normal people. "Then this is the first tic on my list."

He looked over at her. Though his eyes were shielded by the black lenses, she knew, from the angle of his head, that they were narrowed with speculation. "You've been here, what, around a month, and you haven't gone for ribs?"

"No. Will I be arrested?"

"You a vegetarian?"

"No, and I like ribs."

"Honey, you haven't had ribs yet if you haven't had Memphis ribs. Don't your parents live down here? I thought I'd met them once."

"My father and his wife, yeah. Will and Jolene Dooley."

"And no ribs?"

"I guess not. Will *they* be arrested?"

"They might, if it gets out. But I'll give you, and them, a break and keep quiet about it for the time being."

"Guess we'll owe you."

"Heartbreak Hotel" moved into "Shake, Rattle, and Roll." This was her father's music, she thought. It was odd, and kind of sweet, to be driving along, tapping her foot, on the way to Memphis listening to the music her father had listened to as a teenager.

"What you do is you take the kids to the Reunion for ribs," Logan told her. "You can walk over to Beale from there, take in the show. But before you eat, you go by the Peabody so they can see the ducks. Kids gotta see the ducks."

"My father's taken them."

"That might keep him out of the slammer."

"Whew." It was easier than she'd thought it would be, and she felt foolish knowing she'd prepared several avenues for small talk. "Except for the time you moved north, you've always lived in the Memphis area?"

"That's right."

"It's strange for me, knowing I was born here, but having no real memory of it. I like it here, and I like to think—overlooking the lack of ribs to date—that there's a connection for me here. Of course, I haven't been through a summer yet—that I can remember—but I like it. I love working for Roz."

"She's a jewel."

Because she heard the affection in his tone, she shifted toward him a bit. "She thinks the same of you. In fact, initially, I thought the two of you were . . ."

His grin spread. "No kidding?"

"She's beautiful and clever, and you've got a lot in common. You've got a history."

"All true. Probably the history makes anything like that weird. But thanks."

"I admire her so much. I like her, too, but I have such admiration for everything she's accomplished. Single-handedly. Raising her family, maintaining her home, building a business from the ground up. And all the while doing it her own way, calling her own shots."

"Is that what you want?"

"I don't want my own business. I thought about it a couple of years ago. But that sort of leap with no parachute and two kids?" She shook her head. "Roz is gutsier than I am. Besides, I realized it wasn't what I really wanted. I like working for someone else, sort of troubleshooting and coming in with a creative and efficient plan for improvement or expansion. Managing is what I do best."

She waited a beat. "No sarcastic comments to that?"

"Only on the inside. That way I can save them up until you tick me off again."

"I can hardly wait. In any case, it's like, I enjoy planting a garden from scratch—that blank slate. But more, I like taking one that's not planned very well, or needs some shaping up, and turning it around."

She paused, frowned. "Funny, I just remembered. I had a dream about a garden a few nights ago. A really strange dream with . . . I don't know, something spooky about it. I can't quite get it back, but there was something . . . this huge, gorgeous blue dahlia. Dahlias are a particular favorite of mine, and blue's my favorite color. Still, it shouldn't have been there, didn't belong there. I hadn't planted it. But there it was. Strange."

"What did you do with it? The dahlia?"

"Can't remember. Luke woke me up, so my garden and the exotic dahlia went poof." And the room, she thought, the room had been so cold. "He wasn't feeling well, a little tummy distress."

"He okay now?"

"Yeah." Another point for his side, Stella thought. "He's fine, thanks."

"How about the tooth?"

Uh-oh, second point. The man remembered her baby'd had a loose tooth. "Sold to the Tooth Fairy for a crisp dollar bill. Second one's about to wiggle out. He's got the cutest little lisp going on right now."

"His big brother teach him how to spit through the hole yet?"

She grimaced. "Not to my knowledge."

"What you don't know . . . I bet it's still there—the magic dahlia—blooming in dreamland."

"That's a nice thought." *Kill it.* God, where did that come from? she wondered, fighting off a shudder. "It was pretty spectacular, as I recall."

She glanced around as he pulled into a parking lot. "Is this it?"

"It's across the road. This is like the visitors' center, the staging area. We get our tickets inside, and they take groups over in shuttles."

He turned off the engine, shifted to look at her. "Five bucks says you're a convert when we come back out."

"An Elvis convert? I don't have anything against him now."

"Five bucks. You'll be buying an Elvis CD, minimum, after the tour."

"That's a bet."

* * *

IT WAS SO MUCH SMALLER THAN SHE'D IMAGINED. She'd pictured something big and sprawling, something mansionlike, close to the level of Harper House. Instead, it was a relatively modest-sized home, and the rooms—at least the ones the tour encompassed—rather small.

She shuffled along with the rest of the tourists, listening to Lisa Marie Presley's recorded memories and observations through the provided headset.

She puzzled over the pleated fabric in shades of curry, blue, and maroon swagged from the ceiling and covering every inch of wall in the cramped, pool-table-dominated game room. Then wondered at the waterfall, the wild-animal prints and tiki-hut accessories all crowned by a ceiling of green shag carpet in the jungle room.

Someone had lived with this, she thought. Not just someone, but an icon—a man of miraculous talent and fame. And it was sweet to listen to the woman who'd been a child when she'd lost her famous father, talk about the man she remembered, and loved.

The trophy room was astonishing to her, and immediately replaced her style quibbles with awe. It seemed like miles of walls in the meandering hallways were covered, cheek by jowl, with Elvis's gold and platinum records. All that accomplished, all that earned in fewer years, really, than she'd been alive.

And with Elvis singing through her headset, she admired his accomplishments, marveled over his elaborate, splashy, and myriad stage costumes. Then was charmed by his photographs, his movie posters, and the snippets of interviews.

YOU LEARNED A LOT ABOUT SOMEONE WALKING through Graceland with her, Logan discovered. Some snickered over the dated and debatably tacky decor. Some stood glassy-eyed with adoration for the dead King. Others bopped along, rubbernecking or chatting, moving on through so they could get it all in and push on to the souvenir shops. Then they could go home and say, been there, done that.

But Stella looked at everything. And listened. He could tell she was listening carefully to the recording, the way her head would cock just an inch to the right. Listening soberly, he thought, and he'd bet a lot more than five bucks that she followed the instructions on the tape, pressing the correct number for the next segment at exactly the proper time.

It was kind of cute actually.

When they stepped outside to make the short pilgrimage to Elvis's poolside grave, she took off her headphones for the first time.

"I didn't know all that," she began. "Nothing more than the bare basics, really. Over a billion records sold? It's beyond comprehension, really. I certainly can't imagine what it would be like to *do* all that and . . . what are you grinning at?"

"I bet if you had to take an Elvis test right now, you'd ace it."

"Shut up." But she laughed, then sobered again when she walked through the sunlight with him to the Meditation Garden, and the King's grave.

There were flowers, live ones wilting in the sun, plastic ones fading in it. And the little gravesite beside the swimming pool seemed both eccentric and right. Cameras snapped around them now, and she heard someone quietly sobbing.

"People claim to have seen his ghost, you know, back there." Logan gestured. "That is, if he's really dead."

"You don't believe that."

"Oh, yeah, Elvis left the building a long time ago."

"I mean about the ghost."

"Well, if he was going to haunt any place, this would be it."

They wound around toward the shuttle pickup. "People are awfully casual about ghosts around here."

It took him a minute. "Oh, the Harper Bride. Seen her yet?"

"No, I haven't. But that may only be because, you know, she doesn't exist. You're not going to tell me you've seen her."

"Can't say I have. Lot of people claim to, but then some claim to have seen Elvis eating peanut-butter-and-banana sandwiches at some diner ten years after he died."

"Exactly!" She was so pleased with his good sense, she gave him a light punch on the arm. "People see what they want to see, or have been schooled to see, or expect to. Imaginations run wild, especially under the right conditions or atmosphere. They ought to do more with the gardens here, don't you think?"

"Don't get me started."

"You're right. No shop talk. Instead, I'll just thank you for bringing me. I don't know when I'd've gotten around to it on my own."

"What'd you think?"

"Sad and sweet and fascinating." She passed her headphones back to the attendant and stepped on the shuttle. "Some of the rooms were, let's say, unique in decor."

Their arms bumped, brushed, stayed pressed to each other in the narrow confines of the shuttle's seats. Her hair skimmed along his shoulder until she shoved it back. He was sorry when she did.

"I knew this guy, big Elvis fan. He set about duplicating Graceland in his house. Got fabric like you saw in the game room, did his walls and ceilings."

She turned to face him, stared. "You're kidding."

He simply swiped a finger over his heart. "Even put a scar on his pool table to match the one on Elvis's. When he talked about getting those yellow appliances—"

"Harvest gold."

"Whatever. When he starting making noises about putting those in, his wife gave him notice. Her or Elvis."

Her face was alive with humor, and he stopped hearing the chatter of other passengers. There was something about her when she smiled, full out, that blew straight through him.

"And which did he choose?"

"Huh?"

"Which did he choose? His wife or Elvis?"

"Well." He stretched out his legs, but couldn't really shift his body away from hers. The sun was blasting through the window beside her, striking all that curling red hair. "He settled on re-creating it in his basement, and was trying to talk her into letting him put a scale model of the Meditation Garden in their backyard."

She laughed, a delightful roll of sound. When she dropped her head back on the seat, her hair tickled his shoulder again. "If he ever does, I hope we get the job."

"Count on it. He's my uncle."

She laughed again, until she was breathless. "Boy, I can't wait to meet your family." She angled around so she could face him. "I'm going to confess the only reason I came today was because I didn't want to spoil a nice gesture by saying no. I didn't expect to have fun."

"It wasn't a nice gesture so much as a spur of the moment thing. Your hair smelled good, and that clouded my better judgment."

Humor danced over her face as she pushed her hair back. "And? You're supposed to say you had fun, too."

"Actually, I did."

When the shuttle stopped, he got up, stepped back so she could slide out and walk in front of him. "But then, your hair still smells good, so that could be it."

She shot him a grin over her shoulder, and damn it, he felt that clutch in the belly. Usually the clutch meant possibilities of fun and enjoyment. With her, he thought it meant trouble.

But he'd been raised to follow through, and his mama

would be horrified and shocked if he didn't feed a woman he'd spent the afternoon with.

"Hungry?" he asked when he stepped down after her.

"Oh . . . Well, it's too early for dinner, too late for lunch. I really should—"

"Walk on the wild side. Eat between meals." He grabbed her hand, and that was such a surprise she didn't think to protest until he'd pulled her toward one of the on-site eateries.

"I really shouldn't take the time. I told Roz I'd be back around four."

"You know, you stay wrapped that tight for any length of time, you're going to cut your circulation off."

"I'm not wrapped that tight," she objected. "I'm responsible."

"Roz doesn't have a time clock at the nursery, and it doesn't take that long to eat a hot dog."

"No, but . . ." Liking him was so unexpected. As unexpected as the buzz along her skin at the feel of that big, hard hand gripping hers. It had been a long while since she'd enjoyed a man's company. Why cut it short?

"Okay." Though, she realized, her assent was superfluous, as he'd already pulled her inside and up to the counter. "Anyway. Since I'm here, I wouldn't mind looking in the shops for a minute. Or two."

He ordered two dogs, two Cokes and just smiled at her.

"All right, smart guy." She opened her purse, dug out her wallet. And took out a five-dollar bill. "I'm buying the CD. And make mine a Diet Coke."

She ate the hot dog, drank the Coke. She bought the CD. But unlike every other female he knew, she didn't have some religious obligation to look at and paw over everything in the store. She did her business and was done—neat, tidy, and precise.

And as they walked back to his truck, he noticed she glanced at the readout display of her cell phone. Again.

"Problem?"

"No." She slipped the phone back into her bag. "Just

checking to see if I had any messages." But it seemed everyone had managed without her for an afternoon.

Unless something was wrong with the phones. Or they'd lost her number. Or—

"The nursery could've been attacked by psychopaths with a petunia fetish." Logan opened the passenger-side door. "The entire staff could be bound and gagged in the propagation house even as we speak."

Deliberately, Stella zipped her bag closed. "You won't think that's so funny if we get there and that's just what happened."

"Yes, I will."

He walked around the truck, got behind the wheel.

"I have an obsessive, linear, goal-oriented personality with strong organizational tendencies."

He sat for a moment. "I'm glad you told me. I was under the impression you were a scatterbrain."

"Well, enough about me. Why—"

"Why do you keep doing that?"

She paused, her hands up in her hair. "Doing what?"

"Why do you keep jamming those pins in your hair?"

"Because they keep coming out."

To her speechless shock, he reached over, tugged the loosened bobby pins free, then tossed them on the floor of his truck. "So why put them in there in the first place?"

"Well, for God's sake." She scowled down at the pins. "How many times a week does someone tell you you're pushy and overbearing?"

"I don't count." He drove out of the lot and into traffic. "You've got sexy hair. You ought to leave it alone."

"Thanks very much for the style advice."

"Women don't usually sulk when a man tells them they're sexy."

"I'm not sulking, and you didn't say I was sexy. You said my hair was."

He took his eyes off the road long enough to give her an up-and-down glance. "Rest of you works, too."

Okay, something was wrong when that sort of half-assed compliment had heat balling in her belly. Best to return to safe topics. "To return to my question before I was so oddly interrupted, why did you go into landscape design?"

"Summer job that stuck."

She waited a beat, two. Three. "Really, Logan, must you go on and on, boring me with details?"

"Sorry. I never know when to shut up. I grew up on a farm."

"Really? Did you love it or hate it?"

"Was used to it, mostly. I like working outside, and don't mind heavy, sweaty work."

"Blabbermouth," she said when he fell silent again.

"Not that much more to it. I didn't want to farm, and my daddy sold the farm some years back, anyway. But I like working the land. It's what I like, it's what I'm good at. No point in doing something you don't like or you're not good at."

"Let's try this. How did you know you were good at it?"

"Not getting fired was an indication." He didn't see how she could possibly be interested, but since she was pressing, he'd pass the time. "You know how you're in school, say in history, and they're all Battle of Hastings or crossing the Rubicon or Christ knows? In and out," he said, tapping one side of his head, then the other. "I'd jam it in there long enough to skin through the test, then poof. But on the job, the boss would say we're going to put cotoneasters in here, line these barberries over there, and I'd remember. What they were, what they needed. I liked putting them in. It's satisfying, digging the hole, prepping the soil, changing the look of things. Making it more pleasing to the eye."

"It is," she agreed. "Believe it or not, that's the same sort of deal I have with my files."

He slanted her a look that made her lips twitch. "You say. Anyway, sometimes I'd get this idea that, you know, those cotoneasters would look better over there, and instead of barberries, golden mops would set this section off. So I angled off into design."

"I thought about design for a while. Not that good at it," she said. "I realized I had a hard time adjusting my vision to blend with the team's—or the client's. And I'd get too hung up in the math and science of it, and bogged down when it came time to roll over into the art."

"Who did your landscaping up north?"

"I did. If I had something in mind that took machines, or more muscle than Kevin and I could manage, I had a list." She smiled. "A very detailed and specific list, with the design done on graph paper. Then I hovered. I'm a champion hoverer."

"And nobody shoved you into a hole and buried you?"

"No. But then, I'm very personable and pleasant. Maybe, when the time comes and I find my own place, you could consult on the landscaping design."

"I'm not personable and pleasant."

"Already noted."

"And isn't it a leap for an obsessive, linear, detail freak to trust me to consult when you've only seen one of my jobs, and that in its early stages?"

"I object to the term 'freak.' I prefer 'devotee.' And it happens I've seen several of your jobs, complete. I got some of the addresses out of the files and drove around. It's what I do," she said when he braked at a Stop sign and stared at her. "I've spent some time watching Harper work, and Roz, as well as the employees. I made it a point to take a look at some of your completed jobs. I like your work."

"And if you hadn't?"

"If I hadn't, I'd have said nothing. It's Roz's business, and *she* obviously likes your work. But I'd have done some quiet research on other designers, put a file together and presented it to her. That's my job."

"And here I thought your job was to manage the nursery and annoy me with forms."

"It is. Part of that management is to make sure that all

employees and subcontractors, suppliers and equipment are not only suitable for In the Garden but the best Roz can afford. You're pricey," she added, "but your work justifies it."

When he only continued to frown, she poked a finger into his arm. "And men don't usually sulk when a woman compliments their work."

"Huh. Men never sulk, they brood."

But she had a point. Still, it occurred to him that she knew a great deal about him—personal matters. How much he made, for instance. When he asked himself how he felt about that, the answer was, Not entirely comfortable.

"My work, my salary, my prices are between me and Roz."

"Not anymore," she said cheerfully. "She has the last word, no question, but I'm there to manage. I'm saying that, in my opinion, Roz showed foresight and solid business sense in bringing you into her business. She pays you very well because you're worth it. Any reason you can't take that as a compliment and skip the brooding phase?"

"I don't know. What's she paying you?"

"That *is* between her and me, but you're certainly free to ask her." The *Star Wars* theme erupted in her purse. "Gavin's pick," she said as she dug it out. The readout told her the call came from home. "Hello? Hi, baby."

Though he was still a little irked, he watched everything about her light up. "You *did*? You're amazing. Uh-huh. I absolutely will. See you soon."

She closed the phone, put it back in her purse. "Gavin aced his spelling test."

"Yay."

She laughed. "You have *no* idea. I have to pick up pepperoni pizza on the way home. In our family, it's not a carrot at the end of the stick used as motivation—or simple bribery—it's pepperoni pizza."

"You bribe your kids?"

"Often, and without a qualm."

"Smart. So, they're getting along in school?"

"They are. All that worry and guilt wasted. I'll have to set it aside for future use. It was a big move for them—new place, new school, new people. Luke makes friends easily, but Gavin can be a little shy."

"Didn't seem shy to me. Kid's got a spark. Both of them do."

"Comic book connection. Any friend of Spidey's, and so on, so they were easy with you. But they're both sliding right along. So I can scratch traumatizing my sons by ripping them away from their friends off my Things to Worry About list."

"I bet you actually have one."

"Every mother has one." She let out a long, contented sigh as he pulled into the lot at the nursery. "This has been a really good day. Isn't this a great place? Just look at it. Industrious, attractive, efficient, welcoming. I envy Roz her vision, not to mention her guts."

"You don't seem deficient in the guts department."

"Is that a compliment?"

He shrugged. "An observation."

She liked being seen as gutsy, so she didn't tell him she was scared a great deal of the time. Order and routine were solid, defensive walls that kept the fear at bay.

"Well, thanks. For the observation, and the afternoon. I really appreciated both." She opened the door, hopped out. "And I've got a trip into the city for ribs on my list of must-dos."

"You won't be sorry." He got out, walked around to her side. He wasn't sure why. Habit, he supposed. Ingrained manners his mother had carved into him as a boy. But it wasn't the sort of situation where you walked the girl to her door and copped a kiss good night.

She thought about offering her hand to shake, but it seemed stiff *and* ridiculous. So she just smiled. "I'll play the CD for the boys." She shook her bag. "See what they think."

"Okay. See you around."

He started to walk back to his door. Then he cursed under his breath, tossed his sunglasses on the hood, and turned back. "Might as well finish it out."

She wasn't slow, and she wasn't naive. She knew what he intended when he was still a full stride away. But she couldn't seem to move.

She heard herself make some sound—not an actual word—then his hand raked through her hair, his fingers cupping her head with enough pressure to bring her up on her toes. She saw his eyes. There were gold flecks dusted over the green.

Then everything blurred, and his mouth was hard and hot on hers.

Nothing hesitant about it, nothing testing or particularly friendly. It was all demand, with an irritable edge. Like the man, she thought dimly, he was doing what he intended to do, was determined to see it through, but wasn't particularly pleased about it.

And still her heart rammed into her throat, throbbing there to block words, even breath. The fingers of the hand that had lifted to his shoulder in a kind of dazed defense dug in. They slid limply down to his elbow when his head lifted.

With his hand still caught in her hair, he said, "Hell."

He dragged her straight up to her toes again, banded an arm around her so that her body was plastered to his. When his mouth swooped down a second time, any brains that hadn't already been fried drained out of her ears.

He shouldn't have thought of kissing her. But once he had, it didn't seem reasonable to walk away and leave it undone. And now he was in trouble, all wound up in that wild hair, that sexy scent, those soft lips.

And when he deepened the kiss, she let out this sound, this catchy little moan. What the hell was a man supposed to do but want?

Her hair was like a maze of madly coiled silk, and that

pretty, curvy body of hers vibrated against him like a well-tuned machine, revving for action. The longer he held her, the more he tasted her, the dimmer the warning bells sounded to remind him he didn't want to get tangled up with her. On any level.

When he managed to release her, to step back, he saw the flush riding along her cheeks. It made her eyes bluer, bigger. It made him want to toss her over his shoulder and cart her off somewhere, anywhere at all where they could finish what the kiss had started. Because the urge to do so was an ache in the belly, he took another step back.

"Okay." He thought he spoke calmly, but couldn't be sure with the blood roaring in his ears. "See you around."

He walked back to the truck, got in. Managed to turn over the engine and shove into reverse. Then he hit the brakes again when the sun speared into his eyes.

He sat, watching Stella walk forward, retrieve the sunglasses that had bounced off the hood and onto the gravel. He lowered the window as she stepped to it.

His eyes stayed on hers when he reached out to take them from her. "Thanks."

"Sure."

He slipped them on, backed out, turned the wheel and drove out of the lot.

Alone, she let out a long, wheezing breath, sucked in another one; and let that out as she ordered her limp legs to carry her to the porch.

She made it as far as the steps before she simply lowered herself down to sit. "Holy Mother of God," she managed.

She sat, even as a customer came out, as another came in, while everything inside her jumped and jittered. She felt as though she'd fallen off a cliff and was even now, barely—just barely—clinging to a skinny, crumbling ledge by sweaty fingertips.

What was she supposed to do about this? And how could she figure it out when she couldn't think?

So she wouldn't try to figure it out until she could think. Getting to her feet, she rubbed her damp palms on the thighs of her pants. For now, she'd go back to work, she'd order pizza, then go home to her boys. Go home to normal.

She did better with normal.

ten

HARPER SPADED THE DIRT AT THE BASE OF THE clematis that wound its way up the iron trellis. It was quiet on this edge of the garden. The shrubs and ornamental trees, the paths and beds separated what he still thought of as the guest house from the main.

Daffodils were just opening up, with all that bright yellow against the spring green. Tulips would be coming along next. They were one of his favorite things about this leading edge of spring, so he'd planted a bed of bulbs right outside the kitchen door of his place.

It was a small converted carriage house and according to every female he'd ever brought there, it was charming. "Dollhouse" was the usual term. He didn't mind it. Though he thought of it more as a cottage, like a groundskeeper's cottage with its whitewashed cedar shakes and pitched roof. It was comfortable, inside and out, and more than adequate for his needs.

There was a small greenhouse only a few feet out the back door, and that was his personal domain. The cottage was just far enough from the house to be private, so he didn't have to feel weird having overnight guests of the female persuasion. And close enough that he could be at the main house in minutes if his mother needed him.

He didn't like the idea of her being alone, even with David on hand. And thank God for David. It didn't matter that she was self-sufficient, the strongest person he knew. He just didn't like the idea of his mother rattling around in that big old house alone, day after day, night after night.

Though he certainly preferred that to having her stuck in it with that asshole she'd married. Words couldn't describe how he despised Bryce Clerk. He supposed having his mother fall for the guy proved she wasn't infallible, but it had been a hell of a mistake for someone who rarely made one.

Though she'd given him the boot, swiftly and without mercy, Harper had worried how the man would handle being cut off—from Roz, the house, the money, the whole ball.

And damned if he hadn't tried to break in once, the week before the divorce was final. Harper didn't doubt his mother could've handled it, but it hadn't hurt to be at hand.

And having a part in kicking the greedy, cheating, lying bastard out on his ass couldn't be overstated.

But maybe enough time had passed now. And she sure as hell wasn't alone in the house these days. Two women, two kids made for a lot of company. Between them and the business, she was busier than ever.

Maybe he should think about getting a place of his own.

Trouble was, he couldn't think of a good reason. He loved this place, in a way he'd never loved a woman. With a kind of focused passion, respect, and gratitude.

The gardens were home, maybe even more than the house, more than his cottage. Most days he could walk out his front door, take a good, healthy hike, and be at work.

God knew he didn't want to move to the city. All that noise, all those people. Memphis was great for a night out—a club, a date, meeting up with friends. But he'd suffocate there inside a month.

He sure as hell didn't want suburbia. What he wanted was right where he was. A nice little house, extensive gardens, a greenhouse and a short hop to work.

He sat back on his heels, adjusted the ball cap he wore to keep the hair out of his eyes. Spring was coming. There was nothing like spring at home. The way it smelled, the way it looked, even the way it sounded.

The light was soft now with approaching evening. When the sun went down, the air would chill, but it wouldn't have that bite of winter.

When he was done planting here, he'd go in and get himself a beer. And he'd sit out in the dark and the cool, and enjoy the solitude.

He took a bold yellow pansy out of the cell pack and began to plant.

He didn't hear her walk up. Such was his focus that he didn't notice her shadow fall over him. So her friendly "Hey!" nearly had him jumping out of his skin.

"Sorry." With a laugh, Hayley rubbed a hand over her belly. "Guess you were a million miles away."

"Guess." His fingers felt fat and clumsy all of a sudden, and his brain sluggish. She stood with the setting sun at her back, so when he squinted up at her, her head was haloed, her face shadowed.

"I was just walking around. Heard your music." She nodded toward the open windows where REM spilled out. "I saw them in concert once. Excellent. Pansies? They're a hot item right now."

"Well, they like the cool."

"I know. How come you're putting them here? You've got this vine thing happening."

"Clematis. Likes its roots shaded. So you . . . you know, put annuals over them."

"Oh." She squatted down for a closer look. "What color is the clematis?"

"It's purple." He wasn't sure pregnant women should squat. Didn't it crowd things in there? "Ah, you want a chair or something?"

"No, I'm set. I like your house."

"Yeah, me too."

"It's sort of storybook here, with all the gardens. I mean, the big house is amazing. But it's a little intimidating." She grimaced. "I don't mean to sound ungrateful."

"No, I get you." It helped to keep planting. She didn't *smell* pregnant. She smelled sexy. And that had to be wrong. "It's a great place, and you couldn't get my mother out of it with dynamite and wild mules. But it's a lot of house."

"Took me a week to stop walking about on tiptoe and wanting to whisper. Can I plant one?"

"You don't have any gloves. I can get—"

"Hell, I don't mind a little dirt under my nails. A lady was in today? She said it's like good luck for a pregnant woman to plant gardens. Something about fertility, I guess."

He didn't want to think about fertility. There was something terrifying about it. "Go ahead."

"Thanks. I wanted to say . . ." And it was easier with her hands busy. "Well, just that I know how it might look, me coming out of nowhere, landing on your mama's doorstep. But I'm not going to take advantage of her. I don't want you to think I'd try to do that."

"I've only known one person to manage it, and he didn't manage it for long."

"The second husband." She nodded as she patted the dirt around her plant. "I asked David about him so I wouldn't say something stupid. He said how he'd stuck his hand in the till, and cheated on her with another woman." She chose another pansy. "And when Roz got wind of it, she booted him out so hard and fast he didn't land till he was halfway to Memphis. You gotta admire that, because you know even with a mad on, it had to hurt her feelings. Plus, it's just embarrassing when somebody—oops."

She pressed a hand to her side, and had the blood draining out of Harper's face.

"What? What?"

"Nothing. Baby's moving around. Sometimes it gives me a jolt is all."

"You should stand up. You should sit down."

"Let me just finish this one. Back home, when I started to show? People, some people, just figured I'd got myself in trouble and the boy wouldn't stand up for me. I mean, Jesus, are we in the twenty-first century or what? Anyway, that made me mad, but it was embarrassing, too. I guess that's partly why I left. It's hard being embarrassed all the damn time. There." She patted the dirt. "They look really pretty."

He popped up to help her to her feet. "You want to sit for a minute? Want me to walk you back?"

She patted her belly. "This makes you nervous."

"Looks like."

"Me too. But I'm fine. You'll want to get the rest of those planted before it gets dark." She looked down at the flowers again, at the house, at the gardens surrounding it, and those long, lake-colored eyes seemed to take in everything.

Then they zeroed in on his face and made his throat go dry.

"I really like your place. See you at work."

He stood, rooted, as she walked off, gliding along the path, around the curve of it, into the twilight.

He was exhausted, he realized. Like he'd run some sort of crazed race. He'd just have that beer now, settle himself down. Then he'd finish with the pansies.

WITH THE KIDS OUTSIDE TAKING PARKER FOR HIS after-dinner walk, Stella cleaned up the mess two boys and a dog could make in the kitchen over a pepperoni pizza.

"Next pizza night, I buy," Hayley said as she loaded glasses into the dishwasher.

"That's a deal." Stella glanced over. "When I was carrying Luke, all I wanted was Italian. Pizza, spaghetti, manicotti. I was surprised he didn't pop out singing 'That's Amore.' "

"I don't have any specific cravings. I'll just eat anything." In the wash of the outside floodlights, she could see boys and dog racing. "The baby's moving around a lot. That's normal, right?"

"Sure. Gavin just sort of snuggled and snoozed. I'd have to poke him or sip some Coke to get him moving. But Luke did gymnastics in there for months. Is it keeping you up nights?"

"Sometimes, but I don't mind. It feels like we're the only two people in the world. Just me and him—or her."

"I know just what you mean. But Hayley, if you're awake, worried or just not feeling well, whatever, you can come get me."

The tightness in her throat loosened instantly. "Really? You mean it?"

"Sure. Sometimes it helps to talk to somebody who's been there and done that."

"I'm not on my own," she said quietly, with her eyes on the boys outside the window. "Not like I thought I'd be. Was ready to be—I think." When those eyes filled, she blinked them, rubbed at them. "Hormones. God."

"Crying can help, too." Stella rubbed Hayley's shoulders. "And I want you to tell me if you want someone to go with you to your doctor's appointments."

"He said, when I went in, that everything looks good. Right on schedule. And that I should sign up for the classes, you know? Childbirth classes. But they like you to have a partner."

"Pick me!"

Laughing, Hayley turned. "Really? You're sure? It's a lot to ask."

"I would love it. It's almost as good as having another one of my own."

"Would you? If . . ."

"Yes. Two was the plan, but as soon as Luke was born, I thought, how can I not do this again—and wouldn't it be fun to try for a girl? But another boy would be great." She leaned forward on the counter, looked out the window. "They're terrific, aren't they? My boys."

"They are."

"Kevin was so proud, so in love with them. I think he'd have had half a dozen."

Hayley heard the change in tone, and this time, she rubbed a hand on Stella's shoulder. "Does it hurt to talk about him?"

"Not anymore. It did for a while, for a long while." She picked up the dishrag to wipe the counter. "But now it's good to remember. Warm, I guess. I ought to call those boys in."

But she turned at the sound of heels clicking on wood. When Roz breezed in, Stella's mouth dropped open.

She recalled her first impression of Rosalind Harper had been of beauty, but this was the first time she'd seen Roz exploit her natural attributes.

She wore a sleek, form-fitting dress in a muted copper color that made her skin glow. It, along with ice-pick-heeled sandals, showed off lean, toned legs. A necklace of delicate filigree with a teardrop of citrine lay over her breasts.

"David?" Roz scanned the room, then rolled dark, dramatic eyes. "He's going to make me late."

Stella let out an exaggerated breath. "Just let me say, Wow!"

"Yeah." She grinned, did a little half turn. "I must've been insane when I bought the shoes. They're going to kill me. But when I have to drag myself out to one of these charity deals, I like to make a statement."

"If the statement's 'I'm totally hot,'" Hayley put in, "you hit it dead on."

"That was the target."

"You look absolutely amazing. Sex with class. Every

man there's going to wish he was taking you home tonight."

"Well." With a half laugh, Roz shook her head. "It's great having women in the house. Who knew? I'm going to go nag David. He'll primp for another hour if I don't give his ass a kick."

"Have a wonderful time."

"She sure didn't look like anybody's mother," Stella said under her breath.

WHAT WOULD SHE LOOK LIKE IN TWENTY YEARS? Hayley wondered.

She studied herself in the mirror while she rubbed Vitamin E oil over her belly and breasts. Would she still be able to fix herself up and know she looked good?

Of course, she didn't have as much to work with as Roz. She remembered her grandmother saying once that beauty was in the bones. Looking at Roz helped her understand just what that meant.

She'd never be as stunning as Roz, or as eye-catching as Stella, but she looked okay. She took care of her skin, tried out the makeup tricks she read about in magazines.

Guys were attracted.

Obviously, she thought with a self-deprecating smile as she looked down at her belly.

Or had been. Most guys didn't get the hots for pregnant women. And that was fine, because she wasn't interested in men right now. The only thing that mattered was her baby.

"It's all about you now, kid," she said as she pulled on an oversized T-shirt.

After climbing into bed, plumping up her pillows, she reached for one of the books stacked on her nightstand. She had books on childbirth, on pregnancy, on early-childhood development. She read from one of them every night.

When her eyes began to droop, she closed the book.

Switching off the light, she snuggled down. "'Night, baby," she whispered.

And felt it just as she was drifting off. The little chill, the absolute certainty that she wasn't alone. Her heartbeat quickened until she could hear it in her ears. Gathering courage, she let her eyes open to slits.

She saw the figure standing over the bed. The light-colored hair, the lovely sad face. She thought about screaming, just as she did every time she saw the woman. But she bit it back, braced herself, and reached out.

When her hand passed through the woman's arm, Hayley did let out a muffled scream. Then she was alone, shivering in bed and fumbling for the light.

"I'm not imagining it. I'm not!"

STELLA CLIMBED UP THE STEPSTOOL TO HOOK ANOTHER hanging basket for display. After looking over last year's sales, crunching numbers, she'd decided to increase the number offered by 15 percent.

"I could do that," Hayley insisted. "I'm not going to fall off a stupid stepstool."

"No chance. Hand me up that one. The begonias."

"They're really pretty. So lush."

"Roz and Harper started most of these over the winter. Begonias and impatiens are big-volume sellers. With growers like Roz and Harper, we can do them in bulk, and our cost is low. These are bread-and-butter plants for us."

"People could make up their own cheaper."

"Sure." Stella climbed down, moved the ladder, climbed up again. "Ivy geranium," she decided. "But it's tough to resist all this color and bloom. Even avid gardeners, the ones who do some propagating on their own, have a hard time passing up big, beautiful blooms. Blooms, my young apprentice, sell."

"So we're putting these baskets everywhere."

"Seduction. Wait until we move some of the annuals

outside, in front. All that color will draw the customers. Early-blooming perennials too."

She selected another basket. "I've got this. Page Roz, will you? I want her to see these, and get her clearance to hang a couple dozen in Greenhouse Three with the extra stock. And pick out a pot. One of the big ones that didn't move last year. I want to do one up, put it by the counter. I'll move that sucker. In fact, pick out two. Clean off the discount price. When I'm done, they'll not only move, they'll move at a fat profit."

"Gotcha."

"Make sure one of them's that cobalt glaze," she called out. "You know the one? And don't pick it up yourself."

In her mind, Stella began to plan it. White flowers—heliotrope, impatiens, spills of sweet alyssum, silvery accents from dusty miller and sage. Another trail of white petunias. Damn, she should've told Hayley to get one of the stone-gray pots. Good contrast with the cobalt. And she'd do it up hot. Bold red geraniums, lobelia, verbena, red New Guineas.

She added, subtracted plants in her mind, calculated the cost of pots, stock, soil. And smiled to herself as she hung another basket.

"Shouldn't you be doing paperwork?"

She nearly tipped off the stool, might have if a hand hadn't slapped onto her butt to keep her upright.

"It's not all I do." She started to get down, but realized being on the stool kept her at eye level with him. "You can move your hand now, Logan."

"It doesn't mind being there." But he let it fall, slipped it into his pocket. "Nice baskets."

"In the market?"

"Might be. You had a look on your face when I came in."

"I usually do. That's why it's called a face."

"No, the kind of look a woman gets when she's thinking about how to make some guy drool."

"Did I? Mind?" she added, gesturing to a basket. "You're off the mark. I was thinking how I was going to turn two over-stock pots on the discount rack into stupendous displays and considerable profit."

Even as she hung the basket, he was lifting another, and by merely raising his arm, set it in place. "Showoff."

"Shorty."

Hayley came through the doorway, turned briskly on her heel and headed out.

"Hayley."

"Forgot something," she called out and kept going.

Stella blew out a breath and would've asked for another basket, but he'd already picked one up, hung it. "You've been busy," she said.

"Cool, dry weather the last week."

"If you're here to pick up the shrubs for the Pitt job, I can get the paperwork."

"My crew's out loading them. I want to see you again."

"Well. You are."

He kept his eyes on hers. "You're not dim."

"No, I'm not. I'm not sure—"

"Neither am I," he interrupted. "Doesn't seem to stop me from wanting to see you again. It's irritating, thinking about you."

"Thanks. That really makes me want to sigh and fall into your arms."

"I don't want you to fall into them. If I did, I'd just kick your feet out from under you."

She laid a hand on her heart, fluttered her lashes, and did her best woman of the south accent. "My goodness, all this soppy romance is too much for me."

Now he grinned. "I like you, Red. Some of the time. I'll pick you up at seven."

"What? Tonight?" Reluctant amusement turned to outright panic in a fingersnap. "I can't possibly just go out, spur of the moment. I have two kids."

"And three adults in the house. Any reason you can think of why any or all of them can't handle your boys for a few hours tonight?"

"No. But I haven't *asked*, a concept you appear to be

unfamiliar with. And—" She shoved irritably at her hair. "I might have plans."

"Do you?"

She angled her head, looked down her nose. "I always have plans."

"I bet. So flex them. You take the boys for ribs yet?"

"Yes, last week after—"

"Good."

"Do you know how often you interrupt me in the middle of a sentence?"

"No, but I'll start counting. Hey, Roz."

"Logan. Stella, these look great." She stopped in the center of the aisle, scanning, nodding as she absently slapped her dirty gloves against her already dirt-smeared jeans. "I wasn't sure displaying so many would work, but it does. Something about the abundance of bloom."

She took off her ball cap, stuffed it in the back pocket of her work pants, stuffed the gloves in the other. "Am I interrupting?"

"No."

"Yes," Logan corrected. "But it's okay. You up to watching Stella's boys tonight?"

"I haven't said—"

"Absolutely. It'll be fun. You two going out?"

"A little dinner. I'll leave the invoice on your desk," he said to Stella. "See you at seven."

Tired of standing, Stella sat on the stool and scowled at Roz when Logan sauntered out. "You didn't help."

"I think I did." Reaching up, she turned one of the baskets to check the symmetry of the plants. "You'll go out, have a good time. Your boys'll be fine, and I'll enjoy spending some time with them. If you didn't want to go out with Logan, you wouldn't go. You know how to say no loud enough."

"That may be true, but I might've liked a little more notice. A little more . . . something."

"He is what he is." She patted Stella's knee. "And the good thing about that is you don't have to wonder what he's hiding, or what kind of show he's putting on. He's . . . I can't say he's a nice man, because he can be incredibly difficult. But he's an honest one. Take it from me, there's a lot to be said for that."

eLeveN

THIS, STELLA THOUGHT, WAS WHY DATING WAS VERY rarely worth it. In her underwear, she stood in front of her closet, debating, considering, despairing over what to wear.

She didn't even know where she was going. She *hated* not knowing where she was going. How was she supposed to know what to prepare for?

"Dinner" was not enough information. Was it little-black-dress dinner, or dressy-casual on-sale-designer-suit dinner? Was it jeans and a shirt and jacket dinner, or jeans and a silk blouse dinner?

Added to that, by picking her up at seven, he'd barely left her enough time to change, much less decide what to change into.

Dating. How could something that had been so desired, so exciting and so damn much fun in her teens, so easy and natural in her early twenties, have become such a complicated, often irritating chore in her thirties?

It wasn't just that marriage had spoiled her, or rusted her dating tools. Adult dating was complex and exhausting because the people involved in the stupid date had almost certainly been through at least one serious relationship, and breakup, and carried that extra baggage on their backs. They were already set in their ways, had defined their expectations, and had performed this societal dating ritual so often that they really just wanted to cut to the chase—or go home and watch Letterman.

Add to that a man who dropped the date on your head out of the clear blue, then didn't have the sense to give you some guidelines so you knew how to present yourself, and it was just a complete mess before it started.

Fine, then. *Fine*. He'd just get what he got.

She was stepping into the little black dress when the connecting bathroom door burst open and Gavin rushed in. "Mom! I finished my homework. Luke didn't, but I did. Can I go down now? Can I?"

She was glad she'd decided on the open-toed slides and no hose, as Parker was currently trying to climb up her leg. "Did you forget something?" she asked Gavin.

"Nuh-uh. I did all the vocabulary words."

"The knocking something?"

"Oh." He smiled, big and innocent. "You look pretty."

"Smooth talker." She bent down to kiss the top of his head. "But when a door's closed, you knock."

"Okay. Can I go down now?"

"In a minute." She walked over to her dresser to put on the silver hoops she'd laid out. "I want you to promise you'll be good for Miss Roz."

"We're going to have cheeseburgers and play video games. She says she can take us in Smackdown, but I don't think so."

"No fighting with your brother." Hope springs, she thought. "Consider this your night off from your mission in life."

"Can I go *down*?"

"Get." She gave him a light slap on the rump. "Remember, I'll have my phone if you need me."

When he rushed out, she slipped on her shoes and a thin black sweater. After a check in the mirror, she decided the accessories took the dress into the could-be-casual, could-be-more area she'd been shooting for.

She picked up her bag and, checking the contents as she went, walked into the next bedroom. Luke was sprawled belly-down on the floor—his favored position—frowning miserably over his arithmetic book.

"Trouble, handsome?"

He lifted his head, and his face was aggrieved in the way only a young boy could manage. "I hate homework."

"Me too."

"Gavin did the touchdown dance, with his fingers in the air, 'cause he finished first."

Understanding the demoralization, she sat on the floor beside him. "Let's see what you've got."

"How come I have to know two plus three, anyway?"

"How else would you know how many fingers you have on each hand?"

His brow beetled, then cleared with a delighted smile. "Five!"

With the crisis averted, she helped him with the rest of the problems. "There, all done. That wasn't so bad."

"I still hate homework."

"Maybe, but what about the touchdown dance?"

On a giggle, he leaped up and did his strut around the room.

And all, she thought, was right in her little world once more.

"How come you're not going to eat here? We're having cheeseburgers."

"I'm not entirely sure. You'll behave for Miss Roz?"

"Uh-huh. She's nice. Once she came out in the yard and threw the ball for Parker. And she didn't even mind when it got slobbered. Some girls do. I'm going down now, okay? 'Cause I'm hungry."

"You bet."

Alone, she got to her feet, automatically picking up the scatter of toys and clothes that hadn't made it back onto the shelf or into the closet.

She ran her fingers over some of their treasures. Gavin's beloved comic books, his ball glove. Luke's favorite truck, and the battered bear he wasn't yet ashamed to sleep with.

The prickle between her shoulder blades had her stiffening. Even under the light sweater her arms broke out in gooseflesh. Out of the corner of her eye, she saw a shape—a reflection, a shadow—in the mirror over the bureau.

When she spun, Hayley swung around the door and into the room.

"Logan's just pulling up in front of the house," she began, then stopped. "You okay? You look all pale."

"Fine. I'm fine." But she pushed a not-quite-steady hand at her hair. "I just thought . . . nothing. Nothing. Besides pale, how do I look?" And she made herself turn to the mirror again. Saw only herself, with Hayley moving toward her.

"Two thumbs up. I just love your hair."

"Easy to say when you don't wake up with it every morning. I thought about putting it up, but it seemed too formal."

"It's just right." Hayley edged closer, tipping her head toward Stella's. "I did the redhead thing once. Major disaster. Made my skin look yellow."

"That deep, dense brown's what's striking on you." And look at that face, Stella thought with a tiny twist of envy. Not a line on it.

"Yeah, but the red's so now. Anyway, I'm going to go on down. I'll keep Logan busy until. You wait just a few more minutes before you head down, then we'll all be back in the kitchen. Big burger feast."

She didn't intend to make an entrance, for heaven's sake. But Hayley had already gone off, and she did want to check her lipstick. And settle herself down.

At least her nerves over this date—it *was* a date this

time—had taken a backseat to others. It hadn't been Hayley's reflection in the mirror. Even that quick glimpse had shown her the woman who'd stood there had blond hair.

Steadier, she walked out, started down the hall. From the top of the steps, she heard Hayley laugh.

"She'll be right down. I guess you know how to make yourself at home. I'm going on back to the kitchen with the rest of the gang. Let Stella know I'll say bye from her to everyone. Y'all have fun."

Was the girl psychic? Stella wondered. Hayley had timed her exit so adroitly that as she walked down the hall, Stella hit the halfway point on the steps.

And Logan's attention shifted upward.

Good black trousers, she noted. Nice blue shirt, no tie, but with a casual sport coat over it. And still he didn't look quite tame.

"Nice," he said.

"Thanks. You, too."

"Hayley said she'd tell everyone you were leaving. You ready?"

"Sure."

She stepped out with him, then studied the black Mustang. "You own a car."

"This is not merely a car, and to call it such is very female."

"And to say that is very sexist. Okay, if it's not a car, what is it?"

"It's a machine."

"I stand corrected. You never said where we were going."

He opened her door. "Let's find out."

HE DROVE INTO THE CITY, WITH MUSIC SHE DIDN'T recognize on low. She knew it was blues—or supposed it was, but she didn't know anything about that area of music. Mentioning that, casually, not only seemed to shock him but kept conversation going through the trip.

She got a nutshell education on artists like John Lee Hooker and Muddy Waters, B. B. King and Taj Mahal.

And it occurred to her after they'd crossed into the city, that conversation between them never seemed to be a problem. After he parked, he shifted to take a long look at her. "You sure you were born down here?"

"It says so on my birth certificate."

He shook his head and climbed out. "Since you're that ignorant of the blues, you better check it again."

He took her inside a restaurant where the tables were already crowded with patrons and the noise level high with chatter. Once they were seated, he waved the waiter away. "Why don't we just wait on drinks until you know what you want to eat. We'll get a bottle of wine to go with it."

"All right." Since it seemed he'd nixed the pre-dinner conversation, she opened her menu.

"They're known for their catfish here. Ever had it?" he asked.

She lifted her gaze over the top of her menu, met his. "No. And whether or not that makes me a Yankee, I'm thinking I'll go for the chicken."

"Okay. You can have some of mine to give you a sample of what you've been missing. There's a good California Chardonnay on their wine list that'll go with both the fish and the bird. It's got a nice finish."

She set her menu down, leaned forward. "Do you really know that, or are you just making it up?"

"I like wine. I make it a point to know what I like."

She sat back when he motioned the waiter over. Once they'd ordered, she angled her head. "What are we doing here, Logan?"

"Speaking for myself, I'm going to have a really fine catfish dinner and a glass of good wine."

"We've had some conversations, mostly business-oriented."

"We've had some conversations, and some arguments," he corrected.

"True. We had an outing, an enjoyable one, which ended on a surprisingly personal note."

"I do like listening to you talk sometimes, Red. It's almost like listening to a foreign language. Are you laying all those things down like pavers, trying to make some sort of path from one point to the next?"

"Maybe. The fact is, I'm sitting here with you, on a date. That wasn't my intention twenty-four hours ago. We've got a working relationship."

"Uh-huh. And speaking of that, I still find your system mostly annoying."

"Big surprise. And speaking of that, you neglected to put that invoice on my desk this afternoon."

"Did I?" He moved a shoulder. "I've got it somewhere."

"My point is—"

She broke off when the waiter brought the wine to the table, turned the label toward Logan.

"That's the one. Let the lady taste it."

She bided her time, then picked up the glass holding the testing sip. She sampled, lifted her eyebrows. "It's very good . . . has a nice finish."

Logan grinned. "Then let's get started on it."

"The point I was trying to make," she began again, "is that while it's smart and beneficial all around for you and me to develop a friendly relationship, it's probably not either for us to take it to any other level."

"Uh-huh." He sampled the wine himself, kept watching her with those big-cat eyes. "You think I'm not going to kiss you again because it might not be smart or beneficial?"

"I'm in a new place, with a new job. I've taken my kids to a new place. They're first with me."

"I expect they would be. But I don't expect this is your first dinner with a man since you lost your husband."

"I'm careful."

"I never would've guessed. How'd he die?"

"Plane crash. Commuter plane. He was on his way back from a business trip. I had the TV on, and there was a bulletin. They didn't give any names, but I knew it was Kevin's plane. I knew he was gone before they came to tell me."

"You know what you were wearing when you heard the bulletin, what you were doing, where you were standing." His voice was quiet, his eyes were direct. "You know every detail about that day."

"Why do you say that?"

"Because it was the worst day of your life. You'll be hazy on the day before, the day after, but you'll never forget a single detail of that day."

"You're right." And his intuition surprised her, touched her. "Have you lost someone?"

"No, not like what you mean, or how you mean. But a woman like you? She doesn't get married, stay married, unless the man's at the center of her life. Something yanks that center out of you, you never forget."

"No, I won't." It was carved into her heart. "That's the most insightful and accurate, and comforting expression of sympathy anyone's given me. I hope I don't insult you by saying it comes as a surprise."

"I don't insult that easy. You lost their father, but you've built a life—looks like a good one—for your kids. That takes work. You're not the first woman I've been interested in who's had children. I respect motherhood, and its priorities. Doesn't stop me from looking across this table and wondering when I'm going to get you naked."

She opened her mouth, closed it again. Cleared her throat, sipped wine. "Well. Blunt."

"Different sort of woman, I'd just go for the mattress." At her strangled half laugh, he lifted his wine. And waited while their first course was served. "But as it is, you're a . . . since we're having this nice meal together I'll say you're a cautious sort of woman."

"You wanted to say tight-ass."

He grinned, appreciating her. "You'll never know. Added to that, we both work for Roz, and I wouldn't do anything to mess her up. Not intentionally. You've got two kids to worry about. And I don't know how tender you might be yet over losing your husband. So instead of my hauling you off to bed, we're having dinner conversation."

She took a minute to think it through. At the root, she couldn't find anything wrong with his logic. In fact, she agreed with it. "All right. First Roz. I won't do anything to mess her up either. So whatever happens here, we agree to maintain a courteous working relationship."

"Might not always be courteous, but it'll be about the work."

"Fair enough. My boys are my priority, first and last. Not only because they have to be," she added, "but because I want them to be. Nothing will change that."

"Anything did, I wouldn't have much respect for you."

"Well." She waited just a moment because his response had not only been blunt again, but was one she appreciated a great deal. "As for Kevin, I loved him very much. Losing him cut me in two, the part that just wanted to lie down and die, and the part that had to go through the grief and the anger and the motions—and live."

"Takes courage to live."

Her eyes stung, and she took one very careful breath. "Thank you. I had to put myself back together. For the kids, for myself. I'll never feel for another man exactly what I felt for him. I don't think I should. But that doesn't mean I can't be interested in and attracted to someone else. It doesn't mean I'm fated to live my life alone."

He sat for a moment. "How can such a sensible woman have an emotional attachment to forms and invoices?"

"How can such a talented man be so disorganized?" More relaxed than she'd imagined, she enjoyed her salad. "I drove by the Dawson job again."

"Oh, yeah?"

"I realize you still have a few finishing touches that have to wait until all danger of frost is over, but I wanted to tell you it's good work. No, that's wrong. It's not. It's exceptional work."

"Thanks. You take more pictures?"

"I did. We'll be using some of them—before and

after—in the landscaping section of the Web site I'm designing."

"No shit."

"None whatsoever. I'm going to make Roz more money, Logan. She makes more, you make more. The site's going to generate more business for the landscaping arm. I guarantee it."

"It's hard to find a downside on that one."

"You know what I envy you most?"

"My sparkling personality."

"No, you don't sparkle in the least. Your muscle."

"You envy my muscle? I don't think it'd look so good on you, Red."

"Whenever I'd start a project at home—back home—I couldn't do it all myself. I have vision—not as creative as yours, maybe, but I can see what I want, and I've got considerable skill. But when it comes to the heavy, manual labor of it, I'm out. It's frustrating because with some of it, I'd really like to do it all myself. And I can't. So I envy you the muscle that means you can."

"I imagine whether you're doing it or directing it, it's done the way you want."

She smiled into her wine. "Goes without saying. I've heard you've got a place not far from Roz's."

"About two miles out." When their main courses were served, Logan cut a chunk off his catfish, laid it on her plate.

Stella stared at it. "Well. Hmmm."

"I bet you tell your kids they don't know if they like something or not until they've tried it."

"One of the advantages of being a grown-up is being able to say things like that without applying them to yourself. But okay." She forked off a tiny bite, geared herself up for the worst, and ate it. "Interestingly," she said after a moment, "it tastes nothing like cat. Or like what one assumes cat might taste like. It's actually good."

"You might just get back some of your southern. We'll have you eating grits next."

"I don't think so. Those I have tried. Anyway, are you doing the work yourself? On your house."

"Most of it. Land's got some nice gentle rises, good drainage. Some fine old trees on the north side. A couple of pretty sycamores and some hickory, with some wild azalea and mountain laurel scattered around. Some open southern exposure. Plenty of frontage, and a small creek running on the back edge."

"What about the house?"

"What?"

"The house. What kind of house is it?"

"Oh. Two-story frame. It's probably too much space for me, but it came with the land."

"It sounds like the sort of thing I'll be looking for in a few months. Maybe if you hear of anything on the market you could let me know."

"Sure, I can do that. Kids doing all right at Roz's?"

"They're doing great. But at some point we'll need to have our own place. It's important they have their own. I don't want anything elaborate—couldn't afford it, anyway. And I don't mind fixing something up. I'm fairly handy. And I'd really prefer it wasn't haunted."

She stopped herself when he sent her a questioning look. Then shook her head. "Must be the wine because I didn't know *that* was in my head."

"Why is it?"

"I saw—thought I saw," she corrected, "this ghost reputed to haunt the Harper house. In the mirror, in my bedroom, just before you picked me up. It wasn't Hayley. She came in an instant later, and I tried to convince myself it had been her. But it wasn't. And at the same time, it could hardly have been anyone else because . . . it's just not possible."

"Sounds like you're still trying to convince yourself."

"Sensible woman, remember." She tapped a finger on the side of her head. "Sensible women don't see ghosts, or hear them singing lullabies. Or feel them."

"Feel them how?"

"A chill, a . . . *feeling*." She gave a quick shudder and tried to offset it with a quick laugh. "I can't explain it because it's not rational. And tonight, that feeling was very intense. Brief, but intense. And hostile. No, that's not right. 'Hostile' is too strong a word. Disapproving."

"Why don't you talk to Roz about it? She could give you the history, as far as she knows it."

"Maybe. You said you've never seen it?"

"Nope."

"Or felt it?"

"Can't say I have. But sometimes when I've been working a job, walking some land, digging into it, I've felt something. You plant something, even if it dies off, it leaves something in the soil. Why shouldn't a person leave something behind?"

It was something to think about, later, when her mind wasn't so distracted. Right now she had to think about the fact that she was enjoying his company. And there was the basic animal attraction to consider. If she continued to enjoy his company, and the attraction didn't fade off, they were going to end up in bed.

Then there were all the ramifications and complications that would entail. In addition, their universe was finite. They worked for the same person in the same business. It wasn't the sort of atmosphere where two people could have an adult affair without everyone around them knowing they were having it.

So she'd have to think about *that*, and just how uncomfortable it might be to have her private life as public knowledge.

After dinner, they walked over to Beale Street to join the nightly carnival. Tourists, Memphians out on the town, couples, and clutches of young people wandered the street lit by neon signs. Music trickled out of doorways, and people flooded in and out of shops.

"Used to be a club along here called the Monarch. Those shoes going to give you any trouble with this?"

"No."

"Good. Great legs, by the way."

"Thanks. I've had them for years."

"So, the Monarch," he continued. "Happened it shared a back alley with an undertaker. Made it easy for the owners to dispose of gunshot victims."

"That's a pretty piece of Beale Street trivia."

"Oh, there's plenty more. Blues, rock—it's the home of both—voodoo, gambling, sex, scandal, bootleg whiskey, pickpockets, and murder."

Music pumped out of a club as he talked, and struck Stella as southern-fried in the best possible way.

"It's all been right here," he continued. "But you oughta just enjoy the carnival the way it is now."

They joined a crowd lining the sidewalk to watch three boys do running flips and gymnastics up and down the center of the street.

"I can do that." She nodded toward one of the boys as he walked on his hands back to their tip box.

"Uh-huh."

"I can. I'm not going to demonstrate here and now, but I certainly can. Six years of gymnastic lessons. I can bend my body like a pretzel. Well, half a pretzel now, but at one time . . ."

"You trying to get me hot?"

She laughed. "No."

"Just a side effect, then. What does half a pretzel look like?"

"Maybe I'll show you sometime when I'm more appropriately dressed."

"You *are* trying to make me hot."

She laughed again and watched the performers. After Logan dropped money in the tip box, they strolled along the sidewalk. "Who's Betty Paige and why is her face on these shirts?"

He stopped dead. "You've got to be kidding."

"I'm not."

"I guess you didn't just live up north, you lived up north in a cave. Betty Paige, legendary fifties pinup and general sex goddess."

"How do you know? You weren't even born in the fifties."

"I make it a point to learn my cultural history, especially when it involves gorgeous women who strip. Look at that face. The girl next door with the body of Venus."

"She probably couldn't walk on her hands," Stella said, and casually strolled away when he laughed.

They walked off the wine, and the meal, meandering down one side of the street and back up the other. He tempted her with a blues club, but after a brief, internal debate she shook her head.

"I really can't. It's already later than I'd planned. I've got a full day tomorrow, and I've imposed on Roz long enough tonight."

"We'll rain-check it."

"And a blues club will go on my list. Got more checks tonight. Beale Street and catfish. I'm practically a native now."

"Next thing you know you'll be frying up the cat and putting peanuts in your Coke."

"Why in the world would I put peanuts in my Coke? Never mind." She waved him away as he drove out of town. "It's a southern thing. How about if I just say I had a good time tonight?"

"That'll work."

It hadn't been complicated, she realized, or boring, or stressful. At least not after the first few minutes. She'd forgotten, or nearly, what it could be like to be both stimulated and relaxed around a man.

Or to wonder, and there was no point pretending she wasn't wondering, what it would be like to have those hands—those big, work-hardened hands—on her.

Roz had left lights on for her. Front porch, foyer, her own bedroom. She saw the gleam of them as they drove up, and found it a motherly thing to do. Or big sisterly, Stella supposed, as Roz wasn't nearly old enough to be her mother.

Her mother had been too busy with her own life and interests to think about little details like front porch lights. Maybe, Stella thought, that was one of the reasons she herself was so compulsive about them.

"Such a beautiful house," Stella said. "The way it sort of glimmers at night. It's no wonder she loves it."

"No place else quite like it. Spring comes in, the gardens just blow you away."

"She ought to hold a house and garden tour."

"She used to, once a year. Hasn't done it since she peeled off that asshole Clerk. I wouldn't bring it up," he said before Stella spoke. "If she wants to do that kind of thing again, she will."

Knowing his style now, Stella waited for him to come around and open her door. "I'm looking forward to seeing the gardens in their full glory. And I'm grateful for the chance to live here a while and have the kids exposed to this kind of tradition."

"There's another tradition. Kiss the girl good night."

He moved a little slower this time, gave her a chance to anticipate. Those sexy nerves were just beginning to dance over her skin when his mouth met hers.

Then they raced in a shivering path to belly, to throat as his tongue skimmed over her lips to part them. His hands moved through her hair, over her shoulders, and down her body to her hips to take a good, strong hold.

Muscles, she thought dimly. Oh, God. He certainly had them. It was like being pressed against warm, smooth steel. Then he moved in so she swayed back and was trapped between the wall of him and the door. Imprisoned there, her blood sizzling as he devastated her mouth, she felt fragile and giddy, and alive with need.

"Wait a minute," she managed. "Wait."

"Just want to finish this out first."

He wanted a great deal more than that, but already knew he'd have to hold himself at a kiss. So he didn't intend to rush through it. Her mouth was sumptuous, and that slight tremor in her body brutally erotic. He imagined himself gulping her down whole, with violence, with greed. Or savoring her nibble by torturous nibble until he was half mad from the flavor.

When he eased back, the drugged, dreamy look in her eyes told him he could do either. Some other time, some other place.

"Any point in pretending we're going to stop things here?"

"I can't—"

"I don't mean tonight," he said when she glanced back at the door.

"Then, no, there'd be no point in that."

"Good."

"But I can't just jump into something like this. I need to—"

"Plan," he finished. "Organize."

"I'm not good at spontaneity, and spontaneity—this sort—is nearly impossible when you have two children."

"Then plan. Organize. And let me know. I'm good at spontaneity." He kissed her again until she felt her knees dissolve from the knee down.

"You've got my numbers. Give me a call." He stepped back. "Go on inside, Stella. Traditionally, you don't just kiss the girl good night, you wait until she's inside before you walk off wondering when you'll have the chance to do it again."

"Good night then." She went inside, drifted up the stairs, and forgot to turn off the lights.

She was still floating as she started down the hall so the singing didn't register until she was two paces away from her sons' bedroom.

She closed the distance in one leap. And she *saw*, she saw the silhouette, the glint of blond hair in the nightlight, the gleam of eyes that stared into hers.

The cold hit her like a slap, angry and sharp. Then, it, and she, were gone.

On unsteady legs, she rushed between the beds, stroked Gavin's hair, Luke's. Laid her hands on their cheeks, then their backs as she'd done when they were infants. A nervous mother's way to assure herself that her child breathed.

Parker rolled lazily over, gave a little greeting growl, a single thump of his tail, then went back to sleep.

He senses me, smells me, knows me. Is it the same with her? Why doesn't he bark at her?

Or am I just losing my mind?

She readied for bed, then took a blanket and pillow into their room. She laid down between her sons and passed the rest of the night between them, guarding them against the impossible.

twelve

IN THE GREENHOUSE, ROZ WATERED FLATS OF ANNUals she'd grown over the winter. It was nearly time to put them out for sale. Part of her was always a little sad to know she wouldn't be the one planting them. And she knew that not all of them would be tended properly.

Some would die of neglect, others would be given too much sun, or not enough. Now they were lush and sweet and full of potential.

And hers.

She had to let them go, the way she'd let her sons go. She had to hope, as with her boys, that they found their potential and bloomed, lavishly.

She missed her little guys. More than she'd realized now that her house had boys in it again with all their chatter and scents and debris. Having Harper close helped, so much at times that it was hard for her not to lean too heavily on him, not to surround him with need.

But he'd passed the stage when he was just hers. Though he lived within shouting distance, and they often worked together side by side, he would never be just hers again.

She had to content herself with occasional visits, with

phone calls and e-mails from her other sons. And with the knowledge that they were happy building their own lives.

She'd rooted them, and tended them, nurtured and trained. And let them go.

She wouldn't be one of those overbearing, smothering mothers. Sons, like plants, needed space and air. But oh, sometimes she wanted to go back ten years, twenty, and just hold on to those precious boys a little bit longer.

And sentiment was only going to make her blue, she reminded herself. She switched off the water just as Stella came into the greenhouse.

Roz drew a deep breath. "Nothing like the smell of damp soil, is there?"

"Not when you're us. Look at these marigolds. They're going to fly out the door. I missed you this morning."

"I wanted to get here early. I've got that Garden Club meeting this afternoon. I want to put together a couple dozen six-inch pots as centerpieces."

"Good advertising. I just wanted to thank you again for watching the boys for me last night."

"I enjoyed it. A lot. Did you have a good time?"

"I really did. Is it going to be a problem for you if Logan and I see each other socially?"

"Why would it be?"

"In a work situation . . ."

"Adults should be able to live their own lives, just like in any situation. You're both unattached adults. I expect you'll figure out for yourself if there's any problem with you socializing."

"And we're both using 'socializing' as a euphemism."

Roz began pinching back some petunias. "Stella, if you didn't want to have sex with a man who looks like Logan, I'd worry about you."

"I guess you've got nothing to worry about, then. Still, I want to say . . . I'm working for you, I'm living in your house, so I want to say I'm not promiscuous."

"I'm sure you aren't." She glanced up briefly from her

work. "You're too careful, too deliberate, and a bit too bound up to be promiscuous."

"Another way of calling me a tight-ass," Stella muttered.

"Not precisely. But if you were promiscuous, it would still be your business and not mine. You don't need my approval."

"I want it—because I'm working for you and living in your house. And because I respect you."

"All right, then." Roz moved on to impatiens. "You have it. One of the reasons I wanted you to live in the house was because I wanted to get to know you, on a personal level. When I hired you, I was giving you a piece of something very important to me, personally important. So if I'd decided, after the first few weeks, that you weren't the sort of person I could like and respect, I'd have fired you." She glanced back. "No matter how competent you were. Competent just isn't that hard to find."

"Thanks. I think."

"I think I'll take in some of these geraniums that are already potted. Saves me time and trouble, and we've got a good supply of them."

"Let me know how many, and I'll adjust the inventory. Roz, there was something else I wanted to talk to you about."

"Talk away," Roz invited as she started to select her plants.

"It's about the ghost."

Roz lifted a salmon-pink geranium, studied it from all sides. "What about her?"

"I feel stupid even talking about this, but . . . have you ever felt threatened by her?"

"Threatened? No. I wouldn't use a word that strong." Roz set the geranium in a plastic tray, chose another. "Why?"

"Because, apparently, I've seen her."

"That's not unexpected. The Harper Bride tends to

show herself to mothers, and young boys. Young girls, occasionally. I saw her myself a few times when I was a girl, then fairly regularly once the boys started coming along."

"Tell me what she looks like."

"About your height." As she spoke, Roz continued to select her geraniums for the Garden Club. "Thin. Very thin. Mid- to late twenties at my guess, though it's hard to tell. She doesn't look well. That is," she added with an absent smile, "even for a ghost. She strikes me as a woman who had a great deal of beauty, but was ill for some time. She's blond, and her eyes are somewhere between green and gray. And very sad. She wears a gray dress—or it looks gray, and it hangs on her as if she'd lost weight."

Stella let out a breath. "That's who I saw. What I saw. It's too fantastic, but I *saw*."

"You should be flattered. She rarely shows herself to anyone outside the family—or so the legend goes. You shouldn't feel threatened, Stella."

"But I did. Last night, when I got home, and went in to check on the boys. I heard her first. She sings some sort of lullaby."

" 'Lavender's Blue.' It's what you could call her trademark." Taking out small clippers, Roz trimmed off a weak side stem. "She's never spoken that I've heard, or heard of, but she sings to the children of the house at night."

" 'Lavender's Blue.' Yes, that's it. I heard her, and rushed in. There she was, standing between their beds. She looked at me. It was only for a second, but she looked at me. Her eyes weren't sad, Roz, they were angry. There was a blast of cold, like she'd thrown something at me in temper. Not like the other times, when I'd just felt a chill."

Interested now, Roz studied Stella's face. "I felt as if I'd annoyed her a few times, on and off. Just a change of tone. Very like you described, I suppose."

"It happened."

"I believe you, but primarily, from most of my experiences, she's always been a benign sort of presence. I always took those temper snaps to be a kind of moodiness. I expect ghosts get moody."

"You expect ghosts get moody," Stella repeated slowly. "I just don't understand a statement like that."

"People do, don't they? Why should that change when they're dead?"

"Okay," Stella said after a moment. "I'm going to try to roll with all this, like it's not insanity. So, maybe she doesn't like me being here."

"Over the last hundred years or so, Harper House has had a lot of people live in it, a lot of houseguests. She ought to be used to it. If you'd feel better moving to the other wing—"

"No. I don't see how that would make a difference. And though I was unnerved enough last night to sleep in the boys' room with them, she wasn't angry with them. It was just me. Who was she?"

"Nobody knows for sure. In polite company, she's referred to as the Harper Bride, but it's assumed she was a servant. A nurse or governess. My theory is one of the men in the house seduced her, maybe cast her off, especially if she got pregnant. There's the attachment to children, so it seemed most logical she had a connection to kids. It's a sure bet she died in or around the house."

"There'd be records, right? A family Bible, birth and death records, photographs, tintypes, whatever."

"Oh, tons."

"I'd like to go through them, if it's all right with you. I'd like to try to find out who she was. I want to know who, or what, I'm dealing with."

"All right." Clippers still in hand, Roz set a fist on her hip. "I guess it's odd no one's ever done it before, including myself. I'll help you with it. It'll be interesting."

"THIS IS SO AWESOME." HAYLEY LOOKED AROUND the library table, where Stella had arranged the photograph albums, the thick Bible, the boxes of old papers, her laptop, and several notebooks. "We're like the Scooby gang."

"I can't believe you saw her, too, and didn't say anything."

Hayley hunched up her shoulders and continued to wander the room. "I figured you'd think I'd wigged. Besides, except for the once, I only caught a glimpse, like over here." She held up a hand at the side of her head. "I've never been around an actual ghost. This is completely cool."

"I'm glad someone's enjoying herself."

She really was. As she and her father had both loved books, they'd used their living room as a kind of library, stuffing the shelves with books, putting in a couple of big, squishy chairs.

It had been nice, cozy and nice.

But this was a *library*. Beautiful bookcases of deep, dark wood flanked long windows, then rose up and around the walls in a kind of platform where the long table stood. There had to be hundreds of books, but it didn't seem overwhelming, not with the dark, restful green of the walls and the warm cream granite of the fireplace. She liked the big black candlesticks and the groupings of family pictures on the mantel.

There were more pictures scattered around here and there, and *things*. Fascinating things like bowls and statues and a dome-shaped crystal clock. Flowers, of course. There were flowers in nearly every room of the house. These were tulips with deep, deep purple cups that sort of spilled out of a wide, clear glass vase.

There were lots of chairs, wide, butter-soft leather chairs, and even a leather sofa. Though a chandelier dripped from the center of the tray ceiling, and even the bookcases lit up, there were lamps with those cool shades that looked like stained glass. The rugs were probably really old, and so interesting with their pattern of exotic birds around the borders.

She couldn't imagine what it must have been like to

have a room like this, much less to know just how to decorate it so it would be—well, gorgeous was the only word she could think of—and yet still be as cozy as the little library she'd had at home.

But Roz knew. Roz, in Hayley's opinion, was the absolute bomb.

"I think this is my favorite room of the house," she decided. "Of course, I think that about every room after I'm in it for five minutes. But I really think this wins the prize. It's like a picture out of *Southern Living* or something, but the accent's on *living*. You wouldn't be afraid to take a nap on the couch."

"I know what you mean." Stella set aside the photo album she'd looked through. "Hayley, you have to remember not to say anything about this to the kids."

"Of course, I won't." She came back to the table, and finally sat. "Hey, maybe we could do a séance. That would be so spooky and great."

"I'm not that far gone yet," Stella replied. She glanced over as David came in.

"Ghost hunter snacks," he announced and set the tray on the table. "Coffee, tea, cookies. I considered angel food cake, but it seemed too obvious."

"Having fun with this?"

"Damn right. But I'm also willing to roll up my sleeves and dive into all this stuff. It'll be nice to put a name to her after all this time." He tapped a finger on Stella's laptop. "And this is for?"

"Notes. Data, facts, speculation. I don't know. It's my first day on the job."

Roz came in, carting a packing box. There was a smudge of dust on her cheek and silky threads of cobwebs in her hair. "Household accounts, from the attic. There's more up there, but this ought to give us a start."

She dumped the box on the table, grinned. "This should be fun. Don't know why I haven't thought of it before. Where do y'all want to start?"

"I was thinking we could have a séance," Hayley began. "Maybe she'll just tell us who she is and why her spirit's, you know, trapped on this plane of existence. That's the thing with ghosts. They get trapped, and sometimes they don't even know they're dead. How creepy is that?"

"A séance." David rubbed his hands together. "Now where did I leave my turban?"

When Hayley burst into throaty laughter, Stella rapped her knuckles on the table. "If we could control the hilarity? I thought we'd start with something a little more mundane. Like trying to date her."

"I've never dated a ghost," David mused, "but I'm up for it."

"Get her time period," Stella said with a slanted look for David. "By what she's wearing. We might be able to pinpoint when she lived, or at least get an estimate."

"Discovery through fashion." Roz nodded as she picked up a cookie. "That's good."

"Smart," Hayley agreed. "But I didn't really notice what she had on. I only got a glimpse."

"A gray dress," Roz put in. "High-necked. Long sleeves."

"Can any of us sketch?" Stella asked. "I'm all right with straight lines and curves, but I'd be hopeless with figures."

"Roz is your girl." David patted Roz on the shoulder.

"Can you draw her, Roz? Your impression of her?"

"I can sure give it a shot."

"I bought notebooks." Stella offered one and made Roz smile.

"Of course you did. And I bet your pencils are all nicely sharpened, too. Just like the first day of school."

"Hard to write with them otherwise. David, while she's doing that, why don't you tell us your experiences with . . . I guess we'll call her the Harper Bride for now."

"Only had a few, and all back when I was a kid, hanging out here with Harper."

"What about the first time?"

"You never forget your first." He winked at her, and

after sitting, poured himself coffee. "I was bunking in with Harper, and we were pretending to be asleep so Roz didn't come in and lower the boom. We were whispering—"

"They always thought they were," Roz said as she sketched.

"I think it was spring. I remember we had the windows open, and there was a breeze. I'd have been around nine. I met Harper in school, and even though he was a year behind me, we hit it off. We hadn't known each other but a few weeks when I came over to spend the night. So we were there, in the dark, thinking we were whispering, and he told me about the ghost. I thought he was making it up to scare me, but he swore all the way up to the needle in his eye that it was true, and he'd seen her lots of times.

"We must've fallen asleep. I remember waking up, thinking somebody had stroked my head. I thought it was Roz, and I was a little embarrassed, so I squinted one eye open to see."

He sipped coffee, narrowing his eyes as he searched for the memory. "And I saw her. She walked over to Harper's bed and bent over him, the way you do when you kiss a child on the top of the head. Then she walked across the room. There was a rocking chair over in the corner. She sat down and started to rock, and sing."

He set the coffee down. "I don't know if I made some sound, or moved, or what, but she looked right at me. She smiled. I thought she was crying, but she smiled. And she put her finger to her lips as if to tell me to hush. Then she disappeared."

"What did you do?" Hayley whispered the question, reverently.

"I pulled the covers over my head, and stayed under till morning."

"You were afraid of her?" Stella prompted.

"Nine-year-old, ghost—and I have a sensitive nature, so sure. But I didn't stay afraid. In the morning it seemed like a dream, but a nice one. She'd stroked my hair and sung to me. And she was pretty. No rattling chains or bloodless howls. She seemed a little like an angel, so I wasn't afraid of her. I told Harper about it in the morning, and he said we must be brothers, because none of his other friends got to see her."

He smiled at the memory. "I felt pretty proud of that, and looked forward to seeing her again. I saw her a few more times when I was over. Then, when I was about thirteen the—we'll say visitations—stopped."

"Did she ever speak to you?"

"No, she'd just sing. That same song."

"Did you only see her in the bedroom, at night?"

"No. There was this time we all camped out back. It was summer, hot and buggy, but we nagged Roz until she let all of us sleep out there in a tent. We didn't make it through the night 'cause Mason cut his foot on a rock. Remember that, Roz?"

"I do. Two o'clock in the morning, and I'm packing four kids in the car so I can take one of them to the ER for stitches."

"We were out there before sunset, out near the west edge of the property. By ten we were all of us half sick on hot dogs and marshmallows, and had spooked ourselves stupid with ghost stories. Lightning bugs were out," he murmured, closing his eyes. "Past midsummer then, and steamy. We'd all stripped down to our underwear. The younger ones fell asleep, but Harper and I stayed up for a while. A long while. I must've conked out, because the next thing I knew, Harper was shaking my shoulder. 'There she is,' he said, and I saw her, walking in the garden."

"Oh, my God," Hayley managed, and edged closer to David as Stella continued to type. "What happened then?"

"Well, Harper's hissing in my ear about how we should go follow her, and I'm trying to talk him out of it without sacrificing my manhood. The other two woke up, and Harper said he was going, and we could stay behind if we were yellow coward dogs."

"I bet that got you moving," Stella commented.

"Being a yellow coward dog isn't an option for a boy in

the company of other boys. We all got moving. Mason couldn't've been but six, but he was trotting along at the rear, trying to keep up. There was moonlight, so we could see her, but Harper said we had to hang back some, so she didn't see us.

"I swear there wasn't a breath of air that night, not a whisper of it to stir a leaf. She didn't make a sound as she walked along the paths, through the shrubs. There was something different about her that night. I didn't realize what it was until long after."

"What?" Breathless, Hayley leaned forward, gripped his arm. "What was different about her that night?"

"Her hair was down. Always before, she'd had it up. Sort of sweet and old-fashioned ringlets spiraling down from the top of her head. But that night it was down, and kind of wild, spilling down her back, over her shoulders. And she was wearing something white and floaty. She looked more like a ghost that night than she ever did otherwise. And I was afraid of her, more than I was the first time, or ever was again. She moved off the path, walked over the flowers without touching them. I could hear my own breath pant in and out, and I must've slowed down because Harper was well ahead. She was going toward the old stables, or maybe the carriage house."

"The carriage house?" Hayley almost squealed it. "Where Harper lives?"

"Yeah. He wasn't living there then," he added with a laugh. "He wasn't more than ten. It seemed like she was heading for the stables, but she'd have to go right by the carriage house. So, she stopped, and she turned around, looking back. I know I stopped dead then, and the blood just drained out of me."

"I guess!" Hayley said, with feeling.

"She looked crazy, and that was worse than dead somehow. Before I could decide whether to run after Harper, or hightail it like a yellow coward dog, Mason screamed. I thought somehow she'd gotten him, and damn near screamed myself. But Harper came flying back. Turned out

Mason had gashed his foot open on a rock. When I looked back toward the old stables, she was gone."

He stopped, shuddered, then let out a weak laugh. "Scared myself."

"Me, too," Hayley managed.

"He needed six stitches." Roz scooted the notebook toward Stella. "That's how she looks to me."

"That's her." Stella studied the sketch of the thin, sad-eyed woman. "Is this how she looked to you, David?"

"Except that one night, yeah."

"Hayley?"

"Best I can tell."

"Same for me. This shows her in fairly simple dress, nipped-in waist, high neck, front buttons. Okay, the sleeves are a little poufed down to the elbow, then snug to the wrist. Skirt's smooth over the hips, then widens out some. Her hair's curly, lots of curls that are scooped up in a kind of topknot. I'm going to do an Internet search on fashion, but it's obviously after the 1860s, right? Scarlett O'Hara hoop skirts were the thing around then. And it'd be before, say, the 1920s and the shorter skirts."

"I think it's near the turn of the century," Hayley put in, then shrugged when gazes shifted to her. "I know a lot of useless stuff. That looks like what they called hourglass style. I mean, even though she's way thin, it looks like that's the style. Gay Nineties stuff."

"That's good. Okay, let's look it up and see." Stella tapped keys, hit Execute.

"I gotta pee. Don't find anything important until I get back." Hayley dashed out, as fast as her condition would allow.

Stella scanned the sites offered, and selected one on women's fashion in the 1890s.

"Late Victorian," she stated as she read and skimmed pictures. "Hourglass. These are all what I'd think of as more stylish, but it seems like the same idea."

She moved to the end of the decade, and over into the early twentieth century. "No, see, these sleeves are a lot bigger at the shoulder. They're calling them leg-o'-mutton, and the bodices on the daywear seem a little sleeker."

She backtracked in the other direction. "No, we're getting into bustles here. I think Hayley may have it. Somewhere in the 1890s."

"Eighteen-nineties?" Hayley hurried back in. "Score one for me."

"Not so fast. If she was a servant," Roz reminded them, "she might not have been dressed fashionably."

"Damn." Hayley mimed erasing a scoreboard.

"But even so, we could say between 1890 and, what, 1910?" Stella suggested. "And if we go with that, and an approximate age of twenty-five, we could estimate that she was born between 1865 and 1885."

She huffed out a breath. "That's too much scope, and too much margin for error."

"Hair," David said. "She may have been a servant, may have had secondhand clothes, but there'd be nothing to stop her from wearing her hair in the latest style."

"Excellent." She typed again, picked through sites. "Okay, the Gibson Girl deal—the smooth pompadour—was popularized after 1895. If we take a leap of faith, and figure our heroine dressed her hair stylishly, we'd narrow this down to between 1890 and 1895, or up to, say '98 if she was a little behind the times. Then we'd figure she died in that decade, anyway, between the ages of . . . oh, let's say between twenty-two and twenty-six."

"Family Bible first," Roz decided. "That should tell us if any of the Harper women, by blood or marriage, and of that age group, died in that decade."

She dragged it in front of her. The binding was black leather, ornately carved. Someone—Stella imagined it was Roz herself—kept it dusted and oiled.

Roz paged through to the family genealogy. "This goes back to 1793 and the marriage of John Andrew Harper to Fiona MacRoy. It lists the births of their eight children."

"Eight?" Hayley widened her eyes and laid a hand on her belly. "Holy God."

"You said it. Six of them lived to adulthood," Roz continued. "Married and begat, begat, begat." She turned the thin pages carefully. "Here we've got several girl children born through Harper marriages between 1865 and 1870. And here, we've got an Alice Harper Doyle, died in childbirth October of 1893, at the age of twenty-two."

"That's awful," Hayley said. "She was younger than me."

"And already gave birth twice," Roz stated. "Tough on women back then, before Margaret Sanger."

"Would she have lived here, in this house?" Stella asked. "Died here?"

"Might have. She married Daniel Francis Doyle, of Natchez, in 1890. We can check the death records on her. I've got three more who died during the period we're using, but the ages are wrong. Let's see here, Alice was Reginald Harper's youngest sister. He had two more, no brothers. He'd have inherited the house, and the estate. A lot of space between Reggie and each of his sisters. Probably miscarriages."

At Hayley's small sound, Roz looked up sharply. "I don't want this to upset you."

"I'm okay. I'm okay," she said again and took a long breath. "So Reginald was the only son on that branch of the family tree?"

"He was. Lots of cousins, and the estate would've passed to one of them after his death, but he had a son—several daughters first, then the boy, in 1892."

"What about his wife?" Stella put in. "Maybe she's the one."

"No, she lived until 1925. Ripe age."

"Then we look at Alice first," Stella decided.

"And see what we can find on servants during that period. Wouldn't be a stretch for Reginald to have diddled around with a nurse or a maid while his wife was breeding. Seeing as he was a man."

"Hey!" David objected.

"Sorry, honey. Let me say he was a Harper man, and

lived during a period where men of a certain station had mistresses and didn't think anything of taking a servant to bed."

"That's some better. But not a lot."

"Are we sure he and his family lived here during that period?"

"A Harper always lived in Harper House," Roz told Stella. "And if I remember my family history, Reginald's the one who converted from gaslight to electricity. He'd have lived here until his death in . . ." She checked the book. "Nineteen-nineteen, and the house passed to his son, Reginald Junior, who'd married Elizabeth Harper McKinnon—fourth cousin—in 1916."

"All right, so we find out if Alice died here, and we go through records to find out if there were any servants of the right age who died during that period." Using her notebook now, Stella wrote down the points of the search. "Roz, do you know when the—let's call them sightings for lack of better. Do you know when they began?"

"I don't, and I'm just realizing that's odd. I should know, and I should know more about her than I do. Harper family history gets passed down, orally and written. But here we have a ghost who as far as I know's been wandering around here for more than a century, and I know next to nothing about her. My daddy just called her the Harper Bride."

"What do you know about her?" Stella readied herself to take notes.

"What she looks like, the song she sings. I saw her when I was a girl, when she came in my room to sing that lullaby, just as she's reputed to have done for generations before. It was . . . comforting. There was a gentleness about her. I tried to talk to her sometimes, but she never talked back. She'd just smile. Sometimes she'd cry. Thanks, sweetie," she said when David poured her more coffee. "I didn't see her through my teenage years, and being a teenage girl I didn't think about her much. I had my mind on other things. But I remember the next time I saw her."

"Don't keep us in suspense," Hayley demanded.

"It was early in the summer, end of June. John and I hadn't been married very long, and we were staying here. It was already hot, one of those hot, still nights where the air's like a wet blanket. But I couldn't sleep, so I left the cool house for the hot garden. I was restless and nervy. I thought I might be pregnant. I wanted it—we wanted it so much, that I couldn't think about anything else. I went out to the garden and sat on this old teak glider, and dreamed up at the moon, praying it was true and we'd started a baby."

She let out a little sigh. "I was barely eighteen. Anyway, while I sat there, she came. I didn't see or hear her come, she was just there, standing on the path. Smiling. Something in the way she smiled at me, something about it, made me know—absolutely know—I had child in me. I sat there, in the midnight heat and cried for the joy of it. When I went to the doctor a couple weeks later, I already knew I was carrying Harper."

"That's so nice." Hayley blinked back tears. "So sweet."

"I saw her off and on for years after, and always saw her at the onset of a pregnancy, before I was sure. I'd see her, and I'd know there was a baby coming. When my youngest hit adolescence, I stopped seeing her regularly."

"It has to be about children," Stella decided, underlining "pregnancy" twice in her notes. "That's the common link. Children see her, women with children, or pregnant women. The died-in-childbirth theory is looking good." Immediately she winced. "Sorry, Hayley, that didn't sound right."

"I know what you mean. Maybe she's Alice. Maybe what she needs to pass over is to be acknowledged by name."

"Well." Stella looked at the cartons and books. "Let's dig in."

* * *

She dreamed again that night, with her mind full of ghosts and questions, of her perfect garden with the blue dahlia that grew stubbornly in its midst.

A weed is a flower growing in the wrong place.

She heard the voice inside her head, a voice that wasn't her own.

"It's true. That's true," she murmured. "But it's so beautiful. So strong and vivid."

It seems so now, but it's deceptive. If it stays, it changes everything. It will take over, and spoil everything you've done. Everything you have. Would you risk that, risk all, for one dazzling flower? One that will only die away at the first frost?

"I don't know." Studying the garden, she rubbed her arms as her skin pricked with unease. "Maybe I could change the plan. I might be able to use it as a focal point."

Thunder boomed and the sky went black, as she stood by the garden, just as she'd once stood through a stormy evening in her own kitchen.

And the grief she'd felt then stabbed into her as if someone had plunged a knife into her heart.

Feel it? Would you feel it again? Would you risk that kind of pain, for this?

"I can't breathe." She sank to her knees as the pain radiated. "I can't breathe. What's happening to me?"

Remember it. Think of it. Remember the innocence of your children and hack it down. Dig it out. Before it's too late! Can't you see how it tries to overshadow the rest? Can't you see how it steals the light? Beauty can be poison.

She woke, shivering with cold, with her heart beating against the pain that had ripped awake with her.

And knew she hadn't been alone, not even in dreams.

thirteen

On her day off, Stella took the boys to meet her father and his wife at the zoo. Within an hour, the boys were carting around rubber snakes, balloons, and chowing down on ice cream cones.

Stella had long since accepted that a grandparent's primary job was to spoil, and since fate had given her sons only this one set, she let them have free rein.

When the reptile house became the next objective, she opted out, freely handing the controls of the next stage to Granddad.

"Your mom's always been squeamish about snakes," Will told the boys.

"And I'm not ashamed to admit it. You all just go ahead. I'll wait."

"I'll keep you company." Jolene adjusted her baby-blue ball cap. "I'd rather be with Stella than a boa constrictor any day."

"Girls." Will exchanged a pitying look with each of his grandsons. "Come on, men, into the snake pit!"

On a battle cry, the three of them charged the building.

"He's so good with them," Stella said. "So natural and

easy. I'm so glad we're living close now, and they can see each other regularly."

"You couldn't be happier about it than we are. I swear that man's been like a kid himself the last couple of days, just waiting for today to get here. He couldn't be more proud of the three of you."

"I guess we both missed out on a lot when I was growing up."

"It's good you're making up for it now."

Stella glanced at Jolene as they walked over to a bench. "You never say anything about her. You never criticize."

"Sugar pie, I bit my tongue to ribbons more times than I can count in the last twenty-seven years."

"Why?"

"Well, honey, when you're the second wife, and the stepmama on top of that, it's the smartest thing you can do. Besides, you grew up to be a strong, smart, generous woman raising the two most handsome, brightest, most charming boys on God's green earth. What's the point of criticizing?"

She does you, Stella thought. "Have I ever told you I think you're the best thing that ever happened to my father?"

"Maybe once or twice." Jolene pinked prettily. "But I never mind hearing it repeated."

"Let me add, you're one of the best things that ever happened to me. And the kids."

"Oh, now." This time Jolene's eyes filled. "Now you've got me going." She dug in her purse, dug out a lace hankie. "That's the sweetest thing. The sweetest thing." She sniffled, tried to dab at her eyes and hug Stella at the same time. "I just love you to pieces. I always did."

"I always felt it." Tearing up herself, Stella pushed through her own purse for a more mundane tissue. "God, look at the mess we've made of each other."

"It was worth it. Sometimes a good little cry's as good as some sex. Do I have mascara all down my face?"

"No. Just a little . . ." Stella used the corner of her tissue to wipe away a smear under Jolene's eye. "There. You're fine."

"I feel like a million tax-free dollars. Now, tell me how you're getting on before I start leaking again."

"Work-wise it couldn't be better. It really couldn't. We're about to hit the spring rush dead-on, and I'm so revved for it. The boys are happy, making friends at school. Actually, between you and me, I think Gavin's got a crush on this little curly-headed blond in his class. Her name's Melissa, and the tips of his ears get red when he mentions her."

"That's so sweet. Nothing like your first crush, is there? I remember mine. I was crazy for this boy. He had a face full of freckles and a cowlick. I just about died with joy the day he gave me a little hop-toad in a shoe box."

"A toad."

"Well, honey, I was eight and a country girl, so it was a thoughtful gift all in all. He ended up marrying a friend of mine. I was in the wedding and had to wear the most god-awful pink dress with a hoop skirt wide enough I could've hidden a horse under it and rode to the church. It was covered with ruffles, so I looked like a human wedding cake."

She waved a hand while Stella rolled with laughter. "I don't know why I'm going on about that, except it's the sort of traumatic experience you never forget, even after more than thirty years. Now they live on the other side of the city. We get together every now and then for dinner. He's still got the freckles, but the cowlick went, along with most of his hair."

"I guess you know a lot of the people and the history of the area, since you've lived here all your life."

"I guess I do. Can't go to the Wal-Mart, day or night, without seeing half a dozen people I know."

"What do you know about the Harper ghost?"

"Hmm." Jolene took out a compact and her lipstick and freshened her face. "Just that she's always roamed around there, or at least as far back as anybody can remember. Why?"

"This is going to sound insane, especially coming from me, but . . . I've seen her."

"Oh my goodness." She snapped the compact closed. "Tell me everything."

"There isn't a lot to tell."

But she told her what there was, and what she'd begun to do about it.

"This is so exciting! You're like a detective. Maybe your father and I could help. You know how he loves playing on that computer of his. Stella!" She clamped a hand on Stella's arm. "I bet she was *murdered*, just hacked to death with an ax or something and buried in a shallow grave. Or dumped in the river—pieces of her. I've always thought so."

"Let me just say—ick—and her ghost, at least is whole. Added to that, our biggest lead is the ancestor who died in childbirth," Stella reminded her.

"Oh, that's right." Jolene sulked a moment, obviously disappointed. "Well, if it turns out it's her, that'd be sad, but not nearly as thrilling as murder. You tell your daddy all about this, and we'll see what we can do. We've both got plenty of time on our hands. It'll be fun."

"It's a departure for me," Stella replied. "I seem to be doing a lot of departing from the norm recently."

"Any of that departing have to do with a man? A tall, broad-shouldered sort of man with a wicked grin?"

Stella's eyes narrowed. "And why would you ask?"

"My third cousin, Lucille? You met her once. She happened to be having dinner in the city a couple nights ago and told me she saw you in the same restaurant with a very good-looking young man. She didn't come by your table because she was with her latest beau. And he's not altogether divorced from his second wife. Fact is, he hasn't been altogether divorced for a year and a half now, but that's Lucille for you."

Jolene waved it away. "So, who's the good-looking young man?"

"Logan Kitridge."

"Oh." It came out in three long syllables. "That *is* a good-looking young man. I thought you didn't like him."

"I didn't not like him, I just found him annoying and difficult to work with. We're getting along a little better at work, and somehow we seem to be dating. I've been trying to figure out if I want to see him again."

"What's to work out? You do or you don't."

"I do, but . . . I shouldn't ask you to gossip."

Jolene wiggled closer on the bench. "Honey, if you can't ask me, who can you ask?"

Stella snickered, then glanced toward the reptile house to be sure her boys weren't heading out. "I wondered, before I get too involved, if he sees a lot of women."

"You want to know if he cats around."

"I guess that's the word for it."

"I'd say a man like that gets lucky when he has a mind to, but you don't hear people saying, 'That Logan Kitridge is one randy son of a gun.' Like they do about my sister's boy, Curtis. Most of what you hear about Logan is people—women mostly—wondering how that wife of his let him get loose, or why some other smart woman hasn't scooped him up. You thinking about scooping?"

"No. No, definitely not."

"Maybe he's thinking about scooping you up."

"I'd say we're both just testing the ground." She caught sight of her men. "Here come the Reptile Hunters. Don't say anything about any of this in front of the boys, okay?"

"Lips are sealed."

IN THE GARDEN OPENED AT EIGHT, PREPARED FOR ITS advertised spring opening as for a war. Stella had mustered the troops, supervised with Roz the laying out of supplies. They had backups, seasoned recruits, and the field of combat was—if she said so herself—superbly organized and displayed.

By ten they were swamped, with customers swarming

the showrooms, the outside areas, the public greenhouses. Cash registers rang like church bells.

She marched from area to area, diving in where she felt she was most needed at any given time. She answered questions from staff and from customers, restacked wagons and carts when the staff was too overwhelmed to get to them, and personally helped countless people load purchases in their cars, trucks, or SUVs.

She used the two-way on her belt like a general.

"Miss? Do you work here?"

Stella paused and turned to the woman wearing baggy jeans and a ragged sweatshirt. "Yes, ma'am, I do. I'm Stella. How can I help you?"

"I can't find the columbine, or the foxglove or . . . I can't find half of what's on my list. Everything's changed around."

"We did do some reorganizing. Why don't I help you find what you're looking for?"

"I've got that flat cart there loaded already." She nodded toward it. "I don't want to have to be hauling it all over creation."

"You're going to be busy, aren't you?" Stella said cheerfully. "And what wonderful choices. Steve? Would you take this cart up front and tag it for Mrs . . . I'm sorry?"

"Haggerty." She pursed her lips. "That'd be fine. Don't you let anybody snatch stuff off it, though. I spent a good while picking all that out."

"No, ma'am. How are you doing, Mrs. Haggerty?"

"I'm doing fine. How's your mama and your daddy?"

"Doing fine, too," Steve lifted the handle of her cart. "Mrs. Haggerty's got one of the finest gardens in the county," he told Stella.

"I'm putting in some new beds. You mind my cart, Steve, or I'll come after you. Now where the hell's the columbine?"

"It's out this way. Let me get you another cart, Mrs. Haggerty."

Stella grabbed one on the way.

"You that new girl Rosalind hired?"

"Yes, ma'am."

"From up north."

"Guilty."

She pursed her lips, peered around with obvious irritation. "You sure have shuffled things around."

"I know. I hope the new scheme will save the customer time and trouble."

"Hasn't saved me any today. Hold on a minute." She stopped, adjusting the bill of her frayed straw hat against the sun as she studied pots of yarrow.

"That achillea's good and healthy, isn't it? Does so well in the heat and has a nice long blooming season."

"Wouldn't hurt to pick up a few things for my daughter while I'm here." She chose three of the pots, then moved on. As they did, Stella chatted about the plants, managed to draw Mrs. Haggerty into conversation. They'd filled the second cart and half of a third by the time they'd wound through the perennial area.

"I'll say this, you know your plants."

"I can certainly return the compliment. And I envy you the planting you've got ahead of you."

Mrs. Haggerty stopped, peering around again. But this time with speculation. "You know, the way you got things set up here, I probably bought half again as much as I planned on."

This time Stella offered a wide, wide smile. "Really?"

"Sneaky. I like that. All your people up north?"

"No, actually my father and his wife live in Memphis. They're natives."

"Is that so. Well. Well. You come on by and see my gardens sometime. Roz can tell you where to find me."

"I'd absolutely love to. Thanks."

BY NOON STELLA ESTIMATED SHE'D WALKED TEN miles.

By three, she gave up wondering how many miles she'd walked, how many pounds she'd lifted, how many questions she'd answered.

She began to dream about a long, cool shower and a bottomless glass of wine.

"This is wild," Hayley managed as she dragged wagons away from the parking area.

"When did you take your last break?"

"Don't worry, I've been getting plenty of sit-down time. Working the counter, chatting up the customers. I wanted to stretch my legs, to tell you the truth."

"We're closing in just over an hour, and things are slowing down a bit. Why don't you find Harper or one of the seasonals and see about restocking?"

"Sounds good. Hey, isn't that Mr. Hunky's truck pulling in?"

Stella looked over, spotted Logan's truck. "Mr. Hunky?"

"When it fits, it fits. Back to work for me."

It should have been for her, too. But she watched as Logan drove over the gravel, around the mountains formed by huge bags of mulch and soil. He climbed out one side of the truck, and his two men piled out the other. After a brief conversation, he wandered across the gravel lot toward her.

So she wandered across to him.

"Got a client who's decided on that red cedar mulch. You can put me down for a quarter ton."

"Which client?"

"Jameson. We're going to swing back by and get it down before we knock off. I'll get the paperwork to you tomorrow."

"You could give it to me now."

"Have to work it up. I take time to work it up, we're not going to get the frigging mulch down today. Client won't be happy."

She used her forearm to swipe at her forehead. "Fortunately for you I don't have the energy to nag."

"Been busy."

"There's no word for what we've been. It's great. I'm betting we broke records. My feet feel like a couple of smoked sausages. By the way, I was thinking I'd like to come by, see your house."

His eyes stared into hers until she felt fresh pricks of heat at the base of her spine. "You could do that. I've got time tonight."

"I can't tonight. Maybe Wednesday, after we close? If Roz is willing to watch the boys."

"Wednesday's no problem for me. Can you find the place all right?"

"Yeah, I'll find it. About six-thirty?"

"Fine. See you."

As he walked back to his truck, Stella decided it was the strangest conversation she'd ever had about sex.

THAT EVENING, AFTER HER KIDS WERE FED, AND engaged in their play hour before bed, Stella indulged in that long shower. As the aches and fatigue of the day washed away, her excitement over it grew.

They'd kicked *ass*! she thought.

She was still a little concerned about overstock in some areas, and what she saw as understock in others. But flushed with the day's success, she told herself not to question Roz's instincts as a grower.

If today was any indication, they were in for a rock-solid season.

She pulled on her terry-cloth robe, wrapped her hair in a towel, then did a kind of three-step boogie out of the bathroom.

And let out a short, piping scream at the woman in her bedroom doorway.

"Sorry. Sorry." Roz snorted back a laugh. "Flesh and blood here."

"God!" Since her legs had gone numb, Stella sank onto the side of the bed. "*God!* My heart just about stopped."

"I got something that should start it up again." From behind her back, Roz whipped out a bottle of champagne.

"Dom Perignon? Woo, and two hoos! Yes, I think I detect a beat."

"We're going to celebrate. Hayley's across in the sitting room. And I'm giving her half a glass of this. No lectures."

"In Europe pregnant women are allowed, if not encouraged, to have a glass of wine a week. I'm willing to pretend we're in France if I get a full glass of that."

"Come on over. I sent the boys down to David. They're having a video game contest."

"Oh. Well, I guess that's all right. They've got a half hour before bath and bed. Is that caviar?" she asked when she stepped into the sitting room.

"Roz says I can't have any." Hayley leaned over and sniffed the silver tray with its silver bowl of glossy black caviar. "Because it's not good for the baby. I don't know as I'd like it, anyway."

"Good. More for me. Champagne and caviar. You're a classy boss, Ms. Harper."

"It was a great day. I always start off the first of the season a little blue." She popped the cork. "All my babies going off like that. Then I get too busy to think about it." She poured the glasses. "And by the end I'm reminded that I got into this to sell and to make a profit—while doing something I enjoy doing. Then I come on home and start feeling a little blue again. But not tonight."

She passed the glasses around. "I may not have the figures and the facts and the data right at my fingertips, but I know what I know. We've just had the best single day ever."

"Ten percent over last year." Stella lifted her glass in a toast. "I happen to have facts and data at my fingertips."

"Of course you do." With a laugh, Roz stunned Stella by throwing an arm around her shoulders, squeezing once, then pressing a kiss to her cheek. "Damn right you do. You did a hell of a job. Both of you. Everyone. And it's fair to say, Stella, that I did myself and In the Garden a favor the day I hired you."

"Wow!" She took a sip to open her throat. "I won't argue with that." Then another to let the wine fizz on her tongue before she went for the caviar. "However, as much as I'd love to take full credit for that ten percent increase, I can't. The stock is just amazing. You and Harper are exceptional growers. I'll take credit for five of the ten percent."

"It was fun," Hayley put in. "It was crazy a lot of the time, but fun. All those people, and the noise, and carts sailing out the door. Everybody seemed so happy. I guess being around plants, thinking about having them for yourself, does that."

"Good customer service has a lot to do with those happy faces. And you"—Stella tipped her glass to Hayley—"have that knocked."

"We've got a good team." Roz sat, wiggled her bare toes. They were painted pale peach today. "We'll take a good overview in the morning, see what areas Harper and I should add to." She leaned forward to spread caviar on a toast point. "But tonight we'll just bask."

"This is the best job I've ever had. I just want to say that." Hayley looked at Roz. "And not just because I get to drink fancy champagne and watch y'all eat caviar."

Roz patted her arm. "I should bring up another subject. I've already told David. The calls I've made about Alice Harper Doyle's death certificate? Natchez," she said. "According to official records, she died in Natchez, in the home she shared with her husband and two children."

"Damn." Stella frowned into her wine. "I guess it was too easy."

"We'll just have to keep going through the household records, noting down the names of the female servants during that time period."

"Big job," Stella replied.

"Hey, we're good." Hayley brushed off the amount of work. "We can handle it. And, you know, I was thinking. David said they saw her going toward the old stables, right? So maybe she had a thing going with one of the stablehands. They got into a fight over something, and he killed her. Maybe an accident, maybe not. Violent deaths are supposed to be one of the things that trap spirits."

"Murder," Roz speculated. "It might be."

"You sound like my stepmother. I talked to her about it," Stella told Roz. "She and my father are willing and able to help with any research if we need them. I hope that's all right."

"It's all right with me. I wondered if she'd show herself to one of us, since we started looking into it. Try to point us in the right direction."

"I had a dream." Since it made her feel silly to talk about it, Stella topped off her glass of champagne. "A kind of continuation of one I had a few weeks ago. Neither of them was very clear—or the details of them go foggy on me. But I know it—they—have to do with a garden I've planted, and a blue dahlia."

"Do dahlias come in blue?" Hayley wondered.

"They do. They're not common," Roz explained, "but you can hybridize them in shades of blue."

"This was like nothing I've ever seen. It was . . . electric, intense. This wildly vivid blue, and huge. And she was in the dream. I didn't see her, but I felt her."

"Hey!" Hayley pushed herself forward. "Maybe her name was Dahlia."

"That's a good thought," Roz commented. "If we're researching ghosts, it's not a stretch to consider that a dream's connected in some way."

"Maybe." Frowning, Stella sipped again. "I could hear her, but I couldn't see her. Even more, I could feel her, and there was something dark about it, something frightening. She wanted me to get rid of it. She was insistent, angry, and, I don't know how to explain it, but she was *there*. How could she be in a dream?"

"I don't know," Roz replied. "But I don't care for it."

"Neither do I. It's too . . . intimate. Hearing her inside my head that way, whispering." Even now, she shivered.

"When I woke up, I knew she'd been there, in the room, just as she'd been there, in the dream."

"It's scary," Hayley agreed. "Dreams are supposed to be personal, just for ourselves, unless we want to share them. Do you think the flower had something to do with her? I don't get why she wants you to get rid of it."

"I wish I knew. It could've been symbolic. Of the gardens here, or the nursery. I don't know. But dahlias are a particular favorite of mine, and she wanted it gone."

"Something else to put in the mix." Roz took a long sip of champagne. "Let's give it a rest tonight, before we spook ourselves completely. We can try to carve out some time this week to look for names."

"Ah, I've made some tentative plans for Wednesday after work. If you wouldn't mind watching the boys for a couple of hours."

"I think between us we can manage them," Roz agreed.

"Another date with Mr. Hunky?"

With a laugh, Roz ate more caviar. "I assume that would be Logan."

"According to Hayley," Stella stated. "I was going to go by and see his place. I'd like a firsthand look at how he's landscaping it." She downed more champagne. "And while that's perfectly true, the main reason I'm going is to have sex with him. Probably. Unless I change my mind. Or he changes his. So." She set down her empty glass. "There it is."

"I'm not sure what you'd like us to say," Roz said after a moment.

"Have fun?" Hayley suggested. Then looked down at her belly. "And play safe."

"I'm only telling you because you'd know anyway, or suspect, or wonder. It seems better not to dance around it. And it doesn't seem right for me to ask you to watch my kids while I'm off . . . while I'm off without being honest about it."

"It is your life, Stella," Roz pointed out.

"Yeah." Hayley took the last delicious sip of her champagne. "Not that I wouldn't be willing to hear the details. I think hearing about sex is as close as I'm getting to it for a long time. So if you want to share . . ."

"I'll keep that in mind. Now I'd better go down and round up my boys. Thanks for the celebration, Roz."

"We earned it."

As Stella walked away, she heard Roz's questioning "Mr. Hunky?" And the dual peals of female laughter.

fourteen

GUILT TUGGED AT STELLA AS SHE BUZZED HOME TO clean up before her date with Logan. No, not date, she corrected as she jumped into the shower. It wasn't a date unless there were plans. This was a drop-by.

So now they'd had an outing, a date, and a drop-by. It was the strangest relationship she'd ever had.

But whatever she called it, she felt guilty. She wasn't the one giving her kids their evening meal and listening to their day's adventures while they ate.

It wasn't that she had to be with them every free moment, she thought as she jumped back out of the shower again. That sort of thing wasn't good for them—or for her. It wasn't as if they'd starve if she wasn't the one to put food in front of them.

But still, it seemed awfully selfish of her to give them over to someone else's care just so she could be with a man.

Be intimate with a man, if things went as she expected.

Sorry, kids, Mom can't have dinner with you tonight. She's going to go have some hot, sweaty sex.

God.

She slathered on cream as she struggled between anticipation and guilt.

Maybe she should put it off. Unquestionably she was rushing this step, and that wasn't like her. When she did things that weren't like her, it was usually a mistake.

She was thirty-three years old, and entitled to a physical relationship with a man she liked, a man who stirred her up, a man, who it turned out, she had considerable in common with.

Thirty-three. Thirty-four in August, she reminded herself and winced. Thirty-four wasn't early thirties anymore. It was mid-thirties. Shit.

Okay, she wasn't going to think about that. Forget the numbers. She'd just say she was a grown woman. That was better.

Grown woman, she thought, and tugged on her robe so she could work on her face. Grown, single woman. Grown, single man. Mutual interests between them, reasonable sense of companionship. Intense sexual tension.

How could a woman think straight when she kept imagining what it would be like to have a man's hands—

"Mom!"

She stared at her partially made-up face in the mirror. "Yes?"

The knocking was like machine-gun fire on the bathroom door.

"Mom! Can I come in? Can I? Mom!"

She pulled open the door herself to see Luke, rosy with rage, his fists bunched at his side. "What's the matter?"

"He's *looking* at me."

"Oh, Luke."

"With the face, Mom. With . . . the . . . *face.*"

She knew the face well. It was the squinty-eyed, smirky sneer that Gavin had designed to torment his brother. She knew damn well he practiced it in the mirror.

"Just don't look back at him."

"Then he makes the noise."

The noise was a hissing puff, which Gavin could keep up for hours if called for. Stella was certain that even the most hardened CIA agent would crack under its brutal power.

"All right." How the hell was she supposed to gear herself up for sex when she had to referee? She swung out of the bath, through the boys' room and into the sitting room across the hall, where she'd hoped her sons could spend the twenty minutes it took her to get dressed companionably watching cartoons.

Foolish woman, she thought. Foolish, foolish woman.

Gavin looked up from his sprawl on the floor when she came in. His face was the picture of innocence under his mop of sunny hair.

Haircuts next week, she decided, and noted it in her mental files.

He held a Matchbox car and was absently spinning its wheels while cartoons rampaged on the screen. There were several other cars piled up, lying on their sides or backs as if there'd been a horrendous traffic accident. Unfortunately the miniature ambulance and police car appeared to have had a nasty head-on collision.

Help was not on the way.

"Mom, your face looks crooked."

"Yes, I know. Gavin, I want you to stop it."

"I'm not doing anything."

She felt, actually felt, the sharp edges of the shrill scream razor up her throat. Choke it back, she ordered herself. Choke it back. She would *not* scream at her kids the way her mother had screamed at her.

"Maybe you'd like to not do anything in your room, alone, for the rest of the evening."

"I wasn't—"

"Gavin!" She cut off the denial before it dragged that scream out of her throat. Instead her voice was full of weight and aggravation. "Don't look at your brother. Don't hiss at your brother. You know it annoys him, which is exactly why you do it, and I want you to stop."

Innocence turned into a scowl as Gavin rammed the last car into the tangle of disabled vehicles. "How come I always get in trouble?"

"Yes, how come?" Stella shot back, with equal exasperation.

"He's just being a baby."

"I'm not a baby. You're a dickhead."

"Luke!" Torn between laughter and shock, Stella rounded on Luke. "Where did you hear that word?"

"Somewhere. Is it a swear?"

"Yes, and I don't want you to say it again." Even when it's apt, she thought as she caught Gavin making the face.

"Gavin, I can cancel my plans for this evening. Would you like me to do that, and stay home?" She spoke in calm, almost sweet tones. "We can spend your play hour cleaning your room."

"No." Outgunned, he poked at the pileup. "I won't look at him anymore."

"Then if it's all right with you, I'll go finish getting ready."

She heard Luke whisper, "What's a dickhead?" to Gavin as she walked out. Rolling her eyes to the ceiling, she kept going.

"THEY'RE AT EACH OTHER TONIGHT," STELLA WARNED Roz.

"Wouldn't be brothers if they weren't at each other now and then." She looked over to where the boys, the dog, and Hayley romped in the yard. "They seem all right now."

"It's brewing, under the surface, like a volcano. One of them's just waiting for the right moment to spew over the other."

"We'll see if we can distract them. If not, and they get out of hand, I'll just chain them in separate corners until you get back. I kept the shackles I used on my boys. Sentimental."

Stella laughed, and felt completely reassured. "Okay.

But you'll call me if they decide to be horrible brats. I'll be home in time to put them to bed."

"Go, enjoy yourself. And if you're not back, we can manage it."

"You make it too easy," Stella told her.

"No need for it to be hard. You know how to get there now?"

"Yes. That's the easy part."

She got in her car, gave a little toot of the horn and a wave. They'd be fine, she thought, watching in the rearview as her boys tumbled onto the ground with Parker. She couldn't have driven away if she wasn't sure of that.

It was tougher to be sure she'd be fine.

She could enjoy the drive. The early-spring breeze sang through the windows to play across her face. Tender green leaves hazed the trees, and the redbuds and wild dogwoods teased out blooms to add flashes of color.

She drove past the nursery and felt the quick zip of pride and satisfaction because she was a part of it now.

Spring had come to Tennessee, and she was here to experience it. With her windows down and the wind streaming over her, she thought she could smell the river. Just a hint of something great and powerful, contrasting with the sweet perfume of magnolia.

Contrasts, she supposed, were the order of the day now. The dreamy elegance and underlying strength of the place that was now her home, the warm air that beat the calendar to spring while the world she'd left behind still shoveled snow.

Herself, a careful, practical-natured woman driving to the bed of a man she didn't fully understand.

Nothing seemed completely aligned any longer. Blue dahlias, she decided. Her life, like her dreams, had big blue dahlias cropping up to change the design.

For tonight at least, she was going to let it bloom.

She followed the curve of the road, occupying her mind with how they would handle the weekend rush at the nursery.

Though "rush," she admitted, wasn't precisely the word. No one, staff or customer, seemed to rush—unless she counted herself.

They came, they meandered, browsed, conversed, ambled some more. They were served, with unhurried graciousness and a lot more conversation.

The slower pace sometimes made her want to grab something and just get the job done. But the fact that it often took twice as long to ring up an order than it should—in her opinion—didn't bother anyone.

She had to remind herself that part of her duties as manager was to blend efficiency with the culture of the business she managed.

One more contrast.

In any case, the work schedule she'd set would ensure that there were enough hands and feet to serve the customers. She and Roz had already poured another dozen concrete planters, and would dress them tomorrow. She could have Hayley do a few. The girl had a good eye.

Her father and Jolene were going to take the boys on Saturday, and *that* she couldn't feel guilty about, as all involved were thrilled with the arrangement.

She needed to check on the supply of plastic trays and carrying boxes, oh, and take a look at the field plants, and . . .

Her thoughts trailed off when she saw the house. She couldn't say what she'd been expecting, but it hadn't been this.

It was gorgeous.

A little run-down, perhaps, a little tired around the edges, but beautiful. Bursting with potential.

Two stories of silvered cedar stood on a terraced rise, the weathered wood broken by generous windows. On the wide, covered porch—she supposed it might be called a veranda—were an old rocker, a porch swing, a high-backed bench. Pots and baskets of flowers were arranged among them.

On the side, a deck jutted out, and she could see a short span of steps leading from it to a pretty patio.

More chairs there, more pots—oh, she was falling in love—then the land took over again and spread out to a lovely grove of trees.

He was doing shrubberies in the terraces—Japanese andromeda with its urn-shaped flowers already in bud, glossy-leaved bay laurels, the fountaining old-fashioned weigela, and a sumptuous range of azalea just waiting to explode into bloom.

And clever, she thought, creeping the car forward, clever and creative to put phlox and candytuft and ground junipers on the lowest terrace to base the shrubs and spill over the wall.

He'd planted more above in the yard—a magnolia, still tender with youth, and a dogwood blooming Easter pink. On the far side was a young weeping cherry.

Some of these were the very trees he'd hammered her over moving the first time they'd met. Just what did it say about her feelings for him that it made her smile to remember that?

She pulled into the drive beside his truck and studied the land.

There were stakes, with thin rope riding them in a kind of meandering pattern from drive to porch. Yes, she saw what he had in mind. A lazy walkway to the porch, which he would probably anchor with other shrubs or dwarf trees. Lovely. She spotted a pile of rocks and thought he must be planning to build a rock garden. There, just at the edge of the trees, would be perfect.

The house needed its trim painted, and the fieldstone that rose from its foundation repointed. A cutting garden over there, she thought as she stepped out, naturalized daffodils just inside the trees. And along the road, she'd do ground cover and shrubs, and plant daylilies, maybe some iris.

The porch swing should be painted, too, and there should be a table there—and there. A garden bench near the weeping cherry, maybe another path leading from there to around the back. Flagstone, perhaps. Or pretty stepping-stones with moss or creeping thyme growing between them.

She stopped herself as she stepped onto the porch. He'd have his own plans, she reminded herself. His house, his plans. No matter how much the place called to her, it wasn't hers.

She still had to find hers.

She took a breath, fluffed a hand through her hair, and knocked.

It was a long wait, or it seemed so to her while she twisted her watchband around her finger. Nerves began to tap-dance in her belly as she stood there in the early-evening breeze.

When he opened the door, she had to paint an easy smile on her face. He looked so *male*. The long, muscled length of him clad in faded jeans and a white T-shirt. His hair was mussed; she'd never seen it any other way. There was too much of it, she thought, to be tidy. And tidy would never suit him.

She held out the pot of dahlias she'd put together. "I've had dahlias on the mind," she told him. "I hope you can use them."

"I'm sure I can. Thanks. Come on in."

"I love the house," she began, "and what you're doing with it. I caught myself mentally planting—"

She stopped. The door led directly into what she supposed was a living room, or family room. Whatever it was, it was completely empty. The space consisted of bare drywall, scarred floors, and a smoke-stained brick fireplace with no mantel.

"You were saying?"

"Great views." It was all she could think of, and true enough. Those generous windows brought the outdoors in. It was too bad *in* was so sad.

"I'm not using this space right now."

"Obviously."

"I've got plans for it down the road, when I get the time, and the inclination. Why don't you come on back before you start crying or something."

"Was it like this, when you bought it?"

"Inside?" He shrugged a shoulder as he walked back through a doorway into what might have been a dining room. It, too, was empty, its walls covered with faded, peeling wallpaper. She could see brighter squares on it where pictures must have hung.

"Wall-to-wall carpet over these oak floors," he told her. "Leak upstairs had water stains all over the ceiling. And there was some termite damage. Tore out the walls last winter."

"What's this space?"

"Haven't decided yet."

He went through another door, and Stella let out a whistle of breath.

"Figured you'd be more comfortable in here." He set the flowers on a sand-colored granite counter and just leaned back to let her look.

It was his mark on the kitchen, she had no doubt. It was essentially male and strongly done. The sand tones of the counters were echoed in the tiles on the floor and offset by a deeper taupe on the walls. Cabinets were a dark, rich wood with pebbled-glass doors. There were herbs growing in small terra-cotta pots on the wide sill over the double sinks, and a small stone hearth in the corner.

Plenty of workspace on the long L of the counter, she calculated, plenty of eating space in the diagonal run of the counter that separated the kitchen area from a big, airy sitting space where he'd plopped down a black leather couch and a couple of oversized chairs.

And best of all, he'd opened the back wall with glass. You would sit there, Stella thought, and be a part of the gardens he was creating outside. Step through to the flagstone terrace and wander into flowers and trees.

"This is wonderful. Wonderful. Did you do it yourself?"

Right at the moment, seeing that dreamy look on her

face, he wanted to tell her he'd gathered the sand to make the glass. "Some. Work slows down in the winter, so I can deal with the inside of the place when I get the urge. I know people who do good work. I hire, or I barter. Want a drink?"

"Hmm. Yes. Thanks. The other room has to be your formal dining room, for when you entertain, or have people over for dinner. Of course, everyone's going to end up in here. It's irresistible."

She wandered back into the kitchen and took the glass of wine he offered. "It's going to be fabulous when you're done. Unique, beautiful, and welcoming. I love the colors you've picked in here."

"Last woman I had in here said they seemed dull."

"What did she know?" Stella sipped and shook her head. "No, they're earthy, natural—which suits you and the space."

She glanced toward the counter, where there were vegetables on a cutting board. "And obviously you cook, so the space needs to suit you. Maybe I can get a quick tour along with this wine, then I'll let you get to your dinner."

"Not hungry? I got some yellowfin tuna's going to go to waste, then."

"Oh." Her stomach gave a little bounce. "I didn't intend to invite myself to dinner. I just thought . . ."

"You like grilled tuna?"

"Yes. Yes, I do."

"Fine. You want to eat before or after?"

She felt the blood rush to her cheeks, then drain out again. "Ah . . ."

"Before or after I show you around?"

There was enough humor in his voice to tell her he knew just where her mind had gone. "After." She took a bracing sip of wine. "After. Maybe we could start outside, before we lose the light."

He took her out on the terrace, and her nerves eased back again as they talked about the lay of his land, his plans for it.

She studied the ground he'd tilled and nodded as he spoke of kitchen gardens, rock gardens, water gardens. And her heart yearned.

"I'm getting these old clinker bricks," he told her. "There's a mason I know. I'm having him build a three-sided wall here, about twenty square feet inside it."

"You're doing a walled garden? God, I am going to cry. I always wanted one. The house in Michigan just didn't work for one. I promised myself when I found a new place I'd put one in. With a little pool, and stone benches and secret corners."

She took a slow turn. A lot of hard, sweaty work had already gone into this place, she knew. And a lot of hard, sweaty work was still to come. A man who could do this, would do it, wanted to do this, was worth knowing.

"I envy you—and admire you—every inch of this. If you need some extra hands, give me a call. I miss gardening for the pleasure of it."

"You want to come by sometime, bring those hands and the kids, I'll put them to work." When she just lifted her eyebrows, he added. "Kids don't bother me, if that's what you're thinking. And there's no point planning a yard space where kids aren't welcome."

"Why don't you have any? Kids?"

"Figured I would by now." He reached out to touch her hair, pleased that she hadn't bothered with pins. "Things don't always work out like you figure."

She walked with him back toward the house. "People often say divorce is like death."

"I don't think so." He shook his head, taking his time on the walk back. "It's like an end. You make a mistake, you fix it, end it, start over from there. It was her mistake as well as mine. We just didn't figure that out until we were already married."

"Most men, given the opportunity, will cheerfully trash an ex."

"Waste of energy. We stopped loving each other, then we stopped liking each other. That's the part I'm sorry about," he added, then opened the wide glass door to the kitchen. "Then we stopped being married, which was the best thing for both of us. She stayed where she wanted to be, I came back to where I wanted to be. It was a couple years out of our lives, and it wasn't all bad."

"Sensible." But marriage was a serious business, she thought. Maybe the most serious. The ending of it should leave some scars, shouldn't it?

He poured more wine into their glasses, then took her hand. "I'll show you the rest of the house."

Their footsteps echoed as they moved through empty spaces. "I'm thinking of making a kind of library here, with work space. I could do my designs here."

"Where do you do them now?"

"Out of the bedroom mostly, or in the kitchen. Whatever's handiest. Powder room over there, needs a complete overhaul, eventually. Stairs are sturdy, but need to be sanded and buffed up."

He led her up, and she imagined paint on the walls, some sort of technique, she decided, that blended earthy colors and brought out the tones of wood.

"I'd have files and lists and clippings and dozens of pictures cut out of magazines." She slanted him a look. "I don't imagine you do."

"I've got thoughts, and I don't mind giving them time to stew a while. I grew up on a farm, remember? Farm's got a farmhouse, and my mama loved to buy old furniture and fix it up. Place was packed with tables—she had a weakness for tables. For now, I'm enjoying having nothing much but space around."

"What did she do with all of it when they moved? Ah, someone mentioned your parents moved to Montana," she added when he stopped to give her a speculative look.

"Yeah, got a nice little place in Helena. My daddy goes fly-fishing nearly every damn day, according to my mama, anyway. And she took her favorite pieces with her, filled a frigging moving van with stuff. She sold some, gave some to my sister, dumped some on me. I got it stored. Gotta get around to going through it one of these days, see what I can use."

"If you went through it, you'd be able to decide how you want to paint, decorate, arrange your rooms. You'd have some focal points."

"Focal points." He leaned against the wall, just grinned at her.

"Landscaping and home decorating have the same basic core of using space, focal points, design—and you know that very well or you couldn't have done what you did with your kitchen. So I'll shut up now."

"Don't mind hearing you talk."

"Well, I'm done now, so what's the next stop on the tour?"

"Guess this would be. I'm sort of using this as an office." He gestured to a door. "And I don't think you want to look in there."

"I can take it."

"I'm not sure I can." He tugged her away, moved on to another door. "You'll get all steamed up about filing systems and in and out boxes or whatever, and it'll screw up the rhythm. No point in using the grounds as foreplay if I'm going to break the mood by showing you something that'll insult your sensibilities."

"The grounds are foreplay?"

He just smiled and drew her through a door.

It was his bedroom and, like the kitchen, had been finished in a style that mirrored him. Simple, spacious, and male, with the outdoors blending with the in. The deck she'd seen was outside atrium doors, and beyond it the spring green of trees dominated the view. The walls were a dull, muted yellow, set off by warm wood tones in trim, in floor, in the pitched angles of the ceiling, where a trio of skylights let in the evening glow.

His bed was wide. A man of his size would want room there, she concluded. For sleeping, and for sex. Black iron head- and footboards and a chocolate-brown spread.

There were framed pencil drawings on the walls, gardens in black and white. And when she moved closer, she saw the scrawled signature at the lower corner. "You did these? They're wonderful."

"I like to get a visual of projects, and sometimes I sketch them up. Sometimes the sketches aren't half bad."

"These are a lot better than half bad, and you know it." She couldn't imagine those big, hard hands drawing anything so elegant, so lovely and fresh. "You're a constant surprise to me, Logan. A study of contrasts. I was thinking about contrasts on the way over here tonight, about how things aren't lined up the way I thought they would be. Should be."

She turned back to him, gestured toward his sketches. "These are another blue dahlia."

"Sorry—not following you. Like the one in your dream?"

"Dreams. I've had two now, and neither was entirely comfortable. In fact, they're getting downright scary. But the thing is the dahlia, it's so bold and beautiful, so unexpected. But it's not what I planned. Not what I imagined. Neither is this."

"Planned, imagined, or not, I wanted you here."

She took another sip of wine. "And here I am." She breathed slow in and out. "Maybe we should talk about . . . what we expect and how we'll—"

He moved in, pulled her against him. "Why don't we plant another blue dahlia and just see what happens."

Or we could try that, she thought when his mouth was on hers. The low tickle in her belly spread, and the needy part of her whispered, Thank God, inside her head.

She rose on her toes, all the way up, like a dancer on point, to meet him. And angling her body more truly to his, let him take the glass out of her hand.

Then his hands were in her hair, fingers streaming through it, clutching at it, and her arms were locked around him.

"I feel dizzy," she whispered. "Something about you makes me dizzy."

His blood fired, blasting a bubbling charge of lust straight to his belly. "Then you should get off your feet." In one quick move he scooped her up in his arms. She was, he thought, the sort of woman a man wanted to scoop up. Feminine and slight and curvy and soft. Holding her made him feel impossibly strong, uncommonly tender.

"I want to touch you everywhere. Then start right back at the beginning and touch you everywhere again." When he carried her to the bed, he felt sexy little tremors run through her. "Even when you annoy me, I want my hands on you."

"You must want them on me all the time, then."

"Truer words. Your hair drives me half crazy." He buried his face in it as he lowered the two of them to the bed.

"Me too." Her skin sprang to life with a thousand nerves as his lips wandered down to her throat. "But probably for different reasons."

He bit that sensitive skin, lightly, like a man helping himself to a sample. And the sensation rippled through her in one long, sweet stream. "We're grown-ups," she began.

"Thank God."

A shaky laugh escaped. "What I mean is we . . ." His teeth explored the flesh just above her collarbone in that same testing nibble, and had a lovely fog settling over her brain. "Never mind."

He touched, just as he'd told her he wanted to. A long, smooth stroke from her shoulders down to her fingertips. A lazy pass over her hips, her thigh, as if he were sampling her shape as he'd sampled her flavor.

Then his mouth was on hers again, hot and greedy. Those nerve endings exploded, electric jolts as his hands, his lips ran over her as if he were starved now for each separate taste. Hard hands, rough at the palms, rushed over her with both skill and desperation.

Just as she'd imagined. Just as she'd wanted.

Desires she'd ruthlessly buried broke the surface and screamed into life. Riding on the thrill, she dragged at his shirt until her hands found the hot, bare skin and dug in.

Man and muscle.

He found her breast, had her arching in delicious pleasure as his teeth nipped over shirt and bra to tantalize the flesh beneath, to stir the blood beneath into feverish, pulsing life. Everything inside her went full, and ripe, and ready.

As senses awakened, slashing one against the other in an edgy tangle of needs, she gave herself over to them, to him. And she yearned for him, for that promise of release, in a way she hadn't yearned for in so long. She wanted, craved, the heat that washed through her as the possessive stroke of those labor-scarred hands, the demanding crush of those insatiable lips, electrified her body.

She wanted, craved, all these quivering aches, these madly churning needs and the freedom to meet them.

She rose with him, body to body, moved with him, flesh to flesh. And drove him toward delirium with that creamy skin, those lovely curves. In the softening light, she looked beyond exquisite lying against the dark spread—that bright hair tumbled, those summer-blue eyes clouded with pleasure.

Passion radiated from her, meeting and matching his own. And so he wanted to give her more, and take more, and simply drown himself in what they brought to each other. The scent of her filled him like breath.

He murmured her name, savoring and exploiting as they explored each other. And there was more, he discovered, more than he'd expected.

Her heart lurched as those rugged hands guided her up, over, through the steep rise of desire. The crest rolled through her, a long, endless swell of sultry heat. She arched up again, crying out as she clamped her arms around him, pulses galloping.

Her mouth took his in a kind of ravenous madness, even as her mind screamed—Again!

He held on, held strong while she rode the peak, and the thrill her response brought him made him tremble. He ached, heart, mind, loins, ached to the point of pain.

And when he could bear it no longer, he drove into her.

She cried out once more, a sound of both shock and triumph. And she was already moving with him, a quick piston of hips, as her hands came up to frame his face.

She watched him, those blue eyes swimming, those lush lips trembling with each breath as they rose and fell together.

In the whole of his life, he'd never seen such beauty bloom.

When those eyes went blind, when they closed on a sobbing moan, he let himself go.

HE WAS HEAVY. VERY HEAVY. STELLA LAY STILL beneath Logan and pondered the wonder of being pinned, helplessly, under a man. She felt loose and sleepy and utterly relaxed. She imagined there was probably a nice pink light beaming quietly out of her fingers and toes.

His heart was thundering still. What woman wouldn't feel smug and satisfied knowing she'd caused a big, strong man to lose his breath?

Cat-content, she stroked her hands over his back.

He grunted, and rolled off of her.

She felt immediately exposed and self-conscious. Reaching out, she started to give the spread a little tug, to cover herself at least partially. Then he did something that froze her in place, and had her heart teetering.

He took her hand and kissed her fingers.

He said nothing, nothing at all, and she stayed very still while she tried to swallow her heart back into place.

"Guess I'd better feed you now," he said at length.

"Ah, I should call and make sure the boys are all right."

"Go ahead." He sat up, patting her naked thigh before he rolled out of bed and reached for his jeans. "I'll go get things started in the kitchen."

He didn't bother with his shirt, but started out. Then he stopped, turned and looked at her.

"What?" She lifted an arm, casually, she hoped, over her breasts.

"I just like the way you look there. All mussed and flushed. Makes me want to muss and flush you some more, first chance I get."

"Oh." She tried to formulate a response, but he was already sauntering off. And whistling.

fifteen

THE MAN COULD COOK. WITH LITTLE HELP FROM Stella, Logan put together a meal of delicately grilled tuna, herbed-up brown rice, and chunks of sautéed peppers and mushrooms. He was the sort of cook who dashed and dumped ingredients in by eye, or impulse, and seemed to enjoy it.

The results were marvelous.

She was an adequate cook, a competent one. She measured everything and considered cooking just one of her daily chores.

It was probably a good analogy for who they were, she decided. And another reason why it made little sense for her to be eating in his kitchen or being naked in his bed.

The sex had been . . . incredible. No point in being less than honest about it. And after good, healthy sex she should've been feeling relaxed and loose and comfortable. Instead she felt tense and tight and awkward.

It had been so intense, then he'd just rolled out of bed and started dinner. They might just as easily have finished a rousing match of tennis.

Except he'd kissed her fingers, and that sweet, affectionate gesture had arrowed straight to her heart.

Her problem, her problem, she reminded herself. Over-analyzing, over-compensating, over-something. But if she didn't analyze something how did she know what it was?

"Dinner okay?"

She broke out of her internal debate to see him watching her steadily, with those strong jungle-cat eyes. "It's terrific."

"You're not eating much."

Deliberately she forked off more tuna. "I've never understood people who cook like you, like they do on some of the cooking shows. Tossing things together, shaking a little of this in, pinches of that. How do you know it's right?"

If that was really what she'd been thinking about with her mouth in that sexy sulk, he'd go outside and eat a shovelful of mulch. "I don't know. It usually is, or different enough to be right some other way."

Maybe he couldn't get inside her head, but he had to figure whatever was in there had to do with sex, or the ramifications of having it. But they'd play it her way for the moment. "If I'm going to cook, and since I don't want to spend every night in a restaurant, I'm going to cook, I want to enjoy it. If I regimented it, it'd start to piss me off."

"If I don't regiment it to some extent, I get nervous. Is it going to be too bland, or overly spiced? Overcooked, underdone? I'd be a wreck by the time I had a meal on the table." Worry flickered over her face. "I don't belong here, do I?"

"Define here."

"Here, here." She gestured wide with both arms. "With you, eating this really lovely and inventive meal, in your beautifully designed kitchen in your strangely charming and neglected house after relieving some sort of sexual insanity upstairs in your I'm-a-man-and-I-know-it bedroom."

He sat back and decided to clear the buzz from his head with a long drink of wine. He'd figured her right, he decided, but he just never seemed to figure her enough. "I've never heard that definition of here before. Must come from up north."

"You know what I mean," she fired back. "This isn't . . . It isn't—"

"Efficient? Tidy? Organized?"

"Don't take that placating tone with me."

"That wasn't my placating tone, it was my exasperated tone. What's your problem, Red?"

"You *confuse* me."

"Oh." He shrugged a shoulder. "If that's all." And went back to his meal.

"Do you think that's funny?"

"No, but I think I'm hungry, and that I can't do a hell of a lot about the fact that you're confused. Could be I don't mind all that much confusing you, anyway, since otherwise you'd start lining things up in alphabetical order."

Those bluebell eyes went to slits. "A, you're arrogant and annoying. B, you're bossy and bullheaded. C—"

"C, you're contrary and constricting, but that doesn't bother me the way it once did. I think we've got something interesting between us. Neither one of us was looking for it, but I can roll with that. You pick it apart. Hell if I know why I'm starting to like that about you."

"I've got more to risk than you do."

He sobered. "I'm not going to hurt your kids."

"If I believed you were the sort of man who would, or could, I wouldn't be with you on this level."

"What's 'this level'?"

"Evening sex and kitchen dinners."

"You seemed to handle the sex better than the meal."

"You're exactly right. Because I don't know what you expect from me now, and I'm not entirely sure what I expect from you."

"And this is your equivalent of tossing ingredients in a pot."

She huffed out a breath. "Apparently you understand me better than I do you."

"I'm not that complicated."

"Oh, please. You're a maze, Logan." She leaned forward until she could see the gold flecks on the green of his eyes. "A goddamn maze without any geometric pattern. Professionally, you're one of the most creative, versatile, and knowledgeable landscape designers I've ever worked with, but you do half of your designing and scheduling on the fly, with little scraps of papers stuffed into your truck or your pockets."

He scooped up more rice. "It works for me."

"Apparently, but it shouldn't work for anyone. You thrive in chaos, which this house clearly illustrates. Nobody should thrive in chaos."

"Now wait a minute." This time he gestured with his fork. "Where's the chaos? There's barely a frigging thing in the place."

"Exactly!" She jabbed a finger at him. "You've got a wonderful kitchen, a comfortable and stylish bedroom—"

"Stylish?" Mortification, clear as glass, covered his face. "Jesus."

"And empty rooms. You should be tearing your hair out wondering what you're going to do with them, but you're not. You just—just—" She waved her hand in circles. "Mosey along."

"I've never moseyed in my life. Amble sometimes," he decided. "But I never mosey."

"Whatever. You know wine and you read comic books. What kind of sense does that make?"

"Makes plenty if you consider I *like* wine and comic books."

"You were married, and apparently committed enough to move away from your home."

"What's the damn point in getting married if you're not ready and willing to do what makes the other person happy? Or at least try."

"You loved her," Stella said with a nod. "Yet you walked

away from a divorce unscarred. It was broken, too bad, so you ended it. You're rude and abrupt one minute, and accommodating the next. You knew why I'd come here tonight, yet you went to the trouble to fix a meal—which was considerate and, and civilized—there, put *that* in the C column."

"Christ, Red, you kill me. I'd move on to D, and say you're delicious, but right now it's more like demented."

Despite the fact he was laughing, she was wound up and couldn't stop. "And we have incredible, blow-the-damn-roof-off sex, then you bounce out of bed as if we'd been doing this every night for years. I can't keep up."

Once he decided she'd finished, he picked up his wine, drank thoughtfully. "Let's see if I can work my way back through that. Though I've got to tell you, I didn't detect any geometric pattern."

"Oh, shut up."

His hand clamped over hers before she could shove back from the table. "No, you just sit still. It's my turn. If I didn't work the way I do? I wouldn't be able to do what I do, and I sure as hell wouldn't love it. I found that out up north. My marriage was a failure. Nobody likes to fail, but nobody gets through life without screwing up. We screwed it up, didn't hurt anybody but ourselves. We took our lumps and moved on."

"But—"

"Hush. If I'm rude and abrupt it's because I feel rude and abrupt. If I'm accommodating, it's because I want to be, or figure I have to be at some point."

He thought, What the hell, and topped off his wine. She'd barely touched hers. "What was next? Oh, yeah, you being here tonight. Yeah, I knew why. We're not teenagers, and you're a pretty straightforward woman, in your way. I wanted you, and made that clear. You wouldn't come knocking on my door unless you were ready. As for the meal, there are a couple of reasons for that. One, I like to eat. And two, I wanted you here. I wanted to be with you here, like this. Before, after, in between. However it worked out."

Somewhere, somehow, during his discourse, her temper had ebbed. "How do you make it all sound sane?"

"I'm not done. While I'm going to agree with your take on the sex, I object to the word 'bounce.' I don't bounce anymore than I mosey. I got out of bed because if I'd breathed you in much longer, I'd have asked you to stay. You can't, you won't. And the fact is, I don't know that I'm ready for you to stay anyway. If you're the sort who needs a lot of postcoital chat, like 'Baby, that was amazing'—"

"I'm not." There was something in his aggravated tone that made her lips twitch. "I can judge for myself, and I destroyed you up there."

His hand slid up to her wrist, back down to her fingers. "Any destruction was mutual."

"All right. Mutual destruction. The first time with a man, and I think this holds true for most women, is as nerve-racking as it is exciting. It's more so afterward if what happened between them touched something in her. You touched something in me, and it scares me."

"Straightforward," he commented.

"Straightforward, to your maze. It's a difficult combination. Gives us a lot to think about. I'm sorry I made an issue out of all of this."

"Red, you were born to make issues out of every damn thing. It's kind of interesting now that I'm getting used to it."

"That may be true, and I could say that the fact your drummer certainly bangs a different tune's fairly interesting, too. But right now, I'm going to help you clean up your kitchen. Then I have to get home."

He rose when she did, then simply took her shoulders and backed her into the refrigerator. He kissed her blind and deaf—pent-up temper, needs, frustration, longings all boiled together.

"Something else to think about," he said.

"I'll say."

* * *

ROZ DIDN'T PRY INTO OTHER PEOPLE'S BUSINESS. SHE didn't mind hearing about it when gossip came her way, but she didn't pry. She didn't like—more she didn't permit—others to meddle in her life, and afforded them the same courtesy.

So she didn't ask Stella any questions. She thought of plenty, but she didn't ask them.

She observed.

Her manager conducted business with her usual calm efficiency. Roz imagined Stella could be standing in the whirling funnel of a tornado and would still be able to conduct business efficiently.

An admirable and somewhat terrifying trait.

She'd grown very fond of Stella, and she'd come—unquestionably—to depend on her to handle the details of the business so she herself could focus on the duties, and pleasures, of being the grower. She adored the children. It was impossible for her not to. They were charming and bright, sly and noisy, entertaining and exhausting.

Already, she was so used to them, and Stella and Hayley, being in her house she could hardly imagine them not being there.

But she didn't pry, even when Stella came home from her evening at Logan's with the unmistakable look of a woman who'd been well pleasured.

But she didn't hush Hayley, or brush her aside when the girl chattered about it.

"She won't get specific," Hayley complained while she and Roz weeded a bed at Harper House. "I really like it when people get specific. But she said he cooked for her. I always figure when a man cooks, he's either trying to get you between the sheets, or he's stuck on you."

"Maybe he's just hungry."

"A man's hungry, he sends out for pizza. At least the guys I've known. I think he's stuck on her." She waited, the pause obviously designed for Roz to comment. When there was none, Hayley blew out a breath. "Well? You've known him a long time."

"A few years. I can't tell you what's in his mind. But I can tell you he's never cooked for me."

"Was his wife a real bitch?"

"I couldn't say. I didn't know her."

"I'd like it if she was. A real stone bitch who tore him apart and left him all wounded and resentful of women. Then Stella comes along and gets him all messed up in the head even as she heals him."

Roz sat back on her heels and smiled. "You're awfully young, honey."

"You don't have to be young to like romance. Um . . . your second husband, he was terrible, wasn't he?"

"He was—is—a liar, a cheat, and a thief. Other than that he's charming."

"Did he break your heart?"

"No. He bruised my pride and pissed me off. Which was worse, in my opinion. That's yesterday's news, Hayley. I'm going to plug some *silene armeria* in these pockets," she continued. "They've got a long blooming season, and they'll fill in nice here."

"I'm sorry."

"No need to be sorry."

"It's just that this woman was in this morning, Mrs. Peebles?"

"Oh, yes, Roseanne." After studying the space, Roz picked up her trowel and began to turn the earth in the front of the mixed bed. "Did she actually buy anything?"

"She dithered around for an hour, said she'd come back."

"Typical. What did she want? It wouldn't have been plants."

"I clued in there. She's the nosy sort, and not the kind with what you'd call a benign curiosity. Just comes in for gossip—to spread it or to harvest it. You see her kind most everywhere."

"I suppose you do."

"So, well. She'd gotten word I was living here, and was a family connection, so she was pumping me. I don't pump so easy, but I let her keep at it."

Roz grinned under the brim of her cap as she reached for a plant. "Good for you."

"I figured what she really wanted was for me to pass on to you the news that Bryce Clerk is back in Memphis."

A jerk of her fingers broke off part of the stem. "Is he?" Roz said, very quietly.

"He's living at the Peabody for now and has some sort of venture in the works. She was vague about that. She says he plans to move back permanent, and he's taking office space. Said he looked very prosperous."

"Likely he hosed some other brainless woman."

"You aren't brainless, Roz."

"I was, briefly. Well, it's no matter to me where he is or what he's doing. I don't get burned twice by the same crooked match."

She set the plant, then reached for another. "Common name for these is none-so-pretty. Feel these sticky patches on the stems? They catch flies. Shows that something that looks attractive can be dangerous, or at least a big pain in the ass."

SHE BURIED IT AS SHE CLEANED UP. SHE WASN'T CONcerned with a scoundrel she'd once been foolish enough to marry. A woman was entitled to a few mistakes along the way, even if she made them out of loneliness or foolishness, or—screw it—vanity.

Entitled, Roz thought, as long as she corrected the mistakes and didn't repeat them.

She put on a fresh shirt, skimmed her fingers through her damp hair as she studied herself in the mirror. She could still look good, damn good, if she worked at it. If she wanted a man, she could have one—and not because he assumed she was dim-witted and had a depthless well of money to draw from. Maybe what had happened with Bryce had shaken her confidence and self-esteem for a little while, but she was all right now. Better than all right.

She hadn't needed a man to fill in the pockets of her life before he'd come along. She didn't need one now. Things were back the way she liked them. Her kids were happy and productive, her business was thriving, her home was secure. She had friends she enjoyed and acquaintances she tolerated.

And right now, she had the added interest of researching her family ghost.

Giving her hair another quick rub, she went downstairs to join the rest of the crew in the library. She heard the knock as she came to the base of the stairs, and detoured to the door.

"Logan, what a nice surprise."

"Hayley didn't tell you I was coming?"

"No, but that doesn't matter. Come on in."

"I ran into her at the nursery today, and she asked if I'd come by tonight, give y'all a hand with your research and brainstorming. I had a hard time resisting the idea of being a ghostbuster."

"I see." And she did. "I'd best warn you that our Hayley's got a romantic bent and she currently sees you as Rochester to Stella's Jane Eyre."

"Oh. Uh-oh."

She only smiled. "Jane's still with the boys, getting them settled down for the night. Why don't you go on up to the West wing? Just follow the noise. You can let her know we'll entertain ourselves until she comes down."

She walked away before he could agree or protest.

She didn't pry into other people's business. But that didn't mean she didn't sow the occasional seeds.

Logan stood where he was for a moment, tapping his fingers on the side of his leg. He was still tapping them as he started up the stairs.

Roz was right about the noise. He heard the laughter

and squeals, the stomping feet before he'd hit the top. Following it, he strolled down the hall, then paused in the open doorway.

It was obviously a room occupied by boys. And though it was certainly tidier than his had been at those tender ages, it wasn't static or regimented. A few toys were scattered on the floor, books and other debris littered the desk and shelves. It smelled of soap, shampoo, wild youth, and crayons.

In the midst of it, Stella sat on the floor, mercilessly tickling a pajama-clad Gavin while a blissfully naked Luke scrambled around the room making crazed hooting sounds through his cupped hands.

"What's my name?" Stella demanded as she sent her oldest son into helpless giggles.

"Mom!"

She made a harsh buzzing sound and dug fingers into his ribs. "Try again, small, helpless boy child. What is my name?"

"Mom, Mom, Mom, Mom, Mom!" He tried to wiggle away and was flipped over.

"I can't hear you."

"Empress," he managed on hitching giggles.

"And? The rest, give it all or the torment continues."

"Empress Magnificent of the Entire Universe!"

"And don't you forget it." She gave him a loud, smacking kiss on his cotton-clad butt, and sat back. "And now you, short, frog-faced creature." She got to her feet, rubbing her hands together as Luke screamed in delight.

And stumbled back with a scream of her own when she saw Logan in the doorway. "Oh, my God! You scared me to death!"

"Sorry, just watching the show. Your Highness. Hey, kid." He nodded at Gavin, who lay on the floor. "How's it going?"

"She defeated me. Now I have to go to bed, 'cause that's the law of the land."

"I've heard that." He picked up the bottom half of a pair

of X-Men pj's, lifted an eyebrow at Luke. "These your mom's?"

Luke let out a rolling gut laugh, and danced, happy with his naked state. "Uh-*uh*. They're mine. I don't have to wear them unless she catches me."

Luke started to make a break for the adjoining bath and was scooped up, one-armed, by his mother.

Stronger than she looks, Logan mused as she hoisted her son over her head.

"Foolish boy, you'll never escape me." She lowered him. "Into the pj's, and into bed." She glanced over at Logan. "Is there something . . ."

"I got invited to the . . . get-together downstairs."

"Is it a party?" Luke wanted to know when Logan handed him the pajama bottoms. "Are there cookies?"

"It's a meeting, a grown-up meeting, and if there are cookies," Stella said as she turned down Luke's bed, "you can have some tomorrow."

"David makes really good cookies," Gavin commented. "Better than Mom's."

"If that wasn't true, I'd have to punish you severely." She turned to his bed, where he sat grinning at her, and using the heel of her hand shoved him gently onto his back.

"But you're prettier than he is."

"Clever boy. Logan, could you tell everyone I'll be down shortly? We're just going to read for a bit first."

"Can he read?" Gavin asked.

"I can. What's the book?"

"Tonight we get *Captain Underpants*." Luke grabbed the book and hurried over to shove it into Logan's hands.

"So is he a superhero?"

Luke's eyes widened like saucers. "You don't know about Captain Underpants?"

"Can't say I do." He turned the book over in his hands, but he was looking at the boy. He'd never read to kids before. It might be entertaining. "Maybe I should read it, then I can find out. If that suits the Empress."

"Oh, well, I—"

"Please, Mom! Please!"

At the chorus on either side of her, Stella eased back with the oddest feeling in her gut. "Sure. I'll just go straighten up the bath."

She left them to it, mopping up the wet, gathering bath toys, while Logan's voice, deep and touched with ironic amusement, carried to her.

She hung damp towels, dumped bath toys into a plastic net to dry, fussed. And she felt the chill roll in around her. A hard, needling cold that speared straight to her bones.

Her creams and lotions tumbled over the counter as if an angry hand swept them. The thuds and rattles sent her springing forward to grab at them before they fell to the floor.

And each one was like a cube of ice in her hand.

She'd seen them move. Good God, she'd seen them *move.*

Shoving them back, she swung instinctively to the connecting doorway to shield her sons from the chill, from the fury she felt slapping the air.

There was Logan, with the chair pulled between the beds, as she did herself, reading about the silly adventures of Captain Underpants in that slow, easy voice, while her boys lay tucked in and drifting off.

She stood there, blocking that cold, letting it beat against her back until he finished, until he looked up at her.

"Thanks." She was amazed at how calm her voice sounded. "Boys, say good night to Mr. Kitridge."

She moved into the room as they mumbled it. When the cold didn't follow her, she took the book, managed a smile. "I'll be down in just a minute."

"Okay. See you later, men."

The interlude left him feeling mellow and relaxed. Reading bedtime stories was a kick. Who knew? Captain Underpants. Didn't that beat all.

He wouldn't mind doing it again sometime, especially

if he could talk Mama into letting them read a graphic novel.

He'd liked seeing her wrestling on the floor with her boy. Empress Magnificent, he thought with a half laugh.

Then the breath was knocked out of him. The force of the cold came like a tidal wave at his back, swamping him even as it shoved him forward.

He pitched at the top of the stairs, felt his head go light at the thought of the fall. Flailing out, he managed to grab the rail and, spinning his body, hook his other hand over it while tiny black dots swam in front of his eyes. For another instant he feared he would simply tumble over the railing, pushed by the momentum.

Out of the corner of his eye, he saw a shape, vague but female. And from it he felt a raw and bitter rage.

Then it was gone.

He could hear his own breath heaving in and out, and feel the clamminess of panic sweat down his back. Though his legs wanted to fold on him, he stayed where he was, working to steady himself until Stella came out.

Her half smile faded the minute she saw him. "What is it?" She moved to him quickly. "What happened?"

"She—this ghost of yours—has she ever scared the boys?"

"No. Exactly the opposite. She's . . . comforting, even protective of them."

"All right. Let's go downstairs." He took her hand firmly in his, prepared to drag her to safety if necessary.

"Your hand's cold."

"Yeah, tell me about it."

"You tell me."

"I intend to."

HE TOLD THEM ALL WHEN THEY SAT AROUND THE library table with their folders and books and notes. And he dumped a good shot of brandy in his coffee as he did.

"There's been nothing," Roz began, "in all the years she's been part of this house, that indicates she's a threat. People have been frightened or uneasy, but no one's ever been physically attacked."

"Can ghosts physically attack?" David wondered.

"You wouldn't ask if you'd been standing at the top of the stairs with me."

"Poltergeists can cause stuff to fly around," Hayley commented. "But they usually manifest around adolescent kids. Something about puberty can set them off. Anyway, this isn't that. It might be that an ancestor of Logan's did something to her. So she's paying him back."

"I've been in this house dozens of times. She's never bothered with me before."

"The children." Stella spoke softly as she looked over her own notes. "It centers on them. She's drawn to children, especially little boys. She's protective of them. And she almost, you could say, envies me for having them, but not in an angry way. More sad. But she was angry the night I was going out to dinner with Logan."

"Putting a man ahead of your kids." Roz held up a hand. "I'm not saying that's what I think. We have to think like she does. We talked about this before, Stella, and I've been thinking back on it. The only times I remember feeling anything angry from her was when I went out with men now and again, when my boys were coming up. But I didn't experience anything as direct or upsetting as this. But then, there was nothing to it. I never had any strong feelings for any of them."

"I don't see how she could know what I feel or think."

But the dreams, Stella thought. She's been in my dreams.

"Let's not get irrational now," David interrupted. "Let's follow this line through. Let's say she believes things are serious, or heading that way, between you and Logan. She doesn't like it, that's clear enough. The only people who've felt threatened, or been threatened are the two of you. Why? Does it make her angry? Or is she jealous?"

"A jealous ghost." Hayley drummed her hands on the table. "Oh, that's good. It's like she sympathizes, relates to you being a woman, a single woman, with kids. She'll help you look after them, even sort of look after you. But then you put a man in the picture, and she's all bitchy about it. She's like, you're not supposed to have a nice, standard family—mom, dad, kids—because I didn't."

"Logan and I hardly . . . All he did was read them a story."

"The sort of thing a father might do," Roz pointed out.

"I . . . well, when he was reading to them, I was putting the bathroom back in shape. And she was there. I felt her. Then, well, my things. The things I keep on the counter started to jump. *I* jumped."

"Holy shit," Hayley responded.

"I went to the door, and in the boy's room, everything was calm, normal. I could feel the warmth on the front of me, and this, this raging cold against my back. She didn't want to frighten them. Only me."

But buying a baby monitor went on her list. From now on, she wanted to hear everything that went on in that room when her boys were up there without her.

"This is a good angle, Stella, and you're smart enough to know we should follow it." Roz laid her hands on the library table. "Nothing we've turned up indicates this spirit is one of the Harper women, as has been assumed all these years. Yet someone knew her, knew her when she was alive, knew that she died. So was it hushed up, ignored? Either way, it might explain her being here. If it was hushed up or ignored, it seems most logical she was a servant, a mistress, or a lover."

"I bet she had a child." Hayley laid a hand over her own. "Maybe she died giving birth to it, or had to give it up, and died from a broken heart. It would have been one of the Harper men who got her into trouble, don't you think? Why would she stay here if it wasn't because she lived here or—"

"Died here," Stella finished. "Reginald Harper was head of the house during the period when we think she died. Roz, how the hell do we go about finding out if he had a mistress, a lover, or an illegitimate child?"

sixteen

LOGAN HAD BEEN IN LOVE TWICE IN HIS LIFE. HE'D been in lust a number of times. He'd experienced extreme interest or heavy like, but love had only knocked him down and out twice. The first had been in his late teens, when both he and the girl of his dreams had been too young to handle it.

They'd burned each other and their love out with passion, jealousies, and a kind of crazed energy. He could look back at that time now and think of Lisa Anne Lauer with a sweet nostalgia and affection.

Then there was Rae. He'd been a little older, a little smarter. They'd taken their time, two years of time before heading into marriage. They'd both wanted it, though some who knew him were surprised, not only by the engagement but by his agreement to move north with her.

It hadn't surprised Logan. He'd loved her, and north was where she'd wanted to be. Needed to be, he corrected, and he'd figured, naively as it turned out, that he could plant himself anywhere.

He'd left the wedding plans up to her and her mother,

with some input from his own. He wasn't crazy. But he'd enjoyed the big, splashy, crowded wedding with all its pomp.

He'd had a good job up north. At least in theory. But he'd been restless and dissatisfied in the beehive of it, and out of place in the urban buzz.

The small-town boy, he thought as he and his crew finished setting the treated boards on the roof of a twelve-foot pergola. He was just too small-town, too small-time, to fit into the urban landscape.

He hadn't thrived there, and neither had his marriage. Little things at first, picky things—things he knew in retrospect they should have dealt with, compromised on, overcome. Instead, they'd both let those little things fester and grow until they'd pushed the two of them, not just apart, he thought, but in opposite directions.

She'd been in her element, and he hadn't. At the core he'd been unhappy, and she'd been unhappy he wasn't acclimating. Like any disease, unhappiness spread straight down to the roots when it wasn't treated.

Not all her fault. Not all his. In the end they'd been smart enough, or unhappy enough, to cut their losses.

The failure of it had hurt, and the loss of that once-promising love had hurt. Stella was wrong about the lack of scars. There were just some scars you had to live with.

The client wanted wisteria for the pergola. He instructed his crew where to plant, then took himself off to the small pool the client wanted outfitted with water plants.

He was feeling broody, and when he was feeling broody, he liked to work alone as much as possible. He had the cattails in containers and, dragging on boots, he waded in to sink them. Left to themselves, the cats would spread and choke out everything, but held in containers they'd be a nice pastoral addition to the water feature. He dealt with a trio of water lilies the same way, then dug in the yellow flags. They liked their feet wet, and would dance with color on the edge of the pool.

The work satisfied him, centered him as it always did. It let another part of his mind work out separate problems. Or at least chew on them for a while.

Maybe he'd put a small pool in the walled garden he planned to build at home. No cattails, though. He might try some dwarf lotus, and some water canna as a background plant. It seemed to him it was more the sort of thing Stella would like.

He'd been in love twice before, Logan thought again. And now he could sense those delicate taproots searching inside him for a place to grow. He could probably cut them off. Probably. He probably should.

What was he going to do with a woman like Stella and those two ridiculously appealing kids? They were bound to drive each other crazy in the long term with their different approaches to damn near everything. He doubted they'd burn each other out, though, God, when he'd had her in bed, he'd felt singed. But they might wilt, as he and Rae had wilted. That was more painful, more miserable, he knew, than the quick flash.

And this time there were a couple of young boys to consider.

Wasn't that why the ghost had given him a good kick in the ass? It was hard to believe he was sweating in the steamy air under overcast skies and thinking about an encounter with a ghost. He'd thought he was open-minded about that sort of thing—until he'd come face-to-face, so to speak, with it.

The fact was, Logan realized now, as he hauled mulch over for the skirt of the pool, he hadn't believed in the ghost business. It had all been window dressing or legendary stuff to him. Old houses were supposed to have ghosts because it made a good story, and the south loved a good story. He'd accepted it as part of the culture, and maybe, in some strange way, as something that might happen to someone else. Especially if that someone else was a little drunk, or very susceptible to atmosphere.

He'd been neither. But he'd felt her breath, the ice of it, and her rage, the power of it. She'd wanted to cause him harm, she'd wanted him away. From those children, and their mother.

So he was invested now in helping to find the identity of what walked those halls.

But a part of him wondered if whoever she was was right. Would they all be better off if he stayed away?

The phone on his belt beeped. Since he was nearly done, he answered instead of ignoring, dragging off his filthy work gloves and plucking the phone off his belt.

"Kitridge."

"Logan, it's Stella."

The quick and helpless flutter around his heart irritated him. "Yeah. I've got the frigging forms in my truck."

"What forms?"

"Whatever damn forms you're calling to nag me about."

"It happens I'm not calling to nag you about anything." Her voice had gone crisp and businesslike, which only caused the flutter and the irritation to increase.

"Well, I don't have time to chat, either. I'm on the clock."

"Seeing as you are, I'd like you to schedule in a consult. I have a customer who'd like an on-site consultation. She's here now, so if you could give me a sense of your plans for the day, I could let her know if and when you could meet with her."

"Where?"

She rattled off an address that was twenty minutes away. He glanced around his current job site, calculated. "Two o'clock."

"Fine. I'll tell her. The client's name is Marsha Fields. Do you need any more information?"

"No."

"Fine."

He heard the firm click in his ear and found himself even more annoyed he hadn't thought to hang up first.

* * *

BY THE TIME LOGAN GOT HOME THAT EVENING, HE was tired, sweaty, and in a better mood. Hard physical work usually did the job for him, and he'd had plenty of it that day. He'd worked in the steam, then through the start of a brief spring storm. He and his crew broke for lunch during the worst of it and sat in his overheated truck, rain lashing at the windows, while they ate cold po'boy sandwiches and drank sweet tea.

The Fields job had strong possibilities. The woman ran that roost and had very specific ideas. Since he liked and agreed with most of them, he was eager to put some of them on paper, expand or refine them.

And since it turned out that Marsha's cousin on her mother's side was Logan's second cousin on his father's, the consult had taken longer than it might have, and had progressed cheerfully.

It didn't hurt that she was bound to send more work his way.

He took the last curve of the road to his house in a pleasant frame of mind, which darkened considerably when he saw Stella's car parked behind his.

He didn't want to see her now. He hadn't worked things out in his head, and she'd just muck up whatever progress he'd made. He wanted a shower and a beer, a little quiet. Then he wanted to eat his dinner with ESPN in the background and his work spread out on the kitchen table.

There just wasn't room in that scenario for a woman.

He parked, fully intending to shake her off. She wasn't in the car, or on the porch. He was trying to determine if going to bed with him gave a woman like her the notion that she could waltz into his house when he wasn't there. Even as he'd decided it wouldn't, not for Stella, he heard the watery hiss of his own garden hose.

Shoving his hands in his pockets, he wandered around the side of the house.

She was on the patio, wearing snug gray pants—the sort that stopped several inches above the ankle—and a loose blue shirt. Her hair was drawn back in a bright, curling tail, which for reasons he couldn't explain he found desperately sexy. As the sun had burned its way through the clouds, she'd shaded her eyes with gray-tinted glasses.

She looked neat and tidy, careful to keep her gray canvas shoes out of the wet.

"It rained today," he called out.

She kept on soaking his pots. "Not enough."

She finished the job, released the sprayer on the hose, but continued to hold it as she turned to face him. "I realize you have your own style, and your own moods, and that's your business. But I won't be spoken to the way you spoke to me today. I won't be treated like some silly female who calls her boyfriend in the middle of the workday to coo at him, or like some anal business associate who interrupts you to harangue you about details. I'm neither."

"Not my girlfriend or not my business associate?"

He could see, quite clearly, the way her jaw tightened when she clenched her teeth. "If and when I contact you during the workday, it will be for a reason. As it most certainly was this morning."

She was right, but he didn't have to say so. "We got the Fields job."

"Hooray."

He bit the inside of his cheek to hold back the grin at her sour cheer. "I'll be working up a design for her, with a bid. You'll get a copy of both. That suit you?"

"It does. What doesn't—"

"Where are the kids?"

It threw her off stride. "My father and his wife picked them up from school today. They're having dinner there, and spending the night, as I have a birthing class with Hayley later."

"What time?"

"What time what?"

"Is the class?"

"At eight-thirty. I'm not here for small talk, Logan, or to be placated. I feel very strongly that—" Her eyes widened, then narrowed as she stepped back. He'd stepped forward, and there was no mistaking the tone of that slow smile.

"Don't even think about it. I couldn't be less interested in kissing you at the moment."

"Then I'll kiss you, and maybe you'll get interested."

"I mean it." She aimed the hose like a weapon. "Just keep your distance. I want to make myself perfectly clear."

"I'm getting the message. Go ahead and shoot," he invited. "I sweated out a gallon today, I won't mind a shower."

"Just stop it." She danced back several steps as he advanced. "This isn't a game, this isn't funny."

"I just get stirred right up when your voice takes on that tone."

"I don't have a tone."

"Yankee schoolteacher. I'm going to be sorry if you ever lose it." He made a grab, and instinctively she tightened her fist on the nozzle. And nailed him.

The spray hit him mid-chest and had a giggle bubbling out of her before she could stop it. "I'm not going to play with you now. I'm serious, Logan."

Dripping, he made another grab, feinted left. This time she squealed, dropped the hose, and ran.

He snagged her around the waist, hauled her off her feet at the back end of the patio. Caught somewhere between shock and disbelief, she kicked, wiggled, then lost her breath as she landed on the grass on top of him.

"Let me go, you moron."

"Don't see why I should." God, it felt good to be horizontal. Better yet to have her horizontal with him. "Here you are, trespassing, watering my pots, spouting off lectures." He rolled, pinning her. "I ought to be able to do what I want on my own land."

"Stop it. I haven't finished fighting with you."

"I bet you can pick it up where you left off." He gave her a playful nip on the chin, then another.

"You're wet, you're sweaty, I'm getting grass stains on my—"

The rest of the words were muffled against his mouth, and she would have sworn the water on both of them went to steam.

"I can't—we can't—" But the reasons why were going dim. "In the backyard."

"Wanna bet?"

He couldn't help wanting her, so why was he fighting it? He wanted the solid, sensible core of her, and the sweet edges. He wanted the woman obsessed with forms who would wrestle on the floor with her children. He wanted the woman who watered his pots even while she skinned him with words.

And the one who vibrated beneath him on the grass when he touched her.

He touched her, his hands possessive as they molded her breasts, as they roamed down her to cup her hips. He tasted her, his lips hungry on her throat, her shoulder, her breast.

She melted under him, and even as she went fluid seemed to come alive with heat, with movement.

It was insane. It was rash and it was foolish, but she couldn't stop herself. They rolled over the grass, like two frenzied puppies. He smelled of sweat, of labor and damp. And, God, of man. Pungent and gorgeous and sexy.

She clamped her hands in that mass of waving hair, already showing streaks from the sun, and dragged his mouth back to hers.

She nipped his lip, his tongue.

"Your belt." She had to fight to draw air. "It's digging—"

"Sorry."

He levered up to unbuckle it, then just stopped to look at her.

Her hair had come out of its band; her eyes were sultry, her skin flushed. And he felt those roots take hold.

"Stella."

He didn't know what he might have said, the words were jumbled in his brain and tangled with so much feeling he couldn't translate them.

But she smiled, slow and sultry as her eyes. "Why don't I help you with that?"

She flipped open the button of his jeans, yanked down the zipper. Her hand closed over him, a velvet vise. His body was hard as steel, and his mind and heart powerless.

She arched up to him, her lips skimmed over his bare chest, teeth scoring a hot little line that was a whisper away from pain.

Then she was over him, destroying him. Surrounding him.

She heard birdsong and breeze, smelled grass and damp flesh. And heliotrope that wafted on the air from the pot she'd watered. She felt his muscles, taut ropes, the broad plane of his shoulders, the surprisingly soft waves of his hair.

And she saw, as she looked down, that he was lost in her.

Throwing her head back, she rode, until she was lost as well.

SHE LAY SPRAWLED OVER HIM, DAMP AND NAKED AND muzzy-headed. Part of her brain registered that his arms were clamped around her as if they were two survivors of a shipwreck.

She turned her head to rest it on his chest. Maybe they'd wrecked each other. She'd just made wild love with a man in broad daylight, outside in the yard.

"This is insane," she murmured, but couldn't quite convince herself to move. "What if someone had come by?"

"People come by without an invitation have to take potluck."

There was a lazy drawl to his voice in direct opposition to his grip on her. She lifted her head to study. His eyes were closed. "So this is potluck?"

The corners of his mouth turned up a little. "Seems to me this pot was plenty lucky."

"I feel sixteen. Hell, I never did anything like this when I was sixteen. I need my sanity. I need my clothes."

"Hold on." He nudged her aside, then rose.

Obviously, she thought, it doesn't bother him to walk around outside naked as a deer. "I came here to talk to you, Logan. Seriously."

"You came here to kick my ass," he corrected. "Seriously. You were doing a pretty good job of it."

"I hadn't finished." She turned slightly, reached out for her hairband. "But I will, as soon as I'm dressed and—"

She screamed, the way a woman screams when she's being murdered with a kitchen knife.

Then she gurgled, as the water he'd drenched her with from the hose ran into her astonished mouth.

"Figured we could both use some cooling off."

It simply wasn't in her, even under the circumstances, to run bare-assed over the grass. Instead, she curled herself up, knees to breast, arms around knees, and cursed him with vehemence and creativity.

He laughed until he thought his ribs would crack. "Where'd a nice girl like you learn words like that? How am I supposed to kiss that kind of mouth?"

She seared him with a look even when he held the hose over his own head and took an impromptu shower. "Feels pretty good. Want a beer?"

"No, I don't want a beer. I certainly don't want a damn beer. I want a damn towel. You insane idiot, now my clothes are wet."

"We'll toss 'em into the dryer." He dropped the hose, scooped them up. "Come on inside, I'll get you a towel."

Since he sauntered across the patio to the door, still unconcerned and naked, she had no choice but to follow.

"Do you have a robe?" she asked in cold and vicious tones.

"What would I do with a robe? Hang on, Red."

He left her, dripping and beginning to shiver in his kitchen.

He came back a few minutes later, wearing ratty gym pants and carrying two huge bath sheets. "These ought to do the trick. Dry off, I'll toss these in for you."

He carried her clothes through a door. Laundry room, she assumed as she wrapped one of the towels around her. She used the other to rub at her hair—which would be hopeless, absolutely hopeless now—while she heard the dryer click on.

"Want some wine instead?" he asked as he stepped back in. "Coffee or something."

"Now you listen to me—"

"Red, I swear I've had to listen to you more than any woman I can remember in the whole of my life. It beats the living hell out of me why I seem to be falling in love with you."

"I don't like being . . . Excuse me?"

"It was the hair that started it." He opened the refrigerator, took out a beer. "But that's just attraction. Then the voice." He popped the top and took a long drink from the bottle. "But that's just orneriness on my part. It's a whole bunch of little things, a lot of big ones tossed in. I don't know just what it is, but every time I'm around you I get closer to the edge."

"I—you—you think you're falling in love with me, and your way of showing it is to toss me on the ground and carry on like some sex addict, and when you're done to drench me with a hose?"

He took another sip, slower, more contemplative, rubbed a hand over his bare chest. "Seemed like the thing to do at the time."

"Well, that's very charming."

"Wasn't thinking about charm. I didn't say I wanted to

be in love with you. In fact, thinking about it put me in a lousy mood most of the day."

Her eyes narrowed until the blue of them was a hot, intense light. "Oh, really?"

"Feel better now, though."

"Oh, that's fine. That's lovely. Get me my clothes."

"They're not dry yet."

"I don't care."

"People from up north are always in a hurry." He leaned back comfortably on the counter. "There's this other thing I thought today."

"I don't care about that either."

"The other thing was how I've only been in love—the genuine deal—twice before. And both times it . . . let's not mince words. Both times it went to shit. Could be this'll head the same way."

"Could be we're already there."

"No." His lips curved. "You're pissed and you're scared. I'm not what you were after."

"I wasn't after anything."

"Me either." He set the beer down, then killed her temper by stepping to her, framing her face with his hands. "Maybe I can stop what's going on in me. Maybe I should try. But I look at you, I touch you, and the edge doesn't just get closer, it gets more appealing."

He touched his lips to her forehead, then released her and stepped back.

"Every time I figure some part of you out, you sprout something off in another direction," she said. "I've only been in love once—the genuine deal—and it was everything I wanted. I haven't figured out what I want now, beyond what I have. I don't know, Logan, if I've got the courage to step up to that edge again."

"Things keep going the way they are for me, if you don't step up, you might get pushed."

"I don't push easily. Logan." It was she who stepped to him now, and she took his hand. "I'm so touched that you'd tell me, so churned up inside that you might feel that way about me. I need time to figure out what's going on inside me, too."

"It'd help," he decided after a moment, "if you could work on keeping the pace."

HER CLOTHES WERE DRY BUT IMPOSSIBLY WRINKLED, her hair had frizzed and was now, in Stella's opinion, approximately twice its normal volume.

She dashed out of the car, mortified to see both Hayley and Roz sitting on the glider drinking something out of tall glasses.

"Just have to change," she called out. "I won't be long."

"There's plenty of time," Hayley called back, and pursed her lips as Stella raced into the house. "You know," she began, "what it means when a woman shows up with her clothes all wrinkled to hell and grass stains on the ass of her pants?"

"I assume she went by Logan's."

"Outdoor nookie."

Roz choked on a sip of tea, wheezed in a laugh. "Hayley. Jesus."

"You ever do it outdoors?"

Roz only sighed now. "In the dim, dark past."

STELLA WAS SHARP ENOUGH TO KNOW THEY WERE talking about her. As a result, the flush covered not only her face but most of her body as she ran into the bedroom. She stripped off her clothes, threw them into a hamper.

"No reason to be embarrassed," she muttered to herself as she threw open her armoire. "Absolutely none." She dug out fresh underwear and felt more normal after she put it on.

And reaching for her blouse, felt the chill.

She braced, half expecting a vase or lamp to fly across the room at her this time.

But she gathered her courage and turned, and she saw the Harper Bride. Clearly, for the first time, clearly, though the dusky light slipped through her as if she were smoke. Still, Stella saw her face, her form, the bright ringlets, the shattered eyes.

The Bride stood at the doorway that connected to the bath, then the boys' room.

But it wasn't anger Stella saw on her face. It wasn't disapproval she felt quivering on the air. It was utter and terrible grief.

Her own fear turned to pity. "I wish I could help you. I want to help." With her blouse pressed against her breasts, Stella took a tentative step forward. "I wish I knew who you were, what happened to you. Why you're so sad."

The woman turned her head, looked back with swimming eyes to the room beyond.

"They're not gone," Stella heard herself say. "I'd never let them go. They're my life. They're with my father and his wife—their grandparents. A treat for them, that's all. A night where they can be pampered and spoiled and eat too much ice cream. They'll be back tomorrow."

She took a cautious second step, even as her throat burned dry. "They love being with my father and Jolene. But it's so quiet when they're not around, isn't it?"

Good God, she was talking to a ghost. Trying to draw a ghost into conversation. How had her life become so utterly strange?

"Can't you tell me something, anything that would help? We're all trying to find out, and maybe when we do . . . Can't you tell me your name?"

Though Stella's hand trembled, she lifted it, reached out. Those shattered eyes met hers, and Stella's hand passed through. There was cold, and a kind of snapping shock. Then there was nothing at all.

"You can speak," Stella said to the empty room. "If you can sing, you can speak. Why won't you?"

Shaken, she dressed, fought her hair into a clip. Her

heart was still thudding as she did her makeup, half expecting to see that other heartbroken face in the mirror.

Then she slipped on her shoes and went downstairs. She would leave death behind, she thought, and go prepare for new life.

seventeen

THE PACE MIGHT HAVE BEEN SLOW, BUT THE HOURS were the killer. As spring turned lushly green and temperatures rose toward what Stella thought of as high summer, garden-happy customers flocked to the nursery, as much, she thought, to browse for an hour or so and chat with the staff and other customers as for the stock.

Still, every day flats of bedding plants, pots of perennials, forests of shrubs and ornamental trees strolled out the door.

She watched the field stock bagged and burlapped, and scurried to plug holes on tables by adding greenhouse stock. As mixed planters, hanging baskets, and the concrete troughs were snapped up, she created more.

She made countless calls to suppliers for more: more fertilizers, more grass seed, more root starter, more everything.

With her clipboard and careful eye she checked inventory, adjusted, and begged Roz to release some of the younger stock.

"It's not ready. Next year."

"At this rate, we're going to run out of columbine, astilbes, hostas—" She waved the board. "Roz, we've sold out a good thirty percent of our perennial stock already. We'll be lucky to get through May with our current inventory."

"And things will slow down." Roz babied cuttings from a stock dianthus. "If I start putting plants out before they're ready, the customer's not going to be happy."

"But—"

"These dianthus won't bloom till next year. Customers want bloom, Stella, you know that. They want to plug it in while it's flowering or about to. They don't want to wait until next year for the gratification."

"I do know. Still . . ."

"You're caught up." With her gloved hand, Roz scratched an itch under her nose. "So's everyone else. Lord, Ruby's beaming like she's been made a grandmother again, and Steve wants to high-five me every time I see him."

"They love this place."

"So do I. The fact is, this is the best year we've ever had. Weather's part of it. We've had a pretty spring. But we've also got ourselves an efficient and enthusiastic manager to help things along. But end of the day, quality's still the byword here. Quantity's second."

"You're right. Of course you're right. I just can't stand the thought of running out of something and having to send a customer somewhere else."

"Probably won't come to that, especially if we're smart enough to lead them toward a nice substitution."

Stella sighed. "Right again."

"And if we do need to recommend another nursery . . ."

"The customers will be pleased and impressed with our efforts to satisfy them. And this is why you're the owner of a place like this, and I'm the manager."

"It also comes down to being born and bred right here. In a few more weeks, the spring buying and planting season will be over. Anyone who comes in after mid-May's going to be looking mostly for supplies, or sidelines, maybe a basket or planter already made up, or a few plants to replace something that's died or bloomed off. And once that June heat hits, you're going to want to be putting what we've got left of spring and summer bloomers on sale before you start pushing the fall stock."

"And in Michigan, you'd be taking a big risk to put anything in before mid-May."

Roz moved to the next tray of cuttings. "You miss it?"

"I want to say yes, because it seems disloyal otherwise. But no, not really. I didn't leave anything back there except memories."

It was the memories that worried her. She'd had a good life, with a man she'd loved. When she'd lost him that life had shattered—under the surface. It had left her shaky and unstable inside. She'd kept that life together, for her children, but in her heart had been more than grief. There'd been fear.

She'd fought the fear, and embraced the memories.

But she hadn't just lost her husband. Her sons had lost their father. Gavin's memory of him was dimmer—dimmer every year—but sweet. Luke was too young to remember his father clearly. It seemed so unfair. If she moved forward in her relationship with Logan while her boys were still so young . . .

It was a little like no longer missing home, she supposed. It seemed disloyal.

As she walked into the showroom, she spotted a number of customers with wagons, browsing the tables, and Hayley hunkering down to lift a large strawberry pot already planted.

"Don't!"

Her sharp command had heads turning, but she marched right through the curious and, slapping her hands on her hips, glared at Hayley. "Just what do you think you're doing?"

"We sold the point-of-purchase planters. I thought this one here would be good out by the counter."

"I'm sure it would. Do you know how pregnant you are?"

Hayley glanced down at her basketball belly. "Kind of hard to miss."

"You want to move a planter, then you ask somebody to move it for you."

"I'm strong as an ox."

"And eight months pregnant."

"You listen to her, honey." One of the customers patted Hayley on the arm. "You don't want to take chances. Once that baby pops out, you'll never stop hauling things around. Now's the time to take advantage of your condition and let people spoil you a little bit."

"I've got to watch her like a hawk," Stella said. "That lobelia's wonderful, isn't it?"

The woman looked down at her flatbed. "I just love that deep blue color. I was thinking I'd get some of that red salvia to go beside it, maybe back it up with cosmos?"

"Sounds perfect. Charming and colorful, with a whole season of bloom."

"I've got some more room in the back of the bed, but I'm not sure what to put in." She bit her lip as she scanned the tables loaded with options. "I wouldn't mind some suggestions, if you've got the time."

"That's what we're here for. We've got some terrific mixed hollyhocks, tall enough to go behind the cosmos. And if you want to back up the salvia, I think those marigolds there would be fabulous. And have you seen the perilla?"

"I don't even know what it is," the woman said with a laugh.

Stella showed her the deep-purple foliage plant, had Hayley gather up several good marigolds. Between them, they filled another flatbed.

"I'm glad you went with the alyssum, too. See the way

the white pops the rest of your colors? Actually, the arrangement there gives you a pretty good idea what you'll have in your garden." Stella nodded toward the flatbeds. "You can just see the way those plants will complement each other."

"I can't wait to get them in. My neighbors are going to be *green* with envy."

"Just send them to us."

"Wouldn't be the first time. I've been coming here since you opened. Used to live about a mile from here, moved down toward Memphis two years ago. It's fifteen miles or more now, but I always find something special here, so I keep coming back."

"That's so nice to hear. Is there anything else Hayley or I can help you with? Do you need any starter, mulch, fertilizer?"

"Those I can handle on my own. But actually"—she smiled at Hayley—"since this cart's full, if you'd have one of those strong young boys cart that pot out to the counter—and on out to my car after—I'll take it."

"Let me arrange that for you." Stella gave Hayley a last telling look. "And you, behave yourself."

"Y'all sisters?" the woman asked Hayley.

"No. She's my boss. Why?"

"Reminded me of my sister and me, I guess. I still scold my baby sister the way she did you, especially when I'm worried about her."

"Really?" Hayley looked off toward where Stella had gone. "I guess we sort of are, then."

WHILE SHE AGREED THAT EXERCISE WAS GOOD FOR expectant mothers, Stella wasn't willing to have Hayley work all day and then walk close to half a mile home at this stage of her pregnancy. Hayley groused, but every evening Stella herded her to the car and drove her home.

"I *like* walking."

"And after we get home and you have something to eat, you can take a nice walk around the gardens. But you're not walking all that way, and through the woods alone, on my watch, kid."

"Are you going to be pestering me like this for the next four weeks?"

"I absolutely am."

"You know Mrs. Tyler? The lady who bought all those annuals we helped her with?"

"Mmm-hmm."

"She said how she thought we were sisters because you give me grief like she does her baby sister. At the time, I thought that was nice. Now, it's irritating."

"That's a shame."

"I'm taking care of myself."

"Yes, and so am I."

Hayley sighed. "If it's not you giving me the hairy eye, it's Roz. Next thing, people'll start thinking she's my mama."

Stella glanced down to see Hayley slip her feet out of her shoes. "Feet hurt?"

"They're all right."

"I've got this wonderful foot gel. Why don't you use it when we get home, and put your feet up for a few minutes?"

"I can't hardly reach them anymore. I feel . . ."

"Fat and clumsy and sluggish," Stella finished.

"And stupid and bitchy." She pushed back her damp bangs, thought about whacking them off. Thought about whacking all her hair off. "And hot and nasty."

When Stella reached over, bumped up the air-conditioning, Hayley's eyes began to sting with remorse and misery. "You're being so sweet to me—everyone is—and I don't even appreciate it. And I just feel like I've been pregnant my whole life and I'm going to stay pregnant forever."

"I can promise you won't."

"And I . . . Stella, when they showed that video at birthing class and we watched that woman go through it? I don't see how I can do that. I just don't think I can."

"I'll be there with you. You'll be just fine, Hayley. I'm not going to tell you it won't be hard, but it's going to be exciting, too. Thrilling."

She turned into the drive. And there were her boys, racing around the yard with the dog and Harper in what seemed to be a very informal game of Wiffle ball.

"And so worth it," she told her. "The minute you hold your baby in your arms, you'll know."

"I just can't imagine being a mama. Before, I could, but now that it's getting closer, I just can't."

"Of course you can't. Nobody can really imagine a miracle. You're allowed to be nervous. You're supposed to be."

"Then I'm doing a good job."

When she parked, the boys ran over. "Mom, Mom! We're playing Wiffle Olympics, and I hit the ball a *million* times."

"A million?" She widened her eyes at Luke as she climbed out. "That must be a record."

"Come on and play, Mom." Gavin grabbed her hand as Parker leaped up to paw at her legs. "Please!"

"All right, but I don't think I can hit the ball a million times."

Harper skirted the car to get to Hayley's side. His hair curled damply from under his ball cap, and his shirt showed stains from grass and dirt. "Need some help?"

She couldn't get her feet back in her shoes. They felt hot and swollen and no longer hers. Cranky tears flooded her throat. "I'm pregnant," she snapped, "not handicapped."

She left her shoes on the mat as she struggled out. Before she could stop herself, she slapped at Harper's offered hand. "Just leave me be, will you?"

"Sorry." He stuffed his hands in his pockets.

"I can't breathe with everybody hovering around me night and day." She marched toward the house, trying hard not to waddle.

"She's just tired, Harper." Whether it was hovering or not, Stella watched Hayley until she'd gotten inside. "Tired and out of sorts. It's just being pregnant."

"Maybe she shouldn't be working right now."

"If I suggested that, she'd explode. Working keeps her mind busy. We're all keeping an eye on her to make sure she doesn't overdo, which is part of the problem. She feels a little surrounded, I imagine."

"Mom!"

She held up a hand to her impatient boys. "She'd have snapped at anybody who offered her a hand just then. It wasn't personal."

"Sure. Well, I've got to go clean up." He turned back to the boys, who were already squabbling over the plastic bat. "Later. And next time I'm taking you both down."

THE AFTERNOON WAS SULTRY, A SLY HINT OF THE summer that waited just around the corner. Even with the air-conditioning, Stella sweltered in her little office. As a surrender to the weather, she wore a tank top and thin cotton pants. She'd given up on her hair and had bundled it as best she could on top of her head.

She'd just finished outlining the next week's work schedule and was about to update one of her spreadsheets when someone knocked on her door.

"Come in." Automatically, she reached for the thermos of iced coffee she'd begun to make every morning. And her heart gave a little jolt when Logan stepped in. "Hi. I thought you were on the Fields job today."

"Got rained out."

"Oh?" She swiveled around to her tiny window, saw the sheets of rain. "I didn't realize."

"All those numbers and columns can be pretty absorbing."

"To some of us."

"It's a good day to play hookey. Why don't you come out and play in the rain, Red?"

"Can't." She spread her arms to encompass her desk. "Work."

He sat on the corner of it. "Been a busy spring so far. I don't figure Roz would blink if you took a couple hours off on a rainy afternoon."

"Probably not. But I would."

"Figured that, too." He picked up an oddly shaped and obviously child-made pencil holder, examined it. "Gavin or Luke?"

"Gavin, age seven."

"You avoiding me, Stella?"

"No. A little," she admitted. "But not entirely. We've been swamped, here and at home. Hayley's only got three weeks to go, and I like to stick close."

"Do you think you could manage a couple of hours away, say, Friday night? Take in a movie?"

"Well, Friday nights I usually try to take the kids out."

"Good. The new Disney flick's playing. I can pick y'all up at six. We'll go for pizza first."

"Oh, I . . ." She sat back, frowned at him. "That was sneaky."

"Whatever works."

"Logan, have you ever been to the movies with a couple of kids on a Friday night?"

"Nope." He pushed off the desk and grinned. "Should be an experience."

He came around the desk and, cupping his hands under her elbows, lifted her straight out of the chair with a careless strength that had her mouth watering. "I've started to miss you."

He touched his mouth to hers, heating up the contact as he let her slide down his body until her feet hit the floor. Her arms lifted to link around his neck, banding there for a moment until her brain engaged again.

"It looks like I've started to miss you, too," she said as she stepped back. "I've been thinking."

"I just bet you have. You keep on doing that." He tugged at a loose lock of her hair. "See you Friday."

She sat down again when he walked out. "But I have trouble remembering what I'm thinking."

HE WAS RIGHT. IT WAS AN EXPERIENCE. ONE HE HANdled, in Stella's opinion, better than she'd expected. He didn't appear to have a problem with boy-speak. In fact, during the pizza interlude she got the feeling she was odd man out. Normally she could hold her own in intense discussions of comic books and baseball, but this one headed to another level.

At one point she wasn't entirely sure the X-Men's Wolverine hadn't signed on to play third base for the Atlanta Braves.

"I can eat fifty pieces of pizza," Luke announced as the pie was divvied up. "And after, five *gallons* of popcorn."

"Then you'll puke!"

She started to remind Gavin that puke wasn't proper meal conversation, but Logan just plopped a slice on his own plate. "Be smarter to puke after the pizza to make room for the popcorn."

The wisdom and hilarity of this sent the boys off into delighted gagging noises.

"Hey!" Luke's face went mutinous. "Gavin has more pepperoni on his piece. I have two and he has three!"

As Gavin snorted and set his face into the look, Logan nodded. "You know, you're right. Doesn't seem fair. Let's just fix that." He plucked a round of pepperoni off Gavin's piece and popped it into his own mouth. "Now you're even."

More hilarity ensued. The boys ate like stevedores, made an unholy mess, and were so overstimulated by the time they got to the theater, she expected them to start a riot.

"You've got to remember to be quiet during the movie," she warned. "Other people are here to see it."

"I'll try," Logan said solemnly. "But sometimes I just can't help talking."

The boys giggled all the way to the concession counter.

She knew some men who put on a show for a woman's children—to get to the woman. And, she thought as they settled into seats with tubs of popcorn, she knew some who sincerely tried to charm the kids because they were an interesting novelty.

Still, he seemed to be easy with them, and you had to give a man in his thirties points for at least appearing to enjoy a movie with talking monkeys.

Halfway through, as she'd expected, Luke began to squirm in his seat. Two cups of pop, she calculated, one small bladder. He wouldn't want to go, wouldn't want to miss anything. So there'd be a short, whispered argument.

She leaned toward him, prepared for it. And Logan beat her to it. She didn't hear what he said in Luke's ear, but Luke giggled, and the two of them rose.

"Be right back," he murmured to Stella and walked out with his hand over Luke's.

Okay, that was it, she decided as her eyes misted. The man was taking her little boy to pee.

She was a goner.

TWO VERY HAPPY BOYS PILED INTO THE BACK OF Logan's car. As soon as they were strapped in, they were bouncing and chattering about their favorite parts of the movie.

"Hey, guys." Logan slipped behind the wheel, then draped his arm over the seat to look in the back. "You might want to brace yourselves, 'cause I'm gonna kiss your mama."

"How come?" Luke wanted to know.

"Because, as you might have observed yourselves, she's pretty, and she tastes good."

He leaned over, amusement in his eyes. When Stella would have offered him a cheek, he turned her face with one hand and gave her a soft, quick kiss on the mouth.

"You're not pretty." Luke snorted through his nose. "How come she kissed you?"

"Son, that's because I'm one fine-looking hunk of man." He winked into the rearview mirror, noted that Gavin was watching him with quiet speculation, then started the engine.

LUKE WAS NODDING OFF WHEN THEY GOT TO THE house, his head bobbing as he struggled to stay awake.

"Let me cart him up."

"I can get him." Stella leaned in to unbuckle his seat belt. "I'm used to it. And I don't know if you should go upstairs again."

"She'll have to get used to me." He nudged Stella aside and hoisted Luke into his arms. "Come on, pizza king, let's go for a ride."

"I'm not tired."

" 'Course not."

Yawning, he laid his head on Logan's shoulder. "You smell different from Mom. And you got harder skin."

"How about that?"

Roz wandered into the foyer as they came in. "Well, it looks like everyone had a good time. Logan, why don't you come down for a drink once you settle those boys down. I'd like to talk to the both of you."

"Sure. We'll be right down."

"I can take them," Stella began, but he was already carrying Luke up the stairs.

"I'll just get us some wine. 'Night, cutie," Roz said to Gavin, and smiled at Stella's back as she followed Logan.

He was already untying Luke's Nikes. "Logan, I'll do that. You go on down with Roz."

He continued to remove the shoes, wondering if the nerves he heard in her voice had to do with the ghost or with him. But it was the boy standing beside her, unusually silent, who had his attention.

"Go ahead and settle him in, then. Gavin and I want to have a little conversation. Don't we, kid?"

Gavin jerked a shoulder. "Maybe. I guess."

"He needs to get ready for bed."

"Won't take long. Why don't you step into my office?" he said to Gavin, and when he gestured toward the bathroom, he saw the boy's lip twitch.

"Logan," Stella began.

"Man talk. Excuse us." And he closed the door in her face.

Figuring it would be easier on them both if they were more eye-to-eye, Logan sat on the edge of the tub. He wasn't sure, but he had to figure the boy was about as nervous as he was himself.

"Did me kissing your mama bother you?"

"I don't know. Maybe. I saw this other guy kiss her once, when I was little. She went out to dinner with him or something, and we had a babysitter, and I woke up and saw him do it. But I didn't like him so much because he smiled *all* the time." He demonstrated, spreading his lips and showing his teeth.

"I don't like him either."

"Do you kiss all the girls because they're pretty?" Gavin blurted out.

"Well, now, I've kissed my share of girls. But your mama's special."

"How come?"

The boy wanted straight answers, Logan decided. So he'd do his best to give them. "Because she makes my heart feel funny, in a good kind of way, I guess. Girls make us feel funny in lots of ways, but when they make your heart feel funny, they're special."

Gavin looked toward the closed door and back again. "My dad kissed her. I remember."

"It's good you do." He had an urge, one that surprised him, to stroke a hand over Gavin's hair. But he didn't think it was the right time, for either of them.

There was more than one ghost in this house, he knew.

"I expect he loved her a lot, and she loved him. She told me how she did."

"He can't come back. I thought maybe he would, even though she said he couldn't. I thought when the lady started coming, he could come, too. But he hasn't."

Could there be anything harder for a child to face, he wondered, than losing a parent? Here he was, a grown man, and he couldn't imagine the grief of losing one of his.

"Doesn't mean he isn't watching over you. I believe stuff like that. When people who love us have to go away, they still look out for us. Your dad's always going to look out for you."

"Then he'd see you kiss Mom, because he'd watch over her, too."

"I expect so." Logan nodded. "I like to think he doesn't mind, because he'd know I want her to be happy. Maybe when we get to know each other some better, you won't mind too much either."

"Do you make Mom's heart feel funny?"

"I sure hope so, because I'd hate to feel like this all by myself. I don't know if I'm saying this right. I never had to say it before, or think about it. But if we decide to be happy together, all of us, your dad's still your dad, Gavin. Always. I want you to understand I know that, and respect that. Man-to-man."

"Okay." He smiled slowly when Logan offered a hand. When he shook it, the smile became a grin. "Anyway, I like you better than the other guy."

"Good to know."

Luke was tucked in and sleeping when they came back in. Logan merely lifted his eyebrows at Stella's questioning look, then stepped back as she readied Gavin for bed.

Deliberately he took her hand as they stepped into the hall. "Ask him if you want to know," he said before she could speak. "It's his business."

"I just don't want him upset."

"He seem upset to you when you tucked him in?"

"No." She sighed. "No."

At the top of the stairs, the cold blew through them. Protectively, Logan's arm came around her waist, pulling her firmly to his side. It passed by, with a little lash, like a flicked whip.

Seconds later, they heard the soft singing.

"She's angry with us," Stella whispered when he turned, prepared to stride back. "But not with them. She won't hurt them. Let's leave her be. I've got a baby monitor downstairs, so I can hear them if they need me."

"How do you sleep up here?"

"Well, strangely enough. First it was because I didn't believe it. Now it's knowing that in some strange way, she loves them. The night they stayed at my parents', she came into my room and cried. It broke my heart."

"Ghost talk?" Roz asked. "That's just what I had in mind." She offered them wine she'd already poured. Then pursed her lips when Stella switched on the monitor. "Strange to hear that again. It's been years since I have."

"I gotta admit," Logan said with his eyes on the monitor, "creeps me out some. More than some, to tell the truth."

"You get used to it. More or less. Where's Hayley?" she asked Roz.

"She was feeling tired—and a little blue, a little cross, I think. She's settled in upstairs with a book and a big tall glass of decaffeinated Coke. I've already talked to her about this, so . . ." She gestured to seats. On the coffee table was a tray of green grapes, thin crackers, and a half round of Brie.

She sat herself, plucked a grape. "I've decided to do something a little more active about our permanent houseguest."

"An exorcism?" Logan asked, sending a sideways glance toward the monitor and the soft voice singing out of it.

"Not quite that active. We want to find out about her history and her connection to this house. Seems to me we're not making any real progress, mostly because we can't really figure out a direction."

"We haven't been able to spend a lot of time on it," Stella pointed out.

"Another reason for outside help. We're busy, and we're amateurs. So why not go to somebody who knows what to do and has the time to do it right?"

"Concert's over for the night." Logan gestured when the monitor went silent.

"Sometimes she comes back two or three times." Stella offered him a cracker. "Do you know somebody, Roz? Someone you want to take this on?"

"I don't know yet. But I've made some inquiries, using the idea that I want to do a formal sort of genealogy search on my ancestry. There's a man in Memphis whose name's come up. Mitchell Carnegie. Dr. Mitchell Carnegie," she added. "He taught at the university in Charlotte, moved here a couple of years ago. I believe he taught at the University of Memphis for a semester or two and may still give the occasional lecture. Primarily, he writes books. Biographies and so on. He's touted as an expert family historian."

"Sounds like he might be our man." Stella spread a little Brie on a cracker for herself. "Having someone who knows what he's doing should be better than us fumbling around."

"That would depend," Logan put in, "on how he feels about ghosts."

"I'm going to make an appointment to see him." Stella lifted her wineglass. "Then I guess we'll find out."

eighteen

THOUGH HE FELT LIKE HE WAS TAKING HIS LIFE IN his hands, Harper followed instructions and tracked Hayley down at the checkout counter. She was perched on a stool, a garden of container pots and flats around her, ringing out the last customers. Her shirt—smock? tunic? he didn't know what the hell you called maternity-type clothes—was a bright, bold red.

Funny, it was the color that brought her to mind for him. Vivid, sexy red. Those spiky bangs made her eyes seem enormous, and there were big silver hoops in her ears that peeked and swung through her hair when she moved.

With the high counter blocking the target area, you could hardly tell she was pregnant. Except her eyes looked tired, he thought. And her face was a little puffy—maybe weight gain, maybe lack of sleep. Either way, he didn't figure it was the sort of thing he should mention. The fact was, everything and anything that came out of his mouth these days, at least when he was around her, was the wrong thing.

He didn't expect their next encounter to go well either.

But he'd promised to throw himself on the sword for the cause.

He waited until she'd finished with the customers and, girding his loins, he approached the counter.

"Hey."

She looked at him, and he couldn't say her expression was particularly welcoming. "Hey. What're you doing out of your cave?"

"Finished up for the day. Actually my mother just called. She asked if I'd drive you on home when I finished."

"Well, *I'm* not finished," she said testily. "There are at least two more customers wandering around, and Saturday's my night to close out."

It wasn't the tone she'd used to chat up the customers, he noted. He was beginning to think it was the tone she reserved just for him. "Yeah, but she said she needed you at home for something as soon as you could, and to have Bill and Larry finish up and close out."

"What does she want? Why didn't she call me?"

"I don't know. I'm just the messenger." And he knew what often happened to the messenger. "I told Larry, and he's helping the last couple of stragglers. So he's on it."

She started to lever herself off the stool, and though his hands itched to help her, he imagined she'd chomp them off at the wrists. "I can walk."

"Come on. Jesus." He jammed his hands in his pockets and gave her scowl for scowl. "Why do you want to put me on the spot like that? If I let you walk, my mama's going to come down on me like five tons of bricks. And after she's done flattening me, she'll ream you. Let's just go."

"Fine." The truth was, she didn't know why she was feeling so mean and spiteful, and tired and achy. She was terrified something was wrong with her or with the baby, despite all the doctor's assurances to the contrary.

The baby would be born sick or deformed, because she'd . . .

She didn't know what, but it would be her fault.

She snatched her purse and did her best to sail by Harper and out the door.

"I've got another half hour on the clock," she complained and wrenched open the door of his car. "I don't know what she could want that couldn't wait a half hour."

"I don't know either."

"She hasn't seen that genealogy guy yet."

He got in, started the car. "Nope. She'll get to it when she gets to it."

"You don't seem all that interested, anyway. How come you don't come around when we have our meetings about the Harper Bride?"

"I guess I will, when I can think of something to say about it."

She smelled vivid, too, especially closed up in the car with him like this. Vivid and sexy, and it made him edgy. The best that could be said about the situation was the drive was short.

Amazed he wasn't sweating bullets, he swung in and zipped in front of the house.

"You drive a snooty little car like this that fast, you're just begging for a ticket."

"It's not a snooty little car. It's a well-built and reliable sports car. And I wasn't driving that fast. What the hell is it about me that makes you crawl up my ass?"

"I wasn't crawling up your ass; I was making an observation. At least you didn't go for red." She opened the door, managed to get her legs out. "Most guys go for the red, the flashy. The black's probably why you don't have speeding tickets spilling out of your glove compartment."

"I haven't had a speeding ticket in two years."

She snorted.

"Okay, eighteen months, but—"

"Would you stop arguing for five damn seconds and come over here and help me out of this damn car? I can't get up."

Like a runner off the starting line, he sprinted around

the car. He wasn't sure how to manage it, especially when she was sitting there, red in the face and flashing in the eyes. He started to take her hands and tug, but he thought he might . . . jar something.

So he leaned down, hooked his hands under her armpits, and lifted.

Her belly bumped him, and now sweat did slide down his back.

He felt what was in there move—a couple of hard bumps.

It was . . . extraordinary.

Then she was brushing him aside. "Thanks."

Mortifying, she thought. She just hadn't been able to shift her center of gravity, or dig down enough to get out of a stupid car. Of course, if he hadn't insisted she get in that boy toy in the first place, she wouldn't have been mortified.

She wanted to eat a pint of vanilla fudge ice cream and sit in a cool bath. For the rest of her natural life.

She shoved open the front door, stomped inside.

The shouts of *Surprise!* had her heart jumping into her throat, and she nearly lost control of her increasingly tricky bladder.

In the parlor pink and blue crepe paper curled in artful swags from the ceiling, and fat white balloons danced in the corners. Boxes wrapped in pretty paper and streaming with bows formed a colorful mountain on a high table. The room was full of women. Stella and Roz, all the girls who worked at the nursery, even some of the regular customers.

"Don't look stricken, girl." Roz strolled over to wrap an arm around Hayley's shoulders. "You don't think we'd let you have that baby without throwing you a shower, do you?"

"A baby shower." She could feel the smile blooming on her face, even as tears welled up in her eyes.

"You come on and sit down. You're allowed one glass of David's magical champagne punch before you go to the straight stuff."

"This is . . ." She saw the chair set in the center of the

room, festooned with voile and balloons, like a party throne. "I don't know what to say."

"Then I'm sitting beside you. I'm Jolene, darling, Stella's stepmama." She patted Hayley's hand, then her belly. "And I never run out of things to say."

"Here you go." Stella stepped over with a glass of punch.

"Thanks. Thank you so much. This is the nicest thing anyone's ever done for me. In my whole life."

"You have a good little cry." Jolene handed her a lace-edged hankie. "Then we're going to have us a hell of a time."

They did. Ooohing and awwing over impossibly tiny clothes, soft-as-cloud blankets, hand-knit booties, cooing over rattles and toys and stuffed animals. There were foolish games that only women at a baby shower could enjoy, and plenty of punch and cake to sweeten the evening.

The knot that had been at the center of Hayley's heart for days loosened.

"This was the best time I ever had." Hayley sat, giddy and exhausted, and stared at the piles of gifts Stella had neatly arranged on the table again. "I know it was all about me. I liked that part, but everyone had fun, don't you think?"

"Are you kidding?" From her seat on the floor, Stella continued to meticulously fold discarded wrapping paper into neat, flat squares. "This party rocked."

"Are you going to save all that paper?" Roz asked her.

"She'll want it one day, and I'm just saving what she didn't rip to shreds."

"I couldn't help it. I was so juiced up. I've got to get thank-you cards, and try to remember who gave what."

"I made a list while you were tearing in."

"Of course she did." Roz helped herself to one more glass of punch, then sat and stretched out her legs. "God. I'm whipped."

"Y'all worked so hard. It was all so awesome." Feeling

herself tearing up again, Hayley waved both hands. "Everyone was—I guess I forgot people could be so good, so generous. Man, look at all those wonderful things. Oh, that little yellow gown with the teddy bears on it! The matching hat. And the baby swing. Stella, I just can't thank you enough for the swing."

"I'd have been lost without mine."

"It was so sweet of you, both of you, to do this for me. I just had no idea. I couldn't've been more surprised, or more grateful."

"You can guess who planned it out," Roz said with a nod at Stella. "David started calling her General Rothchild."

"I have to thank him for all the wonderful food. I can't believe I ate two pieces of cake. I feel like I'm ready to explode."

"Don't explode yet, because we're not quite done. We need to go up, so you can have my gift."

"But the party was—"

"A joint effort," Roz finished. "But there's a gift I hope you'll like upstairs."

"I snapped at Harper," Hayley began as they helped her up and started upstairs.

"He's been snapped at before."

"But I wish I hadn't. He was helping you surprise me, and I gave him a terrible time. He said I was always crawling up his ass, and that's just what I was doing."

"You'll tell him you're sorry." Roz turned them toward the west wing, moved passed Stella's room, and Hayley's. "Here you are, honey."

She opened the door and led Hayley inside.

"Oh, God. Oh, my God." Hayley pressed both hands to her mouth as she stared at the room.

It was painted a soft, quiet yellow, with lace curtains at the windows.

She knew the crib was antique. Nothing was that beautiful, that rich unless it was old and treasured. The wood gleamed, deep with red highlights. She recognized the layette as one she'd dreamed over in a magazine and had known she could never afford.

"The furniture's a loan while you're here. I used it for my children, as my mama did for hers, and hers before her, back more than eighty-five years now. But the linens are yours, and the changing table. Stella added the rug and the lamp. And David and Harper, bless their hearts, painted the room, and hauled the furniture down from the attic."

As emotions swamped her, Hayley could only shake her head.

"Once we bring your gifts up here, you'll have yourself a lovely nursery." Stella rubbed Hayley's back.

"It's so beautiful. More than I ever dreamed of. I—I've been missing my father so much. The closer the baby gets, the more I've been missing him. It's this ache inside. And I've been feeling sad and scared, and mostly just sorry for myself."

She used her hands to rub the tears from her cheeks. "Now today, all this, it just makes me feel . . . It's not the things. I love them, I love everything. But it's that you'd do this, both of you would do this for us."

"You're not alone, Hayley." Roz laid a hand on Hayley's belly. "Neither one of you."

"I know that. I think, well, I think, we'd have been okay on our own. I'd've worked hard to make sure of it. But I never expected to have real family again. I never expected to have people care about me and the baby like this. I've been stupid."

"No," Stella told her. "Just pregnant."

With a half laugh, Hayley blinked back the rest of the tears. "I guess that accounts for a lot of it. I won't be able to use that excuse too much longer. And I'll never, I'll just never be able to thank you, or tell you, or repay you. Never."

"Oh, I think naming the baby after us will clear the decks," Roz said casually. "Especially if it's a boy. Rosalind Stella might be a little hard for him to handle in school, but it's only right."

"Hey, I was thinking Stella Rosalind."

Roz arched a brow at Stella. "This is one of those rare cases when it pays to be the oldest."

THAT NIGHT, HAYLEY TIPTOED INTO THE NURSERY. Just to touch, to smell, to sit in the rocking chair with her hands stroking her belly.

"I'm sorry I've been so nasty lately. I'm better now. We're going to be all right now. You've got two fairy godmothers, baby. The best women I've ever known. I may not be able to pay them back for all they've done for us, not in some ways. But I swear, there's nothing either of them could ask that I wouldn't do. I feel safe here. It was stupid of me to forget that. We're a team, you and me. I shouldn't've been afraid of you. Or for you."

She closed her eyes and rocked. "I want to hold you in my arms so much they hurt. I want to dress you in one of those cute little outfits and hold you, and smell you, and rock you in this chair. Oh, God, I hope I know what I'm doing."

The air turned cold, raising gooseflesh on her arms. But it wasn't fear that had her opening her eyes; it was pity. She stared at the woman who stood beside the crib.

Her hair was down tonight, golden blond and wildly tangled. She wore a white nightgown, muddy at the hem. And there was a look of—Hayley would have said madness—in her eyes.

"You didn't have anyone to help you, did you?" Her hands trembled a bit, but she kept stroking her belly, kept her eyes on the figure, kept talking.

"Maybe you didn't have anyone to be there with you when you were afraid like I've been. I guess I might've gone crazy, too, all on my own. And I don't know what I'd do if anything happened to my baby. Or how I'd stand it, if something happened to take me away from him—her. Even if I were dead I couldn't stand it. So I guess I understand, a little."

At her words, Hayley heard a keening sound, a sound that made her think of a soul, or a mind, shattering.

Then she was alone.

ON MONDAY, HAYLEY SAT PERCHED ON HER STOOL once more. When her back ached, she ignored it. When she had to call for a relief clerk so she could waddle to the bathroom, again, she made a joke out of it.

Her bladder felt squeezed down to the size of a pea.

On the way back, she detoured outside, not only to stretch her legs and back but to see Stella.

"Is it okay if I take my break now? I want to hunt down Harper and apologize." She'd spent all morning dreading the moment, but she couldn't put it off any longer. "He wasn't anywhere to be found on Sunday, but he's probably back in his cave now."

"Go ahead. Oh, I just ran into Roz. She called that professor. Dr. Carnegie? She has an appointment to see him later this week. Maybe we'll make some progress in that area."

Then she narrowed her eyes on Hayley's face. "I tell you what, one of us is going with you to your doctor's appointment tomorrow. I don't want you driving anymore."

"I still fit behind the wheel." Barely.

"That may be, but either Roz or I will take you. And I'm thinking it's time you go part-time."

"You might as well put me in the loony bin as take work away from me now. Come on, Stella, a lot of women work right up to the end. Besides, I'm sitting on my butt most all day. Best thing about finding Harper is walking."

"Walk," Stella agreed. "Don't lift. Anything."

"Nag, nag, nag." But she said it with a laugh as she started toward the grafting house.

Outside the greenhouse she paused. She'd practiced

what she wanted to say. She thought it best to think it all through. He'd accept her apology. His mama had raised him right, and from what she'd seen he had a good heart. But she wanted, very much, for him to understand she'd just been in some sort of mood.

She opened the door. She loved the smell in here. Experimentation, possibilities. One day, she hoped either Harper or Roz would teach her something about this end of the growing.

She could see him down at the end, huddled over his work. He had his headphones on and was tapping one foot to whatever beat played in his ears.

God, he was so cute. If she'd met him in the bookstore, before her life had changed, she'd have hit on him, or worked it around so he'd hit on her. All that dark, messed-up hair, the clean line of jaw, the dreamy eyes. And those artistic hands.

She'd bet he had half a dozen girls dangling on a string, and another half dozen waiting in line for a chance.

She started down toward him and was surprised enough to pull up short when his head snapped up, and he swung around to her.

"Christ on a crutch, Harper! I thought I was going to startle you."

"What? What?" His eyes were dazzled as he dragged off his headset. "What?"

"I didn't think you could hear me."

"I—" He hadn't. He'd smelled her. "Do you need something?"

"I guess I do. I need to say I'm sorry for jumping down your throat every time you opened your mouth the last couple of weeks. I've been an awful bitch."

"No. Well, yeah. It's okay."

She laughed and edged closer to try to see what he was doing. It just looked like he had a bunch of stems tied together. "I guess I had the jumps. What am I going to do, how am I going to do it? Why do I have to feel so fat and ugly all the time?"

"You're not fat. You could never be ugly."

"That's awful nice of you. But being pregnant doesn't affect my eyesight, and I know what I see in the mirror every damn day."

"Then you know you're beautiful."

Her eyes sparkled when she smiled. "I must've been a pitiful case if you're obliged to flirt with a pregnant woman who's got a bad disposition."

"I'm not—I wouldn't." He wanted to, at the very least. "Anyway, I guess you're feeling better."

"So much better. Mostly I was feeling sorry for myself, and I just hate that poor-me crap. Imagine your mama and Stella throwing me a baby shower. I cried all over myself. Got Stella going, too. But then we had the best time. Who knew a baby shower could rock?" She pressed both hands to her belly and laughed. "You ever met Stella's step-mama?"

"No."

"She's just a hoot and a half. I laughed till I thought I'd shoot the baby right out then and there. And Mrs. Haggerty—"

"Mrs. Haggerty? Our Mrs. Haggerty was there?"

"Not only, but she won the song title game. You have to write down the most song titles with 'baby' in it. You'll never guess one she wrote down."

"Okay. I give."

" 'Baby Got Back.' "

Now he grinned. "Get out. Mrs. Haggerty wrote down a rap song?"

"Then rapped it."

"Now you're lying."

"She *did.* Or at least a couple lines. I nearly peed my pants. But I'm forgetting why I'm here. There you were, just trying to help with the best surprise I ever had, and I was bitching and whining. Crawling up your ass, just like you said. I'm really sorry."

"It's no big. I have a friend whose wife had a baby a few

months ago. I swear you could see fangs growing out of her mouth toward the end. And I think her eyes turned red a couple times."

She laughed again, pressed a hand to her side. "I hope I don't get that bad before . . ."

She broke off, a puzzled expression covering her face as she felt a little snap inside. Heard it, she realized. Like a soft, echoing ping.

Then water pooled down between her legs.

Harper made a sound of his own, like that of a man whose words were strangled off somewhere in his throat. He sprang to his feet, babbling as Hayley stared down at the floor.

"Uh-oh," she said.

"Um, that's okay, that's all right. Maybe I should . . . maybe you should . . ."

"Oh, for heaven's sake, Harper, I didn't just pee on the floor. My water broke."

"What water?" He blinked, then went pale as a corpse. "*That* water. Oh, God. Oh, Jesus. Oh, shit. Sit. Sit, or . . . I'll get—"

An ambulance, the marines.

"My mother."

"I think I'd better go with you. We're a little early." She forced a smile so she wouldn't scream. "Just a couple of weeks. I guess the baby's impatient to get out and see what all the fuss is about. Give me a hand, okay? Oh, Jesus, Harper, I'm scared to death."

"It's fine." His arm came around her. "Just lean on me. You hurting anywhere?"

"No. Not yet."

Inside he was still pale, and half sick. But his arm stayed steady around her, and when he turned his head, his smile was easy. "Hey." Very gently, he touched her belly. "Happy birthday, baby."

"Oh, my God." Her face simply illuminated as they stepped outside. "This is *awesome*."

* * *

SHE COULDN'T ACTUALLY HAVE THE BABY, BUT STELLA figured she could do nearly everything else—or delegate it done. Hayley hadn't put a hospital bag together, but Stella had a list. A call to David got that ball rolling even as she drove Hayley to the hospital. She called the doctor to let him know the status of Hayley's labor, left a voice mail on her father's cell phone, and a message on his home answering machine to arrange for her own children, and coached Hayley through her breathing as the first contractions began.

"If I ever get married, or buy a house, or start a war, I hope you'll be in charge of the details."

Stella glanced over as Hayley rubbed her belly. "I'm your girl. Doing okay?"

"Yeah. I'm nervous and excited and . . . Oh, wow, I'm having a baby!"

"You're going to have a fabulous baby."

"The books say things can get pretty tricky during transition, so if I yell at you or call you names—"

"Been there. I won't take it personally."

By the time Roz arrived, Hayley was ensconced in a birthing room. The television was on—an old *Friends* episode. Beneath it on the counter was an arrangement of white roses. Stella's doing, she had no doubt.

"How's Mama doing?"

"They said I'm moving fast." Flushed and bright-eyed, Hayley reached out a hand for Roz's. "And everything's just fine. The contractions are coming closer together, but they don't hurt all that much."

"She doesn't want the epidural," Stella told her.

"Ah." Roz gave Hayley's hand a pat. "That'll be up to you. You can change your mind if it gets to be too much."

"Maybe it's silly, and maybe I'll be sorry, but I want to feel it. Wow! I feel that."

Stella moved in, helped her breathe through it. Hayley

sighed out the last breath, closed her eyes just as David strode in.

"This here the party room?" He set down an overnight case, a tote bag, and a vase of yellow daisies before he leaned over the bed to kiss Hayley's cheek. "You're not going to kick me out 'cause I'm a man, are you?"

"You want to stay?" Delighted color bloomed on Hayley's cheeks. "Really?"

"Are you kidding?" From his pocket he pulled a little digital camera. "I nominate myself official photographer."

"Oh." Biting her lip, Hayley rubbed a hand over her belly. "I don't know as pictures are such a good idea."

"Don't you worry, sugar, I won't take anything that's not G-rated. Give me a big smile."

He took a couple of shots, directed Roz and Stella to stand beside the bed and took a couple more. "By the way, Stella, Logan's taking the boys back to his place after school."

"What?"

"Your parents are at some golf tournament. They were going to come back, but I told them not to worry, I'd take care of the kids. Then apparently Logan came by the nursery, ran into Harper—he's coming by shortly."

"Logan?" Hayley asked. "He's coming here?"

"No, Harper. Logan's taking kid duty. He said he'd take them over to his place, put them to work, and not to worry. We're supposed to keep him updated on baby progress."

"I don't know if—" But Stella broke off as another contraction started.

Her job as labor coach kept her busy, but part of her mind niggled on the idea of Logan riding herd on her boys. What did he mean, 'put them to work'? How would he know what to do if they got into a fight—which, of course, they would at some point. How could he watch them properly if he took them to a job site? They could fall into a ditch, or out of a tree, or cut off an appendage, for God's sake, with some sharp tool.

When the doctor came in to check Hayley's progress, she dashed out to call Logan's cell phone.

"Kitridge."

"It's Stella. My boys—"

"Yeah, they're fine. Got them right here. Hey, Gavin, don't chase your brother with that chain saw." At Stella's horrified squeak, Logan's laughter rolled over the phone. "Just kidding. I've got them digging a hole, and they're happy as pigs in mud and twice as dirty. We got a baby yet?"

"No, they're checking her now. Last check she was at eight centimeters dilated and seventy percent effaced."

"I have no idea what that means, but I'll assume it's a good thing."

"It's very good. She's breezing through it. You'd think she had a baby once a week. Are you sure the kids are all right?"

"Listen."

She assumed he'd held out the phone as she heard giggles and her boys' voices raised in excited argument over just what they could bury in the hole. An elephant. A brontosaurus. Fat Mr. Kelso from the grocery store.

"They shouldn't call Mr. Kelso fat."

"We have no time for women here. Call me when we've got a baby."

He hung up, leaving her scowling at the phone. Then she turned and nearly rammed into Harper. Or into the forest of red lilies he balanced in both hands.

"Harper? Are you in there?"

"She okay? What's going on? Am I too late?"

"She's fine. The doctor's just checking on her. And you're in plenty of time."

"Okay. I thought lilies because they're exotic, and she likes red. I think she likes red."

"They're extremely gorgeous. Let me guide you in."

"Maybe I shouldn't. Maybe you should just take them."

"Don't be silly. We've got a regular party going on. She's a sociable girl, and having people with her is taking her mind off the pain. When I left, David had the Red Hot Chili Peppers on a CD player and a bottle of champagne icing down in the bathroom sink.

She steered him in. It was still the Red Hot Chili Peppers, and David turned his camera to the door to snap a picture of Harper peering nervously through a wonder of red lilies.

"Oh! Oh! Those are the most beautiful things I've ever seen!" A little pale, but beaming, Hayley struggled to sit up in bed.

"They'll make a great focal point, too." Stella helped Harper set them on a table. "You can focus on them during contractions."

"The doctor says I'm nearly there. I can start pushing soon."

He stepped up to the bedside. "You okay?"

"A little tired. It's a lot of work, but not as bad as I thought." Abruptly, her hand clamped down on his. "Oh-oh. Stella."

Roz stood at the foot of the bed. She looked at her son's hand holding Hayley's, looked at his face. She felt something inside her tighten, release painfully. Then she sighed and began to rub Hayley's feet as Stella murmured instructions and encouragement.

The pain increased. Stella watched the arc of contractions on the monitor and felt her own belly tighten in sympathy. The girl was made of iron, she thought. She was pale now, and her skin sheathed in sweat. There were times when Hayley gripped Stella's hand so hard she was surprised her fingers didn't snap. But Hayley stayed focused and rode the contractions out.

An hour passed into another, with the contractions coming fast, coming hard, with Hayley chugging through the breathing like a train. Stella offered ice chips and cool cloths while Roz gave the laboring mother a shoulder massage.

"Harper!" General Rothchild snapped out orders. "Rub her belly."

He goggled at her as if she'd asked him to personally deliver the baby. "Do what?"

"Gently, in circles. It helps. David, the music—"

"No, I like the music." Hayley reached for Stella's hand as she felt the next coming on. "Turn it up, David, in case I start screaming. Oh, oh, fuck! I want to push. I want to push it the hell out, *now*!"

"Not yet. Not yet. Focus, Hayley, you're doing great. Roz, maybe we need the doctor."

"Already on it," she said on her way out the door.

When it was time to push, and the doctor sat between Hayley's legs, Stella noted that both men went a little green. She gave Hayley one end of a towel, and took the other, to help her bear down while she counted to ten.

"Harper! You get behind her, support her back."

"I . . ." He was already edging for the door, but his mother blocked him.

"You don't want to be somewhere else when a miracle happens." She gave him a nudge forward.

"You're doing great," Stella told her. "You're amazing." She nodded when the doctor called for Hayley to push again. "Ready now. Deep breath. Hold it, and push!"

"God almighty." Even with the babble of voices, David's swallow was audible. "I've never seen the like. I've gotta call my mama. Hell, I gotta send her a truckload of flowers."

"Jesus!" Harper sucked in a breath along with Hayley. "There's a head."

Hayley began to laugh, with tears streaming down her face. "Look at all that hair! Oh, God, oh, Lord, can't we get him the rest of the way out?"

"Shoulders next, honey, then that's it. Another good push, okay? Listen! He's already crying. Hayley, that's your baby crying." And Stella was crying herself as with a last desperate push, life rushed into the room.

"It's a girl," Roz said softly as she wiped the dampness from her own cheeks. "You've got a daughter, Hayley. And she's beautiful."

"A girl. A little girl." Hayley's arms were already reaching. When they laid her on her belly so Roz could cut the cord, she kept laughing even as she stroked the baby from head to foot. "Oh, just *look* at you. Look at you. No, don't take her."

"They're just going to clean her up. Two seconds." Stella bent down to kiss the top of Hayley's head. "Congratulations, Mom."

"Listen to her." Hayley reached back, gripped Stella's hand, then Harper's. "She even sounds beautiful."

"Six pounds, eight ounces," the nurse announced and carried the wrapped bundle to the bed. "Eighteen inches. And a full ten on the Apgar."

"Hear that?" Hayley cradled the baby in her arms, kissed her forehead, her cheeks, her tiny mouth. "You aced your first test. She's looking at me! Hi. Hi, I'm your mama. I'm so glad to see you."

"Smile!" David snapped another picture. "What name did you decide on?"

"I picked a new one when I was pushing. She's Lily, because I could see the lilies, and I could smell them when she was being born. So she's Lily Rose Star. Rose for Rosalind, Star for Stella."

NINETEEN

EXHAUSTED AND EXHILARATED, STELLA STEPPED INTO the house. Though it was past their bedtime, she expected her boys to come running, but had to make do with an ecstatic Parker. She picked him up, kissed his nose as he tried to bathe her face.

"Guess what, my furry little pal? We had a baby today. Our first girl."

She shoved at her hair, and immediately got the guilts. Roz had left the hospital before she had, and was probably upstairs dealing with the kids.

She started toward the steps when Logan strolled into the foyer. "Big day."

"The biggest," she agreed. She hadn't considered he'd be there, and was suddenly and acutely aware that her duties as labor coach had sweated off all of her makeup. In addition, she couldn't imagine she was smelling her freshest.

"I can't thank you enough for taking on the boys."

"No problem. I got a couple of good holes out of them. You may need to burn their clothes."

"They've got more. Is Roz up with them?"

"No. She's in the kitchen. David's back there whipping something together, and I heard a rumor about champagne."

"More champagne? We practically swam in it at the hospital. I'd better go up and settle down the troops."

"They're out for the count. Have been since just before nine. Digging holes wears a man out."

"Oh. I know you said you'd bring them back when I called to tell you about the baby, but I didn't expect you to put them to bed."

"They were tuckered. We had ourselves a manly shower, then they crawled into bed and were out in under five seconds."

"Well. I owe you big."

"Pay up."

He crossed to her, slid his arms around her and kissed her until her already spinning head lifted off her shoulders.

"Tired?" he asked.

"Yeah. But in the best possible way."

He danced his fingers over her hair, and kept his other arm around her. "How's the new kid on the block and her mama?"

"They're great. Hayley's a wonder. Steady as a rock through seven hours of labor. And the baby might be a couple weeks early, but she came through like a champ. Only a few ounces shy of Gavin's birth weight, though it took me twice as long to convince him to come out."

"Make you want to have another?"

She went a few shades more pale. "Oh. Well."

"Now I've scared you." Amused, he slung an arm around her shoulder. "Let's go see what's on the menu with that champagne."

HE HADN'T SCARED HER, EXACTLY. BUT HE HAD MADE her vaguely uneasy. She was just getting used to having a relationship, and the man was making subtle hints about babies.

Of course, it could have been just a natural, offhand remark under the circumstances. Or a kind of joke.

Whatever the intent, it got her thinking. Did she want more children? She'd crossed that possibility off her list when Kevin died and had ruthlessly shut down her biological clock. Certainly she was capable, physically, of having another child. But it took more than physical capability, or should, to bring a child into the world.

She had two healthy, active children. And was solely and wholly responsible for them—emotionally, financially, morally. To consider having another meant considering a permanent relationship with a man. Marriage, a future, sharing not only what she had but building more, and in a different direction.

She'd come to Tennessee to visit her own roots, and to plant her family in the soil of her own origins. To be near her father, and to allow her children the pleasure of being close to grandparents who wanted to know them.

Her mother had never been particularly interested, hadn't enjoyed seeing herself as a grandmother. It spoiled the youthful image, Stella thought.

If a man like Logan had blipped onto her mother's radar, he'd have been snapped right up.

And if that's why Stella was hesitating, it was a sad state of affairs. Undoubtedly part of it, though, she decided. Otherwise she wouldn't be thinking it.

She hadn't disliked any of her stepfathers. But she hadn't bonded with them either, or they with her. How old had she been the first time her mother had remarried? Gavin's age, she remembered. Yes, right around eight.

She'd been plucked out of her school and plunked down in a new one, a new house, new neighborhood, and dazed by it all while her mother had been in the adrenaline rush of having a new husband.

That one had lasted, what? Three years, four? Somewhere between, she decided, with another year or so of upheaval while her mother dealt with the battle and debris of divorce, another new place, a new job, a new start.

And another new school for Stella.

After that, her mother had stuck with *boyfriends* for a long stretch. But that itself had been another kind of upheaval, having to survive her mother's mad dashes into love, her eventual bitter exit from it.

And they were always bitter, Stella remembered.

At least she'd been in college, living on her own, when her mother had married yet again. And maybe that was part of the reason that marriage had lasted nearly a decade. There hadn't been a child to crowd things. Yet eventually there'd been another acrimonious divorce, with the split nearly coinciding with her own widowhood.

It had been a horrible year, in every possible way, which her mother had ended with yet one more brief, tumultuous marriage.

Strange that even as an adult, Stella found she couldn't quite forgive being so consistently put into second or even third place behind her mother's needs.

She wasn't doing that with her own children, she assured herself. She wasn't being selfish and careless in her relationship with Logan, or shuffling her kids to the back of her heart because she was falling in love with him.

Still, the fact was it was all moving awfully fast. It would make more sense to slow things down a bit until she had a better picture.

Besides, she was going to be too busy to think about marriage. And she shouldn't forget he hadn't asked her to marry him and have his children, for God's sake. She was blowing an offhand comment way out of proportion.

Time to get back on track. She rose from her desk and started for the door. It opened before she reached it.

"I was just going to find you," she said to Roz. "I'm on my way to pick up the new family and take them home."

"I wish I could go with you. I nearly postponed this

meeting so I could." She glanced at her watch as if considering it again.

"By the time you get back from your meeting with Dr. Carnegie, they'll be all settled in and ready for some quality time with Aunt Roz."

"I have to admit I want my hands on that baby. So, now, what've you been fretting about?"

"Fretting?" Stella opened a desk drawer to retrieve her purse. "Why do you think I've been fretting about anything?"

"Your watch is turned around, which means you've been twisting at it. Which means you've been fretting. Something going on around here I don't know about?"

"No." Annoyed with herself, Stella turned her watch around. "No, it's nothing to do with work. I was thinking about Logan, and I was thinking about my mother."

"What does Logan have to do with your mother?" As she asked, Roz picked up Stella's thermos. After opening it and taking a sniff, she poured a few swallows of iced coffee in the lid.

"Nothing. I don't know. Do you want a mug for that?"

"No, this is fine. Just want a taste."

"I think—I sense—I'm wondering . . . and I already sound like an ass." Stella took a lipstick from the cosmetic bag in her purse, and walking to the mirror she'd hung on the wall, she began to freshen her makeup. "Roz, things are getting serious between me and Logan."

"As I've got eyes, I've seen that for myself. Do you want me to say *and*, or do you want me to mind my own business?"

"And. I don't know if I'm ready for serious. I don't know that he is, either. It's surprising enough it turned out we like each other, much less . . ." She turned back. "I've never felt like this about anyone. Not this churned up and edgy, and, well, fretful."

She replaced the lipstick and zipped the bag shut. "With Kevin, everything was so clear. We were young and in love, and there wasn't a single barrier to get over, not really. It wasn't that we never fought or had problems, but it was all relatively simple for us."

"And the longer you live, the more complicated life gets."

"Yes. I'm afraid of being in love again, and of crossing that line from this is mine to this is ours. That sounds incredibly selfish when I say it out loud."

"Maybe, but I'd say it's pretty normal."

"Maybe. Roz, my mother was—is—a mess. I know, in my head, that a lot of the decisions I've made have been because I knew they were the exact opposite of what she'd have done. That's pathetic."

"I don't know that it is, not if those decisions were right for you."

"They were. They have been. But I don't want to step away from something that might be wonderful just because I know my mother would leap forward without a second thought."

"Honey, I can look at you and remember what it was like, and the both of us can look at Hayley and wonder how she has the courage and fortitude to raise that baby on her own."

Stella let out a little laugh. "God, isn't that the truth?"

"And since it's turned out the three of us have connected as friends, we can give each other all kinds of support and advice and shoulders to cry on. But the fact is, each one of us has to get through what we get through. Me, I expect you'll figure this out soon enough. Figuring out how to make things come out right's what you do."

She set the thermos lid on the desk, gave Stella two light pats on the cheek. "Well, I'm going to scoot home and clean up a bit."

"Thanks, Roz. Really. If Hayley's doing all right once I get them home, I'll leave David in charge. I know we're shorthanded around here today."

"No, you stay home with her and Lily. Harper can handle things here. It's not every day you bring a new baby home."

* * *

AND THAT WAS SOMETHING ROZ CONSIDERED AS SHE hunted for parking near Mitchell Carnegie's downtown apartment. It had been a good many years since there had been an infant in Harper House. Just how would the Harper Bride deal with that?

How would they all deal with it?

How would she herself handle the idea of her firstborn falling for that sweet single mother and her tiny girl? She doubted that Harper knew he was sliding in that direction, and surely Hayley was clueless. But a mother knew such things; a mother could read them on her son's face.

Something else to think about some other time, she decided, and cursed ripely at the lack of parking.

She had to hoof it nearly three blocks and cursed again because she'd felt obliged to wear heels. Now her feet were going to hurt, *and* she'd have to waste more time changing into comfortable clothes once this meeting was done.

She was going to be late, which she deplored, and she was going to arrive hot and sweaty.

She would have loved to have passed the meeting on to Stella. But it wasn't the sort of thing she could ask a manager to do. It dealt with her home, her family. She'd taken this particular aspect of it for granted for far too long.

She paused at the corner to wait for the light.

"Roz!"

The voice on the single syllable had her hackles rising. Her face was cold as hell frozen over as she turned and stared at—stared through—the slim, handsome man striding quickly toward her in glossy Ferragamos.

"I thought that was you. Nobody else could look so lovely and cool on a hot afternoon."

He reached out, this man she'd once been foolish enough to marry, and gripped her hand in both of his. "Don't you look gorgeous!"

"You're going to want to let go of my hand, Bryce, or you're going to find yourself facedown and eating sidewalk. The only one who'll be embarrassed by that eventuality is yourself."

His face, with its smooth tan and clear features, hardened. "I'd hoped, after all this time, we could be friends."

"We're not friends, and never will be." Quite deliberately, she took a tissue out of her purse and wiped the hand he'd touched. "I don't count lying, cheating sons of bitches among my friends."

"A man just can't make a mistake or find forgiveness with a woman like you."

"That's exactly right. I believe that's the first time you've been exactly right in your whole miserable life."

She started across the street, more resigned than surprised when he fell into step beside her. He wore a pale gray suit, Italian in cut. Canali, if she wasn't mistaken. At least that had been his designer of the moment when she'd been footing the bills.

"I don't see why you're still upset, Roz, honey. Unless there are still feelings inside you for me."

"Oh, there are, Bryce, there are. Disgust being paramount. Go away before I call a cop and have you arrested for being a personal annoyance."

"I'd just like another chance to—"

She stopped then. "That will never happen in this lifetime, or a thousand others. Be grateful you're able to walk the streets in your expensive shoes, Bryce, and that you're wearing a tailored suit instead of a prison jumpsuit."

"There's no cause to talk to me that way. You got what you wanted, Roz. You cut me off without a dime."

"Would that include the fifteen thousand, six hundred and fifty-eight dollars and twenty-two cents you transferred out of my account the week before I kicked your sorry ass out of my house? Oh, I knew about that one, too," she said when his face went carefully blank. "But I let that one go, because I decided I deserved to pay something for my own stupidity. Now you go on, and you stay out of my way, you stay out of my sight, and you stay out of my hearing, or I promise you, you'll regret it."

She clipped down the sidewalk, and even the "Frigid bitch" he hurled at her back didn't break her stride.

But she was shaking. By the time she'd reached the right address her knees and hands were trembling. She hated that she'd allowed him to upset her. Hated that the sight of him brought any reaction at all, even if it was rage.

Because there was shame along with it.

She'd taken him into her heart and her home. She'd let herself be charmed and seduced—and lied to and deceived. He'd stolen more than her money, she knew. He'd stolen her pride. And it was a shock to the system to realize, after all this time, that she didn't quite have it back. Not all of it.

She blessed the cool inside the building and rode the elevator to the third floor.

She was too frazzled and annoyed to fuss with her hair or check her makeup before she knocked. Instead she stood impatiently tapping her foot until the door opened.

He was as good-looking as the picture on the back of his books—several of which she'd read or skimmed through before arranging this meeting. He was, perhaps, a bit more rumpled in rolled-up shirtsleeves and jeans. But what she saw was a very long, very lanky individual with a pair of horn-rims sliding down a straight and narrow nose. Behind the lenses, bottle-green eyes seemed distracted. His hair was plentiful, in a tangle of peat-moss brown around a strong, sharp-boned face that showed a black bruise along the jaw.

The fact that he wasn't wearing any shoes made her feel hot and overdressed.

"Dr. Carnegie?"

"That's right. Ms. . . . Harper. I'm sorry. I lost track of time. Come in, please. And don't look at anything." There was a quick, disarming smile. "Part of losing track means I didn't remember to pick up out here. So we'll go straight back to my office, where I can excuse any disorder in the name of the creative process. Can I get you anything?"

His voice was coastal southern, she noted. That easy

drawl that turned vowels into warm liquid. "I'll take something cold, whatever you've got."

Of course, she looked as he scooted her through the living room. There were newspapers and books littering an enormous brown sofa, another pile of them along with a stubby white candle on a coffee table that looked as if it might have been Georgian. There was a basketball and a pair of high-tops so disreputable she doubted even her sons would lay claim to them in the middle of a gorgeous Turkish rug, and the biggest television screen she'd ever seen eating up an entire wall.

Though he was moving her quickly along, she caught sight of the kitchen. From the number of dishes on the counter, she assumed he'd recently had a party.

"I'm in the middle of a book," he explained. "And when I come up for air, domestic chores aren't a priority. My last cleaning team quit. Just like their predecessors."

"I can't imagine why," she said with schooled civility as she stared at his office space.

There wasn't a clean surface to be seen, and the air reeked of cigar smoke. A dieffenbachia sat in a chipped pot on the windowsill, withering. Rising above the chaos of his desk was a flat-screen monitor and an ergonomic keyboard.

He cleaned off the chair, dumping everything unceremoniously on the floor. "Hang on one minute."

As he dashed out, she lifted her brows at the half-eaten sandwich and glass of—maybe it was tea—among the debris on his desk. She was somewhat disappointed when with a crane of her neck she peered around to his monitor. His screen saver was up. But that, she supposed, was interesting enough, as it showed several cartoon figures playing basketball.

"I hope tea's all right," he said as he came back.

"That's fine, thank you." She took the glass and hoped it had been washed sometime in the last decade. "Dr. Carnegie, you're killing that plant."

"What plant?"

"The dieffenbachia in the window."

"Oh? Oh. I didn't know I had a plant." He gave it a baffled look. "Wonder where that came from? It doesn't look very healthy, does it?"

He picked it up, and she saw, with horror, that he intended to dump it in the overflowing wastebasket beside his desk.

"For God's sake, don't just throw it out. Would you bury your cat alive?"

"I don't have a cat."

"Just give it to me." She rose, grabbed the pot out of his hand. "It's dying of thirst and heat, and it's rootbound. This soil's hard as a brick."

She set it beside her chair and sat again. "I'll take care of it," she said, and her legs were an angry slash as she crossed them. "Dr. Carnegie—"

"Mitch. If you're going to take my plant, you ought to call me Mitch."

"As I explained when I contacted you, I'm interested in contracting for a thorough genealogy of my family, with an interest in gathering information on a specific person."

"Yes." All business, he decided, and sat at his desk. "And I told you I only do personal genealogies if something about the family history interests me. I'm—obviously—caught up in a book right now and wouldn't have much time to devote to a genealogical search and report."

"You didn't name your fee."

"Fifty dollars an hour, plus expenses."

She felt a quick clutch in the belly. "That's lawyer steep."

"An average genealogy doesn't take that long, if you know what you're doing and where to look. In most cases, it can be done in about forty hours, depending on how far back you want to go. If it's more complicated, we could arrange a flat fee—reevaluating after that time is used. But as I said—"

"I don't believe you'll have to go back more than a century."

"Chump change in this field. And if you're only dealing with a hundred years, you could probably do this yourself. I'd be happy to direct you down the avenues. No charge."

"I need an expert, which I'm assured you are. And I'm willing to negotiate terms. Since you took the time out of your busy schedule to speak to me, I'd think you'd hear me out before you nudge me out the door."

All business, he thought again, and prickly with it. "That wasn't my intention—the nudging. Of course I'll hear you out. If you're not in any great rush for the search and report, I may be able to help you out in a few weeks."

When she inclined her head, he began to rummage on, through, under the desk. "Just let me . . . how the hell did that get there?"

He unearthed a yellow legal pad, then mined out a pen. "That's Rosalind, right? *As You Like It*?"

A smile whisked over her mouth. "As in Russell. My daddy was a fan."

He wrote her name on the top of the pad. "You said a hundred years back. I'd think a family like yours would have records, journals, documents—and considerable oral family history to cover a century."

"You would, wouldn't you? Actually, I have quite a bit, but certain things have led me to believe some of the oral history is either incorrect or is missing details. I will, however, be glad to have you go through what I do have. We've already been through a lot of it."

"We?"

"Myself, and other members of my household."

"So, you're looking for information on a specific ancestor."

"I don't know as she was an ancestor, but I am certain she was a member of the household. I'm certain she died there."

"You have her death record?"

"No."

He shoved at his glasses as he scribbled. "Her grave?"

"No. Her ghost."

She smiled serenely when he blinked up at her. "Doesn't a man who digs into family histories believe in ghosts?"

"I've never come across one."

"If you take on this job, you will. What might your fee be, Dr. Carnegie, to dig up the history and identity of a family ghost?"

He leaned back in his chair, tapping the pen on his chin. "You're not kidding around."

"I certainly wouldn't kid around to the tune of fifty dollars an hour, plus expenses. I bet you could write a very interesting book on the Harper family ghost, if I were to sign a release and cooperate."

"I just bet I could," he replied.

"And it seems to me that you might consider finding out what I'm after as a kind of research. Maybe I should charge you."

His grin flashed again. "I have to finish this book before I actively take on another project. Despite evidence to the contrary, I finish what I start."

"Then you ought to start washing your dishes."

"Told you not to look. First, let me say that in my opinion the odds of you having an actual ghost in residence are about, oh, one in twenty million."

"I'd be happy to put a dollar down at those odds, if you're willing to risk the twenty million."

"Second, if I take this on, I'd require access to all family papers—personal family papers, and your written consent for me to dig into public records regarding your family."

"Of course."

"I'd be willing to waive my fee for, let's say, the first twenty hours. Until we see what we've got."

"Forty hours."

"Thirty."

"Done."

"And I'd want to see your house."

"Perhaps you'd like to come to dinner. Is there any day next week that would suit you?"

"I don't know. Hold on." He swiveled to his computer, danced his fingers over keys. "Tuesday?"

"Seven o'clock, then. We're not formal, but you will need shoes." She picked up the plant, then rose. "Thank you for your time," she said, extended a hand.

"Are you really going to take that thing?"

"I certainly am. And I have no intention of giving it back and letting you take it to death's door again. Do you need directions to Harper House?"

"I'll find it. Seems to me I drove by it once." He walked her to the door. "You know, sensible women don't usually believe in ghosts. Practical women don't generally agree to pay someone to trace the history of said ghost. And you strike me as a sensible, practical woman."

"Sensible men don't usually live in pigsties and conduct business meetings barefoot. We'll both have to take our chances. You ought to put some ice on that bruise. It looks painful."

"It is. Vicious little . . ." He broke off. "Got clipped going up for a rebound. Basketball."

"So I see. I'll expect you Tuesday, then, at seven."

"I'll be there. Good-bye, Ms. Harper."

"Dr. Carnegie."

He kept the door open long enough to satisfy his curiosity. He was right, he noted. The rear view was just as elegant and sexy as the front side, and both went with that steel-spined southern belle voice.

A class act, top to toe, he decided as he shut the door.

Ghosts. He shook his head and chuckled as he wound his way through the mess back to his office. Wasn't that a kick in the ass.

twenty

LOGAN STUDIED THE TINY FORM BLINKING IN A patch of dappled sunlight. He'd seen babies before, even had his share of personal contact with them. To him, newborns bore a strange resemblance to fish. Something about the eyes, he thought. And this one had all that black hair going for her, so she looked like a human sea creature. Sort of exotic and otherworldly.

If Gavin had been around, and Hayley out of hearing distance, he'd have suggested that this particular baby looked something like the offspring of Aquaman and Wonder Woman.

The kid would've gotten it.

Babies always intimidated him. Something about the way they looked right back at you, as if they knew a hell of a lot more than you did and were going to tolerate you until they got big enough to handle things on their own.

But he figured he had to come up with something better than an encounter between superheros, as the mother was standing beside him, anticipating.

"She looks as if she might've dropped down from Venus, where the grass is sapphire blue and the sky a bowl of gold dust." True enough, Logan decided, and a bit more poetic than the Aquaman theory.

"Aw, listen to you. Go ahead." Hayley gave him a little elbow nudge. "You can pick her up."

"Maybe I'll wait on that until she's more substantial."

With a chuckle, Hayley slipped Lily out of her carrier. "Big guy like you shouldn't be afraid of a tiny baby. Here. Now, make sure you support her head."

"Got long legs for such a little thing." And they kicked a bit in transfer. "She's picture pretty. Got a lot of you in her."

"I can hardly believe she's mine." Hayley fussed with Lily's cotton hat, then made herself stop touching. "Can I open the present now?"

"Sure. She all right in the sun like this?"

"We're baking the baby," Hayley told him as she tugged at the shiny pink ribbon on the box Logan had set on the patio table.

"Sorry?"

"She's got a touch of jaundice. The sun's good for her. Stella said Luke had it too, and they took him out in the sunshine for a little while a few times a day." She went to work on the wrapping paper. "Seems like she and Roz know everything there is to know about babies. I can ask the silliest question and one of them knows the answer. We're blessed, Lily and I."

Three women, one baby. Logan imagined Lily barely got out a burp before one of them was rushing to pick her up.

"Logan, do you think things happen because they're meant to, or because you make them happen?"

"I guess I think you make them happen because they're meant to."

"I've been thinking. There's a lot of thinking time when you're up two or three times in the middle of the night. I just wanted—needed—to get gone when I left Little Rock, and I headed here because I hoped Roz might give me a job. I could just as well have headed to Alabama. I've got closer kin there—blood kin—than Roz. But I came here, and I think I was meant to. I think Lily was supposed to be born here, and have Roz and Stella in her life."

"We'd all be missing out on something if you'd pointed your car in another direction."

"This feels like family. I've missed that since my daddy died. I want Lily to have family. I think—I know—we'd have been all right on our own. But I don't want things to just be all right for her. All right doesn't cut it anymore."

"Kids change everything."

Her smile bloomed. "They do. I'm not the same person I was a year ago, or even a week ago. I'm a mother." She pulled off the rest of the wrapping and let out a sound Logan thought of as distinctly female.

"Oh, what a sweet baby-doll! And it's so soft." She took it out of the box to cradle it much as Logan was cradling Lily.

"Bigger than she is."

"Not for long. Oh, she's so pink and pretty, and look at her little hat!"

"You pull the hat, and it makes music."

"Really?" Delighted, Hayley pulled the peaked pink hat, and "The Cradle Song" tinkled out. "It's perfect." She popped up to give Logan a kiss. "Lily's going to love her. Thank you, Logan."

"I figured a girl can't have too many dolls."

He glanced over as the patio door slammed open. Parker scrambled out a foot ahead of two shouting, racing boys.

They'd been this small once, he realized with a jolt. Small enough to curl in the crook of an arm, as helpless as, well, a fish out of water.

They ran to Logan as Parker sped in circles of delirious freedom.

"We saw your truck," Gavin announced. "Are we going to go work with you?"

"I knocked off for the day." Both faces fell, comically, and the buzz of pleasure it gave him had him adjusting his weekend plans. "But I've got to build me an arbor tomorrow, out in my yard. I could use a couple of Saturday slaves."

"We can be slaves." Luke tugged on Logan's pant leg. "I know what an arbor is, too. It's a thing stuff grows on."

"There you go, then, I've got a couple of expert slaves. We'll see what your mama says."

"She won't mind. She has to work 'cause Hayley's on turnkey."

"Maternity," Hayley explained.

"Got that."

"Can I see her?" Luke gave another tug.

"Sure." Logan crouched down with the baby in his arms. "She sure is tiny, isn't she?"

"She doesn't do anything yet." Gavin frowned thoughtfully as he tapped a gentle finger on Lily's cheek. "She cries and sleeps."

Luke leaned close to Logan's ear. "Hayley feeds her," he said in a conspirator's whisper, "with milk out of her *booby*."

With an admirably straight face, Logan nodded. "I think I heard about that somewhere. It's a little hard to believe."

"It's *true*. That's why they have them. Girls. Guys don't get boobies because they can't make milk, no matter how much they drink."

"Huh. That explains that."

"Fat Mr. Kelso's got boobies," Gavin said and sent his brother into a spasm of hilarity.

Stella stepped to the door and saw Logan holding the baby with her boys flanking him. All three of them had grins from ear-to-ear. The sun was shimmering down through the scarlet leaves of a red maple, falling in a shifting pattern of light and shadow on the stone. Lilies had burst into bloom in a carnival of color and exotic shapes. She could smell them, and the early roses, freshly cut grass, and verbena.

She heard birdsong and the giggling whispers of her boys, the delicate music of the wind chime hung from one of the maple's branches.

Her first clear thought as she froze there, as if she'd walked into an invisible frame of a picture was, Uh-oh.

Maybe she'd said it out loud, as Logan's head turned toward her. When their eyes met, his foolish grin transformed into a smile, easy and warm.

He looked too big crouched there, she thought. Too big, too rough with that tiny child in his arms, too *male* centered between her precious boys.

And so . . . dazzling somehow. Tanned and fit and strong.

He belonged in a forest, beating a path over rocky ground. Not here, in this elegant scene with flowers scenting the air and a baby dozing in the crook of his arm.

He straightened and walked toward her. "Your turn."

"Oh." She reached for Lily. "There you are, beautiful baby girl. There you are." She laid her lips on Lily's brow, and breathed in. "How's she doing today?" she asked Hayley.

"Good as gold. Look here, Stella. Look what Logan bought her."

Yeah, a female thing, Logan mused as Stella made nearly the identical sound Hayley had over the doll. "Isn't that the most precious thing?"

"And watch this." Hayley pulled the hat so the tune played out.

"Mom. Mom." Luke deserted Logan to tug on his mother.

"Just a minute, baby."

They fussed over the doll and Lily while Luke rolled his eyes and danced in place.

"I think Lily and I should go take a nap." Hayley tucked the baby in her carrier, then lifted it and the doll. "Thanks again, Logan. It was awfully sweet of you."

"Glad you like it. You take care now."

"Dolls are lame," Gavin stated, but he was polite enough to wait until Hayley was inside.

"Really?" Stella reached over to flick the bill of his baseball cap over his eyes. "And what are those little people you've got all over your shelves and your desk?"

"Those aren't dolls." Gavin looked as horrified as an eight-year-old boy could manage. "Those are action figures. Come *on*, Mom."

"My mistake."

"We want to be Saturday slaves and build an arbor." Luke pulled on her hand and to get her attention. "Okay?"

"Saturday slaves?"

"I'm building an arbor tomorrow," Logan explained. "Could use some help, and I got these two volunteers. I hear they work for cheese sandwiches and Popsicles."

"Oh. Actually, I was planning to take them to work with me tomorrow."

"An *arbor*, Mom." Luke gazed up pleadingly, as if he'd been given the chance to build the space shuttle and then ride it to Pluto. "I never, ever built one before."

"Well . . ."

"Why don't we split it up?" Logan suggested. "You take them on in with you in the morning, and I'll swing by and get them around noon."

She felt her stomach knot. It sounded normal. Like parenting. Like family. Dimly, she heard her boys begging and pleading over the buzzing in her ears.

"That'll be fine," she managed. "If you're sure they won't be in your way."

He cocked his head at the strained and formal tone. "They get in it, I just kick them out again. Like now. Why don't you boys go find that dog and see what he's up to, so I can talk to your mama a minute?"

Gavin made a disgusted face. "Let's go, Luke. He's probably going to kiss her."

"Why, I'm transparent as glass to that boy," Logan said. He tipped her chin up with his fingers, laid his lips on hers, and watched her watch him. "Hello, Stella."

"Hello, Logan."

"Are you going to tell me what's going on in that head of yours, or do I have to guess?"

"A lot of things. And nothing much."

"You looked poleaxed when you came outside."

" 'Poleaxed.' Now there's a word you don't hear every day."

"Why don't you and I take a little walk?"

"All right."

"You want to know why I came by this afternoon?"

"To bring Lily a doll." She walked along one of the paths with him. She could hear her boys and the dog, then the quick thwack of Luke's Wiffle bat. They'd be fine for a while.

"That, and to see if I could sponge a meal off Roz, which was a roundabout way of having a meal with you. I don't figure I'm going to be able to pry you too far away from the baby for a while yet."

She had to smile. "Apparently I'm transparent, too. It's so much fun having a baby in the house. If I manage to steal her away from Hayley for an hour—and win out over Roz—I can play with her like, well, a doll. All those adorable little clothes. Never having had a girl, I didn't realize how addicting all those little dresses can be."

"When I asked you if Lily made you want another, you panicked."

"I didn't panic."

"Clutched, let's say. Why is that?"

"It's not unusual for a woman of my age with two half-grown children to clutch, let's say, at the idea of another baby."

"Uh-huh. You clutched again when I said I wanted to take the kids to my place tomorrow."

"No, it's just that I'd already planned—"

"Don't bullshit me, Red."

"Things are moving so fast and in a direction I hadn't planned to go."

"If you're going to plan every damn thing, maybe I should draw you a frigging map."

"I can draw my own map, and there's no point in being annoyed. You asked." She stopped by a tower of madly climbing passionflower. "I thought things were supposed to move slow in the south."

"You irritated me the first time I set eyes on you."

"Thanks so much."

"That should've given me a clue," he continued. "You were an itch between my shoulder blades. The one in that spot you can't reach and scratch away no matter how you contort yourself. I'd've been happy to move slow. Generally, I don't see the point in rushing through something. But you know, Stella, you can't schedule how you're going to fall in love. And I fell in love with you."

"Logan."

"I can see that put the fear of God in you. I figure there's one of two reasons for that. One, you don't have feelings for me, and you're afraid you'll hurt me. Or you've got plenty of feelings for me, and they scare you."

He snapped off a passionflower with its white petals and long blue filaments, stuck it in the spiraling curls of her hair. A carelessly romantic gesture at odds with the frustration in his voice. "I'm going with number two, not only because it suits me better, but because I know what happens to both of us when I kiss you."

"That's attraction. It's chemistry."

"I know the frigging difference." He took her shoulders, held her still. "So do you. Because we've both been here before. We've both been in love before, so we know the difference."

"That may be right, that may be true. And it's part of why this is too much, too fast." She curled her hands on his forearms, felt solid strength, solid will. "I knew Kevin a full year before things got serious, and another year before we started talking about the future."

"I had about the same amount of time with Rae. And here we are, Stella. You through tragedy, me through circumstance. We both know there aren't any guarantees, no matter how long or how well you plan it out beforehand."

"No, there aren't. But it's not just me now. I have more than myself to consider."

"You come as a package deal." He rubbed his hands up and down her arms, then stepped away. "I'm not dim, Stella. And I'm not above making friends with your boys to get you. But the fact is, I like them. I enjoy having them around."

"I know that." She gave his arms a squeeze, then eased back. "I know that," she repeated. "I can tell when someone's faking. It's not you. It's me."

"That's the goddamnedest thing to say."

"You're right, but it's also true. I know what it's like to be a child and have my mother swing from man to man. That's not what we're doing here," she said, lifting her hands palms out as fresh fury erupted on his face. "I know that, too. But the fact is, my life centers on those boys now. It has to."

"And you don't think mine can? If you don't think I can be a father to them because they didn't come out of me, then it is you."

"I think it takes time to—"

"You know how you get a strong, healthy plant like this to increase, to fill out strong?" He jerked a thumb toward the passionflower vine. "You can layer it, and you end up with new fruit and flower. By hybridizing it, it gets stronger, maybe you get yourself a new variety out of it."

"Yes. But it takes time."

"You have to start. I don't love those boys the way you do. But I can see how I could, if you gave me the chance. So I want the chance. I want to marry you."

"Oh, God. I can't—we don't—" She had to press the heel of her hand on her heart and gulp in air. But she couldn't seem to suck it all the way into her lungs. "Marriage. Logan. I can't get my breath."

"Good. That means you'll shut up for five minutes. I love you, and I want you and those boys in my life. If anybody had suggested to me, a few months ago, that I'd want to take on some fussy redhead and a couple of noisy kids,

I'd've laughed my ass off. But there you go. I'd say we could live together for a while until you get used to it, but I know you wouldn't. So I don't see why we don't just do it and start living our lives."

"Just do it," she managed. "Like you just go out and buy a new truck?"

"A new truck's got a better warranty than marriage."

"All this romance is making me giddy."

"I could go buy a ring, get down on one knee. I figured that's how I'd deal with this, but I'm into it now. You love me, Stella."

"I'm beginning to wonder why."

"You've always wondered why. It wouldn't bother me if you keep right on wondering. We could make a good life together, you and me. For ourselves." He jerked his head in the direction of the smack of plastic bat on plastic ball. "For the boys. I can't be their daddy, but I could be a good father. I'd never hurt them, or you. Irritate, annoy, but I'd never hurt any of you."

"I know that. I couldn't love you if you weren't a good man. And you are, a very good man. But marriage. I don't know if it's the answer for any of us."

"I'm going to talk you into it sooner or later." He stepped back to her now, twined her hair around his finger in a lightning change of mood. "If it's sooner, you'd be able to decide how you want all those bare rooms done up in that big house. I'm thinking of picking one and getting started on it next rainy day."

She narrowed her eyes. "Low blow."

"Whatever works. Belong to me, Stella." He rubbed his lips over hers. "Let's be a family."

"Logan." Her heart was yearning toward him even as her body eased away. "Let's take a step back a minute. A family's part of it. I saw you with Lily."

"And?"

"I'm heading toward my middle thirties, Logan. I have an eight- and a six-year-old. I have a demanding job. A career, and I'm going to keep it. I don't know if I want to have more children. You've never had a baby of your own, and you deserve to."

"I've thought about this. Making a baby with you, well, that would be a fine thing if we both decide we want it. But it seems to me that right now I'm getting the bonus round. You, and two entertaining boys that are already housebroken. I don't have to know everything that's going to happen, Stella. I don't want to know every damn detail. I just have to know I love you, and I want them."

"Logan." Time for rational thinking, she decided. "We're going to have to sit down and talk this out. We haven't even met each other's families yet."

"We can take care of that easy enough, at least with yours. We can have them over for dinner. Pick a day."

"You don't have any *furniture*." She heard her voice pitch, and deliberately leveled herself again. "That's not important."

"Not to me."

"The point is we're skipping over a lot of the most basic steps." And at the moment, all of them were jumbled and muzzy in her mind.

Marriage, changing things for her boys once more, the possibility of another child. How could she keep up?

"Here you are talking about taking on two children. You don't know what it's like to live in the same house as a couple of young boys."

"Red, I *was* a young boy. I tell you what, you go ahead and make me a list of all those basic steps. We'll take them, in order, if that's what you need to do. But I want you to tell me, here and now, do you love me?"

"You've already told me I do."

He set his hands on her waist, drew her in, drew her up in the way that made her heart stutter. "Tell me."

Did he know, could he know, how huge it was for her to say the words? Words she'd said to no man but the one she'd lost. Here he was, those eyes on hers, waiting for the simple acknowledgment of what he already knew.

"I love you. I do, but—"

"That'll do for now." He closed his mouth over hers and rode out the storm of emotion raging inside him. Then he stepped back. "You make that list, Red. And start thinking what color you want on those living room walls. Tell the boys I'll see them tomorrow."

"But . . . weren't you going to stay for dinner?"

"I've got some things to do," he said as he strode away. "And so do you." He glanced over his shoulder. "You need to worry about me."

ONE OF THE THINGS HE HAD TO DO WAS WORK OFF the frustration. When he'd asked Rae to marry him, it was no surprise for either of them and her acceptance had been instant and enthusiastic.

Of course, look where that had gotten them.

But it was hard on a man's ego when the woman he loved and wanted to spend his life with countered every one of his moves with a block of stubborn, hardheaded *sense*.

He put in an hour on his cross-trainer, sweating, guzzling water, and cursing the day he'd had the misfortune to fall in love with a stiff-necked redhead.

Of course, if she wasn't stiff-necked, stubborn, and sensible, he probably wouldn't have fallen in love with her. That still made the whole mess her fault.

He'd been happy before she'd come along. The house hadn't seemed empty before she'd been in it. Her and those noisy kids. Since when had he voluntarily arranged to spend a precious Saturday off, a solitary Saturday at his own house with a couple of kids running around getting into trouble?

Hell. He was going to have to go out and pick up some Popsicles.

He was a doomed man, he decided as he stepped into the shower. Hadn't he already picked the spot in the backyard for a swing set? Hadn't he already started a rough sketch for a tree house?

He'd started thinking like a father.

Maybe he'd liked the sensation of holding that baby in his arms, but having one wasn't a deal breaker. How was either one of them supposed to know how they'd feel about that a year from now?

Things happen, he thought, remembering Hayley's words, because they're meant to happen.

Because, he corrected as he yanked on fresh jeans, you damn well made them happen.

He was going to start making things happen.

In fifteen minutes, after a quick check of the phone book, he was in his car and heading into Memphis. His hair was still wet.

WILL HAD BARELY STARTED ON HIS AFTER-DINNER decaf and the stingy sliver of lemon meringue pie Jolene allowed him when he heard the knock on the door.

"Now who the devil could that be?"

"I don't know, honey. Maybe you should go find out."

"If they want a damn piece of pie, then I want a bigger one."

"If it's the Bowers boy about cutting the grass, tell him I've got a couple of cans of Coke cold in here."

But when Will opened the door, it wasn't the gangly Bowers boy, but a broad-shouldered man wearing an irritated scowl. Instinctively, Will edged into the opening of the door to block it. "Something I can do for you?"

"Yeah. I'm Logan Kitridge, and I've just asked your daughter to marry me."

"Who is it, honey?" Fussing with her hair, Jolene walked up to the door. "Why it's Logan Kitridge, isn't it? We met you a time or two over at Roz's. Been some time back, though. I know your mama a little. Come on in."

"He says he asked Stella to marry him."

"Is that so!" Her face brightened like the sun, with her

eyes wide and avid with curiosity. "Why, that's just marvelous. You come on back and have some pie."

"He didn't say if she'd said yes," Will pointed out.

"Since when does Stella say anything as simple as yes?" Logan demanded, and had Will grinning.

"That's my girl."

They sat down, ate pie, drank coffee, and circled around the subject at hand with small talk about his mother, Stella, the new baby.

Finally, Will leaned back. "So, am I supposed to ask you how you intend to support my daughter and grandsons?"

"You tell me. Last time I did this, the girl's father'd had a couple of years to grill me. Didn't figure I'd have to go through this part of it again at my age."

"Of course you don't." Jolene gave her husband a little slap on the arm. "He's just teasing. Stella can support herself and those boys just fine. And you wouldn't be here looking so irritated if you didn't love her. I guess one question, if you don't mind me asking, is how you feel about being stepfather to her boys."

"About the same way, I expect, you feel being their stepgrandmother. And if I'm lucky, they'll feel about me the way they do about you. I know they love spending time with you, and I hear their Nana Jo bakes cookies as good as David's. That's some compliment."

"They're precious to us," Will said. "They're precious to Stella. They were precious to Kevin. He was a good man."

"Maybe it'd be easier for me if he hadn't been. If he'd been a son of a bitch and she'd divorced him instead of him being a good man who died too young. I don't know, because that's not the case. I'm glad for her that she had a good man and a good marriage, glad for the boys that they had a good father who loved them. I can live with his ghost, if that's what you're wondering. Fact is, I can be grateful to him."

"Well, I think that's just smart." Jolene patted Logan's hand with approval. "And I think it shows good character, too. Don't you, Will?"

On a noncommittal sound, Will pulled on his bottom lip. "You marry my girl, am I going to get landscaping and such at the family rate?"

Logan's grin spread slowly. "We can make that part of the package."

"I've been toying with redoing the patio."

"First I've heard of it," Jolene muttered.

"I saw them putting on one of those herringbone patterns out of bricks on one of the home shows. I liked the look of it. You know how to handle that sort of thing?"

"Done a few like it. I can take a look at what you've got now if you want."

"That'd be just fine." Will pushed back from the table.

twenty-one

STELLA CHEWED AT IT, STEWED OVER IT, AND WORRIED about it. She was prepared to launch into another discussion regarding the pros and cons of marriage when Logan came to pick up the boys at noon.

She knew he was angry with her. Hurt, too, she imagined. But oddly enough, she knew he'd be by—somewhere in the vicinity of noon—to get the kids. He'd told them he would come, so he would come.

A definite plus on his side of the board, she decided. She could, and did, trust him with her children.

They would argue, she knew. They were both too worked up to have a calm, reasonable discussion over such an emotional issue. But she didn't mind an argument. A good argument usually brought all the facts and feelings out. She needed both if she was going to figure out the best thing to do for all involved.

But when he hunted them down where she had the kids storing discarded wagons—at a quarter a wagon—he was perfectly pleasant. In fact, he was almost sunny.

"Ready for some man work?" he asked.

With shouts of assent, they deserted wagon detail for more interesting activities. Luke proudly showed him the plastic hammer he'd hooked in a loop of his shorts.

"That'll come in handy. I like a man who carries his own tools. I'll drop them off at the house later."

"About what time do you think—"

"Depends on how long they can stand up to the work." He pinched Gavin's biceps. "Ought to be able to get a good day's sweat out of this one."

"Feel mine! Feel mine!" Luke flexed his arm.

After he'd obliged, given an impressed whistle, he nodded to Stella. "See you."

And that was that.

So she chewed at it, stewed over it, and worried about it for the rest of the day. Which, not being a fool, she deduced was exactly what he'd wanted.

THE HOUSE WAS ABNORMALLY QUIET WHEN SHE GOT home from work. She wasn't sure she liked it. She showered off the day, played with the baby, drank a glass of wine, and paced until the phone rang.

"Hello?"

"Hi there, is this Stella?"

"Yes, who—"

"This is Trudy Kitridge. Logan's mama? Logan said I should give you a call, that you'd be home from work about this time of day."

"I . . . oh." Oh, God, oh, God. Logan's *mother*?

"Logan told me and his daddy he asked you to marry him. Could've knocked me over with a feather."

"Yes, me, too. Mrs. Kitridge, we haven't decided . . . or I haven't decided . . . anything."

"Woman's entitled to some time to make up her mind, isn't she? I'd better warn you, honey, when that boy sets his mind on something, he's like a damn bulldog. He said you wanted to meet his family before you said yes or no. I think that's a sweet thing. Of course, with us living out here now, it's not so easy, is it? But we'll be coming back sometime during the holidays. Probably see Logan for Thanksgiving, then our girl for Christmas. Got grandchildren in Charlotte, you know, so we want to be there for Christmas."

"Of course." She had no idea, no idea whatsoever what to say. How could she with no time to prepare?

"Then again, Logan tells me you've got two little boys. Said they're both just pistols. So maybe we'll have ourselves a couple of grandchildren back in Tennessee, too."

"Oh." Nothing could have touched her heart more truly. "That's a lovely thing to say. You haven't even met them yet, or me, and—"

"Logan has, and I raised my son to know his own mind. He loves you and those boys, then we will, too. You're working for Rosalind Harper, I hear."

"Yes. Mrs. Kitridge—"

"Now, you just call me Trudy. How you getting along down there?"

Stella found herself having a twenty-minute conversation with Logan's mother that left her baffled, amused, touched, and exhausted.

When it was done, she sat limply on the sofa, like, she thought, the dazed victim of an ambush.

Then she heard Logan's truck rumble up.

She had to force herself not to dash to the door. He'd be expecting that. Instead she settled herself in the front parlor with a gardening magazine and the dog snoozing at her feet as if she didn't have a care in the world.

Maybe she'd mention, oh so casually, that she'd had a conversation with his mother. Maybe she wouldn't, and let him stew over it.

And all right, it had been sensitive and sweet for him to arrange the phone call, but for God's *sake*, couldn't he have given her some warning so she wouldn't have spent the first five minutes babbling like an idiot?

The kids came in with all the elegance of an army battalion on a forced march.

"We built a *whole* arbor." Grimy with sweat and dirt,

Gavin rushed to scoop up Parker. "And we planted the stuff to grow on it."

"Carol Jessmint."

Carolina Jessamine, Stella interpreted from Luke's garbled pronunciation. Nice choice.

"And I got a splinter." Luke held out a dirty hand to show off the Band-Aid on his index finger. "A *big* one. We thought we might have to hack it out with a *knife.* But we didn't."

"Whew, that was close. We'll go put some antiseptic on it."

"Logan did already. And I didn't cry. And we had submarines, except he says they're poor boys down here, but I don't see why they're poor because they have *lots* of stuff in them. And we had Popsicles."

"And we got to ride in the wheelbarrow," Gavin took over the play-by-play. "And I used a real hammer."

"Wow. You had a busy day. Isn't Logan coming in?"

"No, he said he had other stuff. And look." Gavin dug in his pocket and pulled out a wrinkled five-dollar bill. "We each got one, because he said we worked so good we get to be cheap labor instead of slaves."

She couldn't help it, she had to laugh. "That's quite a promotion. Congratulations. I guess we'd better go clean up."

"Then we can eat like a bunch of barnyard pigs." Luke put his hand in hers. "That's what Logan said when it was time for lunch."

"Maybe we'll save the pig-eating for when you're on the job."

They were full of Logan and their day through bathtime, through dinner. And then were too tuckered out from it all to take advantage of the extra hour she generally allowed them on Saturday nights.

They were sound asleep by nine, and for the first time in her memory, Stella felt she had nothing to do. She tried to read, she tried to work, but couldn't settle into either.

She was thrilled when she heard Lily fussing.

When she stepped into the hall, she saw Hayley heading down, trying to comfort a squalling Lily. "She's hungry. I thought I'd curl up in the sitting room, maybe watch some TV while I feed her."

"Mind company?"

"Twist my arm. It was lonely around here today with David off at the lake for the weekend, and you and Roz at work, the boys away." She sat, opened her shirt and settled Lily on her breast. "There. That's better, isn't it? I put her in that baby sling I got at the shower, and we took a nice walk."

"It's good for both of you. What did you want to watch?"

"Nothing, really. I just wanted the voices."

"How about one more?" Roz slipped in, walked over to Lily to smile. "I wanted to take a peek at her. Look at her go!"

"Nothing wrong with her appetite," Hayley confirmed. "She smiled at me today. I know they say it's just gas, but—"

"What do they know?" Roz sprawled in a chair. "They inside that baby's head?"

"Logan asked me to marry him."

She didn't know why she blurted it out—hadn't known it was pushing from her brain to her tongue.

"Holy cow!" Hayley exploded, then immediately soothed Lily and lowered her voice. "When? How? Where? This is just awesome. This is the biggest of the big news. Tell us everything."

"There's not a lot of every anything. He asked me yesterday."

"After I went inside to put the baby down? I just knew something was up."

"I don't think he meant to. I think it just sort of happened, then he was irritated when I tried to point out the very rational reasons we shouldn't rush into anything."

"What are they?" Hayley wondered.

"You've only known each other since January," Roz began, watching Stella. "You have two children. You've each been married before and bring a certain amount of baggage from those marriages."

"Yes." Stella let out a long sigh. "Exactly."

"When you know you know, don't you?" Hayley argued. "Whether it's five months or five years. And he's great with your kids. They're nuts about him. Being married before ought to make both of you understand the pitfalls or whatever. I don't get it. You love him, don't you?"

"Yes. And yes to the rest, to a point, but . . . it's different when you're young and unencumbered. You can take more chances. Well, if you're not me you can take more chances. And what if he wants children and I don't? I have to think about that. I have to know if I'm going to be able to consider having another child at this stage, or if the children I do have would be happy and secure with him in the long term. Kevin and I had a game plan."

"And your game was called," Roz said. "It isn't an easy thing to walk into another marriage. I waited a long time to do it, then it was the wrong decision. But I think, if I could have fallen, just tumbled into love with a man at your age, one who made me happy, who cheerfully spent his Saturday with my children, and who excited me in bed, I'd have walked into it, and gladly."

"But you just said, before, you gave the exact reasons why it's too soon."

"No, I gave the reasons you'd give—and ones I understand, Stella. But there's something else you and I understand, or should. And that is that love is precious, and too often stolen away. You've got a chance to grab hold of it again. And I say lucky you."

SHE DREAMED AGAIN OF THE GARDEN, AND THE BLUE dahlia. It was ladened with buds, fat and ripe and ready to burst into bloom. At the top, a single stunning flower swayed electric in the quiet breeze. Her garden, though no longer tidy and ordered, spread out from its feet in waves and flows and charming bumps of color and shape.

Then Logan was beside her, and his hands were warm and rough as he drew her close. His mouth was strong and exciting as it feasted on hers. In the distance she could hear her children's laughter, and the cheerful bark of the dog.

She lay on the green grass at the garden's edge, her senses full of the color and scent, full of the man.

There was such heat, such pleasure as they loved in the sunlight. She felt the shape of his face with her hands. Not fairy-tale handsome, not perfect, but beloved. Her skin shivered as their bodies moved, flesh against flesh, hard against soft, curve against angle.

How could they fit, how could they make such a glorious whole, when there were so many differences?

But her body merged with his, joined, and thrived.

She lay in the sunlight with him, on the green grass at the edge of her garden, and hearing the thunder of her own heartbeat, knew bliss.

The buds on the dahlia burst open. There were so many of them. Too many. Other plants were being shaded, crowded. The garden was a jumble now, anyone could see it. The blue dahlia was too aggressive and prolific.

It's fine where it is. It's just a different plan.

But before she could answer Logan, there was another voice, cold and hard in her mind.

His plan. Not yours. His wants. Not yours. Cut it down, before it spreads.

No, it wasn't her plan. Of course it wasn't. This garden was meant to be a charming spot, a quiet spot.

There was a spade in her hand, and she began to dig.

That's right. Dig it out, dig it up.

The air was cold now, cold as winter, so that Stella shuddered as she plunged the spade into the ground.

Logan was gone, and she was alone in the garden with the Harper Bride, who stood in her white gown and tangled hair, nodding. And her eyes were mad.

"I don't want to be alone. I don't want to give it up."

Dig! Hurry. Do you want the pain, the poison? Do you want it to infect your children? Hurry! It will spoil everything, kill everything, if you let it stay.

She'd get it out. It was best to get it out. She'd just plant it somewhere else, she thought, somewhere better.

But as she lifted it out, taking care with the roots, the flowers went black, and the blue dahlia withered and went to dust in her hands.

KEEPING BUSY WAS THE BEST WAY NOT TO BROOD. And keeping busy was no problem for Stella with the school year winding down, the perennial sale at the nursery about to begin, and her best saleswoman on maternity leave.

She didn't have time to pick apart strange, disturbing dreams or worry about a man who proposed one minute, then vanished the next. She had a business to run, a family to tend, a ghost to identify.

She sold the last three bay laurels, then put her mind and her back into reordering the shrub area.

"Shouldn't you be pushing papers instead of camellias?"

She straightened, knowing very well she'd worked up a sweat, that there was soil on her pants, and that her hair was frizzing out of the ball cap she'd stuck on. And faced Logan.

"I manage, and part of managing is making sure our stock is properly displayed. What do you want?"

"Got a new job worked up." He waved the paperwork, and the breeze from it made her want to moan out loud. "I'm in for supplies."

"Fine. You can put the paperwork on my desk."

"This is as far as I'm going." He shoved it into her hand. "Crew's loading up some of it now. I'm going to take that Japanese red maple, and five of the hardy pink oleanders."

He dragged the flatbed over and started to load.

"Fine," she repeated, under her breath. Annoyed, she glanced at the bid, blinked, then reread the client information.

"This is my father."

"Uh-huh."

"What are you doing planting oleander for my father?"

"My job. Putting in a new patio, too. Your stepmama's already talking about getting new furniture for out there. And a fountain. Seems to me a woman can't see a flat surface without wanting to buy something to put on it. They were still talking about it when I left the other night."

"You—what were *you* doing there?"

"Having pie. Gotta get on. We need to get started on this if I'm going to make it home and clean up before this dinner with the professor guy tonight. See you later, Red."

"Hold it. You just hold it. You had your mother call me, right out of the blue."

"How's it out of the blue when you said you wanted us to meet each other's families? Mine's a couple thousand miles away right now, so the phone call seemed the best way."

"I'd just like you to explain . . ." Now she waved the papers. "All this."

"I know. You're a demon for explanations." He stopped long enough to grab her hair, crush his mouth to hers. "If that doesn't make it clear enough, I'm doing something wrong. Later."

"THEN HE JUST WALKED AWAY, LEAVING ME STANDING there like an idiot." Still stewing hours later, Stella changed Lily's diaper while Hayley finished dressing for dinner.

"You said you thought you should meet each other's families and stuff," Hayley pointed out. "So now you talked to his mama, and he talked to your daddy."

"I know what I said, but he just went tromping over

there. And he had her call me without letting me know first. He just goes off, at the drop of a hat." She picked up Lily, cuddled her. "He gets me stirred up."

"I kinda miss getting stirred up that way." She turned sideways in the mirror, sighed a little over the post-birth pudge she was carrying. "I guess I thought, even though the books said different, that everything would just spring back where it was after Lily came out."

"Nothing much springs after having a baby. But you're young and active. You'll get your body back."

"I hope." She reached for her favorite silver hoops while Stella nuzzled Lily. "Stella, I'm going to tell you something, because you're my best friend and I love you."

"Oh, sweetie."

"Well, it's true. Last week, when Logan came by to bring Lily her doll, and you and the boys came outside? Before I went in and he popped the big Q? You know what the four of you looked like?"

"No."

"A family. And I think whatever your head's running around with, in your heart you know that. And that that's the way it's going to be."

"You're awfully young to be such a know-it-all."

"It's not the years, it's the miles." Hayley tossed a cloth over her shoulder. "Come here, baby girl. Mama's going to show you off to the dinner guests before you go to sleep. You ready?" she asked Stella.

"I guess we'll find out."

They started toward the stairs, with Stella gathering her boys on the way, and met Roz on the landing.

"Well, don't we all look fine."

"We had to wear new shirts," Luke complained.

"And you look so handsome in them. I wonder if I can be greedy and steal both these well-dressed young men as my escorts." She held out both her hands for theirs. "It's going to storm," she said with a glance out the window. "And look here, I believe that must be our Dr. Carnegie, and right on time. What in the world is that man driving? It looks like a rusty red box on wheels."

"I think it's a Volvo." Hayley moved in to spy over Roz's shoulder. "A really old Volvo. They're like one of the safest cars, and so dopey-looking, they're cool. Oh, my, look at that!" Her eyebrows lifted when Mitch got out of the car. "Serious hottie alert."

"Good God, Hayley, he's old enough to be your daddy."

Hayley just smiled at Roz. "Hot's hot. And he's hot."

"Maybe he needs a drink of water," Luke suggested.

"And we'll get one for Hayley, too." Amused, Roz walked down to greet her first guest.

He brought a good white wine as a hostess gift, which she approved of, but he opted for mineral water when she offered him a drink. She supposed a man who drove a car manufactured about the same time he'd been born needed to keep his wits about him. He made appropriate noises over the baby, shook hands soberly with the boys.

She gave him points for tact when he settled into small talk rather than asking more about the reason she wanted to hire him.

By the time Logan arrived, they were comfortable enough.

"I don't think we'll wait for Harper." Roz got to her feet. "My son is chronically late, and often missing in action."

"I've got one of my own," Mitch said. "I know how it goes."

"Oh, I didn't realize you had children."

"Just the one. Josh is twenty. He goes to college here. You really do have a beautiful home, Ms. Harper."

"Roz, and thank you. It's one of my great loves. And here," she added as Harper dashed in from the kitchen, "is another."

"Late. Sorry. Almost forgot. Hey, Logan, Stella. Hi, guys." He kissed his mother, then looked at Hayley. "Hi. Where's Lily?"

"Sleeping."

"Dr. Carnegie, my tardy son, Harper."

"Sorry. I hope I didn't hold you up."

"Not at all," Mitch said as they shook hands. "Happy to meet you."

"Why don't we sit down? It looks like David's outdone himself."

An arrangement of summer flowers in a long, low bowl centered the table. Candles burned, slim white tapers in gleaming silver, on the sideboard. David had used her white-on-white china with pale yellow and green linens for casual elegance. A cool and artful lobster salad was already arranged on each plate. David sailed in with wine.

"Who can I interest in this very nice Pinot Grigio?"

The doctor, Roz noted, stuck with mineral water.

"You know," Harper began as they enjoyed the main course of stuffed pork, "you look awfully familiar." He narrowed his eyes on Mitch's face. "I've been trying to figure it out. You didn't teach at the U of M while I was there, did you?"

"I might have, but I don't recall you being in any of my classes."

"No. I don't think that's it anyway. Maybe I went to one of your lectures or something. Wait. Wait. I've got it. Josh Carnegie. Power forward for the Memphis Tigers."

"My son."

"Strong resemblance. Man, he's a killer. I was at the game last spring, against South Carolina, when he scored thirty-eight points. He's got moves."

Mitch smiled, rubbed a thumb over the fading bruise on his jaw. "Tell me."

Conversation turned to basketball, boisterously, and gave Logan the opportunity to lean toward Stella. "Your daddy says he's looking forward to seeing you and the boys on Sunday. I'll drive you in, as I've got an invitation to Sunday dinner, too."

"Is that so?"

"He likes me." He picked up her free hand, brushed his lips over his fingers. "We're bonding over oleanders."

She didn't try to stop the smile. "You hit him where it counts."

"You, the kids, his garden. Yeah, I'd say I got it covered. You write that list for me yet, Red?"

"Apparently you're doing fine crossing things off without consulting me."

His grin flashed. "Jolene thinks we should go traditional and have a June wedding."

When Stella's mouth dropped open, he turned away to talk to her kids about the latest issues of Marvel Comics.

Over dessert, a rustling, then a long, shrill cry sounded from the baby monitor standing on the buffet. Hayley popped up as if she were on springs. "That's my cue. I'll be back down after she's fed and settled again."

"Speaking of cues." Stella rose as well. "Time for bed, guys. School night," she added even before the protests could be voiced.

"Going to bed before it's dark is a gyp," Gavin complained.

"I know. Life is full of them. What comes next?"

Gavin heaved a sigh. "Thanks for dinner, it was really good, and now we have to go to bed because of stupid school."

"Close enough," Stella decided.

"'Night. I liked the finger potatoes 'specially," Luke said to David.

"Want a hand?" Logan called out.

"No." But she stopped at the doorway, turned back and just looked at him a moment. "But thanks."

She herded them up, beginning the nightly ritual as thunder rumbled in. And Parker scooted under Luke's bed to hide from it. Rain splatted, fat juicy drops, against the windows as she tucked them in.

"Parker's a scaredy-cat." Luke snuggled his head in the pillow. "Can he sleep up here tonight?"

"All right, just for tonight, so he isn't afraid." She lured him out from under the bed, and stroking him as he trembled, laid him in with Luke. "Is that better now?"

"Uh-huh. Mom?" He broke off, petting the dog, and exchanging a long look with his brother.

"What? What are you two cooking up?"

"You ask her," Luke hissed.

"Nuh-uh. You."

"You."

"Ask me what? If you've spent all your allowances and work money on comics, I—"

"Are you going to marry Logan?" Gavin blurted out.

"Am I—where did you get an idea like that?"

"We heard Roz and Hayley talking about how he asked you to." Luke yawned, blinked sleepily at her. "So are you?"

She sat on the side of Gavin's bed. "I've been thinking about it. But I wouldn't decide something that important without talking to both of you. It's a lot to think about, for all of us, a lot to discuss."

"He's nice, and he plays with us, so it's okay if you do."

Stella let out a laugh at Luke's rundown. All right, she thought, maybe not such a lot to discuss from certain points of view.

"Marriage is a very big deal. It's a really big promise."

"Would we go live in his house?" Luke wondered.

"Yes, I suppose we would if . . ."

"We like it there. And I like when he holds me upside down. And he got the splinter out of my finger, and it hardly hurt at all. He even kissed it after, just like he's supposed to."

"Did he?" she murmured.

"He'd be our stepdad." Gavin drew lazy circles with his finger on top of his sheet. "Like we have Nana Jo for a stepgrandmother. She loves us."

"She certainly does."

"So we decided it'd be okay to have a stepdad, if it's Logan."

"I can see you've given this a lot of thought," Stella managed. "And I'm going to think about it, too. Maybe we'll talk about it more tomorrow." She kissed Gavin's cheek.

"Logan said Dad's always watching out for us."

Tears burned the back of her eyes. "Yes. Oh, yes, he is, baby."

She hugged him, hard, then turned to hug Luke. "Good night. I'll be right downstairs."

But she walked through to her room first to catch her breath, compose herself. Treasures, she thought. She had the most precious treasures. She pressed her fingers to her eyes and thought of Kevin. A treasure she'd lost.

Logan said Dad's always watching out for us.

A man who would know that, would accept that and say those words to a young boy was another kind of treasure.

He'd changed the pattern on her. He'd planted a bold blue dahlia in the middle of her quiet garden. And she wasn't digging it out.

"I'm going to marry him," she heard herself say, and laughed at the thrill of it.

Through the next boom of thunder, she heard the singing. Instinctively, she stepped into the bath, to look into her sons' room. She was there, ghostly in billowing white, her hair a tangle of dull gold. She stood between the beds, her voice calm and sweet, her eyes insane as she stared through the flash of lightning at Stella.

Fear trickled down Stella's back. She stepped forward, and was shoved back by a blast of cold.

"No." She raced forward again, and hit a solid wall. "No!" She battered at it. "You won't keep me from my babies." She flung herself against the frigid shield, screaming for her children who slept on, undisturbed.

"You bitch! Don't you touch them."

She ran out of the room, ignoring Hayley, who raced down toward her, ignoring the clatter of feet on the stairs. She knew only one thing. She had to get to her children, she had to get through the barrier and get to her boys.

At a full run she hit the open doorway, and was knocked back against the far wall.

"What the hell's going on?" Logan grabbed her, pushing her aside as he rushed the room himself.

"She won't let me in." Desperate, Stella beat her fists against the cold until her hands were raw and numb. "She's got my babies. Help me."

Logan rammed his shoulder against the opening. "It's like fucking steel." Rammed it again as Harper and David hit it with him.

Behind them, Mitch stared into the room, at the figure in white, who glowed now with a wild light. "Name of God."

"There has to be another way. The other door." Roz grabbed Mitch's arm and pulled him down the hall.

"This ever happen before?"

"No. Dear God. Hayley, keep the baby away."

Frantic, her hands throbbing from pounding, Stella ran. Another way, she thought. Force wouldn't work. She could beat against that invisible ice, rage and threaten, but it wouldn't crack.

Oh, please, God, her babies.

Reason. She would try reason and begging and promises. She dashed out into the rain, yanked open the terrace doors. And though she knew better, hurled herself at the opening.

"You can't have them!" she shouted over the storm. "They're mine. Those are my children. My life." She went down on her knees, ill with fear. She could see her boys sleeping still, and the hard, white light pulsing from the woman between them.

She thought of the dream. She thought of what she and her boys had talked about shortly before the singing. "It's not your business what I do." She struggled to keep her voice firm. "Those are my children, and I'll do what's best for them. You're not their mother."

The light seemed to waver, and when the figure turned, there was as much sorrow as madness in her eyes. "They're not yours. They need me. They need their mother. Flesh and blood."

She held up her hands, scraped and bruised from the beating. "You want me to bleed for them? I will. I am." On her knees, she pressed her palms to the cold while the rain sluiced over her.

"They belong to me, and there's nothing I won't do to keep them safe, to keep them happy. I'm sorry for what happened to you. Whatever it was, whoever you lost, I'm sorry. But you can't have what's mine. You can't take my children from me. You can't take me from my children."

Stella pushed her hand out, and it slid through as if slipping through ice water. Without hesitation, she shoved into the room.

She could see beyond her, Logan still fighting to get through, Stella pressed against the other doorway. She couldn't hear them, but she could see the anguish on Logan's face, and that his hands were bleeding.

"He loves them. He might not have known until tonight, but he loves them. He'll protect them. He'll be a father to them, one they deserve. This is my choice, our choice. Don't ever try to keep me from my children again."

There were tears now as the figure flowed across the room toward the terrace doors. Stella laid a trembling hand on Gavin's head, on Luke's. Safe, she thought as her knees began to shake. Safe and warm.

"I'll help you," she stated firmly, meeting the grieving eyes again. "We all will. If you want our help, give us something. Your name, at least. Tell me your name."

The Bride began to fade, but she lifted a hand to the glass of the door. There, written in rain that dripped like tears, was a single word.

Amelia

When Logan burst through the door behind her, Stella spun toward him, laid a hand quickly on his lips. "Ssh. You'll wake them."

Then she buried her face against his chest and wept.

epilogue

"AMELIA." STELLA SHIVERED, DESPITE THE DRY clothes and the brandy Roz had insisted on. "Her name. I saw it written on the glass of the door just before she vanished. She wasn't going to hurt them. She was furious with me, was protecting them from me. She's not altogether sane."

"You're all right?" Logan stayed crouched in front of her. "You're sure?"

She nodded, but she drank more brandy. "It's going to take a little while to come down from it, but yes, I'm okay."

"I've never been so scared." Hayley looked toward the stairs. "Are you sure all the kids are safe?"

"She would never hurt them." Stella laid a reassuring hand on Hayley's. "Something broke her heart, and her mind, I think. But children are her only joy."

"You'll excuse me if I find this absolutely fascinating, and completely crazy." Mitch paced back and forth across the floor. "If I hadn't seen it with my own eyes—" He shook his head. "I'm going to need all the data you can put together, once I'm able to get started on this."

He stopped pacing, stared at Roz. "I can't rationalize it. I saw it, but I can't rationalize it. An . . . I'll call it an entity, for lack of better. An entity was in that room. The room was sealed off." Absently he rubbed his shoulder where he'd rammed against the solid air. "And she was inside it."

"It was more of a show than we expected to give you on

your first visit," Roz said, and poured him another cup of coffee.

"You're very cool about it," he replied.

"Of all of us here, I've lived with her the longest."

"How?" Mitch asked.

"Because this is my house." She looked tired, and pale, but there was a battle light in her eyes. "Her being here doesn't change that. This is my house." She took a little breath and a sip of brandy herself. "Though I'll admit that what happened tonight shook me, shook all of us. I've never seen anything like what happened upstairs."

"I have to finish the project I'm working on, then I'm going to want to know everything you have seen." Mitch's eyes scanned the room. "All of you."

"All right, we'll see about arranging that."

"Stella ought to lie down," Logan said.

"No, I'm fine, really." She glanced toward the monitor, listened to the quiet hum. "I feel like what happened tonight changed something. In her, in me. The dreams, the blue dahlia."

"Blue dahlia?" Mitch interrupted, but Stella shook her head.

"I'll explain when I feel a little steadier. But I don't think I'll be having them anymore. I think she'll let it alone, let it grow there because I got through to her. And I believe, absolutely, it was because I got through mother to mother."

"My children grew up in this house. She never tried to block me from them."

"You hadn't decided to get married when your sons were still children," Stella announced, and watched Logan's eyes narrow.

"Haven't you missed some steps?" he asked.

She managed a weary smile. "Not any important ones, apparently. As for the Bride, maybe her husband left her, or she was pregnant by a lover who deserted her, or . . . I don't know. I can't think very clearly."

"None of us can, and whether or not you think you're

fine, you're still pale." Roz got to her feet. "I'm going to take you upstairs and put you to bed."

She shook her head when Logan started to protest. "You're all welcome to stay as long as you like. Harper?"

"Right." Understanding his cue, and his duty, he got to his feet. "Can I get anyone another drink?"

Because she was still unsteady, Stella let Roz take her upstairs. "I guess I am tired, but you don't have to come up."

"After a trauma like that, you deserve a little pampering. I imagine Logan would like the job, but tonight I think a woman's the better option. Go on, get undressed now," Roz told her as she turned down the bed.

As the shock eased and made room for fatigue, Stella did what she was told, then slipped through the bathroom to take a last look at her children for the night. "I was so afraid. So afraid I wouldn't get to my boys."

"You were stronger than she was. You've always been stronger."

"Nothing's ever ripped at me like that. Not even . . ." Stella moved back to her room, slipped into bed. "The night Kevin died, there was nothing I could do. I couldn't get to him, bring him back, stop what had already happened, no matter how much I wanted to."

"And tonight you could do something, and did. Women, women like us at any rate, we do what has to be done. I want you to rest now. I'll check on you and the boys myself before I go to bed. Do you want me to leave the light on?"

"No, I'll be fine. Thanks."

"We're right downstairs."

In the quiet dark, Stella sighed. She lay still, listening, waiting. But she heard nothing but the sound of her own breathing.

For tonight—at least for tonight—it was over.

When she closed her eyes, she drifted to sleep.

Dreamlessly.

* * *

SHE EXPECTED LOGAN TO COME BY THE NURSERY THE next day. But he didn't. She was certain he would come by the house before dinner. But he didn't.

Nor did he call.

She decided that after the night before he'd needed a break. From her, from the house, from any sort of drama. How could she blame him?

He'd pounded his hands, his big, hard hands, bloody from trying to get to her boys, then to her. She knew all she needed to know about him now, about the man she'd grown to love and respect.

Knew enough to trust him with everything that was hers. Loved him enough to wait until he came to her.

And when her children were in bed, and the moon began to rise, his truck rumbled up the drive to Harper House.

This time she didn't hesitate, but dashed to the door to meet him.

"I'm glad you're here." She threw her arms around him first, held tight when his wrapped around her. "So glad. We really need to talk."

"Come on out first. I got something in the truck for you."

"Can't it wait?" She eased back. "If we could just sit down and get some things aired out. I'm not sure I made any sense last night."

"You made plenty of sense." To settle it, he gripped her hand, pulled her outside. "Seeing as after you scared ten years off my life, you said you were going to marry me. Didn't have the opportunity to follow through on that then, the way things were. I've got something to give you before you start talking me to death."

"Maybe you don't want to hear that I love you."

"I can take time for that." Grabbing her, he lifted her off her feet and circled them both to the truck. "You going to organize my life, Red?"

"I'm going to try. Are you going to disorganize mine?"

"No question about it." He lowered her until her lips met his.

"Hell of a storm last night—in every possible sense," she said as she rested her cheek against his. "It's over now."

"This one is. There'll be others." He took her hands, kissed them, then just looked down at her in the dusky light of the moon.

"I love you, Stella. I'm going to make you happy even when I irritate the living hell out of you. And the boys . . . Last night, when I saw her in there with them, when I couldn't get to them—"

"I know." Now she lifted his hands to kiss his raw, swollen knuckles. "One day, when they're older, they'll fully appreciate how lucky they are to have had two such good men for fathers. I know how lucky I am to love and be loved by two such good men."

"I figured that out when I started falling for you."

"When was that?"

"On the way to Graceland."

"You don't waste time."

"That's when you told me about the dream you'd had."

Her heart fluttered. "The garden. The blue dahlia."

"Then later, when you said you'd had another, told me about it, it just got me thinking. So . . ." He reached into the cab of the truck, took out a small pot with a grafted plant. "I asked Harper if he'd work on this."

"A dahlia," she whispered. "A blue dahlia."

"He's pretty sure it'll bloom blue when it matures. Kid's got a knack."

Tears burned into her eyes and smeared her voice. "I was going to dig it up, Logan. She kept pushing me to, and it seemed she was right. It wasn't what I'd put there, wasn't what I'd planned, no matter how beautiful it was. And when I did, when I dug it up, it died. It was so stupid of me."

"We'll dig this one in instead. We can plant this, you and me, and the four of us can plant a garden around it. That suit you?"

She lifted her hands, cupped his face. "It suits me."

"That's good, because Harper worked like a mad scientist on it, shooting for a deep, true blue. I guess we'll wait and see what we get when it blooms."

"You're right." She looked up at him. "We'll see what we get."

"He gave me the go-ahead to name it. So it'll be Stella's Dream."

Now her heart swirled into her eyes. "I was wrong about you, Logan. You're perfect after all."

She cradled the pot in her arm as if it were a child, precious and new. Then taking his hand, she linked fingers so they could walk in the moon-drenched garden together.

In the house, in the air perfumed with flowers, another walked. And wept.

Can't get enough of Nora Roberts?
Try the #1 *New York Times* bestselling
In Death series, by Nora Roberts
writing as J. D. Robb.

Turn the page to see where it began . . .

NAKED IN DEATH

SHE WOKE IN THE DARK. THROUGH THE SLATS ON THE window shades, the first murky hint of dawn slipped, slanting shadowy bars over the bed. It was like waking in a cell.

For a moment she simply lay there, shuddering, imprisoned, while the dream faded. After ten years on the force, Eve still had dreams.

Six hours before, she'd killed a man, had watched death creep into his eyes. It wasn't the first time she'd exercised maximum force, or dreamed. She'd learned to accept the action and the consequences.

But it was the child that haunted her. The child she hadn't been in time to save. The child whose screams had echoed in the dreams with her own.

All the blood, Eve thought, scrubbing sweat from her face with her hands. Such a small little girl to have had so much blood in her. And she knew it was vital that she push it aside.

Standard departmental procedure meant that she would spend the morning in Testing. Any officer whose discharge of weapon resulted in termination of life was required to undergo emotional and psychiatric clearance before resuming duty. Eve considered the tests a mild pain in the ass.

She would beat them, as she'd beaten them before.

When she rose, the overheads went automatically to low setting, lighting her way into the bath. She winced once at her reflection. Her eyes were swollen from lack of sleep, her skin nearly as pale as the corpses she'd delegated to the ME.

Rather than dwell on it, she stepped into the shower, yawning.

"Give me one oh one degrees, full force," she said and shifted so that the shower spray hit her straight in the face.

She let it steam, lathered listlessly while she played through the events of the night before. She wasn't due in Testing until nine, and would use the next three hours to settle and let the dream fade away completely.

Small doubts and little regrets were often detected and could mean a second and more intense round with the machines and the owl-eyed technicians who ran them.

Eve didn't intend to be off the streets longer than twenty-four hours.

After pulling on a robe, she walked into the kitchen and programmed her AutoChef for coffee, black; toast, light. Through her window she could hear the heavy hum of air traffic carrying early commuters to offices, late ones home. She'd chosen the apartment years before because it was in a heavy ground and air pattern, and she liked the noise and crowds. On another yawn, she glanced out the window, followed the rattling journey of an aging airbus hauling laborers not fortunate enough to work in the city or by home 'links.

She brought the *New York Times* up on her monitor and scanned the headlines while the faux caffeine bolstered her system. The AutoChef had burned her toast again, but she ate it anyway, with a vague thought of springing for a replacement unit.

She was frowning over an article on a mass recall of droid cocker spaniels when her telelink blipped. Eve shifted to communications and watched her commanding officer flash onto the screen.

"Commander."

"Lieutenant." He gave her a brisk nod, noted the still-wet hair and sleepy eyes. "Incident at Twenty-seven West Broadway, eighteenth floor. You're primary."

Eve lifted a brow. "I'm on Testing. Subject terminated at twenty-two thirty-five."

"We have override," he said, without inflection. "Pick up your shield and weapon on the way to the incident. Code Five, Lieutenant."

"Yes, sir." His face flashed off even as she pushed back from the screen. Code Five meant she would report directly to her commander, and there would be no unsealed interdepartmental reports and no cooperation with the press.

In essence, it meant she was on her own.

BROADWAY WAS NOISY AND CROWDED, A PARTY THAT ROWDY guests never left. Street, pedestrian, and sky traffic were miserable, choking the air with bodies and vehicles. In her old days in uniform she remembered it as a hot spot for wrecks and crushed tourists who were too busy gaping at the show to get out of the way.

Even at this hour steam was rising from the stationary and portable food stands that offered everything from rice noodles to soy dogs for the teeming crowds. She had to swerve to avoid an eager merchant on his smoking Glida-Grill, and took his flipped middle finger as a matter of course.

Eve double-parked and, skirting a man who smelled worse than his bottle of brew, stepped onto the sidewalk. She scanned the building first, fifty floors of gleaming metal that knifed into the sky from a hilt of concrete. She was propositioned twice before she reached the door.

Since this five-block area of West Broadway was affectionately termed Prostitute's Walk, she wasn't surprised. She flashed her badge for the uniform guarding the entrance.

"Lieutenant Dallas."

"Yes, sir." He skimmed his official CompuSeal over the door to keep out the curious, then led the way to the bank of elevators. "Eighteenth floor," he said when the doors swished shut behind them.

"Fill me in, Officer." Eve switched on her recorder and waited.

"I wasn't first on the scene, Lieutenant. Whatever happened upstairs is being kept upstairs. There's a badge inside waiting for you. We have a homicide, and a Code Five in number eighteen-oh-three."

"Who called it in?"

"I don't have that information."

He stayed where he was when the elevator opened. Eve stepped out and was alone in a narrow hallway. Security cameras tilted down at her, and her feet were almost soundless on the worn nap of the carpet as she approached 1803. Ignoring the hand plate, she announced herself, holding her badge up to eye level for the peep cam until the door opened.

"Dallas."

"Feeney." She smiled, pleased to see a familiar face. Ryan Feeney was an old friend and former partner who'd traded the street for a desk and a top-level position in the Electronics Detection Division. "So, they're sending computer pluckers these days."

"They wanted brass, and the best." His lips curved in his wide, rumpled face, but his eyes remained sober. He was a small, stubby man with small, stubby hands and rust-colored hair. "You look beat."

"Rough night."

"So I heard." He offered her one of the sugared nuts from the bag he habitually carried, studying her, and measuring if she was up to what was waiting in the bedroom beyond.

She was young for her rank, barely thirty, with wide brown eyes that had never had a chance to be naive. Her doe-brown hair was cropped short, for convenience rather than style, but suited her triangular face with its razor-edge cheekbones and slight dent in the chin.

She was tall, rangy, with a tendency to look thin, but Feeney knew there were solid muscles beneath the leather jacket. But Eve had more—there was also a brain, and a heart.

"This one's going to be touchy, Dallas."

"I picked that up already. Who's the victim?"

"Sharon DeBlass, granddaughter of Senator DeBlass."

Neither meant anything to her. "Politics isn't my forte, Feeney."

"The gentleman from Virginia, extreme right, old money. The granddaughter took a sharp left a few years back, moved to New York and became a licensed companion."

"She was a hooker." Dallas glanced around the apartment. It was furnished in obsessive modern—glass and thin chrome, signed holograms on the walls, recessed bar in bold red. The wide mood screen behind the bar bled with mixing and merging shapes and colors in cool pastels.

Neat as a virgin, Eve mused, and cold as a whore. "No surprise, given her choice of real estate."

"Politics makes it delicate. Victim was twenty-four, Caucasian female. She bought it in bed."

Eve only lifted a brow. "Seems poetic, since she'd been bought there. How'd she die?"

"That's the next problem. I want you to see for yourself."

As they crossed the room, each took out a slim container, sprayed their hands front and back to seal in oils and fingerprints. At the doorway, Eve sprayed the bottom of her boots to slicken them so that she would pick up no fibers, stray hairs, or skin.

Eve was already wary. Under normal circumstances there would have been two other investigators on a homicide scene, with recorders for sound and pictures. Forensics would have been waiting with their usual snarly impatience to sweep the scene.

The fact that only Feeney had been assigned with her

meant that there were a lot of eggshells to be walked over.

"Security cameras in the lobby, elevator, and hallways," Eve commented.

"I've already tagged the discs." Feeney opened the bedroom door and let her enter first.

It wasn't pretty. Death rarely was a peaceful, religious experience to Eve's mind. It was the nasty end, indifferent to saint and sinner. But this was shocking, like a stage deliberately set to offend.

The bed was huge, slicked with what appeared to be genuine satin sheets the color of ripe peaches. Small, soft-focused spotlights were trained on its center where the naked woman was cupped in the gentle dip of the floating mattress.

The mattress moved with obscenely graceful undulations to the rhythm of programmed music slipping through the headboard.

She was beautiful still, a cameo face with a tumbling waterfall of flaming red hair, emerald eyes that stared glassily at the mirrored ceiling, long, milk-white limbs that called to mind visions of *Swan Lake* as the motion of the bed gently rocked them.

They weren't artistically arranged now, but spread lewdly so that the dead woman formed a final X dead-center of the bed.

There was a hole in her forehead, one in her chest, another horribly gaping between the open thighs. Blood had splattered on the glossy sheets, pooled, dripped, and stained.

There were splashes of it on the lacquered walls, like lethal paintings scrawled by an evil child.

So much blood was a rare thing, and she had seen much too much of it the night before to take the scene as calmly as she would have preferred.

She had to swallow once, hard, and force herself to block out the image of a small child.

"You got the scene on record?"

"Yep."

"Then turn that damn thing off." She let out a breath after Feeney located the controls that silenced the music. The bed flowed to stillness. "The wounds," Eve murmured, stepping closer to examine them. "Too neat for a knife. Too messy for a laser." A flash came to her—old training films, old videos, old viciousness.

"Christ, Feeney, these look like bullet wounds."

Feeney reached into his pocket and drew out a sealed bag. "Whoever did it left a souvenir." He passed the bag to Eve. "An antique like this has to go for eight, ten thousand for a legal collection, twice that on the black market."

Fascinated, Eve turned the sealed revolver over in her hand. "It's heavy," she said half to herself. "Bulky."

"Thirty-eight caliber," he told her. "First one I've seen outside of a museum. This one's a Smith and Wesson, Model Ten, blue steel." He looked at it with some affection. "Real classic piece, used to be standard police issue up until the latter part of the twentieth. They stopped making them in about twenty-two, twenty-three, when the gun ban was passed."

"You're the history buff." Which explained why he was with her. "Looks new." She sniffed through the bag, caught the scent of oil and burning. "Somebody took good care of this. Steel fired into flesh," she mused as she passed the bag back to Feeney. "Ugly way to die, and the first I've seen it in my ten years with the department."

"Second for me. About fifteen years ago, Lower East Side, party got out of hand. Guy shot five people with a twenty-two before he realized it wasn't a toy. Hell of a mess."

"Fun and games," Eve murmured. "We'll scan the collectors, see how many we can locate who own one like this. Somebody might have reported a robbery."

"Might have."

"It's more likely it came through the black market." Eve glanced back at the body. "If she's been in the business for a few years, she'd have discs, records of her clients, her trick books." She frowned. "With Code Five, I'll have to do the door-to-door myself. Not a simple sex crime," she said with a sigh. "Whoever did it set it up. The antique weapon, the wounds themselves, almost ruler-straight down the body, the lights, the pose. Who called it in, Feeney?"

"The killer." He waited until her eyes came back to him. "From right here. Called the station. See how the bedside unit's aimed at her face? That's what came in. Video, no audio."

"He's into showmanship." Eve let out a breath. "Clever bastard, arrogant, cocky. He had sex with her first. I'd bet my badge on it. Then he gets up and does it." She lifted her arm, aiming, lowering it as she counted off, "One, two, three."

"That's cold," murmured Feeney.

"He's cold. He smooths down the sheets after. See how neat they are? He arranges her, spreads her open so nobody can have any doubts as to how she made her living. He does it carefully, practically measuring, so that she's perfectly aligned. Center of the bed, arms and legs equally apart. Doesn't turn off the bed 'cause it's part of the show. He leaves the gun because he wants us to know right away he's no ordinary man. He's got an ego. He doesn't want to waste time letting the body be discovered eventually. He wants it now. That instant gratification."

"She was licensed for men and women," Feeney pointed out, but Eve shook her head.

"It's not a woman. A woman wouldn't have left her looking both beautiful and obscene. No, I don't think it's a woman. Let's see what we can find. Have you gone into her computer yet?"

"No. It's your case, Dallas. I'm only authorized to assist."

"See if you can access her client files." Eve went to the dresser and began to carefully search drawers.

Expensive taste, Eve reflected. There were several items of real silk, the kind no simulation could match. The bottle of scent on the dresser was exclusive, and smelled, after a quick sniff, like expensive sex.

The contents of the drawers were meticulously ordered,

lingerie folded precisely, sweaters arranged according to color and material. The closet was the same.

Obviously the victim had a love affair with clothes and a taste for the best and took scrupulous care of what she owned.

And she'd died naked.

"Kept good records," Feeney called out. "It's all here. Her client list, appointments—including her required monthly health exam and her weekly trip to the beauty salon. She used the Trident Clinic for the first and Paradise for the second."

"Both top-of-the-line. I've got a friend who saved for a year so she could have one day for the works at Paradise. Takes all kinds."

"My wife's sister went for it for her twenty-fifth anniversary. Cost damn near as much as my kid's wedding. Hello, we've got her personal address book."

"Good. Copy all of it, will you, Feeney?" At his low whistle, she looked over her shoulder, glimpsed thc small gold-edged palm computer in his hand. "What?"

"We've got a lot of high-powered names in here. Politics, entertainment, money, money, money. Interesting, our girl has Roarke's private number."

"Roarke who?"

"Just Roarke, as far as I know. Big money there. Kind of guy that touches shit and turns it into gold bricks. You've got to start reading more than the sports page, Dallas."

"Hey, I read the headlines. Did you hear about the cocker spaniel recall?"

"Roarke's always big news," Feeney said patiently. "He's got one of the finest art collections in the world. Arts and antiques," he continued, noting when Eve clicked in and turned to him. "He's a licensed gun collector. Rumor is he knows how to use them."

"I'll pay him a visit."

"You'll be lucky to get within a mile of him."

"I'm feeling lucky." Eve crossed over to the body to slip her hands under the sheets.

"The man's got powerful friends, Dallas. You can't afford to so much as whisper he's linked to this until you've got something solid."

"Feeney, you know it's a mistake to tell me that." But even as she started to smile, her fingers brushed something between cold flesh and bloody sheets. "There's something under her." Carefully, Eve lifted the shoulder, eased her fingers over.

"Paper," she murmured. "Sealed." With her protected thumb, she wiped at a smear of blood until she could read the protected sheet.

ONE OF SIX

"It looks hand printed," she said to Feeney and held it out. "Our boy's more than clever, more than arrogant. And he isn't finished."

Eve spent the rest of the day doing what would normally have been assigned to drones. She interviewed the victim's neighbors personally, recording statements, impressions.

She managed to grab a quick sandwich from the same Glida-Grill she'd nearly smashed before, driving across town. After the night and the morning she'd put in, she could hardly blame the receptionist at Paradise for looking at her as though she'd recently scraped herself off the sidewalk.

Waterfalls played musically among the flora in the reception area of the city's most exclusive salon. Tiny cups of real coffee and slim glasses of fizzling water or champagne were served to those lounging on the cushy chairs and settees. Headphones and discs of fashion magazines were complimentary.

The receptionist was magnificently breasted, a testament to the salon's figure-sculpting techniques. She wore a snug, short outfit in the salon's trademark red, and an incredible coif of ebony hair coiled like snakes.

Eve couldn't have been more delighted.

"I'm sorry," the woman said in a carefully modulated voice as empty of expression as a computer. "We serve by appointment only."

"That's okay." Eve smiled and was almost sorry to puncture the disdain. Almost. "This ought to get me one." She offered her badge. "Who works on Sharon DeBlass?"

The receptionist's horrified eyes darted toward the waiting area. "Our clients' needs are strictly confidential."

"I bet." Enjoying herself, Eve leaned companionably on the U-shaped counter. "I can talk nice and quiet, like this, so we understand each other—Denise?" She flicked her gaze down to the discreet studded badge on the woman's breast. "Or I can talk louder, so everyone understands. If you like the first idea better, you can take me to a nice quiet room where we won't disturb any of your clients, and you can send in Sharon DeBlass's operator. Or whatever term you use."

"Consultant," Denise said faintly. "If you'll follow me."

"My pleasure."

And it was.

Outside of movies or videos, Eve had never seen anything so lush. The carpet was a red cushion your feet could sink blissfully into. Crystal drops hung from the ceiling and spun light. The air smelled of flowers and pampered flesh.

She might not have been able to imagine herself there, spending hours having herself creamed, oiled, pummeled, and sculpted, but if she were going to waste such time on vanity, it would certainly have been interesting to do so under such civilized conditions.

The receptionist showed her into a small room with a hologram of a summer meadow dominating one wall. The quiet sound of birdsong and breezes sweetened the air.

"If you'd just wait here."

"No problem." Eve waited for the door to close then, with an indulgent sigh, she lowered herself into a deeply cushioned chair. The moment she was seated, the monitor beside her blipped on, and a friendly, indulgent face that could only be a droid's beamed smiles.

"Good afternoon. Welcome to Paradise. Your beauty needs and your comfort are our only priorities. Would you like some refreshment while you wait for your personal consultant?"

"Sure. Coffee, black, coffee."

"Of course. What sort would you prefer? Press *C* on your keyboard for the list of choices."

Smothering a chuckle, Eve followed instructions. She spent the next two minutes pondering over her options, then narrowed it down to French Riviera or Caribbean Cream.

The door opened again before she could decide. Resigned, she rose and faced an elaborately dressed scarecrow.

Over his fuchsia shirt and plum-colored slacks, he wore an open, trailing smock of Paradise red. His hair, flowing back from a painfully thin face, echoed the hue of his slacks. He offered Eve a hand, squeezed gently, and stared at her out of soft doe eyes.

"I'm terribly sorry, Officer. I'm baffled."

"I want information on Sharon DeBlass." Again, Eve took out her badge and offered it for inspection.

"Yes, ah, Lieutenant Dallas. That was my understanding. You must know, of course, our client data is strictly confidential. Paradise has a reputation for discretion as well as excellence."

"And you must know, of course, that I can get a warrant, Mr.—?"

"Oh, Sebastian. Simply Sebastian." He waved a thin hand, sparkling with rings. "I'm not questioning your authority, Lieutenant. But if you could assist me, your motives for the inquiry?"

"I'm inquiring into the motives for the murder of DeBlass." She waited a beat, judged the shock that shot into his eyes and drained his face of color. "Other than that, my data is strictly confidential."

"Murder. My dear God, our lovely Sharon is dead? There must be a mistake." He all but slid into a chair, letting his head fall back and his eyes close. When the monitor offered him refreshment, he waved a hand again. Light shot from his jeweled fingers. "God, yes. I need a brandy, darling. A snifter of Trevalli."

Eve sat beside him, took out her recorder. "Tell me about Sharon."

"A marvelous creature. Physically stunning, of course, but it went deeper." His brandy came into the room on a silent automated cart. Sebastian plucked the snifter and took one deep swallow. "She had flawless taste, a generous heart, rapier wit."

He turned the doe eyes on Eve again. "I saw her only two days ago."

"Professionally?"

"She had a standing weekly appointment, half day. Every other week was a full day." He whipped out a butter yellow scarf and dabbed at his eyes. "Sharon took care of herself, believed strongly in the presentation of self."

"It would be an asset in her line of work."

"Naturally. She only worked to amuse herself. Money wasn't a particular need, with her family background. She enjoyed sex."

"With you?"

His artistic face winced, the rosy lips pursing in what could have been a pout or pain. "I was her consultant, her confidant, and her friend," Sebastian said stiffly and draped the scarf with casual flare over his left shoulder. "It would have been indiscreet and unprofessional for us to become sexual partners."

"So you weren't attracted to her, sexually?"

"It was impossible for anyone not to be attracted to her sexually. She . . ." He gestured grandly. "Exuded sex as others might exude an expensive perfume. My God." He took another shaky sip of brandy. "It's all past tense. I can't believe it. Dead. Murdered." His gaze shot back to Eve. "You said murdered."

"That's right."

"That neighborhood she lived in," he said grimly. "No one could talk to her about moving to a more acceptable location. She enjoyed living on the edge and flaunting it all under her family's aristocratic noses."

"She and her family were at odds?"

"Oh definitely. She enjoyed shocking them. She was such a free spirit, and they so . . . ordinary." He said it in a tone that indicated ordinary was more mortal a sin than murder itself. "Her grandfather continues to introduce bills that would make prostitution illegal. As if the past century hasn't proven that such matters need to be regulated for health and crime security. He also stands against procreation regulation, gender adjustment, chemical balancing, and the gun ban."

Eve's ears pricked. "The senator opposes the gun ban?"

"It's one of his pets. Sharon told me he owns a number of nasty antiques and spouts off regularly about that outdated right to bear arms business. If he had his way, we'd all be back in the twentieth century, murdering each other right and left."

"Murder still happens," Eve murmured. "Did she ever mention friends or clients who might have been dissatisfied or overly aggressive?"

"Sharon had dozens of friends. She drew people to her, like . . ." He searched for a suitable metaphor, used the corner of the scarf again. "Like an exotic and fragrant flower. And her clients, as far as I know, were all delighted with her. She screened them carefully. All of her sexual partners had to meet certain standards. Appearance, intellect, breeding, and proficiency. As I said, she enjoyed sex, in all of its many forms. She was . . . adventurous."

That fit with the toys Eve had unearthed in the apartment. The velvet handcuffs and whips, the scented oils and hallucinogens. The offerings on the two sets of colinked virtual reality headphones had been a shock even to Eve's jaded system.

"Was she involved with anyone on a personal level?"

"There were men occasionally, but she lost interest quickly. Recently she'd spoken about Roarke. She'd met him at a party and was attracted. In fact, she was seeing him for dinner the very night she came in for her consultation. She'd wanted something exotic because they were dining in Mexico."

"In Mexico. That would have been the night before last."

"Yes. She was just bubbling over about him. We did her hair in a gypsy look, gave her a bit more gold to the skin—full body work. Rascal Red on the nails, and a charming little temp tattoo of a red-winged butterfly on the left buttock. Twenty-four-hour facial cosmetics so that she wouldn't smudge. She looked spectacular," he said, tearing up. "And she kissed me and told me she just might be in love this time. 'Wish me luck, Sebastian.' She said that as she left. It was the last thing she ever said to me."

Three women learn that the heart of their historic home holds a mystery of years gone by, as #1 *New York Times* bestselling author Nora Roberts brings her In the Garden trilogy to a captivating conclusion.

A Harper has always lived at Harper House, the centuries-old mansion just outside of Memphis. And for as long as anyone alive remembers, the ghostly Harper Bride has walked the halls, singing lullabies at night . . .

Hayley Phillips came to Memphis hoping for a new start, for herself and her unborn child. She wasn't looking for a handout from her distant cousin Roz, just a job at her thriving In the Garden nursery. What she found was a home surrounded by beauty and the best friends she's ever had—including Roz's son Harper. To Hayley's chagrin, she has begun to dream about Harper—as much more than a friend . . .

If Hayley gives in to her desire, she's afraid the foundation she's built with Harper will come tumbling down. And that wouldn't be the only consequence, since her dreams are tangled up with Roz and the nursery. Hayley will have to put the past behind her to know her own heart again—and to decide whether she's willing to risk it.

Turn the page for a complete list of titles by Nora Roberts and J. D. Robb from Berkley . . .

Nora Roberts

HOT ICE
SACRED SINS
BRAZEN VIRTUE
SWEET REVENGE
PUBLIC SECRETS
GENUINE LIES
CARNAL INNOCENCE
HONEST ILLUSIONS
DIVINE EVIL
PRIVATE SCANDALS
HIDDEN RICHES
TRUE BETRAYALS
MONTANA SKY
SANCTUARY
HOMEPORT
THE REEF
RIVER'S END
CAROLINA MOON
THE VILLA
MIDNIGHT BAYOU
THREE FATES
BIRTHRIGHT
NORTHERN LIGHTS
BLUE SMOKE
ANGELS FALL
HIGH NOON
TRIBUTE
BLACK HILLS
THE SEARCH
CHASING FIRE
THE WITNESS
WHISKEY BEACH
THE COLLECTOR
TONIGHT AND ALWAYS
THE LIAR
THE OBSESSION

Series

Irish Born Trilogy
BORN IN FIRE
BORN IN ICE
BORN IN SHAME

Dream Trilogy
DARING TO DREAM
HOLDING THE DREAM
FINDING THE DREAM

Chesapeake Bay Saga
SEA SWEPT
RISING TIDES
INNER HARBOR
CHESAPEAKE BLUE

Gallaghers of Ardmore Trilogy
JEWELS OF THE SUN
TEARS OF THE MOON
HEART OF THE SEA

Three Sisters Island Trilogy
DANCE UPON THE AIR
HEAVEN AND EARTH
FACE THE FIRE

Key Trilogy
KEY OF LIGHT
KEY OF KNOWLEDGE
KEY OF VALOR

In the Garden Trilogy
BLUE DAHLIA
BLACK ROSE
RED LILY

Circle Trilogy
MORRIGAN'S CROSS
DANCE OF THE GODS
VALLEY OF SILENCE

Sign of Seven Trilogy
BLOOD BROTHERS
THE HOLLOW
THE PAGAN STONE

Bride Quartet
VISION IN WHITE
BED OF ROSES
SAVOR THE MOMENT
HAPPY EVER AFTER

The Inn BoonsBoro Trilogy
THE NEXT ALWAYS
THE LAST BOYFRIEND
THE PERFECT HOPE

The Cousins O'Dwyer Trilogy
DARK WITCH
SHADOW SPELL
BLOOD MAGICK

The Guardians Trilogy
STARS OF FORTUNE
BAY OF SIGHS
ISLAND OF GLASS

Ebooks by Nora Roberts

Cordina's Royal Family

AFFAIRE ROYALE
COMMAND PERFORMANCE
THE PLAYBOY PRINCE
CORDINA'S CROWN JEWEL

The Donovan Legacy

CAPTIVATED
ENTRANCED
CHARMED
ENCHANTED

The O'Hurleys

THE LAST HONEST WOMAN
DANCE TO THE PIPER
SKIN DEEP
WITHOUT A TRACE

Night Tales

NIGHT SHIFT
NIGHT SHADOW
NIGHTSHADE
NIGHT SMOKE
NIGHT SHIELD

The MacGregors

PLAYING THE ODDS
TEMPTING FATE
ALL THE POSSIBILITIES
ONE MAN'S ART
FOR NOW, FOREVER
REBELLION/IN FROM THE COLD
THE MACGREGOR BRIDES
THE WINNING HAND
THE MACGREGOR GROOMS
THE PERFECT NEIGHBOR

The Calhouns

COURTING CATHERINE
A MAN FOR AMANDA
FOR THE LOVE OF LILAH
SUZANNA'S SURRENDER
MEGAN'S MATE

Irish Legacy

IRISH THOROUGHBRED
IRISH ROSE
IRISH REBEL

LOVING JACK
BEST LAID PLANS
LAWLESS

BLITHE IMAGES
SONG OF THE WEST
SEARCH FOR LOVE
ISLAND OF FLOWERS
THE HEART'S VICTORY
FROM THIS DAY
HER MOTHER'S KEEPER
ONCE MORE WITH FEELING
REFLECTIONS
DANCE OF DREAMS
UNTAMED
THIS MAGIC MOMENT
ENDINGS AND BEGINNINGS
STORM WARNING
SULLIVAN'S WOMAN
FIRST IMPRESSIONS
A MATTER OF CHOICE

LESS OF A STRANGER
THE LAW IS A LADY
RULES OF THE GAME
OPPOSITES ATTRACT
THE RIGHT PATH
PARTNERS
BOUNDARY LINES
DUAL IMAGE
TEMPTATION
LOCAL HERO
THE NAME OF THE GAME
GABRIEL'S ANGEL
THE WELCOMING
TIME WAS
TIMES CHANGE
SUMMER LOVE
HOLIDAY WISHES

Nora Roberts & J. D. Robb

REMEMBER WHEN

J. D. Robb

NAKED IN DEATH
GLORY IN DEATH
IMMORTAL IN DEATH
RAPTURE IN DEATH
CEREMONY IN DEATH
VENGEANCE IN DEATH
HOLIDAY IN DEATH
CONSPIRACY IN DEATH
LOYALTY IN DEATH
WITNESS IN DEATH
JUDGMENT IN DEATH
BETRAYAL IN DEATH
SEDUCTION IN DEATH
REUNION IN DEATH
PURITY IN DEATH
PORTRAIT IN DEATH
IMITATION IN DEATH
DIVIDED IN DEATH
VISIONS IN DEATH
SURVIVOR IN DEATH
ORIGIN IN DEATH
MEMORY IN DEATH
BORN IN DEATH
INNOCENT IN DEATH
CREATION IN DEATH
STRANGERS IN DEATH
SALVATION IN DEATH
PROMISES IN DEATH
KINDRED IN DEATH
FANTASY IN DEATH
INDULGENCE IN DEATH
TREACHERY IN DEATH
NEW YORK TO DALLAS
CELEBRITY IN DEATH
DELUSION IN DEATH
CALCULATED IN DEATH
THANKLESS IN DEATH
CONCEALED IN DEATH
FESTIVE IN DEATH
OBSESSION IN DEATH
DEVOTED IN DEATH
BROTHERHOOD IN DEATH
APPRENTICE IN DEATH

Anthologies

FROM THE HEART
A LITTLE MAGIC
A LITTLE FATE

MOON SHADOWS
(with Jill Gregory, Ruth Ryan Langan, and Marianne Willman)

The Once Upon Series

(with Jill Gregory, Ruth Ryan Langan, and Marianne Willman)

ONCE UPON A CASTLE
ONCE UPON A STAR
ONCE UPON A DREAM
ONCE UPON A ROSE
ONCE UPON A KISS
ONCE UPON A MIDNIGHT

SILENT NIGHT
(with Susan Plunkett, Dee Holmes, and Claire Cross)

OUT OF THIS WORLD
(with Laurell K. Hamilton, Susan Krinard, and Maggie Shayne)

BUMP IN THE NIGHT
(with Mary Blayney, Ruth Ryan Langan, and Mary Kay McComas)

DEAD OF NIGHT
(with Mary Blayney, Ruth Ryan Langan, and Mary Kay McComas)

THREE IN DEATH

SUITE 606
(with Mary Blayney, Ruth Ryan Langan, and Mary Kay McComas)

IN DEATH

THE LOST
(with Patricia Gaffney, Mary Blayney, and Ruth Ryan Langan)

THE OTHER SIDE
(with Mary Blayney, Patricia Gaffney, Ruth Ryan Langan, and Mary Kay McComas)

TIME OF DEATH

THE UNQUIET
(with Mary Blayney, Patricia Gaffney, Ruth Ryan Langan, and Mary Kay McComas)

MIRROR, MIRROR
(with Mary Blayney, Elaine Fox, Mary Kay McComas, and R. C. Ryan)

DOWN THE RABBIT HOLE
(with Mary Blayney, Elaine Fox, Mary Kay McComas, and R. C. Ryan)

Also available . . .

THE OFFICIAL NORA ROBERTS COMPANION
(edited by Denise Little and Laura Hayden)

NORA ROBERTS

RED LILY

JOVE
New York

A JOVE BOOK
Published by Berkley
An imprint of Penguin Random House LLC
375 Hudson Street, New York, New York 10014

ISBN: 9780515139402

Jove mass-market edition / December 2005
Berkley trade paperback edition / March 2014

Printed in the United States of America
21 23 24 22

Cover design by Steven Ferlauto

To Kayla, child of my child,
and all those lights who've yet to shine
when this was written.

Grafting and budding involve joining two separate plants so that they function as one, creating a strong, healthy plant that has only the best characteristics of its two parents.

American Horticultural Society
Plant Propagation

Youth fades; love droops, the leaves of friendship fall;
a mother's secret hope outlives them all.

Oliver Wendell Holmes

PROLOGUE

Memphis

January 1893

SHE WAS DESPERATE, DESTITUTE, AND DEMENTED.

Once she'd been a beautiful woman, a clever woman with one towering ambition. Luxury. She'd achieved it, using her body to seduce and her mind to calculate. She became the mistress of one of the wealthiest and most powerful men in Tennessee.

Her house had been a showplace, decorated at her whim—and with Reginald's money. There'd been servants to do her bidding, a wardrobe to rival the most sought-after courtesan in Paris. Jewelry, amusing friends, a carriage of her own.

She'd given gay parties. She'd been envied and desired.

She, the daughter of a biddable housemaid, had all her avaricious heart had desired.

She'd had a son.

It had changed her, that life she hadn't wanted to carry

inside her. It had become the center of her world, the single thing she loved more than herself. She planned for her son, dreamed of him. Sang to him while he lay sleeping in her womb.

She delivered him into the world with pain, such pain, but with joy, too. The joy of knowing when the pain was done, she would hold her precious son in her arms.

They told her she delivered a girl child. They told her the baby was stillborn.

They lied.

She'd known it even then, even when she was wild with grief, even when she sank into the pit of despair. Even when she went mad, she knew it for a lie. Her son lived.

They'd stolen her baby from her. Held him for ransom. How could it be otherwise when she could *feel* his heart beat as truly as she felt her own?

But it hadn't been the midwife and doctor who'd taken her child. Reginald had taken what was hers, using his money to buy the silence of those who served him.

How she remembered the way he'd stood in her parlor, coming to her only after her months of grief and worry. Done with her, she thought as she buttoned the gray dress with trembling fingers. Finished now that he had what he had wanted. A son, an heir. The one thing his cold-blooded wife hadn't been able to provide.

He'd used her, then taken her single treasure, as if he had the *right*. Offering her money and a voyage to England in exchange.

He would pay, he would pay, he would pay, her mind repeated as she groomed herself. But not with money. Oh no. Not with money.

She was all but penniless now, but she would find a way. Of course she would find a way, once she had her darling James back in her arms.

The servants—rats and sinking ships—had stolen some of her jewelry. She *knew* it. She'd had to sell most of the rest, and had been cheated in the price. But what could she expect from the thin-lipped scarecrow of a jeweler? He was a man, after all.

Liars and cheats and thieves. Every one of them.

They would *all* pay before she was finished.

She couldn't find the rubies—the ruby and diamond bracelet, heart-shaped stones, blood and ice, that Reginald had given her as a token when he'd learned she was pregnant.

It was a trinket, really. Too delicate, too *small* for her tastes. But she *wanted* it, and tore through the messy maze of her bedroom and dressing area in search.

Wept like a child when she found a sapphire brooch instead. As the tears dried, as her fingers closed around the pin, she forgot the bracelet and her desperate desire for it. Forgot that she'd been searching for it. Now she smiled at the sparkle of rich blue stones. It would be enough to provide a start for her and James. She would take him away, to the country perhaps. Until she felt well again, strong again.

It was all very simple, really, she decided with a ghastly smile as she studied herself in the glass. The gray dress was quiet, dignified—the proper tone for a mother. If it hung on her, drooping at the bodice, it couldn't be helped. She had no servants now, no dressmakers to fuss with alterations. She would get her figure back once she and James found their pretty country cottage.

She'd dressed her blond hair in top curls and, with considerable regret, eschewed rouge. A quiet look was better, she concluded. A quiet look was soothing to a child.

She would simply go get him now. Go to Harper House and take back what was hers.

The drive out of the city to the grand Harper mansion was long, cold, and costly. She no longer had a carriage of her own, and soon, very soon, Reginald's agents would come back to the house and remove her as they'd threatened already.

But it was worth the price of a private carriage. How else could she bring her James back to Memphis, where she would carry him up the stairs to his nursery, lay him tenderly in his crib, and sing him to sleep?

"Lavender's blue, dilly dilly," she sang softly, twisting her thin fingers together as she stared out at the winter trees that lined the road.

She'd brought the blanket she'd ordered him from Paris, and the sweet little blue cap and booties. In her mind he was a newborn still. In her shattered mind the six months since his birth didn't exist.

The carriage rolled down the long drive, and Harper House, in all its glory, stood commanding the view.

The yellow stone, the white trim were warm and graceful against the harsh gray sky. Its three stories were proud and strong, accented by trees and shrubs, a rolling lawn.

She'd heard that peacocks had once wandered the estate, flashing their jeweled tails. But Reginald hadn't cared for their screaming calls, and had done away with them when he'd become master.

He ruled like a king. And she'd given him his prince. One day, one day, her son would usurp the father. She would rule Harper House with James. Her sweet, sweet James.

Though the windows of the great house were blank and glazed by the sun—secret eyes staring out at her—she imagined living there with her James. Saw herself tending him there, taking him for walks in the gardens, hearing his laughter ring in the halls.

One day, of course, that's how it would be. The house

was his, so in turn, the house was hers. They would live there, happily, only the two of them. As it was meant to be.

She climbed out of the carriage, a pale, thin woman in an ill-fitting gray dress, and walked slowly toward the front entrance.

Her heart thudded at the base of her throat. James was waiting for her.

She knocked, and because her hands refused to be still, folded them tightly at her waist.

The man who answered wore dignified black, and though his gaze swept over her, his face revealed nothing.

"Madam, may I assist you?"

"I've come for James."

His left eyebrow lifted, the barest fraction. "I'm sorry, Madam, there is no James in residence. If you're inquiring about a servant, the entrance is in the rear."

"James is not a servant." How *dare* he? "He is my son. He is your master. I've come for him." She stepped defiantly through the doorway. "Fetch him immediately."

"I believe you have the wrong house, Madam. Perhaps—"

"You won't keep him from me. James! James! Mama is here." She dashed toward the steps, scratched and bit when the butler took her arm.

"Danby, what is the problem here?" A woman, again in servant black, bustled down the wide hall.

"This . . . woman. She's overwrought."

"To say the least. Miss? Please, Miss, I'm Havers, the housekeeper. You must calm yourself, and tell me what is the matter."

"I've come for James." Her hands trembled as she lifted them to smooth her curls. "You must bring him to me this instant. It's time for his nap."

Havers had a kind face, and added a gentle smile. "I see. Perhaps you could sit for a moment and compose yourself."

"Then you'll bring James? You'll give me my son."

"In the parlor? There's a nice fire. It's cold today, isn't it?" The look she gave Danby had him releasing his hold. "Here now, let me show you in."

"It's a trick. Another trick." Amelia bolted for the stairs, screaming for James as she ran. She made it to the second floor before she collapsed on weak legs.

A door opened, and the mistress of Harper House stepped out. She knew it was Reginald's wife. Beatrice. She'd seen her at the theater once, and in the shops.

She was beautiful, sternly so, with eyes like chips of blue ice, a slender blade of a nose, and plump lips that were curled now in disgust. She wore a morning dress of deep rose silk, with a high collar and tightly cinched waist.

"Who is this creature?"

"I'm sorry, ma'am." Havers, swifter of foot than the butler, reached the door of the sitting room first. "She didn't give her name." Instinctively, she knelt to drape an arm around Amelia's shoulders. "She seems to be in some distress and chilled right through."

"James." Amelia reached up, and Beatrice deliberately swept her skirts aside. "I've come for James. My son."

There was a flicker over Beatrice's face before her lips clamped into a tight line. "Bring her in here." She turned, strode back into the sitting room. "And wait."

"Miss." Havers spoke quietly as she helped the trembling woman to her feet. "Don't be afraid now, no one's going to hurt you."

"Please get my baby." Her eyes pleaded as she gripped Havers's hand. "Please bring him to me."

"There now, go on in, talk to Mrs. Harper. Ma'am, shall I serve tea?"

"Certainly not," Beatrice snapped. "Shut the door."

She walked to a pretty granite hearth and turned so the

fire smoldered behind her, and her eyes stayed cold when the door shut quietly.

"You are—were," she corrected with a curl of her lips, "one of my husband's whores."

"I'm Amelia Connor. I've come—"

"I didn't ask your name. It holds no interest for me, nor do you. I had assumed that women of your ilk, those who consider themselves mistresses rather than common trollops, had enough wit and style not to step their foot into the home of what they like to call their protector."

"Reginald. Is Reginald here?" She looked around, dazedly taking in the beautiful room with its painted lamps and velvet cushions. She couldn't quite remember how she came to be here. All the frenzy and fury had drained out of her, leaving her cold and confused.

"He is not at home, and you should consider yourself fortunate. I'm fully aware of your . . . relationship, and fully aware he terminated that relationship, and that you were handsomely recompensed."

"Reginald?" She saw him, in her fractured mind, standing in front of a hearth—not this one, no not this one. Her hearth, her parlor.

Did you think I'd allow someone like you to raise my son?

Son. Her son. James. "James. My son. I've come for James. I have his blanket in the carriage. I'll take him home now."

"If you think I'll give you money to ensure your silence on this unseemly matter, you're very mistaken."

"I . . . I came for James." A smile trembled on her lips as she stepped forward, arms outstretched. "He needs his mama."

"The bastard you bore, and that was forced on me is called Reginald, after his father."

"No, I named him James. They said he was dead, but I

hear him crying." Concern covered her face as she looked around the room. "Do you hear him crying? I need to find him, sing him to sleep."

"You belong in an asylum. I could almost pity you." Beatrice stood, the fire snapping at her back. "You have no more choice in this matter than I. But I, at least, am innocent. I am his *wife.* I have borne his children, children born within the bounds of marriage. I have suffered the loss of children, and my behavior has been above reproach. I have turned a blind eye, a deaf ear on the affairs of my husband, and given him not one cause for complaint. But I gave him no son, and that, *that* is my mortal sin."

Color rushed into her cheeks now, all fury. "Do you think I want your brat foisted on me? The bastard son of a whore who will call me mother? Who will inherit this?" She threw her hands out. "All of this. I wish he had died in your womb, and you with him."

"Give him to me, give him back to me. I have his blanket." She looked down at her empty hands. "I have his blanket. I'll take him away."

"It's done. We're prisoners in the same trap, but at least you deserve the punishment. I've done nothing."

"You can't keep him; you don't want him. You can't have him." She rushed forward, eyes wild, lips peeled. And the blow cracked across her cheek, knocking her back and to the floor.

"You will leave this house." Beatrice spoke quietly, calmly, as though giving a servant some minor duty. "You will never speak of this, or I will see to it that you're put in the madhouse. My reputation will not be smeared by your ravings, I promise you. You will never come back here, never set foot in Harper House or on Harper property. You will never see the child—that will be your punishment, though it can never be enough in my mind."

"James. I will live here with James."

"You are mad," Beatrice said with the faintest hint of amusement. "Go back to your whoring. I'm sure you'll find a man who'll be happy to plant another bastard in your belly."

She strode to the door, flung it open. "Havers!" She waited, ignoring the wailing sobs behind her. "Have Danby remove this thing from the house."

BUT SHE DID COME BACK. THEY CARRIED HER OUT, ordered the driver to take her away. But she came back, in the cold night. Her mind was broken to pieces, but she managed the trip this last time, driving in a stolen wagon, her hair drenched from the rain, her white nightdress clinging to her.

She wanted to kill them. Kill them all. Slash them to ribbons, hack them to pieces. She could carry her James away then, in her bloody hands.

But they would never let her. She would never take her baby into her arms. Never see his sweet face.

Unless, unless.

She left the wagon while shadows and moonlight slid over Harper House, while the black windows gleamed and all inside slept.

The rain had stopped; the sky had cleared. Mists twined over the ground, gray snakes that parted for her bare, frozen feet. The hem of her gown trailed over the wet and mud as she wandered. Humming, singing.

They would pay. They would pay dearly.

She had been to the voodoo woman, and knew what had to be done. Knew what would be done to secure all she wanted, forever. For always.

She walked through the gardens, brittle with winter, and to the carriage house to find what she needed.

She was singing as she carried it with her, as she walked in the damp air toward the grand house with its yellow stones alit with moonlight.

"Lavender's blue," she sang. "Lavender's green."

one

Harper House
July 2005

TIRED DOWN THROUGH THE MARROW, HAYLEY YAWNED until her jaw cracked. Lily's head was heavy on her shoulder, but every time she stopped rocking, the baby would squirm and whimper, and those little fingers would clutch at the cotton tank Hayley was sleeping in.

Trying to sleep in, Hayley corrected and murmured hushing noises as she sent the rocker creaking again.

She knew it was somewhere in the vicinity of four in the morning, and she'd already been up twice before to rock and soothe her fretful daughter.

She'd tried at about the two A.M. mark to snuggle the baby into bed with her so they'd both get some sleep. But Lily would have nothing but the rocker.

So Hayley rocked and dozed, rocked and yawned, and wondered if she'd ever get eight straight again in this lifetime.

She didn't know how people did it. Especially single mothers. How did they cope? How did they stand up under all the demands on heart, mind, body—wallet?

How would she have managed it all if she'd been completely on her own with Lily? What kind of life would they have had if she had no one to help with the worry, the sheer drudgery, the fun and the foolishness? It was terrifying to think of it.

She'd been so ridiculously optimistic and confident, and *stupid,* she thought now.

Sailing along, she remembered, nearly six months pregnant, quitting her job, selling most of her things and packing up that rattletrap car to head out.

God, if she'd known then what she knew now, she'd never have done it.

So maybe it was good she hadn't known. Because she wasn't alone. Closing her eyes, she rested her cheek on Lily's soft, dark hair. She had friends—no, family—people who cared about her and Lily and were willing to help.

They didn't just have a roof over their heads, but the gorgeous roof of Harper House. She had Roz, distant cousin and then only through marriage, who'd offered her a home, a job, a chance. She had Stella, her best friend in the world to talk to, bitch to, learn from.

Both Roz and Stella had been single parents—and they'd coped, she reminded herself. They'd better than coped, and Stella had had two young boys to raise alone. Roz *three*.

And here she was wondering how she'd ever manage one, even with all the help only an offer away.

There was David, running the house, cooking the meals. And just being wonderfully David. What if she had to cook every night after work? What if she had to do all the shopping, the cleaning, the hauling, the *everything* in addition to holding up her end at her job and caring for a fourteen-month-old baby?

Thank God she didn't have to find out.

There was Logan, Stella's gorgeous new husband, who was willing to tinker around with her car when it acted up. And Stella's little guys, Gavin and Luke, who not only liked to play with Lily but were giving Hayley a hint of the sort of things she had coming in the next few years.

There was Mitch, so smart and sweet, who liked to scoop Lily up and cart her around on his shoulders while she laughed. He'd be officially here all the time now, she thought, once he and Roz got back from their honeymoon.

It had been so nice, so much fun, to watch both Stella and Roz fall in love. She'd felt a part of it all—the excitement, the changes, the expansion of her new family circle.

Of course, Roz's marriage meant Hayley'd have to stop dragging her feet on finding a place of her own. Newlyweds were entitled to privacy.

She wished there was a place close by. Even on the estate. Like the carriage house. Harper's house. She sighed a little as she rubbed a hand over Lily's back.

Harper Ashby. Rosalind Harper Ashby's firstborn, and one delicious piece of eye candy. Of course she didn't think about him that way. Much. He was a friend, a co-worker, and her baby girl's first crush. From all appearances, that love affair was mutual.

She yawned again, lulled like the baby by the rhythm of the rocking and the early-morning quiet.

Harper was, well, just flat-out amazing with Lily. Patient and funny, easy and loving. Secretly she thought of him as Lily's surrogate father—without the benefits of smoochies with Lily's mother.

Sometimes she played pretend—and what was the harm in that?—and the surrogate part of father didn't apply. The smoochies did. After all, what red-blooded American girl—currently very sex-deprived girl—wouldn't fantasize now and again about the tall, dark, and ridiculously handsome type, especially when he came with a killer grin, heart-melting brown eyes, and a pinchable butt?

Not that she'd ever pinched it. But in theory.

Plus he was completely smart. He knew everything there was to know about plants and flowers. She loved to watch him working in the grafting house at In the Garden. The way his hands held a knife or tied raffia.

He was teaching her, and she appreciated it. Appreciated it too much to indulge herself and take a nice hungry bite out of him.

But imagining doing it didn't hurt a thing.

She eased the rocker to a stop, held her breath and waited. Lily's back continued to rise and fall steadily under her hand.

Thank God.

She got up slowly, moving toward the crib with the stealth and purpose of a woman making a prison break. With her arms aching, her head fuzzy with fatigue, she leaned over the crib and gently, inch by inch laid Lily on the mattress.

Even as she draped the blanket over her, Lily began to stir. Her head popped up, and she began wailing.

"Oh, Lily, please, come on, baby." Hayley patted, rubbed, swaying on her feet. "Ssh now, come on. Give your mama a little break."

The patting seemed to work—as long as she kept her hand on Lily's back, the little head stayed down. So Hayley sank to the floor, stuck her arm through the crib slats. And patted. And patted.

And drifted off to sleep.

* * *

IT WAS THE SINGING THAT WOKE HER. HER ARM WAS asleep, and stayed that way when her eyes opened. The room was cold; the section of the floor where she sat beside the crib a square of ice. Her arm prickled from shoulder to fingertip as she shifted to keep a protective hand on Lily's back.

The figure in the gray dress sat in the rocker, softly singing the old-fashioned lullaby. Her eyes met Hayley's, but she continued to sing, continued to rock.

The jolt of shock cleared the fuzziness from Hayley's head, and had her heart taking one hard leap into her throat.

Just what did you say to a ghost you hadn't seen for several weeks? she wondered. Hey, how are you? Welcome home? Just what was the proper response, especially when the ghost in question was totally whacked?

Hayley's skin was slicked with cold when she pushed slowly to her feet so she could stand between the rocker and the crib. Just in case. Because it felt as if a few thousand needles were lodged in her arm, she cradled it against her body, rubbing it briskly.

Note all the details, she reminded herself. Mitch would want all the details.

She looked pretty calm for a psychotic ghost, Hayley decided. Calm and sad, the way she had the first time Hayley had seen her. But she'd also seen her with crazed, bulging eyes.

"Um. She had to get some shots today. Inoculations. She's always fussy the night after she gets them. But I think she's settled down now. In time to get up again in a couple of hours, so she'll probably be cranky for the babysitter until she gets her nap. But . . . but she should sleep now, so you could go."

The figure faded away seconds before the singing.

* * *

DAVID FIXED HER BLUEBERRY PANCAKES FOR BREAK-fast. She'd told him not to cook for her or Lily while Roz and Mitch were gone, but he always did. Since he looked so cute fussing in the kitchen, she didn't try very hard to discourage him.

Besides, the pancakes were awesome.

"You've been looking a little peaky." David gave her cheek a pinch; then repeated the gesture on Lily to make her giggle.

"Haven't been sleeping much lately. Had a visitor last night."

She shook her head when his eyebrows rose, and his mouth curved into a leer. "Not a man—too sad for my bad luck. Amelia."

Amusement faded immediately, replaced by concern as he slid into the breakfast nook across from her. "Was there trouble? Are you all right?"

"She was just sitting in the rocker, singing. And when I told her Lily was fine, that she could go, she did. It was completely benign."

"Maybe she's settled down again. We can hope. Have you been worried about that?" He took a careful study of her face, noted the smudges under the soft blue eyes, the pallor beneath the carefully applied blush on her cheeks. "Is that why you haven't been sleeping?"

"Some, I guess. Things were pretty wild around here for a few months. Our gooses were constantly getting bumped. Now this lull. It's almost creepier."

"You've got Daddy David right down here." He reached over to pat her hand, his long, concert pianist's fingers giving it a little extra rub. "And Roz and Mitch will be back today. The house won't feel so big and empty."

She let out a long breath, relieved. "You felt that way, too. I didn't want to say, didn't want you to feel like you weren't enough company or something. 'Cause you are."

"You, too, my treasure. But we've gotten spoiled, haven't we? Had a houseful for a year around here." He glanced toward the empty seats at the table. "I miss those kids."

"Aw, you softie. We still see them, everybody, all the time, but it's weird, having everything so quiet."

As if she understood, Lily launched her sip-cup so that it slapped the center island and thudded on the floor.

"Atta girl," David told her.

"And you know what else?" Hayley rose to retrieve the cup. She was tall and lanky, and much to her disappointment, her breasts had reverted to their pre-pregnancy size. She thought of them as an A-minus cup. "I think I'm getting in some sort of mood. I don't mean rut, exactly, because I love working at the nursery, and I was just thinking last night—when Lily woke up for the millionth time—how lucky I am to be here, to be able to have all these people in our lives."

She spread her arms, let them fall. "But, I don't know, David, I feel sort of . . . blah."

"Need shopping therapy."

She grinned and got a washcloth to wipe Lily's syrupy face. "It is the number-one cure for almost everything. But I think I want a change. Something bigger than new shoes."

Deliberately, he widened his eyes, let his jaw go slack. "There's something bigger?"

"I think I'm going to cut my hair. Do you think I should cut my hair?"

"Hmm." He cocked his head, studied her with his handsome blue eyes. "It's gorgeous hair, that glossy mahogany. But I absolutely loved it the way you wore it when you first moved here."

"Really?"

"All those different lengths. Tousled, casual, kicky. Sexy."

"Well . . ." She ran her hand down it. She'd grown it out, nearly to her shoulders. An easy length to pull back for work or motherhood. And maybe that was just the problem. She'd started taking the easy way because she'd stopped finding the time or making the effort to worry about how she looked.

She wiped Lily off, freed her from the high chair so she could wander around the kitchen. "Maybe I will then. Maybe."

"And toss in the new shoes, sweetie. They never fail."

IN HIGH SUMMER BUSINESS SLOWED AT THE GARDEN center. It never trickled down too far at In the Garden, but in July, the heady late winter through spring rush was long over. Wet heat smothered west Tennessee, and only the most avid of gardeners would suffer through it to pump new life into their beds.

Taking advantage of it, and her mood, Hayley wheedled a salon appointment, and an extra hour off from Stella.

When she drove back into work after her extended lunch break, it was with a new do, *two* new pair of shoes, and a much happier attitude.

Trust David, she decided.

She loved In the Garden. Most days, she didn't feel as if she was going to work at all. There couldn't be a better quality in a job than that, in her opinion.

She enjoyed just looking at the pretty white building that looked more like someone's well-tended home than a business, with the seasonal beds spreading out from its porch, and the pots full of colorful blooms by its door.

She liked the industry across the wide gravel lot—the

stacks of peat and mulch, the pavers and landscape timbers. The greenhouses that were full of plants and promises, the storage buildings.

When it was busy with customers, winding along the paths, pulling wagons or flatbeds full of plants and pots—everyone full of news or plans—it was more like a small village than a retail space.

And she was a part of it all.

She stepped in, and did a turn for Ruby, the white-haired clerk who manned the counter.

"Don't you look sassy," Ruby commented.

"I feel sassy." She ran her fingers through her short shaggy hair, then let it fall again. "I haven't done anything new with my hair in a *year.* More. I almost forgot what it was like to sit in a beauty parlor and have somebody do me."

"Things do slide with a new baby. How's our best girl doing?"

"Fussy last night after her shots. But she bounced back this morning. My butt was dragging. Pumped now though." To prove it, she flexed her arms to show little bumps of biceps.

"Good thing. Stella wants everything watered, and I do mean everything. And we're waiting on a big delivery of new planters. They'll need to be stickered and shelved once they come in."

"I'm your girl."

She started outside in the thick, drowsy heat, soaking the bedding plants, the annuals and perennials who'd yet to find a home. They made her think of those awkward kids in school who never got picked for the team. As a result, she had a soft spot for them and wished she had a place where she could dig them into the soil, let them bloom, let them find their potential.

One day she would have a place. She'd plant gardens,

take what she'd learned here and put it to use. Make something beautiful, something special. There would have to be lilies, naturally. Red lilies, like the ones Harper brought to her when she was in labor with Lily. A big, splashy pool of red lilies, bold and fragrant that would come back year after year and remind her how lucky she was.

Sweat trickled down the back of her neck, and water dampened her canvas skids. The gentle spray annoyed the gang of bees covering the sedum. So, come back when I'm finished, she thought as they flew off with an annoyed buzz. We're all after the same thing here.

She moved slowly, half dreaming, down the tables holding the picked-over stock.

And if one day she had a garden, and there was Lily playing on the grass. With a puppy, she decided. There should be a puppy, all fat and soft and frisky. If she was able to have all that, couldn't she add a man? Someone who loved her and Lily, someone funny and smart who made her heart beat just a little faster when he looked at her?

He could be handsome. What was the point of a fantasy if the guy wasn't great-looking? Tall, he would be tall, with good shoulders and long legs. Brown eyes, deep delicious brown, and lots of thick dark hair she could get her hands into. Good cheekbones, the kind you just wanted to nibble your way along until you got to that strong, sexy mouth. And then—

"Jesus, Hayley, you're drowning that coreopsis."

She jerked, whipping the sprayer, then on a little yip of distress whipped it back again. But not before the water hit Harper dead-on.

Gut shot, she thought, torn between embarrassment and inappropriate giggles. He looked down at his soaked shirt, his jeans with a kind of grim resignation.

"Got a license for that thing?"

"I'm sorry! I'm so sorry. But you shouldn't sneak up behind me that way."

"I didn't sneak anywhere. I walked."

His voice was aggravated, but so Memphian, she thought, where she knew hers hit twang when she was excited or upset. "Well, walk louder next time. I really am sorry though. I guess my mind was wandering."

"This kind of heat, it's easy for the mind to wander, then lie down to take a nap." He pulled the wet shirt away from his belly. His eyes crinkled at the corners when he narrowed them. "What did you do to your hair?"

"What?" Instinctively she reached up, pulled her fingers through it. "I had it cut. Don't you like it?"

"Yeah, sure. It's fine."

Her finger itched on the trigger of the sprayer. "Please, stop. That kind of flattery'll just go to my head."

He smiled at her. He had such a great smile—sort of slow, so that it shifted the angles of his face and lit up in those deep, dark brown eyes—she nearly forgave him.

"I'm heading home, for a bit anyway. Mama's back."

"They're back? How are they? Did they have a good time? And you don't know yet because you haven't been home. Tell them I can't wait to see them, and that everything's fine over here, and Roz shouldn't worry and come over and start in working when she's barely walked in the door. And—"

He cocked his hip, hooked a thumb in the front pocket of his ancient jeans. "Should I be writing any of this down?"

"Oh, go on then." But she laughed as she waved him away. "I'll tell them myself."

"See you later."

He walked off, the man of her daydreams, dripping a little.

She really had to get her mind off Harper, she warned herself. Get it off and keep it off. He wasn't for her, and she knew it. She walked over to give the potted shrubs and climbers a good soak.

She wasn't even sure she wanted anybody to be for her—right now, anyway. Lily was number one priority, and after Lily came her job. She wanted her baby happy, healthy, and secure. And she wanted to learn more, do more at the nursery. The more she learned, the less it would be a job, and the more it would be a career.

Pulling her weight was fine, but she wanted to do more.

After Lily, her work, and the family she'd made here, came the fascinating and spooky task of identifying Amelia, the Harper Bride—and laying her to rest.

Most of that fell to Mitch. He was the genealogist, and along with Stella the most organized mind of the bunch. And wasn't it cool that he and Roz had found each other, fallen in love, after Roz had hired him to research the family tree to try to find where Amelia fit in? Not that Amelia had cared for the falling-in-love part. Boy, she'd been a stone bitch about it.

She might get mean again, too, Hayley thought. Now that they were married and Mitch was living at Harper House. She'd been quiet for a while, but it didn't mean she'd stay quiet.

If and when the whirlwind resumed, Hayley intended to be ready for it.

two

HAYLEY WALKED INTO HARPER HOUSE—AH, THE blessed *cool*—with Lily on her hip. She set Lily on her feet, then dumped her purse and the diaper bag on the bottom step so they'd be handy for her to carry up. Up's where she wanted to go. She wanted to shower for, oh, two or three days ought to do it, then drink an ice cold beer, straight down.

But before she did anything, she wanted Roz.

Even as she thought it, Roz came out of the parlor. She and Lily gave mutual cries of delight. Lily changed direction, and as she headed toward Roz, Roz closed the distance and scooped her up.

"There's my sweet potato." She gave Lily a fierce hug, nuzzled her neck, then with a grin for Hayley, looked back at the baby and listened with amazement to the excited and incomprehensible babbling. "Why, I can't believe all that happened in just one week! Don't know what I'd do if you weren't here to catch me up on all the local gossip." She grinned at Hayley again. "And how's your mama?"

"I'm fine. I'm great." Hayley dashed over to lock them both in a hug. "Welcome home. We missed you."

"Good. I like being missed. And look at this." She flipped her fingers over Hayley's hair.

"I just did it. Just today. Woke up with a bug up my butt. Oh, you look so beautiful."

"Listen to you."

But it was true, always true. And now a weeklong honeymoon in the Caribbean had added a dewy glow to innate beauty. Sun had turned the creamy skin pale gold so that Roz's long, dark eyes seemed even deeper. The short, straight hair capped a face with the sort of classic, timeless beauty Hayley knew she could only envy.

"I like that cut," Roz commented. "It looks so young and easy."

"Gave my morale a boost. Lily and I had a rough night. She got her shots yesterday."

"Mmm." Roz gave Lily an extra hug. "No fun there. Let's see if we can make up for it. Come on in here, baby girl," Roz said, snuggling Lily again as she went back in the parlor. "See what we got you."

The first thing Hayley saw was a life-sized doll with a mop of red hair and a sweet and foolish smile.

"Oh, she's so cute! And almost as big as Lily."

"That was the idea. Mitch spotted her before I did, and nothing would do but we bring her home to Lily. What do you think, sweetie?"

Lily poked the doll in the eye a couple of times, pulled its hair, then was happy to sit on the floor and get acquainted.

"It's the kind of doll she'll name in a year or so, then keep in her room till college. Thank you, Roz."

"We're not done. There was this little shop, and they had the most adorable dresses." She began to pull them out of the bag while Hayley goggled. Soft smocked cotton, ruched lace, embroidered denim. "And look at these rompers. Who could resist?"

"They're wonderful. They're beautiful. You'll spoil her."

"Well, of course."

"I don't know what to . . . She doesn't have any grand—anybody to spoil her like this."

Roz arched a brow, folded a romper. "You can say the G word, Hayley. I won't faint in horror. I like to think of myself as her honorary grandmother."

"I'm so lucky. We're so lucky."

"Then why are you tearing up?"

"I don't know. All this stuff's been going on in my head lately." She sniffled, heeled a hand under her eyes to rub away the dampness. "Where I am, how I got here, how it might've been for us if I'd been on my own with Lily the way I thought I'd be."

"Might've beens don't get you very far."

"I know. I'm just so glad I came to you. I was thinking last night that I should start looking for a place."

"A place to what?"

"Live."

"Something wrong with this place?"

"It's the most beautiful house I've ever seen." And here she was, Hayley Phillips from Little Rock, living in it, living in a house that had a parlor furnished with beautiful antiques and deep rich cushions, with generous windows that opened up to acres of more beauty.

"I was thinking I should look for a place, but I don't want to. At least, well, not right now." She looked down, watched Lily struggle to carry the doll around the room. "But I want you to tell me, and I know we're good enough friends that you will, when you want me to start looking."

"All right. That settled then?"

"Sure."

"Don't you want to see what we brought you?"

"I got something, too?" Hayley's lake blue eyes went bright with anticipation. "I *love* presents. I'm not ashamed to say it."

"I hope you like this one." She took a box out of the bag, offered it.

Wasting no time, Hayley took off the top. "Oh, oh! They're gorgeous."

"I thought the red coral would suit you best."

"I *love* them!" She took the earrings out of the box and holding them to her ears rushed to one of the antique mirrors on the wall to study how they looked. The trios of delicate and exotic red balls swayed from a glittery triangle of silver. "They're wonderful. God, I have something from Aruba. I can't believe it."

She dashed back to give a chuckling Roz a hug. "They're just beautiful. Thank you, thank you. I can hardly wait to wear them."

"You can give them a test drive tonight if you want. Stella, Logan, and the boys will be over. David tells me we're having a welcome-home dinner."

"Oh, but you'll be tired."

"Tired? What am I, eighty? I just got back from vacation."

"Honeymoon," Hayley corrected with a smirk. "Bet you didn't get a lot of rest either."

"We slept in every morning, you smart-ass."

"In that case, we'll party. Lily and I'll go upstairs and get ourselves all clean and pretty."

"I'll give you a hand up with all these things."

"Thanks. Roz?" Everything inside her had settled down to a glow. "I'm really glad you're home."

* * *

IT WAS SO MUCH FUN TO PUT ON HER NEW EARRINGS, to dress Lily in one of her pretty new outfits, to fuss a little over both herself and her daughter. She shook her head just for the pleasure of feeling the way her hair fell and her earrings swung.

There now, she thought, not feeling dull and blah anymore. Since she was feeling celebratory, she capped it off with new shoes. The thin-heeled strappy black sandals were impractical and unnecessary. Which made them perfect.

"And they were on sale," she told Lily. "Gotta say, they've got to be more fun than Prozac or whatever."

It felt great to wear a dress—a short dress—and sexy shoes. A new haircut. Red lipstick.

She gave a turn for the mirror and struck a pose. Maybe she had a skinny build, but there was nothing much she could do about that. Still, she wore clothes pretty well, if she did say so. Kind of like a clothes hanger. Add new hair, new earrings, new shoes, and you had something.

"Ladies and gentlemen, I do believe I'm back."

DOWNSTAIRS, HARPER WAS SPRAWLED IN A CHAIR, sipping a beer and watching the way Mitch touched his mother—her hair, her arm—while they related some of the highlights of their trip for Logan and Stella and the boys.

He'd heard some of it already when he'd buzzed home for an hour that afternoon. He wasn't really listening. He was just watching, and thinking it was good, it was time his mother had someone so obviously besotted with her.

He was happy for her—and relieved. No matter how

well his mother could take care of herself, and God knew she could do just that, it was a comfort to know she had a smart, able man at her side.

After what had happened last spring, if Mitch hadn't moved in, he'd have done so himself. And that might've been a little sticky with Hayley living there.

It was more . . . comfortable, he decided, for everybody, if he continued to live in the carriage house. It might not have been much distance geographically, but psychologically it did the job.

"I told him he was crazy," Roz continued, gesturing with her wine in one hand, patting the other on Mitch's thigh. "Windsurfing? Why in God's name would we want to teeter around on a little hunk of wood with a sail attached? But he just had to try it."

"I tried it once." Stella sat, her curling mass of red hair spilling over her shoulders. "Spring break in college. It was fun once I got the hang of it."

"So I hear." Mitch's mutter had Roz grinning.

"He'd get up on the thing, and in two seconds, splash. Get up, and wait, I think he's got it. Splash."

"I had a defective board," Mitch claimed, and poked Roz in the ribs.

"Of course you did." Roz rolled her eyes. "One thing you can say about our Mitchell is he's game. I don't know how many times he hauled himself out of the drink and back on that board."

"Six hundred and fifty-two."

"How about you?" Logan, big and built and rugged beside Stella, gestured toward Roz with his beer.

"Oh, well, I don't like to brag," Roz said and examined her fingernails.

"Yes, she does." Mitch gulped down club soda, stretched out his long, long legs. "Oh, yes, she does."

"But I enjoyed the experience quite a lot."

"She just . . ." Mitch sailed his hand through the air to illustrate. "Sailed off as if she'd been born on one of the damn things."

"We Harpers do tend to have excellent athletic abilities and superior balance."

"But she doesn't like to brag," Mitch pointed out, then glanced over at the click of heels on hardwood.

Harper did the same, and felt his reputed superior balance falter.

She looked frigging amazing. The skinny little red dress, the mile-high shoes combined to make her legs look endless. The sort of legs a man could imagine cruising over for miles and miles. Her hair was so damn sexy that way, and her mouth was all hot and red.

She had a baby on her hip, he reminded himself. He shouldn't be thinking about what he'd like to do to that mouth, that body when she was carrying Lily. It had to be wrong.

Across the room, Logan let out a long, low whistle that had Hayley's face lighting up.

"Hello, beautiful. You look good enough to eat. You look good, too, Hayley."

At that, she gave one of those husky rolls of laughter, and hip-swayed over to drop Lily in Logan's lap. "Just for that."

"How about some wine?" Roz offered.

"To tell you the truth, I've been wanting a cold beer."

"I'll get it." Harper all but sprang out of his chair, and was heading out of the parlor before she could respond. He hoped the trip to the kitchen and back would bring his blood pressure back to normal.

She was a cousin, sort of, he reminded himself. And an employee. His mother's houseguest. A mother. Any one of those reasons meant hands-off. Tally them up, and it put Hayley way off-limits. Added to that, she didn't think of him that way, not even close.

A guy made a move on a woman under those circumstances, he was just asking to screw up a nice, pleasant friendship.

He got out a beer, got out a pilsner. As he was pouring, he heard the squeal, and the rapid clip of heels on wood. He glanced over and spotted Lily running, with Hayley scrambling behind her.

"She want a beer, too?"

With a laugh, Hayley started to scoop Lily up, only to have her baby girl go red in the face and arch away. "You. Like always."

"That's my girl." He hoisted her up, gave her a toss. The mutinous little face went sugar sweet and bright with smiles. Pretending to pout, Hayley finished pouring her beer.

"Shows where I am in her pecking order."

"You got the beer, I got the kid."

Lily wrapped an arm around Harper's neck, dipped her head to rest it on his cheek. Hayley nodded, lifted her glass. "Looks like."

IT WAS WONDERFUL TO HAVE EVERYONE AROUND THE table again, the whole Harper House family, as Hayley thought of them, sitting together, diving into David's honey-glazed ham.

She'd missed having a big family. Growing up, it had been just Hayley and her father. Not that she'd felt deprived, she thought, not in any way. She and her father had been a team, a unit, and he was—had been—the kindest, funniest, warmest man she'd ever known.

But she'd missed having meals like this, a full table, lots

of voices—even the arguments and drama that went hand-in-hand in her mind with big families.

Lily would grow up with that, because Roz had welcomed them. So Lily would have a lifetime of meals like this one, full of aunts and uncles and cousins. Grandparents, she thought, stealing a glance toward Roz and Mitch. And when Roz's other sons, or Mitch's son, came to visit, it would just add to the rich family stew.

One day, Roz's sons, and Mitch's Josh, would get married. Probably have a herd of kids between them.

She shifted her gaze toward Harper and ordered herself to ignore the little ache that came from thinking of him married, making babies with some woman whose face she couldn't see.

Of course, she'd be beautiful, that was a given. Probably blonde and built and blue-blooded. The bitch.

Whoever she turned out to be, whatever she looked like or *was* like, Hayley determined she'd make friends. Even if it killed her.

"Something wrong with the potatoes?" David murmured beside her.

"Hmm. No. They're awesome."

"Just wondered why you looked like you were forcing down some bad-tasting medicine, sugar."

"Oh, just thought about something I'm going to have to do, and won't like. Life's full of them. But that doesn't include eating these potatoes. In fact, I was wondering if you could show me how to cook some things. I can cook pretty good. Daddy and I split that chore, and we were both okay with the basics—I could even get a little fancy now and then. But Lily's growing up on your cooking, so I ought to be able to fix it for her myself when need be."

"Hmm, a kitchen apprentice. One I can mold into my own likeness. Love to."

When Lily began to drop the bits of food still on her tray delicately to the floor, Hayley popped up. "Guess who's done."

"Gavin, why don't you and Luke take Lily outside and play awhile?"

"Oh." Hayley shook her head at Stella's suggestion. "I don't want them to have to mind her."

"We can do it," Gavin piped up. "She likes to chase the ball and the Frisbee."

"Well . . ." At nearly ten, Gavin was tall for his age. And at just-turned-eight, Luke was right behind him. They could—and had—handled Lily at play on the backyard grass. "I don't mind if you don't, and she'd love it. But when you're tired of her, you just bring her back."

"And as a reward, ice cream sundaes later."

David's announcement got a couple of cheers.

When playtime was over, the sundaes devoured, Hayley carried Lily up to get her ready for bed, and Stella brought the boys up to the sitting room they'd once shared to watch television.

"Roz and Mitch want an Amelia talk," Stella told her. "I didn't know if you'd gotten the word."

"No, but that's fine. I'll be down as soon as she is."

"Need any help?"

"Not this time, but thanks. Her eyes are already drooping."

It was nice, she thought, to hear the muted crash and boom of some sort of space war on the sitting room television and the bright chatter of the boys' commentary on the action. She'd missed those noises since Stella had gotten married.

She settled Lily in for the night—hopefully—checked the monitor and the night-light. Then left the door ajar as she returned downstairs.

She found the adults in the library, the most usual meeting spot for ghost talk. The sun had yet to set, so the room was washed with light that was just hinting of pink. Through the glass, the summer gardens were ripe, sumptuous, spears of lavender foxglove dancing over pools of white impatiens, brightened with elegant drips of hot-pink fuschia.

She spotted the soft, fuzzy green of betony, the waxy charm of begonias, the inverted cups of purple coneflowers with their prickly brown heads.

She'd missed her evening walk with Lily, she remembered, and promised herself she'd take her daughter out for a stroll through the gardens the next day.

Out of habit, she crossed to the table where a baby monitor stood beside a vase of poppy-red lilies.

Once she was assured it was on, she tuned in to the rest of the room.

"Now that we're all here," Mitch began, "I thought I should bring you up-to-date."

"You're not going to break my heart and tell us you researched during your honeymoon," David put in.

"Your heart's safe, but we did manage to find some time to discuss various theories here and there. The thing is, I had a couple of e-mails from our contact in Boston. The descendant of the Harper housekeeper during Reginald and Beatrice's reign here."

"She find something?" Harper had chosen the floor rather than one of the seats, and now folded himself from prone to sitting.

"I've been feeding her what we know, and told her what we found in Beatrice Harper's journal, regarding your great-grandfather, Harper. The fact that he wasn't her son, but in fact Reginald's son with his mistress—whom we have to assume was Amelia. She hasn't had any luck, yet, digging up any letters or diaries from Mary Havers—the housekeeper. She has found photographs, and is getting us copies."

Hayley looked toward the second level of the library, to the table loaded with books, Mitch's laptop. And the board beside it that was full of photos and copies of letters and journal entries. "What will that do for us?"

"The more visuals, the better," he said. "She's also been talking to her grandmother, who's not doing very well, although she does have some lucid moments. The grandmother claims to recall her mother and a cousin who also worked here at the time talk about their days at Harper House. Lots of talk about the parties and the work. She also recalls her cousin talking about the young master, that's how she referred to Reginald Jr. And saying the stork got rich delivering that one. That her mother told her to hush, that blood money and curses aside, the child was innocent. When she asked what she meant, her mother wouldn't speak of it, except to say she'd done her duty by the Harper family, and would have to live with it. But the happiest day of her life had been when she'd walked out the door of this house for the last time."

"She knew my grandfather had been taken from his mother." Roz reached down, touched a hand to Harper's shoulder. "And if this woman is remembering correctly, it sounds as though Amelia wasn't willing to give him up."

"Blood money and curses," Stella repeated. "Who was paid, and what was cursed?"

"There would have been a doctor or a midwife, perhaps both, attending Amelia during the birth." Mitch spread his hands. "Almost certainly they'd have been paid off. Some of the servants here might have been bribed."

"I know that's awful," Hayley said. "But you wouldn't call that blood money, would you? Hush money more like."

"Bull's-eye," Mitch told her. "If there was blood money, where was the blood?"

"Amelia's death." Logan shifted, leaned forward. "She haunts here, so she died here. You haven't been able to find any record of that, so we have to assume it was covered up. Easiest way to cover something up is money."

"I agree." Stella nodded. "But how did she get here? There's no mention of Amelia in any of Beatrice's journals. No mention of Reginald's mistress by name, or of her coming to Harper House. She wrote about the baby, and how she felt about Reginald bringing him here, expecting her to pretend she'd given birth to him. Wouldn't she have been just as outraged, and written of that, if he'd established Amelia in the house?"

"He wouldn't have." Hayley spoke quietly. "From everything we've learned about him, he wouldn't have brought a woman of her class, one he considered a convenience, a means to an end, into the house he was so proud of. He wouldn't have wanted her around his son—the one he was passing as legitimate. It'd be a constant reminder."

"That's a good point." Harper stretched out his legs, crossed them at the ankles. "But if we believe she died here, then we have to believe she *was* here."

"Maybe she passed as a servant," Stella suggested. She gestured, and her wedding ring glinted gold in the softening light. "If Beatrice didn't know her, what she looked like, Amelia might have managed to get a position in the house, so she'd be close to her son. She sings to the children of the house, she's obsessed with the children here, in her way. Wouldn't she have been even more so with her own child?"

"It's a possibility," Mitch commented. "We haven't found her through the household records, but it's a possibility."

"Or she came here to try to get him." Roz looked at Stella, at Hayley. "A mother, frantic, desperate, and not completely balanced. She sure as hell didn't go crazy after she died. I'm not willing to stretch credulity that far. Doesn't it play that she would have come here, and something went terribly wrong? We have to consider that if she came here, she might have been murdered. Blood money to cover up the crime."

"So the house is cursed." Harper lifted a shoulder. "And she haunts it until, what, she's avenged? How?"

"Maybe just recognized," Hayley corrected. "Given her due, I guess. You're her blood," she said to Harper. "Maybe it's going to take Harper blood to put her to rest."

"I have to say that sounds logical." David gave a little shudder. "And creepy."

"We're a bunch of rational adults sitting around talking about a ghost," Stella reminded him. "It doesn't get much more creepy."

"I saw her last night."

At Hayley's statement all eyes turned to her. "And you didn't tell us?" Harper demanded.

"I told David this morning," she shot back. "And I'm telling everybody now. I didn't want to say anything in front of the kids."

"Let's get this on record." Mitch rose to go to the table for his tape recorder.

"It wasn't that much of a big."

"We agreed last spring after the last two violent apparitions, that everything goes on the record." He came back to sit again, and set the recorder on the table. "Tell us."

Talking on tape made her feel self-conscious, but she related everything.

"I hear her singing sometimes, but usually when I go in to check, she's gone. You know she's been there. Sometimes I hear her in the boys' room—Gavin's and Luke's old room. Sometimes she's crying. And once I thought . . ."

"Thought what?" Mitch prompted.

"I thought I might've seen her walking outside. The night y'all left on your honeymoon, after we had the wedding party here? I woke up—had a little more wine than I should, I guess—and I had a little headache. So I took some aspirin, checked on Lily. I thought I saw someone, out the window. There was enough moonlight that I could make out the blond hair, the white dress. It appeared like she was going toward the carriage house. But when I opened the doors, to go out on the terrace and get a better look, she was gone."

"Didn't we have an agreement, starting after Mama finally decided to clue us in about nearly being drowned in the bathtub, that we put everything on record?" Anger simmered in Harper's voice. "We don't wait a damn week to make an announcement."

"Harper," Roz said dryly. "That horse is dead. Don't start beating it again."

"We had an agreement."

"I didn't know for sure." Hayley's back went up, and it reflected in her tone as she glared down at Harper. "I still don't. Just because I thought I saw a woman walking toward your place didn't mean she was a ghost. Could just as likely—more likely—have been flesh and blood. What was I supposed to do, Harper, call you over at the carriage house and ask if you were getting a bootie call?"

"Jesus Christ."

"Well, there you are." Pleased, she nodded decisively. "It's not like you never have female company over there."

"Fine, fine. Just FYI, I didn't have female company—flesh and blood variety—that night. Next time, follow through."

"Class," Mitch said mildly, and gave a professorial tap of pencil on notebook. "Can you tell us any more about what you saw, Hayley?"

"Honestly, it was only a few seconds. I was just standing there, hoping the aspirin would kick in before morning, and I caught a movement. I saw a woman—a lot of blond or light hair, and she was wearing white. My first thought was Harper got lucky."

"Oh, man," was Harper's muttered comment.

"Then I thought about Amelia, but when I went out to see better, she was gone. I only mention it because if it was her, and I guess it was, that's twice I've seen her in about a week. And that's a lot for me."

"You were the only woman in the house during that week," Logan pointed out. "She's been more likely to show herself to women."

"That makes sense." And made her feel better.

"Added to that, it was the night after Mitch and I were married," Roz said. "She'd have been miffed."

"And it's the second time we've got a firsthand report of her walking toward the carriage house. There's something there," Mitch said to Harper.

"She's not letting me know about it. So far."

"Meanwhile we keep looking. We believe she lived in this area, so our best bet is Reginald kept her in one of his properties." Mitch lifted his hands. "I'm still pursuing that avenue."

"If we find out her name, her whole name," Hayley asked him, "would you be able to research her the way you did the Harper family?"

"It'd give me a start."

"Maybe she'll tell us, if we just find the right way to ask. Maybe . . ." She trailed off when singing came through the monitor. “She’s with Lily, and she’s early tonight. I’m just going to go up and check.”

“I’ll go with you.” Harper got to his feet.

She didn’t argue. Even after more than a year, the sound of that sad voice sent a chill up her spine. As was her habit, she’d flicked lights on in her wing so she wouldn’t have to come back up in the dark. They reassured her now, as the sun was nearly set, as did the sounds of Luke and Gavin playing in the sitting room.

“You know, if you’re uneasy being over here alone, you could move into the other wing, closer to Mama and Mitch.”

“Just what the newly married couple need. Me and a baby as chaperones. Anyway, I’m mostly used to it. She’s not stopping.” She dropped her voice to a whisper. “She almost always stops before I get to the door.”

Instinctively she reached for Harper’s hand as she eased open the door she always left off the latch.

It was cold, but she’d expected that. Even after Amelia was gone, the chill would linger. Yet Lily was never disturbed by it. Her breath puffed out, a little startled cloud when she heard the distinctive creak of the rocker.

That was a new one, Hayley thought. Oh boy.

She sat in the rocker, wearing her gray dress. Her hands lay quiet in her lap as she sang. Her voice was pretty, unschooled but light and tuneful. Comforting, as a voice singing lullabies should be.

But when she turned her head, when she looked toward the door, Hayley’s blood ran as cold as the air in the room.

It wasn’t a smile on her face, but a grimace. Her eyes bulged, and were rimmed with violent red.

This is what they do. This is what they give.

As she spoke—thought—the form began to disintegrate. Flesh melted away to bone until what sat in the chair was a skeleton that rocked in rags.

Then even that was gone.

"Please tell me you saw that." Hayley's voice trembled. "Heard that."

"Yeah." With his hand firm on hers, he drew Hayley across the room to the crib. "Warmer here. Feel it? It's warm around the crib."

"She's never done anything to scare Lily. Still, I don't want to leave, go down again. I'd just feel better if I stayed close tonight. You can tell the others what happened?"

"I can bunk up here tonight. Take one of the guest rooms."

"It's all right." She arranged Lily's blanket more securely. "We'll be all right."

He tugged her hand, gestured so that she went back out into the hall with him. "That was a first, right?"

"A definite first for me. It's going to give me nightmares."

"You sure you're going to be okay?" He touched his hand to her cheek, and it flitted through her mind that was another first. They were standing close, her hand in his, his fingers on her cheek.

All she had to do was say, no. Stay with me.

And then what? She could start something, and ruin everything.

"Yeah. It's not like she's mad at me or anything. No reason to be. We're good, we're fine. You'd better go down, fill the others in."

"You get spooked in the night, call. I'll come."

"Good to know. Thanks."

She slid her hand out of his, eased back, and slipped into her own room.

No, Amelia had no reason to be mad at her, Hayley considered. She had no boyfriend, no husband, no lover. The only man she wanted was off-limits.

"So you can relax," she murmured. "Looks like I'll be going solo for the next little while.

three

He hunted her up the next day, mid-morning. But he had to be sly about it. He knew her well enough to be sure if she thought he was trying to help, to get her mind off things, to give her any sort of break, she'd brush him off.

Hayley Phillips was the original I'm-fine-don't-worry-about-me girl.

Nothing wrong with that, Harper thought. In her place, a lot of women would have been happy to take advantage of his mother's generosity, or at least to take that generosity for granted. Hayley did neither, and he respected that. He could admire her stand—to a point. But plenty of times, to his mind, that point tripped over into just mule-headed stubborn.

So he kept it casual, even when he had to poke into two greenhouses, work his way to the main building before he found her setting up a new display of houseplants.

She was wearing one of the nursery's bib aprons over black camp shorts and a V-necked tank. There was damp soil on the apron, and on her forearm. Only repressed lust could be responsible for him finding it so absurdly sexy.

"Hey, how's it going?"

"Not too bad. Had ourselves a little run on dish gardens. Customer just came in and bagged five as centerpieces for her sorority reunion lunch. And I talked her into taking the sago palm for her own sunroom."

"Nice going. Guess you're busy then."

She glanced over her shoulder. "Not too. Stella wants to make up more dish gardens, but she's tied up with Logan, which isn't as sexy as it sounds. Big job came in, and she's locked him in the office until she gets all the details for the contract. Last I walked by, he wasn't all that happy about it."

"Ought to be at it for a while then. I was going to do some chip-budding. Could use some help, but—"

"Really? Can I do it? I can take one of the two-ways in case Ruby or Stella need me."

"I could use another pair of hands."

"Mine'll be right back. Hold on."

She dashed through the double glass doors, and was back in thirty seconds, shed of the apron and hitching a two-way to her waistband. And giving him a quick peek at smooth belly skin.

"I read up some, but I can't remember which is the chip-budding."

"It's an old method," he told her as they started out. "More widely used now than it used to be. What we're going to do is work some of the field stock, some of the ornamentals. Mid-summer's the time for it."

Heat hit like a wet wall. "This sure is mid-summer."

"We'll start on magnolias." He picked up a bucket of

water he'd left outside the door. "They never stop being popular."

They walked over gravel, between greenhouses, and headed out to the fields. "Things stay quiet last night?"

"Not a peep after that little show we were treated to. I'm hoping she doesn't plan an encore of that trick. Gross, you know?"

"She sure knows how to get your attention anyway. Okay, here's what we do first." He stopped in front of a tall, leafy magnolia. "I'm going to pick some ripe shoots, this season's wood. You want one not much thicker than a pencil with well-developed buds. See this one?"

With an ungloved hand, he reached up, gently drew a shoot down.

"Okay, then what?"

"I clip it off." He drew pruners out of his tool bag. "See here, where the base is starting to go woody? That's what we're looking for. You don't want green shoots, they're too weak yet."

After he'd cut it, Harper put the shoot in the water bucket. "We keep it wet. If it dries out, it won't unite. Now you pick one."

She started to move around the tree, but he caught her hand. "No, it's better to work on the sunny side of the tree."

"Okay." She rolled her bottom lip between her teeth as she searched, selected. "How about this one?"

"Good. Here, make the cut."

She took the pruners, and since he was close he could smell the scent she wore—always light with a surprising kick—along with the garden green.

"How many are you doing?"

"About a dozen." He stuck his hands in his pockets as he leaned in to watch her, smell her. And told himself he was suffering for a good cause. "Go ahead, pick another."

"I don't get out in the field much." She drew down another shoot, looked toward Harper and got his nod. "It's different out here. Different than selling and displaying, talking to customers."

"You're good at that."

"Yeah, I am, but being out here, it's getting your hands into the thing. Stella knows all this stuff, and Roz, she knows everything. I like to learn. You sell better the more you know."

"I'd rather ram that shoot in my eye than have to sell every day."

She smiled as she worked. "But you're a loner at heart, aren't you? I'd go crazy holed up in the grafting house day after day like you. I like seeing people, and having them talk to me about what they're looking for and why. I like selling, too. 'Here, you take this pretty thing, and give me the money.' "

She laughed as she put another shoot in the bucket. "That's why you and Roz need somebody like me, so you can squirrel away in your caves and work with the plants for hours, and I can sell them."

"Seems to be working."

"That's a dozen, even. What next?"

"Over here, what we've got is rooted shoots I got from stool-grown stock plants."

"Stooling, I know what that is." She stared down at the nursery bed and its line of straight, slim shoots. "Um, you hill the ground up to stimulate rooting, and cut them back hard in the winter, then you take the roots from the what-doyoucallit, parent plant, and plant them out."

"You have been reading up."

"I like to learn."

"Shows." And was just one more click for him. He'd never found a woman who'd interested him physically, emotionally, who shared his love of gardening. "Okay. We use a sharp, clean knife. We're going to trim off all the leaves from the budstick—the shoots we just cut. But we'll leave just a little stub, just about an eighth of an inch of the petiole—the leaf stalk."

"I know what a petiole is," she muttered, and watched Harper demonstrate before she took her turn.

Good hands, she thought. Quick, skilled, sure. Despite—or maybe because of the nicks and calluses—they were elegantly male.

She thought they reflected who he was perfectly, that combination of privileged background and working-class.

"Cut the soft tip from the top, see? Now watch." He angled around so she could see, and their heads bent close together. "We want the first bud at the base, that's where we're going to cut into the stem, just a little below there. See how you have to angle the cut, going down, then another above, behind the bud toward that first cut. And . . ." Gently, holding the chip by the leaf stalk, he held it out.

"I can do that."

"Go ahead." He slipped the bud chip into a plastic bag, and watched her work.

She was careful, which was a relief to him, and he heard her whispering his instructions to herself with every move.

"I did it!"

"Nice job. Let's get the rest."

He did seven in the time it took her to do three, but she didn't mind. He showed her how to stand astride the rootstock to remove the sideshoots and leaves from the bottom twelve inches.

She knew it was a maneuver, and really, she'd probably feel guilty about it later, but she deliberately fumbled her first attempt.

"No, you need to position it between your legs, more like this."

As she'd hoped, he came over to stand behind her, in a nice vertical spoon, his arms coming around, making her belly dance as his hands closed over her wrists.

"Bend down a little, loosen at the knees. That's it. Now . . ." He guided her hand for the cut. "Just a sliver of the bark," he murmured, and his breath breezed along her ear. "See, there's the cambium. You want to leave a lip at the base where the chip will layer."

He smelled like the trees, sort of hot and earthy. His body felt so firm pressed against hers. She wished she could turn around, just turn so they were pressed front to front. She'd only have to rise up on her toes for their mouths to line up.

It was a maneuver, and *shame* on her, but she looked over her shoulder, looked dead into his eyes. And smiled. "Is that better?"

"Yeah. Better. A lot."

As she'd hoped, his gaze skimmed down, lingered on her mouth. Classic move, she thought. Classic results.

"I'll . . . show you how to do the rest."

He looked blank for a moment, like a man who'd forgotten what he was doing in the middle of a task. She couldn't have been more delighted.

Then he stepped back, reached in his tool bag for the grafting tape.

That had been so nice, she mused. Line to line, heat to heat, for just a few seconds. Of course now she was all churned up, but it felt good, felt fine to have everything swimming around inside her.

But as penance for her calculation, she behaved herself, played the eager student as she positioned the bud chip on the stock so the cambium layers met as snugly as her body had met Harper's.

She bound the chip to stock using the tape around and over the bud as instructed.

"Good. Perfect." He still felt a little breathless, and the palms of his hands were damp enough that he wiped them on the knees of his jeans. "In six weeks, maybe two months, the chip will have united, and we'll take off the tape. Late next winter, we'll cut the top of the stock, just above this bud, and during the spring the grafted bud will send out a shoot, and we're off and running."

"It's fun, isn't it? How you can take a little something from one, a little something from another, put them together and make more."

"That's the plan."

"Will you show me some of the other techniques sometime? Like what you do in the grafting house?" Her body was angled, her head bent over the next rootstock. "Roz and Stella showed me some of the propagation techniques. I've done some flats by myself. I'd like to try something in the grafting house."

Alone with her there, in all that moist heat. He'd probably drown in a pool of his own lust.

"Sure, sure. No problem."

"Harper?" She knelt to join chip bud with rootstock. "Did you ever think, when your mama started this place, it'd be what it is?"

He had to focus, on her words, on the work, and ignore—or at least suffer through—his body's reaction to her.

Lily's mama, he reminded himself. A guest in his home. An employee. Could it be any more complicated?

Jesus, God. Help.

"Harper?"

"Sorry." He wrapped grafting tape. "I did." When he looked up, looked around, beyond the fields and nursery beds, to the greenhouses, and sheds, he calmed. "I guess I could see it because it was what I wanted, too. And I know when Mama puts her mind to something, puts her back into it, she's going to make it work."

"What if she hadn't wanted it, or put her mind to it? What would you be doing?"

"Just what I'm doing. If she hadn't decided on this I'd've started it myself. And because I wanted it, she'd've got on board, so I guess we'd have pretty much what we have here."

"She's the best, isn't she? It's good that you know that, that you understand how lucky you are. I see that between you. You don't take each other for granted. I hope Lily and I have that one day."

"Seems like you already do."

She smiled at that, and rose to go to the next rootstock. "Do you think you and Roz are the way you are with each other, to each other—and your brothers, too—because you didn't have a daddy most of your life? I mean, I think I was closer to my own daddy because it was just the two of us than I might've been otherwise. I've wondered about that."

"Maybe." His hair, a thick tangle of black, fell forward as he worked. He shook it back, momentarily annoyed he'd forgotten a hat. "I remember her and my father, how they were together. It was special. She's got something like that with Mitch—not the same. I guess it's never the same, not supposed to be. But they've got something good and special. That's what she deserves."

"Do you ever think about finding somebody? Somebody good and special?"

"Me?" His head whipped up, and he narrowly missed slicing his own finger with the knife. "No. No. Well, eventually. Why? Do you?"

He heard her sigh as she moved down the nursery bed. "Eventually."

* * *

WHEN THEY WERE FINISHED, AND SHE HAD GONE, Harper walked back to the pond. He emptied out his pockets, tossed his sunglasses on the grass. Then dived in.

It had been something he'd done—with or without clothes—since childhood. There was nothing like a quick dip into the pond to cool you down on a sticky summer day.

He'd been on the point of kissing her. More than, he admitted, and sank under the surface, along the lily pads and yellow flags. It had been more than a kiss—even a hot and greedy one—that had run through his mind when he'd had his hands on her.

He had to put that aside—well off to the side—as he had been for more than a year now. She looked to him for friendship. God help him, she probably thought of him as a kind of brother.

So he'd just have to keep tamping down his less than brotherly feelings until he beat out the last of the sparks. Or burned up.

Best thing for him to do was get himself back into circulation. He was spending too much time at home, and too much of that time alone. Maybe he'd go into the city tonight, make some calls, meet some friends. Better yet, make a date. Have dinner, listen to music. Charm himself into some willing female's bed.

The trouble was, he couldn't think of any particular female he wanted to be with, over dinner, with music, or in the bed. That right there, it seemed to him, illustrated his pitiful state of affairs. Or lack of them.

He just wasn't in the mood to do the dance that ended up between the sheets. He couldn't bring himself to call another woman, put on the show, go through the pretense, when the woman he wanted was sleeping in his own house.

And as far out of his reach as the moon.

He pulled himself out of the water, shook like a dog. Maybe he'd go into town though. He picked up the rest of his things, shoving them in his dripping pockets. See if any of his unattached friends felt like catching a movie, eating some barbecue, hitting a club. Something, anything, to take his mind somewhere else for a night.

BUT WHEN HE GOT HOME, HE WASN'T IN THE MOOD TO go out. He made excuses to himself: It was too hot, he was too tired, he didn't feel like the drive. What he really wanted was a cool shower and a cold beer. He was pretty sure there was a frozen pizza buried with the leftovers David was always giving him. There was a ballgame on TV.

What else did he need?

A long warm body with miles of leg and smooth skin. Luscious lips and big blue eyes.

Since that wasn't on the menu, he decided to drop the temperature of the shower to cold.

His hair was still dripping and he wore nothing but ancient cutoffs when he wandered into the kitchen for that beer.

Like the rest of the house, it was small-scale. He didn't need big, he'd grown up in big. And he liked the charm and convenience of his little rooms. He thought of the converted two-story carriage house as a kind of country cottage. The way it sat away from the main house, surrounded by the gardens with their curving paths, shaded by old trees, gave it the kind of solitude and privacy that suited him. And kept him close enough to the main house that he could be on hand if his mother needed him.

If he wanted company, all he had to do was stroll over. If he didn't, he stayed put. More often than not, he admitted, he stayed put.

He remembered when he'd decided to move in, and his biggest decorating plan had been to paint all the walls white and be done with it. Both his mother and David had been all over him like white on rice for that one.

They'd been right, he had to admit it. He liked the silvery sage walls in his kitchen and the stone gray counters, the distressed wood of the cabinets. He supposed the color had inspired him to juice the place up a little with the pieces of old pottery or china sitting around, the herbs growing on the windowsill.

It was a nice space, even if he was just eating a sandwich over the sink. He liked standing here, looking out at his own little greenhouse, and the explosion of the summer gardens.

The hydrangeas were as big as soccerballs this year, he noted, and the infusion of iron he'd given them turned them a strong, unearthly blue. Maybe he'd cut a few, plunk them down somewhere in the house.

Butterflies were massing around the garden he and his mother had planted to lure them. A flurry of colorful wings flashed over the welcoming bloom of purple coneflower, the sunny coreopsis, fragrant verbena, and the reliable asters. Backing them was the elegant dance of daylilies.

Maybe he'd cut a few of those, too, and take them over to the house so Lily could have them in her room. She liked flowers, liked when he took her walking in the gardens so she could touch them.

And her eyes, blue like her mama's, got so big and serious when he recited the names. Just like she was taking it all in, filing it away.

Christ, who'd have thought he'd be so gone on a kid?

But it was so cool the way she'd march along with her little hand in his, then stop and reach up, that pretty face turned to his, that pretty face full of light because she knew he'd swing her up. Then the way she'd hook her arm around his neck, or pat his hair. It just killed him.

It was amazing to love, to be loved in that open, uncomplicated way.

He took a pull of the beer, then opened the freezer to look for the pizza. He heard the quick knock on the front door seconds before it opened.

"Hope I'm interrupting an orgy," David called out. He strolled in, cocked his head at Harper. "What, no dancing girls?"

"They just left."

"I see they ripped your clothes off first."

"You know how it is with dancing girls. Wanna beer?"

"Tempting, but no. I'm saving myself for an exceptional Grey Goose martini. Night off, heading into Memphis to meet some people. Why don't you cover up that manly chest and come along?"

"Too hot."

"I'm driving, got AC. Go on, put on some dancing shoes. We're going to check out some clubs."

Harper pointed his beer toward his friend. "Every time I check out some clubs with you, somebody hits on me. And they're not always female."

"You heartbreaker. I'll protect you, throw myself bodily on anyone who tries to pat your ass. What're you going to do, Harp, stew around here with a beer and Kraft's mac and cheese?"

"Kraft's mac and cheese is the packaged dinner of champions. But I'm going with frozen pizza tonight. Besides, there's a game on."

"You *are* breaking my heart. Harper, we're young, we're hot. You're straight, I'm gay, which means we cover all available ground and double our chances of getting lucky. Between us we can cut a mighty swath down Beale Street. Don't you remember, Harp?" He took Harper by the shoulders, gave him a dramatic shake. "Don't you remember how once we ruled?"

He had to grin. "Those were the days."

"These are still the days."

"Don't you remember how once we puked our guts up in the gutter?"

"Sweet, sweet memories." David hitched himself up to sit on the counter, took Harper's beer for one sip. "Should I be worried about you?"

"No. Why?"

"When's the last time you had your pipes cleaned?"

"Jesus, David." He took a gulp of beer.

"Used to be a time when the nubiles were lined up three deep on the path to your door. Now the closest you come to a bang is nuking Kraft's in the mike."

It was too close to the truth for comfort. "I'm on sabbatical. I guess I got tired of it," he said with a shrug. "Besides, things have been pretty busy and intense around here for a while. The business with the Bride, especially finding out she was like my great-great-grandmother. Somebody screwed with her, messed her up. Careless, you know, callous, the way it's playing out. I don't want to be careless anymore."

"You never were." Soberly now, David boosted himself down. "How long have we been friends? Almost for fucking ever. I've never known you to be careless with anyone. If you're talking sex, you're the only person I know who stays friendly with a lover once the heat blows off. You're not careless with people, Harper. And just because Reginald was a bastard—most likely—doesn't mean you're doomed to be."

"No, I know. I'm not obsessing about it or anything. Just

sort of taking stock. Just chilling awhile until I figure out what I want for the next phase."

"You want company, I can take you up on that beer and whip up something considerably less revolting than frozen pizza."

"I like frozen pizza." He'd do it, Harper thought. He'd blow off his plans, just to hang, to be a pal. "Go, there's a martini with your name on it." He slapped a hand on David's shoulder to lead him to the front door. "Eat, drink, make Barry."

"Got my cell phone if you change your mind."

"Thanks." He opened the door, leaned on the jamb. "But while you're steaming along Beale, I'm going to be sitting in the cool, watching the Braves trounce the Mariners."

"Pitiful, son, just pitiful."

"And drinking beer in my underwear, which cannot be overstated." He broke off, felt the punch straight to the belly when Hayley and Lily came around a turn of the garden.

"Now that's a pretty sight."

"Yeah. They look good." The baby wore some sort of romper thing, pink and white stripes, with a little pink bow in her hair—dark hair, like her mother's. She looked sweet as a candy stick.

And Mama—tiny blue shorts, a yard of leg, bare feet. Some skinny little white top and wraparound shades. A different kind of candy altogether. Maybe it was sweet, but it was sure as hell hot.

He tipped up the beer to cool his throat, and Lily spotted them. She let out something between a yell and a squeal—all delight—and pulling away from Hayley made a beeline toward the carriage house as fast as her little legs could manage.

"Slow down, sweet potato." David moved forward to

scoop her up, give her a toss. She patted his face with both of her hands, gabbled at him, then reached for Harper.

"As always, I'm day-old paté when you're around."

"Hand her over," Harper hitched her onto his hip where she kicked her legs with joy and beamed at him. "Hey, pretty girl."

In response, she tilted her head to lay it on his shoulder.

"What a flirt," Hayley commented as she walked up. "Here we are having a nice walk, having a little girl-talk, she spots a couple of handsome men, and blows me off."

"Why don't you leave her with Harper, put on a party dress and drive on into Memphis with me?"

"Oh, I—"

"Sure." Harper kept his voice carefully neutral as he jiggled Lily. "She can hang with me. You can bring that Portacrib thing over and I'll put her down when she's tired."

"That's nice, I appreciate it. But it's been a long day. I don't think I'm up for a trip to Memphis."

"Fuds and duds, Lily." David leaned over to kiss her. "I'm surrounded by fuds and duds. I'm flying solo then, and I better get started. See y'all."

"I don't mind watching her if you want to get out awhile."

"No. I'm going to put her down pretty soon, then curl on up myself. Why aren't you going?"

"Too hot," he said, decided it was the easiest catchall excuse.

"Isn't it? And you're letting all the cool out. Come on, Lily."

But when she tried to take the baby, Lily squirmed away and clung to Harper like ivy to a tree. The sound she made was distinctly *da-da.*

The flush glowed on Hayley's cheeks even as she gave a weak laugh. "She doesn't mean anything. Those D sounds are the easiest to make, is all. Lots of things are da-da these days. Come on, Lily."

This time her arms circled Harper's neck like a noose, and she started to wail.

"You want to come in for a while?"

"No, no." She spoke quickly now, a tumble of words. "We were just taking a little walk, nearly done with it, and she has to have a bath before bedtime."

"I'll walk back with you." He turned his head, kissed Lily's cheek then whispered in her ear so she laughed and snuggled against him.

"She can't have everything she wants."

"She'll have to learn that soon enough." He reached behind him, and shut the door.

SHE MANAGED BATH AND BEDTIME, KEPT HERSELF distracted with Lily's needs until the baby was asleep.

She tried to read, she tried TV. Too restless for either, she plugged in a yoga tape she'd bought at the mall and gave it a spin. She went down for cookies. She put on music, then turned it off.

By midnight, she was still edgy and unsettled, so gave up and went out on the terrace to take in the warm night.

The lights were on in the carriage house. His bedroom light, she assumed. She'd never been up to the second floor, or what he called the loft. Where he slept. Where he was probably in bed right now, reading a book. Naked.

She should never have walked that way with Lily. All those directions to take, and she'd headed straight toward the carriage house. As besotted as her daughter.

God, she'd nearly melted at the knees when she'd come around that turn in the path and seen him.

Leaning against the doorjamb, wearing nothing but those ragged old cutoffs. Hard chest, golden tan, his hair all curly and damp. That lazy smile on his face as he'd taken a sip from a bottle of beer.

He'd looked so sexy—a freaking billboard for sexy, framed in that cottage doorway, surrounded by flowers, sultry in the heat. She'd been amazed she'd been able to get reasonable words out of her throat when she'd been tingling the whole time, inside and out, while they'd stood there.

And she had no business tingling around Harper. It really had to stop. Why couldn't it go back to the way it used to be? When she'd been pregnant, she'd felt comfortable around him. Even the first months after Lily's birth she'd been easy in his company. When had it started to change on her?

She didn't know, she couldn't pinpoint it. It just was.

And couldn't be. Lily wasn't the only one who couldn't have everything she wanted.

four

SHE FELT ODD AND OUT OF SORTS AT WORK. AS IF HER skin was too small, her head too heavy. Too much yoga for the novice, she decided. Too much work, not enough sleep. Maybe she should take a little vacation. She could get the time off, and she could afford a few days. She could drive back to Little Rock, visit some of her old friends and coworkers. Show Lily off.

But it would eke into the vacation fund she'd started to take Lily to DisneyWorld for her third birthday. Still, how much would it cost, really? A few hundred dollars, and the change of scene might do her good.

She swiped the back of her hand over her forehead. The air in the greenhouse felt too close, too thick. Her fingers as she tried to arrange dish gardens were too fat and clumsy. She didn't see why she got stuck with this job. Stella could've done it, or Ruby. Then she could work the counter—a monkey could work the counter this time of year, she thought irritably.

She should have had the day off. It wasn't as if they needed her. She should have been home, in the cool, relaxing for a damn change. But here she was, sweating and dirty, stuffing plants into bowls because Stella said so. Orders, orders, orders. When was she going to be able to do what she wanted, when she wanted?

They looked down on her because she didn't have the bloodline, she didn't have the education, she didn't have the fancy background that made them all so *important*. But she was just as good as they were. Better. She was better because she'd made her own way. She'd clawed her way up from nothing because—

"Hey, hey! You're breaking the roots on that ludisia."

"What?" She stared down at the plant, and her fingers went limp as Stella snatched it from them. "I'm sorry. Did I kill it? I don't know what I was thinking."

"It's okay. You looked upset. What's wrong?"

"Nothing. I don't know." She shook herself, and flushed with the shame of her own thoughts. "The heat's making me irritable, headachy, I guess. I'm sorry I haven't got these done. I can't seem to concentrate."

"It's okay. I came back to give you a hand anyway."

"I can do it. You don't have to take the time."

"Hayley, you know how I like to play in the dirt when I can. Here." She reached into the cooler under the workbench, took out two bottles of water. "Take five."

What had she been thinking before? she wondered as she took a long pull from the bottle. Nasty, petty thoughts. She didn't understand why her mind would have come up with such mean things. She didn't feel that way. But for a minute or two she had, and it made her feel ugly now.

"I don't know what's wrong with me, Stella."

Frowning, Stella laid her hand on Hayley's brow in the classic mother's gesture. "Maybe you're coming down with a summer cold."

"No, I think it's more the blahs. Not even the blues, just the blahs. They keep sneaking up on me, and I don't know why. I've got the most beautiful baby in the world. I love my job. I've got good friends."

"You can have all that, and still get the blahs." Stella took an apron off a hook, studying Hayley as she tied it on. "You haven't dated in more than a year."

"Closer to two." And that called for another long drink of water. "I've thought about it. I've been asked out a few times. You know Mrs. Bentley's son, Wyatt? He was in a few weeks ago, buying her a hanging basket for her birthday, and he was flirting pretty hard. Asked me if I'd like to have dinner sometime."

"He's pretty cute."

"Yeah, he's got that sexy jock thing going for him, and I thought about it, then I just didn't want to go to all the bother, and I edged back."

"I seem to remember you pushing me out the door when I talked about not wanting to go to all the bother when Logan first asked me out."

"I did, didn't I?" She smiled a little. "I've got such a big mouth."

Before Stella selected plants, she tightened the band that held her mass of curling red hair into a tail. "Maybe you're just a little nervous on the board? You know, taking that dive into the dating pool again."

"I've never been nervous about dating. It's one of my primary skills. I like going out. And I know if I wanted to, you or Roz, or David would take care of Lily." The knowledge brought on another stab of guilt for the resentful thoughts that had wormed into her mind. "I know she'd be fine, so that's no excuse. I just can't seem to get myself in gear."

"Maybe you just haven't met somebody who makes you want to oil the gears and get them moving again."

"I guess . . . maybe." She took another long drink, braced herself. "The thing is, Stella . . ."

When the silence dragged on, Stella glanced up from the pot she was building. "What's the thing?"

"First you gotta promise, *swear* that you won't tell anybody. Even Logan. You can't say anything."

"All right."

"You absolutely swear?"

"I'm not going to spit in my palm, Hayley. You'll have to take my word for it."

"Okay. Okay." She walked down the aisle between tables, then back again. "The thing is, I like Harper."

Stella nodded encouragement. "Sure. So do I."

"No!" Frustrated, mortified to hear herself say it out loud, Hayley set the water down and clamped her hands over her face. "God."

It took her a minute for the light to shine. "Oh," Stella said with her eyes going wide. "Oh. Oh," she repeated drawing out the syllable. Then she pursed her lips. "Oh."

"If that's the best you can do, I'm going to have to hit you."

"I'm trying to take it in. Absorb it."

"It's crazy. I know it's crazy." Hayley dropped her hands. "I know it's not right, it's not even on the table. But I . . . forget I said anything. Just highlight and hit delete."

"I didn't say it was crazy, it's just unexpected. As far as not being right, I don't follow you."

"He's Roz's son. Roz, the woman who took me in off the street."

"Oh, you mean when you were penniless, naked, and

suffering from some rare, debilitating disease? It was saintly of her to take you in, clothe you and spoon-feed you broth night after night."

"I'm allowed to exaggerate when I'm being a fool," Hayley snapped. "She did take me in, she gave me a job. She gave me and Lily a home, and here I am imagining how I can get naked and sweaty with her firstborn."

"If you're attracted to Harper—"

"I want to bite his ass. I want to pour honey all over his body then lick it off an inch at a time. I want to—"

"Okay, okay." Stella held out one hand, laid the other on her heart. "Please don't put any more of those images in my head. We'll just agree you've got the hots for him."

"Major hots. And I can't do anything about it because we're friends. Look how screwed up things got for Ross and Rachel. Of course Monica and Chandler's a different story, but—"

"Hayley."

"And I know this isn't a television show," she muttered over Stella's roll of laughter. "But you know how life imitates art? Besides, he doesn't think about me that way."

"The honey-licking way?"

Hayley's eyes went blurry. "Oh God, now I've got that image in my head."

"Serves you right. Anyway, are you sure he doesn't think of you that way?"

"He hasn't made a move, has he? It's not like there haven't been opportunities. And what if I made a move on him, and he was just, like, horrified or something?"

"What if he wasn't?"

"That could be even worse. We'd have ourselves some wild jungle sex, then after we'd both be . . ." She lifted her hands into the air, waved them wildly. "Oh God, what've I done, and all awkward with each other. And I'd have to take Lily and move to Georgia or somewhere. And Roz would never want to speak to me again."

"Hayley." Stella patted her on the shoulder. "This is just my impression, just my opinion, but I'm fairly sure Roz knows Harper has sex."

"You know what I mean. It's different when he's having sex with women she doesn't know."

"Oh yes, I'm sure she's perfectly delighted that her son has sex with strangers. Strangers to her, anyway," she added with a laugh. "And naturally she'd be appalled to learn that he might be intimate with a woman she knows and loves. Yes, that would be a real knife in the heart."

"It's a kind of betrayal."

"It's no kind of betrayal. He's a grown man, Hayley, and his choices in relationships are his own business. Roz would be the first to say so, and the first—without a doubt—to tell you she doesn't want to be one of the angles in this triangle you've formed."

"Well, maybe, but—"

"Maybe, maybe, but, but." Stella waved them all aside with such enthusiasm, Hayley had to duck and blink. "If you're interested in Harper, you should let him know. See what happens. Besides, I think he's had a crush on you from the get-go."

"He has not."

Stella shrugged. "Just my opinion, just my impression."

"Really?" The quick bump under her heart at the idea was painful and nice. "I don't know. I think if he has a crush on anybody, it's Lily. But I could think about maybe giving it a little push, see what happens."

"Positive thinking. Now, let's get these dish gardens done."

"Stella." Hayley poked a finger in the dirt. "You swear you won't say anything about this to Roz."

"Oh, for God's sake." Stella held out her palm and, mimicking the sacred rite she'd seen her sons perform, spat in it.

When offered the hand Stella held out, Hayley stared at it, and said: "Eeuuww."

IT MADE HER FEEL BETTER. HAVING SOMEBODY ELSE know what she was thinking and feeling took a weight off. Especially when that somebody else was Stella. Who hadn't been shocked, Hayley reminded herself. Surprised, sure, but not shocked, so that was good.

Just as it was good to take a couple of days and think about it. In fact, she was thinking about it, a little dreamily, when with Lily down for the night, she stretched out on the sitting room couch to unwind with some TV.

Idly, she channel surfed and decided how nice it was to have nothing to do for an hour. Still, reruns, repeats, and other summer dreck, she decided, wasn't what she wanted for a lazy hour of entertainment.

She flipped to an old black-and-white movie, something she didn't recognize. It seemed like some kind of romantic drama, where everyone wore gorgeous clothes and went dancing every night at elaborate clubs where they had orchestras and voluptuous girl singers.

Everybody drank highballs.

Why did they call them highballs? she wondered, yawning as she snuggled down. Because the glasses were tall, okay, but why were the glasses called balls? She should look it up sometime.

What would it be like to wear those incredible gowns and glide around a dance floor with everything all Art Deco and glittering? He'd be wearing a tuxedo, of course. She bet Harper looked awesome in a tux.

And what if they'd both come with someone else, but then they saw each other. Through all that silk and shine, their eyes met. And they just knew.

They'd dance, and everything else would wash away. That's the way it was in black-and-white. It didn't have to be complicated; whatever separated you could be vanquished or overcome. Then it all washed away except the two of you together as the end music swelled.

And when it did, you'd be in each other's arms, your face tipped up to his as your lips came together in that movie-perfect kiss. The kind you felt all the way down to the soles of your feet, the kind that meant you'd love each other forever.

Soft, soft kiss, so tender as his hand brushed over your hair, then deepening, heating just a bit when your arms locked around his neck. Up on your toes so your body leaned to his.

Line, angle, curve, all beautifully fitted.

Then after it faded to black, his hands moved over you, touching where it tingled and ached. Stroking over silk and skin so that your mouths met now with little gasps and moans.

The taste of that kiss was so potent, so powerful, the flavor of it streamed through your whole system, woke everything up, made everything swell.

And everywhere you'd felt cold and tired warmed again because you wanted, and were wanted.

Candles were flickering. Smoke and shadows. Flowers scented the room. Lilies, it had to be lilies. The flowers he'd brought her, bold and red and passionate. His eyes, deep brown, depthless brown, told her everything she wanted. That she was beautiful to him, and precious.

When they undressed each other, her gown melted away into a pool of glittery white against the black of his jacket.

Skin to skin, at last. Smooth and soft. Gold dust and milk. His shoulders under her hands, the length of his back, so she could feel those muscles tense as she aroused him.

The way he touched her, with such need, filled her with excitement so that when he gathered her up in his arms—oh—she was quivering for him. He laid her on the bed, the big white bed with sheets as soft as water, then sank into it with her.

His lips skimmed her throat, captured her breast so appetites quickened, and the tug, that long, liquid pull in her belly made her moan out his name.

Candlelight. Firelight. Flowers. Not lilies, but roses. His hands were smooth—a gentleman's hands. Rich hands. She stretched under them, arched, adding throaty purrs. Men liked their whores to make noise. She stroked her hand along the length of him. Ready, more than ready, she thought. But she'd tease him a bit longer. It was wives who lay passive, who let men do what they willed, to have done with it.

That's why they came to her, why they needed her. Why they paid.

She brought her shoulders off the mound of pillows, so her curling mane of golden hair spilled back. And she rolled with him, lush breasts and hips to entice, rolled him over on the bed to slither her way down, to nip and lick her way down his body to do what his cold-blooded, prim-mouthed wife would never do.

His grunts and gasps were her satisfaction.

His hands were in her hair now, gripping, twisting while she pleasured him. His body was trim, and she could gain some enjoyment from it, but had he been fat as a pig she'd have convinced him he was a god to her. It was so easy.

When she straddled him, looked down at his handsome face, saw the greedy desperation in his eyes, she smiled.

She took him into her, fast and hard and thought that nothing fit so well inside her as did a rich man's cock.

Hayley bolted up from the sofa as if she'd been shot out of a cannon. Her heart clanged, hammer to anvil, in her chest. Her breasts felt heavy as if, oh God, as if they'd been fondled. Her lips tingled. Panicked, she grabbed at her hair and nearly wept with relief when she felt her own.

Someone laughed, and had her stumbling back, rapping up against the couch and nearly spilling onto it again. The television, she saw as she crossed her arms protectively over her breasts. Just the television, sophisticated drama in black-and-white.

And oh, God, what had happened to her?

Not a dream, or not just a dream. It couldn't have been.

She dashed out of the room to check on Lily. Her baby slept, snuggled with her stuffed dog.

Ordering herself to calm, she went downstairs. But when she reached the library, she hesitated. Mitch sat at the library table, tapping away at the keyboard of his laptop. She didn't want to disturb him, but she had to check. She had to be sure. Waiting until morning just wasn't in the cards.

She stepped inside. "Mitch?"

"Hmm? What? Where?" He looked up, blinked behind his hornrims. "Hi."

"I'm sorry. You're working."

"Just some e-mail. Do you need something?"

"I just wanted to . . ." She wasn't shy, and she wasn't prudish, but she wasn't sure how to comfortably relate what she'd just experienced to her employer's husband. "Um, do you think Roz is busy?"

"Why don't I call up and see?"

"I don't want to bother her if . . . Yes, yes, I do. Could you ask her to come down?"

"All right." He reached for the phone to dial the bedroom extension. "Something happened."

"Yeah. Sort of. Maybe." To settle one point, she walked to the second level, behind the table and studied the pictures on Mitch's work board.

She stared at the copy of the photograph of a man in formal dress—strong features, dark hair, cool eyes.

"This is Reginald Harper, right? The first one."

"That's right. Roz, can you come down to the library. Hayley's here. She needs to talk to you. Right." He hung up. "She'll be right down. Do you want something—some water, some coffee?"

She shook her head. "No, thanks. I'm okay, just feeling a little weirded out. Ah, when Stella first came here, when she was living here, she had dreams. That's when it really started, right? I mean, before that there were . . . incidents. Sightings. But nothing much ever happened—at least not that Roz heard of—that was dangerous. Regarding The Bride, I mean."

"That seems to be the case. There's been a kind of escalation, which seemed to start when Stella moved in with her boys."

"And I came a few weeks after. So it was the three of us here, living in Harper House." Her skin still felt chilled. She rubbed her bare arms and wished for a sweatshirt. "I was pregnant, Stella had the boys, and Roz, well, Roz is bloodline."

He nodded. "Keep going."

"Stella had the dreams. Intense dreams, which we have to believe were somehow plugged into her subconscious by Amelia. That's not a very scientific way of putting it, but—"

"It's good enough."

"And when Stella and Logan—" She broke off as Roz came in. "I'm sorry I dragged you down here."

"It's all right. What happened?"

"Finish your thought out first," Mitch suggested. "Line it up."

"Okay, well, Stella and Logan got involved, and Amelia didn't like it. Stella's dreams got more disturbing, more pointed, and there were violent incidents, culminating in how she blocked us all out of the boys' room that night—that first night you came here, Mitch."

"I'll never forget it."

"She told us her name that night," Roz commented. "Stella got through to her, and she gave us her first name."

"Yeah. Wouldn't you say she's left Stella be pretty much since then? She'd have told us if she had dreams still, or if anything happened to her directly."

"The focus transferred to Roz," Mitch said.

"Yeah." Pleased they seemed to be traveling the same road, Hayley nodded. "And it was even more intense, right? Like waking dreams, Roz?"

"Yes, and an escalation of violent behavior."

"The closer you got to Mitch, the crazier she got. That's the kind of thing that pisses her off. She nearly killed you. She rode to the rescue, you could say, when you were in trouble, when push came to shove, but before that she attacked you. But since then, since you and Mitch got engaged, got married, she's backed off."

"Apparently, at least for the moment." Roz stepped over, ran a hand down Hayley's arm. "She's moving on you now, isn't she?"

"I think so. I think that the three of us being in the house—you and Stella and me—maybe that pushed her out of pattern." She looked toward Mitch, lifting her hands. "I don't know how to put it, exactly, but things really got rolling then, and the ball seems to pick up bulk and speed, if you get me."

"I do, and it's interesting. The three of you—three women at varying stages of life—all unattached at the point you came together. Your connection made a connection to her, we could say. And as Stella, then Roz became emotionally, romantically involved, it caused Amelia's behavior to deteriorate."

"Honey, did she hurt you?"

"No." Hayley pressed her lips together, then looked from Roz to Mitch. "I know we're supposed to, like, report anything, so Mitch has it on record. I just don't know how to say all this. At least not delicately. It's a little bit embarrassing."

"You want me to step out?" Mitch asked her. "So you can talk to Roz about it?"

"No, that's just dumb—of me, I mean. She'll just tell you anyway." To brace herself, Hayley blew out a long breath. "Okay, so I was taking an hour to relax, watch some TV upstairs in the sitting room. And there was this old movie on, and I was daydreaming, I guess. All those fabulous clothes, you know, and the beautiful lighting, and the fancy clubs where people went out to dance and all. I was imagining what it would be like, how I'd be all dressed up, and I'd see someone."

She trailed off a moment. She didn't have to say the someone was Harper. That didn't have to be relevant.

"Anyway, we'd dance, and fall in love, and have that big movie kiss? You know what I mean."

Roz smiled. "Absolutely."

"Well, then I guess I was drifting off some, and I was thinking about what happens after The End? Thinking about sex, I guess," she said and cleared her throat. "Just a fantasy thing, candlelight and flowers and a big white bed, being in love. Making love." She lowered her head, put it in her hands. "This is mortifying."

"Don't be silly. Healthy girl like you didn't think about

sex, I'd be worried." Roz gave her shoulder a little shake.

"It was nice. Romantic and exciting. Then, it changed. Or I changed. And it was calculating. I was thinking about how I'd do these things. I could feel the skin and the form and the heat. There were roses. I could smell roses, but I had lilies in the fantasy, and now there were roses, and firelight. And his hands were different—soft and smooth. Rich, that's what I thought. And I thought the guy's wife wouldn't do what I'd do, and that's why he came to me. How he'd pay. And I felt my hair, and I could see it. Long and blond and curly. I saw it when it fell over my face, not like I was watching, but like I was there. It *was* me. And I saw him. His face."

She turned to the board and pointed at Reginald. "His face. He was inside me, and I saw his face."

She let out another long breath. "So."

After a moment of silence, Roz spoke. "I don't think it would be that unusual for your mind to weave that sort of thing together, Hayley. We all spend a lot of time thinking about these people, trying to put it all together. We know she was his mistress, we know she bore him a child, so we know they had sex. And for her, we can assume or at least speculate that it was, at least in part, a kind of business arrangement."

"You know how your body feels when you've been fooling around? Physically. Not just the buzz you get from a sex dream, but how you feel physically when you've been with a guy. Maybe I haven't been with one since before Lily was born, but you don't forget how it feels. And that's where I was when I woke up, or came out of it. Roz, I smelled those roses. I know how his body was shaped."

She had to take a breath, had to swallow hard. "I felt him inside me. Inside her, I guess, but it was like being her while it was happening. She liked being with someone handsome and skilled. It wouldn't have mattered if he'd been ugly as homemade sin and a dud in bed, but this was like a bonus. Rich was the bottom line—the rest was icing. I know that, because I was right inside her head. Or she was in mine. I didn't imagine it."

"I believe you," Mitch told her.

"We believe you," Roz corrected. "You're the closest to her age when she died, at least the age we think she was. Maybe she's relating to that, to you, and trying to go through you to tell us what it was like for her."

"Possibly." Mitch tipped back in the chair when Roz arched her brows at him. "It could give us more insight on her, on what happened and why. What else can you tell us about her?"

"Well, I don't think she got that much of a rush out of sex—from the power, the control, yeah, but not the rest of it. It's just what she did, and from his, um, response, she was good at what she did. Her body was a lot better than mine."

With a sheepish smile, she held her hands in front of her breasts to mime someone well-endowed. "And she was cold inside. The whole time they were doing it, she was thinking about what she'd get out of him. There was a derision—that's the best way to describe it—for the wives of men like him. I guess that's about it."

"Hardly her best side. Or maybe it is, from her point of view," Mitch considered. "She was in charge, doing what she'd chosen to do. Young, beautiful, desired by a powerful man and controlling that man through sex. Interesting."

"Creepy's what it was. And if I get to have sex, I'd like to have it with my own body. But anyway, I feel better, getting all that out. I think I'll go back up, maybe do some yoga. I don't think she's going to bother me while I'm trying to twist myself into the warrior position or whatever. Thanks for hearing me out."

"Anything else happens, I want to hear it," Roz told her.

"That's a promise."

Roz waited until Hayley was gone, then turned to Mitch. "We're going to have to worry about her, aren't we?"

"Let's not skip straight to worry." He took her hand. "Let's start with we'll keep an eye out for her."

five

From Stella's kitchen window, Hayley could see the spread of the back gardens, the patio, the arbor, the treehouse Logan and the boys had built snugged into the branches of a sycamore.

She watched Logan push Lily on a red swing that hung from another branch while the boys tossed an old ball for Parker to chase.

It was, she thought, a kind of moving portrait of summer evening. The sort of lazy contentment that only comes on breathless summer days right before the kids are called in for supper and the porch light goes on. Yellow glows to chase the moths away and to shine a circle that says: We're home.

She remembered, so clearly, what it was to be a child in August, to love the heat, to rush through it to snatch every drop of the sun before it went down.

Now, she hoped, she was learning what it was to be a mother. To be on the other side of the screen door. To be the one who turned on the porch light.

"Do you get used to it, or do you still look out sometimes like this, and think 'I'm the luckiest woman in the world.' "

Stella moved over to the window, smiled. "Both. You want to sit out on the patio with this lemonade?"

"In a minute. I didn't want to talk about this at work. Not just because it's at work, but because it's still on the Harper estate. And she's on the estate. She can't come here."

"Roz told me what happened." Stella laid a hand on Hayley's shoulder.

"I didn't tell her that it was Harper. I mean when I was fantasizing, I was with Harper. I'm just not going to tell her I was fantasizing about getting naked with her son."

"I think that's a judicious edit at this point. Has anything happened since?"

"No, nothing. And I don't know whether to hope something does or something doesn't." She watched Logan field the mangled slobbery ball that rolled his way, then toss it, sending dog and boys on a mad chase while Lily bounced in the swing and clapped her hands.

"I can tell you this, if I have to star in someone's life and times, I'd rather take a turn in yours."

"I believe in being a good and true friend, Hayley, but I'm not letting you have sex with Logan."

Hayley snorted out a laugh, then gave Stella an elbow nudge. "Spoilsport, and though I wasn't going there, I bet—wow."

Stella's smile was lazy as a cat's. "You bet right."

"Anyway. I was just thinking how it would be to have someone as crazy about me as Logan is about you. Toss in a couple of great kids, a beautiful home you've made together, and who needs fantasies?"

"You'll have what you're looking for one day, too."

"Listen to me, you'd think I was the redheaded stepchild. I don't know what's wrong with me lately." She rolled her shoulders as if shrugging off a weight. "I keep catching myself doing a poor-me routine. It's not like me, Stella. I'm happy. And even when I'm not, I look for a way to make myself happy. I don't brood and bitch. Or hardly."

"No, you don't."

"Maybe I've got a thing for Harper, but a little frustration's not enough to bring me down. Next time you hear me feeling sorry for myself, give me a good smack."

"Sure. What are friends for?"

SHE MEANT IT, TOO. SHE WASN'T THE TYPE TO SIT around ticking off the negatives of her life to see if she could make them outweigh the positives. If something was wrong, something was missing, she acted. Fix the problem and move ahead. Or if the problem couldn't be fixed, she found the best way to live with it.

When her mother had left, she'd been sad and scared and hurt. But there'd been nothing she could do to bring her back. So she'd done without—and done pretty damn well, Hayley thought as she drove back to Harper House.

She'd learned how to help make a home, and she and her father had had a good life. They'd been happy; she'd been loved. And she'd been useful.

She'd done well in school. She'd gotten a job to help with expenses. She knew how to work, and how to enjoy the work. She liked to learn, and to sell people things that made them happy.

If she'd stayed in Little Rock, at the bookstore, she'd have made manager. She'd have earned it.

Then her father had died. That had blasted a hole in the foundation of her life, and had shaken her like nothing before or since. He'd been her rock, as she'd been his. Nothing had felt steady or sure when he'd died, and her grief had been a constant raw ache.

So she'd turned to a friend—that's all he'd been really, she admitted as she turned down the drive to Harper House. A nice boy, a comfort.

Lily had come from that, and she wasn't ashamed of it. Maybe comfort wasn't love, but it was a positive act, a giving one. How could she have paid that kindness back by pushing the boy into marriage, or responsibility when he'd already moved on by the time she'd realized she was pregnant?

She hadn't wallowed—or hardly. She hadn't cursed God or man, for long. She'd accepted responsibility for her own actions, as she'd been taught, and had made the choice that was right for her.

To keep the child, and raise the child on her own.

Hadn't worked out quite that way, though, she thought with a smile as she parked. Little Rock, the bookstore, the house she'd shared with her father had no longer been her comfort zones once she'd started to show. Once the looks and the questions and the murmurs had begun.

So, fresh start.

She climbed out of the car, rounded it to open the back door and unhook Lily from her car seat.

Sell everything that could be sold, pack up the rest. Positive, move forward. All she'd expected by coming here to Roz was the possibility of a job. What she'd been given was family.

Just more proof, to her mind, that good things happened

when you took steps, when you worked for them—and when you were lucky enough to find people who'd give you a chance to do your best.

"That's what we are, Lily." She hoisted Lily up, covered her face with kisses. "We're a couple of lucky girls."

She swung the diaper bag over her shoulder, bumped the car door shut with her hip. But as she started toward the house an idea bloomed.

Maybe it was time to try her luck again.

Sit around waiting for things to happen and nothing much did. But act, you either failed or succeeded. Either was better than standing still.

She strolled around the house, taking her time, just to see if she could talk herself out of it. But the idea was planted now, and she couldn't find a good enough reason to uproot it.

Maybe he'd be shocked or stunned or even appalled. Well, that would be his problem. At least she'd know *something* and stop wondering all the damn time.

As she rounded the curve in the path, she set Lily down, and let her little girl trot toward Harper's front door.

Maybe he wasn't home, out with some woman. Or worse, had some woman in *his* home. Okay, that would be bad, but she'd deal with it.

It was time she dealt with it.

Though the dark wasn't deep yet, the path lights were glowing, those pretty soft green lanterns speared at the edges of the brick to guide the way. A few early lightning bugs blinked on and off, on and off over the heads of flowers, and out beyond to the roll of grass to lose themselves in the shadows of the woods.

She drew in the perfume of heliotrope, sweet peas, roses, and the more pungent aroma of earth. All of those scents, along with the different tones of growing green would forever make her think of Harper, and this place.

She caught up with Lily, knocked. On impulse she stepped back and to the side, leaving her little girl clapping her hands at Harper's front door. Where the porch light was on, a glowing circle of yellow.

When the door opened, she heard Lily give her greeting—something between hi and hey and a cry of pleasure.

"Look what I found at my front door."

From her vantage point, Hayley could see Lily's arms go up; and Harper's come down. When he scooped her up, Lily was already babbling in her excited and incomprehensible language.

"Is that right? Just thought you'd drop by to say hi? Maybe you ought to come in and have a cookie, but we'd better find your mama first."

"She's right here." Laughing, Hayley stepped over to the door. "Sorry, but it was so cute. You know she can't walk by your place without wanting to see you, so I thought I'd knock and let her stand there on her own."

She reached out, but as usual when Harper was involved, Lily shook her head and wrapped herself around her favorite man.

"I mentioned the C word. Why don't you come in and I'll dig one out for her."

"You're not busy?"

"No. Was just thinking about getting a beer and doing some paperwork. Just as soon postpone the paperwork part of it."

"I always like coming in here." She glanced around the living room as he carried Lily back toward the kitchen. "You're pretty tidy, too, for a single straight guy."

"Comes from living with Mama, I guess." With Lily on his hip, he reached in a cupboard and got out the box of animal crackers he kept on hand for her. "Now how'd these get here?"

He opened the box, let her dig one out. "Want a beer?"

"I wouldn't mind. I stopped off at Stella's after work. Ended up having burgers on the grill, but I passed on the wine. I don't like sipping when I'm driving, even just a little when I've got Lily in the car."

He offered her a beer, got one for himself. "How you doing?" When she only angled her head, he shrugged. "Word spreads. I heard about what happened. In any case, it's something we're all involved in, so word should spread."

"It's a little embarrassing to have word of my sex dreams spreading."

"It wasn't like that. Besides, nothing wrong with a good sex dream."

"I'd as soon the next one I have be all my own idea." She tipped back the beer, watching him. "You look a little like him, you know."

"Sorry?"

"Reginald, especially now that I've seen him in what you could call a more intimate situation. Something more personal than an old photograph. You've got the same coloring, and the same shape to your face—your mouth. His build's not as good as yours."

"Oh. Well." He lifted his beer, drank deep.

"He was slim, but soft. Like his hands. And he was older than you, a little gray in the hair. And some hard lines coming in around the mouth, out from the eyes. But still, very handsome, very virile."

She got Lily's sip-cup of juice and her music cube out of the diaper bag. Bribing her, she lifted her away from Harper and set her on the floor.

"You got better shoulders, and no pudge right here." She poked her finger into his belly.

"Okay."

Lily sat down with her music cube, playing with it so it switched from "This Old Man" to "Bingo."

"I noticed all that," Hayley said, "seeing as we were all naked and sweaty."

"I bet."

"I especially noticed the resemblance—the similarities and the differences because when I started out fantasizing—my own part of it—it was with you."

"It was . . . what?"

Okay, a little shocked, but more confused, she decided, and moved in. "It started with you, something like this."

She slid a hand around to the back of his neck, rose up on her toes. She stopped, her lips a whisper from his, to savor that instant when the breath catches and the heart stumbles. Then she closed the distance.

Soft, as she'd imagined it would be soft. And warm. His hair was a silky weight on the back of her hand, and his body such a pleasure to press against.

He'd gone so still, but for his heart that slammed against hers. Then she felt his hand on her back, the fist he made as he gathered her shirt in his fingers.

On the floor, Lily's music cube was a jubilant crash of sound.

She made herself ease back. One step at a time, she reminded herself. Though her belly was quivering, she did her best to take a casual sip of beer while he stared at her with those dark eyes.

"So, what do you think?"

He lifted a hand, then dropped it again. "I appear to have lost the capability for rational thought."

"When you get it back, you'll have to let me know."

She turned to gather the baby's things.

"Hayley." He reached out, grabbed her by the waistband of her jeans and tugged. "Uh-uh."

Her belly jumped, joyfully. She glanced over her shoulder. "Which means?"

"The short way of saying you don't walk in here, kiss me like that, then walk out again. Question. Was that a demonstration to catch me up with what's happening with Amelia, or was it something else?"

"I've been wondering what it would be like, so I decided to find out."

"Okay." He turned her around, glanced down to be sure Lily was still occupied, then backed her into the counter.

His hands were at her hips when his mouth met hers. As his tongue dipped in, an intimate taste, those hands slid up, cruising over her, setting off little charges under her skin.

Then he stepped back, rubbed a thumb over her tingling lips. "I've been wondering what it would be like, too. So I guess we both know."

"Looks like," she managed.

Since Lily came over to tug at his pants, Harper boosted her up on his hip. "I guess it's complicated."

"Yeah, it is. Very. We'll need to take it slow, think it all the way through."

"Sure. Or we can say screw that and I can come to your room later tonight."

"I . . . I want to say yes. I'm thinking yes," she said on a rush. "Yes is screaming inside my head and I don't know why yes isn't coming out of my mouth. It's exactly what I want."

"But." He nodded. "It's okay. We should give it a little time. Be sure."

"Be sure," she repeated, and hurried to pick up Lily's things. "I need to go, or I'll forget about a little time and being sure, because, *man,* you sure can kiss. And I need to get Lily ready for bed. I don't want to mess things up, Harper. I so don't want to mess things up."

"We won't."

"We can't." She took Lily, though the baby cried pitifully at being pried away from Harper. "I'll see you at work."

"Sure, but I can walk you back."

"No." She hurried toward the door with Lily struggling and crying in her arms. "She'll be okay."

The crying escalated into a full-blown temper tantrum with kicking legs, stiffly arched back, and ear-piercing shrieks. "For God's sake, Lily, you'll see him again tomorrow. It's not like he's going off to war."

The diaper bag slipped off her shoulder to weigh like an anchor on her arm while her sweet baby morphed into a red-faced demon from hell. Tiny, hard-toed walking shoes punched bruises into her hip, her belly, her thighs as she struggled to cart twenty pounds of fury through the dragging summer heat.

"I'd like to've stayed, too, you know." Frustration sharpened her voice. "But we can't, that's just the way it is, so you're going to have to deal."

Sweat dripped into her eyes, blurred her vision so that for a moment, the grand old house seemed to be floating like a mirage. An illusion she'd never reach.

It would just keep swimming farther away, because it wasn't real. Not for her. She'd never really belong there. It would be better, smarter, easier if she packed up, moved on. The house and Harper were one in the same—things that could never be hers. As long as she stayed here, *she* was the illusion.

"Well, what's all this?"

She saw Roz through the shimmer of heat, the daze of

twilight, and felt her own body sway as everything snapped back into focus. A sly tongue of nausea curled in her stomach. Then Lily, tears streaming, all but launched herself out of her arms and into Roz's.

"She's mad at me," Hayley said weakly, and tears stung her own eyes as Lily wrapped her arms around Roz's neck and wept into her shoulder.

"Won't be the last time." Roz rubbed Lily's back, going into that instinctive side-to-side rocking motion as she studied Hayley's face. "What set her off?"

"She saw Harper. She wanted to stay with him."

"It's hard leaving your best guy."

"She needs a bath and bed. Should've had them already. I'm sorry we bothered you. I guess they could hear her screaming clear down to Memphis."

"You didn't bother me. She's not the first baby I've heard in a temper, and she won't be the last."

"I'll take her up."

"I got her." Roz turned to take the steps up to the second floor. "You frazzled each other out. That's what happens when babies want one thing and their mama knows they need something different. Then you end up feeling guilty because they act like it's the end of their world, and you're the one who pulled the rug out."

A tear spilled over, and Hayley rubbed it away. "I hate letting her down."

"And how did you let her down by doing what's best for her? This baby's tired," Roz said as she opened the door to the nursery, turned on the lamp. "And sweaty. She needs her bath, a nightie, and a little quiet time. Go on, get her bath started. I'll get her clothes off."

"That's all right, I can—"

"Honey, you've got to learn to share."

Since Roz was already carrying a now calm Lily away,

Hayley moved into the bathroom. She ran the water, adding the bubbles Lily liked to splash in, the rubber duck and frogs. And caught herself swallowing back tears a half dozen times.

"I got myself a naked baby," she heard Roz say. "Yes, I do. And look at that belly, just calling out to be tickled."

Lily's laughter had Hayley sniffling back more tears as Roz stepped in.

"Why don't you go have yourself a shower? You're hot and you're blue. Lily and I'll have some fun in the tub."

"I don't want you to have to do all this."

"You've been around long enough to know I don't offer to do something if I don't want to do it. Go on. Clean up, cool down."

"All right." Since she feared she'd burst into tears at any moment, she fled.

SHE WAS CLEANER, AND SHE WAS COOLER, IF NOT A great deal steadier when she came back to find Roz putting a little cotton nightgown on a sleepy Lily.

The nursery smelled like powder and sweet soap, and her baby was calm.

"And here's your mama come to give you good night kisses." She lifted Lily, and the baby stretched out her arms to Hayley. "Come on over to the sitting room when you're done putting her down."

"Okay." She held Lily close, breathing in her hair, her skin. "Thanks, Roz."

She stood where she was, holding her little girl, letting the embrace center her. "Mama's sorry, baby. I'd give you the world if I could. The whole wide world and a silver box to put it in."

There were kisses, and quiet murmurs as she laid Lily

down in the crib with her little dog to cuddle. Leaving a low light burning, she slipped out of the room and down the hall to the sitting room.

"I got us some bottled water out of your stash." Roz held one out. "That do for you?"

"Perfect. Oh, Roz, I feel so stupid. I don't know what I'd do without you."

"You'd do fine. Better with me, but then everybody does." Roz sat, stretched out her legs. Her feet were bare tonight, and her toes painted a gumdrop pink. "You keep beating yourself up because your child had herself a tantrum, you're going to be permanently black and blue before you're thirty."

"I knew she was tired. I should've brought her straight into the house instead of letting her visit Harper."

"And I bet she enjoyed the visit as much as he did. Now she's sleeping peaceful in her crib, and no harm done."

"I'm not a terrible mother, am I?"

"You're certainly not anything of the sort. That baby is happy and healthy and loved. She has a sweet disposition. She also knows what she wants when she wants it, and that's a sign of character in my opinion. She's got a right to a temper, hasn't she, same as anybody else?"

"Boy, she's sure got one. I don't know what's wrong with me, Roz." Hayley set the bottle down without drinking. "I'm emotional and bitchy one minute, on top of the world the next. You'd think I was pregnant again, except there's no possibility of that unless the Second Coming's scheduled some time soon."

"That might be your answer right there. You're young and healthy. You've got needs, and they're not being met. Sex is important."

"Maybe, but it's not easily, or safely come by for somebody in my situation."

"I know what that's like, too. You know if you're interested in dating again, you have all manner of willing baby-sitters."

"I know."

"Actually, Hayley, I think sex might be one of the keys to Amelia."

"I'm sorry, Roz, I'd do most anything to help, but I have to draw the line at having sex with Amelia. Ghost, female, psycho. That's a full three strikes."

"There's our girl," Roz said with a laugh. "Mitch and I were talking about what happened to you the other evening, sort of expanding on our theories. Sex is what Amelia used to get what she wanted in life. It was her commodity. In any case, that's our conclusion: She was Reginald's mistress. And it was how, obviously, she conceived a child."

"Well, maybe she loved him. Amelia. It's possible she was seduced by him, in love with him. We really only have Beatrice's viewpoint of her from the journals, and she wouldn't be an objective source."

"Good point, and yes, possible." Roz took a thoughtful sip of water. "But that still points to sex. Even if she was in love and being used, it came down to sex. Reginald went to her for his pleasure, and his purposes. To conceive a male heir. It's not far-fetched to assume Amelia's view of sex is far from healthy."

"Okay."

"Then we come into it, the three of us, living together in this house. Stella hears her, sees her—not that unusual as there were children involved. But there's Logan, and not just an emotional spark between them, but a sexual one. And the episodes begin to escalate. We move to me and Mitch, another sexual contact, and more escalation. Now you."

"I'm not having sex." Yet, she thought. Oh boy.

"You're thinking about it. You're considering it. As Stella was. As I was."

"So . . . you think her focus is on me, the sexual energy kind of thing being the magnet. And things will escalate again."

"I think that may be, and particularly if that sexual energy becomes tied together with genuine affection. With love."

"If I got involved with someone, emotionally, sexually, she could hurt them. Or Lily. She could—"

"Now wait." Roz laid a hand over Hayley's. "She's never hurt a child. Never in all these years. There's absolutely no reason to think she might cause Lily any harm. But you're another matter."

"She could hurt me, or try. I get that." Hayley let out a shaky breath. "So I have to make sure she doesn't. She could hurt someone else, too. You or Mitch, David, any of us. And if there was someone I cared about, someone I wanted, he'd be the most likely target, wouldn't he?"

"Maybe. But I know you can't live your life on maybes. You have a right to your life. Hayley, I don't want you to feel obligated to stay here, or to keep working at In the Garden."

"You want me to leave?"

"I don't." Roz's hand gripped tighter. "On a purely selfish level, I want you here. You're the daughter I never had, that's the God's truth. And that child in the other room is one of the brightest lights of my life. It's because of what you mean to me I'm telling you to go."

Hayley took a deep breath as she rose, first to cross to the window. To look out over the summer gardens, so bold and bright in the hazy dark. And beyond them, to the carriage house, with the porch light glowing.

"My mama left us. Daddy and I weren't enough to keep her. She didn't love us enough. When he died, I didn't even know where to write and tell her. She'll never see her granddaughter. That's a shame for her, I think. But not for Lily. Lily has you. I've got you. I'll go if you tell me to. I'll get another place, get another job. And I'll stay away from Harper House for as long as it takes. But you need to tell me something first, and I know you'll tell me the truth because that's what you do."

"All right."

She turned back, met Roz's eyes. "If you were standing here where I am, having to decide whether to leave people you love—especially when you might be able to help—to leave a place you love, work you love. And you had to decide that because maybe something might happen. Maybe you might have trouble, have to face something hard along the way. What would you do, Roz?"

Roz got to her feet. "I guess you're staying."

"I guess I am."

"David made peach pie."

"Oh my God."

Roz held out a hand. "Let's go have a big sinful slice, and I'll tell you about the flower shop I'm thinking of adding on next year."

IN THE CARRIAGE HOUSE, HARPER RAIDED HIS STASH of leftovers. And thought of Hayley while he ate some of David's fried chicken.

She'd gone and changed the playing field, and he wasn't quite sure what to do with the ball. He'd spent the last year and a half suppressing his feelings and urges when it came to Hayley, and assuming—from her attitude, from every damn signal—that she considered him a friend. Even, God help him, a kind of surrogate brother.

He'd done his best to fill that role.

Now she'd come waltzing in, and put the moves on him. Kissed the brains right out of his head, to the tune of—what the hell was it?—"Bingo."

He was never going to be able to hear that ridiculous song again without getting hot.

What the hell was he supposed to do now, ask her out? He was good at asking women out. It was normal, but there was nothing normal about all of this, not when he'd convinced himself she wasn't interested that way. That he shouldn't be.

Add that they worked together. That she lived in the main house with his mother, for God's sake. Then there was Lily to consider. It sliced him in two, the way she'd cried for him when Hayley had taken her home. What if he and Hayley got together, and something went wrong? Would it spill over onto Lily?

He'd have to make certain it didn't, that's all. He'd have to be careful, take it slow and easy.

Which crossed out any idea brewing in the back of his mind about going over to Hayley's room after dark and letting nature take its course.

He cleaned up the kitchen, as was his habit, then went up to the loft that held his bedroom, a bath, and a small room he used as an office. He spent an hour on paperwork, ordering his mind back to the business at hand every time it drifted toward Hayley.

He switched on ESPN, picked up a book, and indulged in one of his favorite solo evening activities. Reading between innings. Somewhere in the eighth, with Boston down two and the Yankees with a runner on second, he drifted off.

He dreamed that he and Hayley were making love in Fenway Park, rolling naked over the infield grass while the game played on around them. Somehow he knew the batter had a count of three and two, even as Hayley locked those long legs around him, as he sank into her. Into that heat, into those soft blue eyes.

The crash woke him, and his dreaming mind heard the joyful crack of ball on bat. He thought home run even as he sat up, shaking his head to toss off sleep.

Jesus! He rubbed his hands over his face. Weird, very weird, even if it did combine two of his favorite activities. Sports and sex. Amused at himself, he started to toss the book aside.

The second crash from downstairs was like a bullet shot, and no dream.

He was on his feet in a fingersnap and grabbing the Louisville Slugger he'd had since his twelfth birthday as he rushed out of the room.

His first thought was that Bryce Clerk, his mother's ex-husband, had gotten out of jail and was back to cause more trouble. He'd be sorry for it, Harper thought grimly as he gripped the bat. His blood was up as he charged toward the fury of crashing and banging.

He slapped on the lights in time to see a plate come winging toward him. Instinct had him swinging for the fences. The plate shattered, shooting out shards.

Then there was utter silence.

The room he'd washed up before going upstairs looked as though it had been set upon by a particularly destructive gang of vandals. Broken dishes littered the floor along with spilled beer and the jagged remains of the bottles it had come from. His refrigerator door hung open, with all the contents pulled out. His counters and walls were covered with what looked like a nasty mix of ketchup and mustard.

There was no one there but himself. And he could see his own breath in the chill that had yet to fade out of the air.

"Son of a bitch." He scooped a hand through his hair. "Son of a goddamn bitch."

She'd used ketchup—at least he hoped it was that benign condiment rather than the blood it resembled—to write her message on the wall.

I will not rest

He studied the mess. "You're not the only one."

SIX

MITCH ADJUSTED HIS GLASSES AND LOOKED MORE closely at the photographs. Harper had been thorough, he thought, getting pictures from every angle, taking close-ups and wide angles.

The boy had a steady hand and a cool head.

But . . .

"You should've called us when this happened."

"It was one in the morning. What was the point? This is what it looked like."

"What it looks like is you pissed her off. Any ideas?"

"No."

Mitch spread the photos out, adjusting their order, while David looked over his shoulder. "You clean that shit up?" David asked Harper.

"Yeah." Temper seemed to vibrate off the blades of his tensed shoulders. "She got every damn dish in the place."

"No great loss there. They were ugly anyway. What are those?" David snatched one of the pictures up. "Twinkies? What are you, twelve? Harper." His face a picture of pity, David shook his head. "I worry about you."

"I happen to like Twinkies."

Mitch held up a hand. "Snack choices aside—"

"Twinkies are bombs of sugar and fat and preservatives." Interrupting Mitch, David tried for a pinch at Harper's waist.

"Cut it out." But the move, as designed, pushed a little humor through the wall of Harper's temper.

"Girls," Mitch said mildly. "To get back to the matter at hand. This is another change of pattern. She's never, to your knowledge, come into the carriage house, or caused you any particular trouble." He looked to Harper for confirmation.

"No." A glance at the photos he'd taken brought back the shock, the fury, and the *time* it had taken to deal with the destruction. "And this is a hell of a debut."

"Your mother's going to have to know about this."

"Yeah, yeah." Still steaming, Harper paced to the back door, scowled out at the morning haze. He'd waited, deliberately, until he'd seen his mother head out for her morning run. "I value my life, don't I? But I wanted us to go over this first, before we bring her into it." He glanced up at the ceiling, where he imagined Hayley was getting started on the day. "Or any of them."

"Strategizing to protect the womenfolk?" David said in an exaggerated drawl. "Not that I don't agree, son, but Roz isn't going to care for that." He jerked a thumb toward the ceiling. "She won't either."

"I don't want them going postal over it, that's all. If we could downplay it some. It was just dishes and kitchen crap."

"A personal attack, Harper, not on you but on your property, in your home. That's how it is, and that's how they'll see it." Mitch waved a hand at him before he could speak. "We've dealt with worse, all of us, and we'll deal with this. The important thing is to figure out why it happened."

"Maybe it's because she's crazy," Harper snapped back.

"That might be a small, contributing factor."

"Takes after his mama when he's riled up," David offered. "Mean and stubborn."

"I've noticed. She's been seen walking in the direction of the carriage house in the past." Mitch leaned a hip on the table. "You saw her yourselves when you were kids. We can assume she did, at some point in her life, go there. We can assume it was after Reginald Harper brought their love child here to pass him off as his legitimate heir."

"And we can assume she was crazy as a crack monkey," David added. "From the way she looked."

"Yet, from what we know she's never bothered with the place since Harper's lived there. How long?"

"Shit, I don't know." He shrugged, drummed his fingers on the thighs of his ragged work pants. "Since college. Six, seven years."

"But she goes in now, destructively. She may be crazy, but there's a reason. Everything she's done has a root and a reason. Have you brought anything in there recently? Anything new?"

"Ah, no." But the idea made him pause and consider instead of stew. "Plants. I rotate plants, but I've done that for years. And the usual stuff, you know, groceries, CDs, clothes. Nothing particular or unusual."

"Anyone?"

"Sorry?"

"Have you had anyone over who hasn't been there before? A woman?"

"No."

"Now that's just sad." David swung an arm around Harper's shoulders. "Losing your touch?"

"My touch is still gold. Just been a little busy."

"And before it happened, you were?"

"Watching the game upstairs in the bedroom, reading. Zonked out, and the next I know it's crash, boom, bang."

He heard Lily's happy call and winced. "Damn it, here they come. Mitch, let's put those away, put this all away until—"

He broke off, cursing himself for not moving faster, when Lily ran in just ahead of Hayley. She zipped straight for him, all grins and upstretched arms.

"She heard your voice," Hayley said as he picked Lily up. "Her face just lit."

"His touch is gold," David said dryly, "with toddlers."

"It's sure her favorite way to start the morning." She went to the refrigerator for juice, and when she turned with the bottle and Lily's cup in her hands, spotted the photographs. "What's all this?"

"It's nothing. Just a little late-night adventure."

"Good God, what a mess! You have a party and not invite us?" Then she blinked, and paled as she leaned closer. "Oh. Oh, Amelia. Are you all right? Are you hurt?" She dropped Lily's cup as she swung toward him. "Harper, did she hurt you?"

"No. No." He patted the hand she was running over his face, his arm. "It's just dishes."

David bent to retrieve the plastic cup, wiggled his eyebrows at Mitch on the way up, and said, "Aha," under his breath.

"But look at your things." She snatched up a photo. "Your sweet little kitchen. What is *wrong* with her? Why does she have to be so damn mean?"

"Being dead probably ticks her off some. I think Lily wants her juice."

"All right, all right. If it's not one thing it's six others with her—Amelia, not Lily. I'm getting fed up." She poured the juice, secured the lid, then handed it to Lily. "There you are, baby. Just what are we going to do about this?" she demanded as she rounded on Mitch.

"Innocent bystander," he reminded her and held up his hands.

"We all are, aren't we? But that doesn't mean a damn to her, apparently. Bitch." She sat down, folded her arms.

"Feel better?" David asked her, and poured her some coffee.

"I don't know what I feel."

"Just dishes." Harper settled Lily in her highchair. "And according to David, ugly ones."

Hayley worked up a smile. "They weren't too ugly. I'm sorry, Harper." She touched his hand. "I'm so sorry."

"Sorry about what?" Roz asked as she came in.

"There's the bell for round two." David gestured with the coffeepot. "I think I'll make crepes."

SHE COULDN'T CONCENTRATE. HAYLEY WENT THROUGH the routine of waiting on customers, ringing up sales on automatic. When she didn't think she could stand making inane chat with another living soul, she went into Stella's office to throw herself on her mercy.

"Give me some manual labor, will you? Something hot and sweaty. Get me off the counter, please. I keep feeling this bitch attack coming on, and I don't want one to spew onto the customers."

Stella pushed back in her chair to give Hayley the once-over. "Why don't you take a break instead?"

"I stop doing, I'll start thinking. Then I'll start seeing those pictures of Harper's kitchen in my head again."

"I know it's upsetting, Hayley, but—"

"It's my fault."

"How is Harper's kitchen getting trashed your fault? And did you have anything to do with the broken vase in my living room, because no one in my house is taking responsibility. At the moment, I Dunno is taking the rap."

"I Dunno is the classic whipping boy."

"Between him and Not Me, nothing is safe, nothing is sacred."

Blowing out a breath, Hayley dropped into a chair. "All right, I will take a break, just for a minute. Can you take one, too, talk to me?"

"Sure." Stella swung away from the spreadsheet on her computer monitor.

"When I left your place last night I went to Harper's. I talked myself into taking some action, making a move, going up a step, you know? He wants to think of me as Cousin Hayley, or Lily's mama, or whatever the hell he thinks, fine. But I'll give him a taste and see what he thinks of that."

"Woo-hoo. And?"

"I laid one on him. Standing right there in his kitchen, moved in and gave him one of those here's-what-you're-missing-so-why-don't-you-come-get-it kisses."

Stella's lips quivered up into a smile. "And did he? Come and get it?"

"You could say. The kiss he gave me back was more of the since-you-opened-the-gate-I'm-galloping-right-on-in variety. He's got a really amazing mouth. I sort of figured he did, but having a couple of good samples made me realize I'd underestimated. Considerably."

"That's good, isn't it? It's what you wanted."

"It's not about what I want. Or maybe it is." She pushed back to her feet, but there was nowhere to pace in the tiny office. "Maybe that's just the point. In his kitchen, Stella. I kissed him in his kitchen, and a few hours later, she's in there wrecking the place. It doesn't take a math whiz to put that two and two together. I opened the gate, all right, but she's the one who came in."

"You're mixing metaphors. I'm not saying you're entirely wrong," she added, and stretched out from the chair to open her little cooler for bottled water. "But I am going to say it's not your fault. She's a volatile presence, Hayley, and none of us is responsible for her actions, or what happened to her."

"No, but try telling her that. Thanks," she said when Stella handed her one of the bottles.

"What we're doing is trying to find out, maybe to make it as right as it can be made, but we have to live our lives while we do."

"It's about sexual energy and emotional attachments. That's what Roz thinks, and I think she's on to something."

"You told Roz about you and Harper."

She took a long, deep drink. "No, no, I mean in general. And there isn't any 'me and Harper,' not really. Roz and Mitch think it's the sexual buzz and the developing emotions that get her stirred up, at least in part. So I've got to work off some of this buzz and these feelings."

"Even if you could, you're not taking Harper's buzz or feelings into account."

"I can take care of that. It's when they're directed at me. Otherwise, she'd've slapped at him before." Her fingers tightened on the bottle, but she caught herself before the gesture pushed water over the lip. "You can bet he's done more than kiss a woman in his kitchen in that house before last night, and she didn't get bent out of shape."

"Again, no argument. But if it does connect to you and Harper, then it must mean something. Maybe something important. The way Logan and I, the way Mitch and Roz mean something important to each other."

"I can't think about that. Not now. I just want to work off this edge. Give me something physical."

"I want all the excess stock cleared out of greenhouse one, brought around front for a display. One table for annuals, one for perennials, and marked thirty percent off."

"I'll get right on it. Thanks."

"Be sure to remember you thanked me when you collapse from heat exhaustion," Stella called out.

SHE LOADED FLATS AND POTS ON A FLATBED CART AND hauled them around to the front of the building. It took her four trips. She muscled over the tables she wanted, positioning them where they'd be most likely to catch the eye of someone driving by. Possible impulse sales, she decided.

She still had to stop from time to time, talk to customers or direct them, but for the most part, she was blessedly left alone.

The air was close and heavy, the sort that brewed itself into thunderstorms. She hoped it did. She'd relish a bitching good storm. It would suit her mood exactly.

Still, the work kept her mind busy. She played the game of identifying and reciting the name of each specimen as she unloaded. Pretty soon she might be as good as Roz or Stella at recognizing plants. And she was pretty sure by the time she finished the work, she'd be too worn out to think about anything.

"Hayley. Been looking for you." Harper's brows drew together as he got closer. "What the hell are you doing?"

"Working." She swiped a forearm over her sweaty brow. "That's what I do around here."

"It's too hot for this kind of work, and the air quality's in the toilet today. Get inside."

"You're not my boss."

"Technically I am as I'm part owner of this place."

She was a little breathless, and the damn sweat kept dribbling into her eyes. It only made her more irritable. "Stella told me to set this up, and I'm setting it up. She's my immediate supervisor."

"Of all the stupid—" He broke off, strode inside.

And straight into Stella's office. "What the hell's wrong with you, sending Hayley out in this heat hauling stock around?"

"Good God, is she still at it?" Alarmed, she pushed back from her desk. "I had no idea she'd—"

"Give me a goddamn bottle of water."

Stella grabbed one out of her cooler. "Harper, I never thought she'd—"

But he held up a hand to cut her off. "Don't. Just don't."

He marched out again, stormed outside, straight to Hayley. She took a swat at him when he grabbed her arm, but he pulled her away from the front of the building.

"Let go. What do you think you're doing?"

"Getting you into the shade for a start." He propelled her around the back, through tables and potted shrubs, between greenhouses, until he came to the shaded banks of the pond.

"Sit. Drink."

"I don't like you this way."

"Right back at you. Now drink that water, and consider yourself lucky I don't just toss you in the pond to cool you off. I expected better of Stella," he said when Hayley glugged down water. "But the fact is, even though this is her second summer, she's a Yankee. You were born and raised down here. You know what this kind of heat can do."

"And I know how to handle it. And don't you blame Stella for anything." But she had to admit, now that she'd stopped, she felt a little queasy and light-headed. Giving in, she stretched out flat on the grass. "Maybe I overdid it. I got caught up, is all." She turned her head, looked over at him. "But I don't like being pushed around, Harper."

"I don't like pushing people around, but sometimes they need it." He pulled off his fielder's cap and waved it at her face to stir the air and cool her. "And since your color's several shades under fire engine now, I'd say you did."

It was hard to argue when it felt so good to stretch out on the grass, and so sweet to have him fanning her with his sweaty old cap.

The sun was behind him, but filtered through the high, thickly leaved branches so that it dappled over him, made him look romantic and handsome sitting in the summer shade.

All that dark hair, curling a bit at the ends from the heat and humidity. And those long, chocolate brown eyes were so . . . delicious. The blades of his cheekbones, the full, sexy shape of his mouth.

She could lie here, she thought, for hours just looking at him. The idea was foolish enough to make her smile.

"You get away with it, this once. I had a lot on my mind, and good, sweaty work helps me deal with it."

"I got another way to deal with it." He leaned down, then stopped, cocked his head when she brought her hand up between them.

"We're on the clock here."

"I thought we were on a break."

"Work environment." The work, however draining, had done the trick. She'd made her decision. It wasn't about what she wanted, but about what was right. "Besides, I realized that sort of thing isn't a good idea."

"What sort of thing?"

"The you and me sort." She sat up, shook her hair back and made sure she smiled at him. It would drop the base out of her world if they stopped being friends. "I like you, Harper. You mean a lot to me, to Lily, and I want to stay friends. We add sex to that, sure, it'd be nice for a while, but then it'd just get awkward and sticky."

"It doesn't have to."

"Odds are." She touched his knee, gave it a brisk rub. "I was just in a mood yesterday. I liked kissing you. It was nice."

"Nice?"

"Sure." Because she knew that expression on his face—or rather the lack of expression—meant he was angry and fighting it back, she bumped up the smile several degrees. "Kissing a good-looking guy's always nice. But I've got to think beyond that kind of thing, and the best thing for me is to leave things just the way they are."

"Things aren't the way they were. You already changed that."

"Harper, a couple of smoochies between friends isn't such a big." She patted his hand, started to get up, but he clamped his fingers around her wrist.

"It was more than that."

His temper was winning, she could see it. And from the few times she'd watched it fly, she knew it was formidable. Better he was mad, she thought quickly. Better for him that he was mad or disgusted or even hurt for the short term.

"Harper, I know you're probably not used to having a woman put on the brakes, but I'm not going to sit here and argue about whether I'm going to have sex with you."

"It's more than that."

More. And that single word had her heart trembling. "It isn't. And I don't want it to be."

"What's this, some kind of game? You came to me, you moved on me. And now it's that was nice, but I'm not interested?"

"That's the nutshell. I've got to get back to work."

His voice stayed calm and cool; a dangerous sign. "I know what you felt when I had my hands on you."

"Well, for God's sake, Harper, of course I felt something. I haven't had any action in months."

His fingers tightened, then released. Let her go. "So, you were just cruising for a fuck buddy."

It wasn't her heart that bumped this time, but her belly. "I did something on impulse I realized I shouldn't have done. You want to make it crude, go ahead."

Her vision wavered, so she seemed to be looking at him through a rippling wave of heat. The anger inside her spiked up, so acute it all but scored her throat. "Men always take it down to fucking, lying and cheating and buying their way to it. And once they have, the woman's no more than a whore to be used again or tossed away. It's men who are the whores, plotting and planning their way to the next rut."

Her eyes had changed. He couldn't say how, but he knew he wasn't looking at her through them. The heat of his temper froze in fear. "Hayley—"

"Is this what you want, Master Harper?" With a sly smile, she cupped her breasts, caressed them. "And this?" She slid a hand between her legs. "What will you pay?"

He took her shoulders, gave her a quick shake. "Hayley. Stop it."

"Do you want me to play the lady? I'm so good at it. Good enough to be used to breed."

"No." He needed to stay calm, though he could feel his own fingers tremble. "I want you exactly the way you are.

Hayley." He gripped her chin, kept his eyes focused on hers. "I'm talking to you. We've got things to do around here, then you've got to go get Lily. You don't want to be late picking up Lily."

"What? Hey." Frowning, she pushed at his hand. "I said I didn't . . ."

"What did you say?" He moved his hands back to her shoulders, rubbed them gently up and down. "Tell me what you just said to me."

"I said . . . I said I did something on impulse. I said—Oh God." The color drained out of her face. "I didn't. I didn't mean—"

"Do you remember?"

"I don't know. I don't feel right." She pressed a clammy hand to her belly as nausea rolled. "I feel a little sick."

"Okay. I'm going to get you home."

"I didn't mean those things, Harper. I was upset." Her knees wobbled when he helped her to her feet. "I say stupid things when I'm upset, but I didn't mean them. I don't know where that came from."

"That's all right." His tone was grim as he took her weight to walk her around the front. "I do."

"I don't understand." She wanted to lie on the grass again, lie in the shade until her head stopped spinning.

"We'll get you home first, then we'll talk about it."

"I have to tell Stella—"

"I'll tell her. I didn't bring my car. Where are your keys?"

"Um. In my purse, behind the counter. Harper, I really feel . . . off."

"In the car." He opened the door, nudged her in. "I'll get your purse."

Stella was behind the counter when he hurried in. "Hayley's purse. I'm taking her home."

"Oh, Harper, is she sick? I'm so sorry. I—"

"It's not that. I'll explain later." He snatched the purse out of Stella's hand. "Tell Mama, tell her to come. Tell her I need her home."

Though she protested she was feeling better, he all but carried her in the house, then jerked his chin at David. "Get her something. Tea."

"What's the matter with our girl?"

"Just get the tea, David. And Mitch. Get Mitch. Come on, lie down in here."

"Harper, I'm not sick. Exactly. I just got overheated or something." But it was hard to argue with a man who plopped you down on a sofa.

"It's the 'or something' part that worries me. You're still pale." He ran his knuckles down her cheek.

"It could be because I'm completely embarrassed by what came out of my mouth. I shouldn't have said those things, Harper, even if I was mad."

"You weren't that mad." He looked around as Mitch came into the room.

"What's going on?"

"We had . . . a thing."

"Hey, baby, what's the matter?" Mitch walked to the sofa, crouched down.

"Just the heat." The sick weakness was passing, and let her work up an embarrassed smile. "Made me a little crazy."

"It wasn't the heat," Harper corrected. "And you're not the one who's crazy. Mama's on her way. We're going to wait for her."

"You didn't drag Roz away from work over this? Just how bad do you want me to feel?"

"Quiet down," Harper ordered.

"Look, I don't blame you for being mad at me, but I'm not going to lie here and—"

"Yes, you are. Lily doesn't have to be fetched for a couple hours. One of us will go get her."

Since her only response was a dropped jaw, he turned as David brought a tea tray into the room. "You can get Lily from the sitter's, can't you?"

"No problem."

"Since she's my daughter, I'm the one who picks her up, or delegates," Hayley snapped.

"Color's coming back," Harper observed. "Drink your tea."

"I don't want any damn tea."

"There now, sugar, it's nice green tea." David soothed as he set the tray down and poured. "Be a good girl now."

"I wish y'all would stop fussing and making me feel like an idiot." She sulked, but took the cup. "But since you ask, David, I will." She continued to sulk as she sipped, then cursed under her breath when she heard Roz come through the front door.

"What's the matter? What happened?"

"Harper's on some sort of rampage," Hayley said.

"Harper, you rampaging again?" Roz rubbed her hand over his arm as she brushed by him to study Hayley. "When are you going to grow out of these things?"

"Roz, I'm sorry for all this trouble," Hayley began. "I got a little overheated and wonky, is all. I'll put in extra time tomorrow to make up for today."

"Oh good, then I won't have to fire you. Now somebody tell me what the hell's going on."

"First, she was working herself up to a good case of heat exhaustion," Harper told her.

"I overdid just a little, which isn't the same as—"

"Didn't I tell you to quiet down once already?"

She set the cup down with a snap of china on china. "I

don't know where you get off taking that tone with me."

The glance he sent her was as mild, and as formidable, as his tone. "Since it's not working, I'll just tell you to shut the hell up. I got her into the shade, got some water in her," he continued. "We talked a couple minutes, then we had an argument. In the middle of it, it wasn't her talking anymore. It was Amelia."

"No. Just because I said things I shouldn't have—"

"Hayley, it wasn't you saying them. She sounded different," he told Mitch. "Different tonal quality, you could say. And the accent was pure Memphis. Not a trace of Arkansas in it. And her eyes, I don't know how to explain it exactly. They were older. Colder."

Everything inside Hayley sank and shivered. "It's not possible."

"You know it is. You know it happened."

"All right." Roz sat beside Hayley. "What did happen, Hayley, from your point of view?"

"I wasn't feeling quite right—the heat. Then Harper and I got into an argument. He just pushed my buttons, that's all, and I slapped back. I said things. I said . . ."

Her hand shook, groped for Roz's. "Oh God, oh God. I felt—away, detached. I don't know how to say it. And at the same time, I was filled with all this rage. I didn't know what I was saying. It was like I stopped saying anything. Then he was saying my name, and I was irritated. For a minute I couldn't remember. My—my brain felt a little dull, like it does when you first wake up from a nap. And I felt a little queasy."

"Hayley." Mitch spoke gently. "Has this happened before?"

"No. I don't know. Maybe." She closed her eyes a moment. "I've been having these thoughts, these moods, that don't seem like me. A lot of bitchiness, but it just seemed like I was feeling bitchy, that's all. God, what am I going to do?"

"Stay calm," Harper advised. "And we'll figure it out."

"Easy for you to say," she shot back. "You're not possessed by a psychopathic ghost."

seven

"A LITTLE LIKE OLD TIMES," STELLA COMMENTED AS she settled down in the upstairs sitting room with Roz and Hayley. And a bottle of cool white wine.

"I should be getting Lily her supper."

Roz poured the wine, then chose one of the sugared green grapes from the platter David had put together. "Hayley, you not only know she'll be fed, but that she'll handle all those men just fine."

"And it's good practice for Logan. We're thinking maybe we'll try to have a baby."

"Really?" For the first time in hours Hayley felt pure pleasure. "I think that's great. You'll make a beautiful baby, and Gavin and Luke would just love having another brother or a sister."

"Still in the talking stage, but we're leaning toward the acting on it stage."

"Feeling better?" Roz asked Hayley.

"Yeah. A lot. Sorry I cracked on you."

"I think we can make allowances. And give you some leeway. You didn't want to talk about what Mitch called the trigger—what you and Harper were arguing about. You needed your panic time and your weepy time, and you've had them."

"And then some. Nothing clears men out of the room faster than female hysterics."

"Which, I believe, was something you wanted anyway." Roz raised her brows and popped another grape. "You didn't want to discuss this with Mitch. Not what you argued about, or what you said to Harper—or rather what Amelia said."

Rather than meet Roz's eyes, Hayley kept hers fixed on the platter as if the cure for cancer was coded in among the glossy grapes and strawberry flowers. "I don't see what's important about what was said. The important thing is it happened. I think we should all—"

"That's enough nonsense." Roz's voice was mild as May. "Everything's important, every detail. I haven't pushed Harper on this, but I will. I'd prefer to hear it from you and it's been each one of us most intimately involved with this thing. So suck up your pride or whatever it is, Hayley, and spill it."

"I'm sorry. I took advantage of you."

"And how did you do that?"

Hayley took a bracing gulp of wine. "I hit on Harper."

"And?"

"And?" That stumped her for a minute. "You took me into your home, me and Lily. You treat us like family. More than. You—"

"And don't make me regret it by putting strings around it that I never tied on. Harper's a grown man, and makes his own decisions about a number of things, including the women in his life. If you hit on him I have no doubt he knew how to block or hit back."

As Hayley remained silent, Roz settled back with her wine, tucked her legs up, sipped. "And unless I don't know or understand my son as well as I think, I'd bet on the latter."

"It happened in the kitchen. I made it happen. Just kissing," Hayley said quickly when she realized how it sounded. "I mean Lily was right there and it was the first time . . ."

"The kitchen," Roz murmured.

"Yes, yes. You see?" She shuddered. "And that same night, she tore his kitchen apart. So I realized this wasn't something that could happen just because I've got the . . . because I'm attracted to Harper. I told him that I wasn't interested after all, and I probably hurt his feelings. But it's better his feelings get hurt than something else happen."

"Mmm-hmm." Roz nodded as she watched Hayley over the rim of her glass. "I don't imagine he took it well."

"Not exactly, so I was like, what's the big deal." She set her glass down so she could gesture freely with both hands. "Then he said something deliberately crude, and it upset me. Because it wasn't like that. It was just a kiss—well, two," she corrected. "But it wasn't like we stripped down naked and had monkey sex on the kitchen floor."

"Difficult when Lily was there," Roz commented.

"Yeah, but even so, I'm not like that, even though I got pregnant with Lily the way I did. And it might seem like I'm a big ho, but—"

"It doesn't seem," Stella cut in. "Not for a minute. We all know what it is to need someone. Whether for the moment, or for more. Personally, I don't care to hear you talking about a friend of mine that way, or to intimate that I would."

Roz smiled, stirred herself to lean forward and tap her glass to Stella's. "Nice."

"Thanks."

"I forgot where I was," Hayley said after a moment.

"You were arguing with Harper," Stella said helpfully. "You big ho."

It made her laugh, settled her down. "Right. We were arguing, then it happened, the way I said. I sort of faded back, and there were these things coming out of my mouth I didn't put there. About how men are all liars and cheats, and just want to fuck you, and treat you like a whore. It was ugly, and it wasn't true. Especially not about Harper."

"The first thing you have to remember is it wasn't you saying it," Stella reminded her. "And the second is, it fits with what we know of her, and the pattern of her behavior. Men are the enemy, and sex is a trigger."

"During the argument, before Amelia's participation, Harper said something to make you feel cheap."

Hayley picked up her glass again, looked at Roz. "He didn't mean it the way I took it."

"Don't make excuses for my boy." Roz angled her head. "If he was perfect, he wouldn't be mine. The point is, you felt that way, and she moved in."

"Roz, I want you to know, I'm not going to pursue this thing with Harper. This personal thing."

"Is that so?" Roz raised her eyebrows. "What's wrong with him?"

"Nothing." Blinking, Hayley looked to Stella for support and got a smile and a shrug. "Nothing's wrong with him."

"So you're attracted to him, nothing's wrong with you, but you've dumped him before things really got started. Why is that?"

"Well, because he's . . ."

"Mine?" Roz finished. "Then what's wrong with me?"

"Nothing!" At her wit's end, Hayley spread a hand over her face. "I can't even believe how embarrassing this is."

"I expect you and Harper to work this out, and to leave me entirely out of the equation. I will make one observation, as his mother. If he knew you were showing him the door in order to protect him from possible future harm, he'd turn right back around and kick that door in. And I'd applaud the action."

"You won't tell him."

"It's not my place to tell him. It's yours." She pushed to her feet. "Now I'm going downstairs, and I'll discuss this with Mitch over our dinner. Meanwhile, I think you have another hour coming—for sulking time. After that, I expect you to straighten up."

Stella gestured with her glass as Roz walked out, then took a slow, satisfying sip. "She's just frigging terrific, isn't she?"

"You weren't a lot of help," Hayley complained.

"Actually, I was. I agreed with everything she said there at the end, but I didn't mention it. Seems to me, keeping my mouth shut was helpful. Hey, you're doing really well with this sulking hour," she added. "And you're only a couple minutes into it."

"Maybe you should shut up again."

"I love you, Hayley."

"Oh, shit."

"And I'm worried about you. We all are. So we're going to figure this out. Go team and all that. In the meantime you've got to decide what's best for you in regards to Harper. You can't let Amelia drive the train."

"It's tough when she's already highjacked it and put on the engineer's hat. She was inside me, Stella. Somehow."

Stella got up, moved to the couch to sit beside Hayley, to drape her arm over her friend's shoulders.

"I am seriously freaked," Hayley whispered.

"Me, too."

SHE FELT LIKE SHE WAS TIPTOEING ON EGGSHELLS. Only the eggshells were sharp as razor blades. She questioned everything she did or thought or said.

It all seemed like her, she decided as she undressed for bed. She'd tasted the pasta salad, the garden-fresh tomatoes at dinner. It was her head that had throbbed with a tension headache, and her hands that had tucked Lily into the crib.

But just how long could she go on being so hyper-aware of every single action, every breath she took without going a little loopy herself?

There were things she could do, and she was going to start doing them the next day. The first order of business was to weigh down her credit card with the purchase of a laptop. The Internet was probably full of information on possession.

That's what they'd call what had happened to her. Possession.

What she knew about it came out of books, novels mostly. To think she'd enjoyed having her spine tingled with those kind of stories once. Maybe she could take some of the things she'd read and apply it to her situation. Though the one that came first to her mind was Stephen King's *Christine*. She was a woman not a classic car, and come to think of it, the solution of smashing the car to bits didn't seem very practical. Besides, it hadn't really worked anyway.

There was *The Exorcist,* but she wasn't Catholic—and that dealt with demons. Still, she'd be willing to try a priest if things got any worse. In fact, the minute her head spun a three-sixty, she was heading for the nearest church.

She was probably overreacting, she decided, and slipped on a tank and cotton shorts. Just because it happened once didn't mean it would happen again. Especially now that she was aware. She could stop it from happening, probably. Willpower, strength of self.

She needed to do more yoga. Who knew that yoga wasn't the cure for possession?

No, what she was going to do was get some air. The thunderstorm she'd wanted was just starting to lash. The wind was up, and shimmers of lightning were buzzing light against the windows. She'd throw open the terrace doors, let the wind pour in. Then she'd read something light, a nice romantic comedy, and turn her head off for sleep.

She walked to the doors, gave them a big, dramatic yank.

And screamed.

"Jesus! Jesus!" Harper grabbed her before she could let out the next peal. "I'm not an ax murderer. Chill."

"Chill? Chill? You're skulking around, scare my hair white, and I'm supposed to chill?"

"I wasn't skulking. I was just about to knock when you opened the doors. I think you may have cracked my eardrum."

"I hope I did. What are you doing out there? It's just about to storm."

"A couple of things. The first was I saw your light and wanted to see if you were okay."

"Well, I was before you gave me a damn heart attack."

"Good." His gaze drifted down, up again. "Nice outfit."

"Oh stop." Annoyed, she folded her arms over her chest. "It's no less than I might wear running around the yard with the kids."

"Yeah, I've noticed you running around the yard. The second is I was thinking about what happened this afternoon."

"Harper, I haven't been able to think about anything

else for hours." Weary of it, she pushed a hand through her hair, then pressed it to her temple. "I just don't think I *can* think about it any more tonight."

"You don't have to, you just have to answer a question." When he started to step inside, she gave him a good, solid shove back.

"I didn't ask you in. And I don't think it's a good idea for you to be in here when I'm not really dressed."

His eyebrows lifted as he leaned comfortably on the doorjamb. Like he owned the place, she thought. Which, of course, he did.

"Let me point out that you've been here for about a year and a half. During that time I've somehow managed to restrain myself from jumping you. I think I can continue that policy for another few minutes."

"You're feeling pretty snarky, aren't you?"

"I'd say what I'm feeling is pissed off. Especially if you're going to be a drama queen and insist we have this conversation with me standing out here and you standing in there."

The first fat drops began to fall, and he lifted his eyebrows again. Exactly the way his mother did.

"Oh, all right, come in then. No point in you standing out there getting soaked like an idiot."

"Gee, thanks so much."

"And leave those doors open." She jabbed a finger at them because the gesture made her feel more in charge. "Because you're not staying."

"Fine." The wind whipped in through them, chased by a charge of thunder. And he stood, thumbs hooked in the front pockets of ratty jeans, his hip cocked.

She wondered, even through the irritation, why she didn't drool.

"You know," he began, "after I more or less—mostly

less—calmed down about everything, replayed it in my head some, the way you do, something interesting occurred to me."

"You going to make a speech or ask your question?"

He inclined his head, an action that managed to look regal despite the jeans, T-shirt, and bare feet. "You've done a lot of swiping at me since you came here. I've tolerated it pretty well, for certain reasons. I'm about done with that now. But to get back to my point. The interesting thing that occurred to me was timing. Here's how it plays for me. You come over, make your move, I make one back. We have a moment, a couple of them. You want to take it slow, I get that. Then the next time we're together, you're all about now you're not really interested after all, it was just an impulse, no big, and let's just be pals."

"That's right. And if your question is have I changed my mind—"

"It's not. Between those two interludes, I get a visit from our resident crazy, who happens to decide to trash my place. My kitchen to be exact, the scene of interlude one. So my question is, how much did that event play into your role in interlude two?"

"I don't know what you're talking about."

"Well now you're just lying, straight to my face."

Her expression went to pitiful. She could actually feel it move across her face and settle in. "I wish you'd go away, Harper. I'm tired, and I have a headache. It hasn't been the easiest day for me."

"You pulled back because you figured she didn't like us together. Enough that she fired what we could call a warning shot."

"I pulled back because I pulled back. And that should be enough."

"It would be, would have to be, if that were true. If that

was all. I'm not going to push myself on you, on any woman who doesn't want me. I've got too much pride for that, and I was raised better."

He straightened, took another step toward her. "And those are the exact same reasons I don't walk away from a fight anymore than I let somebody stand in front of me if there's trouble."

He angled his head again, rocked on his heels. "So don't even think about getting in my way on this, Hayley, about stepping aside from something to protect me from her."

She cupped her elbows. "You say you won't push, but I feel pushed, so—"

"I've wanted you since the first minute I saw you."

Her arms went limp, simply fell to her sides. "You have not."

"The first moment—it was like being blasted with light. Went straight through me." With his eyes on hers, he tapped a fist on his chest. "I think I stuttered. I could hardly speak."

"Oh God." She pressed a hand to her heart, hoping that would hold it in place. "That's a lousy thing to say to me."

"Maybe." His lips twitched, his eyes warmed. "I'll just follow it up with some lousy behavior then." He reached out, drew her against him.

"Harper, this really isn't something we should—" It was some move, or so she would think when she could think again. With a subtle shift, a tiny bump, they were fitted together. Angle to angle, line to line so that every inch of her body felt the jolt.

"Oh," she murmured. "Uh-oh."

A smile flickered at the corners of his mouth, then that mouth was on hers. Hot and warm and sweet, like liquid sugar. The kiss was a slow, irresistible seduction, a drugging of the senses, as his hands cruised over her, a light and lazy touch. A touch, she thought mistily, of a man confident enough to take his time—sure enough that he had plenty of it.

And his lips rubbed silkily over hers until she'd have sworn she felt her own shimmer.

It was like being gradually, skillfully, thoroughly melted, body and will, heart and mind, until what choice was there really, but surrender?

She moaned for him, that soft, helplessly pleasured sound. And she yielded, degree by erotic degree, until the fingers that had gripped his shoulders went lax.

When he eased back, her eyes were blurred, her lips parted.

"Hayley?"

"Mmm."

"That's not the response of a woman who isn't interested."

She managed to get her hand on his shoulder again, but it wasn't much of a push. "That wasn't really fair."

"Why not?"

"Because . . . that mouth." She couldn't stop her gaze from dropping down to it. "You should need a license to kiss that way."

"Who says I haven't got one?"

"Well, in that case. Do it again, would you?"

"Was planning on it."

It was the same rush with the wind spewing in through the door, and his mouth lighting small, sparkling fires inside her. Little tongues of heat, she thought, that were going to lick their way through her until she simply dissolved.

"Harper." She said it with the kiss, shuddering at the sensation of their lips moving together.

"Hmm?"

"We really have to stop this." She couldn't resist nipping that sexy bottom lip of his, just a little. "Sometime."

"Later is good. Let's say next week."

She had to laugh, but it came out shaky, then ended on a gasp as his mouth slid from hers to find some magic point just under her ear.

"That's good, that's . . . exceptional. But I really think we need to wait, just a . . . Oh." She let her head fall back as his cruising mouth found yet another magical spot. "That's so . . ."

She turned her head to give him better access, and her heavy eyes blinked clear. Widened. "Harper."

When she jerked in his arms, he just shifted his grip. "What? It's not next week yet."

"Harper. Oh God, stop. Look."

Amelia stood in the doorway, the storm raging at her back. Behind her, *through* her, Hayley could see trees whipping in the wind and the bruised fists of clouds that smothered the sky.

Her hair was matted and wild, her white gown streaked with mud that dripped, it seemed to drip, into a filthy pool over her bare and bloodied feet. She carried a long, curved blade in one hand, a rope in the other. And her face was a mask of bitter rage.

"You see her, don't you? You see her." Hayley shuddered now from fear and cold.

"Yeah, I see her." In one easy move, he changed his stance so Hayley was behind him. "You're going to have to get over it," he said to Amelia. "You're dead. We're not."

The force of the blow lifted him off his feet, shot him back five feet to slam against the wall. He tasted blood in his mouth even as he shoved clear again.

"Stop! Stop!" Hayley shouted. Force of will and fear had her pushing against the freezing wind toward Harper.

"He's your great-great-grandbaby. He comes out of you. You sang to him when he was a boy. You can't hurt him now."

She started forward, with no clear idea what she would do if she reached Amelia. Before Harper could yank her back, a gust of wind knocked her off her feet and sent her sprawling. She thought she heard someone scream, in rage or grief. Then there was nothing but the sound of the storm.

"Are you crazy?" Harper dropped down beside her to prop her up.

"No, are you? You're the one whose mouth's bleeding."

He swiped the side of his hand over it. "You hurt?"

"No. She's gone. At least she's gone. Christ, Harper, she had a knife."

"Sickle. And yeah, that's a new one."

"It can't be real, right? I mean, she's not corporeal, so the rest of it isn't real either. She couldn't slice us up with it. You think?"

"No." But he wondered if she could make you imagine you were cut, or do yourself some kind of harm defending yourself.

She stayed on the floor, getting her breath back, leaning on him as she stared through the open doors. "When I first came here, when I was pregnant, she'd come to my room sometimes. It was a little spooky, sure, but there was something comforting, too. The way it seemed she was just looking in on me, seeing if I was okay. And this sense I got, this wistfulness, from her. And now she's—"

She was on her feet and running the instant she heard the singing come through the baby monitor.

She was fast; Harper was faster and got to Lily's door two strides ahead of her. Quick enough to throw out an arm and block her. "It's okay, it's all right. Let's not wake her up."

Lily slept in the crib, curled under her blanket with her stuffed dog. In the rocking chair, Amelia sang. She wore her gray dress, her hair in neat coils, and her face was calm and quiet.

"It's so cold."

"It's not bothering the baby. It never bothered me as a kid. I don't know why."

In her chair, Amelia turned her head to look over. There was sorrow on her face, grief, and, Hayley thought, regret. She continued to sing, low and sweet, but her gaze was on Harper now.

When the song was done, she faded away.

"She was singing to you," Hayley told him. "Some part of her remembers, some part of her knows, and she's sorry. What must it be like, to be insane for a hundred years?"

Together, they crossed to the crib where Hayley fussed with the blanket.

"She's okay, Hayley. Lily's just fine. Come on."

"Sometimes I don't know if I can take it, this roller-coaster ride through the haunted house." She pushed at her hair as they walked back to Hayley's bedroom. "One minute she's knocking us around, and the next, she's singing lullabies."

"Dead lunatic," he pointed out. "Still, maybe it's a way of telling us she might come after you or me, but she won't hurt Lily."

"What if I do? What if she does what she did at the pond, and makes me hurt Lily, or someone else?"

"You won't let that happen. Sit down a minute. You want something? Water or something?"

"No."

He eased her down so they sat on the side of the bed. "She never hurt anybody in this house. Maybe she wanted to. Maybe she even tried, but she never did." He took her hand, and because it still felt chilled, rubbed it between both of his. "That's one thing that would've gotten passed down. A crazy woman attacking a Harper, or even a servant. It would've been reported, and she'd have been taken away, put in jail or an asylum."

"Maybe. What about the sickle, and the rope? That says: I'm gonna tie somebody up and slice them to ribbons."

"Nobody ever got sliced to ribbons in Harper House." He rose to move over and close her terrace doors.

"That you know about."

"Okay, that I know about." He sat again. "We'll pass this on to Mitch. He can look into police records maybe. It's an avenue."

"You've got this calm surface," she said after a moment. "It's deceptive, seeing as there are all these little hot pockets under it. Shows me I don't know you as well as I thought I did."

"Back at you."

She sighed, looked down at her hands as they sat on the side of her bed together. "I can't just sleep with you. I thought I could—at first. Then I thought, I can't go jumping on that. I do and he's going to get hurt. She's going to hurt him." She looked up. "You were right about that."

He only smiled. "Duh."

She gave his arm a swat. "Think you're so clever and smart."

"Only because I am. You can ask my mama, when she's in a good mood."

"You're easy to be around, except when you're not." She studied him, trying to take in all the new things she was learning. "I like that, I guess, finding all those under-the-surface pockets. And God knows you're nice to look at."

"How big a fall are you building me up for?"

"It's not—" She shook her head, rose to wander the room. "I've got all these feelings stored up, and all these needs. It'd be so easy to set them loose on you."

"I don't recall putting up a fight."

"I didn't know you looked at me, not that way. Knowing you did, you do, just adds to everything. I've never been kissed like that in my life, and I've been kissed pretty good now and then. If she hadn't come in here when she did, it's likely we'd be in bed right now, going where that kiss was leading."

"That's no way to make me feel fonder of my great-great-grandmother."

"I'm not feeling so fond of her myself. But it gave me time to think instead of just want." Ordering herself to be sensible, for both of them, she sat on the arm of a chair. "I'm not shy about sex, and I think if you and I were somewhere else, in some other sort of situation, we could be lovers without all these extra complications."

"Why do people always think being lovers shouldn't be complicated?"

She frowned, then shook her head. "Well, that's a question. A good one. I don't know."

"Seems to me," he began, crossing to her. "That there are flings, and that's uncomplicated by design. Nothing wrong with it. But being lovers, going into it thinking about more than a night or two, that should have weight. You've got weight, you've got some complications."

"You're right, I can't say you're not. But there's a lot to consider before we take a step like this. I think we need to be sure it's the right thing for both of us before we take that step. There are things we don't know about each other, and maybe we should."

"How about dinner?"

She stared up at him. "You're hungry?"

"Not now, Hayley. I'm asking you for a date. Have dinner with me. We'll go into the city, have a meal, listen to some music."

Her shoulders relaxed and the tight coil in her belly loosened. “That’d be good.”

“Tomorrow?” he said as he drew her to her feet.

“If your mama or Stella can mind Lily, tomorrow’s fine. Ah, we’ll need to tell them about what happened. About Amelia.”

“In the morning.”

“It’s a little awkward, explaining how you were in here, and what we were doing when—”

“No.” He took her face in his hands, laid his lips on hers. “It’s not. You going to be all right now?”

“Yeah.” She looked over his shoulder to the doors he’d shut. “Storm’s passing, you should go now, in case it decides to rain some more.”

“I’ll bunk in Stella’s old room.”

“You don’t have to do that.”

“We’ll both sleep easier that way.”

SHE DID FEEL BETTER, EVEN THOUGH IT DIDN’T EXactly cajole sleep to imagine him just down the hall. Or to imagine how easy it would be to tiptoe down there, slide into bed beside him.

She had no doubt they’d both sleep a lot easier *that* way.

It was hell being responsible and mature.

Even a bigger hell to realize she cared about him more than she’d bargained for. But that was good, wasn’t it? she thought as she tossed and turned. She wasn’t a slut who hopped into bed with a guy just because he was good-looking and sexy.

Some people might think differently, because of Lily, but it hadn’t been that way. She’d cared for Lily’s father. She’d liked him. Maybe she’d been careless, but it hadn’t been cheap.

And she'd wanted the baby. Maybe not at first, she admitted. But after the panic and pity, the anger and denial, she'd wanted the baby. She'd never wanted anything in her life as much.

Her beautiful baby.

She'd taken nothing from the father, had she? The spineless, selfish bastard who'd used her grief to have his way. That hadn't been stupid. She'd been smart not to tell him, to go away, keep her child to herself. Only hers. Always.

But she could have more, couldn't she? She was thinking about this all the wrong way. Why should she work? Sweat and slave, settle for a room in the great house. She could have it all. Her child would have it all.

He wanted her. She could play this well. Oh yes, who knew better how to play a man. He would come begging before she was done, and she would bind him to her.

When it was done, Harper House would be hers, hers and her child's.

At last.

eight

In the propagation house, Hayley watched Roz set a ceanothus cutting in a rockwood plug. "Are you sure you don't mind watching Lily?"

"Why would I mind? Mitch and I will spend the evening spoiling her rotten while you aren't around to run interference."

"She loves being with you. Roz, I feel so weird about everything."

"I don't know why you'd feel weird about going out on a date with Harper. He's a handsome, charming young man."

"Your young man."

"Yes." Roz smiled as she dipped another cutting in rooting compound. "Aren't I lucky? I also have two other handsome, charming young men, and wouldn't be the least surprised if they had dates tonight."

"It's different with Harper. He's your first, he's your partner. I'm working for you."

"We've been over this, Hayley."

"I know." Just as she knew that impatient tone. "I'm not able to wind myself through it as easy as you, I guess."

"You might if you'd relax, go out, and have a good time." Roz glanced up before sliding the cutting into the plug. "Wouldn't hurt to try to catch a quick nap beforehand, either. See if you can deal with those circles under your eyes."

"I didn't sleep well."

"Not surprising, considering."

The music in the propagation house today was some sort of complicated piano, drenched in romance. Hayley had more skill identifying plants than classical composers, so she just let the music drift around her as she worked.

"I kept having weird dreams, at least I think I did. I can't remember any of them clearly. Roz, are you afraid?"

"Concerned. Here, you do the next one." She stepped back so Hayley could take over. "And angry, too. Nobody slaps at my boy—except me. And if I get the opportunity, I'll tell her so, in no uncertain terms. That's good," she said with a nod as Hayley worked. "This kind of hardwood cutting needs a dry rooting medium or you get rot."

"She may have gotten that sickle and the rope out of the carriage house. I mean all those years ago. Maybe she tried to use them and someone stopped her."

"There are a lot of maybes, Hayley. Since Beatrice didn't mention Amelia again in any of her journals, we may never know all of it."

"And if we don't we may never get her out. Roz, there are people, paranormal experts, who you can hire to clean houses." She glanced up, knitted her brows. "I don't know why you smile at that. It's not such a strange idea."

"I just had an image of a bunch of people running around the house armed with buckets and brooms, and that ray gun sort of thing Bill Murray used in *Ghostbusters.*"

"Proton streams—and I have no idea why I know that. But really, Roz, it's a fringe science and all that, but there are serious and legitimate studies. Maybe we need outside help."

"If it comes to that, we'll see about it."

"I looked up some sites on the Internet."

"Hayley."

"I know, I know, just a contingency."

They both looked over as the door opened. Mitch came in, and something about the look on his face had Hayley holding her breath.

"I think I found her. How soon can you wrap things up here and come home?"

"An hour," Roz decided. "But for God's sake, Mitchell, don't leave it at that. Who was she?"

"Her name was Amelia Connor. Amelia Ellen Connor, born in Memphis, May 12, 1868. No death certificate on record."

"How did you—"

"I'll get into all that at home." He flashed her a wide grin. "Rally your troops, Rosalind. See you there."

"Well, for heaven's sake," she muttered when he walked out. "Isn't that just like a man? I'll finish up here, Hayley. You go tell Harper and Stella to finish up whatever they're doing. Let me think," she said as she pressed fingers to her temple. "Stella can get in touch with Logan if she wants him there, and she'll need to leave Ruby in charge, see that she closes today. Looks like we're taking off a couple hours early."

* * *

AMELIA ELLEN CONNOR. HAYLEY CLOSED HER EYES and thought the name as she stood just inside the foyer of Harper House. Nothing happened, no ghostly revelations or appearances, no sweep of sudden knowledge. She felt a little foolish because she'd been sure *something* would happen if she concentrated on the name while standing inside the house.

She tried saying it out loud, quietly, but got the same results. She'd wanted to be found, Hayley thought. She'd wanted to be acknowledged. All right then.

"Amelia Ellen Connor," she said aloud. "I'm acknowledging you as the mother of Reginald Edward Harper."

But there was nothing but silence in answer, and the scent of David's lemon oil and Roz's summer roses.

Deciding she'd keep the failed experiment to herself, she headed to the library.

Roz and Mitch were already there, with Mitch hammering away at his laptop.

"Says he wants to get some things down while they're fresh in his mind," Roz told her with some exasperation whipping around the edges of her voice. "Stella's in the kitchen with David. Her boys are with their grandparents today. Logan'll be along when he's along. I imagine the same goes for Harper."

"He said he'd come. He just had to finish . . ." She lifted her shoulder. "Whatever."

"Have a seat." Roz waved a hand. "Dr. Carnegie seems determined to keep us in suspense."

"Iced tea and lemon cookies," David announced and he wheeled in a cart just ahead of Stella. "You cracked him yet?" He nodded toward Mitch.

"No, but it's not going to take much more to push me to do just that. Mitch!"

"Five minutes."

"It's such a simple name, isn't it?" Hayley shrugged when Roz looked at her. "Sorry, I was just thinking. Amelia, that's sort of flowy and feminine. But the rest. Ellen Connor. It's solid and simple. You sort of expect the rest to be flowy, too, or a little exotic. Then again, Amelia means industrious—I looked it up."

"Of course you did," Roz said fondly.

"It doesn't sound like that's what it should mean. I think Ellen's a derivative of Helen, and makes me think Helen of Troy, so it's actually more sort of feminine and exotic when you come down to it. And none of that's important."

"Interesting, as always though, to see how your mind works. And here's the rest of our happy few."

"Ran into Harper out front." Logan walked over to kiss Stella. "Sweaty, sorry. Came straight from the job." He picked up a glass of iced tea David had poured and drank every drop.

"So what's the deal?" Harper zeroed in on the cookies, took three, then plopped into a chair. "We've got her name, so what, drum roll?"

"It's pretty impressive Mitch could find her name with the little we had to go on," Hayley shot back.

"Not saying otherwise, just wondering what we do with it."

"First, I'd like to know how he came by it. Mitchell," Roz said with growing impatience. "Don't make me hurt you in front of the children."

"So." Mitch pushed back from the keyboard, took off his glasses to polish them on his shirt. "Reginald Harper owned several properties, including houses. Here in Shelby County, and outside it. Some were rented, of course, investment properties, income. I did find a few, through the old ledgers, that were listed as tenanted through certain periods, but generated no income."

"Cooking the books?" Harper suggested.

"Possibly. Or these residences might have been where he installed mistresses."

"Plural?" Logan took another glass of tea. "Busy boy."

"Beatrice's journal speaks of women, not woman, so it follows. It also follows, as we find him a shrewd, goal-oriented type that as he wanted a son, whatever the cost, he maintained more than one candidate until he got what he was after. But the journals also indicate Amelia was local, so I concentrated on the local properties."

"I doubt he'd list a mistress as a tenant," Roz said.

"No. Meanwhile, I've been scouring the census lists. A lot of names, a lot of years to cover. Then a little lightbulb goes off, and I narrowed it to the years Reginald held those local properties, and before 1892. Still a lot to cull through, but I hit in the 1890 census."

His gaze scanned the room, landed on the cart. "Are those cookies?"

"Jesus, David, get the man some cookies before I have to kill him. What did you hit in 1890?"

"Amelia Ellen Connor, resident of one of Reginald's Memphis houses. One that generated no income from the later half of that year, through March of 1893. One, in fact, he'd listed as untenanted during that period."

"Almost certainly has to be her," Stella said. "It's too neat and tidy not to be."

"She knows her neat and tidy," Logan commented. "In spades."

"If it's not our Amelia, it's one hell of a coincidence." Mitch tossed his glasses onto the table. "Reginald's very careful bookkeeper noted on Reginald's books a number of expenses incurred during the period the property was supposedly empty, and Amelia Connor listed it as her residence on the census. In February of 1893, considerably more expenses were noted dealing with refurbishing in preparation for new tenants, paying tenants. The house was sold, if you're interested, in 1899."

"So we know she lived in Memphis," Hayley began, "at least until a few months after the baby was born."

"More than that. Amelia Ellen Connor." He slipped his glasses back on and read his notes. "Born 1868 to Thomas Edward Connor and Mary Kathleen Connor née Bingham. Though Amelia listed both her parents as deceased, that was only true of her father, who died in 1886. Her mother was alive, and very possibly well, until her death in 1897. She was employed by the Lucerne family as a housemaid at a home on the river, called—"

"The Willows," Roz finished. "I know that house. It's older than this one. It's a bed-and-breakfast now, a very lovely one. It was bought and restored oh, twenty years ago at least."

"Mary Connor worked there," Mitch continued, "and though she listed no children for the census, a check of vital records shows she had a daughter—Amelia Ellen."

"Estranged, I suppose," Stella said.

"Enough that the daughter considered her mother dead, and the mother didn't acknowledge the daughter. There's another interesting bit. There's no record of Amelia having a child, just as there's no record of her death."

"Money can grease wheels or muddy them up," Hayley added.

"What's next?" Logan wondered.

"I'm going to go back over old newspapers, again, keep looking for any mention of her death—unidentified female, that sort of thing. And we'll keep trying to find information through the descendants of servants. I'll see if the people who own The Willows now will let me have a look at any documents or papers from that time."

"I'll smooth the way," Roz offered. "Old family names grease wheels, too."

SHE WAS OUT ON A DATE FOR THE FIRST TIME IN . . . it was really too sad to think about how long. And she looked pretty good, if she did say so herself. The little red top showed off her arms and shoulders, which were nicely toned between hauling Lily, yoga, and digging in the dirt.

There was a great-looking guy sitting across from her in a noisy, energetic Beale Street restaurant. And she couldn't keep her mind on the moment.

"We'll talk about it," Harper said, then picked up the glass of wine she'd ignored and handed it to her. "You'll feel better getting it out than working so hard not to say anything."

"I can't stop thinking about it. Her. I mean she had his baby, Harper, and he just took it. It's not so hard to see why she'd have this hard-on about men."

"Devil's advocate? She sold herself."

"But, Harper—"

"Hold on. She came from a working-class family. Instead of opting to work, she opted to be kept. Her choice, and I got no problem with it. But she traded sex for a house and servants."

"Which gives him the right to take her child?"

"Not saying that, by a long shot. I'm saying it's unlikely she was a rosy-cheeked innocent. She lived in that house, as his mistress, for what, more than a year before she got pregnant."

She wasn't ready to have it all taken down to its lowest level. "Maybe she loved him."

"Maybe she loved the life." He jerked a shoulder.

"I didn't know you were so cynical."

He only smiled. "I didn't know you were so romantic. More than likely, the truth of it hits somewhere in the middle of cynicism and romance, so we'll split the difference."

"Seems fair. I don't always like being fair though."

"Either way it falls, we know this is one screwed-up individual, Hayley. It's pretty likely she was screwed up before this happened. That doesn't mean she deserved it, but I'm betting on a hard edge. It takes one, doesn't it, to list your own mother as dead when she's living a few miles away?"

"Yeah. It doesn't paint a nice picture. I guess part of me wants to see her as a victim, like the heroine, when it's just not that cut and dried."

Deliberately she sipped her wine. "Okay, that's enough. That's all she gets for tonight."

"Fine with me."

"I just have to do one thing."

Harper reached in his pocket. "Here, use my phone."

Laughing, she took it. "I know she's fine with Roz and Mitch. I just want to check."

SHE ATE CATFISH AND HUSH PUPPIES AND DRANK TWO glasses of wine. It was amazing how liberating it was to sit as long as she liked, to talk about whatever came to mind.

"I forgot what this was like." Simply because she could, Hayley lounged back in her chair. "Eating a whole meal without interruptions. I'm glad you finally asked me out."

"Finally?"

"You've had plenty of time," she pointed out. "Then I wouldn't have had to make the first move."

"I liked your first move." He reached over, took her hand.

"It was one of my better ones. Harper." Relaxed, she eased forward, her eyes on his. "Were you really thinking about me that way all this time?"

"I put a lot of effort into not thinking about you that way. It worked some of the time."

"Why did you? Put a lot of effort into it, I mean."

"It seemed . . . rude," was the best he could think of, "to imagine seducing a houseguest, especially a pregnant one. I helped you out of the car once—the day of your baby shower."

"Oh God, I remember." It made her laugh even as she covered her face with her free hand. "I was so awful to you. I felt so hot and fat and miserable."

"You looked amazing. Vital. That was my first impression of you. Light and energy, and well, sex, but I tried to tramp that one out. But that day, when I helped you out, the baby moved. I felt it move. It was . . ."

"Scary?"

"Powerful, and yeah, a little scary. I watched you give birth."

She went still, and flushed to the tips of her ears. "Oh, oh God, I forgot about that." She squeezed her eyes shut. "Oh no."

He grabbed her hands, pulled them toward him to kiss. "It was impossible to describe. After I got over the get-me-the-hell-out-of-here stage, it was just staggering. I saw her born. I've been in love with her ever since."

"I know." Embarrassment faded as her heart swam up into her eyes. "That I know. You never ask about her father."

"It's not my business."

"If we take this any further, it should be. You should at least know. Could we maybe take a walk?"

"Sure."

THEY TURNED AWAY FROM THE LIGHTS AND ACTION of Beale Street and wandered toward the river. Tourists flocked there as well, to stroll through the park or stand and watch the water, but the relative quiet made it easier for her to go back in her mind, and take him with her.

"I didn't love him. I want to say that right off because some people still like to think poor girl, some guy got her in trouble then didn't stand by her. And they think your heart's been broken by some asshole. It wasn't like that."

"Good. It'd be a shame if Lily's father was an asshole."

The laugh bubbled up, made her shake her head. "You're going to make this easier. You've got a way of doing that. He was a nice guy, a grad student I met when I was working at the bookstore back home. We'd flirt with each other, and we hit it off, went out a couple of times. Then my father died."

They crossed the little bridge over the replica of the river, wandered past the couples sitting at stone tables. "I was so lost, so sad."

He slid his arm around her shoulder. "I think if anything happened to my mother, it would be like being blinded. I've got my brothers to hold on to, but I can't imagine the world without her."

"It's like that, like you just can't see. What to do next, what to say next. No matter how kind people are—and they were, Harper, a lot of kind people—you're in the dark. People loved my father, you just had to. So there were neighbors and family and friends, the people I worked with, that he worked with. But still, he was so much the center of my life, I felt alone, just isolated in this void of grief."

"I was a lot younger when my father died, and I guess in some ways it's easier. But I know there's a stage you have to go through, the one where you can't believe anything's ever going to be right again, or solid again."

"Yes, exactly. And when you get through it, start to feel again, it hurts. This guy, he was there for me. He was very sweet, very comforting, and that's how one thing led to another."

She tilted her head to meet his eyes. "Still, we were never more than friends. But it wasn't a fling, it was—"

"Healing."

Her heart warmed. "Yes. He went back to school, and I got on. I didn't realize I was pregnant at first. The signs didn't filter through my head. And when I did . . ."

"You were scared."

She shook her head. "I was *pissed.* I was so mad. Why the hell had this happened to me? Didn't I have enough to deal with? It wasn't like I'd slept around, it wasn't like I hadn't been responsible, so what the hell was this? A joke? God, Harper, I wasn't all soft and shivery. I was enraged. I got around to panic at some point, but I bounced back pretty quick to mad."

"It was a tough spot, Hayley. You were alone."

"Don't pretty it up. I didn't want to be pregnant. I didn't want a baby. I had to work, I had to grieve, and it was about damn time somebody up there gave me a freaking break."

They moved toward the river, and she kept her voice down as she looked out toward the water. "Now I was going to have to get an abortion, and that meant I'd have to figure out how to get some time off work, and pay for it."

"But you didn't."

"I got the literature, and I found a clinic, and then I started thinking maybe it'd be better if I had it then gave it up for adoption. Signed up with one of those agencies. You read so much about these infertile couples pining for a baby. I thought maybe that would be something positive I could do."

He brushed a hand down her hair, spoke softly. "But you didn't do that either."

"I got literature on that kind of thing, started researching. And all the time I was going back and forth, cursing God and so on, I was wondering why this guy wasn't coming back in the store, or calling me. Part of my thinking when I was a little calmer was that I had to tell him, he had to know. I didn't get pregnant by myself, and he'd better take some responsibility, too. Somewhere in all that thinking, it got real. I was going to have a baby. If I had a baby, I wouldn't be alone. That was selfish thinking, and the first time I realized I was leaning toward keeping it. For me."

She breathed deep and faced him. "I decided to keep the baby because I was lonely. That, then, was the heaviest weight on the scale."

He didn't say anything for a moment. "And the grad student?"

"I went to see him, to tell him. Tracked him down at college, all ready to say, oops, look what happened, and here's what I've decided to do so step on up."

A breeze fluttered her hair, and she let it go. Let the damp warm air breathe over her face. "He was glad to see me, a little embarrassed, I think, that he hadn't kept in touch. The thing was, he'd fallen in love with somebody. Big sunbursts of love," she said, throwing her arms out to illustrate. "He was so happy and excited, and when he talked about her he just sent off waves of love."

"So you didn't tell him."

"I didn't tell him. What was I supposed to do? Say, gee, that's nice, glad you found someone who makes your world complete. How do you think she'll feel about the fact that you knocked me up? Too bad you screwed up the rest of your life because you were being a friend to me when I needed one. On top of that, I didn't want him. I didn't want to marry him or anything, so what was the point?"

"He doesn't know about Lily?"

"Another selfish decision, maybe with a little unselfish

best-for-him worked in. I wrestled with it later, when the pregnancy got more real, when I started to show and feel the baby kick around inside me. But I stuck with what I'd done."

She paused a moment. It was harder than she'd known it could be to finish it out, to go on when he was quiet, when the quality of his listening was so complete.

"I know he has a right to know. But that's what I did, and what I'd do again. I heard he married that girl in April, and they moved up to Virginia where his people are from. I think, whatever the reasons were, I did the right thing for all of us. Maybe he'd love Lily, or maybe she'd just be a mistake to him. I don't want to know. Because she was a mistake for me for those first few months, and I hate knowing that. I didn't start to love her, really love her, until I was about five months gone, and then it was like . . . oh, it was like everything in me opened up, and she was filling it. That's when I knew I had to leave home. Give us both a new start, clean slate."

"It was brave, and it was right."

It was so simple, his response, and nothing like what she'd prepared for. "It was crazy."

"Brave," he repeated. He stopped, by deliberate design, next to a patch of small yellow lilies. "And right."

"Turned out right. I was going to name her Eliza. That was the name I had picked out for a girl. Then you brought those red lilies into the room, and they were so beautiful, so bright. When she was born, I thought, she's so beautiful, so bright. She's Lily. So . . ." She let out a long breath. "That's the big circle, from the beginning around to the end."

He leaned down, touched his lips to hers. "The thing about circles? You can keep widening them."

"Is that a way of saying you weren't so bored by my personal soap opera you might want to do this again?"

"One thing you've never done is bore me." He linked his hand with hers so they could continue walking. "And yeah, I'd like to do this again."

"Away from the house. Away from her."

"We can do that. The thing is, Hayley, we live there. We work there. We can't avoid her."

TOO TRUE, HAYLEY THOUGHT WHEN SHE WALKED INTO her bedroom. All the drawers on her dresser hung open. Her clothes from there, from the closet, were all heaped on the bed. She crossed over, lifted a shirt, a pair of jeans. No damage, she noted, so that was something.

There'd been nothing amiss in Lily's room when she'd checked, and that was even more important. Curious, she walked to the bathroom. All of her toiletries had been shoved into a pile on the counter.

"Your way of reminding me this isn't really my place?" she wondered aloud. "That I may be told to pack up and go any time? Maybe you're right. If and when, I'll handle it, so all you managed to do was give me an hour's annoying work before I go to bed."

She began to put away the creams and colognes, the lipsticks and mascaras. Discount brands mostly, with a couple of splurges tossed in. And maybe she did wish she could afford better, just for the fun of it.

The same went for the clothes, she admitted as she went into the bedroom to deal with them. What was wrong with wishing she could afford really good fabrics or designer labels?

It wasn't like she was obsessed with it.

Still, wouldn't it be wonderful to be hanging up fabulous dresses instead of knockoffs and discount rack. Silks and cashmere. It would feel so good against her skin.

Roz had all those incredible clothes, and walked around in old shirts half the time. More than. What was the point in having so much, then taking it for granted? Leaving it hanging when someone else could use it. Use it better, too. Someone younger who knew how to live. Who deserved it, who'd *earned* it instead of just having everything handed to her.

And all those jewels, just going to waste, sitting in a safe when they'd look so beautiful around her throat. Sparkling.

She should just take them, take a few pieces here and there. Who'd know the difference?

Everything she wanted was right here for the taking, so why not . . .

She dropped the shirt she'd been holding. Holding, she realized in front of her the way a woman holds some lovely gown. Swaying in front of the mirror. And thinking of theft.

Not me. Shaking, she stared at her own reflection.

"Not me," she said aloud. "I don't need what you need. I don't want what you want. Maybe you can get inside me, but you can't make me do something like that. You can't."

She dumped the rest of her clothes in a chair, then lay down on the bed fully dressed. And slept with the lights on.

NINE

SHE WAS GLAD TO BE WORKING THE COUNTER, GRATEful to the steady trickle of customers who kept her busy. Amelia didn't appear to be interested in her when she was working. At least not so far.

She'd made a list, documenting every incident she remembered clearly for Mitch's files. She'd noted down the locations: the pond, her bedroom, the nursery. She wasn't absolutely sure, but she thought there had been other times her thoughts weren't really hers. In the garden at Harper House, when she'd been daydreaming at work.

Once it was down on paper, she decided, it didn't seem that enormous.

At least not during the day, when people were around.

She looked over as a new customer came in. Young, good shoes, good haircut. Healthy disposable income, Hayley decided, and hoped to help her dispose of some.

"'Morning. Can I help you find something today?"

"Well, I . . . I'm sorry, I think I've forgotten your name."

"It's Hayley." She narrowed her focus while keeping her expression pleasant. Swingy, streaky blond hair, narrow face, pretty eyes. A little bit shy.

Then her own eyes popped wide. "Jane? Roz's cousin Jane? Holy cow, look at you."

The woman flushed. "I . . . got my hair cut," she told her, and fluffed a hand over the flattering swing.

"I'll say. You look great, totally great."

The last time she'd seen Jane, she'd helped Roz and Stella move the woman's few possessions out of the over-stuffed, overheated city apartment ruled by Clarissa Harper. The woman they'd smuggled out—along with journals Clarissa had nipped out of Harper House—had been dull and dowdy, like a pencil sketch that barely showed up on the paper.

Now her plain, dishwater blond hair had been lightened, highlighted, and shortened to a sassy length that didn't drag down her long, thin face.

Her clothes were simple, but the cotton shirt and breezy cropped pants were a far cry from the dumpy skirt she'd been wearing when she'd made her escape.

"I've gotta say: Wow. You look like you've been on one of those makeover shows. You know, like *What Not to Wear*. And oh boy, what just came out of my mouth was really rude."

"No, it's okay." Her smile spread even as her blush deepened. "I guess I feel made over. Jolene—you know Jolene, Stella's stepmother?"

"Yeah, she's terrific."

"She helped me get the job at the gallery, and the day before I started, she came to my new apartment. She just . . . highjacked me. She said she was my fairy godmother for the day. Before I knew it, I was getting my hair cut, and they were putting aluminum foil in what was left of it. I was too terrified to say no."

"Bet you're glad you didn't."

"I was in a daze. She dragged me out of there to the mall, and said she was going to start me off with three outfits, top to toe. After that, she expected me to fill out the rest of my wardrobe in a like manner."

Her smile wreathed from ear to ear even as her eyes went damp. "It was the most wonderful day of my life."

"That's the sweetest story." Hayley teared up as Jane did. "You deserved a fairy godmother after being kicked around by that wicked witch. You know, historically fairy tales were women's stories, passed orally in a time when women didn't have many rights."

"Um. Oh?"

"Sorry, trivia head. It's just that this is all such a girl thing, I guess. I've got to get Stella."

"I didn't want to interrupt anything. I just hoped to see Cousin Rosalind, and thank her."

"We'll get her, too." Hayley hurried over to Stella's office door. "But Stella's really going to want to see this." She poked her head in without knocking. "You've got to come out here a minute."

"Is there a problem?"

"No, just take my word and come out here."

"Hayley, I've still got half a dozen calls to make before I . . ." She trailed off, automatically putting on her greeting-the-public face when she spotted Jane. "Sorry. Is there something—Oh my God. It's Jane."

"New and improved," Hayley said, then winced. "Sorry."

"Don't be. That's just how I feel."

"Jolene said she'd given you the Jo Special." Delighted,

Stella walked a circle around Jane. "Boy, didn't she just. I love your hair."

"So do I. Your stepmother, she's been so good to me."

"She's enjoyed every minute of it. I've had reports, but I have to say, a picture's worth a thousand. I hope you're doing as well as you look."

"I love my job. I love my apartment. I really love feeling pretty."

"Oh." Stella's eyes filled.

"Same thing happened to me," Hayley said as she got a two-way from behind the counter. "Roz," she said into it, "we need you at checkout."

She clicked it off on Roz's staticky complaint about being busy.

"I don't want to drag her away from her work."

"She'll want to see you. And I want to see her see you. God, this is fun!"

"Tell us what else you've been up to," Stella said.

"Work's number one. I really love it, and I'm learning so much. I've made a couple of friends there."

"Male types?" Hayley wondered.

"I'm not ready for that yet. But there is this man in my building. He's very nice."

"Is he cute? Shoot, customer," Hayley grumbled as one came in through the back with a loaded cart. "Don't talk about anything sexy while I'm busy."

"I thought I'd be embarrassed to see the two of you again." Jane turned to Stella as Hayley waited on the customer.

"Why?"

"That time, when I met you, I was so whiny and horrible."

"You were not, you were scared and upset. For good reason. You were taking a big step, letting us in so Roz could get those journals."

"They belonged to her. Clarissa didn't have the right to take them from Harper House."

"No, she didn't. But it was still a big step for you, to let Roz get them back, to move out, start a new job, a new life. I know how scary that is. So does Hayley."

Jane glanced over her shoulder to where Hayley rang up sales and chatted with her customer. "She doesn't look like she'd be scared of anything. That's what I thought when I met her, and you. That the two of you would never be afraid to stand up for yourselves, never let yourselves get pushed around like I did."

"We all get scared, and we don't always do something so radical and positive about it."

Roz came in, the only sign of irritation the slap of her gardening gloves on her thigh. "Is there a problem?"

"Absolutely not." Stella gestured. "Jane wanted to see you."

Roz's brows lifted, and her smile spread slowly. "Well, well, well. Jolene is a woman of her word. Aren't you just blooming." She stuck her gloves in her back pocket, then lost her breath as Jane threw arms around her. "I'm glad to see you, too."

"Thank you. Thank you so much. I'll never be able to tell you."

"You're welcome."

"I'm so happy."

"I can see that. Feel it, too."

"Sorry." Sniffling, Jane released her. "I didn't intend to do that. I wanted to come, to thank you, and to tell you I'm doing a good job at work. I got a raise already, and I'm making something of myself."

"I can see that, too. I don't have to ask if you've been well. I'm happy for you. And, however small it might be of me, I'm downright delighted to see you looking so pretty, so excited about your life because that must just burn Cousin Rissa's bony ass."

Jane gave a watery laugh. "It does. It has. She came to see me."

"What'd I miss, what'd I miss?" Hayley demanded as she hurried over. "Go back and repeat all the good stuff."

"I think we're just getting to it." Roz angled her head. "So Rissa got her broom out of storage and came to see you?"

"In my apartment. I guess my mother gave her my address, even though I asked her not to. It was about a month ago. I looked through the peephole and saw her. I almost didn't answer the door."

"Who could blame you?" In support, Hayley patted Jane's back.

"But I thought, I can't just sit here like a rabbit hiding in my own apartment. So I opened the door, and don't you know she walked right in, sniffed the air, ordered me to fetch her some sweet tea, then sat down."

"Bless her heart," Roz drawled. "Her ego never withers."

"What floor's that apartment on again?" Hayley squinted as she tried to remember. "Third or fourth, as I recall. She'd've made a nice splat if you'd tossed her out the window."

"I wish I could say I did, but I went and got the tea. I was just quaking. When I came back with it, she said I was an ungrateful, wicked girl, and I could cut off my hair, get myself into some rathole of an apartment, fool some brainless ninny into giving me a job I was certainly unqualified to handle, but it didn't change what I was. She said a number of uncomplimentary things about you, Roz."

"Oh, tell."

"Well, um. Scheming harlot for one."

"I always wanted to be called a harlot. People just don't use the word enough these days."

"That's what started getting my back up. I thought maybe she was entitled to call me ungrateful, because I was." Jane fisted her hands on her hips, jutted her chin in the air. "My apartment's not a rathole, it's just sweet, but with her tastes it might seem like it, and she didn't know Carrie—my boss?—so she might think she's brainless to give me a chance. But she had some nerve calling you names when she's the one who stole from you."

Jane squared her shoulders, gave a decisive nod. "And I said so."

"To her face." Hooting out a laugh, Roz framed Jane's face in her hands. "I couldn't be more proud."

"Her eyes almost bugged out of her head. I don't know where the words came from. I don't have much of a temper, but I was so *mad.* I just cut loose on her, said all the things I hadn't hardly let myself think when I was living with her, and waiting on her hand and foot. How she was mean and spiteful and no one had an ounce of affection for her. How she was a thief and a liar, and she was lucky you hadn't called the police on her."

"Get you." Hayley gave her an elbow nudge. "That's better than tossing her out the window."

"And I wasn't even done."

"Keep right on going," Hayley prompted.

"I said I'd beg on the street before I'd come back and be her whipping girl. Then I told her to get out of my apartment." Jane threw out an arm and pointed. "I gestured, just like this? Sort of over the top, I guess, but I was wound up. She said I'd regret it. I think she might've said I'd rue the day, but I was so stirred up I didn't pay much mind. And she left."

She blew out a breath, waved a hand in front of her face. "Whew."

"Why, Jane, you're a Trojan." Roz took her hand, gave it a squeeze. "Who'd have thought?"

"It didn't end there, exactly. She tried to have me fired."

"That bitch." Hayley's face darkened. "What did she do?"

"She went to Carrie, told her I was a woman of loose morals, how I'd had an affair with a married man, and that I'd stolen from her when she'd graciously taken me into her home. Said she felt it was her Christian duty to warn Carrie about me."

"I've always thought there were special front row seats in hell for Christians such as Clarissa," Roz commented.

"When Carrie called me into her office and told me she'd been there, what she'd said, I was sure I was going to be fired. Instead she asked me how I'd stood living with that horrible old crow. That's what she called her. And the fact that I had told her I had a lot of patience and fortitude, which she thought were good qualities in an employee. Since I had them and had proven I was willing to work hard and learned fast, she was giving me a raise."

"I like Carrie," Hayley decided. "I'd like to buy her a drink."

"THERE'S NOTHING BETTER THAN A HAPPY ENDING." Unless, Hayley decided, it was sitting in the shade on the glider, sipping a cold drink while Lily played on the grass. And Harper swung beside her.

"It's always a happy ending when Cousin Clarissa gets the heave-ho. She used to terrorize me when I was a kid, whenever she came around. Before Mama booted her out."

"Know what Jane said she called your mama?"

"No." The relaxed expression on his face settled into cold stone. "What?"

"A harlot."

"A . . ." The stone broke into a huge, rolling laugh that

had Lily clapping her hands. "A harlot. God, Mama would *love* that."

"She did. You really know her, don't you? It was just such a good morning. Pushed all the bad stuff away awhile. Seeing somebody who'd discovered themselves the way Jane has, or is, I guess. The one time I met her before? She was practically invisible. Now's she's, well, she's pretty hot."

"Yeah? How hot?"

She laughed, elbowed him. "Never you mind. One cousin at a time."

"Exactly what kind of cousins are we anyway? I've never figured it out."

"I think your daddy and mine were third cousins, which makes us fifth. At least, I think. Maybe we're fourth cousins once removed. It could be third cousins, twice removed. I can never get it just right in my head. And there's half blood in there, too with my great-grandmother's second marriage—"

It was probably just as well he stopped her mouth with his. "Kissing cousins covers it," he decided.

"Works for me." Because it did, she leaned in to take his mouth again.

Lily interrupted with a few squawks and babbles, tugging on Harper's legs until he hauled her up. Curling her arm around his neck, she pushed Hayley back.

"Well, I guess that shows me." Amused, Hayley leaned in again, and Lily pushed her back and wrapped tighter to Harper.

"Girls are always fighting over me," he said. "It's a curse."

"I bet. That one you were with last New Year's Eve looked like she could scratch and bite."

He smiled at Lily. "I don't know what she's talking about."

"Oh, yes, you do. The blonde with about a yard of hair and perfect Victoria's Secret breasts."

"Yeah, the breasts are coming back to me."

"That's a terrible thing to say!"

"You started it. Amber," he said with a chuckle as he lifted the baby high over his head to make her laugh.

"Of course. She looked like an Amber."

"She's a corporate lawyer."

"She is not."

"God's truth." He held up a hand like a man taking an oath. "Beautiful doesn't have to mean bimbo, of which you are living proof."

"Good save. Were you serious—and forget that spilled out. I hate when women, or men for that matter, poke into past relationships."

"You showed me yours. Not serious. She didn't want serious, neither did I. She's focused on her career right now."

"You ever been serious?"

"I've approached the parameter of serious a few times. Never crossed over into the zone." He sat Lily between them, snugging her in so she could swing.

Better leave it at that, Hayley told herself. Leave it comfortable with the three of them lazing on the glider with the bees humming in the hazy heat and the flowers bursting through it with bold summer colors.

"This is the best part of summer," she told him. "Evening shade. It seems like you could sit where you are for hours, without a single important thing to do."

"Don't want to get away from here awhile?"

"Not tonight. I wouldn't want to leave Lily two nights running."

"I was thinking we could take her to get some ice cream after dinner."

Surprised, she looked over. Then wondered why she'd

been surprised he'd suggest it. "She'd love that. So would I."

"Then it's a date. In fact, why don't we go out, get a burger and finish it off with ice cream?"

"Even better."

STEAMY JULY MELTED INTO SWELTERING AUGUST, days of white skies and breathless nights. It seemed almost normal, almost peaceful as day blended into day.

"I'm starting to wonder if just finding out her name was enough." Hayley potted up pink and yellow pentas. "Maybe the fact we worked to find it, and how she's Roz's great-grandmother's, satisfied her, calmed her down."

"You think she's done?" Stella asked her.

"I still hear her singing in Lily's room, almost every night. But she hasn't done anything mean. Every once in a while I feel something, or sense something, but it fades away. I haven't done anything weird lately, have I?"

"You were listening to Pink the other day, and talking about getting a tattoo."

"That's not weird. I think we should both get tattoos—a flower theme. I'd get a red lily, and you could get a blue dahlia. I bet Logan would think it was wicked sexy."

"Then let him get the tattoo."

"Just a little one. A girly one."

"I think girly tattoo is an oxymoron."

"Absolutely not," Hayley protested. "Flowers, butterflies, unicorns, that kind of thing. I bet I could talk Roz into getting one."

The idea had Stella tossing back her red curls and laughing. "Tell you what, you talk Roz into getting a tattoo and . . . Nope, I still won't join the party."

"Historically, tattoos are ancient art forms, back to the Egyptians. And they were often used to control the supernatural. Since we've got some heavy supernatural going on, it would be like a talisman, *and* a personal statement."

"My personal statement will be refusing to let some guy named Tank carve a symbol—girly or otherwise—into my flesh. Just call me fussy. Those look good, Hayley. Very sweet."

"Customer wanted sweet, and the yellow and pink are her daughter's wedding colors. These'll make nice centerpieces for the wedding shower. I think I'd shoot for something a little bolder, a little punchier myself. Maybe jewel tones."

"Something you're not telling me?"

"Hmm?"

"Bride colors on your mind?"

"Oh, no." She laughed and set a completed pot aside. "No, nothing like that. We're just, Harper and me, we're just taking it slow. Really, really slow," she added with a huff of breath.

"Isn't that what you wanted?"

"Yeah, I did. I do. I don't know." She blew out another breath, fluttering her bangs. "It's smarter. It's more sensible to take things really easy. There's a lot at stake most people don't have to consider. Like our friendship, and the work, and our connection to Roz. We can't just jump into the sack because I've—we've got an itch."

"But you want to jump into the sack."

Hayley slid her eyes over to Stella's. "I was thinking more dive in, headfirst."

"Why don't you just tell him, Hayley?"

"I made the first move. He's got to make this one. I sure as hell hope he picks up speed pretty soon."

"I'M TRYING NOT TO RUSH HER." IN THE KITCHEN, Harper drained the better part of a can of Coke. He rarely broke for lunch, but early afternoon meant there would be no one in the house but David.

"You've known her going on two years, Harp. That's not just not rushing, that's standing still."

"It was different before. We've only just started seeing each other this way. She said she wanted slow. I think it's killing me."

"I don't think people actually die from sexual frustration."

"Good. I'll be the first. I'll be written up in medical journals posthumously."

"And I'll be able to say I knew him when. Here, eat."

Dubiously, Harper poked at the sandwich David set in front of him. "What is this?"

"Delicious."

Without much interest, Harper picked up the sandwich. "What is this?" he asked again after a sampling bite. "Lamb? Cold lamb?"

"With a touch of nectarine chutney."

"That's . . . pretty damn good. Where do you come up with—no, no, stay on target." He took another bite. "I'm good at reading women, but I can't get a handle on her, on this. It's never been important before—not this way—so I keep clutching."

With his own sandwich, David slid across from him. "It is good you came to me, young student, for I am the master."

"I know. I thought about just walking over one night, maybe with a bottle of wine, knock on her terrace door. The direct approach."

"It's a classic for a reason."

"But she's nervous about Amelia, about having any sort of, you know, encounter, in the house. At least that's my take."

"Is encounter code for hot sex?"

"Damn you, you're too clever for my pitiful ruses. Anyway, I could have her and Lily over for dinner, and after the baby was asleep—a little wine, a little music." He shrugged and felt he was riding around the same circle again.

"There's also a reason why fine hotels have room service and Do Not Disturb signs."

"Room service?"

"Work with me, Harp. You take her out to dinner—fancy dinner. Let's try the Peabody. They have lovely rooms, lovely service, fine food—in-room dining."

Chewing thoughtfully, Harper played it out in his head. "I take her out to dinner—in a hotel room? Don't you think that's a little . . . brilliant," he decided after a moment.

"Yes, I do. Wine, candles, music, the works, all in the elegant privacy of a hotel suite. You'll be bringing her breakfast in bed the next morning."

Harper licked chutney off his thumb. "I'd need a two-bedroom suite for that. Lily."

"Your mama, Mitch, and I would be more than happy to entertain the charming Lily for a night. And to show your amazing forethought—or mine—I'll pack an overnight bag for Hayley. You'll just have to get the room, take her things in, arrange the service, set the scene. Then sweep her up there and off her feet.

"This is a good idea, David. I should've thought of it myself, which just shows how messed up in the head she's got me. I've got to get back, talk Stella into juggling the schedule so I can pull this off. Thanks."

"I'm always here to serve the course of true love, or at least hot hotel sex."

SHE WORE HER RED DRESS. IT WAS THE NICEST SHE had, and she liked the way it looked on her. But she wished he'd given her time to go out and get something new. All their other dates had been casual.

He'd seen her in this dress. The fact was, he'd seen her in everything she owned.

Still, she had great shoes. Roz's cast-off Jimmy Choo's that probably cost three times what the dress did. And worth every penny, Hayley decided as she turned in front of the full-length mirror. Just look what they did for her legs. Sexy instead of skinny, she decided.

Maybe she should wear her hair up. Lips pursed, she scooped it off her neck, angling her head this way and that to check the effect.

"What do you think?" she asked Lily, who was sitting on the floor busily putting a pile of little toys in Hayley's oldest purse. "Up or down? I think I can pull the up-do off, if I keep it sort of tousled. Then I could wear those cool earrings. Let's try it."

When a man said he wanted to take you out to a special dinner, she decided as she pinned and re-pinned, the least you could do was pull out all the stops, appearance-wise.

Right down to the underwear. At least that was new—and purchased recently with the idea that eventually he'd see her in it.

Maybe tonight, if they could extend the evening a little. He could come back here with her. She'd just have to block Amelia out of her mind. Block the idea that Harper's mama was right in the other wing. That her own daughter was in the next room.

Why the hell did it have to be so complicated?

She wanted him. They were both young, free, unattached, healthy. It should be simple.

Becoming lovers should have weight. She remembered Harper's words. Well, the situation had weight. It was time she started thinking of that as a plus instead of a minus.

"I'm the one making it weird, Lily. I can't seem to help it. But I'm going to try."

She put on the earrings, long, flashy gold dangles, considered a necklace and rejected it. The earrings made the show. "Well." She stepped back to do a little turn for her daughter. "What do you think? Does Mama look pretty?"

Lily's response was a mile-wide grin as she dumped everything out of the purse.

"I'll take that as a yes," Hayley said, then turned back to the mirror for one last check.

The breath left her body so fast her head went light.

She wore a red dress, but not the thin-strapped, short-skirted number she'd had for more than two years.

It was long and elaborate, cut low so that her breasts rose up to be framed by the silk with a cascade of rubies and diamonds spilling down over the exposed flesh.

Her hair was piled high in an elaborate confection of shining gold curls with a few arranged to frame a striking face with lush red lips and smoldering gray eyes.

"I'm not you," she whispered. "I'm not."

She turned deliberately away, crouched to pick up scattered toys with trembling fingers. "I know who I am. I know who she is. We aren't the same. We aren't alike."

Chilled with a sudden panic, she spun back again, more than half afraid she'd see Amelia step out of the glass, and become flesh and blood. But she saw only herself now, with her eyes too wide and dark against her pale cheeks.

"Come on, baby." She grabbed Lily, and at the baby's wail of protest, snatched up the old purse, then her own evening bag.

She made herself walk at a reasonable pace, and slowed even that as she approached the stairs. Roz would see the shock on her face, and she didn't want to talk about it. Just for one night she wanted to continue the illusion of normal.

So she took her time, got her breath back, got her features under control. She strolled into the main parlor with Lily on her hip and a smile on her face.

ten

HEAT LIGHTNING SIZZLED IN THE SKY, BROODY BURSTS, as they drove into Memphis. The traffic was as sulky as the night, but Harper seemed immune to it. They might have limped into the city, but the air was cool in the car, and Coldplay simmered out of the speakers.

Every so often he'd take his hand off the wheel to lay it over hers. A casually intimate gesture that made her heart sigh.

She'd been right to say nothing of that vision, or apparition, whatever it had been, in her bedroom mirror. Tomorrow was soon enough.

"I've never had dinner here," she said when he pulled into the hotel's lot. "I bet it's wonderful."

"One of Memphis's finest jewels."

"I've been in the lobby. You can't come to Memphis

without seeing the Peabody's duck walk. It'd be like not seeing Graceland or Beale Street."

"You forgot Sun Records."

"Oh! Isn't that the coolest place?" She shot him a stern look. "And don't think I don't know you're laughing at me."

"Maybe a chuckle. Not an outright laugh."

"Well, anyway, the Peabody's got an awesome lobby. You know they've been doing that duck walk for over seventy-five years."

"Is that a fact?"

She gave him a little shove as they walked toward the hotel. "I guess you know all there is to know about the place, being a native."

"Finding out more all the time." He led her into the lobby.

"Maybe we could have a drink in here before dinner, by the fountain." She imagined something cool and sophisticated to mirror the way she was feeling. A champagne cocktail or a cosmopolitan. "Is there time?"

"We could, but I think you'll like what I have in mind even better." He walked with her toward the elevators.

She glanced back over her shoulder with some regret. All that gorgeous marble and colored glass. "Is there a dining room upstairs? They don't have one on the roof, do they? I've always thought roof-top dining was so elegant. Unless it rains. Or it's windy. Or it's too hot," she added with a laugh. "I think roof-top dining's really elegant in the movies."

He only smiled, nudged her inside ahead of him. "Did I tell you that you look beautiful tonight?"

"You did, but I don't mind certain kinds of repetition."

"You look beautiful." He touched his lips to hers. "You should always wear red."

"And look at you." She ran her fingers down the lapels

of his dark jacket. "All duded up in a suit. The rest of the women in the restaurant won't be able to eat for envying me my good luck."

"If that's the case, we might just have to give them a break." He took her hand as the doors opened, then led her into the hallway. "Come with me."

"What's going on?"

"Something I hope you'll like." He stopped at a door, took out a key. He unlocked the door, opened it, gestured. "After you."

She stepped inside, her breath catching as she saw the spacious room. Her hand fluttered up to her throat as she crossed the black and white checkerboard tiles into a parlor where candles flickered, and red lilies speared lavishly out of glass vases.

The colors were deep and rich, long windows adding the sparkling lights of the city. In front of one, a table was set for two, and a bottle of champagne sat in a gleaming silver bucket.

There was music playing, slow, soft Memphis blues. Stunned, she turned a circle, saw the spiral staircase that led to a second level.

"You . . . you did this?"

"I wanted to be alone with you."

Her heart was still in her throat as she turned to face him. "You did this for me?"

"For both of us."

"This beautiful room—just for us. Flowers and candles, and God, champagne. I'm overwhelmed."

"I want you to be." He stepped to her, took both her hands. "I want tonight to be special, memorable." And brought them to his lips. "Perfect."

"It's sure off to a good start. Harper, no one's ever gone to so much trouble for me. I've never felt more special."

"It's just the start. I ordered dinner already. It'll be up in about fifteen minutes. Plenty of time for us to have that drink. How do you feel about champagne?"

"I feel like I couldn't settle for anything less right now. Thank you." She leaned to him, took his mouth for a long, warm kiss.

"I'd better open that bottle, or I'll forget the lineup of events."

"There's a lineup?"

"More or less." He walked over to lift the bottle from the bucket. "And just so you can relax, I gave Mama the number here. She's got that, your cell, mine, and I made her promise to call if Lily so much as hiccups."

He popped the cork as she laughed. "All right. I'll trust Roz to keep it all under control."

She did a little spin, just couldn't help herself. "I feel like Cinderella. Minus the evil stepsisters, and well, the pumpkin. But other than that, me and Cindy, we're practically twins."

"If the shoe fits."

"I'm going to wallow in this, Harper, I may as well just tell you that. I don't know how sophisticated I can be when I just want to jump up and down, go racing around to look at everything. I bet the bathrooms are amazing. Do you think that fireplace works? I know it's too hot for a fire, but I don't care."

"We'll light it. Here." He handed her a glass, tapped his to it. "To memorable moments."

She held the moment, the glow of it. "And to men who make them happen. Oh, wow," she said after the first sip. "This is really good. Maybe I'm dreaming."

"If you are, I am, too."

"That's all right then."

He touched her, skimming his fingers over the back of

her neck, exposed by her upswept hair. Then with the lightest of pressure eased her toward him. The knock on the door brought on a wry grin.

"Prompt service. I'll get it. Once they've set up dinner, we'll be completely alone."

HE MADE IT ALL HAPPEN, SHE MUSED. THE BIG PICture, the tiny details so the evening unfolded for her like the pages of a storybook. And because of him, she was sitting in an elegant suite, sipping champagne with the romance of candlelight, the shimmer of firelight. Flowers scented the air. There was a lovely meal she could barely taste through the anticipation bubbling in her throat.

Tonight, they would make love.

"Tell me what it was like for you, growing up," she asked him.

"I liked having brothers, even when they pissed me off."

"You're close. I can see that whenever they come to visit. Even though they live away from Memphis, the three of you are like a team."

He topped off her glass. "Did you wish for sibs when you were a kid?"

"I did. I had friends and cousins to play with, but I did. A sister especially. Somebody to tell secrets to in the middle of the night, or even to fight with. You had all that."

"As kids, it was like having a personal gang, especially when David came along."

"Bet the four of you drove Roz crazy."

He grinned, lifted his glass. "We did our best. Summers were long, the way they're supposed to be when you're a kid. Long, hot days, and the yard, the woods, they were the whole world. I remember how it smelled, all green and thick. And this time of year, how you'd hear the cicadas all night."

"I used to leave my window open a little ways at night so I could hear them better. I bet y'all got in plenty of trouble."

"Probably more than our share. You couldn't slip much by Mama. She had this radar, it was a little scary. I remember how she'd be in the garden, or in the house doing something, and I'd come around and she'd just know I'd been doing something I shouldn't've been doing."

She propped an elbow on the table, cupped her chin in her hand. "Name something."

"The most baffling, at least at the time, was when I was with a girl the first time." He drenched one of the strawberries in whipped cream, held it out for her to bite. "I came home having had my first sample of paradise in the backseat of my much-loved Camaro, about six months after my sixteenth birthday. She came into my room the next morning, and put a box of Trojans on my dresser."

With a shake of his head, he polished off the berry. "She said, and I remember this very well, that we'd already talked about sex and responsibility, about being safe and smart and careful, so she assumed that I had used protection, and would continue to do so. Then she asked if I had any questions or comments."

"What did you say?"

"I said, 'No ma'am.' And when she walked out the door, I pulled the covers up over my head and asked God how the hell my mama came to know I'd had sex with Jenny Proctor in my Camaro. It was both mystifying and humiliating."

"I hope I'm like that."

His eyebrows lifted as he coated another berry. "Mystified and humiliated?"

"No. As smart as your mama. As wise as that with Lily."

"Lily's not allowed to have sex until she's thirty, and married a couple of years."

"Goes without saying." She bit into the berry he offered,

mmm'd over it. "What happened to Jenny Proctor?"

"Jenny?" He got a look on his face, a kind of half smile that told her he was looking back. "Why, she just pined away for me. She was forced to go to California to college, and stay out there and marry a screenwriter."

"Poor thing. I shouldn't have any more," she said when he topped off her glass again. "I'm already half buzzed."

"No point in doing things halfway."

Angling her head, she sent him a deliberately provocative look. "Is part of the lineup you talked about getting me loose on champagne so you can have your way with me?"

"It was on the schedule."

"Thank God. Is that event coming up soon, because I don't think I can sit here and look at you much longer without having you touch me."

His eyes darkened as he rose, held out a hand for hers. "Here was my plan. I was going to ask you to dance, so I could get my arms around you, something like this."

She slid into them. "I haven't found a single flaw in your plan so far."

"Then I was going to kiss you, here." He brushed his lips over her temple. "And here." Her cheek. "And here." And her mouth, sinking in slowly and deeply until that meeting of lips was the center of the world.

"I want you so much." She pressed against him, burrowed in. "It takes me over. Take me over, Harper. I'll go crazy if you don't."

He circled her toward the steps, stopped at the base and looked into her eyes. "Come upstairs, and be with me."

With her hand in his, she started up, then let out a breathless laugh. "My knees are shaking. I can't even tell if it's from nerves or excitement. I've imagined myself with you so many times, but I never imagined I'd be nervous."

"We'll go slow. No rush."

Her heart was beginning to trip and stumble, but there was one more thing. "Um, I'm using something—birth control—but I think we should . . . I didn't bring any of those Trojans."

"I'll take care of it."

"Should've figured you'd thought of everything."

"Be prepared."

"Were you a Boy Scout?"

"No, but I dated a few former Girl Scouts."

It made her chuckle, and nearly relax again. "I think . . ."

She trailed off as she stepped into the bedroom. There were candles waiting to be lit, and the lamp on low. The bed was already turned down, with a single red lily resting on the pillow.

The romance of it saturated her.

"Oh, Harper."

"Wait." He walked around the room to light the candles, to turn off the lamp. Then he picked up the flower and offered it. "I brought you these because it's how I think of you, how I've thought of you since the beginning. I've never thought of anyone else the same way."

She stroked the petals over her cheek, breathed in their fragrance, then set the lily aside. "Undress me."

He lifted a hand, nudged the thin strap from her shoulder, laid his lips there. In turn, with her heart beating thickly, she slid the jacket off his.

Then her mouth found his as her fingers opened the buttons of his shirt, as his drew down the zipper at the back of her dress. His hands cruised over her back, and hers spread over his chest. When her dress slithered to the floor, she stepped out of it—then held her breath as he eased back and just looked at her.

She wore flimsy scraps of red that shimmered in the candlelight against her smooth pale skin. And high, high heels with long, long legs. Desire, already impossibly strong, clutched at his belly.

"You're amazing."

"I'm skinny. All angles, no curves."

He shook his head, reached out to trace a finger over the subtle curve of her breast. "Delicate, like a lily stem. Would you take your hair down?"

With her eyes on his, she reached up to pull out the pins, then skimmed her fingers through it. And waited.

"Amazing," he repeated. Taking her hand, he drew her to the bed. "Just sit," he said, then knelt in front of her to slip off her shoes.

His lips trailed up her calf and had her clutching the edge of the bed. "Oh God."

"Let me do the things I've thought about doing." His teeth grazed the back of her knee. "All of them."

There was no thought to deny him, and no words that could surface through the flood of sensation. His tongue slid along her thigh, that mouth burning tiny brands into her flesh even as his hands traveled up, tracing her breasts with his fingers until they ached over her thundering heart.

She shuddered out his name, falling back on the bed as he came to her.

She could hold him close now, touch as she was touched. Taste as she was tasted. The pleasure filled her—the glide of his hands, the heat of his lips, the catch of his breath as they rolled together to find more.

No rush, he'd told her, but he couldn't slow his hands. They wanted to take, and take more. Her breasts in his hands, in his mouth, small and firm and satin smooth, and when he feasted on them she bowed up, exposing the long, slender line of her throat.

At last, she was his.

Her nails bit into his back, scraped down his hips. Tiny

thrilling pains. Then she was over him, her mouth as greedy as his, and her quick, gasping breaths roaring in his head like a storm.

Candlelight sheened over her skin, skin going damp with the heat they fueled through each other. The gold of those flickering lights glowed in the deepening blue of her eyes as he slid his hand over her, found her hot. Found her wet.

The orgasm was like a burst of light, a stunning flash that blinded her, set her body on fire then left it to glow. She felt herself slide toward oblivion, then come back into the bright, bright world of swimming sensations. Her body was awake, alive.

Then his mouth found her and sent her spinning beyond pleasure. It was a roiling heat that built and built, then gushed through her so that she was weak and wavery when he dragged her to her knees.

He looked at her, into her it seemed, so deep she thought he must see everything she was. And his mouth took hers in a kiss that made her heart tremble.

So this was love, she thought. This utter trust and surrender of self. This complete gift of heart that left you open, defenseless. And full of joy.

She touched her hand to his cheek, her lips curving as she shifted, as she wrapped her legs around him. "Yes," she said, and took him into her. "Yes," then arched back with a moan as the beauty swamped her.

He lowered his brow to her shoulder, barely able to breathe as she closed around him. But he drew her back to him, heart against heart. Not close enough, he thought. It could never be close enough.

Her arms locked around him, her mouth found his as they rocked themselves toward the edge, and over.

* * *

THERE WAS PROBABLY SOMETHING MORE RELAXING than sprawling on a big bed, limbs tangled with your lover's after mind-melting sex. But Hayley figured it was probably illegal.

In any case, she'd take this shimmery afterglow.

As far as romantic nights, this one left everything else she'd experienced in the dust. Gliding on it, she curled her body a little closer to his, and smiled dreamily when his hand stroked over her back.

"That was wonderful," she murmured. "You're wonderful. Everything's wonderful. I feel like if I stepped outside right now, this light inside me would blind the entire population of Memphis."

"If you stepped outside right now, you'd be arrested." His hand slipped lower. "Better just stay right here with me."

"You're probably right. Mmm, I feel so loose." She stretched like a cat. "I guess I was pretty blocked up, you know? Self-servicing isn't nearly as satisfying as . . . Oh God, I can't believe I said that."

His shoulders were already shaking as he snorted out a laugh. He hooked an arm firmly around her before she could roll away. "Happy to be . . . at your service."

She buried her face against his shoulder. "Things just jump out of my mouth sometimes. It's not like I'm a sex maniac or anything."

"Well, now you've shattered my dreams."

She cuddled closer, tipped her head up. "It's nice being here like this. I mean just like this," she said, and feathered her fingers through his hair. "All soft and warm, snuggled up in bed. I wish we could just stay, and tonight would just go on and on."

"We can stay, and when tonight stops going on, we can have breakfast right here in bed."

"That sounds amazing, but you know I can't. Lily—"

"Is sound asleep in the Portacrib we moved into my mother's sitting room earlier today." When her eyes widened, he pressed a kiss to her forehead. "Mama was practically rubbing her hands together with glee at the prospect of keeping her overnight.

"Your mama . . ." She pushed up on her elbow. "God, did everybody know about this but me?"

"Pretty much."

"Roz knows we're . . . that's just very strange. But I don't think I should—"

"Mama said to remind you she managed to raise three boys, keep them all alive and out of jail."

"But . . . I'm a terrible mother. I want to stay."

"You're not a terrible mother. You're an awesome mother." He sat up as she did, took her shoulders. "You know Lily's fine, and you know Mama loves having her."

"I do. I do know that, but . . . what if she wakes up and wants me? Okay," she said with a sigh when he just lifted his eyebrows. "If she wakes up, Roz'll handle it. And Lily loves spending time with her, and Mitch. I'm being a cliché."

"But you're such a pretty one."

She looked around the room. Beautiful, sumptuous—absolute freedom. "We can really just stay?"

"I'm hoping you will."

She bit her lip. "I don't have any . . . things, you know? Not even a toothbrush. A hairbrush. I don't have my—"

"David packed you a bag."

"David . . . well, that's all right then. He'd know what I'd want." She felt giddy little bubbles rising up in her throat. "We're just staying?"

"That's the plan. If it's okay with you."

"If it's okay with me?" she repeated, and a gleam came into her eyes as she launched herself at him. "Let me show you what I think about that."

* * *

LATER, SHE CAME RUSHING OUT OF THE BATHROOM. "Harper, did you see these robes? They're so big and soft." She stood rubbing a sleeve against her cheek. "There are two of them, one for each of us."

Lazily, he opened one eye. The woman, he thought, was proving to be insatiable. Praise Jesus. "Nice."

"Everything in here is wonderful."

"Romeo and Juliet suite," he murmured, almost drifting.

"What?"

"The suite. It's the Romeo and Juliet suite."

"Really, but that's . . ." Her brows drew together. "Well, if you think about it, they were a couple of teenage suicides."

On a laugh, he opened his eyes. "Trust you."

"I never saw it as being romantic. Tragic is what it was—and plain stupid. Not the play," she corrected, turning a circle to swirl the robe. "It's brilliant, but those two? Oops, she's dead, I'll drink this poison. Oops, he's dead, I'll stab myself in the heart. I mean, *Jesus,* and I'm babbling."

"What you are," he said, staring at her, "is fascinating."

"I get pretty opinionated about books. But whoever it's named for, the suite's downright awesome. It just makes me want to dance all around it, buck-ass naked."

"I knew I should've brought a camera."

"I wouldn't mind." Holding the robe up like a cape, she swirled once more. "I think it'd be sexy if we took naked pictures of each other. Then when I'm old, and all brittle and wrinkled up, I'd look at myself and remember being young."

She bounced onto the bed. "You got any naked pictures of yourself?"

"Not so far."

"Look at you." She tickled his knee. "You're embarrassed."

"Not entirely." Oh yeah, he thought, she was fascinating. "You got any?"

"Never trusted anybody enough before. And I've got this bony build. But you didn't seem to mind it."

"I think you're beautiful."

He meant it, and wasn't that a miracle? She could see it in his eyes. She'd felt it in his touch. "I feel beautiful tonight." She rose, wrapping the white robe around her. "All plush and lush and decadent."

"Let's order dessert."

She stopped twirling. "Dessert? But it's almost two in the morning."

"They have this amazing invention called twenty-four-hour room service."

"All night? I'm such a rube. But I don't care." She plopped back down on the bed. "Can we eat it up here? In bed?"

"The rules attached to twenty-four-hour room service are if you order after midnight, you're required to eat in bed. Naked."

She grinned wickedly. "Rules are rules."

They lay belly-down, facing each other, with a plate of chocolate-soaked cake between them.

"Probably going to be sick," she said as she ate another mouthful. "But it's so good."

"Here." He stretched out an arm, managed to grab one of the glasses on the floor. "Wash it down."

"I can't believe you ordered another bottle of champagne."

"You can't do naked chocolate cake without champagne. It's declassé."

"If you say so." She drank, then forked up more cake and held it out for him. "You know . . ." She wagged the fork at him. "On the date-o-meter you're going to have to go a ways to top this one. I don't think I can settle for anything less than, oh, a wild weekend in Paris or maybe a quick jet to Tuscany to make love in a vineyard."

"How about a sun-and-sex-soaked sojourn to Bimini."

"Sex-soaked sojourn." She gave a tipsy giggle. "Say that five times fast." On a moan, she rolled over to her back. "If I eat another bite, I believe I'll regret it for the rest of my life."

"Can't have that." He set the plate aside. Then easing forward, closed his mouth over hers in a lingering upside-down kiss.

"Mmm." She rubbed her lips together when he lifted his head. "You taste very potent."

"Got a nice chocolate high going here."

She smiled as he slid down to her, as his hands trailed over her breasts, her torso, her belly. Then gasped when his lips nibbled away.

"Oh my God, Harper."

"I forgot to mention this part of late-night dessert." He shifted, reached out. Swirling a finger through cream and chocolate, he smeared it lightly onto her breast. "Oops. I'd better get that off."

SHE FELT SO SMUG AND COSMOPOLITAN, STEPPING OUT of the elevator into the lobby with her overnight bag. It was nearly noon, and she was just wandering into the day. She'd had breakfast in bed. The fact was, she thought, she'd had about everything in bed that was available in the State of Tennessee.

She imagined even her toenails were glowing as a result.

"I'm going to check out." He nipped a little kiss on her lips. "Why don't you sit down?"

"I'm going to walk around. Look at everything. And I want to pick up a few things in the gift shop."

"Be right back."

She let out a happy sigh. She wanted to remember everything. The people, the fountain, the tidy bellmen, the shiny displays of art and jewelry.

She bought a little quacking duck for Lily, and a silver frame as a thank-you gift for Roz. Then there were the sweet duck-shaped soaps, and the pretty yellow cap that would look so cute on Lily. And . . .

"No man in his right mind turns his back on a woman in a gift shop," Harper said from behind her.

"I can't help it. Everything's so pretty. No," she said when she saw him reach for his wallet. "I'm getting these." She set all her items on the counter, then picked up a canister once it was rung up. "This is for you."

"Duck soap?"

She inclined her head. "To commemorate our stay. We had the best time," she told the clerk.

"I'm glad you enjoyed the hotel. Are you here on business or pleasure?"

"Just pleasure." Hayley gathered the bag. "Just lots and lots of pleasure." She tucked her free hand into Harper's as they strolled back into the lobby. "We'd better get home before Lily forgets what I look like and . . . oh man, just *look* at that bracelet."

The display showcasing a local jeweler glittered and shone, but all Hayley could see was the delicate bracelet with sizzling white diamonds framing gleaming ruby hearts.

"It's drop dead, isn't it? I mean it's elegant, even delicate, and the heart shapes make it romantic, but something about it just says: Hey, I'm an important piece. Maybe because it's an estate piece. Antique jewelry has such a—what's the word I want. Panache," she decided.

"Nice."

"Nice," she said and rolled her eyes at him. "Such a guy. What it is, is stunning. Some of the other pieces in there have bigger stones, more diamonds, whatever, but this is the one that stands out. To me, anyway."

He scanned the name and address of the store. "Let's go get it."

"Sure." She laughed up at him. "Why don't we pick up a new car on the way, too?"

"I like my car. The bracelet would suit you. Rubies would be your stone."

"Harper, paste is my stone."

She tugged his hand, but he continued to study the bracelet. The longer he looked at it, the more clearly he could see it on her. "I'll just talk to the concierge."

"Harper." Distressed now, she stepped back. "I was just looking. That's what we girls do—we look in shop windows."

"I want to buy it for you."

It was more than distress now, and closer to panic. "You can't buy me something like that. It probably costs—I can't even guess."

"Then let's find out."

"Harper, just wait. Just . . . I don't expect you to buy me expensive jewelry. I don't expect you to do things like this." She gestured to encompass the hotel. "It was the most incredible night of my life, but it's not why—Harper, it's not why I'm with you."

"Hayley, if it was why you were with me, you wouldn't be. Last night was for us, and it meant every bit as much to me as it did to you. I've got enough of my mother in me that you should know if I do something like this, it's because I want to. I want to buy this for you, and if it's not out of my range, that's what I'm going to do." He kissed her forehead. "Just hang here a minute."

Speechless, she watched him walk to the concierge desk.

And on the drive home, she continued to be speechless at the way the ruby hearts in their diamond frames glittered on her wrist.

eLeveN

SHE FRETTED FOR THE REST OF THE AFTERNOON, AND lavished attention on Lily. It was a strange and, she imagined, strictly maternal sort of juggling act to balance the fact that she'd missed her baby girl with the fact that she'd had the most wonderful time without her.

Guilt, she thought, came in many forms. By the time Roz got in from work, Hayley had built up a sputtering head of guilt.

"Welcome home." Roz stretched her back, eyed Hayley who stood in the foyer. "Did you have a good time?"

"Yes. Wonderful. Beyond wonderful. I should start out saying you raised the most incredible man."

"That was the goal."

"Roz, I can't thank you enough for keeping Lily that way." Unconsciously, she covered the bracelet on her wrist with her other hand. "It was more than I could expect."

"I enjoyed it. We all did. Where is she?"

"I wore her out," Hayley said with a weak smile. "All but kissed the skin off her bones. She's taking a quick nap. I got you a gift."

"Isn't that sweet." Taking the box, Roz strolled into the parlor to open it. And beamed when she found the frame, already spotlighting a picture of her with Lily. "I love this shot. I'm going to put this on the desk in my sitting room."

"I hope she didn't give you any trouble last night."

"Not a bit. We had ourselves a fine time."

"I—we—Harper. Hell. Can we sit down a minute?"

Obligingly, Roz sat on the sofa, propped her feet on the table. "I wonder if David's made any lemonade? I could drink a gallon."

"I'll go get you some."

Roz waved toward a seat. "I'll get my own in a minute. Tell me what's on your mind."

Hayley sat, stiff-backed, her hands folded in her lap. "I got to know the mothers of some of the guys I dated. We always got along okay. But I never . . . it's so surreal to be good friends with the mother of a man I'm . . . romantically intimate with."

"I'd think, all in all, that would be a bonus."

"It's not that it isn't. I suppose it would be less surreal if I'd gotten to know you, gotten to be friends with you *after* things became—"

"Romantically intimate."

"Yeah. I don't know how to talk to you about it, exactly, because the relationships are all tangled together. But I wanted to say, to tell you, that you raised an amazing individual. I know I did that, but I want to say it again. Harper went to so much trouble, took such care to give me something special. There aren't many like that, at least in my experience."

"He's a very special man. I'm glad you see that, and appreciate it."

"I do. He had this beautiful suite, and flowers and candles. Champagne. No one's ever done anything like that for me. I don't just mean the lavishness, you know? I'd've been fine with a plate of ribs and a motel room. And how crude is that," she muttered, closing her eyes.

"Not crude. Honest. And refreshing."

"What I mean to say is no one's ever taken that time, that care to plan a whole evening with me in mind."

"It's a disconcerting thrill to be swept off your feet."

"Yes." Relief poured through her. "Yes, exactly. My head's still spinning. I wanted you to know that I'd never take advantage of his nature, his consideration."

"He bought you that bracelet."

Hayley jolted, clamped a hand over it. "Yes. Roz—"

"I've been admiring it since I came in. And watching you rub your hand over it, guiltily. As if you'd stolen it."

"I feel like I did."

"Oh, don't be ridiculous." Roz's eyebrows drew together as she waved a hand. "You'll irritate me."

"I didn't ask for it. I told him not to. All I did was admire it in the window, and the next thing you know he's making arrangements with the concierge and the jewelry store. He wouldn't tell me how much it cost."

"I should hope not," she said staunchly. "I raised him better."

"Roz, these are real stones. It's an antique. It's a real antique."

"I've been on my feet most of today. Don't make me get up to get a closer look at it."

Emotions in turmoil, Hayley stepped over, held out her wrist. Roz simply tugged her down on the sofa. "That is a beauty, and certainly suits you. How many ruby hearts are there?"

"I wouldn't count them," she began, then lowered her head at Roz's bland stare. "Fourteen," she confessed. "With ten little diamonds around here, and two between each heart. God, I'm crass."

"No, you're a girl. And one with excellent taste. Don't wear that to work, no matter how much you want to. You'll get it dirty."

"You're not upset?"

"Harper is free to spend his money as he sees fit, and has the good sense to spend it with some discrimination. He gave you a lovely gift. Why don't you just enjoy it?"

"I thought you'd be mad."

"Then you underestimate me."

"I don't. I don't." Tears swam into her eyes as she burrowed against Roz. "I love you. I'm sorry, I'm so twisted up. I'm so happy. I'm so scared. I'm in love with him. I'm in love with Harper."

"Yes, honey." Roz curled an arm around Hayley, and patted gently. "I know."

"You know." Sniffling, Hayley reared back.

"Look at you." Smiling a little, Roz brushed Hayley's hair away from her damp cheeks. "Sitting here crying, happy, scared tears. The kind a woman sheds over some man she's realized she's crazy about, and doesn't know quite how the hell it happened to her."

"I didn't really know until last night. I knew I liked him, that I cared about him, but mostly I thought I wanted to bang him. Then . . . Oh God, oh God, I actually said that." Mortified, she pressed the heels of her hands against her eyes and rubbed. "See why this is surreal? I just told Harper's mother I wanted to bang him."

"I admit, the situation is a bit unique. But I think my sensibilities can handle it."

"It all just opened up inside me last night, everything opened up and poured through. I've never felt like that." Hayley pressed a hand to her heart, and the rubies glittered. "I've never been in love before, not all the way in love. And I thought, when it happened, that this is it, this is how it feels when you fall. Don't tell him." She gripped Roz's hand. "Please don't tell him."

"It's not for me to tell him. It's for you, when you're ready. Love's a gift, Hayley, to be taken and received freely."

"Love's a lie, an illusion created by weak women and conniving men. An excuse for the middle class to breed and their betters to ignore so they can marry within their own station and build more wealth."

Roz felt the shudder run through her, and her breath back up in her lungs. But she straightened, continued to look in the eyes that were no longer only Hayley's. "Is that how you justified the choices you made?"

"I lived very well on my choices." She lifted her arm, smiled as she trailed a finger over the bracelet. "Very well. Better than those I came from. She was content to serve on her knees. I preferred serving on my back. I could have lived here."

She rose, wandering the room. "I should have. So now I am here. Always."

"But you're not happy. What happened? Why are you here, and so unhappy?"

"I made life." She whirled, cupping a hand over her belly. "You know the power of that. Life grew in me, came from me. And he took it. My son." She looked around, those eyes darting. "My son. I came for my son."

"He's gone now, too." Roz rose slowly. "Long ago. My grandfather. He was a good man."

"A baby. My baby. Little boy, sweet, small. Mine. Men, men are liars, thieves, cheats. I should have killed him."

"The child?"

Those eyes glittered, bright and hard as the diamonds on her wrist. "The father. I should have found a way to kill him, all of them. Burned the house to the ground around them, and sent us all to hell."

There was a chill, and the pity Roz had once felt couldn't chip through the ice of it. "What did you do?"

"I came, I came in the night. Quiet as a mouse." She tapped a finger to her lips, then began to laugh. "Gone." She turned a circle, holding her arm high so the rubies and diamonds flashed. "All gone, everything gone. Nothing left for me." Her head cocked, her gaze turned to the monitor, and Lily's waking cries.

"The baby. The baby's crying."

Her head lolled as she slid to the floor.

"Mitch! David!" Roz rushed across the room to drop down beside Hayley.

"Got a little dizzy," Hayley murmured, passing a hand over her face. Then she looked around, groped for Roz's hand. "What? What?"

"It's all right. Just stay down a minute. David." Roz glanced over her shoulder when both men hurried into the room. "Get us some water and the brandy."

"What happened?" Mitch demanded.

"She had a spell, an episode."

"Lily. Lily's crying."

"I'll get her." Mitch, touched Hayley's shoulder. "I'll go get her."

"I remember. I think. Sort of. My head hurts."

"All right, sweetie. Let's get you onto the couch."

"Little queasy," Hayley managed when Roz helped her to her feet. "I didn't feel it coming, Roz. Then it was . . . it was stronger that time. It was more."

David brought both water and brandy, and sitting on Hayley's other side, put a glass of water in her hand. "Here now, baby doll, sip some water."

"Thanks. I'm okay, feeling better. Just a little shaky."

"You're not the only one," Roz said.

"You talked to her."

"We had quite the conversation."

"You asked her questions. I don't know how you held it together like that."

"Have a little brandy," Roz suggested, but Hayley wrinkled her nose.

"I don't like it. I feel better, honest."

"Then I'll have your share." Roz picked up the snifter and took a healthy swallow as Mitch came in with Lily.

"She'll want her juice. She likes a little juice when she gets up from a nap."

"I'll get her some," Mitch told Hayley.

"No, I'll take her in. I'd like to do something normal for a few minutes." She got to her feet, reaching for Lily as Lily reached for her. "There's my baby girl. We'll be right back."

Roz got to her feet when Hayley left the room. "I'm going to call Harper. He'll want to know about this."

"I'd like to know about this myself," Mitch reminded her.

"You'll want your notebook and tape recorder."

"WE WERE JUST SITTING THERE TALKING. I WAS TELLING Roz what a wonderful time I'd had last night, and showing her the bracelet. And—sorry Harper—but I was telling her I felt guilty about you buying it for me. And I guess I got emotional." She sent a pleading look at Roz, clearly begging confidence. "And then she was just there. Like a bang. I'm a little bit vague on it. It was like hearing a conversation—like when you hold a glass to a wall to hear what people are saying in the next room. All sort of tinny and echoing."

"She was amused, in my opinion, in a nasty sort of way," Roz began, and took them through it.

"She was accustomed to receiving gifts for sex." Mitch scribbled in his notebook. "So that's how she'd equate the bracelet Hayley's wearing. She wouldn't understand," he continued, hearing the quiet sound of distress she made, "generosity, or the pleasure of giving for the sake of the gift. When something was given to her, it was an exchange. Never a token of affection."

Hayley nodded and continued to sit on the floor with Lily.

"She came here," he continued. "By her own words she came here at night. She wanted to cause harm to Reginald, perhaps the entire household. Maybe even planned to. But she didn't. We could assume harm came to her here. She said she was here, always."

"Died here." Hayley nodded. "Remains here. Yes. It felt like that. Like I could almost, almost, see what was in her head while it was happening. And that's what it felt like. She died here, and she stays here. And she thinks of the child she had as a baby still. She's the way she was then, and in her mind—I think—so is her son."

"So she relates to, is drawn to, children," Harper finished. "Once they grow up, they're no real substitute for hers. Especially if they happen to grow up into men."

"She came to help me when I needed it," Roz pointed out. "She recognizes the blood connection. Acknowledges it, at least when it suits her. Hayley's heightened emotions brought her out. But then she answered questions, she spoke intelligently."

"So I'm a kind of conduit." Hayley fought back another shudder. "But why me?"

"Maybe because you're a young mother," Mitch suggested. "Close to the age she was when she died, raising a child—something that was denied her. She made life. It was stolen from her. When life is stolen, what's left?"

"Death," Hayley said with a shudder. She stayed where she was when Lily ran over to Harper and lifted her arms to be held. "She's getting stronger, that's how it felt. She likes having a body around her, having her say. She'd like more. She'd like . . ."

She caught herself twisting the bracelet, and stared down at it. "I forgot," she whispered. "Oh God, I forgot. Last night, when I was dressing, checking myself out in the mirror. She was there."

"You had one of these experiences last night?" Harper demanded.

"No. Or not like this one. She was there, instead of me, in the mirror. I wasn't—" She shook her head impatiently. "I was me, all the way, but the reflection was her. I didn't say anything because I just didn't want to go around about it last night. I just wanted to get out awhile, then everything . . . it went out of my mind until now. She wasn't like we've seen her before."

"What do you mean?" Mitch sat, pencil poised.

"She was all dressed up. A red dress, but not like what I was wearing. Fancy gown, low-cut, off the shoulders. Ball gown, I'd guess. She wore a lot of jewels. Rubies and diamonds. The necklace was . . ." She trailed off to stare at the bracelet in speechless shock.

"Rubies and diamonds," she repeated. "She was wearing this. This bracelet. I'm sure of it. When I saw it at the hotel, I was so pulled toward it. I couldn't see anything else in the display. She was wearing this, on her right wrist. It was hers. This was hers."

Mitch left his seat to crouch on the floor by Hayley and examine the bracelet. "I don't know anything about dating jewelry, about eras along this avenue. Harper, did the jeweler give you a history?"

"Circa 1890," he said tightly. "I never thought twice about it."

"Maybe she pushed you to buy it for me." Hayley shoved to her feet. "If she—"

"No. I wanted to give you something. It's as simple as that. If it makes you uncomfortable to have it, or weirds you out, we can keep it in the safe."

Utter trust, she remembered. That was love. "No. It wasn't an exchange, it was a gift." She crossed to him, kissed him lightly on the lips. "So screw her."

"That's my girl."

Lily batted her hand on his cheek until he turned his face to hers, then she bumped her mouth to his.

"Or one of them," he added.

BY EVENING, SHE WAS CALM AGAIN. CALMER STILL when she settled down in the rocking chair with Lily. She prized these moments, when the room was quiet and she could rock her baby to sleep. Sing to her, and though her voice was no prize, Lily seemed to like it.

This was what Amelia craved, maybe what she craved most under the madness. Just these moments of unity and peace, a mother rocking her child to sleep with a lullaby.

She would try to remember that, Hayley promised herself, whenever she got too frightened or too angry. She would try to remember what Amelia had lost, what had been stolen from her.

She tried "Hush, Little Baby," because it pleased her she knew all the words. And Lily's head was usually heavy on her shoulder by the time the song was finished.

She was nearly there when a movement at the doorway had her heart bumping her ribs. Then it stilled when Harper smiled in at her. In the same rusty, sing-song voice she was using for the lullabye, she warned him.

"She won't go down if she sees you in here."

He nodded, lingered another moment, then slipped away.

Humming, she rose to walk to the crib, tucking Lily in with her stuffed dog within cuddling reach. "When you're three, Mama'll get you a real puppy. Okay, when you're two, but that's my final offer. 'Night, baby."

Leaving the night-light glowing, she left the baby sleeping. Harper turned from the terrace doors when she came in.

"That was a pretty picture, you and Lily rocking in the chair. Mama says she used to rock me and my brothers to sleep in that chair."

"It's why it feels so good. A lot of love's sat in that rocker."

"It's cooler tonight, at least a little cooler. Maybe we could sit out for a while."

"All right." She picked up her bedside monitor, and went with him.

In front of the rail, there was a trio of huge copper pots, greening softly in the weather. She'd been charged with selecting and planting the flowers in them this year, and was always thrilled to see the thriving mix of color, shape, and texture.

"I don't mind the heat, not this time of day anyway." She leaned down to sniff a purple bloom. "The sun goes down a little more, the lightning bugs'll come out, and the cicadas'll start singing."

"Gave me a scare when Mama called earlier."

"Guess so."

"So here's the thing." He ran a hand absently along her arm. "You shouldn't stay here after tonight. You can move on over to Logan's tomorrow. Take some time off," he continued as she turned to stare at him.

"Time off?"

"The nursery's the same as Harper House, as far as this goes. Best you steer clear of both for a while. Mitch and I'll see what we can do about tracing the bracelet, for what that's worth."

"Just pack up and move to Stella's, quit work."

"I didn't say quit. Take some time off."

There was such patience in his voice, the sort of patience that raised her hackles like fingernails on a blackboard.

"Some time."

"Yeah. I talked to Mama about that, and to Stella about you staying with them for a while."

"You did? You talked to them about it."

He knew how a woman sounded when she was getting ready to tear a strip out of him. "No point getting your back up. This is the sensible thing to do."

"So you figure the *sensible* thing is for you to make decisions for me, talk them over with other people, then present them to me on a platter?" Deliberately she took a step back, as if to illustrate she stood on her own feet. "You don't tell me what to do, Harper, and I don't leave this house unless Roz shows me the door."

"No one's kicking you out. What's the damn big deal about staying with a friend for a while?"

It sounded so reasonable. It was infuriating. "Because

this is my home now. This is where I live, and the nursery is where I work."

"And it'll still be your home, still be where you live and where you work. For Christ's sake, don't be so pigheaded."

The lash of temper delighted her. It meant she could lash right back. "Don't you swear at me and call me names."

"I'm not—" He bit off the rest of the words, rammed his hands in his pockets to stride up and down the terrace while he fought with his temper. "You said she was getting stronger. Why the hell would you stay here, risk what happens to you, when all you have to do is move a couple miles away? Temporarily."

"How temporarily? Have you figured that out, too? I'm supposed to just sit around at Stella's, twiddling my thumbs until you decide I can come back?"

"Till it's safe."

"How do you know when it'll be safe, if it'll ever be safe. And if you're so damn worried, why aren't you packing up?"

"Because I . . ." He cleared his throat, turned to glare out at the gardens.

"That was a wise move. Choking back any comment that resembled because you're a man. But I saw it on your face." She gave him a hard shove. "Don't think I didn't see what almost came out of your mouth."

"Don't tell me what almost came out of my mouth, and don't put words into it. I want you somewhere I don't have to worry about you."

"Nobody's asking you to worry. I've been taking care of myself for a lot of years now. I'm not so stupid, or so *pig*-*headed* that I'm not concerned about what's been going on. But I'm also smart enough to consider that maybe I'm the last push. Maybe I'm what's going to finish this. Roz *talked* to her, Harper. Next time maybe there'll be answers that tell us just what happened, and what needs to be done to make it right."

"Next time? Listen to yourself. I don't want her touching you."

"It's not your decision, and I'm no quitter. Do you know me so little you'd think I'd just, yes, Harper, and trot along like a nice little puppy?"

"I'm not trying to run your life, goddamn it, Hayley. I'm just trying to protect you."

Of course, he was. And he looked so aggrieved, so frustrated, she had to sympathize. A little. "You can't. Not this way. And the only thing that you're going to accomplish by making plans around me that don't include talking to me first is piss me off."

"There's a news flash. Just give me a week then. Just do this for a week and let me try to—"

"Harper, they took her child away. They drove her mad. Maybe she was heading there anyway, but they sure as hell gave her the last push over the edge. I've been part of this for over a year now. I can't walk away from it."

She lifted her hand, stroked the bracelet she continued to wear. "She showed me this. Somehow. I'm wearing what was hers. You gave it to me. It means something. I have to find out what that is. And I, very much, need to stay here with you." She softened enough to touch his cheek. "You had to know I'd stay. What did your mother say when you said you were going to tell me to go to Stella's?"

He shrugged, walked back to the terrace rail.

"Figured that. And Stella, I imagine said the same."

"Logan agreed with me."

"I bet he did." She moved to him now, wrapped her arms around him, rested her cheek on his back.

He had a good, strong back. Working man, prince of the

castle. What a fascinating combination of both he was. "I appreciate the thought, if not the method. That help any?"

"Not so much."

"How about it's nice that you care enough about me to try to boss me around?"

"It's not bossing you around to—" He broke off with a curse and a sigh when he turned to see her grinning at him. "You're not going to budge."

"Not an inch. I think some of the Ashby blood, even as diluted as it is in me, must have stubborn corpuscles. And I want to be a part of finding the answers to all this, Harper. It's important to me, maybe more important now that I've shared a kind of consciousness with her. Boy, that sounds pretty woo-woo, but I don't know how else to say it."

"How about she invades you?"

Her face sobered. "All right, that's fair. You're still mad, and that's fair, too. I guess I don't mind knowing you're worried enough about me to be mad."

"If you're going to be reasonable about this, it's just going to piss me off more." He laid his hands on her shoulders, rubbed. "I do care about you, Hayley, and I am worried."

"I know. Just remember I care about me, too, and worry enough to be as careful as I can be."

"I'm going to stay with you tonight. I'm not budging about that."

"Good thing that's just where I want you. You know . . ." She slid her hands up his chest, linked them around his neck. "If we start fooling around, she might do something. So I think we ought to test that." She rose on her toes, played her lips over his. "Like an experiment."

"In my line of work I live for experiments."

"Come on inside." She stepped back, caught both his hands in hers. "We'll set up the lab."

* * *

LATER, WHEN THEY LAY TURNED TOWARD EACH OTHER in the dark, she brushed at his hair. "She didn't seem to be interested this time."

"You can't predict a ghost who should be haunting an asylum."

"Guess not." She snuggled closer. "You're a kind of scientist, right?"

"Kind of."

"When scientists are experimenting, they usually have to try more than once, maybe with some slight varieties, over a course of time. I've heard."

"Absolutely."

"So." She closed her eyes, all but purring at the stroke of his hand. "We'll just have to try this again, at some opportunity. Don't you think?"

"I do. And I think I hear opportunity knocking right now."

She opened her eyes, laughed into his. "They don't call that opportunity where I come from."

twelve

David turned the map upside down, and ran a fingertip down a line of road. "We're like detectives. Like Batman and Robin."

"They weren't detectives," Harper corrected. "They were crime fighters."

"Picky, picky. All right, like Nick and Nora Charles."

"Just tell me where I turn, Nora."

"Should be a right in about two miles." David let the map lay on his lap and shifted to enjoy the scenery. "Now that we're so hot on the trail of the mysterious jewels, just what are we going to do if and when we find out where the bracelet originally came from?"

"Knowledge is power." Harper shrugged. "Something like that. And I've had enough of sitting around waiting for something to happen. The jeweler said it came from the Hopkins estate."

"Cream cheese."

"What? You're hungry?"

"Cream cheese," David repeated. "You spread it on smooth and thick. 'My girlfriend really loved the bracelet. She's got a birthday coming up soon, and since it was such a hit with her, I wondered if you had any matching pieces. Something from the same estate? That's the Kent estate, isn't it?' Guy practically fell over himself to give you the information, even if he did try to sell you a couple of gaudy rings. Ethel Hopkins did not have flawless taste. You should've sprung for the earrings, though. Hayley would love them."

"I just bought her a bracelet. Earrings are overkill at this point."

"Your right's coming up. Earrings are never overkill," he added when Harper made the turn. "About a half mile down this road. Should be on the left."

He pulled into a double drive beside a late-model Town Car, then sat tapping his fingers on the steering wheel as he studied the lay of the land.

The house was large and well-kept in an old, well-to-do neighborhood. It was a two-story English Tudor with a good selection of foundation plants, an old oak, and a nicely shaped dogwood in the front. The lawn was trimmed and lushly green, which meant lawn service or automatic sprinklers.

"Okay, what have we got here?" he queried. "Established, upper middle class."

"Ethel's only surviving daughter, Mae Hopkins Ives Fitzpatrick," David read from the notes he'd taken from the courthouse records. "She's seventy-six. Twice married, twice widowed. And you can thank me for digging that up so quickly due to my brilliant observation of Mitch's methods."

"Let's see if we can charm our way in, then get her to tell us if she remembers when her mother came by the bracelet."

They went to the door, rang the bell, and waited in the thick heat.

The woman who opened the door had a short, sleek cap of brown hair, and faded blue eyes behind the lenses of fashionable gold-framed glasses. She was tiny, maybe an inch over five feet, and workout trim in a pair of blue cotton pants and a crisp white camp shirt. There were pearls around her throat, whopping sapphires on the ring fingers of either hand, and delicate gold hoops in her ears.

"You don't look like salesmen to me." She spoke in a raspy voice and kept a hand on the handle of the screened door.

"No, ma'am." Harper warmed up his smile. "I'm Harper Ashby, and this is my friend David Wentworth. We'd like to speak with Mae Fitzpatrick."

"That's what you're doing."

Genetic good luck or, more likely, a skilled plastic surgeon, Harper thought, had shaved a good ten years off her seventy-six. "I'm pleased to meet you, Miz Fitzpatrick. I realize this is an odd sort of intrusion, but I wonder if we might come in and have a word with you?"

The color of her eyes might have been faded, but the expression of them was sharp as a scalpel. "Do I look like the simpleminded sort of woman who lets strange men into her house?"

"No, ma'am." But he had to wonder why a woman who claimed good sense would believe a screened door was any sort of barrier. "If you wouldn't mind then, if I could just ask you a few questions regarding a—"

"Ashby, you said?"

"Yes, ma'am."

"Any relation to Miriam Norwood Ashby?"

"Yes, ma'am. She was my paternal grandmother."

"I knew her a little."

"I can't really claim the same."

"Don't expect so, as she's been dead some time now. You'd be Rosalind Harper's boy then."

"Yes, ma'am, her oldest."

"I've met her a time or two. First time being at her wedding to John Ashby. You have the look of her, don't you?"

"I do. Yes, ma'am."

She slid her eyes toward David. "This isn't your brother."

"A family friend, Miz Fitzpatrick," David said with a full-wattage smile. "I live at Harper House, and work for Rosalind. Perhaps you'd feel more at ease if you contacted Miz Harper before you speak to us. We'd be happy to give you a number where you can reach her, and wait out here while you do."

Instead she opened the screen. "I don't believe Miriam Ashby's grandson is going to knock me unconscious and rob me. Y'all come in."

"Thank you."

The house was as neat and well-tended as its mistress, with polished oak floors and muted green walls. She let them into a generous living room that was furnished in a contemporary, almost minimalistic style.

"I suppose you boys could use a cold drink."

"We don't want to put you to any trouble, Miz Fitzpatrick," Harper told her.

"Sweet tea's simple enough. Have a seat. I'll be with you in a minute."

"Classy," David commented when she left the room. "A bit pared down, but classy."

"The place, or her?"

"Both." He took a seat on the sofa. "Ashby-Harper is a very slick entree. Charm wouldn't have worked on her."

"Interesting she knew my grandmother—she's some younger—and that she was invited to my mother's wedding. All these little intersections. I wonder if one of her ancestors knew Reginald or Beatrice."

"Coincidence is only coincidence if you don't have an open mind."

"Living with a ghost tends to leave it gaping." Harper got to his feet as Mae came back with a tray of glasses. "Let me get that for you. We very much appreciate your time, Miz Fitzpatrick." He set the tray on the coffee table. "I'll try not to take up too much of it."

"Your grandmother was a kindhearted woman. While I didn't know her intimately, your grandfather and my first husband had a small business venture together many years ago. A real estate venture," she added, "that was satisfactorily profitable for all involved. Now, why has her grandson come knocking on my door?"

"It has to do with a bracelet from your mother's estate."

She angled her head with polite interest. "My mother's estate."

"Yes, ma'am. It happens that I bought this bracelet from the jeweler who acquired it from the estate."

"And is there something wrong with the bracelet?"

"No. No, ma'am. I'm hoping you might remember some of the history of it, as I'm very interested in its origins. I'm told it was made sometime around 1890. It's made up of ruby hearts framed in diamonds."

"Yes, I know the piece. I sold it and several others recently as they weren't to my taste and saw no reason to have them sitting in a safety deposit box as they had been since my mother's death some years ago." She sipped her tea as she watched him. "You're curious about its history?"

"Yes, ma'am, I am."

"But not forthcoming with your reasons."

"Oddly enough, I have reason to believe it—or one very like it—was in my family. When I discovered that, I found it interesting and thought satisfying my curiosity would be worth a little time in trying to trace it back."

"Is that so? Now, that I find interesting. The bracelet was given by my grandfather to my grandmother in 1893, as an anniversary gift. It's possible that there was more than one made, in that same design, at the time."

"Yes, possibly."

"There is, however, a story behind it, if you'd like to hear it."

"I really would."

She held out the plate of cookies she'd brought out with the tea, waited until each of the men had taken one. Then she settled back with a hint of a smile on her face. "My grandparents did not have a happy marriage, my grandfather being somewhat of a scoundrel. He enjoyed gambling and shady deals and the company of loose women—according to my grandmother, who lived to the ripe age of ninety-eight, so I knew her quite well."

Rising, she walked to an étagère and took down a photo framed in slim silver.

"My grandparents," she said, passing the photo to Harper. "A formal portrait taken in 1891. You can see, scoundrel or not, he was quite handsome."

"Both are." And, Harper noted, the style of dress, hair, even the photographic tone was similar to the copies of photographs Mitch had pinned to his workboard.

"She's a beauty." David glanced up. "You favor her."

"So I've been told. Physically, and in temperament." Obviously pleased, she took the photo, replaced it. "My grandmother claimed two of the happiest days of her life were her wedding day, when she was too young and foolish to know what she was getting into, and the day she became a widow—some twelve years later, and could enjoy life without the burden of a man who couldn't be trusted."

She sat again, picked up her tea. "A handsome man, as you saw for yourselves. A charming man, by all accounts, and one who had considerable success with the gambling and the shady deals. But my grandmother was a moral sort of woman. One who managed to bend those morals, just enough to enjoy the results of her husband's successes, even as she decried them."

She set down her tea, sat back, obviously relishing her role. "She told the story, often, of discovering—during one of my grandfather's drunken confessions that the anniversary gift—the ruby hearts—had come from a somewhat less than reputable source. He had acquired it in a payoff of a gambling debt from a man who bought jewelry and so forth on the cheap from those unfortunate or desperate enough to have to sell their possessions quickly. Often, more likely, from those who had stolen those possessions and used him as a fence."

She smiled broadly now, no doubt relishing the thought. "It had belonged to a wealthy man's mistress, and was stolen from her by one of the servants after she had been cut off by him. The story, as my grandmother claimed it was told to her, was that the woman had gone raving mad, and had subsequently vanished."

She reached for her tea, sipped. "I always wondered if that story was true."

HARPER WENT TO HIS MOTHER FIRST, AND KNELT DOWN beside her in the gardens at home. Absently, he began to help her weed.

"I heard you took some time off today," she began.

"I had something I wanted to do. Why aren't you wearing a hat?"

"I forgot it. I was only going to come out for a minute, then I got started."

He pulled off the ballcap he wore, tugged it down over her head. "Do you remember how so many times after school, if I was working out here when you came home, you'd sit down beside me, help me weed or plant and tell me your troubles, or your triumphs of the day?"

"I remember you were always here to listen. To me, to Austin and Mason. Sometimes to all three of us at once. How'd you do that?"

"A mother's got an ear for the voices of her children. Like a conductor for each separate instrument in his orchestra, even in the middle of a symphony. What are your troubles, baby boy?"

"You were right about Hayley."

"I make being right a policy. What was I right about exactly?"

"That she wouldn't move over to Logan's because I asked her to."

Under the bill, Roz's eyebrows arched. "Asked her?"

"Asked her, told her." He shrugged. "What's the difference when you've got the person's welfare in mind?"

She let out a husky laugh, patted her dirty hands on his cheeks. "Such a man."

"A minute ago I was your baby boy."

"My baby boy is such a man. I don't see that as a flaw. An amusement sometimes—such as now—a puzzlement now and then, and on rare occasions a damned irritation. Are you fighting? It didn't seem to me you were at odds when you came down to breakfast together this morning."

"No, we're all right. If you don't like me sleeping with her in the house, I get that."

"So you'll respect the sanctity of our home and sleep with her elsewhere?"

"Yeah."

"I slept with men I wasn't married to in Harper House. It's not a cathedral, it's a home. Yours as much as mine. If you're having sex with Hayley, you might as well have it comfortably. And safely," she added with a direct look.

Even after all these years, it made his shoulders hunch. "I buy my own condoms these days."

"I'm glad to hear it."

"And that isn't what I wanted to get into. I traced the bracelet back to Amelia."

Those eyes widened as she sat back on her heels. "You did? That was fast work."

"Fast work, coincidence, lucky break. I'm not sure where it falls. It came from the estate of an Esther Hopkins. She's been dead a few years now, apparently, and her daughter decided to go ahead and sell some of the things she didn't like, or care to keep. Mae Fitzpatrick. She said she knew you."

"Mae Fitzpatrick." Roz closed her eyes and tried to flip through the vast mental files of acquaintances. "I'm sorry, it doesn't seem familiar."

"She was married before. Wait a minute . . . Ives?"

"Mae Ives doesn't ring bells either."

"Well, she said she'd only met you a couple of times. Once was when you married Daddy. She was at your wedding."

"Is that a fact? Well, that's interesting, but not all that surprising. I think between my mama and John's we had everybody in Shelby County and most of Tennessee at the wedding."

"She knew Grandma Ashby."

He sat on the garden path with her and told her of the conversation he'd had with Mae Fitzpatrick.

"Amazing, isn't it," she mused. "All those little angles and curls, and how they fit together."

"I know. Mama, she had it figured. Too well-bred to say it right out, but she put it together, about Reginald Harper being the wealthy protector who'd cast his mistress off. She's likely to talk about it."

"And you think that bothers me? Honey, the fact that my great-grandfather had mistresses, that he kept women, tossed them aside, and lived a life generally rife with infidelity isn't a reflection on me, or you. His behavior isn't our responsibility, which is something I sincerely wish Amelia would realize."

She dug out more weeds. "As to the rest of his behavior, which is beyond deplorable, it's not our fault either. Mitch is writing about it. Unless you and your brothers feel strongly that all of this should be kept as closely within the family as possible, I want him to do this book."

"Why?"

"It's not our fault, it's not our responsibility. That's all true," she said as she sat back to look at him. "But I feel that airing all of this is somehow giving her her due. It's a way to acknowledge an ancestor who, no matter what she did, what she became, was treated shabbily at best, monstrously at worst."

She lifted her hand, pressed her soil-streaked palm to his. "She's our blood."

"Does that make me heartless because I want her gone, I want her ended for what she nearly did to you, for what she's doing now to Hayley?"

"No. It means Hayley and I are closer to your heart. That's enough for today." She swiped her hands on the thighs of her gardening pants. "We're going to boil in this wet heat if we stay out much longer. Come on inside with me. Let's sit in the cool and have a beer."

"Tell me something." He studied the house as they walked down the path. "How did you know that Daddy was the one?"

"Stars in my eyes." She laughed, and despite the heat hooked an arm through his. "I swear, stars in my eyes. I was so young, and he put stars in my eyes. But that was infatuation. I think I knew that he was mine when we talked for hours one night. I snuck out of the house to meet him. God, my daddy would have skinned him alive. But all we did was talk, hour after hour, under a willow tree. He was just a boy, but I knew I'd love him all of my life. And I have. I knew because we sat there, almost till dawn, and he made me laugh, and made me think and dream and tremble. I never thought I'd love again. But I do. It takes nothing away from your father, Harper."

"Mama. I know." He closed a hand over hers. "How did you know with Mitch?"

"I guess I was too cynical for those stars, at least at first. It was slower, and scarier. He makes me laugh and think and dream and tremble. And there was a time during that longer, slower climb that I looked at him, and my heart warmed again. I'd forgotten what it was like to feel that warmth inside the heart."

"He's a good man. He loves you. He watches you when you come into a room, when you walk out of one. I'm glad you found him."

"So am I."

"With Daddy? What willow was it?"

"Oh, it was a big, beautiful old tree, way back, beyond the old stables." She paused, looked toward the ruin, gestured. "John was going to come back sometime soon after, carve our initials in the trunk. But that next night lightning struck it, split it right in two, and—Oh my God."

"Amelia," he said softly.

"It had to be. It never occurred to me before this, but I remember there hadn't been a storm. The servants were talking about the tree and the lightning hitting it when there hadn't been a storm."

"So even then," he said, "she took her shots."

"How mean, how petty of her. I cried over that tree. I fell in love under it, and cried when I watched the groundskeepers clear away the wood and pull the trunk out."

"Don't you wonder if there were other things? Small, violent acts we passed off as nature or some strange quirk, all while we thought of her as benevolent?"

He studied the house now, thought of what it was to him—and what had walked there long before he was born. "She's never been benevolent, not really."

"All that hate and anger stored up. Trapped."

"Leaking now and again, like water through a crack in a dam. It's coming faster and harder now. And we can't put it back in, Mama. What we have to do is empty it out, draw out every drop."

"How?"

"I think we're going to have to break the dam, while we're the ones holding the hammer."

IT WAS TWILIGHT WHEN HAYLEY WANDERED THROUGH the gardens. The baby was asleep, and Roz and Mitch were taking monitor duty. Harper's car was there, so he was *somewhere*. Not in the carriage house, because she'd knocked, then poked her head in and called.

It wasn't as if they were joined at the hip, she reminded herself. But he hadn't stayed for dinner. He'd said he'd had something to do, that he'd be back before dark.

Well, it was nearly dark, and she was just wondering.

Besides, she liked walking in the gardens, in the gloaming. Even under the circumstances. It was soothing, and she could use a little soothing after running the story he'd told her about the bracelet over and over in her head.

They were getting closer to the answers, she was sure of it. But she was no longer sure it would all end quietly once they had them.

Amelia might not be content to give up her last links with this world and pass on—she supposed that was the term—to the next.

She liked inhabiting a body. If you could call it inhabiting. Sharing one? Sliding through one? Whatever it was, Amelia liked it, of that Hayley was sure. Just as she was sure it was something as new for Amelia as it was for herself.

If it happened again—*when,* she corrected, ordering herself to face facts. When it happened again, she was going to fight to stay more aware, to find more control.

And wasn't that what she was doing out here alone, in the half light? No point in pretending to herself this wasn't a deliberate move. A sort of dare. *Come on, bitch.* She wanted to see what she could handle, and how she would handle it when no one else was around to run interference. Or be hurt.

But nothing was happening. She felt completely normal, completely herself.

And was completely herself when sounds out of the shadows made her jump. She stopped, caught in the crosshairs of fight or flight, ears straining. The rhythmic, repetitive sound made her frown as she inched forward.

It sounded . . . but it couldn't be. Still her heart beat like wings as she crept closer, envisioning a ghostly figure digging a grave.

Amelia's grave. It could be. This could be the answer, at last. Reginald had murdered her, then buried her here on the property. She was going to be shown the grave—on unconsecrated ground. They could have it blessed or marked or—well, she'd look up what was done in cases like this.

Then the haunting of Harper House would be over.

She picked her way quietly around the ruins of the stables, edging as close to the building as she dared. Her palms sprang damp, and her breath seemed to rattle in her throat.

She turned the corner of the building, following the sound, prepared to be terrified and amazed.

And saw Harper, his T-shirt stripped off and tossed to the ground, digging a hole.

The lctdown had the breath expelling from her lungs in a frantic whoosh.

"Harper, for Christ's sake, you scared me brainless. What are you doing?"

He continued to spear the blade of the shovel into the ground, tossing the dirt into the pile beside it. Though she was still jittery, she cast her eyes skyward, then marched to him.

"I said—" He jumped a clean foot off the ground when she poked a finger in his back. And even as she yelped in response, he whirled, cocking the shovel over his shoulder like a bat. He managed to check his swing, cursed a blue streak as she stumbled back and fell hard on her ass.

"Jesus, God almighty!" He dragged the headset down to his shoulders. "What the hell are you doing, sneaking around in the dark?"

"I didn't sneak, I called you. If you didn't play that headset so loud you could hear a person when they said something. I thought you were going to brain me with that shovel. I thought . . ."

She began to giggle, tried to snuff it back. "You should've

seen your face. Your eyes were this big." She held up her hands, curling her fingers into wide balls, then dissolved into laughter when he snarled at her.

"Oh, oh, I'm going to wet my pants. Wait." She squeezed her eyes, bounced quickly in place while more giggles bubbled. "Okay, okay, back in control. The least you could do is help me up after you knocked me down."

"I didn't knock you down. Damn near though." He offered a hand, pulled her up.

"I thought you were Reginald, digging Amelia's untimely grave."

Shaking his head, he leaned on the shovel and stared at her. "So you came on around to what, give him a hand?"

"Well, I had to see, didn't I? What in the world are you doing, digging a hole out here in the dark?"

"It's not dark."

"You said it was dark when you yelled at me. What are you doing?"

"Playing third base for the Atlanta Braves."

"I don't see why you're being pissy. I'm the one who fell down and nearly wet her pants."

"Sorry. Did you hurt yourself?"

"No. You planting that tree?" She finally focused in on the slim, young willow. "Why are you planting a tree, Harper, back here and at this time of night?"

"It's for Mama. She told me this story today, about how she snuck out of the house to meet my father one night, and that they sat under a willow that used to be back here, and talked. That's when she fell in love with him. The next day it got hit by lightning. Amelia," he said and dug out another shovelful of dirt. "She didn't put it together before, but you've got to figure the odds. So I'm putting one in for her."

She stood silently for a moment while he eyeballed the hole, then the rootball, then dug some more.

"That's the sweetest thing. That just coats my heart with sweetness, Harper. Can I help, or is it something you want to do alone?"

"Hole's about right. You can help me put it in."

"I never planted a tree before."

"See, you want the hole about three times as wide as the rootball, but no deeper. Get the sides of the hole loose so the roots have room to spread."

He picked up the tree, set it in the hole. "How's that look to you?"

"It looks right, like you said."

"Now you peel the burlap back, from the main stem, then we'll see the original soil line, at least we will if you turn on that flashlight over there, because it is getting dark. Took me a while to get everything I needed for this."

She turned it on, crouched down and aimed. "How's that?"

"Good. See?" He tapped a finger on the mark at the base. "That's the soil line, and we've got the right depth here. We've just got a little bit of roots that need pruning off. Hand me those."

She got the clippers, passed them to him. "You know digging a hole for a tree sounds the same as digging a grave."

He flicked her a look. "Have you ever heard anybody digging a grave?"

"In movies."

"Right. We're going to fill the hole, but we do it little by little and firm the soil down as we do. I don't have any spare gloves. Here."

"No." She waved him back when he started to pull off his work gloves. "A little dirt won't hurt me. Am I doing this right?"

"Yeah, that's good. You just keep filling and firming,

hilling it up toward the base and leaving a kind of shallow moat around the edge of the hole."

"I like the way it feels. The dirt."

"I know what you mean." When they'd finished to his satisfaction, he took out his knife, trimmed off the exposed burlap, then pushed to his feet. "We'll give it plenty of water, pour it into the rim around the mound, see?"

He hauled up one of the buckets he'd filled, nodded when she lifted the other.

"There, you planted a tree."

"Helped plant one anyway." She stepped back, reached out a hand for his. "It looks lovely, Harper. It'll mean a lot to her that you thought to do this."

"It meant something to me to do it." He gave her hand a squeeze, then bent to pick up his tools. "Probably should've waited until next spring, but I wanted to do it now. A kind of nose-thumbing. Go ahead and knock them down, we'll just put them back up. I wanted to do it now."

"You're so angry with her."

"I'm not a kid, charmed by lullabies anymore. I've seen her for what she is."

Hayley shook her head, shivered a little in the close evening air. "I don't think any of us have seen her for what she is. Not yet."

thirteen

THE GRAFTING HOUSE WAS MORE THAN A WORK SPACE for Harper. It was also part playhouse, part sanctuary, and part lab. He could, and often did, lose himself for hours inside its warm, music-filled air, working, experimenting, or just reveling in being the only human among the plants.

A lot of times he preferred the plants to humans. Though he wasn't altogether sure what that said about him, he wasn't all that concerned about it.

He'd found his passion in life, and considered himself fortunate that he could make a living doing something that made him completely happy.

His brothers had to leave home to find theirs. It was the bonus round for him that he'd been able to stay where he loved, and do what he loved.

He had his home, his work, his family. Throughout his adult life he'd had women he'd liked and enjoyed. But none of them had ever made him think, had ever nudged him to consider the next step on the rung of what he'd thought of vaguely as The Future.

He hadn't worried about that either. His vision of marriage was reflected in what he knew his parents had together. Love, dedication, respect, and tempering it all, like an alloy in steel, an unwavering friendship.

He understood his mother had found that a second time, with Mitch. Not so much lightning striking twice as a true and perfect graft that united to make a new and healthy plant.

In his mind, nothing less strong, less important was worth the time or risk.

So he'd enjoyed the women who'd passed through his life, and had never pictured any of them as The One.

Until Hayley.

Now, so much of his world had changed, while other parts of it remained, comfortably, the same.

He'd flipped on Chopin for his plants' enjoyment today. And had P.O.D rocking the party on his headset.

The space might not appear efficient with its groupings of plants in various stages of growth, the buckets of gravel or wood chips, the scatter of tapes and twine, clothespins and labels. There were scraps of burlap, piles of pots, bags of soil, tangles of rubber bands. Trays of knives and clippers. But he knew where to find what he wanted when he needed it.

There might have been times he couldn't put his hands on a pair of matching socks, but he could always put them on the tool he needed.

He walked along, airing the tents and cases that housed his plants, as he did every morning. A few minutes without their covers would dry off any surface moisture that might have condensed on his rootstocks. Fungal disease was always a worry. Still, too much air might dry out the union.

As he aired them, he checked specimens for progress, for any signs of disease or rot. He was particularly pleased with the camellia he'd cleft-grafted over the winter. His specimens would take another year, perhaps two to flower, but he believed they'd be worth the wait.

The work required his passion, but it also required his patience, and his faith.

He made notes to be transcribed to his computer files. There was active, steady growth in the astrophytum seedlings he had protected under a bottle cloche, and the nurse grafts of his clematis looked strong and healthy.

Making the rounds once more, he retented the plants. He'd need to check the pond later to study the water lilies and irises he'd hybridized. A side and personal experiment he hoped would prove rewarding.

Plus, it would give him an excuse to take a cooling dip in the heat of the day.

But for now, he had several cultivars to see to.

He gathered the tools he'd need, then selected a healthy rootstock from his pot-grown lantana, made the oblique cut, then matched it with a scion of viburnum. The girths were similar enough that he was able to use the simple slant of each cut to place them together so the cambiums on each side met truly.

Using elastic bands, he kept the pressure light and even as he bound them together. Judging the graft good, he used grafting wax to seal the joining. He set it in a seed tray, covered the roots and graft with moist soil—his mother's mix—then labeled.

Once he'd repeated the process several times, he tented the tray, and swiveled to his computer to log in the work.

Before he started on the next house specimens, he switched his music to Michelle Branch and pulled a Coke from his cooler.

By the time he'd finished, Michelle had played through and his morning's work was completed.

He gathered a bag of tools and supplies, left his headset behind, and went out to check his field-grown and water plants.

There were a few customers wandering around, scouting out the discounted stock under shade screens or poking into the public greenhouses. He knew if he didn't make his escape quickly, one of them might catch him.

He didn't mind talking plants or directing a customer toward what they were looking for. He just preferred keeping his mind in the game, and right now that game was checking his field plants.

He made it past the portulaca before someone called his name. Should've kept the headset on, he thought, but turned, readying up his customer smile.

The brunette had a curvy little body, which he'd had occasion to see naked several times. At the moment, she was showing it off in belly-baring shorts and a brief top designed to make a man give thanks for August heat.

With a delighted laugh, she bounced up on her toes, clamped her arms around his neck and gave him a loud smack of a kiss. She still tasted of bing cherries, and brought back a flood of equally sweet memories.

Instinctively he gave her a hard hug before stepping back to get a better view. "Dory, what're you doing in town? How've you been?"

"I've been terrific, and I just moved back. Just a couple weeks ago. Got a job with a PR firm here. I got tired of Miami, missed being home, too, I guess."

She'd probably changed her hair from the last time he'd seen her. Women were forever changing their hair. But since he wasn't absolutely sure, he fell back on the standard: "You look great."

"Feel the same. And look at you, all buff and tan. I was going to call you but I wasn't sure you were still living in that sweet little house."

"Yeah, still there."

"I was hoping. I always loved that place. How's your mama, and David, and your brothers, and oh, just everybody." She gave a bubbling laugh, threw out her arms. "I feel like I've been living on Mars for the past three years."

"Everybody's good. Mama got married a few weeks ago."

"I heard. My mama caught me up with some of the local news. I heard you haven't."

"Haven't what? Oh, no."

"I was thinking you and I could do some catching up." Dory trailed a finger down his chest. "I'd love to see your place again. I could pick up some Chinese, a bottle of wine. Like the old days."

"Ah, well . . ."

"A kind of welcome-home and thank-you for you helping me pick out some houseplants for my new place. You'll do that, won't you, Harper? I'd like a few nice ones."

"Sure. I mean, sure I'll help you pick out some plants. But—"

"Why don't we go inside, out of this heat. You can tell me what you've been up to while you help me out. But save some of the good stuff for later."

She took his hand, squeezing it as she tugged him with her. "I've missed seeing you," she continued. "We barely had a chance to talk when I was up for a few days last year. I was going out with that photographer then, remember? I told you."

"Yeah." Vaguely. "And I'm—"

"Well, that is so over. I don't know why I wasted a year of my life on a man so self-centered. It was always about him, you know what I mean? What made me think I wanted to hook up with the artistic, broody type?"

"I—"

"So I shook him and the sand out of my shoes, and here I am."

Inside, she turned and slid her hands in the back pockets of his jeans. An old habit of hers that brought on another memory flash. "I really have missed the hell right out of you. You're glad to see me, aren't you, Harper?"

"Sure. Sure, I am. The thing is, Dory, I'm seeing somebody."

"Oh." Her full bottom lip pouted. "Some serious somebody?"

"Yeah."

"Oh well." She left her hands in his pockets another moment, then drew them out. Gave his ass a little pat. "I guess I figured it would take a lot of luck on my part for you to be flying solo. How long have you been seeing her?"

"Depends. What I mean is, I've known her awhile, but we've only started . . . we've only been involved recently."

"Looks like I should've gotten here sooner. We're still friends, right? Good friends."

"We always were."

"That's what I remembered, and I guess what I missed with Justin, the photographer. We never managed to be friends, and we sure as hell weren't anything close to friends when it fell apart. You, on the other hand. I was telling another friend of mine not long ago how I've never been dumped as sweetly as I was with you."

She laughed, rose on her toes to kiss him lightly. "You're a rare one, Harper."

She stepped back, and seconds later, Hayley came through the glass doors. "I'm sorry, am I interrupting? Is there something I can help you with?"

"No, thanks. Harper's giving me a hand." Dory patted

hers on his arm. "I'm clueless about plants, so I came to the expert."

"Hayley, this is Dory. We went to college together."

"Is that right?" She smiled, widely. "I don't think I've seen you in here before."

"I haven't been, for a long time. I've just moved back from Miami. New job, fresh start, you know how it goes."

"Don't I just," Hayley purred with that wide smile still in place.

"I decided I'd come see Harper, and catch up, and get a few plants to liven up my new apartment. Wait till you see it, Harper, it's a big step up from the hole I rented off-campus back in the day."

"Anything would be. I hope you got rid of that futon."

"I burned it. Harper hated that thing," she said to Hayley. "Even offered to buy me a bed, but all I had was this tiny little place—just one room. If I had three people over, we were so crammed together we were halfway to an orgy."

"Those were the days," Harper said, and made Dory laugh.

"Weren't they? Well, you'd better show me what I'm going to need, or I'll keep you talking the rest of the day."

"I'll just leave y'all alone." Hayley backed out the doors.

She got back to work, but made certain she wasn't on checkout duty when Dory was ready to pay for the plants Harper selected for her. But she could hear Dory laugh—a particularly grating laugh, in her opinion—as she stocked shelves across the room.

Harper leaned on the counter through the process, she noted out of the corner of her eye. And just look how he wore that lazy smile of his while they talked about mutual friends and the good old days.

And damn if that Dory didn't keep touching him. Little pats and pokes in between her hair flips. The steam began to rise from her belly up to her throat as Harper pulled the cart of potted plants out to Dory's car.

Hayley decided she really needed to check the stock of the shelves by the window. And if a person happened to look out while they were working, it wasn't spying. It was glancing.

Enough of a glance that she saw Harper lean down and exchange a liplock with his college buddy.

Bastard.

Then he waved her off before strolling around the side of the building like he wasn't a low-life cheating scum. Worse, the sort that did his low-life cheating right in front of her face.

You'd think he'd have the courtesy, the good breeding, to at least do it behind her back.

Well, that was just fine. She wasn't going to let it matter. She wasn't going to give a single wrinkled, balled-up damn.

And she wasn't going outside to kick him in his two-timing balls either. She was just going out to see if any customers needed her assistance.

That's what she got paid for. Not for flirting, not for spending half the day reminiscing. And certainly not for kissing customers before she waved bye-bye.

She was nearly to the grafting house when she saw him out in the field. He was already crouched down, examining grafts on the magnolias she'd helped him graft and plant weeks before.

He flicked her a glance and a smile as she approached. "Take a look. These are coming along. Couple of weeks we can remove the tape."

"If you say so."

"Yeah, they're looking good. I need to check some of the other ornamentals. I think we're going to have some nice weeping pears and cherries for next season. Have I shown you the fruiting pears I did? The dwarfs?"

"No. Did your friend get what she was after?"

"Hmm. Yeah." He rose, walked across to check the balance of the canopies on his weepers. "Kept it simple," he said absently as he studied the tree. "Low maintenance. What I did here was use *pyrus communis* for stock—three-year-olds, and grafted three pendulas. You gotta make sure you get the spacing right, so you produce a nice shape."

"And you know all about shapes."

"Yeah. I like chip-budding these. I did these two springs ago, and these this spring. See how they develop?"

"I see how a lot of things develop. I was surprised you didn't go with her, carry the plants to her door."

"Who? Oh, Dory?" He flipped Hayley an absent look as sarcasm sailed, visibly, over his head. "She'll be able to handle it. A couple trips."

He continued to walk, continued to examine.

"Here? For these weeping cherries, I used a semi-dwarfing rootstock. Should make a nice specimen tree for smaller spaces. 'Round October, I'm going to take some ripe shoots from the Colt stock. What you do is bundle them, and drop them root-end down in a trench in the nursery bed, and hill 'em up so they're about three-quarters buried. Then next spring, we'll lift the bundles, plant the cuttings, and by summer they'll be ready to use for rootstocks."

"That's all just fascinating, Harper. Did you spend all that time with Dory lecturing her on how to make a damn rootstock?"

"Huh." His distraction was evident on his face as he glanced around. "She's not interested in this kind of work. She's in public relations."

"Private ones from what I saw."

"What?"

"I was about to come back and suggest the two of you get a room. You ought to know better than to make out in one of the retail areas."

This time his mouth dropped open. "*What?* We weren't. We were just—"

"Those doors are glass, Harper, in case you've forgotten. I saw you, and you ought to have more respect for your workplace than to fool around in one of the public areas during working hours. But as you're the boss, I guess you can do what the hell you like."

"My mother's the boss, and I wasn't fooling around anywhere. Dory and I are old friends. We were just—"

"Kissing, touching, flirting, making dates. It's unprofessional, in my opinion, to do that during work hours. But it's downright rude to do it in front of me."

"Behind your back would be better?"

Because it echoed her own nasty thoughts, her eyes went hot, searing like suns. "Let me just say, fuck you, Harper."

Since it was as good an exit line as she could think of when her brain was ready to explode, she turned on her heel. And spun right back when he grabbed her arm.

He didn't look distracted now, she noted. He looked ice-cold mad. "I wasn't flirting or making dates."

"Just kissing and touching then."

"I kissed her because she's a friend, a good one, who I haven't seen in a while. I kissed her the way you kiss a friend. Which is nothing like this, for instance."

He gave her a yank that threw her off balance so her body collided with his. Then was scooped up, pulled in. He got a fistful of her hair, gave it a quick tug. And had his mouth crushed to hers.

Not sweetly, not warmly, but with the stark heat of raw temper. She struggled, shocked that she was clamped so hard and tight she couldn't fight her way free. A thread of fear snaked through her anger, and began to tighten just before he let her go.

"That's how I kiss women I don't feel friendly toward."

"You think you have the right to treat me that way?"

"As much as you do to accuse me of doing something, of being something I'm not. I don't cheat and I don't lie, and I'm not going to apologize for my behavior. If you want to know something about my relationship with Dory, or anyone else, past or present, then ask. But don't come tearing into me with accusations."

"I saw—"

"Maybe you saw what you were ready to see. That's on you, Hayley. Now I've got work. If you've got any more to say about this, then say it after hours."

He strode off toward the pond, leaving her no choice, as she saw it, but to storm away in the opposite direction.

"Then he had the nerve, the *nerve* to snap at me and act like I was in the wrong." Hayley paced back and forth on Stella's front porch while Lily raced over the lawn after Parker. "Acting like I've got a dirty mind or that I'm some crazy jealous witch because I have a reasonable and legitimate complaint about him slobbering all over another woman. And in front of my face."

"Before you said she was slobbering over him."

"It was mutual slobbering. And when I walked in on them, after seeing all this going on through the door, he acts like it's nothing. He doesn't even have the grace to look embarrassed or nervous."

"So you said." Twice, Stella thought, but she understood the nature of female friendship and didn't mention the repetition. "Sweetie, we've both known Harper for some time now. Don't you think he would've looked embarrassed if he'd been caught doing something he shouldn't?"

"I guess I just don't mean enough to him for it to embarrass him."

"Now stop. That's not true."

"It feels true." Hayley slumped to the steps. "It feels awful."

"I know." Sitting beside her, Stella wrapped her arm around her shoulders. "I know it does. I'm so sorry you were hurt."

"He doesn't even care."

"Yes, he does. Maybe what you saw hit you wrong because of the way you feel about him."

"Stella, he *kissed* her."

"He's kissed me, too."

"It's not the same."

"If you hadn't met me before, and you saw him kiss me, what would you think?"

"Before or after I mentally ripped your lungs out through your nose?"

"Ouch. I'm not saying it didn't look bad, but that you might have, possibly, misinterpreted. I'm saying that because I know Harper, and because of his reaction."

"You're saying I overreacted."

"I'm saying, if I were you, I'd want to find out for sure."

"He slept with her. Okay, okay," she muttered when Stella stared at her. "Before, and before is before, blah blah. But she was so pretty. She had a great body, and those dark, exotic eyes. And this sheen, you know, this polish. Oh, hell."

"You're going to go talk to him."

"I guess."

"Want me to keep Lily while you do?"

"No." Hayley let out a long sigh. "She needs her supper

soon, and besides, if I take her with me we're not as likely to yell at each other."

"All right. You can call me if you want, let me know how it goes. Or you can just come back over. I'll break out the Ben and Jerry's."

"Way I'm feeling, I'll need a full quart."

SHE HAD LILY'S HAND IN HERS WHEN SHE KNOCKED on the door of the carriage house. He hadn't been long out of the shower, she noted when he answered. His hair was still damp. But if the grim set of his face was any barometer, it hadn't cooled him off.

"I'd like to talk to you." She said it briskly. "If you have the time."

He simply bent down to pick up Lily who'd already wrapped her arms around his leg. He turned, without a word for Hayley, and carried the baby back toward the kitchen. "Hey, pretty girl. Look what we got here."

One-handed, he opened a cupboard, took out a couple of plastic bowls, then rooted through a drawer for a big plastic spoon. He set them, and Lily, on the floor where she immediately went to town banging.

"Want a drink?" he said to Hayley.

"No, no, I don't. I want to ask you—"

"I'm having a beer. You want any milk or juice for Lily?"

"I didn't bring her sippy cup."

"I have one."

"Oh." The fact that he did threw her off, made her heart start to melt. "She could have a little juice. You have to dilute it."

"I've seen the routine." He fixed the juice, handed it to Lily, then got out a beer. "So?" He took a long gulp.

"I wanted to ask—No, I wanted to say that I know we

haven't made any sort of commitment to each other. But sleeping with someone is a form of commitment to me, enough of one that it's insulting to see the person I'm sleeping with kissing and flirting with another woman. And I don't find that unreasonable."

He took another pull, slowly, thoughtfully. "You know if you'd put it that way to begin with, you wouldn't have insulted me, or pissed me off. I'm going to repeat that I was flirting with Dory, but not the way you mean."

"If you come on to all women the way—"

"Or coming on to her. And be careful or you'll piss me off again. If you want to know what was going on, why don't you ask?"

"I don't like being in this position."

"Well, neither do I. If that's the way you want to leave it, I need to throw something together for dinner. I missed lunch."

"Fine." She started to bend down for Lily, then stopped. "Why are you so hard?"

"Why are you so mistrustful?"

"I *saw* you. She had her arms around you. She put her hands in your damn pockets and felt your ass. You weren't exactly fighting her off, Harper."

"Okay, you've got a point. It was something she used to do, and I didn't think much about it when she did it today. I was thinking more how I was going to tell her I couldn't pick things up with her, couldn't see her beyond the friendship thing because I was with somebody else."

"How long does it take to say that?"

"A little longer than it might otherwise if a woman's got her hands on your ass." She opened her mouth, but the way his eyebrows shot up had her closing it again, and waiting. "Right or wrong, Hayley. But I did tell her, before you came through the door."

"Before? But . . . you didn't even miss a beat, Harper. And the two of you were all . . ." She waved a hand, trying to find the phrase. "Touchy. And you kissed her when you went out to the car."

His eyes narrowed. "You were watching us."

"No. Yes. So what?"

"Too bad you didn't manage to slip a listening device on me, then this conversation wouldn't be necessary."

She folded her arms and met his insult straight-on. "I'm not apologizing for my behavior either."

"Fine. First, why should I have missed a beat? I wasn't doing anything to feel guilty about. Next, Dory's a touchy kind of person. She makes contact with people, which is probably why she's good in PR. And yeah, I kissed her before she left. I'll probably kiss her next time I see her. I like her. We have a history. We met in high school, ended up in college together—and ended up being an item for about a year. In college, Hayley, for Christ's sake. When we stopped being an item, we stayed friends. If you can manage to whip some of the green out of your vision, you'd probably end up being friends with her, too."

"I don't like being jealous. I've never really been jealous before, and I don't like it."

"If you'd heard our conversation out by her car, you'd have heard her tell me that she hoped you and I would come into the city, have drinks, so she could get to know you. She said it was good to see me, and good to see me happy. I said pretty much the same, and I kissed her goodbye."

"It's just . . . you looked like a couple."

"We're not. That's what you and I are. That's what I feel," he said when she only stared at him. "That's what I want. I don't know what I've done to make you doubt me, or that."

"You've never actually said . . ."

He stepped to her, caught her face in his hands. "I don't want to be with anyone but you. You're the only one, Hayley. Is that clear enough?"

"Yeah." She laid her hand on his, turned her head so that her lips pressed to his palm.

"So we're good now?"

"It looks like. Um, you told her you were seeing someone. I mean me?"

"I didn't have to. When you walked back out, she punched me in the arm. She said, 'She's taller than me, she's thinner than me, and she's got better hair.' What is it about your breed and hair?"

"Never mind that. What else did she say?"

"That it was bad enough I was blowing her off, but it had to be over somebody who looked like you. I figured it for some sort of twisted girl compliment."

"A nice one. Now I feel guilty. I bet I would like her, and that's just a little bit irritating." She brooded a minute, then beamed. "But I'll get over it. I'm not going to apologize, exactly, because—hey, hands on your ass. But I'll offer to cook you dinner."

"Sold," he said without hesitation.

"Got anything in mind?"

"Nothing. Surprise me. Us," he corrected and scooped Lily up to hang her upside down. "I'll get shortie here out of your hair. We have some havoc to wreak in the other room."

And just like that, she thought, her life was back on level. With the sounds of growling from Harper, and wild giggles from Lily rolling out of the living room, Hayley opened the refrigerator to examine the contents.

Pitiful, she decided. A total guy assortment of beer, soft drinks, bottled water, what appeared to be an ancient fried chicken leg, two eggs, a stick of butter and a small, moldy hunk of cheese.

She opened the freezer, and hit the payload. Several carefully labeled containers of leftovers. David to the rescue. But it was a shame she couldn't actually cook something, impress Harper.

Who's pitiful? He flaunts another woman in your face and you grovel. Now cooking for him, like a servant. Women are nothing but servants to men. Their conveniences.

He lies as all men lie, and you believe because you're weak and foolish.

Make him pay. They should all pay.

"No." She said it softly when she found herself standing in front of the open freezer door. "No. Those weren't my thoughts. And I won't have them in my head."

"You say something?" Harper called out.

"No. No," she said more calmly.

There was nothing to say. Nothing to think. She would put a meal together and they'd eat. Like a couple. Or even, just a little bit, like a family.

The three of them. Only the three of them.

fourteen

Feeling so settled was just a little spooky to Harper's mind. They'd taken to having dinner together in the evenings. Sitting together in the kitchen, Lily strapped in the highchair he'd carted over from the main house, he and Hayley at the table with a meal, and conversation seemed so easy it made him nervous.

They were drifting into something solid, like a boat sailing toward shore in a light wind. He wasn't sure whether when they hit it, they'd end up bruised and battered or safe and sound.

Did she seem edgy, too, under the casual? he wondered. Or was he projecting his own jitters?

It was all so normal, this eating together at the end of the day, talking about work or Lily's latest accomplishment. Yet twined through the respite was an intensity, a feeling. A here we are, and here we'll stay—at least for the night.

How much did he, did both of them, want to keep the "at least" in the mix?

"I was thinking," he began, "that if things are slow inside tomorrow, I could show you how to hybridize."

"I know a little. Roz walked me through a snapdragon."

"I was thinking a lily. They're a good specimen for it, and we could try one. I was thinking we could try for a mini, something in a kind of candy pink. And name it for Lily."

Her face switched on to glow. "Really? Like create a new specimen, for her? Oh, Harper, that would be so awesome."

"I thought pink—but a strong pink—and we could try for a hint of red blushing the petals. Red's your color, so it'd be like Hayley's Lily. I was thinking."

"You're going to make me cry."

"Spend some time hand-pollinating and you might just cry. It's not an instant-gratification deal."

"I'd really like to try."

"Then we'll work on it. What do you think of that, shortie?" he asked Lily. "Want your own flower?"

She picked up a green bean with two delicate fingers and dropped it with some care on the floor.

"I bet she likes the flower more than her vegetables. That's her signal she's done." Hayley rose. "I'll clean her up."

"I could do it. Give her a bath."

With a laugh, Hayley removed the highchair tray. "Ever given a toddler a bath?"

"No, but I've had a few. Just fill up the tub, dump her in, hand her the soap. Then go back and dry her off after I've had another beer. Just kidding," he said when Hayley's eyes bugged out. He unstrapped Lily, hitched her up. "Your mama thinks I'm a bath moron. We'll show her."

"Oh, but—"

"Stay with her at all times. Don't even turn your back.

Warm water, not hot. Blah, blah, blah," he continued as he walked away. Over his shoulder, Lily happily waved bye-bye.

She checked on them three times, but tried to be subtle about it.

By the time she'd finished dealing with the kitchen, Lily was running around, all pink and powdered and wearing nothing but her Huggies. Some men, she decided, were natural with children. Harper seemed to be one of them.

"What's next on her agenda?"

"I usually let her play for another hour or so, tires her out. Then maybe we'll read a book—or part of one—if she'll sit still long enough. Harper, don't you want to get rid of us?"

"No. I'm hoping you'll stay. I can set that portable deal up in the spare room. We'll hear her if she wakes up. Then you could be with me." He took Hayley's hands, leaned in to take her lips. "I want you to be with me tonight."

"Harper . . ." She eased away, then hurried after Lily. "Wait," she said, and stopped in the living room when Lily made a beeline for a pile of plastic trucks and cars. "Where'd they come from?"

"They were mine. Some things you keep."

She imagined Harper as a little boy, playing with his trucks and making engine noises, much as her baby was doing now. "Harper, this is so hard."

"What's hard?"

"Not falling dead stupid in love with you."

He said nothing for a moment, then turned her around to face him. "What if you did?"

"That's what I don't know. See, that's what I don't know." Her voice hitched, and she swallowed to even it out. "There's a lot tangled up in this. We only started being with each other a few weeks ago, and there's all this stuff happening. I don't know what you want, what you're looking for."

"I'm still figuring it out."

"That's fine for you, Harper. I mean it really is, it's just fine. But what if I love you? I love you, and you figure out what you want is a trip to Belize and six months bumming on the beach? I've got Lily to consider. I can't—"

"Hayley, if I wanted to be a beach bum, I think I'd know it by now."

"You know what I'm talking about."

"Okay, yeah. What if I fall for you, what if I love you and you decide you want to go back to Little Rock with Lily and open your own nursery?"

"I couldn't—"

He held up a hand. "Sure you could. It's the kind of risk people take when they get involved this way. Maybe you'll fall, and maybe the other person won't want what you're looking for."

"So we're sensible? Take it a day at a time."

"We could. We could do that."

"What if I don't want to be sensible?" she fired back. "What if I want to stand here right now and tell you I'm in love with you? What are you going to do about it?"

"I'm not sure since it's pissing you off."

"Of course I'm pissed off." She threw up her arms. "I'm in love with you, damn it, Harper, and you want to be sensible, take it a day at a time. And from where I'm standing your way just sucks sideways."

He considered himself a fairly laid-back sort of man, albeit one with a dangerous temper, which he was careful to control most of the time. How, he wondered, had he fallen so completely for a women whose moods tended to bounce around like a pinball?

Proved, he supposed, that there was no logic in love.

"Instead of going off, you should listen. I said we could be sensible. We could take it a day at a time. But since I'm in love with you right back, I'm not so crazy about that idea either."

"You go around doing romantic stuff, movie-time romantic stuff. And then the sweet things like giving my little girl a bath, and I'm supposed to stay sensible? I mean, what do you expect, Harper, what do you expect when you . . ."

She caught her breath, then took a long one while he just looked at her, that lazy half smile on his face. "What was that part after how I should listen?"

"I said I was in love with you right back."

"Oh. Oh." She crouched when Lily brought her one of the trucks. "That's nice, honey. Why don't you go get it?" She rolled the truck across the room, got back up. "You're not saying that because I'm being bitchy?"

"Generally, my policy doesn't include telling a woman I'm in love with her when she's being bitchy. Fact is, I haven't said it to anyone before, because it's the kind of thing that has weight. Should have weight. So you're the first."

"It's not because you're so stuck on Lily?"

He cast his eyes to heaven. "For Christ's sake."

"I'm picking it apart." She held her hands up, wagged them. "I hear myself. I'm just breathless. You make me so happy I've been miserable."

"Yeah, I can see how that works. Completely not."

"I've been so scared." On a laugh, she threw her arms around him. "I was so scared that I'd fall for you, then we'd end up being friends like that woman who came into the nursery the other day. I'm not going to be friends with you, Harper, if this doesn't work out." She reared back, then pressed her mouth hard to his. "I'm going to hate you forever."

"Good. I think."

She sighed, long and deep, as she laid her cheek to his. "What do we do now?"

"Since it's a first for me, I'd like to ride on it awhile. It's some pretty heady stuff. More immediately, I'd say we'll play with Lily. Tire her out good, so that after you put her to bed I can take you to mine."

"I like that plan."

BY THE TIME SHE'D SETTLED LILY DOWN, HARPER HAD music on. She knew he was rarely without it. Though it was just dusk, he had candles flickering in his bedroom. And flowers—a touch she'd rarely seen in another man, but had come to expect from him.

"She okay?" he asked her.

"Fine. She goes down pretty easy, doesn't always stay that way through the night though."

"Then we should take advantage of the quiet." He slid his hands down her arms, then back up the sides of her body. "I love making love with you. Touching you. Watching you when I touch you. The way your body moves with mine."

"Maybe we're just in lust."

"I've been in lust." His lips cruised over her jaw. "Is that what this feels like to you?"

"No." She turned her head so their lips could meet. "Not just."

"I think about you. How you look, how you sound, how you feel. And here we are."

She linked her arms around his neck as he lowered her to the bed. His hands glided down, up, then palmed over her breast.

"You are perfect. Perfect, perfect." He nibbled his way down, then nipped lightly at her nipple through her shirt until she quivered under him.

Then he tugged her shirt down, and took flesh.

More than arousal, she thought even as her body bowed up in response. There was joy fizzing through the excitement, like the bubbles in champagne. He loved her. Harper with the patient hands and ripping temper loved her.

Whatever happened, she was loved. And the love that rose so full and strong inside her was welcomed. There was no gift she treasured more.

To show him, and how she needed to show him, she poured herself into a kiss on a flood of that love.

She surrounded him with it so he felt his heart ache from the brilliance. He loved. It had never come to him before, this stunning surge of emotion that filled heart and soul, gut and mind. This woman, the one who moved with him, merged with him, was the one who sparked it.

He savored the scent and flavor of her skin as the sky deepened to night and a whippoorwill began to sing in the apple tree outside his window.

Inside, the air went soft and thick, throbbing with the sounds of sighs. He felt her rise, tremble, and tremble on the peak, then float down on a moan that was his name. Her skin quivered where he touched and his own warmed as her hands glided over him.

Her lips. He could sink into them until pleasure swirled and shimmered in his mind like mists.

When she rolled over him, rose over him, he could see her face in the candlelight. The glow of it framed by her dark hair, the delicate blue of her eyes deepened with passion.

Her lips reclaimed his, soft, soft even as the kiss deepened. Then the throaty hum as she took him into her. He closed his eyes, riding the sensation as she closed around him.

"This is what you want," she whispered. "What you all want."

The change was like a finger snap, the cold like a sheath of ice. He looked at her, and everything inside him stilled.

"No."

"To penetrate. To bury yourself."

"Stop." Even as she rocked, arousal mixing with horror, he gripped her hips to hold her still.

"Tell her anything. Love. Promises. Lies. As long as you get between her legs." Her thighs clamped him, long, lean vises. Hayley's body, he knew, but not Hayley. Revulsion rose in his throat.

"Stop." He reached up, and what was inside her laughed.

"Shall I make you come? Shall I ride you like a pony until you—"

He shoved her back, and she continued to laugh, sprawled naked in the flickering light.

"Leave her alone." He hauled her back. "You've got no right to her."

"As much as you. More. We're the same, she and I. The same."

"No. You're not. She doesn't look for the easy way. She's warm and strong and honest."

"I could have been." Something else came into her eyes then. Regret, grief, need. "I can be. And I know better than she does what can be done with this body." She pressed it to his, began to whisper erotic suggestions in his ear.

With sick panic burning in his belly, he shook her. "Hayley. Damn it, Hayley. You're stronger than her. Don't let her do this." And though it was still something else that looked at him, though her lips were cold, so cold, he kissed her. Gently. "I love you. Hayley, I love you. Come back to me."

He knew when she did, the instant. And gathered her hard and close while she shivered. "Harper."

"Ssh. It's okay."

"She was— Oh God. It wasn't me. I didn't mean those things. Harper—"

Comfort, he thought, wasn't the answer, not here, not now. "It's you I want." His lips skimmed over her face, and his hands began to stroke her warm once more. "Just you, just me. We won't let her touch this. Look at me."

He gripped her hands in his, and plunged into her. "Look at me," he repeated. "Stay with me."

The cold became heat, the horror became joy. She stayed with him. Linked.

SHE COULDN'T SPEAK, EVEN WHEN HIS HEAD WAS pillowed on her belly and the whippoorwill had given way to the cicadas. So much churned inside her she couldn't separate the shock from the fear, the fear from the shame.

He brushed a kiss over her flesh, then rose.

"I'm going to get us some water, and I'll look in on Lily."

She had to choke back words now. Pleas that he not leave her alone, even for a moment. But that was foolish, and impossible. She couldn't be watched every minute. More, she couldn't bear the idea that he might feel he had to watch her, waiting for Amelia to use her again.

She sat up, drawing her knees up to rest her brow on them.

She stayed that way when he came back, sat on the bed beside her.

"Harper. I don't know what to say."

"It wasn't your fault, let's just get that out of the way. And you pushed her out, or pushed through her, whatever the hell."

"I don't know how you could stand to touch me after."

"You think I'd let her win? You think I'd let her beat us?"

The barely restrained fury in his voice had her lifting

her head. "You . . . you were inside me when she— It's so creepy."

"Here." He nudged the water on her. "Creepy for both of us," he agreed. "And a little incestuous for me. Jesus. Nothing like getting really close to your great-great-grandmother."

"She wasn't thinking of you that way. I don't know if that helps." Fighting off a shudder, she handed the water back to him. "She was . . . I felt like she was seeing him. Reginald. She was—I was—all turned on, you know, then it was like this spit of rage spewing up through that. But the kind that makes it more, sort of more exciting. Darker. Then it was all blurred together. Her and me, him and you. And I was so wound up I couldn't get a grip on anything. Then you said you loved me, you kissed me and I could hold on to that."

"She tried to use us. We didn't let her." He set the water aside before easing her back so he could lie beside her and draw her close. "It's going to be okay."

But even lying beside him, held firm and safe in his arms, she couldn't quite believe it.

IT WAS AWKWARD, BUT HARPER FELT MITCH SHOULD know about any incident involving Amelia. Even if that incident had happened in bed with Hayley.

At least it was a man-to-man sort of thing. If his mother had to have the information, Harper would just as soon have it filtered through his stepfather.

"How long did it last?" Mitch asked.

"Maybe a couple of minutes. Seemed longer, considering the situation, but probably around that."

"She wasn't violent."

"No. But you know . . ." He had to pause a moment and

give his attention fully to the work board in the library. "Rape's not always violent, but it's still . . . Anyway, that's what it felt like, to me. Like a kind of rape. Like a power thing. Got you by the dick, so I'm in charge."

"It fits the kind of personality profile we've been building. She wouldn't get that while what's between you and Hayley is sexual, sex for the sake of sex isn't the driving force. Must've shaken you up."

Harper only nodded. There was still a coating of that raw sickness in his belly. "How much more do we need to know before we can stop this?"

"I wish I could tell you. We have her name, her circumstance. We know your bloodline comes down through her. We know her baby was taken, and we're assuming without her consent. Or that after she gave it, she changed her mind. We know she came here, to Harper House, and we have to believe she died here. Maybe if we find out how, but that's no guarantee."

He'd never counted on guarantees, not in his life or in his work. His father had died when he'd been seven, which had put paid to any sort of traditional family warranty. His work was a series of experiments, calculated risks, learned skills, and sheer luck. None of those guaranteed success.

Harper considered failure a postponement at worst, and another step in the process at best.

But things were considerably different when it involved the woman he loved, and her welfare, her well-being.

He was reminded of that when he found her watering flats.

She wore the cotton shorts and tank that was a kind of summer uniform around the nursery. Her feet were tucked into thin, backless canvas shoes that could take a soaking, and her face was shaded by the bill of one of the nursery's gimme caps.

She looked entirely too sad and thoughtful. The thoughtful part was proven right when she jumped nearly a foot off the ground when he said, "Hey."

"God, you scared me."

"That's what you get for taking side-trips when you're on the clock. Speaking of which, I'm going to start that hybridizing, and could use an assist."

"You still want to do that?"

"Why wouldn't I?"

"I thought maybe when you thought things through, you'd want to keep your distance for a while."

He simply stepped up to her, cautiously nudging the watering wand aside and kissed her. "Guess you're wrong."

"Guess I am. Lucky for me."

"Just come on over when you're done. I already let Stella know I was stealing you for a while."

He spent the time setting up for the work, lining up the tools, the plants he wanted to use. He logged the species, the cultivar, the name and characteristics of the desired plant in his files.

Since headphones wouldn't be an option as he wouldn't be working alone, he switched Beethoven for Loreena McKennitt. He figured his plants would like it fine, and he'd be a lot happier.

When Hayley came in, he was digging out a Coke, so he pulled out two.

"This is pretty exciting."

He handed her the can. "Tell me what you know about hybridizing first."

"Well, it's like you have a mama and a daddy, the parents. Two different plants—they can be the same type or two different . . . What is it?"

"Genera."

"Right. So you want ones with stable characteristics and

you cross them by hand-pollinating. Like pollen from one, seed from the other—like sex."

"Not bad. We're going to use this miniature I've been screening as a parent plant. And this variegated will be the other, the seed parent. See I've had it protected with a bag—that keeps insect pollinators from messing with it, and we're going to remove the stamens now, before it can self-pollinate. I potted these up, brought them in last winter so they could develop."

"You've been thinking about doing this for a while."

"Yeah, since she was born, more or less. Anyway, we work with the pollen parent today. You know how?"

"Roz did it before. I really just watched."

"This time, you try it. I cut this one already, just above the node, see? It's been in water and it's fully open now. See how the anthers are split? They're ready for pollen."

"So, you did the foreplay."

"One of my little skills."

She gave an exaggerated roll of her eyes. "Tell me about it."

"You go next."

"Oh man. I have to pull the petals off, right?"

"Quick, gentle twists, work inward until you see the anthers."

"Here goes."

"That's good," he said as he watched her. "Just be careful to leave the anthers intact. Yeah, nice work, good hands."

"I'm nervous. I hate screwing up."

"You're not." Her fingers were quick and precise as they twisted the petals away. "And if you do, we'll pick another."

"Is that right? Is that okay?"

"What do you see?"

She bit her lip. "The little anthers are all naked."

"Next step." He picked up a clean camel-hair brush.

"You need to collect the pollen. Use this, brush it over the anthers. We'll store it in this dish, keep it dry. See, it's fluffy, so it's ripe. I'll label the dish."

"This is fun. You wouldn't believe how totally I sucked in high school chemistry."

"Just needed a better lab partner. All mine aced. Now we're going to prep the seed parent. See this?" He held up the lily he'd chosen. "We don't want her fully open. We're looking for well-developed but with immature anthers—before self-pollination can happen. We take petals and anthers off her."

"Strip her right down."

"So to speak. No fragments left, they can cause rot fungi, then you're screwed. What we're after is nice exposed stigmas."

"You do that part. Then it's like a team."

"Okay." He twisted off the petals, then reached for his tweezers, skillfully plucking out the anthers. "Now she waits until tomorrow for the pollen. That gives her stigmas time to get sticky. Then we'll transfer the ripe pollen onto the stigmas. You can use a brush, but I like using my finger. There."

He stepped back.

"That's it?"

"That's the first one. Let's do the next. We've got a good dozen seed parents on here. I think we'll try a couple of pollen parents on her. See what we get."

They took turns with the steps. A nice, companionable rhythm, Hayley thought, and a satisfying one. "How did you pick the plants to work with?"

"I've been scoping them out awhile, tracking growth habits and form, color patterns."

"Since she was born."

"Yeah, pretty much."

"Harper, you know how I said if things don't work out with us, I'll hate you for the rest of my life?"

"Yeah, I got that."

"Well, I will, but I'll suck it in—mostly—because I know you love her. You really do."

"She's got me wrapped. I gotta admit. Tomorrow, we'll pollinate, label, log. Then we'll keep an eye on her. Probably take about a week before we see the ovary swelling, if we're successful here."

"Swelling ovaries. Takes me back."

He grinned, kept working. "Couple weeks more, the pod should be formed, then it takes about a month more for the seed to ripen. We'll know it has when the top begins to split."

"Yeah, déjà vu."

"Cut it out. That's just weird."

He moved to his computer, his long fingers tapping keys as he input data. "What we'll do is take the seeds, dry them and plant them late fall. I like to do it that way so it won't germinate until spring."

"We plant them outside?"

"No, in here. Mama's potting soil, four-inch pots, then we put them out. When they're big enough, we'll put them in nursery beds. It'll take another year before they bloom and we see what we've really got."

"Fortunately, I know nothing about a two-year pregnancy."

"Yeah, women get by with nine little months. Blink of an eye."

"You try it, pal."

"I'm a fan of the way things work. So. I've got the records logged, and if things work out, we should eventually see some new flowers, and some of them should have characteristics of each parent." He glanced over the work, nodded. "We'll get what we're after, or if not exactly, hopefully something close enough that we can do another generation, or try a different parent."

"In other words, this could take years."

"Serious hybridizing isn't for weenies."

"I like it. And I like that it's not an overnight kind of deal. You have all this anticipation. And maybe you won't get exactly what you had in mind, but something else. Something, not necessarily better, but just as beautiful."

"Now you're talking the talk."

"I feel good." She stepped back from the worktable. "I was having such a bad day. I kept thinking about what happened last night, circling around and around it, and just feeling sick about the whole thing."

"It wasn't your fault."

"I know—in my head. But somewhere in there I wondered if we'd be able to be easy together again—or at least this soon. If you'd be, I don't know, uncomfortable and I'd be jittery. It seemed like the chance we had to just be in love might've been spoiled."

"Nothing's changed for me."

"I know." They stood side-by-side at the workbench and she tilted her head onto his shoulder. "And I feel calmer knowing it."

"I better let you know I told Mitch what happened."

"Oh." She sucked in a breath, winced. "I guess it had to be done, and better you than me. Was it awful?"

"No. Just a little weird. We spent a lot of time talking about it without making any eye contact."

"I'm not going to think about it," Hayley decided. "I'm just not." She turned just enough to kiss him. "I'd better get on with the work I really get paid for. I'll see you back home."

* * *

AS SHE HUMMED HER WAY THROUGH THE REST OF THE day, Stella passed by, then stopped to put her hands on her hips. "Hybridizing certainly agrees with you."

"Feel great. Step two tomorrow."

"Well, good. You looked a little draggy this morning."

"Didn't sleep very well, but I've got my second wind, and then some." She glanced around to be sure no one was within hearing distance. "We're in love." Grinning, she used the index fingers of both hands to draw a heart in the air. "Me and Harper. Together."

"Wow. News flash."

With a laugh, Hayley continued hauling bags of potting soil from cart to shelf. "I mean really in love. So we said the L word to each other."

"I'm happy for you." She gave Hayley a hug. "Seriously."

"I'm happy for me, too. But there's this . . . I have to tell you about this thing that happened." Cautious, Hayley took another look around, and related the incident to Stella in undertones.

"My God. Are you all right?"

"It was awful, so awful, it still makes my stomach churn. I didn't know how we'd get past it. That was almost worse than the experience itself. But we have. We did. I can't imagine how he must've felt, but he didn't pull back from me."

"He loves you."

"He does. He really does." Miracles everywhere, she thought. "Stella, I always believed I'd fall in love one day, but I never knew it could be like this. Now that I know, I can't imagine not keeping it. You know?"

"I do. You should be happy. You should know this other thing is separate from that. And you and Harper should enjoy this bliss stage because it's very precious."

"I feel like everything in my life has been leading up to

this, to him. The good and the bad. I can take the bad because I know we've found something in each other that really matters. I guess that sounds lame, but—"

"It does not. It sounds happy."

fifteen

THE SECONDHAND LAPTOP WAS A GOOD BUY, AND using it made Hayley feel she was doing something active. An hour or two in research mode may not have garnered her a great deal of new information, at least as applied to her situation, but it assured her she wasn't alone.

There were a lot of people out there who at least believed they'd had experience with ghosts and hauntings. She was already documenting an essential piece of advice from every website she'd visited. But at least with the computer she could type her reports instead of scrawling them in a notebook.

And it was fun to be able to e-mail friends back in Little Rock.

Of course she got caught up in surfing the web, much as she got caught up when scanning books. There was just so much information, so many interesting things. And one invariably led to another so that if she wasn't careful, she'd be up past midnight hunched over the keyboard.

She had her chin propped on her elbow, her mind focused on an on-line report from Toronto of a ghost baby crying, when a hand brushed her shoulder.

She didn't jump, held back a scream. Instead she closed her eyes and spoke in a nearly normal tone. "Please tell me that's a real hand."

"I hope it is as it's attached to my wrist."

"Roz." Hayley let out her breath slowly. "Points for me, right, for not jumping up to cling to the ceiling like a cartoon cat."

"That might've been entertaining." She narrowed her eyes to read the screen. "Ghosthunters dot com?"

"One of many," Hayley told her. "And really, there's some pretty cool stuff. Did you know that one of the traditional ways to discourage ghosts from coming into a room was to stick pins or hammer iron nails around the door? It's like they'd get caught on them and couldn't get in. Of course, if you did it while they were already in, then they couldn't get out."

"I catch you nailing anything into my woodwork, I'll skin you."

"Already figured that. Plus I don't see how it could work." She scooted around, away from the screen. "They say you should talk to the ghost, politely, just ask it to leave. Like: Hey, sorry about your bad luck being dead and all that, but this is my house now and you're disturbing me, so I wonder if you'd mind just moving on."

"I'd say we've tried variations of that."

"Yeah, no go." When Roz sat on the sofa in the sitting room, Hayley understood she hadn't come by just to chat about Amelia. Nerves began to drum. "Of course, they say you should document everything, but Mitch already has us doing that. And take photographs. You can hire a ghost hunter, but I don't guess you want a bunch of strangers in the house."

"You guess right."

"Or you can ask a minister or a priest to bless the house. That couldn't hurt."

"You're afraid."

"More than I was, yeah. But I know this stuff"—she tapped the screen—"isn't really helpful because what we're doing, what we always planned to do was find out who, what, why. And if we did manage just to boot her out, we wouldn't know it all. But I like, well, harvesting information."

"You and Mitch, peas in a pod. Have you documented what happened the other night, with you and Harper?"

"Yes." Heat burned her cheeks. "I haven't, ah, given it to Mitch yet."

"It's very personal. I wouldn't like sharing that sort of personal experience with an outsider."

"You're not. I mean, he's not. Neither of you."

"Anyone, no matter how you love them, is an outsider when it comes to the bed, Hayley. I want you to know I understand that. I also want you to know you've got no need to walk on eggshells with me about this. I waited a couple of days, hoping it wouldn't be quite as touchy a subject."

"I know Harper went to Mitch about it, and I knew Mitch would tell you. I just couldn't, Roz. If it'd been anybody but Harper—not that I'd be with anybody but Harper . . . And I'm already messing this up."

"You're not."

"It's . . . Harper's yours."

"Yes, he is." She propped her feet on the table, her most habitual position. "I knew when he fell in love with you, though you didn't know, and I doubt he did."

"I think maybe it was the night we stayed at the Peabody."

Roz shook her head. "That's romance, and valuable. But that wasn't when. Who held your hand when Lily was born?"

"Oh." Hayley lifted a hand to her throat as it filled. "He did. Harper did, and I think he was almost as scared as I was."

"When I saw, and I understood, my heart ached. Just for a moment. You'll know what I mean when it's Lily's turn. And if you're lucky, as I'm lucky, you'll watch your child fall in love with someone you can love, and respect and admire, be amused by, feel close to. So when your heart aches, it's with happiness, and gratitude."

Tears spilled down her cheeks. "I don't know how I could get any luckier than I already am. You've been so good to me. No, please don't brush it off," she said when Roz shook her head. "It means so much to me. When I came here, I thought I was so smart and strong, so ready. If she kicks me out, I thought, I'll just keep going. I'll find a job, get an apartment, have this baby. I'll be fine. If I'd known what it takes—not just the hours, the effort, but the love and the worry that just fills you up when you have a child, I'd've thrown myself at your feet and begged for help. But all I had to do was ask."

"I gave you a job and a place to stay because you're family, and because of the situation you were in. But that's not why you're still here. You earned your place at In the Garden, and your place in this house. Make no mistake, if you hadn't, I'd have shown you the door."

"I know." And knowing it made Hayley grin. "I wanted to prove myself to you, and I'm proud that I did. But, Roz, because I have Lily, I know what Harper means to you. And part of the reason I'm scared, more scared than I was, is I'm afraid The Bride might hurt him."

"Why do you think that?"

"She saw Reginald in him. Maybe one of the reasons she's moved on to me is because of the feelings that I developed for Harper. When I first met him, I remember thinking, wow, if I was in the market, I'd be all over that one."

When Roz laughed, Hayley flushed. "See what comes out of my mouth?" she demanded. "Jesus, you're his *mother.*"

"Forget that a minute. Keep going."

"Well, see I wasn't in a place in my head, or anywhere else, where I could think seriously about a man, a relationship. I just thought he was hot, then as I got to know him, sweet and funny and smart. I liked him a lot, and I got irritated now and then that he was so cute and I was pregnant and cranky and not at my best. After Lily, I tried to think of him as kind of a brother, or a cousin. Well, he is a cousin, but you know what I mean."

"The way you think of David or Logan, or my other sons."

"Yeah. I really tried to put Harper in that same slot. And there was so much to do and learn, that it was easy to ignore that little low tickle that was going on inside me. You know the one."

"Thank God I do," Roz said with feeling.

"Then it wasn't so easy, and the feelings for him kept getting stronger. It seems to me, when I started to admit them to myself, started to imagine how it could be with him, that's when Amelia started slipping in."

"And the stronger your feelings, the stronger and more demonstrative her objections."

"I'm worried that she'll hurt him, through me. Not seeing Harper, but Reginald. I'm worried I won't be able to stop her."

Roz frowned. "Seems that you're not giving Harper enough credit for being able to handle himself."

"Maybe not. But she's awful strong, Roz. Stronger than she was, I think." Remembering the sensation of having her *self* pushed aside, Hayley inhaled, exhaled, deeply. "And it seems to me she's had a lot of time to think about payback."

"Harper's stronger than she thinks. And so are you."

SHE HOPED ROZ WAS RIGHT. AS SHE LAY SLEEPLESS, with Harper beside her, she hoped she had the grit and the brains to combat the vengeance of a vindictive spirit. Worse, one she felt some sympathy for.

But Harper wasn't responsible for what had happened to her. No one who lived at Harper House now was responsible. There had to be a way, some way, for her to make Amelia understand that. To show her that Harper was not only the child she'd once sung to, but a good, caring man. And nothing like Reginald.

What had he been like, really? Reginald Harper. A man so obsessed with having a son, he would deliberately impregnate a woman not his wife. Whether or not Amelia had consented—and that they couldn't know—it had been a selfish and hurtful act on his part. Then to take the child, to force his own wife to accept it as her own. He couldn't have loved. Not his wife, not Amelia, certainly not the child.

It was no wonder Amelia despised him, and with her spirit or mind, or heart, shattered, that she'd grouped all men along with him.

What had it been like for her? For Amelia?

SHE SAT AT HER DRESSING TABLE, CAREFULLY ROUGING her cheeks by gaslight. Pregnancy had stolen her color. Just one more indignity, after the horrible sickness morning after morning, the widening of her waist, the incessant fatigue.

And yet, there were benefits. So many she hadn't counted

on. She smiled as she added color to her lips. How could she have known Reginald would be so pleased? Or so generous.

She lifted her arm to study the ruby and diamond hearts that circled her wrist. A bit delicate for her taste, really, but you couldn't fault the glimmer.

And he'd hired another maid, given her carte blanche for a new wardrobe to accommodate her changing body. More jewels. More attention.

He visited her three times a week now, and never came empty-handed. Even if it was only to bring her chocolates or candied fruit when she mentioned craving sweets.

How fascinating to know that the prospect of a child could make a man so biddable.

She imagined he'd been very solicitous of his wife, in turn. But then she'd plagued him with girls rather than the son he coveted.

She would give him a son. And in giving, would reap the benefits for the rest of her life.

A bigger house to start, she decided. Clothes, jewels, furs, a new carriage—perhaps a small country house as well. He could afford it. Reginald Harper would spare no expense for his son, even his bastard son, she was sure.

As the mother of that son, she would never have to seek out another protector, never have to flirt and seduce and bargain with the men of wealth and position, offering sex and comfort in exchange for the mode of life she craved. Deserved. Earned.

She rose from the dressing table, and hair shining gold, jewels glittering white and red, gown sweeping silver, she turned in the chevel glass.

This was her exchange now. This bulge of the belly. Look how odd and awkward, how fat and unfashionable she looked, despite the gown. And yet, Reginald doted. He would stroke that bulge, even during passion. And in passion, he was kinder, gentler than she'd ever known him to be. She could almost love him during those times, when his hands were tender instead of demanding. Almost.

But love was not part of the game, and a game was all it was. This bartering pleasure for style. How could she love what was so weak, so deceitful, so arrogant? A ridiculous notion, as ridiculous as feeling pity for the wives they betrayed with her. Women who folded their thin lips and pretended not to know. Who passed her on the street with their noses in the air. Or women like her mother who slaved for them for pennies.

She was meant for bigger things, she thought, and lifted a heavy crystal decanter to stroke scent on her throat. She was meant for silks and diamonds.

When Reginald arrived, she would pout, just a little. And tell him of the diamond broach she'd seen that afternoon. How she would pine without it.

Pining wasn't good for the child. She imagined the broach would be hers within a day.

She gave a light laugh, a little turn.

Then stopped, went still. Her hand trembled as she lifted it to press over her belly.

It had moved.

Inside her a flutter, a stretch. Little wings beating.

The glass reflected her as she stood in her shimmering gown, her fingers spread over the slight bulge as if she would guard what was inside.

Inside her. Alive. Her son.

Hers.

HAYLEY REMEMBERED IT VIVIDLY. EVEN IN THE morning there was nothing of the fragmented or misty quality of a dream.

"It was, I think it was, a kind of a bid for sympathy. More for empathy." She held her cup in both hands as she sipped coffee in the breakfast nook.

"How so?" Mitch had his tape recorder and notebook as she'd requested. "Did she speak directly to you at some point?"

"No, because it wasn't her, it was me. Or it was both of us. I wasn't dreaming so much as I was there. I felt, I saw, I thought. She wasn't just showing me, but reliving. If that makes sense."

"Eat your eggs, sweetie-pie," David urged her. "You look peaked."

She scooped some up obediently. "She was beautiful. Not like the way we've seen her, really. Vibrant and drop-dead—excuse the term. There was so much going through her head—my head—I don't know. Irritation about the changes in her body, the inconvenience, plots and plans to get more out of Reginald, surprise at his reaction to her condition, disgust for men like him, for their wives, envy, greed. It all just kept rolling around in a big mass."

She paused, breathed. "I think she was already a little bit crazy."

"And how was that a bid for sympathy?" Harper asked her. "Why would you feel sorry for someone like that?"

"It was the change. It was feeling the baby move. I felt it, too. That shock of feeling, the sudden realization that there's life inside you. And there's this wave of love along with it. In that moment, the baby was hers. Not a ploy or an inconvenience, but her child, and she loved it." She looked at Roz.

"Yes."

"So she was showing me. I loved my child, wanted it. And the man, the kind of man who'd use a woman like me, took it from me. She was wearing the bracelet. The heart bracelet. And I did feel for her. I don't think she was a good person, certainly not a nice one, and even then, before the rest happened, I don't think she was balanced. But she loved the child, wanted it. I think what she showed me was real, and she showed me because I'd understand it more than anyone else. Yeah, I felt sorry for her."

"Sympathy is fine," Mitch said. "But you can't let down your guard. She's using you, Hayley."

"I know, and I won't. I can feel for her, but I don't have to trust her."

DAYS PASSED, AND SHE WAITED FOR THE NEXT MOVE, the next experience, but August boiled quietly toward September. The most wrenching experience was having her ancient car break down between work and the sitter's, and finally having to accept it was time to replace it.

"It's not just the money," she told Harper as she strolled Lily through the used-car lot. "It's one of my last links to childhood, I guess. My daddy bought that car, secondhand. I learned to drive with it."

"It'll go to a good home."

"Hell, Harper, it's going on the scrap heap, and we both know it. Poor, pitiful old thing. I know I've got to be sensible, too. I can't be hauling Lily around in an unreliable car. I'll be lucky if that salesman who took it off for appraisal doesn't come back and say I owe him just for dumping it on him."

"Just let me handle it."

"I will not." She stopped by a hatchback, kicked its tires. "You know what I hate? I hate that a lot of car salesmen and mechanics and that whole breed treat women who come in like brainless bimbos just because they don't have a penis. Like all the automotive data and know-it-all is stored in their dicks."

"Jesus, Hayley." He had to laugh, even as he winced.

"It's true. So, I've done my research. I know what I want and how much I should have to pay. He doesn't want to deal with me, then I'll just take my business elsewhere."

She stopped by a sedan, braced one hand on the fender and waved the other in front of her face. "God almighty, it's hot. Feel like every fluid in my body's boiled away."

"You look a little pale. Why don't we go inside, sit down for a minute?"

"I'm okay. Just not resting well. Even when I sleep, I feel like I'm on alert, like the first few weeks after Lily was born. Makes me draggy and irritable. So if I end up snapping at you, try to bear with me."

He rubbed the small of her back. "Don't worry about it."

"I appreciate you coming with me today, I really do. But don't feel like you've got to step in."

"Ever bought a car?"

She sent him a sidelong, annoyed look as she continued to push Lily's stroller. "Just because I haven't, doesn't mean I'm some rube down from the hills. I've bought lots of other things, and I can guarantee I know more about negotiating prices than you. Rich boy."

He grinned. "I'm just a working gardener."

"You may work for a living, but you've got a few silver spoons tucked away for rainy days. Now here's what I'm after."

She stopped to study a sturdy-looking five-door Chevy. "It's got plenty of room, but it's not big and bulky, and it's clean. It's bound to get better mileage than my old car and it's not flashy."

She frowned over the listed price. "I'll just get him to come down a bit, and it'll be in my range. Sort of."

"Don't tell him you—"

"Harper."

"Backing off." He shook his head, stuck his hands in his pockets.

And had to saw his tongue in half when the salesman came out, big smiles, and announced the meager offer on the trade-in.

"Oh, is that all?" Hayley widened her baby blues and fluttered her lashes. "I guess sentiment doesn't count, does it? But maybe, maybe you could just ease that up, a little bit, depending on what I buy. This one's pretty. I like the color."

Playing him, Harper realized, noting how she'd bumped up her accent. He went along for the ride as the salesman steered her toward a couple of pricier options, watched her chew her lip, flash her smile, and steer him right back to what she wanted.

Guy's toast, he decided as she finagled the price down, took Lily out of the stroller to sit with her behind the wheel. Harper concluded nobody could resist the pair of them.

Two hours later, they were driving off the lot with Lily dozing in her carseat and Hayley beaming behind the wheel.

" 'Oh, Mr. Tanner, I just don't know a thing about cars. You're so sweet to help me out this way.' " Harper shook his head. "When we were sitting in there doing the paperwork I wanted to warn him to lift up his feet. It was sure getting deep."

"He made a nice sale, got his commission, and I got what I went in for. That's what counts." But she let out a hoot of laughter. "I liked when he tried to bring you into it, showed you under the hood and you just scratched your head like you were looking at a cruise missile or something. I think we made him feel good, like he was giving me what I needed for the price I could pay. And that counts, too. Next time I have to buy, I'd go right back to Mr. Tanner."

"Didn't hurt for you to tear up a couple times."

"That was real. I was sad to sell that old heap—and don't think these car payments aren't going to sting some." More, she thought, it had put an ache in her throat when Mr. Tanner had assumed they were a family.

"If you need some help—"

"Don't go there, Harper." But she reached over to pat his hand, to show she appreciated the offer. "We'll be fine, Lily and me."

"Why don't I take you out to lunch to celebrate then?"

"That's a deal. I'm starving."

They had looked like a family, she thought. A normal young family buying a secondhand car, having lunch in a diner, treating the baby to a cup of ice cream.

But putting them there was rushing it, for all of them. They were a man and a single mother who were romantically involved. Not a unit.

At home, she decided to take advantage of the rest of her day off by curling up with Lily for an afternoon nap.

"We're all right, aren't we, baby?" she murmured as Lily played with her mother's hair, her big eyes heavy, her pretty mouth going slack. "I'm doing right by you? I'm sure trying."

She snuggled down a little closer. "I'm so tired. Got a million things I ought to be doing, but I'm so tired. I'll get them all done sooner or later, right?"

She closed her eyes, started to calculate her finances in her head, juggling funds, changing weekly deposits. But her brain wouldn't focus.

It drifted back to the used-car lot, and Mr. Tanner shaking hands with her before she drove off. How he'd smiled at her and wished her and her charming family well.

Drifted to sitting out on her terrace with Harper, drinking cold wine in the heat-soaked night.

Dancing with him in the shimmering romance of the suite at the Peabody.

Working with him in the grafting house.

Watching him lift Lily onto his shoulders.

It should be easier to be in love, she thought sleepily. It should be simpler. It shouldn't make you want more when love was everything.

She sighed once, and told herself to enjoy what she had, and let the rest come.

And the pain was like knives in the belly, shocking, sharp, and horrid. Her whole body fought against them, and she screamed at the sensation of being ripped in two.

The heat, the pain. Unbearable. How could something so loved, so desired, punish her this way? She would die from it, surely she would die. And never see her son.

Sweat streamed off her, and the utter weariness was nearly as severe as the pain.

Blood and sweat and agony. All for her child, her son. Her world. No price too dear to pay for giving him life.

And as the pain sliced her, sent her tumbling toward the dark, she heard the thin cry of birth.

Hayley woke drenched in sweat, her body still radiating from the pain. And her own child blissfully asleep in the protective crook of her arm.

She eased free, fumbled for the bedside phone.

"Harper? Can you come?"

"Where are you?"

"In my room. Lily's sleeping right here. I can't leave her. We're all right," she said quickly. "We're fine, but something just happened. Please can you come?"

"Two minutes."

She made a wall of pillows around the baby, but knew even then she couldn't leave the room. Lily might roll off somehow, or certainly climb over and fall. But she could pace, even on her weakened legs she could pace.

She flung open the doors even as Harper ran up the steps.

"They told her it was stillborn." She swayed, and her knees nearly folded. "They told her her baby was dead."

SIXTEEN

In the parlor where the light was soft through gauzy curtains and the air was sweet with roses, Harper stood by the front window with his fists balled in his pockets.

"She was wrecked," he said with his back to the room. "She just sort of folded up when I got there, and even when she pulled it together, she looked sick."

"She wasn't hurt." Mitch held up a hand when Harper whirled. "I know how you feel. I do. But she wasn't physically harmed, and that's important."

"This time," he shot back. "It's out of hand. All of this is fucking out of hand."

"Only more reason for us to stick together, and stay calm."

"I'll be calm when she's out of the house."

"Amelia," Logan asked, "or Hayley?"

"Right now? Both."

"You know she can stay with us. And if I were in your shoes, I'd want to pack her up and haul her out. But from what I gather, you tried that once and it didn't work. If you think you've got a better shot at it now, I'll carry her suitcase."

"She won't budge. What the hell is wrong with these women?"

"They feel connected." David spread his hands. "Even when they see Amelia at her worst, they feel attached. Engaged. Right or wrong, Harp, there's a kind of solidarity."

"And it's her home," Mitch added. "As much as yours now, or mine. She won't walk out of it and leave this undone. Any more than you, or I, or any or us." He glanced around the room. "So we finish it."

Logic, even truth, didn't settle Harper's anger, or his worry. "You didn't see her after it happened."

"No, but I've got the gist from what you told me. She matters to me, too, Harper. To all of us."

"All for one, great. I'm for it." His gaze shifted to the parlor doors, and his mind traveled upstairs, to Hayley. "But she's the one on the line."

"Agreed." Mitch leaned forward in his chair to draw Harper's attention back to him. "Let's look at what happened for a minute. Hayley was taken through childbirth, and a traumatic aftermath when Amelia was told the baby was dead. And she went through this while she was napping with Lily. But Lily wasn't disturbed. That tells me that there's no intent to harm or even frighten the baby. If there were, how long do you think it would take Hayley to head out that door?"

"That may be true, but to get whatever it is she wants, Amelia's going to keep using Hayley, and using her hard."

"I agree." Mitch nodded. "Because it works. Because

this way she's feeding us information we might not ever be able to find. We know now that not only was her child taken from her, but that she was told, cruelly, that it was dead. It's hardly a wonder that her mind, which already seemed to be somewhat imbalanced, shattered."

"We can assume she came here for him," Logan suggested. "And died here."

"Well, the kid's dead, too. Dead as she is, dead as disco." Harper slumped into a chair. "She's not going to find him here."

UPSTAIRS, HAYLEY WOKE FROM A LIGHT DOZE. THE curtains were pulled so the light was dim but for a thin chink. She saw Roz sitting, reading a book in that narrow spear of light.

"Lily."

Roz set the book aside and rose. "Stella has her. She took her and the boys over to the other wing to play so you'd have some quiet. How are you feeling?"

"Exhausted. A little raw inside yet." But she sighed, comforted when Roz sat and stroked her hair. "It was harder than when I had Lily, rougher and longer. I know it was only a few minutes, really, but it seemed like hours. Hours and hours of pain and heat. Then this awful muzzy feeling toward the end. They gave her something, and it made her kind of float away, but it was almost worse."

"Laudanum, I imagine. Nothing like a shot of opiate."

"I heard the baby cry." Struggling to relax, Hayley curled on her side, tilting her head up to keep Roz in her line of sight. "You know how it is, no matter what's gone on in those hours before, everything inside you rising up when you hear your baby cry the first time."

"Hers." Roz took Hayley's hand. "Not yours."

"I know, I know, but for that instant he was mine. And that horrible tearing grief, that crazy disbelief when the doctor said it was stillborn, that was mine, too."

"I've never lost a child," Roz told her. "I can't even imagine the pain of it."

"They lied to her, Roz. I guess he paid them, too. They lied, but she knew. She heard the baby cry, and she *knew*. It drove her crazy."

Roz shifted on the bed, angling so she could rest Hayley's head on her lap. And sat in silence, staring at that thin lance of light through the curtains.

"She didn't deserve it," Hayley started.

"No. She didn't deserve it."

"Whatever she was, whatever she did, she didn't deserve to be treated that way. She loved the baby, but . . ."

"But what?"

"It wasn't right, the way she loved it. It wasn't a healthy sort of thing. She wouldn't have been a good mother."

"How do you know?"

"I felt . . ." Obsession, she thought, hunger. Impossible to describe the vastness of it. "It had to be a boy, you see? A girl wouldn't have mattered to her. A girl wouldn't have been just a disappointment, but an outrage. And if she'd had the boy and kept it, she would've twisted it. Not on purpose, but he wouldn't have been the man he was. He wouldn't have been the one who loved his dog and buried it with a marker, and loved your grandmother. And none of this would be the way it is."

She turned her head so that she could look up at Roz. "You, Harper. Nothing would be the same. But it doesn't make it right. It still doesn't make what happened right."

"Wouldn't it be nice if everything balanced in the

world? If right came out on top and wrong was punished. It sure would be simple."

Hayley's lips curved. "Then Justin Terrell, who cheated on me in tenth grade, would be fat and bald and asking people if they want fries with that instead of being part owner of a successful sport's bar and bearing a strong resemblance to Toby McGuire."

"Isn't that just the way?"

"Then again, maybe I'd go to hell for not telling Lily's biological father about her."

"Your motives were pure."

"Mostly. I guess doing what's best isn't always doing what's right. It was best for that baby to be raised here, at Harper House."

"Not the same thing, Hayley. No one's motives were pure, or even mostly, in that case. Lies and deceit, cold cruelty, and selfishness. I shudder to think what might have become of that child had it been a girl. You feeling better now?"

"Lots."

"Why don't I go down, fix you something to eat? I'll bring you food on a tray."

"I'll go down. I know Mitch wants to record all this. I know Harper's probably told him by now, but it's better if I give it to him firsthand. And I think I'll feel better yet when I do."

"If you're sure."

She nodded as she pushed herself up on the bed. "Thanks for sitting with me. It felt good knowing you were here while I slept."

She glanced in the mirror, winced. "I'm going to put on some makeup first. I may be possessed by a ghost, but I don't have to look like one."

"That's my girl. I'll go let Stella know you're up and around."

HAYLEY FIGURED SHE OWED ROZ ANOTHER ONE WHEN she realized everything had been arranged so that just she and Mitch would sit in the library to document the experience.

It was easier, somehow, to talk only to him. He was so smart and scholarly, in a studly kind of way. Sort of Harrison Fordish, in hornrims she decided.

With the leading edge of the fatigue and the shock dulled by a little sleep and a lot of TLC, she felt steadier, and more in control.

In any case, she loved this room. All the books, all those stories, all those words. Gardens outside the windows, big cozy chairs inside.

When she'd first come to Harper House she'd sometimes tiptoe down at night, just to sit in this room—her favorite of all of them—and marvel.

And she liked the way Mitch approached the whole Amelia project. With his work boards, his computer, his files and notes, he made it all rational, doable, grounded.

She studied the board now, with its long lists and columns that comprised Harper's family tree.

"Do you think, after all this is over, you could do a family tree for me?"

"Hmm?"

"Sorry." She glanced back at him, waved a hand. "Mind's wandering."

"It's okay, you've got a lot on it." He put down his notebook, focused his attention on her. "Sure I can do that. You give me the basics you know—father's full name, date and place of birth, your mother's, and we're off and running."

"I'd really like that. It'd be interesting. Harper and I cross a couple generations back, sort of over to the side. Is he awful mad at me?"

"No, honey. Why would he be?"

"He was upset. He wanted to scoop me and Lily right up and haul us to Stella's. I wouldn't go. I can't."

Mitch doodled on a pad. "If I could've gotten Roz out of this house a few months ago, I'd have done it—even if it had taken dynamite."

"Did you fight about it?"

"Not really." Amusement danced in his eyes. "But then I'm older, wiser, and more in tune with the limitations a man faces when dealing with a stubborn woman."

"Am I wrong?"

"That's not for me to say."

"It is if I'm asking you."

"Rock and hard place, kid. That's where you've shoved me." He pushed back, took off his glasses. "I understand exactly how Harper feels and why, and he's not wrong. I respect how you feel and why, and you're not wrong either. How's that?"

She managed a wry smile. "Smart—and no help at all."

"Just another benefit of that older and wiser phase of life. But I'm going to add one thing as a potentially overprotective male. I don't think you should spend a lot of time alone."

"Good thing I like people." When his cell phone rang, she rose. "I'll go on, let you get that."

Because she'd seen Harper outside, she went out the side door. She hoped Stella wouldn't mind a little more time on Lily patrol. She wandered the path toward where he worked in the cutting garden.

Summer still had her world in its sweaty clutches, but the heat was strong and vital. Real. She'd take all the reality she could get. Mammoth blue balls of hydrangeas weighed down the bushes, daylilies speared up with their elegant cheer, and passionflowers twined their arbor in bursts of purple.

The air was thick with fragrance and birdsong, and through it rode the frantic wings of butterflies.

Around the curve Harper stood, legs spread, body slightly bent as his quick, skilled fingers twisted off deadheads, then dropped them in a bag knotted to his belt. At his feet was a small, shallow basket where daisies and snapdragons, larkspur and cosmos already lay.

It was, somehow, so sweepingly romantic—the man, the evening, the sea of flowers—that her heart floated up to her throat and ached there.

A hummingbird, a sapphire and emerald whir, arrowed past him to hover over the feathery cup of a deep red blossom of monarda and drink.

She saw him pause to watch it, going still with his hand on a stem and his other holding a seed head. And she wished she could paint. All those vivid colors of late summer, bold and strong, and the man so still, so patient, stopping his work to share his flowers with a bird.

Love saturated her.

The bird flew off, a small, electric jewel. He watched it, as she watched him.

"Harper."

"The hummingbirds like the bee balm," he said, then took his sheers and clipped a monarda. "But there's enough for all of us. It's a good spreader."

"Harper," she said again and walked up to slide her arms around him, press her cheek to his back. "I know you're worried, and I won't ask you not to be. But please don't be mad."

"I'm not. I came out here to cool off. It usually works. I'm down to irritated and worried."

"I was set to come out here, argue with you." She rubbed her cheek over his shirt. She could smell soap and sweat, both healthy and male. "Then I saw you, and I just don't want to argue. I just don't want to fight. I can't do what you want when everything inside me pulls the other way. Even if it's wrong, I can't."

"I don't have any choice about that." He clipped more flowers for the basket, deadheaded others. "And you don't have any say about this. I'm moving in. I'd rather you and Lily shift over to my place, but it makes more sense for me to move into your room for now since there are two of you and one of me. When this is over, we'll reevaluate."

"Reevaluate."

"That's right." He'd yet to look at her, really look, and now moved off a few paces to cut more blooms. "It's a little hard to figure out where we're going, what we're doing under the circumstances."

"So you figure we'll live together, under the circumstances, and when those circumstances change, we'll take another look at the picture."

"That's right."

Maybe she did feel like arguing. "Ever heard of asking?"

"Heard of it. Not doing it. At the nursery, you work with Stella, Mama, or me, at all times."

"Who suddenly made you the boss of me?"

With steady hands, unerring eye, he just kept working. "One of us will drive back and forth with you."

"One of you coming with me every time I have to pee?"

"If necessary. You've got your mind set on staying, those are the terms."

The hummingbird whizzed back, but this time she wasn't caught by its charm. "Terms? Somebody die and make you king? Listen, Harper—"

"No. This is how it's going to be. You're determined to

stay, see this through. I'm just as determined you'll be looked after. I love you, so that's the end of it."

She opened her mouth, closed it again, and took a calming breath. "If you'd said that—the I love you part—right off, I might've been more open to discussion."

"There is no discussion."

Her eyes narrowed. He'd yet to stop what he was doing and face her fully. "You sure can be a hard-ass when you put your mind to it."

"This didn't take much effort." He reached down, gathered the flowers in the basket, tucking their stems into a casual bouquet. Now he turned, and those long brown eyes met hers. "Here."

She took them, frowned at him over them. "Did you cut these for me?"

The slow, lazy smile moved over his face. "Who else?"

She blew out a breath. He'd added nicotiana to the bouquet, and when she inhaled, she drew in its rich perfume. "It's exasperating, I swear, how you can be pushy one minute and sweet the next. They're really pretty."

"So are you."

"You know, another man might've started off with the flowers, the flattery, and the I-love-yous to soften me up for the rest. But you go at it ass-backwards."

His gaze stayed on hers, steady. "I wasn't worried about softening you up."

"I get that. You're not waiting for me to say, all right, Harper, we'll do this your way. You're just going to make sure I do."

"See how quick you catch on?"

She had to laugh, and clutching the flowers in one hand gave in and linked her arms around his neck. "In case you're interested, I'm glad you're going to be staying with me. Next time I have my spine tingled, I'd as soon you be there."

"I will be."

"If you've got more work to do out here—"

She broke off when Logan strode down the path. "Sorry. Something's up," he said. "Better come on back in."

HAYLEY FELT THE EXCITEMENT, LIKE A HUM IN THE AIR when they stepped back into the library. She took a quick scan first, saw Lily playing cars with Gavin and Luke on the floor by the fireplace David had filled with flowers for the summer months.

Spotting her mother, Lily began to jabber and interrupted her game to come over and show off her dump truck. But the minute Hayley lifted her, Lily stretched out her arms for Harper.

"Everybody's second choice when you're around," Hayley commented as she passed her over.

"She understands I know the fine points of Fisher-Price. It's all right," he added. "I've got her. What's up?" he asked his mother.

"I'm going to let Mitch explain. Ah, David, we can always count on you."

He wheeled in a cart with cold drinks, and finger food for the kids. "Gotta keep body and soul together." He winked at the boys. "Especially around this house."

"Y'all get what you want," Roz ordered. "And let's get settled."

While the wine looked tempting, Hayley opted for the iced tea. Her stomach wasn't quite a hundred percent yet. "Thanks for looking out for my girl," she said to Stella.

"You know I love it. It always amazes me how well the

boys play with her." Stella brushed a hand down Hayley's arm. "How're you feeling?"

"A little off yet, but okay. You know what this is about?"

"Not even a glimmer. Go on and sit. You look worn out."

As she did, Hayley grinned. "You're getting a little southern in your accent. Yankee southern, but it's starting to creep in. Kinda cute."

"Must come from being outnumbered." Because she was concerned with how pale Hayley looked still, she sat on the arm of the chair.

"How long you going to keep us dangling?" Logan complained, and Mitch stood in front of the library table.

Like a teacher, Hayley thought. Sometimes she forgot he'd been one.

"Y'all know I've been in contact for several months with a descendant of the housekeeper who worked here during Reginald and Beatrice Harper's time."

"The Boston lawyer," Harper said and sat on the floor with Lily and her truck.

Mitch nodded. "Her interest has been piqued, and the more she's looked for information, the more people she's spoken with, the more invested she's become."

"Added to that Mitch has been doing a genealogy for her—gratis," Roz added.

"Tit for tat," he said. "And we needed some of the information anyway. Up till now she hasn't been able to find a great deal that applied to us. But today, she got a hit."

"You're killing us here," Stella commented.

"A letter, written by the housekeeper in question. Roni—Veronica, my contact, found a box full of letters in the attic of one of her great-aunts. It's considerable to sort through, to read through. But today, she found one written by Mary Havers to a cousin. The letter was dated January 12, 1893."

"A few months after the baby was born," Hayley added.

"That's right. Most of the letter deals with family business, or the sort of casual conversational observations that you'd expect—particularly in an era when people still wrote conversational letters. But in the body of the letter . . ." He held up papers. "She faxed me copies. I'm going to read the pertinent parts."

"Mom!" Luke's aggrieved voice wailed out. "Gavin's looking at me with the *face.*"

"Gavin, not now. I mean it. Sorry," Stella apologized. She took a deep breath and determined to ignore the whispered argument from behind her. "Keep going."

"Just hold on one minute." Logan rose, walked over to crouch and have a conversation with the boys. There was a cheer, then they scrambled up.

"We're going to take Lily out to play," Gavin announced, and puffed out his chest. "Come on Lily. Wanna go outside?"

Clutching her truck, she deserted Harper, waved bye-bye, and took Gavin's hand. Logan closed the door behind them. "We're going out for ice cream later," he said to Stella as he walked back to his seat.

"Bribery. Good thinking. Sorry, Mitch."

"No problem. This was written to Mary Havers's cousin, Lucille."

Leaning back on the library table, Mitch adjusted his glasses, and read.

" 'I should not be writing of this, but I am so troubled in my heart and in my mind. I wrote to you last summer of the birth of my employers' baby boy. He is a beautiful child, Master Reginald, with such a sweet nature. The nurse Mister Harper hired is very competent and seems both gentle with him and quite attached. To my knowledge, the mistress has never entered the nursery. The nurse reports to Mister Harper, and only Mister Harper. Belowstairs Alice, the nurse, tends to chatter, as girls often do. More than once I have heard her comment that the mistress never sees the child, has never held him, has never asked of his welfare.' "

"Cold bitch," Roz said quietly. "I'm glad she's not a blood ancestor. I'd rather have crazy than cruel." Then she lifted a hand. "Sorry, Mitchell. I shouldn't interrupt."

"It's okay. I've already read this through a couple times, and tend to agree with you. Mary Havers continues," he said.

" 'It is not my place to criticize, of course. However, it would seem unnatural that a mother show no interest in her child, particularly the son who was so desired in this house. It cannot be said that the mistress is a warm woman, or naturally maternal, yet with her girls she is somewhat involved in their daily activities. I cannot count the number of nurses and governesses who have come and gone over the last few years. Mrs. Harper is very particular. Yet, she has never once given Alice instructions on what she expects regarding Master Reginald.

" 'I tell you this, Lucy, because while we both know that often those abovestairs take little interest in the details of the household, unless there is an inconvenience, I suspect there is something troubling in this matter, and I must tell someone my thoughts, my fears.' "

"She knew something wasn't right," Hayley interrupted. "Sorry," she added with a glance around the room. "But you can hear it, even in what she doesn't say."

"She's fond of the baby, too." Stella turned her wineglass around and around in her hands. "Concerned for him. You can hear that, too. Go on, Mitch."

"She writes, 'While I told you of the baby's birth, I did not mention in previous correspondence that there was no sign in the months before that Mrs. Harper was expecting. Her activities, her appearance remained as ever. We who serve are privy to the intimate details of a household and those who live in it. It is unavoidable. There was no preparation for this child. No talk of nursemaids, of layettes, there was no lying-in for Mrs. Harper, no visits from the doctor. The baby was simply here one morning, as if, indeed, the stork had delivered him. While there was some talk belowstairs, I did not allow it to continue, at least in my presence. It is not our place to question such matters.

" 'Yet, Lucille, she has been so separate from this child it breaks the heart. So, yes, I have wondered. There can be little doubt who fathered the boy as he is the image of Mister Harper. His maternity, however, was another matter, at least in my mind.' "

"So they knew." Harper turned to his mother. "She knew, this Havers, and the household knew. And nothing was done."

"What could they do?" Hayley asked, and her voice was thick with emotion. "They were servants, employees. Even if they'd made noise about it, who would listen? They'd have been fired and kicked out, and nothing would have changed here."

"You're right." Mitch sipped from his glass of mineral water. "Nothing would have changed. Nothing did. She wrote more."

He set down his glass, turned the next page. " 'Earlier today a woman came to Harper House. So pale, so thin was she, and in her eyes, Lucy, was something not only desperate but not quite sane. Danby—' That was the butler at the time," Mitch explained. " 'Danby mistook her for someone looking for employment, but she pushed into the house by the front door, something wild in her. She claimed to have come for the baby, for her baby. For her son she called James. She said she heard him crying for her. Even if the child had cried, no one could hear in the entrance hall as he was tucked up in the nursery. I could not turn her away, could not wrest her away as she ran wildly up the stairs, calling for her son. I do not know what I might have done, but the mistress appeared and bade me show the woman up to her sitting room. This poor creature trembled as I led her in. The mistress would allow me to bring no refreshment. I should not have done what I did next, what I have never done in all my years of employment. I listened at the door.' "

"So she did come here." There was pity in Stella's voice as she laid a hand on Hayley's shoulder. "She did come for her baby. Poor Amelia."

" 'I heard the cruel things the mistress said to this unfortunate woman,' " Mitch continued. " 'I heard the cold things she said about the child. Wishing him dead, Lucy, God's pity, wishing him and this desperate woman dead even as she, who called herself Amelia Connor, asked to have the child returned to her. She was refused. She was threatened. She was dismissed. I know now that the master got this child, this son he craved, with this poor woman, his lightskirt, and took the baby from her to foist it on his wife, to raise the boy here as his heir. I understand that the doctor and the midwife who attended this woman were ordered to tell her the child, a girl child, was stillborn.

" 'I have known Mister Harper to be coldly determined in his business, in his private affairs. I have not seen affection between him and his wife, or from him for his daughters. Yet I would not have deemed him capable of such a monstrous act. I would not have believed his wife capable of aligning herself with him. Miss Connor, in her ill-fitting gray dress and shattered eyes, was ordered away, was threatened with the police should she ever come back, ever speak of what was spoken of in that room. I did my duty, Lucille, and showed her from the house. I watched her carriage drive away. I have not been easy in my mind since.

" 'I feel I should try to help her, but what can I do? Is it not my Christian duty to offer some assistance, or comfort at the very least, to this woman? Yet my duty to my employers, those who provide the roof over my head, the food I eat, the money which keeps me independent, is to remain silent. To remember my place.

" 'I will pray that I come to know what is right. I will pray for this young woman who came for the child she birthed, and was turned away.' "

Mitch set the pages down. And there was silence.

Tears slid down Hayley's cheeks. Her head was lowered, as it had been during the last page of Mitch's recital. Now she lifted it, and with her eyes shining with tears, smiled.

"But I came back."

seventeen

"HAYLEY."

"Don't." Mitch stepped forward as Harper sprang off the floor. "Wait."

"I came back," Hayley repeated, "for what was mine."

"But you weren't able to get to the child," Mitch said.

"Wasn't I? Didn't I?" In the chair Hayley lifted her arms, held her palms up. "Aren't I here? Didn't I watch him, didn't I sing him to sleep, night after night? And all the others who came after? They were never rid of me."

"But that's not enough now."

"I want what' s mine! I want my due. I want . . ." Her eyes darted around the room. "Where are the children? Where are they?"

"Outside." Roz spoke quietly. "Playing outside."

"I like the children," Hayley said dreamily. "Who would have guessed? Such messy, selfish creatures. But so sweet, so soft and sweet when they sleep. I like them best when they sleep. I would have shown him the world, my James. The world. And he would never have left me. Do you think I want her pity?" she said in a sudden rage. "A housekeeper? A *servant*? Do you think I want pity from her? Damn her and the rest of them. I should have killed them in their sleep."

"Why didn't you?"

Her gaze shifted, latched on Harper. "There are other ways to damn. So handsome. You are so like him."

"I'm not. I'm yours. The great-grandson of your son."

Her eyes clouded, and her fingers plucked at the thighs of her pants. "James? My James? I watched you. Sweet baby. Pretty little boy. I came to you."

"I remember. What do you want?"

"Find me. I'm lost."

"What happened to you?"

"You know! You did it. You're damned for it. Cursed with my last breath. I will have what's *mine*." Hayley's head fell back, and her hand clutched at her belly before her body shuddered. "God." She breathed out audibly. "Intense."

Harper grabbed her hands, knelt in front of her. "Hayley."

"Yeah." Her eyes were blurred, her face white as paper. "Can I have some water?"

He brought her hands up, pressed his face into them. "You can't keep doing this."

"Just as soon not. She was pissed. Thanks," she said to David as he handed her a glass of water. She drank it down like a woman dying of thirst. "Pissed, then sad, then pissed again—all sort of over the top on the emotional scale. The letter got to her. Well, it got to me."

She turned to Mitch with her hands still caught in Harper's. "I felt so sorry for her, and for the housekeeper. I could see it. You know, how you do when you're reading a book. The house, the people. I could imagine what it would be like if somebody had Lily, and I couldn't do anything to get her back. 'Course the first thing I'd've done was clock Beatrice. The bitch. I guess I was getting pretty worked up, in my head, and she just sort of slid in."

Her fingers tightened on Harper's. "She's twisted up about you. Mostly, she's just twisted altogether, but she remembers you as a baby, as a little boy, she feels love for you because you're her blood. But you're his, too. And you resemble him, sort of. At least that's how it seems to me. It's confusing when it happens."

"You're stronger than she is," Harper told her.

"Saner anyhow. Way."

"You did great." Mitch set his tape recorder aside. "And I'd say you've had enough for today."

"It's been a busy one." She worked up a smile as she looked around the room. "Did I wig everybody out?"

"You could say that. Look, why don't you go up, stretch out," Stella suggested. "Logan will go out, check on the kids. Right?"

"Sure." He stepped over to Hayley first, gave her head a pat. "Go on up, beautiful, take a load off."

"I think I will, thanks." Harper straightened, took her hand to bring her to her feet. "I don't know what I'd do without you guys, I really don't."

Roz waited until they were out of the room. "This is wearing on her. I've never seen her look so tired. Hayley's a bundle of energy most times. Hell, she wears me out just watching her."

"We've got to finish this." Logan walked to the door, opened it. "And soon," he said before he went outside.

"What can we do?" Stella spread her hands. "Waiting and watching doesn't seem like enough. I don't know about the rest of you, but seeing that happen, seeing it, shook me right down to the bone."

"I could go to Boston, help Veronica sort through the papers." Mitch shook his head. "But I'm just not comfortable leaving right now."

"Safety in numbers?" Roz reached out a hand for his, squeezed. "I feel the same. To tell the truth, at this point I don't like David spending so much time alone in the house."

"She doesn't bother me." He'd poured a glass of wine and lifted it now in a half toast. "Maybe because I'm not a blood-related male. Add gay to that and I'm not of much interest to her. You can factor in that she'd see me as a servant. That puts me bottom of the feeding chain."

"A lot she knows," Roz replied. "But that's logical, from her point of view, and does a lot to relieve my mind. Find her. She's said that before."

"Her grave," Mitch put in.

"I think we're all agreed on that." Roz walked over, helped herself to a sip of David's wine. "And how the hell are we supposed to do that?"

LATER, WHEN THE HOUSE WAS QUIET AND LILY SLEPT in her crib, Hayley couldn't settle. "One minute I'm ready to drop, and the next I'm all revved up. I must be really annoying."

"Now that you mention it." With a grin, Harper pulled her down on the sofa beside him. "Why don't we watch the game. I'll raid the kitchen for junk food."

"You want me to sit here and watch baseball?"

"I thought you liked baseball."

"Yeah, but not enough to zone out in front of the TV."

"Okay." He heaved an exaggerated sigh. "I'm about to

make the ultimate sacrifice for my breed. Pick a DVD. We'll watch a movie, even if it's a chick flick."

She eased back. "Really?"

"But you have to make the popcorn."

"You mean you'll sit here and watch a girlie movie without making snide comments?"

"I don't remember agreeing to the second part."

"You know, I like action flicks."

"Now we're talking."

"But I'd love to watch something romancey, with a couple of good weep scenes. Thanks!" She pressed her lips noisily to his, then jumped up. "I'm loading the popcorn with butter." At the door, she stopped and beamed back at him. "I feel better already."

SHE'D NEVER HAD SO MANY UPS AND DOWNS IN HER moods in all of her life. From manic energy to exhaustion, from joy to despair. She ran the gamut, it seemed, every day. And under the swings, the spurts, and the tumbles was an edgy anticipation of what happens next. And when.

When she spiraled down, she struggled to remind herself of what she had. A beautiful child, a wonderful man who loved her, friends, family, a good interesting job. And still, once the spiral began, she couldn't seem to control the fall.

She worried there was something physically wrong with her. A chemical imbalance, a brain tumor. Maybe she was going as crazy as The Bride.

Feeling harassed and overtired, she swung into Wal-Mart on her morning off to pick up diapers, shampoo, a few other basics. She could only thank God to be able to snatch this little window of alone time. Or alone with Lily time, she corrected, as she strapped her daughter in the shopping cart.

At least nobody felt they were obliged to watch her when she was away from Harper House or work. And watching was what they did. Like hawks.

She understood why, God knew she appreciated the concern and care. But that didn't stop her from feeling smothered. She could barely start to brush her teeth without whoever was hovering offering to spread the paste on the brush for her.

She wandered down aisles, listlessly picking up what she needed. Then she detoured into cosmetics, thinking a new lipstick might cheer her up. But the shades seemed too dark or too light, too bold or too dull. Nothing suited her.

She looked so pale and wan these days, she decided if she put anything bright on her lips they'd look as though they walked into the room a foot ahead of her.

New perfume maybe. But every tester she sniffed made her feel slightly queasy.

"Just forget it," she muttered, and glanced back at Lily who was trying to stretch out her arm to reach a spin rack of mascaras and eye pencils.

"Not for a long time yet, young lady. It's fun being a girl though, you'll see. All these toys we get to play with." She chose one of the mascaras herself, tossed it in the cart. "I just can't seem to gear myself up for it right now. We'll just go on, get your diapers. And maybe if you're good, a new board book."

She turned down another aisle, reluctant to leave. Once she did, she'd need to take Lily to the sitter's, go to work. Where somebody would be attached to her hip for the rest of the day.

She wanted to do something normal, damn it. More, she wanted to *feel* like doing something. Anything.

And an absent glance to her right stopped her in her tracks.

Something that was both panic and nausea, with a helping of dull realization spurted into her belly. It continued to rise as she did hasty calculations in her head.

While everything inside her sank, Hayley closed her eyes. She opened them again, looked into Lily's happy face. And reached for the home pregnancy test.

SHE DROPPED LILY OFF, KEPT A SMILE PLASTERED ON her face until she walked out the door to her car. Afraid to do otherwise, she kept her mind blank while she drove home. She wouldn't think, she wouldn't project. She would just go home, take the test. Twice. When it came out negative, which of course it would, she'd hide the packages somewhere until she could dispose of them without anyone knowing she'd had a panic attack.

She wasn't pregnant again. She absolutely couldn't be pregnant again.

She parked, and made certain the boxes were buried at the bottom of her bag and well hidden. But she'd taken two steps into the house when David appeared like some magic genie.

"Hi, sugar, want a hand with that?"

"No." She gripped the bag to her chest like a cache of gold. "No," she repeated more calmly. "I'm just going to take these things up. And I have to pee, if that's all the same to you."

"It is. I often have to pee myself."

Knowing her tone had been nasty, she rubbed a hand over her face. "I'm sorry. I'm in a mood."

"Something else I often have." He pulled an open tube of Life Savers from his pocket, thumbed out a cherry circle. "Open up."

She smiled, obeyed.

"Let's see if that sweetens your mood," he said as he popped the candy into her mouth. "Can't help worrying about you, honey."

"I know. If I'm not back down in fifteen minutes, you can call out the cavalry. Deal?"

"Deal."

She hurried up, then dumped the contents of the bag on her bed—for God's sake, she'd forgotten the diapers. Cursing, she snatched both pregnancy tests and bolted to the bathroom.

For a moment she was afraid she wouldn't be able to pee. Wouldn't that just be her luck? She ordered herself to calm down, took several long breaths. Added a prayer.

Moments later, with the sweetness of cherry candy still on her tongue, she was staring at the stick with PREGNANT reading clear as day in its window.

"No." She gripped the stick, shook it as if it were a thermometer and the action would drop things back down to normal. "No, no, no, no! What *is* this? What are you?" She looked down at herself, rapped a fist lightly below her navel. "Some kind of sperm magnet?"

Undone, she sat on the toilet lid, buried her face in her hands.

THOUGH SHE MIGHT HAVE PREFERRED TO CRAWL INTO the cabinet under the sink, curl up in the dark, and stay there for the next nine months, she didn't have much time to indulge in a pity fest. She washed her face, slapping on cold water to eradicate the signs of her bathroom crying jag.

"Yeah, crying's going to make a difference," she berated herself. "That'll do the trick, all right. It'll change everything so when you look at that *stupid* test again the damn stick will read: Why no, Hayley, you're not pregnant.

You just needed to sit on the toilet and bawl for ten minutes. Idiot."

She sniffled back what felt like another flood of tears and faced herself in the mirror. "You played, now you pay. Deal with it."

A quick makeup session helped. The sunglasses she grabbed out of her purse helped more.

She buried the home pregnancy test boxes in the bottom of her underwear drawer, jumpy as a drug addict hiding his stash.

When she went out, David was already halfway up the stairs.

"I was about to get my bugle."

She stared at him. "What?"

"To call the cavalry, honey. You were longer than fifteen."

"Sorry. I got . . . Sorry."

He started to smile and brush it off, then shook his head. "Nope, not going to pretend I don't know you've been crying. What's the matter?"

"I can't." Even on those two words her voice shook, broke. "I'm going to be late for work."

"Somehow the world will keep turning. What you're going to do is sit right down here in my office." Taking her hand, he tugged until she sat on the steps with him. "And tell Uncle David your troubles."

"I don't have troubles. I'm *in* trouble." She didn't mean to tell him, to tell anyone. Not until she had time to think, to deal. To bury her head in the sand for a few days. But he draped an arm around her shoulders to hug her, and the words leaped out of her mouth.

"I'm pregnant."

"Oh." His hand stroked up and down her arm. "Well, that's something my secret horde of super chocolate truffles won't fix."

She turned her head, pressed her face to his shoulder. "I'm like some sort of fertility bomb, David. What am I going to do? What the hell am I going to do?"

"What's right for you. You're sure now?"

Sniffling, she boosted her butt off the steps, tugged the stick out of her pocket. "What's that say in there?"

"Mmm. The eagle has landed." Gently, he caught her chin in his hand, lifted her face. "How are you feeling?"

"Sick, scared. Stupid! So damn stupid. We used protection, David. It's not like we were a couple of lust-crazed teenagers in the back of a Chevy. I think I have some sort of *über*eggs or something, and they just spit on barriers and *suck* the sperm in."

He laughed, then gave her another squeeze. "Sorry. I know it's not funny to you. Let's calm down here and take a look at the big picture. You're in love with Harper."

"Of course I am, but—"

"He's in love with you."

"Yes, but— Oh, David, we're just getting started on that. On being in love, on being together. Maybe I let myself imagine how it might be down the road some. But we haven't made any plans about the long-term. We haven't talked about it at all."

"That's why sooner comes before later, honey. You'll talk now."

"How can any man in the world not feel trapped when a woman comes up and tells him she's pregnant?"

"You manage to get that way all by yourself?"

"That's not the point."

"Hayley." He drew back, tipped her sunglasses down her nose so he could look into her eyes. "That's exactly the point. With Lily, you did what was right for you, and what you felt in your heart was right for the father, and for the baby. Right or wrong—and personally I think it was right—but either way, I think it was brave. Now you've got to be brave again, do what's right for everybody concerned. You've got to tell Harper."

"I don't know how. I get sick thinking about it."

"Then you might love him, but you're not giving him credit for being the man he is."

"I am, that's the trouble." She stared back down at the stick and the word in that window seemed to scream in her head. "He'll stand up. How will I know if he did because he loves me, or because he feels responsible?"

David leaned over, kissed her temple. "Because you will."

IT ALL SOUNDED GOOD. IT SOUNDED REASONABLE, logical, and adult. But it didn't make it any easier to do what she was about to do.

She wished she could delay it, just ignore it all for a few days. Even pretend it would go away. And that was small and selfish and childish.

When she reached the nursery, she slipped into one of the employee bathrooms to take the second test. She glugged down most of a pint of water, turned the spigot on for good measure. She started to cross her fingers, but told herself not to be a complete ass.

Still, she read the results with eyes squinted half shut.

It didn't change the outcome.

Well, still pregnant, she thought. There was no crying this time, no cursing fate. She simply tucked the stick back in her pocket, opened the door, and prepared to do what needed to be done next. She had to tell Harper.

Why? Why did he have to know? She could go away now, she thought. Pack up and go. The baby was *hers.*

He was rich, he was powerful. He would take the child

and toss her aside. Take her son. For the glory of the great Harper name he would use her like a vessel, then rip away what grew in her.

He had no right to what was hers. No right to what she carried inside her.

"Hayley."

"What?" She jolted like a thief, then blinked at Stella.

She was standing among the shade plants, surrounded by hostas green as Ireland. Yards away from the restroom.

How long had she been standing there, thinking thoughts not her own?

"Are you all right?"

"A little turned around." She drew in a long breath. "I'm sorry I'm late."

"It's all right."

"I'll make it up. But I need . . . I have to talk to Harper. Before I get started I need to talk to him."

"In the grafting house. He wanted to know when you got in. Hayley, I wish you'd tell me what's wrong."

"I need to talk to Harper first." Before she lost her nerve, or her mind.

She hurried away, walking quickly between the tables of plants, across the asphalt skirt, past the greenhouses. Business was picking up, she noted, after the high summer slump. Temperatures were easing off, just a little, and made people think about their fall plantings. Stella's boys were going back to school. Days were getting shorter.

The world didn't stop just because she had a crisis on her hands.

She hesitated outside of the grafting house, struck by the fact that her mind—so full a moment before—was now a complete blank.

There was only one thing to do, she decided. That was to go in.

The house was warm and full of music. It so well suited him, full of plants in various stages of growth and development, smelling of soil and green.

She didn't know the music that played, something with harps and flutes. But she knew whatever it was wouldn't be playing through his headphones.

He was down at the far end, and it seemed like the longest walk of her life. Even when he turned, saw her, and flashed a grin.

"Hey, just who I wanted to see." He made a come-ahead gesture with one hand as he drew his headset off with the other. "Take a look."

"At what?"

"Our babies."

Since he shifted to the plants, he didn't see her jerk in response. "They're right on schedule," he continued. "See, the ovary sections have already swelled."

"They're not the only ones," she mumbled, but moved forward to stand beside him and study the plants they'd grafted a few weeks before.

"See? The pods are fully formed. We give them another three, four weeks for the seeds to ripen. The top'll split. We'll gather the seeds, plant them in pots. Keep 'em outdoors, exposed. And in the spring, they'll germinate. Once they're about three inches, we'll plant them out in nursery beds."

It wasn't procrastinating to stand there talking about a mutual project. It was . . . polite. "Then what?"

"Usually we'll get blooms the second season. Then we'll study and record the differences, the likenesses, the characteristics. What we're hoping for is at least one—and I'm banking on more—mini with a strong pink color, and that blush of red. We get that, we've got Hayley's Lily."

"If we don't."

"Pessimism isn't the gardener's friend, but if we don't, we'll have something else cool. And we'll try again. Anyway, I thought you might want to work with me on a rose, for my mother."

"Oh, um . . ." If it was a girl, should they name her Rose? "That'd be nice. Sweet of you."

"Well, it's Mitch's idea, but the guy couldn't grow a Chia Pet. He wants to try for a black. Nobody's ever managed a true black rose, but I thought we could play around and see what we came up with. It's the right time of year—time to wash down, disinfect, air and dry out this place. Hygiene's a big for this kind of work, and roses are pretty fussy. They're time-consuming, too, but it'd be fun."

He looked so excited, she thought, at the idea of starting something new. Just how would he look when she told him they already had?

"Um, when you do all this, you pick the parents—the pollen plant, the seed plant. Deliberate selection, for specific characteristics."

Her blue eyes, Harper's brown. His patience, her impulse. What would you get?

"Right. You're trying to cross them, to create something with the best—or at least the desired characteristics—of both."

His temper, her stubbornness. Oh God. "People don't work that way."

"Hmm." He turned to his computer, keying data into a file. "No, guess not."

"And with people, they can't always—or don't always—plan it all out like this. They don't always get together and say, hey, let's hybridize."

He shot a laugh over his shoulder. "Now that's a line I never thought to use in a bar, picking up a girl. I'd put it in the file, but since I've already got a girl, it'd be wasted."

"You never used a line on me," she told him. "Anyway, hybridizing's about creating something, a separate something. Not just about the fun and games."

"Hmm. Hey, did I show you the viburnum? Suckering's been a problem, but I'm pretty happy with how it's coming along."

"Harper." Tears wanted to spurt and spill again. "Harper, I'm sorry."

"It's not a big," he said absently. "I know how to deal with suckering."

"I'm pregnant."

There, she thought. She said it. Fast and clean. Like ripping a bandage off a wound.

"You said what?" He stopped typing, slowly swiveled on his stool.

She didn't know how to read his face. Maybe it was because her own vision seemed blurry and half blind. She couldn't read the tone of his voice, not with the roaring going on in her ears.

"I should've known. I should have. I've been so tired, and I missed my period—I just forgot about it—and I've been queasy on and off, and so damn moody. I thought, I didn't think. I thought it was what was happening with Amelia. I didn't put it together. I'm sorry."

The entire burst came out in a disjointed ramble that she could barely comprehend herself. She dropped into silence when he held up a hand.

"Pregnant. You said you were pregnant."

"God, do I have to spell the word out for you?" Not sure if she wanted to weep or rage, she yanked the test stick out of her pocket. "There, read it yourself. P-R-E—"

"Hold it." He took the stick from her, stared at it. "When did you find out?"

"Just today, now. A little while ago. I was in Wal-Mart, getting some things. I forgot Lily's diapers and bought mascara. What kind of a mother am I?"

"Quiet down." He rose, took her shoulders and nudged her onto the stool. "You're all right? I mean it doesn't hurt or anything."

"Of course it doesn't hurt. For Christ's sake."

"Look, don't crawl up my ass." He scrubbed a hand over the back of his neck as he studied her. Much, she thought, as he did his plants-in-progress. "It's my first day on the job. How much are you pregnant?"

"Pretty much all the way."

"Damn it, Hayley, I mean how far along, or whatever you call it?"

"I think about six weeks. Five or six."

"How big is it in there?"

She dragged a hand through her hair. "I don't know. About as big as a kernel of rice."

"Wow." He stared at her belly, laid a hand on it. "Wow. When does it start to move around? When does it get, like, fingers or toes?"

"Harper, can we focus here?"

"I don't know any of this stuff. I want to know. You need to go to the doctor, right?" He grabbed her hand. "We should go now."

"I don't need to go to the doctor now. Harper, what are we going to do?"

"What do you mean what are we going to do. We're going to have a baby. Holy shit!" He plucked her right off the stool and a half a foot off the ground. The face he tilted up to hers was split with a dazzled grin. "We're going to have a baby."

She had to brace her hands on his shoulders. "You're not mad."

"Why would I be mad?"

Now she felt dizzy, overwhelmed, shaken to the core. "Because. Because."

He lowered her, slowly, back onto the stool. And now his voice was careful and cool. "You don't want the baby."

"I don't know. How can I think about what I want? How can I think at all?"

"Pregnancy affects brain waves. Interesting."

"I—"

"But, okay, I'll do the thinking. You go to the doctor so we're sure everything's okay in there. We get married. And next spring we have a baby."

"Married? Harper, people shouldn't get married just because—"

Though he leaned back against the worktable, he still managed to hedge her in. "In my world, where the sky's blue, people who love each other and are having babies get married all the time. Maybe this is a little ahead of our regularly scheduled program, but it's the kind of bulletin you pay attention to."

"We had a regularly scheduled program?"

"I did." He reached over to tuck her hair behind her ears, then tugged gently at the ends. "I want you, you know I do. I want the baby. We're going to do this right, and that's the way it's going to be."

"So you're ordering me to marry you."

"I had planned to charm you into it, at some point a little farther down the road. But since the timing's changed—and pregnancy's jammed your power of thought—we're going this way."

"You're not even upset."

"No, I'm not upset." He paused a moment as if taking stock. "A little scared, a lot awed. Man, Lily's going to love this. Baby brother or sister to torment. Wait till I tell my brothers they're going to be uncles. What till I tell Mama she's going to be a . . ."

"Grandmother," Hayley finished and nodded, subversively pleased to see a flicker of doubt in his eyes at last. "Just how do you think she's going to feel about that?"

"I guess I'll find out."

"I can't—just can't take all this in." She pressed the heels of her hands to her temples as if it would stop her head from spinning. "I don't even know what I'm feeling." Dropping her hands in her lap, she stared at him. "Harper, you don't think this is a mistake?"

"Our baby's not a mistake." He gathered her in, felt her breath give a hitch as she struggled with tears. "But it's one hell of a surprise."

eighteen

He went in and out of a daze for the rest of the day. There was a lot to be considered, worked out, planned. The initial steps were crystal to him, as clear and precise as the initial steps in any graft.

They would get Hayley into the doctor, get her and the baby checked out. He'd start reading up on baby stuff—womb stuff—so that he understood the process, got sharper images in his head of what was going on in there.

They'd get married as soon as possible, but not so fast it had to be something rushed and cold and practical. He didn't want that for Hayley, or when he thought it through, for himself.

He wanted to get married at Harper House. In the gardens he helped tend, in the shadow of the house where he'd grown up. He wanted to make his promises to Hayley there, and he realized, to make them to Lily there, and to this new child who was now the size of a grain of rice.

This was what he wanted, what he had, somehow, been moving toward all of his life. It was something he'd never thought about before, and knew now as surely as he knew his own name.

Hayley and Lily would move into the carriage house. He'd speak to his mother about adding on to it, giving it more space while staying true to the heart and the traditional style.

More space for their children, he thought, so that they, too, could grow up in Harper House, with its gardens, its woods, its history that would be theirs as it was his.

He could see all of that, he could *know* all of that. But what he couldn't see was the child. The child he'd helped create.

A grain of rice? How could something so small be so huge? And already be so loved?

But now there was a step that had to be taken before the others.

He found his mother in the garden, adding a few asters and mums to one of her beds.

She wore thin cotton gloves, soiled with seasons of work. Cropped cotton pants, the color of bluebonnets that were already smudged with the greens and browns of the task she performed. Her feet were bare, and he could see the backless slides she'd stepped out of before she'd knelt at the border.

When he'd been a child, he'd believed her to be invincible, almost supernatural. She knew everything whether you wanted her to or not. She'd had the answers when he'd needed them, had given him hugs—and the occasional licks. Some of which he'd still like to dispute.

Most of all she'd been there, unfailingly been there. In the best times, in the worst, and all the times between.

Now, it would be his turn.

She tilted her head up as he approached, absently brushed the back of her hand over her brow. It struck him how beautiful she was, her hat tipped over her eyes, her face serene.

"Had a good day," she said. "Thought I'd extend it and fluff up this bed. Gonna rain tonight."

"Yeah." Automatically he glanced up at the sky. "Hoping for a nice soaker."

"Your mouth, God's ear." She squinted against the sun as she studied him. "My, don't you have your serious face on. You gonna sit down here so I don't get a crick in my neck?"

He crouched. "I need to talk to you."

"You usually do when you have your serious face on."

"Hayley's pregnant."

"Well." She set down her trowel, very carefully. "Well, well, well."

"She just found out today. She thinks about six weeks. She got the symptoms—I guess you call them symptoms—mixed up with everything else that's going on."

"I can see how that might happen. Is she all right?"

"A little upset, a little scared, I guess."

She reached up, took off his sunglasses, looked into his eyes. "How about you?"

"I've been taking it in. I love her, Mama."

"I know you do. Are you happy, Harper?"

"I'm a lot of things. Happy's one of them. I know this isn't how you'd hoped I would do things."

"Harper, it doesn't matter what I hoped or want." Carefully she selected a blue aster, set it in the hole she'd already dug. Her hands worked, tucking it in, patting the earth as she spoke. "What matters is what you and Hayley want. What matters is that little girl, and the child you've started."

"I want Lily. I want to marry Hayley and make Lily

mine, legally. I want this baby. And I know it might seem like I've just dropped a pill into a glass of water. Pow, instant family, but . . . Don't cry. Please don't cry."

"I'm entitled to cry when my firstborn tells me he's making me a grandmother. I'm damn well entitled to a few tears. Where the hell is my bandanna?"

He pulled it out of her back pocket, handed it to her.

"I've got to sit all the way down a minute." She plopped down on her butt, wiped her eyes, blew her nose. "You know this day's going to come. From the moment you hold your child in your arms, you know. It's not your first thought, even a conscious one, but it's there, this knowledge that the thread's spinning out. Life cycles. Women know them. And gardeners. Harper."

She opened her arms to him. "You're going to be a daddy."

"Yeah." Because he could, he always could, he pressed his face to the strong line of her neck.

"And I'm going to be a grandmama. Two for one." She drew back, kissed his cheeks. "I love that little girl. She's already ours. I want you and Hayley to know I feel that way. That I'm happy for you. Even if you did manage to do this so the new baby arrives during our busiest season."

"Oops. Didn't think of that."

"I forgive you." She laughed, then pulled off her gloves so she could take his hands, flesh to flesh. "You asked her to marry you?"

"Sort of. Mostly I told her she was going to. And don't give me that look."

Her eyebrows stayed raised, her eyes steely. "It's exactly the look you deserve."

"I'm going to take care of it." He looked down at their joined hands, then lifted hers, one by one, to his lips. "I love you, Mama. You set the bar high."

"What bar is that?"

He looked back up, into her eyes. "I couldn't settle for anybody I loved or respected less than I love and respect you."

Tears swam again. "I'm going to need more than that bandanna in a minute."

"I'm going to give her the best I've got. And to start, I'd like to have Grandmama's rings. Grandmama Harper's engagement and wedding rings. You said once when I got married—"

"That's my boy." With her lips curved, she kissed him lightly. "That's the man I raised. I'll get them for you."

ONE OF THE OTHER THINGS HE'D NEVER IMAGINED was how he'd propose to a woman. To *the* woman. A fancy dinner and wine? A lazy picnic? A giant WILL YOU MARRY ME? on the scoreboard screen at a game.

How weak was that?

The best, he decided, was the place and the tone that suited them both.

So he took her for a walk in the gardens at twilight.

"I don't feel right about your mother riding herd on Lily again. I'm pregnant, not handicapped."

"She wanted to. And I wanted an hour alone with you. Don't—don't go there. God, it's getting so I can see what's going on in your head. I'm crazy about Lily, and I'm not going to spend time telling you what's so damn obvious."

"I know. I know you are. I just can't settle into all this. It's not like I went jumping into bed all over two states. But here I am, for the second time."

"No, this time is different. This is the first time. See that flowering plum?"

"I can only tell—or tell sometimes—when they're blooming."

"This one." He stopped, reached up to touch one of the glossy green leaves. "My parents planted this right after I was born. We'll plant one for Lily, and we'll plant one for this baby. But see this one? It's got nearly thirty years on it now, and they planted it for me. I always felt good about that. Always felt this was one of my places, right here. We'll be making other places, you and me, but we'll start here, with one that already is."

He took the box out of his pocket, watched her lips tremble open, her gaze shoot up to his face. "Oh my God."

"I'm not getting down on one knee. I'm not going to feel like an ass when I do this."

"I think it had something to do with him pledging his loyalty. I mean that's why guys started the one-knee thing."

"You'll just have to take my word on mine. I want this life we've started. Not just the baby, but what we've started together. You and me, and Lily, and now this baby. I want to live that life with you. You're the first woman I've loved. You'll be the last."

"Harper, you—you really do take my breath away."

He opened the box, smiled a little when he saw her eyes widen. "This was my grandmother's. Kind of an old-fashioned setting, I guess."

"I—" She had to swallow. "I prefer the word *classic,* or *heirloom.* Or let's get real, woo-hoo. Harper, Roz must—"

"It was promised to me. Given to me to give to you, to the woman I want to spend my life with. I want you to wear it. Marry me, Hayley."

"It's beautiful, Harper. You're beautiful."

"I'm not done."

"Oh." She gave a nervous laugh. "I can't imagine there's more."

"I want you to take my name. I want Lily to take my name. I want the whole package. I can't settle for less."

"Do you know what you're saying?" She laid a hand on his cheek. "What you're doing?"

"Exactly. And you better answer me soon, because I'd hate to spoil this romantic moment by wrestling you to the ground and shoving this ring on your finger."

"It's not going to come to that." She closed her eyes for a moment, thought of flowering plums, of generations of tradition. "I knew you'd ask me to marry you when I told you I was pregnant. You're built that way, to do what's right. What's honorable."

"This isn't—"

"You had your say." She shook her head fiercely. "I'm having mine. I knew you'd ask, and part of the reason I felt sick about all this was because I was afraid I wouldn't know for sure. That you'd ask because you felt it was what you had to do. But I do know, and that's not why. I'll marry you, Harper, and take your name. So will Lily. We'll love you all of our lives."

He took the ring out of the box, slid it on her finger.

"It's too big," he murmured as he lifted her hand to kiss.

"You're not getting it back."

He closed his hand over hers to hold the ring in place. "Just long enough to have it sized."

She managed a nod, then threw herself into his arms. "I love you. I love you, I love you."

With a laugh, he tipped back her head to kiss her. "I was hoping you'd say that."

* * *

SHE FELT A LITTLE AWKWARD GOING IN WITH HARPER to make the announcement to his mother and Mitch, to have David serving champagne. She was allowed half a glass, and had to make due with that for both toasts.

One on the engagement, and one for the baby.

Roz gathered her into a hug, and whispered in her ear. "You and I have to talk. Soon."

"Oh. I guess so."

"How about now? Harper, I'm going to steal your girl for a few minutes. There's something I want to show her."

Without waiting for a response, Roz hooked an arm through Hayley's and led her out of the room and toward the stairs.

"You giving any thought to the sort of wedding you want?"

"I—no. It's so much."

"I'm sure it is."

"Harper . . . he said something about getting married here."

"I was hoping. We could use the ballroom if you want something splashy. Or the gardens and terrace if you want something more intimate. Y'all discuss it and let me know. I'm dying to dive in, and I plan to be very opinionated, so you'll have to watch me like a hawk."

"You're not mad."

"I'm surprised you'd say such a thing to me."

"I'm trying to put myself in your place," Hayley said as they climbed the stairs. "And I can't quite get there."

"That's because you've got your own place. I like having mine to myself." She turned toward her wing.

"I didn't get pregnant on purpose."

At the entrance to her bedroom, Roz paused, looked Hayley squarely in her swimming eyes. "Is that what's going on in your head? Me thinking this is calculated on your part."

"No—not exactly. A lot of people would."

"I'm pleased to say I'm not a lot of people. I'm also a superior judge of character, with only one major stumble in my illustrious career. If I thought less of you, Hayley, you wouldn't be living in my home."

"I thought . . . when you said we had to talk."

"Oh, that's about enough of this business out of you." Roz walked over to the bed, opened the box that sat on it. She lifted out what looked like a pale blue cloud.

"This was Harper's blanket, what I had made for him right after he was born. I had one made for each of my boys, and they're one of the things I saved to pass on. If you have a girl, you'll use something of Lily's or want something new and feminine. But I hope, if you have boy, you'll use this. In either case, you should have this now."

"It's beautiful."

Roz held it against her cheek a moment. "Yes, it is. Harper is one of the great loves of my life. There's nothing I want more on this earth than his happiness. You make him happy. That's more than enough for me."

"I'll be a good wife to him."

"You damn well better be. Are we going to sit down and have a cry now?"

"Oh yeah. Yeah, that'd be good."

WHEN SHE LAY BESIDE HIM IN THE DARK, SHE LIStened to the steady, drumming rain.

"I don't know how I can be so happy and so scared at the same time."

"I'm right there with you."

"This morning, it felt like everything crashed down on my head, like a whole bookcase, and every book smacked me with the hard edge. Now it turns out it was flowers falling, and I'm covered in all these soft petals and perfume."

He took her hand, the left, the one where her thumb kept rubbing along her third finger. The ring was in its box on the dresser. "I'll get it to the jeweler tomorrow."

"I don't know how I'm going to feel about being married to somebody who reads my mind." Then she rolled over onto him, tossed back her hair. "I think I can read yours, too. And it goes something like this."

She lowered her lips to his.

Soft and smooth, that's how she felt with him. Lovely and loose. And most of all, loved. Whatever tried to darken her heart, whatever brewed in the night, she could, she would, hold off and have this time with him.

Safe, secure. Seduced.

She could trust him to hold her, as he did now, with their bodies warm, their lips tender. She could trust herself to be strong with the taste of him teasing her tongue.

They moved together, slow and easy, while the rain drummed musically on the stones of the terrace. Her heart drummed, too. Pleasure and anticipation. She knew him so well. Friend and partner, now lover. Husband.

Overcome, she laid her cheek on his. "I love you, Harper. It seems like I've already loved you forever."

"We've still got forever."

He brushed his fingers over her face, her cheeks, her temples, into her hair. He could see her in the gloomy dark, the shape of her, the gleam of her eyes. Witchy and mysterious in this storm light, but nonetheless his. He could look at her and see the long roll of the future. Touch her, and know the simple beauty of the now.

He sampled her lips, skin, the long line of her throat, the subtle curve of her breast. Her heart beat under it, steady as the rain. And quickened as his mouth possessed.

Slowly, guided by her sighs, he took his hands and lips over her. The narrow torso, so white, so delicate in the dim light, and the jump of muscles as he passed, the quivers, told him she was roused.

He laid his lips, gently, so gently, on her belly, and laid his cheek there just a moment, in wonder of what grew in her. Her hand brushed over his hair, stroked.

"Its middle name has to be Harper," she murmured. "Boy or girl, whatever we choose for the first name, it's important we pass the Harper name on."

He turned his head to press another kiss over their child. "How about Cletis? Cletis Harper Ashby."

He fought to keep his lips from curving against her skin when her hand stilled. "That's a joke, right?"

"Little Cletis, or Hermione, if it's a girl. You just don't see enough Hermiones these days."

He kissed his way back up until his lips hovered over hers.

"You'd be sorry if I fell in love with those names and insisted on them. Wouldn't be so funny then, would it?"

"Maybe Clemm." He dropped little kisses at the corners of her mouth. "Or Gertrude."

Her fingers drilled into his ribs. "Looks like I'm going to have to be sure I'm the one filling out the birth certificate. Especially since I'm thinking we'll stick with flower names. Begonia's my personal favorite."

"But what if it's a girl?"

She grabbed both of his ears and pulled, then gave up on a laugh.

And was laughing when he slipped inside her.

* * *

SHE WAS SO WARM, SO CONTENT, SNUGGLED UP BESIDE him, drifting off to sleep. The patter of rain was music, a lullabye to float away to dreams on.

She imagined herself walking toward him, her long white dress shimmering in the sunlight, lilies, bold and red lying in the crook of her arm, like a child. He would wait for her, wait to take her hand, to make promises. Take the vows that meant forever.

Till death do you part.

No. She shifted with the quiver under her heart. She wanted no mention of death on the day they married. No promises tied to it.

Death brought shadows, and shadows blocked the sun.

Empty promises. Words spoken by rote and never meant to be kept. Clouds over the sun, and the rain turning her white gown to dull, dingy gray.

It was cold, bleak. But there was such heat in her. Hate was a furnace, rage the fire that stoked it.

How strange, how extraordinary that she should feel so alive, so viciously *alive* at last.

The house was dark. A tomb. They were all dead inside. Only her child lived, and would always, ever. Endless. She and her son would live forever, be together until the end of days while the rest rotted.

This was her vengeance. Her only task now.

She had given life. She had grown it inside her own body, had pushed it into the world with a pain akin to madness. It would not be stolen from her. It was hers to keep.

She would bide in that house with her son. And she would be the true mistress of Harper House.

After this night, she and James would never be parted again.

The rain drenched her as she walked, humming her tune as the hem of her soaked nightdress waded through mud.

They would play in the gardens in the bright spring. How he would laugh. Flowers blooming, birds singing, only for them. Tea and cakes, yes, tea and cakes for her precious boy.

Soon, very soon now, an endless spring for them.

She walked through the rain, wading through the crawl of fog. Now and then she thought she heard some sound—voices, laughter, weeping, shouting.

Now and then, she thought she saw some movement out of the corner of her eye. Children playing, an old woman sleeping in a chair, a young man planting flowers.

But they were not of her world, not of the world she sought.

In her world, they would be the shadows.

She walked the paths, or trod over the winter beds, her feet bare and filthy. Her eyes mad moonbeams.

She saw the silhouette of the stables. What she needed would be there, but so would others. Servants, rutting stablehands, dirty grooms.

Instead, she tapped a finger on her lips, as if for silence, but a rolling laugh escaped. Maybe she should burn the stables, set a fire that would rise up in the sky. Oh, how the horses would scream and the men run.

A toasty blaze on an ice-cold night.

She felt that she could light fires with a thought. And thinking, whirled to face Harper House. She could burn it to ash with her mind. Every room bursting with heat. And he, the great Reginald Harper, and all who had betrayed her would perish in the hell she created.

But not the child. No, no, not the child. She pressed both hands to her mouth, banished the thought before the spark flew. It was not the way for her son.

He must come with her. Be with her.

She walked toward the carriage house. Her hair, tangled around her face, dripped into her eyes, but she walked unhurried.

No locks here, she thought at the wide doors. Who would dare trespass on Harper land?

She would.

The door creaked as she pulled it open. Even in the gloom, she could see the shine of the carriages. No dull wheels for the great master. Big, glossy carriages to carry him and his whore-wife, his mewling daughters, wherever they chose to go.

While the mother of his son, the creator of *life,* drove in a stolen wagon.

Oh, he would pay.

She stood in the open doorway, swaying as her mind rolled in circles, buzzing rings of rage and confusion and terrible love. She forgot where she was, what she was, why. Then the purpose looped around once more.

Could she risk a light? Dare she? She must, she must. She couldn't see in the dark.

Not yet.

Though her fingers shook with cold as she lighted a lamp, she didn't feel it. The heat still burned through her, and made her smile as she saw the hank of rope.

There now, that would do, that would do nicely.

She left the lamp burning, the door open as she walked back out into the rain.

WHEN HARPER TURNED, REACHED FOR HER, SHE wasn't there. He half woke, stretching his arm out farther, expecting to meet her skin.

"Hayley?"

He murmured her name, pushed onto his elbow. His first

thought was that she'd gone in to Lily, but he heard nothing from the bedside monitor.

It took him a few seconds longer to realize what he did hear.

The rain was too loud. Pushing up quickly he saw the terrace doors were open. He rolled out, grabbing his jeans.

"Hayley!" He dragged on his jeans, bolted for the door. He saw nothing but the rain and the dark.

Rain pelted him, his heart constricted to an ice chip in his chest. On a panicked oath, he rushed back inside, and into Lily's room.

The baby slept, peacefully. Her mother wasn't there.

He strode back to the bedroom, grabbed the monitor, and, shoving it in his back pocket, went out to find her.

Calling for her, he bolted down the steps. The carriage house, he thought. He'd always believed Amelia had gone there. The night he'd seen her in the garden when he'd been a child, he'd been sure that's where she'd been going.

Her gown had been wet and muddy, he remembered as he ran. As if she'd been in the rain.

He knew his way, even in the dark. There was no turn of the path that wasn't familiar to him. He saw his front door hanging open, felt a trip of relief.

"Hayley!" He slapped on the light as he rushed in.

The floor was wet, and muddy footprints crossed the room, into the kitchen. He knew the house was empty even before he called for her again, before he ran through it, heart thundering, looking for her.

This time he grabbed the phone, speed-dialing as he ran back out.

"Mama, Hayley's gone. She went outside. I can't find her. She's—oh Jesus, I see her. Third floor. She's on the third floor terrace."

He tossed the phone aside and kept running.

She didn't turn when he shouted her name, but continued to cross the terrace like a wraith. His feet skidded on wet stone, and flowers were crushed as he leaped off the path into beds to cut to the stairs leading up.

Lungs burning, heart screaming, he bounded up.

He reached the third level as she flung open a door.

She hesitated when he called out to her, and slowly turned her head to face him. And smiled. "Death for life."

"No."

He made the last leap, grabbed her arm and jerked her inside out of the rain. "No," he said again, and wrapped his arms around her. "Feel me. You know who I am. You know who you are. Feel me."

He tightened his grip when she struggled. Held her close and warm even as her head whipped from side to side and her teeth snapped like a wild dog's.

"I will have my son!"

"You have a daughter. You have Lily. Lily's sleeping. Hayley, stay with us."

And swept her up in his arms when her body sagged.

"I'm cold. Harper, I'm cold."

"It's all right. You're all right." He carried her across the wide ballroom with its ghostly dust sheets as rain lashed windows.

Before he reached the door, Mitch shoved it open. After one quick glance, Mitch let out a breath. "Your mother went to check on Lily. What happened?"

"Not now." With Hayley shivering in his arms, Harper moved by Mitch. "We'll deal with it later. She needs to get warm and dry. The rest will have to wait."

NINETEEN

HE HAD HER BUNDLED IN A BLANKET FROM NECK TO toe, and sat behind her on the bed drying her hair with a towel.

"I don't remember getting up. I don't remember going out."

"Are you warm enough?"

"Yeah." Except for the sheen of ice inside her bones. She wondered if any heat would ever reach that deep in her again. "I don't know how long I was out there."

"You're back now."

She reached back, laid a hand over his. He needed warmth and comfort as much as she did. "You found me."

He pressed a kiss to her damp hair. "I always will."

"You took Lily's monitor." And that, she thought, meant even more. "You remembered to take it. You didn't leave her alone."

"Hayley." He wrapped his arms around her, pressed his cheek to hers. "I won't leave either of you alone." Then laid a hand on her belly. "Any of you. I swear it."

"I know. She doesn't believe in promises, or faith, or love. I do. I believe in us, with everything I've got." She turned her head so her lips could brush his. "I didn't always, but I do now. I have everything. She has nothing."

"You can feel sorry for her? After this? After everything?"

"I don't know what I feel for her. Or about her." It felt so wonderful to be able to lean her head back, rest it on his good, strong shoulder. "I thought I understood her, at least a little. We were both in a kind of similar situation. I mean, getting pregnant, and not wanting the baby at first."

"You're nothing alike."

"Harper, erase the personalities, and your feelings for just a minute. Look at it objectively, like you do at work. Look at the situation. We were both unmarried and pregnant. Not loving the father, not wanting to see our lives changed, burdened even. Then coming to want the baby. In different ways, for different reasons, but coming to want the baby so much."

"Different ways and different reasons," he repeated. "But all right, I can see that, on the surface, there's a pattern."

The door opened. Roz came in with a tray. "I'm not going to disturb you. Harper, you see that she drinks this." After setting the tray at the foot of the bed, Roz skirted around to the side. She took Hayley's face in her hand, kissed her cheek. "You get some rest."

Harper reached out, took Roz's hand for a moment. "Thanks, Mama."

"You need anything, you call."

"She didn't have anyone to take care of her," Hayley said quietly when the door closed behind Roz. "No one to care about her."

"Who did she care about? Who did she care for? Obsession isn't caring," he added before Hayley could speak. He eased away to get up, pour the tea. "What was done to her sucked big-time. No argument, no debate. But you know what? There aren't any heroes in her sad story."

"There should be. There should always be heroes. But no." She took the tea. "She wasn't heroic. Not even tragic, like Juliet. She's just sad. And bitter."

"Calculating," he added. "And crazy."

"That, too. She wouldn't have understood you. I think I know her well enough now to be sure of that. She wouldn't have understood your heart, or your honesty. That's sad, too."

He walked to the doors. He was getting the soaker he'd wished for and could stand there, watch the earth drink in the rain.

"She was always sad." He reached inside, beyond his anger and found the pity. "I could see it even when I was a kid, and she'd be in my room, singing. Sad and lost. Still I felt safe with her, the way you do when you're with someone you know cares about you. She cared, on some level, for me, for my brothers. I guess that has to count for something."

"She still cares, I feel that. She just gets confused. Harper, I can't remember."

She lowered the cup, and emotion swam into her eyes. "Not like I could the other times it happened. I could see, at least a part of me could. I don't know how to explain. But this time, it's mixed up, and I can't see. Not all of it. Why was she going into the ballroom? What did she do there?"

He wanted to tell her to relax, not to think. But how could she? Instead he came back, sat by her. "You went to the carriage house. You must have. The door was open, and I could see where you'd walked back to the kitchen. The floor was wet."

"That's where she went that night, the night she died here. She had to have died here that night. Nothing else makes sense. We saw her that time, you and me. Standing out on the terrace, wet and muddy. She had a rope."

"There could've been rope in the carriage house. Probably was."

"Why would she need a rope to get the baby? To tie up the nursemaid?"

"I don't think that's why she wanted rope."

"She had that sickle thing, too." Bright and gleaming, she remembered. Sharp. "Maybe she was going to kill anyone who tried to stop her. But the rope. What would she do with rope besides tie somebody up?"

Her eyes widened and she set the cup down with a rattle when she read the look in his eyes.

"Oh my God. To kill herself? To hang herself, is that what you're thinking? But why? Why would she come all the way out here? Why would she drag herself through the rain, and hang herself in the ballroom?"

"The nursery was on the third floor back then."

What little color had come back into her cheeks drained again. "The nursery."

No, she thought as the image played in her mind, she might never be truly warm again.

ON HER DAYS OFF, HAYLEY WAS USED TO THE HOURS flying by. The time was so crowded with chores—shopping, laundry, organizing what had gotten disorganized during workdays, caring for Lily and the myriad tasks that turned up—she barely remembered what it was like to have what those who didn't have full-time jobs and a toddler called free time.

Who knew she liked it that way?

Finding herself with time on her hands left her feeling broody and restless. But when the boss ordered you to take the day off, there was no arguing. At least not when the boss was Rosalind Harper.

She'd been banished to Stella's house for the day without even Lily as a distraction. She'd been told to rest, and she'd tried. Really she had. But her usual delight in reading didn't satisfy her; the stack of DVDs Stella had handed her didn't entertain, and the quiet, empty house kept her counting the minutes rather than lulling her into a nap.

She passed some of the time roaming the rooms, rooms she'd helped paint. Stella and Logan had turned it into a home, mixing Stella's flair for detail and style with Logan's sense of space. And the boys, of course, she thought as she paused outside of the room Gavin and Luke shared with its bunk beds and shelves loaded with comic books and trucks. It was a home created with children in mind, lots of light and color, the big yard that bumped right up to kiss the woods. Even with the elegance of gardens—and how could the landscaping be anything but beautiful here—it was a yard where kids and a dog could romp around.

She picked up Parker—the dog had been her only company through the day—and nuzzled him as she walked back downstairs.

Would she be as clever as Stella with a home and family? As loving and smart and sane?

She'd never planned it this way. Stella was the one for plans. She'd just cruised along, happy enough with her job at the bookstore, helping her father tend the little house they shared. Now and again she'd thought about taking a few extra classes in business—to prepare for the vague dream of opening her own bookstore. One day.

She'd thought about falling in love—one day. Most girls did, she imagined. But she hadn't been in any hurry for it, for the big love, and what followed. Permanency, home, kids. The whole minivan, soccer-mom routine had been distant as the moon in her head. Years off. Light-years off.

But things had happened that had pushed her in directions she'd never expected to go. So here she was, not yet twenty-six, pregnant with her second child, working in a field she'd known next to nothing about two years before.

And so stupidly in love she was all but breathing valentines.

Just to ice that cake, a cryptic and certainly psychopathic spirit had decided to borrow her body from time to time.

When Parker wiggled, she set him down, then followed him into the kitchen where he parked himself by the back door and stared holes through it.

"Okay, okay, out you go. Guess I'm not the most sparkling company today."

She let him out, and he pranced across the yard, into the woods as if he had an appointment to keep.

She wandered out herself. It was a pretty day. The rain had freshened things, cooled the air a little. She could take a walk, do some weeding. Or she could stretch out on the patio chaise and see if being outdoors was more conducive to napping.

Without much hope, she cocked the chair back, thought about going back in for a book. And was asleep in minutes.

SHE WOKE A LITTLE FUZZY IN THE BRAIN TO THE SOUND of snoring. Baffled, she pressed a hand to her mouth, but the sound continued. There was a light cotton throw tossed over her, and the table umbrella had been cocked to shade her.

The snoring came from Parker who was flopped on his back beside her chaise, his feet straight up in the air so he looked like a toy dog that had been knocked off its perch.

Her life might've been strange at the moment, but she didn't think a dog could have moved the umbrella or brought her a blanket.

Even as she cleared sleep from her throat and pushed herself up, Stella came out the back door bearing two glasses of iced tea.

"Nice nap?" she asked.

"I don't know. I slept through it. Thanks," she added as she took a glass of tea. "What time . . . Wow." She blinked at her own watch. "I was out for almost two hours."

"Glad to hear it. You look better."

"I hope to God. Where are the kids?"

"Logan picked them up after school. They like going to jobs with him. Gorgeous out, isn't it? The perfect day for drinking tea on the patio."

"Everything okay at the nursery? This kind of weather brings people in."

"And it did. We were busy. Look at those crepe myrtles. I love this yard," she said with a sigh.

"You and Logan have done an amazing job. I was thinking that before. What a good team you are."

"Turns out. Who'd have thought a cranky disorganized know-it-all and an anal-retentive overachiever could find true love and happiness?"

"I did. Right from the start."

"I suppose you did. Smartie. Have you eaten?"

"I wasn't really hungry."

Stella wagged a finger. "Somebody in there might be. I'm going to fix you a sandwich."

"Don't fuss, Stella."

"PB and J?"

With a shake of her head, Hayley gave in. "No fair. You know my weaknesses."

"Sit right there. The fresh air's good for you. I'll be back in a minute."

True to her word, Stella was back not only with the sandwich, but a sprig of purple grapes, bite-size wedges of cheese. And a half a dozen Milano cookies.

Hayley looked at the plate on her lap, then up at Stella. "Will you be my mommy?"

With a laugh, Stella sat on the chaise at Hayley's feet. And began to rub them in a way that had every muscle in Hayley's body sighing in relief. "One of my favorite things about being pregnant was getting pampered once in a while."

"Missed that the first few months the first time out."

"So, you'll make up for it with this one." Stella patted Hayley's leg. "How you feeling—gestating-wise?"

"Good. Tired, you know, and up and down on the emotional scale, but pretty good. Better now," she added after another bite of the sandwich. "And I hate admitting that—a long nap, comfort food, it's doing the job. I'm going to take care of myself, Stella, I promise. I was careful carrying Lily, and I'll be careful this time, too."

"I know you will. Besides, nobody's going to give you a choice."

"I get . . ." She moved her shoulders restlessly. "Funny when everybody's worried about me."

"Then you'll have to get funny, because we can't help it. Not with everything that's going on."

"Last night, it was so . . . I've used all the words before. Strong, strange, bizarre, intense. But this was the most of all of them. Stella, I didn't tell Harper everything. I couldn't."

"What do you mean?"

"I didn't tell him what I felt. He'd wig, the way guys do. I'm counting on you not to."

"Tell me what's going on."

"It's a feeling—and I don't know if it's just stress or if it's real. But I feel. Stella, she wants the baby. This baby." Hayley pressed a hand to her belly.

"How—"

"She can't. No power on this earth, no power anywhere, is strong enough to push me aside. You know, because you've had a child inside you. Harper, he'd freak."

"Explain this to me, so I don't."

"She gets mixed up is the best way I can explain it. From the here and now, to back in her own time. She wavers back and forth. When she's in the now, she wants what I have. This child, the life, the body. Even more, wealth and privilege. She wants the sensations and the payoff. Do you understand?"

"All right, yes."

"She's much more frightening, much more selfish when her mind's in the now. When it's back, when she's caught up in what happened to her, it's like it *is* happening. Then she's just angry and vindictive, so she wants someone to pay for what happened to her. Or she's sad, and pitiable, and she just wants it all to stop. She's tired. Harper thinks she committed suicide."

"I know. We talked a little."

"He thinks she hanged herself in the nursery. Right there while the baby slept. She could've done it. She was lost and crazy enough to have done it."

"I know that, too." Stella rose, walked to the edge of the patio to look out over the yard. "I've been having dreams again."

"What? When?"

"Not here, not at night. Daydreams, you could say. At

work. On Harper ground. Images like before of the dahlia. The blue dahlia. Only it's monstrous. That's how she wants me to see it. Petals like razors, waiting to slice your fingers to ribbons if you touch it. It's not growing out of a garden this time." She turned back; met Hayley's eyes. "But out of a grave. Unmarked, black dirt. The dahlia is the only thing that grows there."

"When did they start?"

"A few days ago."

"Do you think Roz has had them, too?"

"We'll need to ask her."

"Stella, we have to go up to the old nursery."

"Yes." She walked back, took the hand Hayley held out to her. "We will."

IT WAS EASY TO TALK WITHOUT MEN WHEN THE ANnounced activity was wedding planning. Men, Hayley noted, scattered like ants when terms like guest lists and color schemes were mentioned.

So they were able to sit on Stella's patio in the balm of the evening with Lily being passed from one pair of arms to another, or playing in the grass with Parker.

"I didn't think it would be so easy to chase Harper off," Hayley complained. "You'd think he'd want some input into the wedding plans. He's getting married, too."

Roz and Stella exchanged amused looks before Roz reached over, patted Hayley's hand. "Sweet, foolish child."

"I guess it doesn't matter, since that's not what we're doing. But still." Annoyed with herself, Hayley waved her hands. "Anyway. Amelia's been messing with you, too."

"Twice," Roz confirmed. "Both times when I was alone in the propagation house. I'd be working, and then I'd be somewhere else. It's dark, too dark to tell where, and cold.

Very cold. I'm standing over an open grave. When I look down I see her, looking back at me. Her hands are clasped over the stem of a black rose. Or it looks black in the dark."

"Why didn't you tell us?" Stella demanded.

"The same could be asked of you. I intended to tell you, and did tell Mitch. But we've had a few major distractions."

Hayley hauled Lily onto her lap and admired the thick plastic bracelet she played with. "I know that when this first started and I suggested a seance everybody thought it was a joke. But maybe we should try it. The three of us have this connection to her. Maybe if we tried, really tried to communicate, she'd tell us what she wants."

"I'm not pulling out the turban and crystal ball anytime soon," Roz said, definitely. "In any case, I don't think she knows. By that, I mean she wants to be found—and I think she means her grave, or her remains. But she doesn't know where it is."

"We can't be a hundred percent certain it's on Harper property," Stella put in.

"No, we can't. Mitch is doing all he can to find death records, burial records. We don't think there are any for her."

"A secret burial." Hayley nodded. "But she always wants us to know what happened to her. It still pisses her off." She shrugged, smiled a little. "It's one of the things I get, pretty loud and clear. If she was killed, or killed herself, in the house, we need to find out."

"The nursery," Roz stated. "It was still in use when I was born."

"You stayed up there when you were a baby?" Hayley asked.

"So I'm told. At least for the first few months, with the nursemaid. My grandmother didn't approve, Grandmama Harper. Apparently she'd only used it when they were entertaining. She used her considerable influence on my parents until they moved me to a room on the second floor. I never used it for my boys."

"Why?"

Roz pursed her lips and thought over Hayley's question. "First, I didn't want them that far away from me. And yes, I didn't like the feel of the room. Something I couldn't explain, and didn't think about that much at the time."

"The furniture in Lily's room came from there."

"Yes. Once Mason was out of the crib, I had everything taken back up. I took to storing the boys' things in there when they outgrew them. We don't use the third floor as a rule. It's too costly to maintain, and more space than we can practically use. Though I have had parties in the ballroom in the past."

"I'd never been up there," Hayley commented. "Which is strange now that I think about it, because I like going through houses, seeing how they look, picturing them the way they were, that kind of thing. But I never even thought of going up there in all the time I've lived in the house. Stella?"

"No, and you're right, it is odd. The boys had the run of the house for more than a year. You'd think I'd have had to chase them down from there at some point. But I don't think they ever went up either. Even if they did it in secret, Luke would've spilled. He always does."

"I think we should." Hayley looked from one to the other. "I think we have to."

"Tonight?" Stella asked.

"I don't think I can stand to wait. It's driving me crazy."

"If that's what we're going to do, we'll all do it together. The six of us," Roz said. "Not the children. David can keep them downstairs. You have to be sure, Hayley. At this point it seems, of all of us, you're the closest to her."

"I am sure. But not just me, which is something else I

wanted to bring up. Harper. Her feelings for him, about him." A little chilled, Hayley rubbed her arms. "They're awfully mixed, and potent. She loves him—the child of the child of the child sort of thing. And she hates him—a man, a Harper man, Reginald's blood."

She looked at Stella, at Roz. "That combination of feelings, it's powerful. I think maybe more powerful because of the way Harper and I feel about each other."

"Love, sex, kinship, vengeance, grief." Roz nodded. "And insanity."

"His feelings about her are pretty mixed, too." Hayley let out a breath. "I don't know if that matters, but I think all of it, at this point, everything's important. I think we must be getting close to the end of it."

"Hallelujah," Stella announced.

"I know. I want this over. I want to really plan a wedding, and plan for this baby. I want to sit here with the two of you and talk about flowers and music and the kind of dress I'm going to wear."

Roz covered Hayley's hand with hers. "We will."

"Last night, before it happened, it was like I was imagining it, seeing myself in a long white dress and the flowers . . . But I guess that's out." She gave a half shrug as she patted her belly. "I don't guess I'm entitled to a long white dress."

"Honey." Roz gave Hayley's hand a quick squeeze. "Every bride's entitled to a long white dress."

FOOD CAME FIRST, A FAMILY MEAL, THE KIND OF RITUAL that brought them all together where flowers were set and children chattered. Roz had said such things were important, and Hayley could see the purpose of it.

This is who we are, it seemed to say. What we are and

what we'll be regardless of trouble. Maybe because of it.

She'd been given this, this family. A mother, a sister, a lover, brothers and friends. A child who was loved by them, and another child to come.

Whatever it took to keep it whole and safe, she would do.

So she ate. She talked and listened, helped wipe up spills, and buried her nerves under the treasure of normality.

There was talk of flowers and books, of school and books. And here was the talk of wedding plans she'd pined for.

"I guess Hayley told you we'd like to get married here, if that suits you, Mama."

"That's what I like to hear." Roz set her fork aside. "In the gardens? We'll insist the weather stay fine, and have tents as a backup. I intend to roll up my sleeves regarding the flowers. I insist you give me my head there. You'll want lilies, I expect."

"Yes. I want to carry red lilies."

"Bold colors then, toss the pastels. I can work with that. I know you don't want anything too formal, and since we've had two weddings already this year, I think we can iron out the details without much pain and suffering."

"Step away now," Logan advised Harper. "Save yourself. Just say, 'That sounds fine.' And if they give you two choices in anything, don't fall into the trap. Just say, 'They're both great,' and tell her to pick."

"He thinks he's being funny," Stella said dryly. "I'm not kicking him under the table because he's right."

"How come everybody's getting married?" Gavin demanded. "How come we always have to wear ties?"

"Because they like to torture us," Logan told him. "It's the way of women."

"They should have to wear ties, too."

"I'll wear a tie," Stella offered. "You wear high heels."

"I know why people get married," Luke piped up. "So they can sleep in the same bed and make babies. Did you and Mitch make a baby yet?" he asked Roz.

"We already made our quota some time ago. And on that note." Roz pushed away from the table. "I think it's time for you boys to help David clear this up so you can have ice cream in the kitchen."

"All right, troops. Fall in. You, too, Private." Before Hayley could deal with it herself, David moved over to take Lily out of the high chair. "Just because you're short, doesn't mean you can skate out of KP. She likes to help me load the dishwasher," he said to Hayley. "We're fine."

"I just need to talk to you for one minute in the kitchen."

"Clear and stack, gentlemen," he ordered, then carried Lily out of the dining room. "We got this end covered," he said to Hayley. "You don't need to worry."

"No, that's not it. I know Lily's fine with you. It's about the wedding. I need to ask you for something."

He set Lily down, gave her a pot and a spoon to bang. "What do you need?"

"I know this might sound sort of strange, but I think you get to tailor a day like your wedding day to suit you best, don't you?"

"If not that day, what day?"

"That's right. So I was wondering, I was hoping, you'd give me away."

"What?" David's face went utterly blank. "Me?"

"I know you're not old enough to be my daddy, or anything. But I wasn't thinking about it that way. I was thinking how you're one of my best friends, and Harper's, too. How we're like family. And how a day like that's about family. I don't have my daddy, or any blood kin I love the way I love you. So I want you to walk me down the aisle—so to speak—and give me to Harper. It would mean a lot to me."

His eyes went misty as he wrapped his arms around her. "That's the sweetest thing," he crooned. "The damnedest sweetest thing."

"Will you?"

He drew back. "I would be honored." Taking both her hands, he turned them over, kissed her palms. "Extremely."

"Whew. I thought you might think it was silly."

"Not even close. I'm so proud, and touched. And, honey, if you don't go on now, I'm going to embarrass myself in front of my troops."

"Me, too." She sniffled. "Okay. We'll talk about all of it later on." She crouched down to kiss Lily's head, and was largely ignored. "You be good, baby girl."

"Hayley." David drew a breath as she stopped at the door. "Your daddy? He'd be proud, too."

The best she could manage was a nod as she left him.

She brushed away tears as she followed the voices in the parlor, then paused when she heard the temper in Harper's.

"I don't like this idea, not one bit. And I like less the fact that the three of you were off plotting this on your own."

"We womenfolk," Roz said with a sarcasm that dripped so heavy Hayley could feel its weight outside the room.

"The fact that you are women isn't any of my doing," he shot back. "But the fact that *my* woman is pregnant is. I don't take chances on this."

"All right, you have a valid point. But what do you intend to do with her for the next seven, eight months, honey?"

"Protect her."

"You do make it hard to argue."

"Arguing isn't going to help." Mitch's voice of reason cut between them. "We can discuss and debate, and we're unlikely to be in full agreement on all points. But we do have to come to some decisions."

Hayley straightened her spine, and stepped into the room. "I'm sorry. Hard not to overhear. Harper, I was going to ask if we could go outside so I could talk to you, but I think what I have to say needs to be said here, to everyone."

"I've got some things to say you might rather hear in private."

She only smiled. "There'll be plenty of time for you to yell at me in private. A lifetime of it. I know you kept it buttoned till now because of the kids. But I'd like you to hear me out before you say anything more."

She cleared her throat and moved farther into the room. "Earlier today, when I was alone, I was wondering how I'd gotten here. I'd never figured on moving away from where I grew up, having a couple of kids before I figured out where I really wanted to go, really wanted to do. Getting married, having babies, that was going to be later, after I'd made something of myself, had some fun. Here I am, living in another state. I've got a daughter not yet two and another baby on the way. I'm getting married. I'm working in a field I never thought about being in before. How'd I get here? What am I doing here?"

"If you're not happy—"

"Please, just listen. I asked myself that. I've still got choices. There are always choices. So I asked myself, is this what I want, is this where I want to be, what I want to do? And it is. I love you. I didn't know I had all this in me."

She kept her eyes on Harper's, only on Harper's and crossed her hands over her heart. "I didn't know I could love a child the way I do Lily. I didn't know I could love a man the way I love you. If I had every choice in the world, this is the one I'd pick. Being with you, with our children, in this place. Because you see that's one more thing, Harper. I love this house, I love this place. As much as you do. What it is, what it stands for, what it'll be to our children, and theirs."

"I know. My mind traveled that same road. That's why you're the one for me.

"I can't walk away from here. Please don't ask me to do that. I can't walk away from this house, this family, the work I've come to love. The only way I can stay is to try to do this thing, to settle this. Right a wrong, or at least understand it. Maybe I was meant to. Maybe we found each other because *we* were meant to. I don't know if I can do it if you're not with me." She scanned the room. "All of you."

Then she looked at Harper. "Be with me, Harper. Trust me to do what's right. Trust us to do it."

He stepped to her, rested his brow on hers. "I am with you."

twenty

"THERE'S NO GUARANTEE ANYTHING WILL HAPPEN." Mitch slipped a spare tape in his pocket.

"I think I can make it happen. What I mean . . ." Hayley moistened her lips. "I think I can draw her. She wants this—a part of her does, and has for a century."

"And the other part?" Harper asked.

"Wants revenge. When it comes down to it, she'll probably be more inclined to hurt you than me."

"And she can hurt us," Roz pointed out. "We've seen that."

"So we go up there armed with cameras and tape recorders." Logan shook his head.

"We happy few," Mitch stated.

"Well, she's raised the stakes." Logan took Stella's hand. "Since none of us are willing to fold, let's ante up."

"We stay together," Roz said as they started up the

stairs. "No matter what. We've never really confronted her as a group before. I think there's strength in that."

"She always had the upper hand, she always moved first." Harper nodded. "Yeah, we stay together."

When they reached the third floor, Roz turned toward the ballroom. Going with instinct, she stepped forward, pushed the double pocket doors open.

"There were lovely parties here. I remember creeping up at night to watch the dancing."

She reached in to switch on the light. It showered down on the shrouded furniture, and the lovely pattern of the maple floor. "I nearly sold those chandeliers once." She looked up at the dazzling trio of them dripping down from ornate plaster medallions. "Couldn't bring myself to do it, even though it would've made day-to-day living easier. I gave my own parties here, once upon a time. I believe it's time I did so again."

"She came in this way, that night. I'm sure of it." Though her hand was already in Harper's, Hayley tightened her grip. "Don't let go."

"Not a chance."

"She came in the terrace doors. They weren't locked. She could've broken the glass if they had been. She came in, and oh . . . Gilt and crystal, the smell of beeswax and lemon oil. The rain dripping, dripping from the gutters. Turn on the lights."

"I have," Roz said quietly.

"No, she turns on the light. Harper."

"Right here."

"I can see it. I can see it."

The fog rolled in the doors behind her, smoking damp over the glossy floors. Her feet were caked with mud, with blood where she'd trod on stones, and left streaks of that mud, of that blood, where she walked.

Alive still. Heart beating blood.

This, this is how they lived at Harper House. Grand rooms lit by sparkling chandeliers, gilt mirrors on the walls, long, polished tables and potted palms so lush they smelled of the tropics.

She had never been to the tropics. She and James would go one day, one day they'd go and stroll on sugar sand by warm blue water.

But no, but no, their lives were here, in Harper House. They had cast her out, but she would be here. Always here. To dance in this ballroom, lit by crystal drops.

She swayed, a partnerless waltz, her head tilted up flirtatiously. The blade in her hand shooting light from its keen edge.

She would dance here, night after night if she chose. Drink champagne, wear fine jewels. She would teach James to waltz with her. How handsome he would be, wrapped in his soft blue blanket. How sweet a picture they would make. Mother and son.

She must go to him now, go to James, so they could always be together.

She wandered out. Where would the nursery be? In the other wing, of course. Of course. Children and those who tended them didn't belong near grand ballrooms, elegant withdrawing rooms. Smell the house! How rich its perfume. Her son's home. And hers now.

The carpet was soft as fur on her feet. And even so late, even when the house was in bed, the gaslights glowed on low.

Spare no expense! she thought. Money to burn.

Oh, she should burn them all.

At the stairs she paused. They would be sleeping down there, the bastard and his whore. The sleep of the rich and the privileged. She could go down, kill them. Hack them to pieces, bathe in their blood.

Idly, she rubbed her thumb over the curved blade of the sickle, had blood welling red. Would their blood run blue? Harper blood. It would be so lovely to see it, spilling out of their white throats, pooling regally blue on their linen sheets.

But someone might hear. One of the servants could hear, and stop her before her duty was done.

So quiet. She tapped a finger to her cheek, stifled a laugh. Quiet as a mouse.

Quiet as a ghost.

She walked to the other wing, easing doors open if they were closed. Peeking inside.

She knew—it was her mother's heart speaking, she thought—as her trembling hand reached for the latch on the next door. She knew her James slept inside.

A low light burned, and with it she could see the shelves of toys and books, the rocking chair, the small bureaus and the chests.

And there, the crib.

Tears spilled out of her eyes as she crossed to it. There he lay sleeping, her precious son, his dark hair clean and sweet, his plump cheeks rosy with health.

Never had there been a more beautiful baby than her James. So pretty and soft in his crib. He needed to be tended, and rocked, and sung to. Sweet songs for her sweet son.

She'd forgotten his blanket! How could she have forgotten his blanket? Now she would have to use what another had bought him when it came time to carry him off with her.

Gently, so gently, she brushed her fingers over his soft hair and sang his lullaby.

"We'll be together always, James. Nothing will ever part us again."

Sitting on the floor, she went to work.

She used the blade to hack through the rope. It was difficult to form the noose, but she thought she did well. Well enough. Discarding the sickle, she carried a chair, positioned it under the ceiling lamp. And sang softly as she tied the rope to the arms of the lamp.

It held on a strong, testing pull and made her smile.

She pulled out the gris-gris she had in a bag looped around her neck by a ribbon. She'd memorized the chant the voodoo queen had sold her, but she struggled with the words now as she sprinkled the gris-gris in a circle around the chair.

She used the blade to slice open her own palm. And let the blood from her hand drip over the gris-gris, to bind the work.

Her blood. Amelia Ellen Connor. The same blood that ran in her child. A mother's blood, potent magic.

Her hands shook, but she continued to croon as she went to the crib. For the first time since he'd been born, she lifted her child into her arms.

Bloodied his blanket, and his rosy cheek.

Ah, so warm, so sweet! Weeping with joy she cuddled the child against her damp and filthy gown. When he stirred and whimpered, she hugged him only closer.

Hush, hush, my precious. Mama is here now. Mama will never leave you again. His head moved, his mouth sucking as if in search of a nipple. But when with a sob of joy, she tugged her gown below her breast, pressed him there, he arched and let out a cry.

Hush, hush, hush. Don't cry, don't fret. Sweet, sweet baby boy. Sawing her arms back and forth to rock him, she moved to the chair. Mama has you now. She'll never, never let you go. Come with Mama, my darling James. Come with Mama now where you will never know pain or grief. Where we will waltz in the ballroom, have tea and cake in the garden.

She climbed, awkward with his weight, with his wiggles, onto the chair. Even as he wailed, she smiled down at him, and slipped the noose around her neck. Softly singing, she slipped the smaller noose around his.

Now, we're together.

The connecting door opened, a spill of light that had her turning her head, baring her teeth like a tiger protecting her cub.

The sleepy-eyed nursemaid shrieked, her hands flying to her face at the sight of the woman in the filthy white gown, and the baby in her arms, screaming with fear and angry hunger, with a rope around his neck.

"He's mine!"

As she kicked the chair away, the nursemaid sprang forward.

Screams gave way to the cold, and the dark.

Hayley sat on the floor of what had been the nursery, weeping in Harper's arms.

SHE WAS STILL ICY, EVEN IN THE PARLOR WITH A BLANKET over her legs, and the unseasonable fire Mitch had set to blaze in the hearth.

"She was going to kill him," she told them. "She was going to kill the baby. My God, my God, she meant to hang her own child."

"To keep him." Roz stood, staring at the fire. "That's more than madness."

"If the nurse hadn't come in when she did. If she hadn't heard him crying and come in quickly, she would've done it."

"Selfish woman."

"I know, I know." Hayley lifted her hands, rubbed her shoulders. "But she didn't do it to hurt him. She believed they'd be together, and happy, and, oh Jesus. She was broken, in every possible way. Then at the end, when she lost again . . ." Hayley shook her head. "She keeps waiting for him. I think she must see him in every child who comes to Harper House."

"A kind of hell isn't it?" Stella asked. "For madness."

She'd never forget it, Hayley thought. Never. "The nurse, she saved the baby."

"I haven't been able to trace her," Mitch put in. "They had more than one nursemaid during his babyhood, but the timing of this points to a girl named Alice Jameson—which also jibes with Mary Havers's letter to Lucille. Alice left the Harper employ in February of 1893, and I haven't found anything more on her."

"They sent her away." Stella closed her eyes. "That's what they'd have done. Paid her maybe, or just as likely threatened her."

"Both would be my guess," Logan said.

"I'll push on it, do what I can to find her," Mitch promised, and Roz turned to smile at him.

"I'd appreciate it. I wouldn't be here without her, nor would my sons."

"It wasn't what she wanted us to know," Hayley said quietly. "Or not all of it. She doesn't know where she is. Where she's buried. What they did with her. She won't be able to leave, to rest, to pass over, whatever it is, until we find her."

"How?" Stella spread her hands.

"I have an idea on that." Roz scanned faces. "One I think's going to hit this group about fifty-fifty."

"What's the point?" Harper objected. "So Hayley can see her try to hang a baby again?"

"So she, or one of us, can see what happened next. Hopefully. And by we, I mean myself, Hayley, and Stella."

For the first time since they'd started upstairs, Harper released Hayley's hand. He shoved off the couch. "That's a damn stupid idea."

"Don't take that tone with me, Harper."

"It's the only tone I've got when my mother goes crazy. Did you see what just happened up there? The way Hayley walked from the ballroom to the old nursery? The way she talked as if she was watching it happen, and like she was part of what was happening?"

"I saw perfectly well. That's why we have to go back."

"I've got to side with Harper on this, Roz." Logan gave an apologetic shrug. "I don't see sitting down here while three women go up there alone. I don't give a rat's ass if it's sexist."

"I expected as much. Mitch?" Her eyebrows winged up when he sat, frowning at her. "Well, you're about to surprise me again."

"You can't seriously agree with her on this?" Harper whirled around to his stepfather.

"The hell of it, Harper, is that I am. I don't like it, but I see where she's going, and why. And before you take my head off, consider this: They'll do it later, at some point when none of us is around."

"What happened to staying together?"

"It's a man who used her, abused her, stole her child, cast her off. She's been poking at me and Stella again. She won't trust you. Maybe we can convince her to trust us."

"And maybe she'll toss you off the third floor terrace."

"Harper." Roz crossed to him, her smile as thin as a blade. "Anybody gets tossed out of this house, it's going to be her. That's a stone promise. My sympathy for her is at an end. You still have it." She looked over at Hayley. "And that's fine, probably an advantage. But mine is over. What she would have done if not for intervention is unforgivable to me. I will have her out of this house. Can you go back?" she asked Hayley.

"Yes, I can. I want it done. I don't think I'll ever have another easy moment until it is."

"You're asking me to risk you."

"No." Hayley rose to go to Harper. "To believe in me."

"YOU KNOW HOW, IN THE MOVIES, THE STUPID, USUally scantily clad blonde, goes down in the basement alone when she hears a noise, especially if there's a slasher-type killer running around?"

Roz laughed at Hayley as they stood on the third floor landing. "We're not stupid."

"And none of us are blond," Stella added. "Ready?"

They clasped hands and started down the hall.

"The problem with this," Hayley began in a voice that sounded tinny to her ears, "is that if she doesn't know what happened to her after, how will we?"

"One step at a time." Roz gave Hayley's hand a squeeze. "How are you feeling?"

"My heart's beating a mile a minute. Roz, when this is over, can we open this room again? Make it, I don't know, a playroom maybe. Something with light and color."

"A wonderful idea."

"And here we go," Stella declared. They walked in together.

"How did it look before, Hayley?" Roz asked her.

"Um. The crib was over there." She gestured with her chin. "Against the wall. The lights were on low. Gaslights, like in that movie with Ingrid Bergman. The one where Charles Boyer tries to drive her crazy. There was a rocking chair over there, and another, straight-backed chair—the one she used—over there. Shelves here," she pointed, "with toys and books on them. And a . . ."

Her head snapped back, her eyes rolled up white. As she began to choke, her legs buckled.

She heard, through the storm surge in her ears, Roz shout to get her out. But she shook her head wildly.

"Wait, wait. God it *burns*! The baby's screaming, and the maid, the nurse. Don't let go of me."

"We're taking you out," Roz said.

"No, no. Just don't let go. She's dying—it's horrible—and she's so angry." Hayley let her head fall onto Roz's shoulder. "It's dark. It's dark where she is. Was. No light, no air, no hope. She lost. They took him again, and now she's alone. She'll always be alone. She can't see, she can't feel. Everything seems so far away. Very cold, very dark. There are voices, but she can't hear them, only echoes. It's so empty. She's going down, down, so heavy. She can only see the dark. She doesn't know where she is. She just floats away."

She sighed, left her head on Roz's shoulder. "I can't help it, even in this room, I feel sorry for her. She was cold and selfish, calculating. A whore, certainly, in the lowest sense of the word. But she's paid for it, hasn't she? More than a hundred years of being lost, of watching over other people's children and never having more than that one mad moment with her own. She's paid."

"Maybe she has. Are you all right?"

Hayley nodded. "It wasn't like before, not the way I could feel her pulling at me. I was stronger. I need life more than she does. I think she's tired. Almost as tired as we are."

"That may be, too. But you don't let your guard down." Stella looked up where once had hung an armed gaslight chandelier. "Not for a minute."

"Let's go back." Stella rose, helped Hayley to her feet. "You did what you could. We all have."

"It doesn't seem like enough. It was a brutal death. It wasn't quick, and she saw the maid run out with the baby. She reached out her arms for him, even when she was strangling."

"That's not a mother's love, whatever she thought," Roz said.

"No, it's not. It wasn't. But it was all she had." Hayley moistened her lips, wished desperately for water. "She cursed him—Reginald. Cursed them all—the Harpers. She . . . she willed herself to stay here. But she's tired. Part of her, the part that sings lullabies, is so tired and lost."

She let out a sigh, then smiled when she saw Harper pacing the landing. "We've all got so much more than she did. We're fine." She left the other women to go to him. "I guess we didn't get what we were after, but we're fine."

"What happened?"

"I saw her die, and I felt her in the dark. Awful. Dark and cold and alone. Lost." She leaned against him, let him lead her downstairs. "I don't know what happened to her, what they did with her. She was going down in the dark, in the dark and cold."

"Buried?"

"I don't know. It was more . . . floating away in the dark, drifting down where she couldn't see or hear, or find her way out." Unconsciously, she rubbed a hand over her throat, remembering the sensation of the rope biting in. "Maybe it was a soul thing—you know the opposite of the tunnel of light."

"Floating, drifting?" Harper's eyes went sharp. "How about sinking?"

"Ah . . . yeah. I guess."

"The pond," he said and looked at her. "We never thought of the pond."

"THIS IS CRAZY." IN THE HAZY LIGHT OF DAWN, Hayley stood on the bank of the pond. "It could take hours, more. He should have help. We could get other people. Search-and-rescue people."

Roz slid an arm over her shoulders. "He wants to do this. He needs to." She watched while Harper pulled on flippers. "It's time for us to step back, let them do."

The pond looked so dark and deep with the skim of fog rising over its surface. The floating lilies, the spears of cattails and iris greens that had always seemed so charming to her were ominous now, fairy-tale foreign and frightening.

But she remembered how he'd paced the landing while she'd gone up the stairs into the nursery.

"He trusted me," Hayley said quietly. "Now I have to trust him."

Mitch crouched beside Harper, handed him an underwater lamp. "Got everything you need?"

"Yeah. Been a while since I scuba'd." He took deep, steady breaths to expand his lungs. "But it's like sex, you don't forget the moves."

"I can get some students, some friends of my son's who know the moves, too." Like Hayley, Mitch studied the wide, misty surface of the water. "It's a big pond for one man to cover."

"Whatever else she was, she was mine, so it's for me to do. What Hayley said last night about maybe she'd been meant to help find her. I'm feeling the same about this."

Mitch braced a hand on his shoulder. "You keep an eye

on your watch, surface every thirty minutes. Otherwise, your mama's going to toss me in after you."

"Got it." He looked over at Hayley, shot her a grin.

"Hey." She stepped to him, crouched down. With a hand on his cheek she touched her mouth to his. "For luck."

"Take all I can get. Don't worry. I've been swimming in this pond . . ." He glanced up at his mother, and vague memories of his own tiny hands slapping at the water while she held him flashed into his mind. "Well, longer than I can remember."

"I'm not worried."

He kissed her again, tested his mouthpiece. Then, adjusting his mask, slid into the pond.

He'd swum here countless times, he thought as he dived, following the beam of the light through the water. Cooling off on hot summer afternoons, or taking an impulsive dip before work in the morning.

Or bringing a girl back after a date and talking her into a moonlight skinny dip.

He'd splashed with his brothers in this pond, he remembered, playing his light over the muddy bottom before he checked his watch, his compass. His mother had taught them each how to swim here, and he remembered the laughter, the shrieks, and the cool, quiet moments.

Had all that happened over the grave of Amelia?

Mentally, he cut the pond into wedges, like a pie, and methodically began to search each slice.

At thirty minutes, then an hour, he surfaced.

He sat on the edge, feet dangling in while Logan helped him change his tank. "I've covered nearly half. Found some beer cans, soft drink bottles." He tilted his face toward his mother. "And don't look at me, I got more respect."

She reached down, skimmed a hand over his dripping hair. "I should think."

"Somebody'd get me a bag, I'd clean up as I go."

"We'll worry about it later."

"It's not deep, maybe eighteen feet at the deepest point, but the rain's stirred up the mud some, so it's a little murky."

Hayley sat beside him, but he noted she was careful not to dip her toes in the water. "I wish I could go in with you."

"Maybe next year I'll teach you how to scuba." He patted her belly. "Stay up here and take care of Hermione."

He rolled back into the water.

It was tedious work, without any of the adventure or thrill he'd experienced when he'd strapped on tanks on vacations. The strain of peering through the water, training his gaze on the circle of light had a headache brewing.

The sound of nothing but his own breath, sucking in oxygen from the tank, was monotonous and increasingly annoying. He wished it was done, over, and he was sitting in the dry, warm kitchen drinking coffee instead of swimming around in the damn, dark water looking for the remains of a woman who, at this point, just pissed him off.

He was tired, sick and tired of having so much of his life focused on a suicidal crazy woman—one who would have, if left to her own devices, killed her own child.

Maybe Reginald wasn't so much the villain of the piece after all. Maybe he'd taken the kid to protect him. Maybe . . .

There was a burn in his belly, not sickness so much as a hot ball of fury. The sort, Harper realized, that could make a man forget he was fifteen feet or so underwater.

So he rechecked his watch, deliberately, paid more attention to his breathing, and followed the path of his light.

What the hell was the matter with him? Reginald had been a son of a bitch, no question about it. Just as Amelia had been self-centered and whacked. But what had come from that selfish union had been good and strong. Loving. What had come from it mattered.

So this mattered. Finding Amelia mattered.

She was probably buried out in the woods, he decided. But hell, why dig a hole in the ground in winter when you've got a private pond handy? It seemed right, so right he wondered they hadn't thought of it before.

Then again, maybe they hadn't thought of it before because it was lame. People used the pond, even back then. To swim, to fish. Bodies that got dumped in water often resurfaced.

Why risk it?

He moved to another area, skimmed his light.

Nearly another hour passed in the murk, in the wet. He'd have to finish for the day, he decided. Get his tanks refilled and continue tomorrow. Customers would be coming in soon, and nothing put off retail like hearing that some guy was looking for human remains.

He trailed his light through the roots of his water lilies, thought fleetingly that he might try to hybridize a red one. Something that really snapped. He studied the roots, pleased with the health and progress of what he'd begun, and decided to surface.

His light caught something below, and slightly south. He checked his watch, noted he was approaching borrowed time, but he kicked, dived, scanned.

And he saw her, what was left of her. Bones, filthy with mud, tangled with growth. Weighed down, he saw, with a stirring of pity, by bricks and stones, tied to those bones, hands, legs, waist by the rope he imagined she'd hanged herself with.

The rope she'd meant to use on her son.

Still, shouldn't she have surfaced at some point? Why hadn't the rope rotted, those weights shifted? It was basic physics, wasn't it?

But basic physics didn't take ghosts and curses into account.

He paddled a hand in the water, moving closer to her.

The blow knocked him back, sent him somersaulting and ripped the light from his hand.

He was in the dark, with the dead, and running out of air.

He fought not to panic, to let his body go loose and limp so that he would drop to the bottom, and be able to spring off to the surface.

But another wave bowled him over.

He saw her, gliding through the water, her white gown billowing, her hair floating out in tangled ropes. Her eyes were wide with lunacy, her hand reaching out, curled like claws.

He felt them close around his neck, squeeze, though he could see her still, feet away, suspended in the water over her own bones.

He struck out, but there was nothing to fight. He clawed toward the surface, but she held him down as inevitably as the bricks and stones that had carried her to the bottom.

She was killing him, as she'd planned to kill her own child. Maybe that had been the plan all along, he thought dimly. To take a Harper with her.

He thought of Hayley, waiting for him on the surface, of the child she carried. Of the daughter she'd already given him.

He wouldn't give them up.

He looked back down at the bones, tried to find a glimmer of that pity. And he looked at Amelia, eternally mad.

I remember you. He thought it with all his will. *Singing to me. I knew you'd never hurt me. Remember me. The child that came from your child.*

He groped for his diving knife, sliced his palm with the

blade. As she had once sliced hers in madness. His blood dripped and clouded in the murky water between them, and drifted down toward the filthy bones.

That's your blood in me. Connor blood as much as Harper. Amelia to James, James to Robert, Robert to Rosalind, and Rosalind to me. That's why I found you. Let me go. Let me take you home. You don't have to be alone or lost anymore.

When the pressure on his throat released, he fought the urge to kick straight for the surface. He could still see her, and wondered how it was he could see tears flow down her cheeks.

I'll come back for you. I swear it.

He pushed up, and he thought he heard her singing, the light, sweet voice of his childhood. When he looked back, he saw the beam of his light spear out from the bottom, arrow to her so she was illuminated in its shaft.

And watched her fade away like a dream.

Breaking the surface, he ripped his mouthpiece away, sucked in air that burned his scored throat. Sunlight sparkled in his eyes, dazzling them, and through the roaring in his ears there were voices calling his name.

Through the dazzle, he found Hayley standing on the verge, a hand pressed to her belly. On the wrist of that hand, ruby hearts glittered like hope.

He swam through the lilies toward her, swam away from death toward life. Logan and Mitch helped pull him out of the water where he lay on his back, drawing in air, looking into Hayley's eyes.

"I found her."

epilogue

THE SUN FILTERED THROUGH THE LEAVES OF SYCAMORES and oaks and cast pretty patterns of light and shadows on the green of the grass. On the branches birds sang, filling the balmy air with music.

Gravestones stood, marble white, granite gray, carved to mark the dead. On some, flowers lay, petals fading, petals fluttering in the light breeze. Tributes to those who'd passed before.

Harper stood between his mother and Hayley, holding their hands as the casket was lowered.

"I don't feel sad," Hayley declared. "Not anymore. This feels right. More than right, it feels kind."

"She earned the right to be here. Beside her son." Roz looked at the graves, the names. Reginald and Beatrice, Reginald and Elizabeth.

And there, her parents. Their aunts and uncles, cousins,

all links in the long chain of Harpers. "In the spring," she said, "we'll put a marker for her. Amelia Ellen Connor."

"You already have, in a way." Mitch turned his head to kiss her hair. "Burying her son's rattle with her, his picture. Hayley's right. It's kind."

"Without her, I'm not. Without her, Harper, Austin, Mason are not. Nor are the children who come from them. She deserves her place."

"Whatever she did, she deserved better than what was done to her." Stella sighed. "I'm proud I was part of this, of giving her back her name, and I hope, giving her peace." She smiled at Logan, then over at David and all the others. "We were all part of it."

"Tossed in the pond. Discarded." Logan rubbed a hand over the small of Stella's back. "All to protect, what? Reputation."

"She's found now," David added. "You did good, Roz, pushing through the system to have her buried here."

"The Harper name still has the weight to shove the bureaucrats. Truth be told I wanted to give her this nearly as much as I wanted her out of my house, away from what and who I love." She rose up to peck Harper's cheek. "My boy. My brave boy. She owes you most of all."

"I don't think so," he disagreed.

"You went back." Hayley pressed her lips together. "Even after she tried to hurt you, you went back to help bring her out."

"I told her I would. Ashbys keep their word as well as Harpers. I'm both." He picked up a fist of earth, held it over the grave, let it sift through his fingers. "Now it's done."

"What can we say about Amelia?" Roz lifted a red rose. "She was mad—let's be honest. She died badly, and didn't live much better. But she sang to me, and to my children.

Her life gave me mine. So rest now, Great-grandmama." She dropped the rose onto the casket.

In turn the others sent a rose into the grave, and stepped back. "Let's give them a minute alone," Roz said, nodding toward Harper and Hayley.

"She's gone." Hayley closed her eyes, settled her mind. "I can feel it. I knew she was gone before you came up. Knew you'd found her before you told us. It was like the rope tying me to her was cut."

"Happiest day of my life. So far."

"Whatever she needed, she has." She stared down at the casket, at the flowers that lay on it. "I was so afraid, when you were in the pond, that you wouldn't come back to me."

"I wasn't finished with you. Not nearly." He took her shoulders, turned her away from the grave, toward him, toward the sunlight. "We've got a life to live. It's our time now."

He took the ring out of his pocket, slipped it onto her finger. "Fits now. It's yours now." He lowered his lips to hers. "Let's go get married."

"I think that's a great idea."

With their hands clasped, they walked away from death, into love, and life.

In Harper House, the wide halls and gracious rooms were quiet, full of sun, full of memories. Full of past, open to tomorrow.

No one sang there.

But its gardens bloomed.

Can't get enough of Nora Roberts?
Try the #1 *New York Times* bestselling
In Death series, by Nora Roberts
writing as J. D. Robb.

Turn the page to see where it all began . . .

NAKED IN DEATH

SHE WOKE IN THE DARK. THROUGH THE SLATS ON THE window shades, the first murky hint of dawn slipped, slanting shadowy bars over the bed. It was like waking in a cell.

For a moment she simply lay there, shuddering, imprisoned, while the dream faded. After ten years on the force, Eve still had dreams.

Six hours before, she'd killed a man, had watched death creep into his eyes. It wasn't the first time she'd exercised maximum force, or dreamed. She'd learned to accept the action and the consequences.

But it was the child that haunted her. The child she hadn't been in time to save. The child whose screams had echoed in the dreams with her own.

All the blood, Eve thought, scrubbing sweat from her face with her hands. Such a small little girl to have had so much blood in her. And she knew it was vital that she push it aside.

Standard departmental procedure meant that she would spend the morning in Testing. Any officer whose discharge of weapon resulted in termination of life was required to undergo emotional and psychiatric clearance before resuming duty. Eve considered the tests a mild pain in the ass.

She would beat them, as she'd beaten them before.

When she rose, the overheads went automatically to low setting, lighting her way into the bath. She winced once at her reflection. Her eyes were swollen from lack of sleep, her skin nearly as pale as the corpses she'd delegated to the ME.

Rather than dwell on it, she stepped into the shower, yawning.

"Give me one oh one degrees, full force," she said and shifted so that the shower spray hit her straight in the face.

She let it steam, lathered listlessly while she played through the events of the night before. She wasn't due in Testing until nine, and would use the next three hours to settle and let the dream fade away completely.

Small doubts and little regrets were often detected and could mean a second and more intense round with the machines and the owl-eyed technicians who ran them.

Eve didn't intend to be off the streets longer than twenty-four hours.

After pulling on a robe, she walked into the kitchen and programmed her AutoChef for coffee, black; toast, light. Through her window she could hear the heavy hum of air traffic carrying early commuters to offices, late ones home. She'd chosen the apartment years before because it was in a heavy ground and air pattern, and she liked the noise and crowds. On another yawn, she glanced out the window, followed the rattling journey of an aging airbus hauling laborers not fortunate enough to work in the city or by home 'links.

She brought the *New York Times* up on her monitor and scanned the headlines while the faux caffeine bolstered her system. The AutoChef had burned her toast again, but she ate it anyway, with a vague thought of springing for a replacement unit.

She was frowning over an article on a mass recall of droid cocker spaniels when her telelink blipped. Eve shifted to communications and watched her commanding officer flash onto the screen.

"Commander."

"Lieutenant." He gave her a brisk nod, noted the still-wet hair and sleepy eyes. "Incident at Twenty-seven West Broadway, eighteenth floor. You're primary."

Eve lifted a brow. "I'm on Testing. Subject terminated at twenty-two thirty-five."

"We have override," he said, without inflection. "Pick up your shield and weapon on the way to the incident. Code Five, Lieutenant."

"Yes, sir." His face flashed off even as she pushed back from the screen. Code Five meant she would report directly to her commander, and there would be no unsealed interdepartmental reports and no cooperation with the press.

In essence, it meant she was on her own.

BROADWAY WAS NOISY AND CROWDED, A PARTY THAT rowdy guests never left. Street, pedestrian, and sky traffic were miserable, choking the air with bodies and vehicles. In her old days in uniform she remembered it as a hot spot for wrecks and crushed tourists who were too busy gaping at the show to get out of the way.

Even at this hour steam was rising from the stationary and portable food stands that offered everything from rice noodles to soy dogs for the teeming crowds. She had to swerve to avoid an eager merchant on his smoking Glida-Grill, and took his flipped middle finger as a matter of course.

Eve double-parked and, skirting a man who smelled worse than his bottle of brew, stepped onto the sidewalk. She scanned the building first, fifty floors of gleaming metal that knifed into the sky from a hilt of concrete. She was propositioned twice before she reached the door.

Since this five-block area of West Broadway was affectionately termed Prostitute's Walk, she wasn't surprised. She flashed her badge for the uniform guarding the entrance.

"Lieutenant Dallas."

"Yes, sir." He skimmed his official CompuSeal over the door to keep out the curious, then led the way to the bank of elevators. "Eighteenth floor," he said when the doors swished shut behind them.

"Fill me in, Officer." Eve switched on her recorder and waited.

"I wasn't first on the scene, Lieutenant. Whatever happened upstairs is being kept upstairs. There's a badge inside waiting for you. We have a homicide, and a Code Five in number eighteen-oh-three."

"Who called it in?"

"I don't have that information."

He stayed where he was when the elevator opened. Eve stepped out and was alone in a narrow hallway. Security cameras tilted down at her, and her feet were almost soundless on the worn nap of the carpet as she approached 1803. Ignoring the hand plate, she announced herself, holding her badge up to eye level for the peep cam until the door opened.

"Dallas."

"Feeney." She smiled, pleased to see a familiar face. Ryan Feeney was an old friend and former partner who'd traded the street for a desk and a top-level position in the Electronics Detection Division. "So, they're sending computer pluckers these days."

"They wanted brass, and the best." His lips curved in his wide, rumpled face, but his eyes remained sober. He was a small, stubby man with small, stubby hands and rust-colored hair. "You look beat."

"Rough night."

"So I heard." He offered her one of the sugared nuts from the bag he habitually carried, studying her, and measuring if she was up to what was waiting in the bedroom beyond.

She was young for her rank, barely thirty, with wide brown eyes that had never had a chance to be naive. Her doe-brown hair was cropped short, for convenience rather than style, but suited her triangular face with its razor-edge cheekbones and slight dent in the chin.

She was tall, rangy, with a tendency to look thin, but Feeney knew there were solid muscles beneath the leather jacket. But Eve had more—there was also a brain, and a heart.

"This one's going to be touchy, Dallas."

"I picked that up already. Who's the victim?"

"Sharon DeBlass, granddaughter of Senator DeBlass."

Neither meant anything to her. "Politics isn't my forte, Feeney."

"The gentleman from Virginia, extreme right, old money. The granddaughter took a sharp left a few years back, moved to New York and became a licensed companion."

"She was a hooker." Dallas glanced around the apartment. It was furnished in obsessive modern—glass and thin chrome, signed holograms on the walls, recessed bar in bold red. The wide mood screen behind the bar bled with mixing and merging shapes and colors in cool pastels.

Neat as a virgin, Eve mused, and cold as a whore. "No surprise, given her choice of real estate."

"Politics makes it delicate. Victim was twenty-four, Caucasian female. She bought it in bed."

Eve only lifted a brow. "Seems poetic, since she'd been bought there. How'd she die?"

"That's the next problem. I want you to see for yourself."

As they crossed the room, each took out a slim container, sprayed their hands front and back to seal in oils and fingerprints. At the doorway, Eve sprayed the bottom of her boots to slicken them so that she would pick up no fibers, stray hairs, or skin.

Eve was already wary. Under normal circumstances there would have been two other investigators on a homicide scene, with recorders for sound and pictures. Forensics would have been waiting with their usual snarly impatience to sweep the scene.

The fact that only Feeney had been assigned with her meant that there were a lot of eggshells to be walked over.

"Security cameras in the lobby, elevator, and hallways," Eve commented.

"I've already tagged the discs." Feeney opened the bedroom door and let her enter first.

It wasn't pretty. Death rarely was a peaceful, religious experience to Eve's mind. It was the nasty end, indifferent to saint and sinner. But this was shocking, like a stage deliberately set to offend.

The bed was huge, slicked with what appeared to be genuine satin sheets the color of ripe peaches. Small, soft-focused spotlights were trained on its center where the naked woman was cupped in the gentle dip of the floating mattress.

The mattress moved with obscenely graceful undulations to the rhythm of programmed music slipping through the headboard.

She was beautiful still, a cameo face with a tumbling waterfall of flaming red hair, emerald eyes that stared glassily at the mirrored ceiling, long, milk-white limbs that called to mind visions of *Swan Lake* as the motion of the bed gently rocked them.

They weren't artistically arranged now, but spread lewdly so that the dead woman formed a final X dead-center of the bed.

There was a hole in her forehead, one in her chest, another horribly gaping between the open thighs. Blood had splattered on the glossy sheets, pooled, dripped, and stained.

There were splashes of it on the lacquered walls, like lethal paintings scrawled by an evil child.

So much blood was a rare thing, and she had seen much too much of it the night before to take the scene as calmly as she would have preferred.

She had to swallow once, hard, and force herself to block out the image of a small child.

"You got the scene on record?"

"Yep."

"Then turn that damn thing off." She let out a breath after Feeney located the controls that silenced the music. The bed flowed to stillness. "The wounds," Eve murmured, stepping closer to examine them. "Too neat for a knife. Too messy for a laser." A flash came to her—old training films, old videos, old viciousness.

"Christ, Feeney, these look like bullet wounds."

Feeney reached into his pocket and drew out a sealed bag. "Whoever did it left a souvenir." He passed the bag to Eve. "An antique like this has to go for eight, ten thousand for a legal collection, twice that on the black market."

Fascinated, Eve turned the sealed revolver over in her hand. "It's heavy," she said half to herself. "Bulky."

"Thirty-eight caliber," he told her. "First one I've seen outside of a museum. This one's a Smith and Wesson, Model Ten, blue steel." He looked at it with some affection. "Real classic piece, used to be standard police issue up until the latter part of the twentieth. They stopped making them in about twenty-two, twenty-three, when the gun ban was passed."

"You're the history buff." Which explained why he was with her. "Looks new." She sniffed through the bag, caught the scent of oil and burning. "Somebody took good care of this. Steel fired into flesh," she mused as she passed the bag back to Feeney. "Ugly way to die, and the first I've seen it in my ten years with the department."

"Second for me. About fifteen years ago, Lower East Side, party got out of hand. Guy shot five people with a twenty-two before he realized it wasn't a toy. Hell of a mess."

"Fun and games," Eve murmured. "We'll scan the collectors, see how many we can locate who own one like this. Somebody might have reported a robbery."

"Might have."

"It's more likely it came through the black market." Eve glanced back at the body. "If she's been in the business for a few years, she'd have discs, records of her clients, her trick books." She frowned. "With Code Five, I'll have to do the door-to-door myself. Not a simple sex crime," she said with a sigh. "Whoever did it set it up. The antique weapon, the wounds themselves, almost ruler-straight down the body, the lights, the pose. Who called it in, Feeney?"

"The killer." He waited until her eyes came back to him. "From right here. Called the station. See how the bedside unit's aimed at her face? That's what came in. Video, no audio."

"He's into showmanship." Eve let out a breath. "Clever bastard, arrogant, cocky. He had sex with her first. I'd bet my badge on it. Then he gets up and does it." She lifted her arm, aiming, lowering it as she counted off, "One, two, three."

"That's cold," murmured Feeney.

"He's cold. He smooths down the sheets after. See how neat they are? He arranges her, spreads her open so nobody can have any doubts as to how she made her living. He does it carefully, practically measuring, so that she's perfectly aligned. Center of the bed, arms and legs equally apart. Doesn't turn off the bed 'cause it's part of the show. He leaves the gun because he wants us to know right away he's no ordinary man. He's got an ego. He doesn't want to waste time letting the body be discovered eventually. He wants it now. That instant gratification."

"She was licensed for men and women," Feeney pointed out, but Eve shook her head.

"It's not a woman. A woman wouldn't have left her looking both beautiful and obscene. No, I don't think it's a woman. Let's see what we can find. Have you gone into her computer yet?"

"No. It's your case, Dallas. I'm only authorized to assist."

"See if you can access her client files." Eve went to the dresser and began to carefully search drawers.

Expensive taste, Eve reflected. There were several items

of real silk, the kind no simulation could match. The bottle of scent on the dresser was exclusive, and smelled, after a quick sniff, like expensive sex.

The contents of the drawers were meticulously ordered, lingerie folded precisely, sweaters arranged according to color and material. The closet was the same.

Obviously the victim had a love affair with clothes and a taste for the best and took scrupulous care of what she owned.

And she'd died naked.

"Kept good records," Feeney called out. "It's all here. Her client list, appointments—including her required monthly health exam and her weekly trip to the beauty salon. She used the Trident Clinic for the first and Paradise for the second."

"Both top-of-the-line. I've got a friend who saved for a year so she could have one day for the works at Paradise. Takes all kinds."

"My wife's sister went for it for her twenty-fifth anniversary. Cost damn near as much as my kid's wedding. Hello, we've got her personal address book."

"Good. Copy all of it, will you, Feeney?" At his low whistle, she looked over her shoulder, glimpsed the small gold-edged palm computer in his hand. "What?"

"We've got a lot of high-powered names in here. Politics, entertainment, money, money, money. Interesting, our girl has Roarke's private number."

"Roarke who?"

"Just Roarke, as far as I know. Big money there. Kind of guy that touches shit and turns it into gold bricks. You've got to start reading more than the sports page, Dallas."

"Hey, I read the headlines. Did you hear about the cocker spaniel recall?"

"Roarke's always big news," Feeney said patiently.

"He's got one of the finest art collections in the world. Arts and antiques," he continued, noting when Eve clicked in and turned to him. "He's a licensed gun collector. Rumor is he knows how to use them."

"I'll pay him a visit."

"You'll be lucky to get within a mile of him."

"I'm feeling lucky." Eve crossed over to the body to slip her hands under the sheets.

"The man's got powerful friends, Dallas. You can't afford to so much as whisper he's linked to this until you've got something solid."

"Feeney, you know it's a mistake to tell me that." But even as she started to smile, her fingers brushed against something between cold flesh and bloody sheets. "There's something under her." Carefully, Eve lifted the shoulder, eased her fingers over.

"Paper," she murmured. "Sealed." With her protected thumb, she wiped at a smear of blood until she could read the protected sheet.

ONE OF SIX

"It looks hand-printed," she said to Feeney and held it out. "Our boy's more than clever, more than arrogant. And he isn't finished."

#1 *NEW YORK TIMES* BESTSELLING AUTHOR

NORA ROBERTS

"You can't bottle wish fulfillment, but Ms. Roberts certainly knows how to put it on the page."

—The New York Times

For a complete list of titles,
please visit prh.com/noraroberts

#1 *New York Times* bestselling author Nora Roberts presents the second novel of her In the Garden trilogy, as three women must discover the secrets from the past contained within their historic home.

A Harper has always lived at Harper House, the centuries-old mansion just outside of Memphis. And for as long as anyone alive remembers, the ghostly Harper Bride has walked the halls, singing lullabies at night . . .

At forty-seven, Rosalind Harper is a woman whose experiences have made her strong enough to bend without breaking—and to weather any storm. A widow with three grown sons, she survived a disastrous second marriage and built her In the Garden nursery from the ground up. Through the years, In the Garden has become more than just a thriving business—it is a symbol of hope and independence to Roz, and to the two women she shares it with. Newly engaged Stella and new mother Hayley are the sisters of her heart, and together, the three of them are the future of In the Garden.

Hired to investigate Roz's Harper ancestors, Dr. Mitchell Carnegie finds himself just as intrigued by Roz herself. And as they begin to resurrect old secrets, Roz is shocked to find herself falling for the fascinating genealogist—even when he learns more about her than anyone has before . . .

Turn the page for a complete list of titles by Nora Roberts and J. D. Robb from Berkley . . .

Nora Roberts

HOT ICE
SACRED SINS
BRAZEN VIRTUE
SWEET REVENGE
PUBLIC SECRETS
GENUINE LIES
CARNAL INNOCENCE
HONEST ILLUSIONS
DIVINE EVIL
PRIVATE SCANDALS
HIDDEN RICHES
TRUE BETRAYALS
MONTANA SKY
SANCTUARY
HOMEPORT
THE REEF
RIVER'S END
CAROLINA MOON
THE VILLA
MIDNIGHT BAYOU
THREE FATES
BIRTHRIGHT
NORTHERN LIGHTS
BLUE SMOKE
ANGELS FALL
HIGH NOON
TRIBUTE
BLACK HILLS
THE SEARCH
CHASING FIRE
THE WITNESS
WHISKEY BEACH
THE COLLECTOR
TONIGHT AND ALWAYS
THE LIAR
THE OBSESSION

Series

Irish Born Trilogy
BORN IN FIRE
BORN IN ICE
BORN IN SHAME

Dream Trilogy
DARING TO DREAM
HOLDING THE DREAM
FINDING THE DREAM

Chesapeake Bay Saga
SEA SWEPT
RISING TIDES
INNER HARBOR
CHESAPEAKE BLUE

Gallaghers of Ardmore Trilogy
JEWELS OF THE SUN
TEARS OF THE MOON
HEART OF THE SEA

Three Sisters Island Trilogy
DANCE UPON THE AIR
HEAVEN AND EARTH
FACE THE FIRE

Key Trilogy
KEY OF LIGHT
KEY OF KNOWLEDGE
KEY OF VALOR

In the Garden Trilogy
BLUE DAHLIA
BLACK ROSE
RED LILY

Circle Trilogy
MORRIGAN'S CROSS
DANCE OF THE GODS
VALLEY OF SILENCE

Sign of Seven Trilogy
BLOOD BROTHERS
THE HOLLOW
THE PAGAN STONE

Bride Quartet
VISION IN WHITE
BED OF ROSES
SAVOR THE MOMENT
HAPPY EVER AFTER

The Inn BoonsBoro Trilogy
THE NEXT ALWAYS
THE LAST BOYFRIEND
THE PERFECT HOPE

The Cousins O'Dwyer Trilogy
DARK WITCH
SHADOW SPELL
BLOOD MAGICK

The Guardians Trilogy
STARS OF FORTUNE
BAY OF SIGHS
ISLAND OF GLASS

Ebooks by Nora Roberts

Cordina's Royal Family
AFFAIRE ROYALE
COMMAND PERFORMANCE
THE PLAYBOY PRINCE
CORDINA'S CROWN JEWEL

The Donovan Legacy
CAPTIVATED
ENTRANCED
CHARMED
ENCHANTED

The O'Hurleys
THE LAST HONEST WOMAN
DANCE TO THE PIPER
SKIN DEEP
WITHOUT A TRACE

Night Tales
NIGHT SHIFT
NIGHT SHADOW
NIGHTSHADE
NIGHT SMOKE
NIGHT SHIELD

The MacGregors
PLAYING THE ODDS
TEMPTING FATE
ALL THE POSSIBILITIES
ONE MAN'S ART
FOR NOW, FOREVER
REBELLION/IN FROM THE COLD
THE MACGREGOR BRIDES
THE WINNING HAND
THE MACGREGOR GROOMS
THE PERFECT NEIGHBOR

The Calhouns
COURTING CATHERINE
A MAN FOR AMANDA
FOR THE LOVE OF LILAH
SUZANNA'S SURRENDER
MEGAN'S MATE

Irish Legacy
IRISH THOROUGHBRED
IRISH ROSE
IRISH REBEL

LOVING JACK
BEST LAID PLANS
LAWLESS

BLITHE IMAGES
SONG OF THE WEST
SEARCH FOR LOVE
ISLAND OF FLOWERS
THE HEART'S VICTORY
FROM THIS DAY
HER MOTHER'S KEEPER
ONCE MORE WITH FEELING
REFLECTIONS
DANCE OF DREAMS
UNTAMED
THIS MAGIC MOMENT
ENDINGS AND BEGINNINGS
STORM WARNING
SULLIVAN'S WOMAN
FIRST IMPRESSIONS
A MATTER OF CHOICE

LESS OF A STRANGER
THE LAW IS A LADY
RULES OF THE GAME
OPPOSITES ATTRACT
THE RIGHT PATH
PARTNERS
BOUNDARY LINES
DUAL IMAGE
TEMPTATION
LOCAL HERO
THE NAME OF THE GAME
GABRIEL'S ANGEL
THE WELCOMING
TIME WAS
TIMES CHANGE
SUMMER LOVE
HOLIDAY WISHES

Nora Roberts & J. D. Robb

REMEMBER WHEN

J. D. Robb

NAKED IN DEATH
GLORY IN DEATH
IMMORTAL IN DEATH
RAPTURE IN DEATH
CEREMONY IN DEATH
VENGEANCE IN DEATH
HOLIDAY IN DEATH
CONSPIRACY IN DEATH
LOYALTY IN DEATH
WITNESS IN DEATH
JUDGMENT IN DEATH
BETRAYAL IN DEATH
SEDUCTION IN DEATH
REUNION IN DEATH
PURITY IN DEATH
PORTRAIT IN DEATH
IMITATION IN DEATH
DIVIDED IN DEATH
VISIONS IN DEATH
SURVIVOR IN DEATH
ORIGIN IN DEATH
MEMORY IN DEATH
BORN IN DEATH
INNOCENT IN DEATH
CREATION IN DEATH
STRANGERS IN DEATH
SALVATION IN DEATH
PROMISES IN DEATH
KINDRED IN DEATH
FANTASY IN DEATH
INDULGENCE IN DEATH
TREACHERY IN DEATH
NEW YORK TO DALLAS
CELEBRITY IN DEATH
DELUSION IN DEATH
CALCULATED IN DEATH
THANKLESS IN DEATH
CONCEALED IN DEATH
FESTIVE IN DEATH
OBSESSION IN DEATH
DEVOTED IN DEATH
BROTHERHOOD IN DEATH
APPRENTICE IN DEATH

Anthologies

FROM THE HEART
A LITTLE MAGIC
A LITTLE FATE

MOON SHADOWS
(with Jill Gregory, Ruth Ryan Langan, and Marianne Willman)

The Once Upon Series

(with Jill Gregory, Ruth Ryan Langan, and Marianne Willman)

ONCE UPON A CASTLE
ONCE UPON A STAR
ONCE UPON A DREAM
ONCE UPON A ROSE
ONCE UPON A KISS
ONCE UPON A MIDNIGHT

SILENT NIGHT
(with Susan Plunkett, Dee Holmes, and Claire Cross)

OUT OF THIS WORLD
(with Laurell K. Hamilton, Susan Krinard, and Maggie Shayne)

BUMP IN THE NIGHT
(with Mary Blayney, Ruth Ryan Langan, and Mary Kay McComas)

DEAD OF NIGHT
(with Mary Blayney, Ruth Ryan Langan, and Mary Kay McComas)

THREE IN DEATH

SUITE 606
(with Mary Blayney, Ruth Ryan Langan, and Mary Kay McComas)

IN DEATH

THE LOST
(with Patricia Gaffney, Mary Blayney, and Ruth Ryan Langan)

THE OTHER SIDE
(with Mary Blayney, Patricia Gaffney, Ruth Ryan Langan, and Mary Kay McComas)

TIME OF DEATH

THE UNQUIET
(with Mary Blayney, Patricia Gaffney, Ruth Ryan Langan, and Mary Kay McComas)

MIRROR, MIRROR
(with Mary Blayney, Elaine Fox, Mary Kay McComas, and R. C. Ryan)

DOWN THE RABBIT HOLE
(with Mary Blayney, Elaine Fox, Mary Kay McComas, and R. C. Ryan)

Also available . . .

THE OFFICIAL NORA ROBERTS COMPANION
(edited by Denise Little and Laura Hayden)

NORA ROBERTS

BLACK ROSE

JOVE
New York

A JOVE BOOK
Published by Berkley
An imprint of Penguin Random House LLC
375 Hudson Street, New York, New York 10014

ISBN: 9780515138658

Jove mass-market edition / June 2005
Berkley trade paperback edition / February 2014

Printed in the United States of America
31 33 35 34 32

Cover illustration by Yuan Lee
Cover design by Steven Ferlauto

For Stacie
It's wise for a mother to love the woman her son loves.
But it's a lovely gift to like the woman
who becomes your daughter.
Thanks for the gift.

A stock plant is grown purely to provide cutting material. It can be encouraged to produce the best type of growth for cuttings while plants that are grown for garden display can be left untouched.

American Horticultural Society
Plant Propagation

If you would know secrets, look for them in grief or pleasure.

George Herbert

PROLOGUE

Memphis, Tennessee

December 1892

SHE DRESSED CAREFULLY, ATTENDING TO THE DETAILS of her appearance as she hadn't done for months. Her personal maid had run off weeks before, and she had neither the wit nor the will to hire another. So she spent an hour with the curling rods herself—as she had in the years before she'd been kept so lavishly—meticulously coiling and arranging her freshly rinsed hair.

It had lost its bright gold luster over the long, bleary autumn, but she knew what lotions and potions would bring back its shine, what pots of paint to select to put false color in her cheeks, on her lips.

She knew all the tricks of the trade. How else could she have caught the eye of a man like Reginald Harper? How else had she seduced him into making her his mistress?

She would use them again, all of them, Amelia thought, to seduce him once more, and to urge him to do everything that must be done.

He hadn't come, in all this time, in all these months, he hadn't come to her. So she'd been forced to send notes to his businesses, begging him to come, only to be ignored.

Ignored after all she had done, all she had been, all she had lost.

What choice had she had but to send more notes, and to his home? To the grand Harper House where his pale wife reigned. Where a mistress could never walk.

Hadn't she given him all he could ask, all he could want? She'd traded her body for the comfort of this house, the convenience of servants, for the baubles, like the pearl drops she fixed on her ears now.

Small prices to pay for a man of his stature and wealth, and such had been the limits of her ambitions once. A man only, and what he could give her. But he'd given her more than either of them had bargained for. The loss of it was more than she could bear.

Why had he not come to comfort her? To grieve with her?

Had she complained, ever? Had she ever turned him from her bed? Or mentioned even once the other women he kept?

She had given him her youth, and her beauty. And, it seemed, her health.

And he would desert her now? Turn away from her *now*?

They said the baby had been dead at birth. Stillborn, they said. A stillborn girl child that had perished inside her.

But . . . but . . .

Hadn't she felt it move? Felt it kick, and grow vital under her heart? In her heart. This child she hadn't wanted who had become her world. Her life. The son she grew inside her.

The son, the son, she thought now as her fingers plucked at the buttons of her gown, as her painted lips formed the words over and over.

She'd heard him cry. Yes, yes, she was sure of it. Sometimes she heard him cry still, in the night, crying for her to come and soothe him.

But when she went to the nursery, looked in the crib, it was empty. Like her womb was empty.

They said she was mad. Oh, she heard what servants she had left whispering, she saw the way they looked at her. But she wasn't mad.

Wasn't mad, wasn't mad, she told herself as she paced the bedroom she'd once treated like a palace of sensuality.

Now the linens were rarely changed, and the drapes always drawn tight to block out the city. And things went missing. Her servants were thieves. Oh, she knew they were thieves and scoundrels. And spies.

They watched her, and they whispered.

One night they would kill her in her bed. One night.

She couldn't sleep for the fear of it. Couldn't sleep for the cries of her son inside her head. Calling her. Calling her.

But she'd gone to the voodoo queen, she reminded herself. Gone to her for protection, and knowledge. She'd paid for both with the ruby bracelet Reginald had once given her. The stones shaped like bloody hearts against the icy glitter of diamonds.

She'd paid for the gris-gris she kept under her pillow, and in a silk bag over her heart. She'd paid, and dearly, for the raising spell. A spell that had failed.

Because her child lived. This was the knowledge the voodoo queen had given her, and it was worth more than ten thousand rubies.

Her child lived, he lived, and now he must be found. He must be brought back to her, where he belonged.

Reginald must find him, must pay whatever needed to be paid.

Careful, careful, she warned herself as she felt the scream beating at her throat. He would only believe her if she remained calm. He would only heed her if she were beautiful.

Beauty seduced men. With beauty and charm, a woman could have whatever she wanted.

She turned to the mirror and saw what she needed to see. Beauty, charm, grace. She didn't see that the red gown sagged at the breasts, bagged at the hips, and turned her pale skin a sallow yellow. The mirror reflected the tumbling tangle of curls, the overbright eyes, and the harshly rouged cheeks, but her eyes, Amelia's eyes, saw what she had once been.

Young and beautiful, desirable and sly.

So she went downstairs to wait for her lover, and under her breath, she sang.

"Lavender's blue, dilly, dilly. Lavender's green."

In the parlor a fire was burning, and the gaslight was lit. So the servants would be careful, too, she thought with a tight smile. They knew the master was expected, and the master held the purse strings.

No matter, she would tell Reginald they needed to go, all of them, and be replaced.

And she wanted a nursemaid hired for her son, for James, when he was returned to her. An Irish girl, she thought. They were cheerful around babies, she believed. She wanted a cheerful nursery for her James.

Though she eyed the whiskey on the sideboard, she poured a small glass of wine instead. And settled down to wait.

Her nerves began to fray as the hour grew late. She had a second glass of wine, then a third. And when she saw through the window his carriage pull up, she forgot to be careful and calm and flew to the door herself.

"Reginald. Reginald." Her grief and despair sprang out of her like snakes, hissing and coiling. She threw herself at him.

"Control yourself, Amelia." His hands closed over her bony shoulders, nudged her back. "What will the neighbors say?"

He shut the door quickly, then with one steely look had a hovering servant rushing forward to take his hat and walking stick.

"I don't care! Oh, why haven't you come sooner? I've needed you so. Did you get my letters? The servants, the servants lie. They didn't post them. I'm a prisoner here."

"Don't be ridiculous." A momentary disgust flickered over his face as he evaded her next attempt at an embrace. "We agreed you'd never attempt to contact me at my home, Amelia."

"You didn't come. I've been alone. I—"

"I've been occupied. Come now. Sit. Compose yourself."

Still, she clung to his arm as he led her into the parlor. "Reginald. The baby. The baby."

"Yes, yes." He disentangled himself, nudged her into a chair. "It's unfortunate," he said as he moved to the sideboard to pour himself a whiskey. "The doctor said there was nothing to be done, and you needed rest and quiet. I've heard you've been unwell."

"Lies. It's all a lie."

He turned to her, his gaze taking in her face, the ill-fitting gown. "I can see for myself you're not well, Amelia. I think perhaps some sea air. It would do you good." His smile was cool as he leaned back against the mantel. "How would you like an ocean crossing? I think it would be just the thing to calm your nerves and bring you back to health."

"I want my *child*. He's all I need."

"The child is gone."

"No, no, no." She sprang up to clutch at him again. "They stole him. He lives, Reginald. Our child lives. The doctor, the midwife, they planned it. I know it all now, I understand it all. You must go to the police, Reginald. They'll listen to you. You must pay whatever ransom they demand."

"This is madness, Amelia." He pried her hand from his lapel, then brushed at the creases her fingers had caused in the material. "I'll certainly not go to the police."

"Then I will. Tomorrow I'll go to the authorities."

The cold smile faded until his face was hard as stone. "You will do nothing of the kind. You will have a cruise to Europe, and ten thousand dollars to assist you in settling in England. They will be my parting gifts to you."

"Parting?" She groped for the arm of a chair, melted into it as her legs gave way. "You—you would leave me now?"

"There can be nothing more between us. I'll see to it that you're well set, and I believe you'll regain your health with a sea voyage. In London you're bound to find another protector."

"How can I go to London when my son—"

"You will go," he interrupted, then sipped his drink. "Or I will give you nothing. You have no son. You have nothing but what I deem to give you. This house and everything in it, the clothes on your back, the jewels you wear are mine. You'd be wise to remember how easily I can take it all away."

"Take it away," she whispered, and something in his face, something in her fractured mind gave her truth. "You want to get rid of me because . . . you know. It's you who've taken the baby."

He finished his drink as he studied her. Then set the empty glass on the mantel. "Do you think I'd allow a creature like you to raise my son?"

"My son!" She sprang up again, hands curled like claws.

The slap stopped her. In the two years he had been her protector, he had never raised a hand to her.

"Listen to me now, and carefully. I will not have my son known as a bastard, one born of a whore. He will be raised at Harper House, as my legitimate heir."

"Your wife—"

"Does what she is told. As will you, Amelia."

"I'll go to the police."

"And tell them what? The doctor and midwife who attended you will attest that you delivered a stillborn girl, while others will attest my wife delivered a healthy boy. Your reputation, Amelia, will not stand to mine, or theirs. Your own servants will swear to it, and to the fact that you've been ill, and behaving strangely."

"How can you do this?"

"I need a son. Do you think I selected you out of affection? You're young, healthy—or were. You were paid, and paid well for your services. You will be recompensed for this one."

"You won't keep him from me. He's mine."

"Nothing is yours but what I allow you. You would have rid yourself of him, had you been given the opportunity. You'll come nowhere near him, now or ever. You will make the crossing in three weeks. A deposit of ten thousand dollars will be put in your account. Until that time your bills will continue to come to me for payment. It's all you'll get."

"I'll kill you!" she shouted when he started out of the parlor.

At this, for the first time since he'd arrived, he looked amused. "You're pathetic. Whores generally are. Be assured of this, if you come near me or mine, Amelia, I will have you arrested, and put in an asylum for the criminally insane." He gestured for the servant to bring his hat and stick. "You wouldn't find it to your taste."

She screamed, tearing at her hair and her gown; she screamed until blood ran from her flesh from her own nails.

When her mind snapped, she walked up the stairs in her tattered gown, humming a lullaby.

ONE

Harper House

December 2004

DAWN, THE AWAKENING PROMISE OF IT, WAS HER FAvorite time to run. The running itself was just something that had to be done, three days a week, like any other chore or responsibility. Rosalind Harper did what had to be done.

She ran for her health. A woman who'd just had—she could hardly say "celebrated" at this stage of her life—her forty-seventh birthday had to mind her health. She ran to keep strong, as she desired and needed strength. And she ran for vanity. Her body would never again be what it had been at twenty, or even thirty, but, by God, it would be the best body she could manage at forty-seven.

She had no husband, no lover, but she did have an image to uphold. She was a Harper, and Harpers had their pride.

But, Jesus, maintenance was a bitch.

Wearing sweats against the dawn chill, she slipped out of her bedroom by the terrace door. The house was sleeping still. Her house that had been too empty was now occupied again, and rarely completely quiet any longer.

There was David, her surrogate son, who kept her house in order, kept her entertained when she needed entertaining, and stayed out of her way when she needed solitude.

No one knew her moods quite like David.

And there was Stella, and her two precious boys. It had been a good day, Roz thought as she limbered up on the terrace, when she'd hired Stella Rothchild to manage her nursery.

Of course, Stella would be moving before much longer and taking those sweet boys with her. Still, once she was married to Logan—and wasn't that a fine match—they'd only be a few miles away.

Hayley would still be here, infusing the house with all that youth and energy. It had been another stroke of luck, and a vague and distant family connection, that had Hayley, then six-months pregnant, landing on her doorstep. In Hayley she had the daughter she'd secretly longed for, and the bonus of an honorary grandchild with the darling little Lily.

She hadn't realized how lonely she'd been, Roz thought, until those girls had come along to fill the void. With two of her own three sons moved away, the house had become too big, too quiet. And a part of her dreaded the day when Harper, her firstborn, her rock, would leave the guesthouse a stone's throw from the main.

But that was life. No one knew better than a gardener that life never stayed static. Cycles were necessary, for without them there was no bloom.

She took the stairs down at an easy jog, enjoying the way the early mists shrouded her winter gardens. Look how pretty her lambs ear was with its soft silvery foliage covered in dew. And the birds had yet to bother the bright fruit on her red chokeberry.

Walking to give her muscles time to warm, and to give herself the pleasure of the gardens, she skirted around the side of the house to the front.

She increased to a jog on the way down the drive, a tall, willowy woman with a short, careless cap of black hair. Her eyes, a honeyed whiskey brown, scanned the grounds—the towering magnolias, the delicate dogwoods, the placement of ornamental shrubs, the flood of pansies she'd planted only weeks before, and the beds that would wait a bit longer to break into bloom.

To her mind, there were no grounds in western Tennessee that could compete with Harper House. Just as there was no house that could compare with its dignified elegance.

Out of habit, she turned at the end of the drive, jogged in place to study it in the pearly mists.

It stood grandly, she thought, with its melding of Greek Revival and Gothic styles, the warm yellow stone mellow against the clean white trim. Its double staircase rose up to the balcony wrapping the second level, and served as a crown for the covered entryway on the ground level.

She loved the tall windows, the lacy woodwork on the rail of the third floor, the sheer space of it, and the heritage it stood for.

She had prized it, cared for it, worked for it, since it had come into her hands at her parents' death. She had raised her sons there, and when she'd lost her husband, she'd grieved there.

One day she would pass it to Harper as it had passed to her. And she thanked God for the absolute knowledge that he would tend it and love it just as she did.

What it had cost her was nothing compared with what it gave, even in this single moment, standing at the end of the drive, looking back through the morning mists.

But standing there wasn't going to get her three miles done. She headed west, keeping close to the side of the road, though there'd be little to no traffic this early.

To take her mind off the annoyance of exercise, she started reviewing her list of things to do that day.

She had some good seedlings going for annuals that should be ready to have their seed leaves removed. She needed to check all the seedlings for signs of damping off. Some of the older stock would be ready for pricking off.

And, she remembered, Stella had asked for more amaryllis, more forced-bulb planters, more wreaths and poinsettias for the holiday sales. Hayley could handle the wreaths. The girl had a good hand at crafting.

Then there were the field-grown Christmas trees and hollies to deal with. Thank God she could leave that end to Logan.

She had to check with Harper, to see if he had any more of the Christmas cacti he'd grafted ready to go. She wanted a couple for herself.

She juggled all the nursery business in her mind even as she passed In the Garden. It was tempting—it always was—to veer off the road onto that crushed-stone entryway, to take an indulgent solo tour of what she'd built from the ground up.

Stella had gone all out for the holidays, Roz noted with pleasure, grouping green, pink, white, and red poinsettias into a pool of seasonal color in the front of the low-slung house that served as the entrance to the retail space. She'd hung yet another wreath on the door, tiny white lights around it, and the small white pine she'd had dug from the field stood decorated on the front porch.

White-faced pansies, glossy hollies, hardy sage added more interest and would help ring up those holiday sales.

Resisting temptation, Roz continued down the road.

She had to carve out some time, if not today, then certainly later this week, to finish up her Christmas shopping. Or at least put a bigger dent in it. There were holiday parties to attend, and the one she'd decided to give. It had been awhile since she'd opened the house to entertain in a big way.

The divorce, she admitted, was at least partially to blame for that. She'd hardly felt like hosting parties when she'd felt stupid and stung and more than a bit mortified by her foolish, and mercifully brief, union to a liar and a cheat.

But it was time to put that aside now, she reminded herself, just as she'd put him aside. The fact that Bryce Clerk was back in Memphis made it only more important that she live her life, publically and privately, exactly as she chose.

At the mile-and-a-half mark, a point she judged by an old, lightning-struck hickory, she started back. The thin fog had dampened her hair, her sweatshirt, but her muscles felt warm and loose. It was a bitch, she mused, that everything they said about exercise was true.

She spotted a deer meandering across the road, her coat thickened for winter, her eyes on alert by the intrusion of a human.

You're beautiful, Roz thought, puffing a little on that last half mile. Now, stay the hell out of my gardens. Another note went in her file to give her gardens another treatment of repellant before the deer and her pals decided to come around for a snack.

Roz was just making the turn into the drive when she heard muffled footsteps, then saw the figure coming her way. Even with the mists she had no trouble identifying the other early riser.

They both stopped, jogged in place, and she grinned at her son.

"Up with the worms this morning."

"Thought I'd be up and out early enough to catch you." He scooped a hand through his dark hair. "All that celebrating for Thanksgiving, then your birthday, I figured I'd better work off the excess before Christmas hits."

"You never gain an ounce. It's annoying."

"Feel soft." He rolled his shoulders, then his eyes, whiskey brown like hers, and laughed. "Besides, I gotta keep up with my mama."

He looked like her. There was no denying she'd stamped herself on his face. But when he smiled, she saw his father. "That'll be the day, pal of mine. How far you going?"

"How far'd you?"

"Three miles."

He flashed a grin. "Then I'll do four." He gave her a light pat on the cheek as he passed.

"Should've told him five, just to get his goat." She chuckled, and slowing to a cool-down walk, started down the drive.

The house shimmered out of the mists. She thought: Thank God that's over for another day. And she circled around to go in as she'd left.

The house was still quiet, and lovely. And haunted.

She'd showered and changed for work, and had started down the central stairs that bisected the wings when she heard the first stirrings.

Stella's boys getting ready for school, Lily fussing for her breakfast. Good sounds, Roz thought. Busy, family sounds she'd missed.

Of course, she'd had the house full only a couple weeks earlier, with all her boys home for Thanksgiving and her birthday. Austin and Mason would be back for Christmas. A mother of grown sons couldn't ask for better.

God knew there'd been plenty of times when they were growing up that she'd yearned for some quiet. Just an hour of absolute peace where she had nothing more exciting to do than soak in a hot tub.

Then she'd had too much time on her hands, hadn't she? Too much quiet, too much empty space. So she'd ended up marrying some slick son of a bitch who'd helped himself to her money so he could impress the bimbos he'd cheated on her with.

Spilled milk, Roz reminded herself. And it wasn't constructive to dwell on it.

She walked into the kitchen where David was already whipping something in a bowl, and the seductive fragrance of fresh coffee filled the air.

"Morning, gorgeous. How's my best girl?"

"Up and at 'em anyway." She went to a cupboard for a mug. "How was the date last night?"

"Promising. He likes Grey Goose martinis and John Waters movies. We'll try for a second round this weekend. Sit yourself down. I'm making French toast."

"French toast?" It was a personal weakness. "Damn it, David, I just ran three miles to keep my ass from falling all the way to the back of my knees, then you hit me with French toast."

"You have a beautiful ass, and it's nowhere near the back of your knees."

"Yet," she muttered, but she sat. "I passed Harper at the end of the drive. He finds out what's on the menu, he'll be sniffing at the back door."

"I'm making plenty."

She sipped her coffee while he heated up the skillet.

He was movie-star handsome, only a year older than her own Harper, and one of the delights of her life. As a boy he'd run tame in her house, and now he all but ran it.

"David . . . I caught myself thinking about Bryce twice this morning. What do you think that means?"

"Means you need this French toast," he said while he soaked thick slices of bread in his magic batter. "And you've probably got yourself a case of the mid-holiday blues."

"I kicked him out right before Christmas. I guess that's it."

"And a merry one it was, with that bastard out in the cold. I wish it *had* been cold," he added. "Raining ice and frogs and pestilence."

"I'm going to ask you something I never did while it was going on. Why didn't you ever tell me how much you disliked him?"

"Probably the same reason you didn't tell me how much you disliked that out-of-work actor with the fake Brit accent I thought I was crazy about a few years back. I love you."

"It's a good reason."

He'd started a fire in the little kitchen hearth, so she angled her body toward it, sipped coffee, felt steady and solid.

"You know if you could just age twenty years and go straight, we could live with each other in sin. I think that would be just fine."

"Sugar-pie." He slid the bread into the skillet. "You're the only girl in the world who'd tempt me."

She smiled, and resting her elbow on the table, set her chin on her fist. "Sun's breaking through," she stated. "It's going to be a pretty day."

A PRETTY DAY IN EARLY DECEMBER MEANT A BUSY ONE for a garden center. Roz had so much to do she was grateful she hadn't resisted the breakfast David had heaped on her. She missed lunch.

In her propagation house she had a full table covered with seed trays. She'd already separated out specimens too young for pricking off. And now began the first transplanting with those she deemed ready.

She lined up her containers, the cell packs, the individual pots or peat cubes. It was one of her favorite tasks, even more than sowing, this placing of a strong seedling in the home it would occupy until planting time.

Until planting time, they were all hers.

And this year she was experimenting with her own potting soil. She'd been trying out recipes for more than two years now, and believed she'd found a winner, both for indoor and outdoor use. The outdoor recipe should serve very well for her greenhouse purposes.

From the bag she'd carefully mixed, she filled her containers, testing the moisture, and approved. With care she lifted out the young plants, holding them by their seed leaves. Transplanting, she made certain the soil line on the stem was at the same level it had been in the seed tray, then firmed the soil around the roots with experienced fingers.

She filled pot after pot, labeling as she went and humming absently to the Enya playing gently from the portable CD player she considered essential equipment in a greenhouse.

Using a weak fertilizer solution, she watered them.

Pleased with the progress, she moved through the back opening and into the perennial area. She checked the section—plants recently started from cuttings, those started more than a year before that would be ready for sale in a few months. She watered and tended, then moved to stock plants to take more cuttings. She had a tray of anemones begun when Stella stepped in.

"You've been busy." Stella, with her curling red hair bundled back in a tail, scanned the tables. "Really busy."

"And optimistic. We had a banner season, and I'm expecting we'll have another. If Nature doesn't screw around with us."

"I thought you might want to take a look at the new stock of wreaths. Hayley's worked on them all morning. I think she outdid herself."

"I'll take a look before I leave."

"I let her go early, I hope that's all right. She's still getting used to having Lily with a sitter, even if the sitter is a customer and only a half mile away."

"That's fine." She moved on to the catananche. "You know you don't have to check every little thing with me,

Stella. You've been managing this ship for nearly a year now."

"They were excuses to come back here."

Roz paused, her knife suspended above the plant roots, primed for cutting. "Is there a problem?"

"No. I've been wanting to ask, and I know this is your domain, but I wondered if, when things slow down a bit after the holidays, I can spend some time with the propagation. I'm missing it."

"All right."

Stella's bright blue eyes twinkled when she laughed. "I can see you're worried I'll try to change your routine, organize everything my way. I promise I won't. And I won't get in your way."

"You try, I'll just boot you out."

"Got that."

"Meanwhile, I've been wanting to talk to you. I need you to find me a supplier for good, inexpensive soil bags. One pound, five pound, ten, and twenty-five to start."

"For?" Stella asked as she pulled a notebook out of her back pocket.

"I'm going to start making and selling my own potting soil. I've got mixes I like for indoor and outdoor use, and I want to private-label it."

"That's a great idea. Good profit in that. And customers will like having Rosalind Harper's gardening secrets. There are some considerations, though."

"I thought of them. I'm not going to go hog-wild right off. We'll keep it small." With soil on her hands still, she plucked a bottle of water from a shelf. Then, absently wiping her hand on her shirt, twisted the cap. "I want the staff to learn how to bag, but the recipe's my secret. I'll give you and Harper the ingredients and the amounts, but it doesn't go out to the general staff. For right now we'll set up the procedure in the main storage shed. It takes off, we'll build one for it."

"Government regulations—"

"I've studied on that. We won't be using any pesticides, and I'm keeping the nutrient content to below the regulatory levels." Noting Stella continued to scribble on her pad, Roz took a long drink. "I've applied for the license to manufacture and sell."

"You didn't mention it."

"Don't get your feelings hurt." Roz set the bottle aside, dipped a cutting in rooting medium. "I wasn't sure I'd go on and do the thing, but I wanted the red tape out of the way. It's kind of a pet project of mine I've been playing with for a while now. But I've grown some specimens in these mixes, and so far I like what I see. I got some more going now, and if I keep liking it, we're going for it. So I want an idea how much the bags are going to run us, and the printing. I want classy. I thought you could fiddle around with some logos and such. You're good at that. In the Garden needs to be prominent."

"No question."

"And you know what I'd really like?" She paused for a minute, seeing it in her head. "I'd like brown bags. Something that looks like burlap. Old-fashioned, if you follow me. So we're saying, this is good old-fashioned dirt, southern soil, and I'm thinking I want cottage garden flowers on the bag. Simple flowers."

"That says, this is simple to use, and it'll make your garden simple to grow. I'll get on it."

"I can count on you, can't I, to work out the costs, profits, marketing angles with me?"

"I'm your girl."

"I know you are. I'm going to finish up these cuttings, then take off early myself if nothing's up. I want to get some shopping in."

"Roz, it's already nearly five."

"Five? It can't be five." She held up an arm, turned her

wrist, and frowned at her watch. "Well, shit. Time got away from me again. Tell you what, I'm going to take off at noon tomorrow. If I don't, you hunt me down and push me out."

"No problem. I'd better get back. See you back at the house."

WHEN SHE DID GET HOME, IT WAS TO DISCOVER THE Christmas lights were glinting from the eaves, the wreaths shimmered on all the doors, and candles stood shining in all the windows. The entrance was flanked by two miniature pines wrapped in tiny white lights.

She had only to step inside to be surrounded by the holiday.

In the foyer, red ribbon and twinkling lights coiled up the twin banisters, with white poinsettias in Christmas-red pots under the newel posts.

Her great-grandmother's silver bowl was polished to a beam and filled with glossy red apples.

In the parlor a ten-foot Norway spruce—certainly from her own field—ruled the front windows. The mantel held the wooden Santas she'd collected since she'd been pregnant with Harper, with fresh greenery dripping from the ends.

Stella's two sons sat cross-legged on the floor beneath the tree, staring up at it with enormous eyes.

"Isn't it great?" Hayley bounced dark-haired Lily on her hip. "Isn't it awesome?"

"David must've worked like a dog."

"We helped!" The boys jumped up.

"After school we got to help with the lights and everything," the youngest, Luke, told her. "And pretty soon we get to help make cookies, and decorate them and everything."

"We even got a tree upstairs." Gavin looked back at the spruce. "It's not as big as this one, 'cause it's for upstairs. We helped David take it up, and we get to decorate it *ourselves.*" Knowing who was the boss of the house, Gavin looked at her for confirmation. "He said."

"Then it must be true."

"He's cooking up some sort of trim-the-tree buffet in the kitchen." Stella walked over to look at the tree from Roz's perspective. "Apparently, we're having a party. He's already given Logan and Harper orders to be here by seven."

"Then I guess I'd better get myself dressed for a party. Hand over that baby first." She reached out, took Lily from Hayley and nuzzled. "Tree that size, it'll take all of us to dress it up. What do you think of your first Christmas tree, little girl?"

"She's already tried to belly-scoot over to it when I put her on the floor. I can't wait to see what she does when she sees it all decked out."

"Then I'd better get a move on." Roz gave Lily a kiss, handed her back. "It's a bit warm yet, but I think we ought to have a fire. And somebody tell David to ice down some champagne. I'll be down shortly."

It had been too long since there were children in the house for Christmas, Roz thought as she hurried upstairs. And damn if having them there didn't make her feel like a kid herself.

two

ROZ TOOK HER HOLIDAY MOOD SHOPPING. THE NURSery could get along without her for half a day. The fact was, the way Stella managed it, the nursery could get along without her for a week. If she had the urge, she could take herself off on her first real vacation in—how long had it been? Three years, she realized.

But she didn't have the urge.

Home was where she was happiest, so why go to all the trouble of packing, endure the stress of traveling, just to end up somewhere else?

She'd taken the boys on a trip every year when they were growing up. Disney World, the Grand Canyon, Washington, D.C., Bar Harbor, and so on. Little tastes of the country, sometimes chosen at whim, sometimes with great planning.

Then they'd taken that three-week vacation in Europe. Hadn't that been a time?

It had been hard, sometimes frantic, sometimes hysterical, herding three active boys around, but oh, it had been worth it.

She could remember how Austin had loved the whale-watch cruise in Maine, how Mason had insisted on ordering snails in Paris, and Harper had managed to get himself lost in Adventureland.

She wouldn't trade those memories for anything. And she'd seen a nice chunk of the world herself.

Instead of a vacation, she could concentrate on other things. Maybe it was time to start thinking about adding a little florist shop onto the nursery. Fresh-cut flowers and arrangements. Local delivery. Of course, it would mean another building, more supplies, more employees. But it was something to think about for a year or two down the road.

She'd have to go over some figures, see if the business could handle the outlay.

She'd sunk a great deal of her personal resources into the nursery to get it off the ground. But she'd been ready to gamble. Her priorities had been, always, that her children were safe, secure, and well provided for. And that Harper House remain tended, protected, and in the family.

She'd accomplished that. Though there'd been times it had taken a lot of creative juggling and had caused the occasional sleepless night. Perhaps money hadn't been the terrifying issue for her that it often was for single parents, but it had been an issue.

In the Garden hadn't just been a whim, as some thought. She'd needed fresh income and had bargained, gambled, and finagled to get it.

It didn't matter to Roz if people thought she was rich as Croesus or poor as a church mouse. The fact was she was neither, but she'd built a good life for herself and her children with the resources she'd had at hand.

Now, if she wanted to go just a little crazy playing Santa, she'd earned it.

She burned up the mall, indulging herself to the point that she needed to make two trips out to her car with bags.

Seeing no reason to stop there, she headed to Wal-Mart, intending to plow through the toy department.

As usual, the minute she stepped through the doors she thought of a dozen other things she could probably use. Her basket was half loaded, and she'd stopped in the aisles to exchange greetings with four people she knew before she made it to the toy department.

Five minutes later she was wondering if she'd need a second cart. Struggling to balance a couple of enormous boxes on top of the mound of other purchases, she turned a corner.

And rapped smartly into another cart.

"Sorry. I can't seem to . . . oh. Hi."

It had been weeks since she'd seen Dr. Mitchell Carnegie, the genealogist she'd hired—more or less. There had been a few brief phone conversations, some businesslike e-mails, but only a scatter of face-to-face contacts since the night he'd come to dinner. And had ended up seeing the Harper Bride ghost.

She considered him an interesting man and gave him top marks for not hightailing it after the experience they'd all shared the previous spring.

He had, in her opinion, the credentials she needed, along with the spine and the open mind. Best of all he'd yet to bore her in their discussions of family lineage and the steps necessary to identifying a dead woman.

Just now it looked as if he hadn't shaved in the past few days, so there was a dark stubble toughening his face. His bottle-green eyes appeared both tired and harassed. His hair badly needed a trim.

He was dressed much like the first time she'd met him, in old jeans and rolled-up shirtsleeves. Unlike hers, his basket was empty.

"Help me," he said in the tone of a man dangling from a cliff by a sweaty grip on a shaky limb.

"I'm sorry?"

"Six-year-old girl. Birthday. Desperation."

"Oh." Deciding she liked that warm bourbon voice, even with panic sharpening it, Roz pursed her lips. "What's the connection?"

"Niece. Sister's surprise late baby. She had the decency to have two boys before. I can handle boys."

"Well, is she a girly girl?"

He made a sound, as if the limb had started to crack.

"All right, all right." Roz waved a hand and, abandoning her own cart, turned down the aisle. "You could've saved yourself some stress by just asking her mother."

"My sister's pissed at me because I forgot *her* birthday last month."

"I see."

"Look, I forgot everything last month, including my own name a couple of times. I told you I was finishing some revisions on the book. I was on deadline. For God's sake, she's forty-three. One. Or possibly two." Obviously at wit's end, he scrubbed his hands over his face. "Doesn't your breed stop having birthdays at forty?"

"We may stop counting, Dr. Carnegie, but that doesn't mean we don't expect an appropriate gift on the occasion."

"Loud and clear," he responded, watching her peruse the shelves. "And since you're back to calling me Dr. Carnegie, I'd hazard a guess you're on her side. I sent flowers," he added in an aggrieved tone that had her lips twitching. "Okay, late, but I sent them. Two dozen roses, but does she cut me a break?"

He jammed his hands into his back pockets and scowled at Malibu Barbie. "I couldn't get back to Charlotte for Thanksgiving. Does that make me a demon from hell?"

"It sounds like your sister loves you very much."

"She'll be planning my immediate demise if I don't get this gift today, and have it FedExed tomorrow."

She picked up a doll, set it down again. "Then I assume your niece's birthday is tomorrow, and you waited until the eleventh hour to rush out and find something for her."

He said nothing for a moment, then laid a hand on her shoulder so that she looked over, and up at him. "Rosalind, do you want me to die?"

"I'm afraid I wouldn't feel responsible. But we'll find something, then you can get it wrapped up and shoot it off."

"Wrapped. God almighty, it has to be wrapped?"

"Of course it has to be wrapped. And you have to buy a nice card, something pretty and age-appropriate. Hmm. I like this." She tapped a huge box.

"What is it?"

"It's a house-building toy. See, it has all these modular pieces so you can design and redesign your own doll house, with furnishings. It comes with dolls, and a little dog. Fun, and educational. You hit on two levels."

"Great. Good. Wonderful. I owe you my life."

"Aren't you a little out of your milieu?" she asked when he took the box off the shelf. "You live right in the city. Plenty of shops right there."

"That's the problem. Too many of them. And the malls? They're like a labyrinth of retail hell. I have mall fear. So I thought, hey, Wal-Mart. At least everything's all under one roof. I can get the kid taken care of and get . . . what the hell was it? Laundry soap. Yeah, I need laundry soap and something else, that I wrote down . . ." He dug in his pocket, pulled out a PDA. "Here."

"Well, I'll let you get to it then. Don't forget the wrapping paper, ribbon, a big bow, and a pretty card."

"Hold on, hold on." With the stylus he added the other items. "Bow. You can just buy them ready-made and slap it on, right?"

"That will do, yes. Good luck."

"No. Wait, wait." He shoved the PDA back in his pocket, shifted the box. His green eyes seemed calmer now and focused on her. "I was going to get in touch with you anyway. Are you finished in here?"

"Not quite."

"Good. Let me grab what I need, then I'll meet you at the checkout. I'll help you haul your load out to your car, then take you to lunch."

"It's nearly four. A little late for lunch."

"Oh." He looked absently at his watch to confirm the time. "I think time must warp in places like this so you could actually spend the rest of your natural life wandering aimlessly without realizing it. Anyway. A drink then. I'd really like to have a conversation about the project."

"All right. There's a little place called Rosa's right across the way. I'll meet you there in a half hour."

BUT HE WAS WAITING AT THE CHECKOUT. PATIENTLY, from all appearances. Then insisted on helping her load her bags in her car. He took one look at what was already stacked in the back of her Durango and said, "Holy Mother of God."

"I don't shop often, so when I do I make it count."

"I'll say."

"There are less than three weeks left till Christmas."

"I'll have to ask you to shut up." He hefted the last bag inside. "My car's that way." He gestured vaguely toward their left. "I'll meet you."

"Fine. Thanks for the help."

The way he wandered off made her think he wasn't entirely sure just where he'd parked. She thought he should've plugged the location into that little personal data thingy he had in his pocket. The idea made her chuckle as she drove over to the restaurant.

She didn't mind a certain amount of absentmindedness. To her it simply indicated the person probably had a lot in his head, and it took a little longer to find just what he was after. She'd hadn't hired him out of the blue, after all. She'd researched Mitchell Carnegie and had read or skimmed some of his books. He was good at what he did, he was local, and though he was pricey, he hadn't balked—overmuch—about the prospect of researching and identifying a ghost.

She parked, then walked into the lounge area. Her first thought was to order a glass of iced tea, or some coffee. Then she decided, the hell with that. She deserved a nice glass of wine after such a successful shopping expedition.

While she waited for Mitch, she called the nursery on her cell phone to let them know she wouldn't be back in, unless she was needed.

"Everything's fine here," Hayley told her. "You must be buying out the stores."

"I did. Then I happened to run into Dr. Carnegie at Wal-Mart—"

"Dr. Hottie? How come I never run into hunks at Wal-Mart?"

"Your day will come, I'm sure. In any case, we're going to have a drink here and discuss, I assume, our little project."

"Cool. You ought to spin it out over dinner, Roz."

"It's not a date." But she did pull out her lipstick and slide a little pale coral on her lips. "It's an impromptu meeting. If anything comes up, you can give me a call. I should be heading home within the hour anyway."

"Don't worry about a thing. And, hey, you've both got to eat sometime, somewhere, so why not—"

"Here he comes now, so we'll get started. I'll fill everyone in later. Bye now."

Mitch slipped into the booth across from her. "This was handy, wasn't it? What would you like?"

She ordered a glass of wine, and he coffee, black. Then he flipped open the bar menu and added antipasto. "You've got to need some sustenance after a shopping safari like that. How've you been?"

"Very well, thanks. How about you?"

"Good, now that the book's out of my hair."

"I never asked you what it was about."

"A history and study of Charles-Pierre Baudelaire." He waited a beat, noted her questioning lift of brows. "Nineteenth-century poet. Wild man of Paris—druggie, very controversial, with a life full of drama. He was found guilty of blasphemy and obscenity, squandered his inheritance, translated Poe, wrote dark, intense poetry, and, long after his death from a sexually transmitted disease, is looked on by many to be the poet of modern civilization—and others as being one sick bastard."

She smiled. "And which camp do you pitch your tent in?"

"He was brilliant, and twisted. And believe me, you don't want to get me started, so I'll just say he was a fascinating and frustrating subject to write about."

"Are you happy with the work you did?"

"I am. Happier yet," he said as their drinks were served, "not to be living with Baudelaire day and night."

"It's like that, isn't it, like living with a ghost."

"Nice segue." He toasted her with his coffee. "Let me say, first, I appreciate your patience. I'd hoped to have this book wrapped up weeks ago, but one thing led to another."

"You warned me at the start you wouldn't be available for some time."

"Hadn't expected it to be quite this much time. And I've given quite a bit of thought to your situation. Hard not to after that experience last spring."

"It was a more personal introduction to the Harper Bride than I'd planned."

"You've said she's been . . . subdued," he decided, "since then."

"She still sings to the boys and to Lily. But none of us has seen her since that night. And to be frank, it hasn't been patience so much as being swamped myself. Work, home, a wedding coming up, a new baby in the house. And after that night, it seemed like all of us needed a little break."

"I'd like to get started now, really started, if that works for you."

"I suppose it was fate that we ran into each other like this, because I've been thinking the same thing. What will you need?"

"Everything you've got. Hard data, records, journals, letters, family stories. Nothing's too obscure. I appreciate the family photos you had copied for me. It just helps me immerse, you could say, if I have photos, and letters or diaries written in the hands of the people I'm researching."

"No problem. I'll be happy to load you up with more."

"Some of what I've managed so far—between bouts with Baudelaire—is what we'll call a straight job. Starting to chart the basic family tree, getting a feel for the people and the line. Those are the first steps."

"And at the end of the day, something I'll enjoy having."

"I wonder if there's a place I could work in your house. I'd do the bulk in my apartment, but it might be helpful if I had some space on site. The house plays a vital part in the research, and the results."

"That wouldn't be a problem."

"For the Amelia portion of the project, I'd like a list of names. Anyone who's had any sort of contact with her I'll need to interview."

"All right."

"And the written permission we talked about before, for me to access family records, birth, marriage, death certificates, that sort of thing."

"You'll have it."

"And permission to use the research, and what I pull out of it, in a book."

She nodded. "I'd want manuscript approval."

He smiled at her, charmingly. "You won't get it."

"Well, really—"

"I'll be happy to provide you with a copy, when and if, but you won't have approval." He picked up a short, thick breadstick from the wide glass on the table and offered it to her. "What I find, I find; what I write, I write. And *if* I write a book, sell it, you owe me nothing for the work."

She leaned back, drew air deep. His casual good looks, that somewhat shaggy peat-moss brown hair, the charming smile, the ancient high-tops, all disguised a clever and stubborn man.

It was a shame, she supposed, that she respected stubborn, clever men. "And if you don't?"

"We go back to the original terms we discussed at our first meeting. The first thirty hours are gratis, and after that it's fifty an hour plus expenses. We can have a contract drawn up, spelling it all out."

"I think that would be wise."

When the appetizer was served, Roz declined a second glass of wine, absently selected an olive from the plate. "Won't you need permission from anyone you interview as well, if you decide to publish?"

"I'll take care of that. I want to ask, why haven't you done this before? You've lived in that house your whole life and never dug down to identify a ghost who lives there with you. And, let me add, even after my experience, it's hard to believe that sentence just came out of my mouth."

"I don't know exactly. Maybe I was too busy, or too used to her. But I've started to wonder if I wasn't just, well, inoculated. The family never bothered about her. I can give you all sorts of details on my ancestors, strange little family anecdotes, odd bits of history, but when it came to her, nobody seemed to know anything, or care enough to find out. Myself included."

"Now you do."

"The more I thought about what I didn't know, the more, yes, I wanted to find out. And after I saw her again, for myself, that night last June, I need to find out."

"You saw her when you were a child," he prompted.

"Yes. She would come into my room, sing her lullaby. I was never afraid of her. Then, as happens with every child who grows up at Harper House, I stopped seeing her when I was about twelve."

"But you saw her again."

There was something in his eyes that made her think he was wishing for his notebook or a tape recorder. That intensity, the absolute focus that she found unexpectedly sexy.

"Yes. She came back when I was pregnant with each of my boys. But that was more of a sensation of her. As if she were close by, that she knew there was going to be another child in the house. There were other times, of course, but I imagine you want to talk about all that in a more formal setting."

"Not necessarily formal, but I'd like to tape the conversations we have about her. I'm going to start off with some basic groundwork. *Amelia* was the name Stella said she saw written on the window glass. I'll check your family records for anyone named Amelia."

"I've already done that." She lifted a shoulder. "After all, if it was going to be that simple, I thought I might as well wrap it up. I found no one with that name—birth, death, marriage, at least, not in any of the records I have."

"I'll do another search, if it's all the same to you."

"Suit yourself. I expect you'll be thorough."

"Once I get started, Rosalind, I'm a bloodhound. You'll be good and sick of me by the end of this."

"And I'm a moody, difficult woman, Mitchell. So I'll say, same goes."

He grinned at her. "I'd forgotten just how beautiful you are."

"Really?"

Now he laughed. Her tone had been so blandly polite. "It shows what a hold Baudelaire had on me. I don't usually forget something like that. Then again, he didn't have complimentary things to say about beauty."

"No? What did he say?"

" 'With snow for flesh, with ice for heart, I sit on high, an unguessed sphinx begrudging acts that alter forms; I never laugh, I never weep.' "

"What a sad man he must have been."

"Complicated," Mitch said, "and inherently selfish. In any case, there's nothing icy about you."

"Obviously, you haven't talked with some of my suppliers." Or, she thought, her ex-husband. "I'll see about having that contract drawn up, and get you the written permissions you need. As far as work space, I'd think the library would work best for you. Whenever you need it, or want something, you can reach me at one of the numbers I've given you. I swear, we all have a hundred numbers these days. Failing that, you can speak with Harper, or David, with Stella or Hayley, for that matter."

"I'd like to set something up in the next few days."

"We'll be ready. I really should be getting home. I appreciate the drink."

"My pleasure. I owe you a lot more for helping me out with my niece."

"I think you're going to be a hero."

He laid some bills on the table, then rose to take her hand before she could slide out of the booth on her own. "Is anybody going to be home to help you haul in all that loot?"

"I've hauled around more than that on my own, but yes, David will be there."

He released her hand, but walked her out to her car. "I'll be in touch soon," he said when he opened the car door for her.

"I'll look forward to it. You'll have to let me know what you come up with for your sister for Christmas."

Pain covered his face. "Oh, hell, did you have to spoil it?"

Laughing, she shut the door, then rolled down the window. "They have some gorgeous cashmere sweaters at Dillard's. Any brother who sprang for one of those for Christmas would completely erase a forgotten birthday."

"Is that guaranteed? Like a female rule of law?"

"From a husband or lover, it better glitter, but from a brother, cashmere will do the trick. That's a promise."

"Dillard's."

"Dillard's," she repeated, and started the engine. "Bye."

"Bye."

She pulled out, and as she drove away glanced in the rearview mirror to see him standing there, rocking on his heels with his hands in his pockets.

Hayley was right. He was hot.

ONCE SHE GOT HOME, SHE PULLED THE FIRST LOAD out, carried it in the house and directly up the stairs to her wing. After a quick internal debate, she piled bags into her sitting room, then went down for more.

She could hear Stella's boys in the kitchen, regaling David with the details of their day. Better that she got everything inside by herself, upstairs and hidden away before anyone knew she was home.

When she was finished, she stood in the middle of the room, and stared.

Why, she'd gone crazy, obviously. Now that she saw everything all piled up, she understood why Mitch had goggled. She could, easily, open her own store with what she'd bought in one mad afternoon.

How the hell was she going to wrap all of this?

Later, she decided after dragging both hands through her hair. She'd just worry about that major detail later. Right now she was going to call her lawyer, at home—the benefit of knowing him since high school—and get the contract done.

And because they'd gone to high school together, the conversation took twice as long as it might have. By the time she'd finished, put some semblance of order back into her sitting room, then headed downstairs, the house was settled down again.

Hayley, she knew, would be up with Lily. Stella would be with her boys. And David, she discovered, when she found the note on the kitchen counter, was off to the gym.

She nibbled on the potpie he'd left for her, then took a quiet walk around her gardens. The lights were on in Harper's cottage. David would have called him to let him know he'd made potpie—one of Harper's favorites. If the boy wanted some, he knew where to find it.

She slipped back inside, then poured herself another glass of wine with the idea of enjoying it in a long, hot bath.

But when she went back upstairs, she caught a movement in her sitting room. Her whole body tightened as she went to the door, then loosened again when she saw Stella.

"You got my juices up," Roz said.

It was Stella who jolted and spun around with a hand to her heart. "God! You'd think we'd all stop jumping by now. I thought you'd be in here. I came by to see if you'd like to go over the weekly report, and saw this." She swept a hand toward the bags and boxes lining the wall. "Roz, did you just buy the mall?"

"Not quite, but I gave it a good run. And because I did, I'm not much in the mood for the weekly report. What I want is this wine and a long, hot bath."

"Obviously well deserved. We can do it tomorrow. Ah, if you need help wrapping some of this—"

"Sold."

"Just tap me any evening after the kids are in bed. Ah, Hayley mentioned you were having drinks with Mitch Carnegie."

"Yeah. We ran into each other, as it seems everyone in Tennessee does eventually, at Wal-Mart. He's finished his book and appears to be raring to go on our project. He's going to want to interview you, and Hayley among others. That's not going to be a problem, is it?"

"No. I'm raring, too. I'll let you get started on that bath. See you in the morning."

"'Night."

Roz went into her bedroom, closed the door. In the adjoining bath she ran water and scent and froth, then lit candles. For once she wouldn't use this personal time to soak and read gardening or business literature. She'd just lie back and veg.

As an afterthought, she decided to give herself a facial.

In the soft, flickering light, she slipped into the perfumed water. Let out a low, lengthy sigh. She sipped wine, set it on the ledge, then sank nearly to the chin.

Why, she wondered, didn't she do this more often?

She lifted a hand out of the froth, examined it—long, narrow, rough as a brick. Studied her nails. Short, unpainted. Why bother painting them when they'd be digging in dirt all day?

They were good, strong, competent hands. And they looked it. She didn't mind that, or the fact there were no rings on her fingers to sparkle them up.

But she smiled as she raised her feet out. Her toenails now, they were her little foolishness. This week she'd painted them a metallic purple. Most days they'd be buried in work socks and boots, but she knew she had sexy toes. It was just one of those silly things that helped her remember she was female.

Her breasts weren't as perky as they'd once been. She could be grateful they were small, and the sagging hadn't gotten too bad. Yet.

While she didn't worry too much about the state of her hands—they were, after all, tools for her—she was careful about her skin. She couldn't stop all the lines, but she pampered it whenever she could.

She wasn't willing to let her hair go to salt-and-pepper, so she took care of that, too. Just because she was being dragged toward fifty didn't mean she couldn't dig her heels in and try to slow down the damage time insisted on inflicting.

She had been beautiful once. When she'd been a young bride, fresh and innocent and radiantly happy. God, she looked at those pictures now and it was almost like looking at a stranger.

Who had that sweet young girl been?

Nearly thirty years, she thought. And it had gone by in the snap of a finger.

How long had it been since a man had looked at her and told her she was beautiful? Bryce had, certainly, but he'd told her all manner of lies.

But Mitch had said it almost offhand, casually. It made it easier to believe he'd meant it.

And why did she care?

Men. She shook her head and sipped more wine. Why was she thinking of men?

Because, she realized with a half laugh, she had no one to share those sexy toes with. No one to touch her as she liked to be touched, to thrill her. To hold her in the night.

She'd done without those things, and was content. But every now and again, she missed having someone. And maybe she was missing it now, she admitted, because she'd spent an hour talking with an attractive man.

When the water turned tepid, she got out. She was humming as she dried off, creamed her skin, performed her nightly ritual with her moisturizer. Wrapped in her robe, she started into her bedroom.

She felt the chill even before she saw the figure standing in front of her terrace doors.

Not Stella, not this time. The Harper Bride stood in her simple gray gown, her bright hair in a crown of curls.

Roz had to swallow once, then she spoke easily. "It's been some time since you've come to see me. I know I'm not pregnant, so that can't be it. Amelia? Is that your name?"

There was no answer, nor had she expected one. But the Bride smiled, just a brief shadow of a smile, then faded away.

"Well." Standing, Roz rubbed the warmth back into her arms. "I guess I'll assume that's your way of letting me know you approve that we're getting back to work."

She went back to the sitting room and took a calendar she'd begun keeping over the last winter out of her desk. She noted down the sighting on the day's date.

Dr. Carnegie, she assumed, would be pleased she was keeping a record.

three

HE'D NEVER BEEN MUCH OF A GARDENER. THEN AGAIN, he'd lived in apartments most of his life. Still, he liked the look of plants and flowers, and had an admiration for those who knew what to do with them.

Rosalind Harper obviously knew what to do with them.

He'd seen some of the gardens on her estate this past June. But even their graceful beauty had paled next to his encounter with the Harper Bride. He'd always believed in the spirit of a person. Why else would he be so drawn to histories, to genealogies, to all those roots and branches of family trees? He believed that spirit could, and did, have influence and impact for generations, potentially centuries.

But he'd never believed in the tangibility, the physical presence of that spirit.

He knew better now.

It was difficult for someone with Mitch's academic bent to rationalize, then absorb, something as fanciful as ghosts.

But he'd felt and he'd seen. He'd experienced, and there was no denying facts.

So now he was caught up. He could admit it. With his book finally put to bed, he could pour his energies and his time, his skills, into identifying the spirit that had—purportedly—walked the halls of Harper House for more than a century.

A few legalities to get out of the way, then he could dive in.

He turned into the parking area of In the Garden.

Interesting, he thought, that a place that certainly had its prime in spring and summer could look so attractive, so welcoming as December clicked away.

The sky was heavy with clouds that would surely bring a cold, ugly rain before it was done. Still there were things growing. He had no clue what they were, but they looked appealing. Rusty red bushes, lush evergreens with fat berries, silvery green leaves, brightly painted pansies. At least he recognized a pansy when he saw one.

There were industrious-looking piles of material—material he assumed one would need for gardening or landscaping. Long tables on the side that held plants he assumed could handle the chill, a small forest of trees and shrubs.

The low-slung building was fronted with a porch. He saw poinsettias and a small, trim Christmas tree strung with lights.

There were other cars in the lot. He watched a couple of men load a tree with a huge burlapped ball into the back of a truck. And a woman wheel out a red wagon loaded with poinsettias and shopping bags.

He walked up the ramp, crossed the porch to go inside.

There were a lot of wares, he noted. More than he'd expected. Pots, decorative garden stakes, tabletop trees already decorated, books, seeds, tools. Some were put together in gift baskets. Clever idea.

Forgetting his intention of seeking Roz out immediately, he began to wander. When one of the staff asked if he needed help, he just smiled, shook his head, and continued to browse around.

A lot went into putting a place like this together, Mitch mused as he studied shelves of soil additives, time released fertilizer pellets, herbal pest repellents. Time, labor, know-how, and, he thought, courage.

This was no hobby or little enterprise indulged in by a southern aristocrat. This was serious business. Another layer to the woman, he supposed, and he hadn't begun to get to the center of her.

Beautiful, enigmatic Rosalind Harper. What man wouldn't want the chance to peel off those layers and know who she really was?

As it was, he owed his sister and niece a big, sloppy thanks for sending him scrambling out to shop. Running into Roz, seeing her with her shopping cart, having an hour alone with her was the most intriguing personal time he'd had in months.

Hardly a surprise he was hoping for more, and that he'd made this trip to her garden center mainly to study yet another side of her.

He wandered through wide glass doors and found an exotic mass of houseplants. There were tabletop and garden fountains as well, and baskets of ferny and viney things hanging from hooks or standing on pedestals.

Through another set of doors was a kind of greenhouse, with dozens of long wooden tables. Most were empty, but some held plants. The pansies he recognized, and others he didn't. Though, he noted, they were labeled and billed to be winter hardy.

He was debating whether to continue on or go back and ask for Roz when her son Harper came in from the outside.

"Hi. Need some help?" As he walked toward Mitch, recognition crossed his face. "Oh, hey, Dr. Carnegie."

"Mitch. Nice to see you again, Harper," he said as they shook hands.

"You, too. That was some game against Little Rock last week."

"It was. Were you there?"

"Missed the first quarter, but the second half rocked. Josh ruled."

Pride in his son beamed through him. "He had a good game. Missouri this week. I'll have to catch that one on ESPN."

"Same here. You see your son, tell him I said that three-pointer in the last five minutes was a thing of beauty."

"I'll do that."

"You looking for something, or someone?"

"Someone. Your mother, actually." You have her eyes, he thought. Her mouth, her coloring. "I was taking a little tour before I hunted her up." As he looked around, Mitch slipped his hands in his pockets. "This is a hell of a place you've got here."

"Keeps us busy. I just left her in the propagation house. I'll take you back."

"Appreciate it. I guess I didn't think this kind of business would have so much going on this late in the year."

"Always something going on when you're dealing with gardening and landscaping." Mirroring Mitch's stance, Harper scanned the area. "Holiday stuff's big now, and we're working on getting plants ready for March."

When they stepped outside, Mitch stopped, hooked his thumbs in his jacket pockets. Low, long greenhouses spread, separated into two areas by a wide space where more tables stood under a screened shelter. Even now he could see a field where someone worked a machine to dig up a pine—or a spruce, or a fir. How could you tell the difference?

He caught a glimpse of a little pond, and a small stream, then the woods that shielded the business from the main house, and the main house from the business.

"I've got to say, wow. I didn't expect anything this expansive."

"Mom doesn't do things halfway. We started a little smaller, added on two more greenhouses and an additional space in the retail area a couple years ago."

More than a business, Mitch realized. This was a life. "It must take an incredible amount of work."

"It does. You've gotta love it."

"Do you?"

"Yeah. That's my castle over there." Harper gestured. "Grafting house. Mostly, I deal with grafting and propagation. But I get pulled out for other things, like the Christmas tree end this time of year. In fact, I was grabbing ten before I head out to the field when I ran into you."

As the rain began to fall, Harper nodded toward one of the greenhouses. "That's the propagation area. Since we've got Stella, Mom spends most of her time in there."

"Then I can find her from here. Why don't you go on, catch what you've got left of your break."

"Better get right out in the field." As the rain fell, Harper pulled the bill of his cap lower on his head. "Get those trees up before the rain scares the customers away. Just go ahead in. See you later."

Harper set off at a jog, and had made the turn toward the field when Hayley rushed up to him from the opposite direction. "Wait! Harper, wait a minute."

He stopped, lifting the bill a bit to get a better look at her. She was wearing a short red denim jacket over jeans, and one of the In the Garden caps Stella had ordered for employees.

"Jesus, Hayley, get inside. This rain's going to cut loose big-time any minute."

"Was that Dr. Carnegie?"

"Yeah. He was looking for the boss."

"You took him to the propagation house?" Her voice pitched up over the increasing drum of rain. "Are you just stupid?"

"What? He's looking for Mom, she's in the propagation house. I just left her there five minutes ago."

"So you just take him there, say go right in?" She made wild gestures with both hands. "Without letting her *know*?"

"Know what?"

"That he's here, for God's sake. And now he's going in, and she's all dirty and sweaty, with no makeup on and in her grubbiest clothes. You couldn't stall him for five damn minutes to give her some warning?"

"About what? She looks like she always does. What's the damn difference?"

"If you don't know, you are stupid. And it's too late now. One of these days, Harper Ashby, you're going to have use of the single brain men pass around among them."

"What the hell," he grumbled after she'd given him a punch on the arm and dashed inside again.

MITCH DUCKED INTO THE PROPAGATION HOUSE OUT of the rain. If he'd thought the houseplant section seemed exotic, it was nothing compared to this. The place seemed alive with plants in various stages of growth. The humid warmth was almost tropical, and with the rain pattering it seemed he'd walked into some sort of fantasy cave.

The air was pungent with green and brown—plants and soil. Music twined along with the scents. Not classical, he noted. Not quite New Age. Something oddly and appealingly between.

He saw tables and tools, buckets and bags. Shallow black containers holding delicate growing things.

And he saw Roz at the far end, on the side. Her back was to him as she worked.

She had a gorgeous neck. It was an odd thought, and, he admitted, probably a foolish one. But again, facts were facts. She wore her hair short and straight and to his mind, the style showed off that long, lovely neck perfectly.

Then again, all of her was rather long and lovely. Arms, legs, torso. At the moment that intriguing body was camouflaged in baggy pants and a shapeless sweatshirt she'd pushed up at the sleeves. But he remembered, very well, that willowy figure.

Just as he remembered, even before she heard his approach and turned, that her eyes were long as well. Long lidded and in a fascinating shade of deep, deep amber.

"I'm sorry. I'm interrupting."

"That's all right. I didn't expect to see you here."

"I got the paperwork, and thought I'd ride out and let you know it's signed, sealed, and on its way back to your lawyer. Plus, it gave me a chance to see your place. I'm impressed. Even though I don't know squat about gardening, I'm majorly impressed."

"Thank you."

He glanced down at her worktable. There were pots, some empty yet, some filled with soil and small green leaves. "What's going on here?"

"I'm potting up some seedlings. Celosia—cockscomb."

"I have no idea what that is."

"I'm sure you've seen them." She brushed a hand absently over her cheek, transferring a smudge of soil. "In bloom they're like small feather dusters in bold colors. Red's very popular."

"Okay. And you put them in these little pots because?"

"Because they don't like their roots disturbed after they're established. I pot them young, then they'll be blooming for our spring customers, and only have to tolerate that last transplanting. And I don't imagine you're all that interested."

"Didn't think I would be. But this is like a whole new world. What's this here?"

She raised her eyebrows. "All right, then. That's matthiola, also called gillyflower or stock. It's very fragrant. Those there with the yellowish green leaves? They'll be double-flowered cultivars. These will flower for spring. Customers prefer to buy in bloom, so I plan my propagation to give them plenty of blooms to choose from. This section is for annuals. I do perennials back there."

"Is it a gift, or years of study? How do you come to know what to do, how to recognize the . . . cockscomb from the gillyflower at this stage?"

"It's both, and a love of it with considerable hands-on experience thrown in. I've been gardening since I was a child. I remember my grandmother—on the Harper side—putting her hands over mine to show me how to press the soil around a plant. What I remember best about her is in the gardens at Harper House."

"Elizabeth McKinnon Harper, wife to Reginald Harper, Jr."

"You have a good memory."

"I've been skimming over some of the lists. What was she like?"

It made her feel soft, and a little sentimental, to be asked. "Kind, and patient, unless you riled her up. Then she was formidable. She went by Lizzie, or Lizzibeth. She always wore men's pants, and an old blue shirt and an odd straw hat. Southern women of a certain age always wear odd straw hats to garden. It's the code. She smelled of the eucalyptus and pennyroyal she'd make up into a bug repellant. I use her recipe for it still."

She picked up another pot. "I still miss her, and she's been gone nearly thirty years now. Fell asleep in her glider on a hot summer day in July. She'd been deadheading in the garden, and sat down to rest. She never woke up. I think that's a very pleasant way to pass."

"How old was she?"

"Well, she claimed to be seventy-six, but in fact, according to the records she was eighty-four. My daddy was a late baby for her, as I was for him. I broke that Harper family tradition by having my children young."

"Did she ever talk to you about the Harper Bride?"

"She did." As she spoke, Roz continued with her potting. "Of course, she was a McKinnon by birth and wasn't raised in the house. But she claimed to have seen the Bride when she'd come to live here, when my great-grandfather passed. My grandfather Harper grew up at Harper House, of course, and if we were right in dating Amelia, would have been a baby around the time she died. But he passed when I was about eight, and I don't recall him ever speaking of her."

"How about your parents, or other relatives?"

"Are we on the clock here, Doctor?"

"Sorry."

"No, I don't mind." She labeled the new potted plant, reached for another. "My daddy never said much, now that I think about it. Maybe it's a thing with the Harper men, or men in general. My mother was a dramatic sort of female, one who enjoyed the illusion of turmoil in her life. She claimed to have seen the Bride often, and with great stress. But then, Mama was always stressed about something."

"Did either she or your grandmother keep a journal, any sort of diary?"

"Yes, both of them. Another fine old tradition I haven't followed. My grandmother moved into the guesthouse when my father married and brought his own bride home. After she died, he cleaned out her things. I recall asking him about her journals, but he said they were gone. I don't know what became of them. As for my mother's, I have hers. You're welcome to them, but I doubt you'll find anything pertinent."

"Just the same. Aunts, uncles, cousins?"

"Oh, legions. My mother's sister, who married some British lord or earl—third marriage—a few years ago. She lives in Sussex, and we don't see each other often. She has children from her first two marriages, and they have children. My father was an only child. But his father had four sisters, older sisters—Reginald's daughters."

"Yeah, I've got their names on my list."

"I don't remember them at all. They each had children. Let's see, that would be my cousins Frank and Esther—both gone years now—and their children, of course. Ah, Lucerne, Bobby, and Miranda. Bobby was killed in World War II. Lucerne and Miranda are both gone now, too. But they all had children, and some of them have children now. Then there's Owen, Yancy, ah . . . Marylou. Marylou's still living, down in Biloxi where she suffers from dementia and is tended by her children, best they can. Yancy, I couldn't say. He ran off to join a carnival years back, and no one heard from him again. Owen's a fire-and-brimstone minister, last I heard, in Macon, Georgia. He wouldn't talk to you about ghosts, I can promise you."

"You never know."

She made a noncommittal sound as she worked. "And my cousin Clarise, who never married. She has managed to live to a ripe age. Too sour not to. She's living in a retirement village, other side of the city. She doesn't speak to me."

"Because?"

"You do ask questions."

"Part of the process."

"I'm not sure I remember exactly why she stopped speaking to me. I recall she didn't appreciate that my grandparents left everything to me and my daddy. But they were *my* grandparents, after all. My father's parents, while she was only a niece to them. She came to visit here when the boys were young. I believe that's when she cut me off, or we cut each other off, which is more accurate. She didn't care for my style of raising the boys, and I didn't care for her criticism of them, or me."

"Before the family rift, do you recall if she ever talked to you about the Bride?"

"I don't, no. Cousin Rissy's conversations mostly consisted of complaints or her own irritable observations. And I know damn well she pilfered things from the house. Little bits and pieces. I can't say I'm sorry we're not on speaking terms."

"Will she talk to me?"

Thoughtfully, Roz turned to him, studied his face. "She might, especially if she thinks I'd prefer she didn't. If you decide to go see the dried-up old bat, be sure you take her flowers, and chocolate. You spring for Godiva and she'll be very impressed with you. Then you turn on the charm. Be sure to call her Miss Harper, until she says otherwise. She uses the family name, and is very formal about everything. She'll ask about your people. If you happen to have any ancestors who fought in the War Between the States, be sure to mention it. Any Yankees in your tree, disavow them."

He had to laugh. "I get the type. I have a great-aunt who's on the same page."

She reached under the worktable to a cooler, took out two bottles of chilled water. "You look hot. I'm so used to it, I don't notice."

"Working in all this humidity every day must be what gives your skin that English rose look." Absently he reached out, flicked a finger over her cheek. When her brows shot up again, he eased back, just a step.

"Sorry. You had a little dirt . . ."

"Something else I'm used to."

"So . . ." He reminded himself to keep his hands otherwise occupied. "I guess from what I saw the other day, you're ready for Christmas."

"Near enough. You?"

"Not even close, though I owe you big—once again—for the gift for my sister."

"You went for the cashmere, then."

"Something the salesgirl called a twinset, and she said no woman could have too many of them."

"Absolutely true."

"Okay. So, I'm going to put some effort into the rest of it over the next few days. Get the tree out, fight with the lights."

"Get it out?" A look that might have been pity, might have been derision covered her face. "I assume that means you've got a fake tree."

His hands slid into his pockets, his smile spread slowly. "It's simplest. Apartment life."

"And from the state of that dieffenbachia, probably for the best."

"State of the what?"

"The plant you were slowly murdering. The one I took when I came to your place to meet you the first time."

"Oh. Oh, right." When she'd been wearing that lady suit, he thought, and those high heels that had made her legs look ten feet long. "How's it doing?"

"It's just fine now, and don't think I'll be giving it back."

"Maybe I could just visit it sometime."

"That could be arranged. We're having a holiday party at the house, a week from Saturday. Nine o'clock. You're welcome to come, if you like. And bring a guest, of course."

"I'd like that. Would you mind if I went over to the house now, took a look at the library? Get a ground floor started?"

"No, that'll be fine. I'll just call David and let him know you're coming."

"Good. I'll go on, then, and get out of your way. I appreciate the time."

"I've plenty of it."

He didn't see how. "I'll call you later, then. You have a strong place here, Rosalind."

"Yes, I do."

When he'd gone out, she set her tools aside to drink deeply from the water bottle. She wasn't a silly young girl who was flustered and giddy at the touch of a man's hand on her skin. But it had felt strange and oddly sweet, that careful brush of his fingers over her cheek, and that look in his eyes when he touched her.

English rose, she thought and let out a half laugh. Once, long ago, she might have appeared that fragile and dewy. She turned and studied one of her healthy stock plants. She was much more like that now, sturdy and strong.

And that, she thought as she got back to work, was just fine with her.

DESPITE THE STEADY RAIN, MITCH TOOK A WALK around the buildings, and gained even more respect for Roz and what she'd built. And built almost single-handedly, he thought. The Harper money may have given her a cushion, he decided, but it took more than funds to create all this.

It took guts and vision and hard work.

Had he actually made that lame, clichéd comment about her skin? English rose, he thought now and shook his head. Like she hadn't heard that one before.

In any case, it wasn't even particularly apt. She was no delicate English rose. More a black rose, he decided, long and slender and exotic. A little haughty, a lot sexy.

He'd learned a lot about her life, just from that conversation in her work space. A lot about her. She'd lost someone she'd loved very much—her grandmother—at a tender age. She hadn't been very close with her parents. And had lost them as well. Her relatives were far-flung, and it didn't appear she had close relations with any of them.

Other than her sons, she had no one.

And after her husband's death, she'd had only herself to depend on, only herself to turn to while she raised three boys.

But he'd detected no sense of pity, certainly no weakness in her.

Independent, direct, strong. But there was humor there, and a good heart. Hadn't she helped him out when he'd been floundering over a toy for a little girl? And hadn't she been amused by his dilemma?

Now that he'd begun to get a good sense of her, he only wanted to know more.

What was the deal with the second husband and the divorce, for instance? None of his business, of course, but he could justify the curiosity. The more he knew, the more he knew. And it wouldn't be difficult to find out. People just loved to talk.

All you had to do was ask the questions.

On impulse, he detoured back into the center. There were a few customers debating over the poinsettias and some sort of cactus-looking plant that was loaded with pink blossoms. Mitch had barely raked a hand through his wet hair when Hayley arrowed in his direction.

"Dr. Carnegie! What a nice surprise."

"Mitch. How are you, Hayley, and the baby?"

"We both couldn't be better. But look at you, you're soaked! Can I get you a towel?"

"No, I'm fine. I couldn't resist walking around, looking the place over."

"Oh." She beamed at him, all innocence. "Were you looking for Roz?"

"Found her. I'm about to head over to the house, get a sense of my work space there. But I thought maybe I'd pick up one of those tabletop trees. The ones that're already decorated."

"Aren't they sweet? Really nice for a small space, or an office."

"A lot nicer than the old artificial one I fight to put together every year."

"And they smell just like Christmas." She steered him over. "You see one you like?"

"Ah . . . this one's fine."

"I just love all the little red bows and those tiny Santas. I'll get you a box for it."

"Thanks. What are those?"

"Those are Christmas cacti. Aren't they beautiful? Harper grafts them. He's going to show me how one of these days. You know, you should have one. They're so celebrational. And they bloom for Christmas and Easter."

"I'm not good with plants."

"Why, you don't have to do much of anything for it." She set those big baby blue eyes on him. "You live in an apartment, don't you? If you take the tree, a Christmas cactus, a couple of poinsettias, you'll be all decorated for the holidays. You can have company over, and be set."

"I don't know how much attention Josh is going to pay to a cactus."

She smiled. "Maybe not, but you must have a date over for a holiday drink, right?"

"Ah . . . I've been pretty busy with the book."

"A handsome single man like you must have to beat the ladies off with a stick."

"Not lately. Um—"

"You should have a wreath for the door, too."

"A wreath." He began to feel slightly desperate as she took his arm.

"Let me show you what we've got. I made some of these myself. See this one here? Just smell that pine. What's Christmas without a wreath on the door?"

He knew when he was outgunned. "You're really good at this, aren't you?"

"You bet," she said with a laugh and selected a wreath. "This one goes so well with your tree."

She talked him into the wreath, three windowsill-size poinsettias, and the cactus. He looked bemused and a little dazed as she rang it all up and boxed his purchases.

And when he left, Hayley knew what she wanted to know.

She dashed into Stella's office.

"Mitch Carnegie's not seeing anybody."

"Was he recently blinded?"

"Come on, Stella, you know what I mean. He doesn't have a sweetie." She drew off her cap, raked her fingers through her oak-brown hair she was wearing long enough to pull back into a stubby tail.

"And he just spent a good half hour in the propagation house with Roz before he came in here to buy a tabletop tree. Harper sent him in there without even letting her know. Just go right on in while she's working and doesn't even have time to swipe on some lipstick."

"Just sent him in? What is Harper, stupid?"

"Exactly what I asked him—Harper, that is. Anyway, then he—Mitch—came in all wet because he'd been walking around the place checking it out. He's going over to the house for a while now."

"Hayley." Stella turned from her computer. "What are you cooking?"

"Just observing, that's all. He's not seeing anybody, she's not seeing anybody." She lifted her hands, pointing both index fingers, then wiggled them toward each other.

"Now they're both going to be seeing a lot of each other. And besides being a hottie, he's so cute. I talked him into buying a wreath, three mini poinsettias, and a Christmas cactus as well as the tree."

"Go, Hayley."

"But see, he didn't know how to say no, that was the cute part. If Roz doesn't go for him, I might myself. Okay, no." She laughed at Stella's bland stare. "He's old enough to be my daddy and blah blah blah, but he's just perfect for Roz. I'm telling you, I know this stuff. Wasn't I right about you and Logan?"

Stella sighed as she looked at the aquamarine he'd given her as an engagement ring. "I can't argue about that. And while I'm going to say, firmly, that observing's all we should do, I can't deny this may be a lot of fun to watch."

four

As a rule when he was working, Mitch remembered to clean his apartment when he ran out of places to sit, or coffee cups. Between projects he was slightly better at shoveling out, or at least rearranging the debris.

He hired cleaning services. In fact, he hired them routinely. They never lasted long, and the fault—he was willing to admit—was largely his.

He'd forget which day he'd scheduled them and, invariably, pick that day to run errands, do research, or meet his kid for a quick game of Horse or one-on-one. There was probably something Freudian about that, but he didn't want to think too deeply about it.

Or he'd remember, and the team would come in, goggle at the job facing them. And he'd never see them again.

But a man had to—or at least should—make an effort for the holidays. He spent an entire day hauling out, scrubbing down, and sweeping up, and was forced to admit that if he were being paid to do the job, he'd quit, too.

Still, it was nice to have some order back in his apartment, to actually be able to see the surface of tables, the cushions of chairs. Though he didn't hold out much hope he'd keep them alive for the long-term, the plants Hayley had talked him into added a nice holiday touch.

And the little tree, well, that was ingenious. Now instead of dragging the box out of storage, fighting with parts, cursing the tangle of lights only to discover half of them didn't work anyway, all he had to do was set the cheerful tree on the Hepplewhite stand by his living room window and plug the sucker in.

He hung the wreath on the front door, set the blooming cactus on his coffee table, and the three little poinsettias on the top of the toilet tank. It worked for him.

By the time he'd showered, dragged on jeans and a shirt, his date for the evening was knocking at the door.

Barefoot, his hair still damp, Mitch crossed the living room to answer. And grinned at the only person he loved without reservation.

"Forget your key?"

"Wanted to make sure I had the right place." Joshua Carnegie tapped a finger on the greenery. "You've got a wreath on your door."

"It's Christmas."

"I heard a rumor about that." He walked in, and his eyes, the same sharp green shade as his father's, widened.

He was taller than Mitch by a full inch, but spread the height on the same lanky frame. His hair was dark, and it was shaggy. Not because he forgot haircuts like his father, but because he wanted it that way.

He wore a hooded gray sweatshirt and baggy jeans.

"Wow. You find a new cleaning service? Do they get combat pay?"

"No, haven't had a chance. Besides, I think I've ripped through all the cleaning services in western Tennessee."

"You cleaned up?" Lips pursed, Josh took a brief tour of the living room. "You've got a plant—with flowers on it."

"You're taking that with you."

"I am."

"I'll kill it. I've already heard it gasping. I can't be responsible."

"Sure." Josh pulled absently on his ear. "It'll jazz up the dorm. Hey. You got this little tree going on. And candles."

"It's Christmas," Mitch repeated, even as Josh leaned down to sniff the fat red candle.

"Smelly candles. Plus, if I'm not mistaken, you vacuumed." Eyes narrowed he looked back at his father. "You've got a woman."

"Not on me, no. More's the pity. Want a Coke?"

"Yeah." With a shake of his head, Josh started toward the bathroom. "Gotta use the john. We getting pizza?"

"Your choice."

"Pizza," Josh called out. "Pepperoni and sausage. Extra cheese."

"My arteries are clogging just hearing that," Mitch called out as he pulled two cans of Coke out of the refrigerator. From experience, he knew his son could steam through most of a pie on his own and still stay lean as a greyhound.

Oh, to be twenty again.

He speed-dialed the local pizza parlor, ordered a large for Josh, and a medium veggie-style for himself.

When he turned, he saw Josh leaning against the jamb, feet crossed at the ankles of his Nike Zooms. "You've got flowers in the john."

"Poinsettias. Christmas. Deal."

"You've got a woman. If you haven't bagged one, you've got one in the sights. So spill."

"No woman." He tossed one of the cans to Josh. "Just a clean apartment with a few holiday touches."

"We have ways of making you talk. Where'd you meet her? Is she a babe?"

"Not talking." Laughing, Mitch popped the can.

"I'll get it out of you."

"Nothing to get." Mitch walked by him into the living room. "Yet."

"Ah-ha!" Josh followed him in, plopped down on the couch, propped his feet on the coffee table.

"I repeat: Not talking. And that's a premature *ah-ha*. Anyway, I'm just feeling a little celebrational. Book's done, which means a check will be in the mail shortly. I'm starting on a new, interesting project—"

"Already? No decompressing?"

"I've had this one dangling awhile, and I want to get on it full steam. It's better than thinking about Christmas shopping."

"Why do you have to think about it? It's still a couple weeks away."

"Now, that's my boy." Mitch raised his Coke in toast. "So how are your mother and Keith?"

"Good. Fine." Josh took a long swallow from his can. "She's all jazzed up about the holidays. You know how it is."

"Yeah, I do." He gave Josh an easy slap on the knee. "It's not a problem, Josh. Your mom wants you home for the holidays. That's the way it should be."

"You could come. You know you could come."

"I know, and I appreciate it. But it'd be better if I just hang out here. We'll have our Christmas deal before you leave. It's important to her to have you there. She's entitled. It's important for you, too."

"I don't like thinking about you being alone."

"Just me and my cup of gruel." It was a sting, it always was. But it was one he'd earned.

"You could go to Grandma's."

"Please." Exaggerated pain covered Mitch's face, rang in his voice. "Why would you wish that on me?"

Josh smirked. "You could wear that reindeer sweater she got you a couple years ago."

"Sorry, but there's a nice homeless person who'll be sporting that this holiday season. When do you head out?"

"Twenty-third."

"We can do our thing the twenty-second if that works for you."

"Sure. I've just got to juggle Julie. She's either going to Ohio to her mother's, or L.A. to her father's. It's seriously messed up. They're both doing the full court press on her, laying on the guilt and obligation crap, and she's all, 'I don't want to see either one of them.' She's either crying or bitchy, or both."

"We parents can certainly screw up our children."

"You didn't." He took another drink, then turned the can around in his hands. "I don't want to get all Maury Povich or whatever, but I wanted to say that you guys never made me the rope in your personal tug-of-war. I've sort of been thinking about that, with all this shit Julie's going through. You and Mom, you never hung that trip on me. Never made me feel like I had to choose or ripped on each other around me. It sucks when people do. It sucks long."

"Yeah, it does."

"I remember, you know, before you guys split. It was rugged all around. But even then, neither of you used me as a hammer on the other. That's what's going on with Julie, and it makes me realize I was lucky. So I just wanted to say."

"That's a . . . That's a good thing to hear."

"Well, now that we've had this Hallmark moment, I'm getting another Coke. Pregame show should be coming on."

"I'm on that." Mitch picked up the remote. He wondered what stars had shone on him to give him the gift of such a son.

"Hey, man! Salt and vinegar chips!"

Hearing the bag rip, and the knock on the door, Mitch grinned, and rising, took out his wallet to pay for the pizza.

"I DON'T GET IT, STELLA. I JUST DON'T GET IT." Hayley paced Stella's room while the boys splashed away in the adjoining bath.

"The sexy black shoes that will kill my feet, or the more elegant pumps?"

When Stella stood, one of each pair on either foot, Hayley stopped pacing long enough to consider them. "Sexy."

"I was afraid of that. Well." Stella took them both off, replaced the rejected pair in her closet. Her outfit for the evening was laid out on the bed, the jewelry she'd already selected was in a tray on the dresser.

Now all she had to do was settle the boys down for the night, get dressed, deal with her hair, her makeup. Check the boys again, check the baby monitors. And . . . Hayley's pacing and muttering distracted her enough to have her turn.

"What? Why are you so nervous? Do you have a date going on for tonight's party I don't know about?"

"No. But it's dates I'm talking about. Why would Roz tell Mitch to bring a date? Now he probably will, because he'll think if he doesn't, he'll look like a loser. And they'll both miss a golden opportunity."

"I missed something." She hooked on her earrings, studied the results. "How do you know Roz told him to bring a date? How do you find this stuff out?"

"It's a gift of mine. Anyway, what's up with her? Here's this perfectly gorgeous and available man, and she invites him for tonight—points there. But then tells him he can bring somebody. Jeez."

"She'd have considered it the polite thing to do, I guess."

"You can't be polite in the dating wars, for God's sake." On a long huff, Hayley plopped down on the foot of the bed, then lifted her legs out to examine her own shoes. "You know, *date*'s from the Latin—or maybe it's Old English. Anyway, it comes from *data*—and it's a *female* part of speech. Female, Stella. We're supposed to take the controls."

Since she hadn't yet started her makeup, Stella was free to press her fingers to her eyes. "How? How do you know that kind of thing? Nobody knows that kind of thing."

"I was a bookseller for years, remember. I read a lot. I don't know why I retain the weird stuff. But anyway, it's a holiday party here—her house. And you know she'll look amazing. And now he'll show up with some woman and screw everything up."

"I don't actually think there's anything to screw up at this point."

Hayley tugged at her hair in frustration. "But there *could* be. I just know it. You watch, you just watch them tonight and see if you don't get the vibe."

"All right, I will. But now I've got to get the kids out of the tub and into bed. Then I have to get dressed, and strap on my sexy shoes with the single goal of driving Logan crazy."

"Want a hand? With the kids, not with driving Logan crazy. Lily's already sleeping."

"No, you'll get wet or wrinkled, and you look fantastic. I wish I could wear that shade of red. Talk about sexy."

Hayley looked down at the short siren-red slip dress. "You don't think it's too . . ."

"No, I think it's exactly."

"Well, I'll go down, see if I can give David a hand with the caterer and all. Then I can get his take on the outfit. He rules in fashion."

Roz was already downstairs, checking details and second-guessing herself. Maybe she should have opened the third-floor ballroom and held the party there. It was a gorgeous space, so elegant and graceful. But the main level, with its hive of smaller rooms, the fires burning, was warmer and more friendly somehow.

Space wasn't a problem, she assured herself as she checked the positioning of tables, chairs, lamps, candles. And she liked throwing open the rooms this way, knowing people would wander from here to there, admiring the home she loved.

It was a clear night, so they could spill onto the terraces, too. There were heaters if it got too chilly, and more tables, more seating, more candles and all those festive lights in the trees, the luminaries along the garden paths.

And you'd think, for heaven's sake, that it was the first party she'd given in her life.

Been awhile, though, since she'd held anything this expansive. Because of that, the attrition rate on her guest list had been very low. She was going to be packed.

Avoiding the caterers and extra staff bustling around, she slipped outside. Yes, the lights were lovely, and fun, she decided. And she liked the poinsettia tree she'd created out of dozens of white plants.

Harper House was designed for entertaining, she reminded herself. She'd been shirking her duty there, and denying herself, she supposed, the pleasure of socializing with people she enjoyed.

She turned when she heard the door open. David stepped out, holding two flutes of champagne.

"Hello, beautiful. Can I interest you in a glass of champagne?"

"You can. Though I should be inside, helping with the madhouse."

"Under control." He tapped his glass to hers. "Another twenty minutes, and it'll be perfect. And look at us! Aren't we gorgeous?"

She laughed, slipped her hand into his. "You always are."

"And you, my treasure." Still holding her hand, he stepped back. "You just shimmer."

She'd chosen a gown of dull silver in a long, narrow column with an off-the-shoulder neckline that would showcase her great-grandmother's rubies.

She brushed her fingertips over the platinum necklace with its spectacular ruby drops. "I don't have many opportunities to wear the Harper rubies. This seemed the night for them."

"And a treat they are for the eyes plus they do amazing things for your collarbone. But I was talking about you, my incandescent beauty. Why don't we run away to Belize?"

Champagne and David, the perfect combination to make her feel bubbly and relaxed. "I thought it was going to be Rio."

"Not until Carnival. It's going to be a wonderful party, Roz. You just put all the other crap out of your mind."

"You read me, don't you?" She shook her head, staring into the gardens as she sipped champagne. "Last time I threw one of these holiday bashes, I walked upstairs into the bedroom to change my bracelet because the clasp was loose, and what do I find but my husband nibbling on one of our guests instead of the canapés."

She took a longer, deeper sip. "A singularly mortifying moment in my life."

"Hell with that. You handled it, didn't you? I still don't know how you managed to step back out, leave them there, to get through the rest of the party and wait until everyone was gone before you pitched the son of a bitch out on his ear."

His voice heated up on the rant, his fury for her lighting little fires. "You've got balls of steel, Roz. And I mean that in the best possible way."

"It was self-serving, not courageous or ballsy." She shrugged it off, or tried to. "Causing a scene with a house full of guests would only have been more humiliating."

"In your place, I'd've scratched both of them blind, then chased them out the door brandishing one of your great-great . . . however many greats-granddaddy's muskets."

She let out a little sigh, sipped again. "That would've been satisfying, and damn if I don't wish I'd thought of the musket after the guests had gone. Well, we didn't let him spoil that evening, and we won't let him spoil this one."

She polished off the champagne and turned to David with the determined look of a woman prepared for battle. "Let's get the rest of these candles lit, put some music on. I'm ready for a party."

YES, IT WAS GOOD TO OPEN THE HOUSE AGAIN. To have wine and music, good food, good friends. She listened to snippets of gossip, political debates, discussions on sports and the arts as she moved from group to group, from room to room.

She hooked her arm through her old friend Will Dooley's, who was also Stella's father, and Roz's landscaper, Logan Kitridge's future father-in-law. "You slipped by me."

"Just got here." He brushed his lips over her cheek. "Jo kept changing her shoes. She just went upstairs with Hayley. Said she had to peek at the baby."

"I'll find her. Lose your fiancée, Logan?"

"She's everywhere." He shrugged, sipped from his pilsner. "Woman can't rest until she's checked every detail personally. Nice party, Roz."

"Oh, you hate parties."

Now Logan grinned, a quick grin that added charm to his rugged looks. "A lot of people. But the food's first-rate, the beer's cold, and my date's the most beautiful woman in the world. Tough to complain. Don't tell her daddy, but I plan to lure her out to the gardens later to neck."

He winked at Will, then shifted his gaze. "Your Dr. Carnegie just came in. Seems to be looking for you—or somebody."

"Oh?" Roz glanced around, and those expressive eyebrows lifted. He'd worn a suit, stone gray, that flattered his lean build. He'd gotten a haircut since the last time she'd seen him, she noted, and was looking a little more *GQ* than professorial.

She could admit, to herself at least, that it was a treat to study him either way.

Still, he seemed slightly befuddled with the crowd, and shook his head when one of the efficient servers offered him a glass from a tray of champagne.

"Excuse me just a minute," she said to Will and Logan.

She started to wind her way through the room, and broke her stride when his gaze skimmed over, then locked on her face.

She felt a little bump under her heart, and a quickening of pulse she found both baffling and embarrassing.

He just hones in, she thought. Those eyes just zeroed right on in so she felt—anyone would feel—that she was the only person in the room. A good trick in a space jammed with people and noise, and just a little disconcerting.

But her expression was easy and friendly as she walked to him.

"I'm so glad you could come."

"When you throw a party, you mean it. I could see the lights from a mile away. You don't actually know all these people, do you?"

"Never seen them before in my life. What can I get you to drink?"

"Club soda, lime."

"There's a bar set up over here." To guide him, she laid a hand on his arm. "Let's get you fixed up."

"Thanks. Listen, I have something for you. A gift."

He dug into his pocket as they crossed to the bar, then offered her a small wrapped box.

"That's completely unnecessary, and awfully sweet."

"Just a thanks for bailing me out with the gift for my niece." He ordered his drink. "You look . . . *amazing* is the word that springs to mind, with *spectacular* coming right behind it."

"Thank you."

"From head." His gaze skimmed down to her silver-heeled sandals—and the ruby-red toenails. "To toe."

"My mama always said a woman wasn't groomed unless her toenails were painted. It's one of the few pieces of advice she gave me I agreed with. Should I open this now?"

He'd barely glanced at the rubies, though his amateur antiquer's eye judged them to be vintage. But the toes. The toes were terrific.

"What?"

"The gift." She smiled. It was hard not to be pleased, and a little bit smug, when a man was enraptured by your feet. "Should I open it now?"

"Oh, no, I wish you wouldn't. If you open it later, and you hate it, you'll have time to prepare a polite lie."

"Don't be silly. I'm opening it now."

She tugged off the ribbon, lifted the top. Inside was a miniature clock, framed in silver filigree. "It's lovely. It's really lovely."

"Antiquing's a hobby of mine. Makes sense, considering. I figured with this house, you'd enjoy old things. There's an inscription on the back. It got to me."

She turned it over and read.

L, Count the hours. N

"Lovely, and romantic. It's wonderful, Mitch, and certainly more than I deserve for picking out a toy."

"It made me think of you." When she lifted her head, he shook his. "That put a cynical look in your eye. But fact's fact. I saw it, thought of you."

"Does that happen often?"

"My thinking of you?"

"No, thinking of someone and buying her a charming gift."

"From time to time. Not in some time, actually. Does it happen often on your end?"

She smiled a little. "Not in some time. Thank you, very much. I want to put this upstairs. Why don't I introduce you to . . . oh, there's Stella. Nobody can steer you through a party better than our Stella."

"Mitch." Stella held out a hand for him. "It's good to see you again."

"And you. You're blooming," he said. "It must be love."

"I can confirm that."

"And how are your boys?"

"They're great, thanks. Conked out upstairs, and . . . oh." She broke off when she saw the little clock. "Isn't that sweet? So romantic and female."

"Lovely, isn't it?" Roz agreed. "It was a gift, for a very small favor."

"You wouldn't say small if you'd been on the receiving end of the phone call I got from my sister and my niece," Mitch told her. "I'm not only officially forgiven, I'm currently enjoying favorite-uncle status."

"Well then, obviously I deserve this. Stella, show Mitch around, will you? I just want to put this upstairs."

"Sure." And Stella noted the way Mitch's gaze followed Roz out of the room.

"One question before we make the rounds. Is she seeing anyone?"

"No, she's not."

He grinned as he took Stella's arm. "How about that?"

Roz mingled her way to the foyer, then started upstairs. It reminded her that she'd walked up these stairs at another party, with the voices and the music and lights behind her. And she'd stepped into the end of a relationship.

She wasn't naive. She knew very well Mitch was asking her if she was interested in beginning a relationship, and was laying some groundwork so she would be. What was strange was that her answer wasn't a flat no. What was strange, Roz thought as she walked to her bedroom, was not knowing the answer.

She slipped into the room to set the romantic little clock on her dresser. She couldn't stop the smile as she traced the frame. A very thoughtful gift, she thought, and yes, her cynical side added that it was a very clever gift. Then again, a woman who'd been through two marriages was bound to have a healthy dose of cynicism.

A relationship with him might be interesting, even entertaining, and God knew she was due for some passion in her life. But it would also be complicated, possibly intense. And potentially sticky with the work she'd hired him to do.

She was allowing the man to write a book that involved her family history, and would certainly involve herself to some extent. Did she really want to become intimate with someone who could, if things burned out, slap her, and her family, in print?

Her experience with Bryce warned her that when things went bad, things got worse.

A lot to consider, she mused. Then she raised her eyes to the mirror.

She saw not only herself, her skin flushed, her eyes bright from her own thoughts, but the pale figure behind her.

Her breath caught, but she didn't jolt. She didn't spin around. She simply stood as she was, her eyes linked with Amelia's in the glass.

"Twice in so many weeks," she said calmly. "You, I imagine, would tell me to brush him off. You don't like men much, do you, Amelia? Boys, yes, children, but men are a different kettle. No one but a man puts that kind of anger in a woman. I know. Was it one of my blood who put that anger in you?"

There was no answer, none expected.

"Let me finish this one-sided conversation by saying I have to think for myself, decide for myself, just as I always have. If I let Mitchell into my life, into my bed, the consequences, and the pleasure, will be on me."

She took a slow breath. "But I'll make you one promise. Whatever I do, or don't, we won't stop looking for the answers for you. Not now that we've started."

Even as the figure began to fade, Roz felt something brush her hair, like a soft stroke of fingers that warmed even as it chilled.

She had to steady herself, pressing both hands to the top of the dresser. Then she meticulously freshened her lipstick, dabbed a bit more scent on her throat. And started back to the party.

She thought a ghostly caress would be enough of a shock for one night, but she had another, harder shock, as she reached the bottom of the stairs.

Bryce Clerk stood in her foyer.

The rage spewed through her, hot and horrid, and had a vision of herself flashing through her brain. Of leaping down the stairs, spitting out all the bitter insult and fury as she beat him senseless, and threw him out the door.

For an instant, that vision was so sharp, so clear, that the rest, the reality around her, blurred and vanished. She heard nothing but the pounding blood in her ears.

He beamed up at her as he helped a woman she knew from the garden club with her wrap. Roz clutched the newel post until control clamped down over temper and she was marginally sure her hand wouldn't bunch into a fist and fly out.

She took the last step. "Mandy," she said.

"Oh, Roz!" Amanda Overfield giggled, kissed both of Roz's cheeks in a couple of quick pecks. She was Harper's age, Roz knew, a silly, harmless, and wealthy young woman. Recently divorced herself, she'd only relocated in Memphis the previous summer. "Your house is just *gorgeous*. I know we're awfully late, but we got . . ." She giggled again, and set Roz's teeth on edge. "It doesn't matter. I'm so glad you asked me to come. I've been dying to see your home. Where are my manners? Let me introduce you to my date. Rosalind Harper, this is Bryce Clerk."

"We've met."

"Roz. You look spectacular, as always."

He started to lean down, as if to kiss her. She knew conversations nearby had died off, knew people were watching, listening. Waiting.

She spoke very softly. "Touch me, and I'll kick your balls right up into your throat."

"I'm an invited guest in your home." Bryce's voice was smooth, and lifted enough to reach interested ears. She watched him fix an expression of injured shock on his face. "Rudeness doesn't become you."

"I don't understand." Hands clasped together, Mandy looked from one to the other. "I don't understand."

"I'm sure you don't. Mandy, why don't you and your escort come out front with me a moment?"

She heard the vicious curse behind her, fought valiantly not to wince. She turned, and again kept her voice low. "Harper. Don't. Please."

When she shifted her body to block his, Harper's gaze snapped from Bryce to his mother. "Once and for all."

"I'm going to take care of it. Let me take care of it." She rubbed a hand over his arm, felt his muscles quivering. "Please."

"Not alone."

"Two minutes." She kissed his cheek, whispered in his ear. "He wants a scene. We won't give it to him. He gets nothing from us. Two minutes, baby."

She turned. "Mandy? Let's get a little air, all right?" She took the woman by the arm.

Bryce held his ground. "This is ungracious of you, Rosalind. You're embarrassing yourself, and your guests. I'd hoped we could be civil, at least."

"I suppose your hopes are dashed then."

She saw the change in his face as he looked over her shoulder. She followed his direction, noted that Mitch stood beside Harper now, and that Logan and David were both moving into the foyer. Their expressions were far less *civil*, she decided, than hers.

"Who's the asshole?" Mitch's question was barely a mutter, but Roz heard it, just as she heard Harper's answer.

"Bryce Clerk. The garbage she tossed out a few years ago."

Roz drew Mandy outside. Bryce was an idiot, she thought, and he might've enjoyed an altercation, a public one, with Harper. But he wouldn't take on several strong, angry men, even for the pleasure of embarrassing her in her own home.

She was proven right as he walked stiffly out the door behind her. Roz shut it.

"Mandy, this is my ex-husband. The one I found upstairs, at a similar party, with his hands all over the naked breasts of a mutual acquaintance."

"That's a damn lie. There was nothing—"

Her head whipped around. “You’re free to tell Mandy your side of things, when you’re not standing on my doorstep. You are not welcome here. You will never be welcome here. If you come onto my property again, I will call the police and have you arrested for trespassing. And you can bet your lying, cheating ass I will prosecute. Now you have one minute, and one minute only, to get in your car and get off my land.”

She turned, smiled now into Mandy’s shocked face. “Mandy, you’re certainly welcome to come in, to stay. I’ll arrange for you to be taken home later if you like.”

“I think I should . . . I, ah, guess I should go.”

“All right, then. I’ll see you next month at the meeting. Merry Christmas.”

She stepped back, but didn’t open the door. “I believe you’re down to about forty seconds now before I go inside and contact the police.”

“Everyone in there knows what you are now,” Bryce shot out at her as he pulled Mandy toward his car.

“I’m sure they do.”

She waited until he’d gunned the engine, until he’d sped off.

Only then did she press a hand to her sick stomach, and squeeze her eyes shut until she could bank back the trembling rage and embarrassment.

She took two deep breaths, lifted her head high, then walked back into the house.

She smiled, brilliantly, then held out a hand for Harper’s.

“Well,” she said, giving his hand a squeeze as she scanned curious faces, “I could use a drink.”

five

WHEN THE PARTY WAS OVER, AND THE GUESTS ON THEIR way home, Roz couldn't settle. She knew better than to go up to her rooms, where she would just pace and rehash and twist herself up over this personal humiliation.

Instead, she made herself a big mug of coffee and took it out on the patio to enjoy the cool and the solitude. With the heaters humming and the lights still twinkling, she sat down to sip, to enjoy and maybe to brood just a little.

Harper was angry with her, she knew. Angry because she'd held him off from physically ejecting Bryce from the house. He was still young enough—and bless his heart, he was a man on top of it—to believe that brute force could solve this particular problem. And he loved her enough to chain his temper down because she'd asked.

At least this time he'd managed to chain it down.

The single other time Bryce had attempted to enter Harper House without invitation, she'd been too shocked to hold Harper off. Or David, for that matter. Bryce had been thrown out on his cheating ass, and she was small enough to gain some satisfaction from the way her boy had hauled the man out. But what had it solved?

Bryce had accomplished then just what he'd accomplished this round. He'd upset her.

How long, she wondered, just how goddamn long was she supposed to pay for one stupid, reckless mistake?

When she heard the door open behind her, Roz tensed up. She didn't want to rehash this nasty little business with David or Harper, didn't want a man to pat her head and tell her not to worry.

She wanted to sit and brood alone.

"I don't know about you, but I could use some chocolate."

Surprised, Roz watched Stella set a tray on the table. "I thought you'd gone up to bed."

"I always like to decompress a little after a big party. Then there was the matter of these chocolate truffles, just sitting out there in the kitchen, calling my name."

She'd brewed tea, Roz noted, and remembered Stella wasn't one for late-night coffee. And she'd arranged the leftover truffles on a pretty plate.

"Hayley would be down, too, but Lily woke up. She must be cutting a tooth, because she's fussing. It's beautiful out here. Middle of December, and it's just so beautiful. Not even much of a bite to the air yet."

"Did you practice the small talk, decide you'd open with the weather?"

There had been a time when that aloof tone would have had Stella easing back. But those days were over. "I always figure the weather's a good starter, especially for a couple of gardeners. I was going to segue into how spectacular the poinsettias are this year, but I guess we'll skip that part."

She selected a truffle, bit in. "But the chocolate was just a natural, all around. God, whoever invented these should be canonized."

"Ask Hayley. If she doesn't know who made the first chocolate truffle, she'll find out." Since the chocolate was there, Roz couldn't come up with a good reason not to have one.

"I've been here nearly a year now," Stella began.

"Is this your way of leading up to asking for a raise?"

"No, but good idea. I've worked for you for nearly a year, lived in the same house with you. The second part is certainly longer than I intended."

"No point in moving somewhere else, then moving again when you and Logan get married."

"No, and I appreciate you understanding that, and making it easy for me not to shuffle my kids around. The fact is, even though I'm looking forward to getting married, and moving into Logan's place—especially now that I've been getting my hands on it—I'll miss being here. So will the boys."

"It's nice to hear."

"Even with everything that went on last spring, maybe in some ways because of it, I'm attached to this house. And to you."

"That's nice to hear, too. You have a sweet heart to go with that orderly mind of yours, Stella."

"Thanks." She sat back in her chair, cupping her tea in both hands. Her flower-blue eyes were directly on Roz's. "Living with and working for you for nearly a year, I know your mind and heart. At least as much as I can. One of the things I know is that despite your generosity, your hospitality, you're a very private woman. And I know I'm stepping into that private area when I say I'm sorry about what happened tonight. I'm sorry and I'm angry and just a little bit stunned that some asshole would walk into your home, uninvited and unwelcomed, for the purpose of embarrassing you."

When Roz said nothing, Stella took a long breath. "So,

if you're in the mood to eat truffles and trash the son of a bitch, I'd be happy to listen. If you'd rather sit out here alone, and let it fester, then I'll take my tea and half these chocolates upstairs."

For a moment, Roz just sat, sipping her coffee. Then she thought, what the hell, and had another chocolate. "You know, having lived here all my life, I have a number of friends, and a bevy, we could say, of acquaintances. But I haven't had what you might call close, important female friends. There's a reason for that—"

She lifted a finger, wagged it before Stella could speak. "The reason being my own preference to an extent, and that having its roots in being widowed young. So many of my social circle, in the female area, became just a little wary. Here I was, young, attractive, fairly well off—and available. Or so they assumed. In the other camp were those eager, just innately, to pair me up with a man. A friend, a brother, a cousin, whatever. I found both of those attitudes annoying. As a result, I got out of the habit of having close women friends. So I'm a little rusty. I consider you a friend, the best I have of the female persuasion."

"Since I feel the same about you, I wish you'd let me help you. Even if it's only to say really nasty things about that fucking Bryce Clerk and bring you chocolate."

"Why, Stella." Roz's voice was as creamy as the truffles. "I believe that's the first time in this entire year I've heard you say fuck."

Stella flushed a little, the curse of redheads. "I reserve it for special occasions."

"This is certainly that." Roz tipped her head back and studied the stars. "He didn't do it to embarrass me. That was just a side benefit."

"Then why? Did he think, could he actually be stupid enough to think you'd have let him come in and party?"

"He may have thought my need to maintain image would give him a pass, and if I had, just a little more grease to oil the gears of whatever moneymaking plots and plans he has going."

"If so, he couldn't know you very well to have underestimated you like that."

"He knows enough that he got exactly what he was after tonight. The young woman he had on his arm? She's very wealthy, and very silly. Chances are she'll feel some sympathy, even some outrage on his behalf over tonight."

"Then she's more than silly. She's bone stupid."

"Maybe, but he's an accomplished liar, and slick as a snake. I'm not silly or stupid, and I fell for it."

"You loved him, so—"

"Oh, honey, I didn't love him. Thank God for that." She shuddered at the thought of it. "I enjoyed the attention, the flattery, and initially at least, the romance and sex of it. Added to that I had a raging case of empty nest, so I was ripe for plucking. My own fault that I went and married him instead of sleeping with him until I got bored, or saw what was under that pretty exterior."

"I don't know if that makes it worse or better," Stella said after a moment.

"Neither do I, but it is what it is. In any case, he wanted to remind me he exists, that he can and does swim in the same social pond. He wanted, primarily, for me to be upset and to think about him. Mission accomplished. He has a need for attention, to have attention focused on him—for better or worse. The worst punishment I can give him is to ignore him, which I've done, fairly successfully, since he came back to Memphis. Tonight was a way, a very clever way, of shoving himself in my face, in my own home, in front of my guests."

"I wish I'd gotten there quicker. I was nearly at the other end of the house when I heard the rumbles. But I don't see how anyone could get any sort of satisfaction out of being turned away, in public, the way I heard you turned him away."

"You don't know Bryce. He'll dine off the incident for weeks. Center of attention, and he has a smooth way." Her short, unpainted nails tapped against her teacup. "Before he's done, he'll be the underdog. All he'd done was try to mend fences, to come by to wish me well, it being the holidays and all. And what had I done but rebuffed him, and humiliated his date—an invited guest."

She stopped a moment to suck back the fresh rage. "People will say: 'My goodness, how cold and hard, how ungracious and rude of her.' "

"Then people are idiots."

"Yes, indeed they are. Which is why I rarely socialize with them. And why I've been so particular in my friends. And why I'm very grateful to have one who would sit out here with me at this time of night, eating chocolate truffles while I feel sorry for myself."

She let out a long breath. "And damned if I don't feel better. Let's go on up. Get some sleep. We're going to have us a busy day tomorrow, with the gossip sniffers slinking in along with the regular customers."

SOME WOULD HAVE CALLED IT BURYING HERSELF IN work. Roz called it doing what needed to be done and enjoying every minute of it. She loved winter chores, loved closing herself in for hours, even days in a greenhouse and starting new life, nurturing it along. Her seedlings, and cuttings, sprouts started by layering or leaf buds. She loved the smell of rooting compound and damp, and watching the stages of progress.

There were pests and problems to guard against here, just as there were in life. When she caught signs of downy mildew or rusts, she snipped off the infected leaves, sprayed the plants. She checked air circulation, adjusted temperature.

Any cuttings that showed signs of rot or virus were systematically removed and discarded. She would not allow infection here, any more than she allowed it in her life.

It soothed her to work, and to remember that. She had cut Bryce off, discarded him, rid her life of *that* infection. Maybe not quite soon enough, maybe she hadn't been quite vigilant enough, so even now she was forced to guard and control.

But she was strong, and the life she'd built was strong enough to withstand these small, annoying invasions.

Thinking of that, she finished her list of tasks for the day, then sought out Harper.

She slipped into his grafting house, knowing he wouldn't hear her right away, not with Beethoven soaring for the plants, and whatever music he'd chosen for himself that day booming in his headset.

She took a moment, a moment that made her feel tender, to watch him work. Old sweatshirt, older jeans, grubby boots—he'd have been out in the field off and on that day, she realized.

He'd gotten a haircut recently, so all that glossy black fell in a sleeker, more ordered style. She wondered how long that would last? If she knew her boy—and she did—he'd forget about that little grooming task for weeks until he ended up grabbing a piece of raffia to tie his hair back while he worked.

He was so competent, so creative here. Each of her sons had his own talent, his own direction—she'd made sure of it—but only Harper had inherited her abiding love for gardening.

She moved down through the tables crowded with plants and tools and mediums to watch him skillfully graft a miniature rose.

When he'd finished the specimen, reached for the can of Coke that was always nearby, she moved into his line of vision.

She saw him focus on her as he sipped.

"Nice job," she said. "You don't often do roses."

"Experimenting with these. Thought we might be able to have a section for container-grown miniatures. Working on a climbing mini, and some ground-cover specimens. Want a Coke?"

"No, thanks." He was so much *her*, she thought. How many times had she heard that polite, cool tone come out of her own mouth when she was irritated. "I know you're upset with me, Harper."

"No point in me being upset."

"Point isn't, well, the point, is it?" She wanted to stroke his shoulders, rub her cheek to his. But he'd stiffen, just as she would if someone touched her before she was ready to be touched.

"You're angry with the way I handled things last night. With the way I wouldn't let you handle them."

"Your choice." He jerked a shoulder. "And I'm not mad at you. I'm disappointed in you, that's all."

If he'd taken his grafting knife and stabbed it into her heart, she'd have felt less pain, less shock. "Harper."

"Did you have to be so goddamn polite? Couldn't you have given him what he deserved right then and there instead of brushing me back and taking it outside?"

"What good would—"

"I don't give a *shit* about what good, Mama." The infamous Harper temper smoldered in his eyes. "He deserved to have his clock cleaned, right on the spot. You should've let me stand up for you. But it had to be your way, with me standing there doing nothing. So what is the damn point?"

She wanted to turn away, to take a moment to compose herself, but he deserved better. He deserved face-to-face. "There's no one in this world who can hurt me the way you can."

"I'm not trying to hurt you."

"No, you're not. You wouldn't. That's how I know just how angry you are. And how I can see where it comes from. Maybe I was wrong." She lifted her hands to rub them over her face. "I don't know, but it's the only way I know. I had to get him out of the house. I'm asking you to understand that I *had* to get him out of our house, quickly and before he'd smeared it all again."

She dropped her hands, and her face was naked with regret. "I brought him into our home, Harper. I did that, you didn't."

"That doesn't mean you're to blame, for Christ's sake, or that you have to handle something like that by yourself. If you can't depend on me to help you, to stand up for you—"

"Oh, God, Harper. Here you are, sitting in here thinking I don't need you when half the time I'm worried I need you too much for your own good. I don't know what I'd do without you, that's the God's truth. I don't want to fight with you over him." Now she pressed her fingers to her eyes. "He's nothing but a bully."

"And I'm not a little boy you have to protect from bullies anymore, Mama. I'm a man, and it's my job now to protect you. Whether you want it or not. And whether you damn well need it or not."

She dropped her hands again, nearly managed a smile this time. "I guess that's telling me."

"He comes to the door again, you won't stop me."

She drew a breath, then framed his face with her hands. "I know you're a man. It pains me sometimes, but I know you're a man with his own life, his own ways. I know you're a man, Harper, who'll stand beside me when I ask, even though you'd rather stand in front of me and fight the battle."

Though she knew she wasn't quite forgiven, she pressed a kiss to his forehead. "I'm going on home to work in the garden. Don't stay mad at me too long."

"Probably won't."

"There's some of that baked ham left over from the party. Plenty of side dishes, too, if you wanted to come by and forage for dinner."

"Might."

"All right, then. You know where to find me."

WITH GARDENS AS EXTENSIVE AS HERS, THERE WAS always some chore to do. Since she wanted work, Roz hauled mulch, checked her compost, worked with the cuttings and seedlings she grew for her personal use in the small greenhouse at home.

Then grabbing gloves and her loppers, she headed out to finish up some end-of-the-year pruning.

When Mitch found her, she was shoving small branches into a little chipper. It rattled hungrily as it chewed, with its dull red paint looking industrious.

As she did, he thought, in her dirt-brown and battered jacket, the black cap, thick gloves, and scarred boots. There were shaded glasses hiding her eyes, and he wondered if she wore them against the beam of sunlight, or as protection against flying wood chips.

He knew she couldn't hear him over the noise of the chipper, so took a moment just to watch her. And let himself meld the sparkling woman in rubies with the busy gardener in faded jeans.

Then there was the to-the-point woman in a business suit who'd first come to his apartment. Roz of the tropical greenhouse with a smudge of soil on her cheek. And the casual, friendly Roz who'd taken the time to help him select a child's toy.

Lots of angles to her, he decided, and likely more than he'd already seen. Strangely enough, he was attracted to every one of them.

With his thumbs hooked in his front pockets, he moved

into her line of vision. She glanced up from under the brim of the ballcap, then switched off the machine.

"You don't need to stop on my account," he told her. "It's the first time I've seen one of those things in action except in *Fargo*."

"This one isn't quite up to disposing of a body, but it does the job for garden chores."

She knew *Fargo*, he thought, ridiculously pleased. It was a sign they had some common ground. "Uh-huh." He peered down where most of a branch had gone inside. "So you just shove stuff in there, and chop, chop, chop."

"More or less."

"Then what do you do with what's left?"

"Enough branches and leaves and such, you get yourself a nice bag of mulch."

"Handy. Well, I didn't mean to interrupt, but David said you were out here. I thought I'd come by, get in a couple hours of research."

"That's fine. I didn't figure you'd have much time to spare on it until after the holidays."

"I've got time. I'm getting copies of official records, and I need to make some notes from your family Bible, that sort of thing. Get some order before I can dig down below the surface."

He brushed a good-sized wood chip from her shoulder and wished she'd take off the sunglasses. Her eyes just killed him.

"And I'd like to set up times for those interviews, for after the holidays."

"All right."

He stood, his hands in the pockets of his leather jacket. He was stalling, he knew, but she smelled so damn good. Just a hint of secret female under the woody scent. "Funny, I didn't think much went on in a garden this time of year."

"Something goes on every time of year."

"And I'm holding you up. Listen, I wanted to see if you were all right."

"I'm fine. Just fine."

"It'd be stupid for me to pretend I didn't hear murmurs about what was behind that scene last night. Or what would have been a scene if you hadn't handled things so . . . adroitly."

"Adroitly's how I prefer handling things, whenever possible."

"And if you're going to get your back up when a conversation between us touches on the personal, it's going to be tough to research your family history."

Because he was watching carefully, because he was learning to read her, he saw the annoyance flick over her face before she composed it. "Last night has nothing whatsoever to do with my family history."

"I disagree. It involves you, and this . . . thing going on in your house involves you."

She might kick him out as . . . adroitly as she had Bryce Clerk, but if so, it would be because he was honest and up-front.

"I'm going to pry, Roz. That's what you've hired me to do, and I won't always pry gently. If you want me to move forward with this, you'll have to get used to it."

"I fail to see what my regrettable and thankfully brief second marriage could have to do with the Harper Bride."

He didn't have to see her eyes clearly to know they'd chilled. He heard it in her voice. "Bride. Whether or not she was one, she's referred to as such through your family lore. When she . . . manifested herself," he decided, "last spring—in spades—you said she'd never bothered with you when you'd socialized with men, or when you'd married—as she had with Stella."

"Stella has small children. My children are grown."

"Doesn't make them less your children."

Her shoulders relaxed, then she bent to scoop up some smaller twigs and toss them in the mouth of the chipper. "No, of course, it doesn't."

"So, we can theorize that she didn't feel threatened by Bryce—and what the hell kind of name is that anyway? Stupid. Or that she considered your maternal duties done, and didn't care what you did regarding your sex life. Or that after a certain point, she stops showing herself to whoever's living in the house."

"It can't be three, as I've seen her recently."

"Since June?"

"Just a few days ago, and then again last night."

"Interesting. What were you doing, what was she doing? I should have my notebook."

"It was nothing. She was there, then she wasn't. I don't expect you to solve the puzzle of why she comes, or to whom. I want you to find out who she was."

"One puzzle's connected to the other. I really want some time to talk to you. And this is obviously not it. Maybe we can have dinner, next evening you're free."

"It's not necessary for you to buy me dinner to get an interview."

"It might be enjoyable to buy you dinner. If you have strong objections to mixing business and pleasure, I'm going to be sorry to wait to ask you out until I'm finished with this project."

"I don't date anymore, Mitch. I gave it up."

"The word *date* always makes me feel like I'm back in college. Or worse, high school." He took a chance and reached out to slide her glasses down her nose. Looked directly into her eyes. "We could just say that I'm interested in spending time with you on a social level."

"That says *date* to me." But she smiled before she scooted the glasses back in place. "Not that I don't appreciate it."

"We'll settle for an interview for now. I'm going to be in and out the next couple of weeks, so you can let me know when you've got time to sit down for an extended period. Otherwise, you can call me at home, and we'll set it up."

"That's fine."

"I'll go in, get some work done. Let you get back to yours."

When he started to walk away, she reached for the switch on the chipper.

"Roz? Any time you change your mind about dinner, you just let me know."

"I'll be sure to do that." She switched on the machine, pushed the branch in.

SHE WORKED UNTIL SHE LOST THE LIGHT, THEN STOWED her tools before climbing the steps to the second-floor terrace and her outside door.

She wanted an endless hot shower, soft clothes, then a cold glass of wine. No, she thought. A martini. One of David's amazing, icy martinis with the fancy olives he squirreled away. Then she'd make a sandwich out of that glorious leftover ham. Maybe she'd spend most of the evening playing with sketches and ideas for the florist expansion. Then there were the bag selections Stella had gotten for her, for the in-house potting soil.

Dates, she thought as she shed her clothes and turned on the shower. She didn't have time, certainly didn't have the inclination to date at this stage of her life. Even if the offer had come from a very attractive, intelligent, and intriguing man.

One who'd ask her out when she was covered with wood chips.

Why couldn't they just have sex and clear the air?

Because she wasn't built that way, she admitted. And wasn't that too damn bad. There had to be a little more . . . something before she stripped down, literally and figuratively, with a man.

She liked him, well enough, she thought as she tipped her head back and let the hot water beat on her face, her shoulders. She appreciated the way he'd reacted last spring when there'd been trouble, admired—now that she had the distance to look back—the way he'd leaped in without hesitation, without investment.

Some men would have run the other way, and would certainly have dismissed the idea of working for her, in a house haunted by what they now knew could be a dangerous spirit.

And well, she'd been charmed, really, at the way he'd been so flummoxed over buying a child's gift—and how much he'd wanted to find the right thing. It was a point in his favor.

If she were keeping score.

If she wanted to dip her toe in the dating pool again, it would probably be with someone like him. Someone she could have conversations with, someone who attracted and interested her.

And it didn't hurt that he was what Hayley termed a hottie.

Then again, look what happened last time.

It was a stupid woman who'd use anyone like Bryce as a yardstick. She *knew* that, so why couldn't she stop? The fact that she was doing it was a sort of victory for Bryce, wasn't it? If she could do nothing else about it, she could and would work on pushing him out of her thoughts.

Prick.

All right, she thought as she switched the water off again and reached for a towel. Maybe she'd consider—just consider—going out to dinner with Mitch. Just to prove to herself that she wasn't letting Bryce affect her life in any way.

A little dinner out, some conversation, a mix of business and pleasure. That wouldn't be so bad, when she drummed up the energy for it. She wouldn't mind seeing him on a personal level. In fact, it might help all around if she got to know him better.

She'd think about it.

After wrapping the towel around her body, she reached automatically for her lotion. And her hand froze inches from the bottle.

Written in the steam of the bathroom mirror were two words.

Men Lie!

SIX

Roz put men, family ghosts, and messages written in steam out of her mind. Her sons were home.

The house was full of them, their voices, their energy, their debris. Once, the piles of shoes, the hats, the *things* they'd leave scattered around had driven her slightly crazy. Now she loved seeing the evidence of them. Once, she'd longed for an ordered, quiet house, and now reveled in the noise and confusion.

They'd be gone soon enough, back to the lives they were building. So she would treasure every minute of the two days she had her family under one roof again.

And wasn't it fun to see her sons with Stella's boys, or watch Harper lift a fussy Lily and cuddle her in his arms? It made up for finding herself at the head of this mixed generational train.

"I want to thank you for letting Logan stay tonight." Stella settled onto the sofa beside Roz.

"It's Christmas Eve. We generally have room at the inn."

"You know what I mean, and *I* know it's probably fussy

and anal and silly, but I really want our first Christmas in his—*our*—house to be when we're official."

"I think it's sweet and sentimental, and selfishly I'm glad everyone's here tonight." She watched Hayley scoop Lily up as the baby made a crawling beeline for the tree. "Glad to have children in the house tonight. Austin!" she called out as her middle son began to juggle three apples he'd plucked out of a bowl. "Not in the parlor."

"That tune's so familiar, I can add the music." A tall, narrow-hipped young man with his father's wavy blond hair, he winked at Gavin while giving the apples one more rotation. "Not in the parlor, Austin, not in the parlor," he sang, making Stella's sons roll with laughter before he tossed them each an apple, and took a bite out of the third.

"Here, Mama, have some wine." Her youngest, Mason, sat on the arm of the sofa and handed her a glass. There was a wicked twinkle in his blue eyes that warned Roz trouble was coming. "Austin, you know the parlor is sacred ground. You don't want to be juggling in here. Especially something like, say, shoes."

"You can juggle shoes!" Awestruck, Luke goggled at Austin.

"I can juggle anything. I have amazing talent and dexterity."

"But sadly, I wasn't able to talk him into running off and joining the circus when he was eight." Harper took Lily when she leaned away from Hayley and held out her chubby arms to him.

"Can you juggle mine?" Luke asked.

"Hand one over."

"Austin." Resigned, Roz sighed and sipped her wine. "You break anything, you're grounded."

"Why, another familiar tune. Let's see, I need a challenge. Logan, looks to me like that shoe's big enough to house a family of four. Let's have it."

"I give you my shoe, you get grounded, I get fired. Call me a coward, but I'll soon have two growing boys to feed." He reached down to poke Gavin in the ribs. "And they eat like pigs."

"Oink." Showing off, Gavin grabbed a cookie from a tray and stuffed it whole in his mouth. "Oink."

"Oh, go ahead, Logan." Roz waved a hand. "He won't be satisfied otherwise."

"Let's see, one more." His gaze scanned, landed on Hayley. "Look at those pretty, delicate feet. How about it, sweetheart?"

Hayley laughed. "They're about as delicate as banana boats." But she slipped her shoe off.

"Harper, move your grandmother's Baccarat there to safer ground," Roz ordered, "so your brother can show off."

"I prefer the term *perform.*"

"I recall a performance that cost Mama a lamp," Harper commented as he moved heirlooms. "And got all three of us—and you, too, David, if memory serves—KP duty."

"In my salad days," Austin claimed. After giving the trio of varied footwear a few testing tosses, he began to juggle. "As you can see, I've sharpened my skills since that regrettable incident."

"Fortunate to have a fallback career," Mason told him. "You can take that act down to Beale Street."

The circling shoes had Lily giggling and bouncing on Harper's hip. For herself, Roz just held her breath until Austin took his bow.

He tossed a shoe back to a delighted Luke. "Can you teach me?"

"Me, too!" Gavin insisted.

"She's going to say 'not in the parlor,'" Austin announced even as Roz opened her mouth. "We'll work in a lesson tomorrow—outside—keep us all safe from Mama's wrath."

"She's the boss of everybody," Luke told him solemnly.

"No flies on you. Since nobody's seen fit to throw money, I'll have to settle for a beer."

He strolled over to hand Logan his shoe, then walked to Hayley. "All right, Cinderella, let's see if this fits."

He made a production out of slipping it back on her foot, then grinned at Harper over Hayley's head. "Shoe fits." He took her hand, kissed it. "We'll just have to get ourselves married when I get back from the kitchen."

"That's what they all say." But she gave him a flirting sweep with her eyes.

"Why don't you get me a beer while you're at it?" Mason asked.

"If I'm taking orders, what can I get everyone?"

After a scatter of requests, he looked over at Harper again. "Why don't you give me a hand fetching the supplies?"

"Sure." He passed Lily back to Hayley, and followed his brother out of the room.

"Can't miss this," Mason whispered to his mother, then strolled out behind them.

"PRETTY THING, ISN'T SHE, OUR COUSIN HAYLEY?" Austin commented.

"You've always had a keen knack for stating the obvious."

"Then I'll keep my streak going by saying I think she's soft on me."

"And an infallible way of misjudging women."

"Hold on," Mason told them. "I've got to find something to write on so I can keep score."

"She's got the prettiest mouth. Not that you'd notice, big brother, since it's not something growing out of a pot." He took out a beer, had a swig from the bottle even as Harper got out pilsners.

"And the only way you'd get your fat lips on hers is if she has a seizure and requires mouth-to-mouth."

"He shoots, he scores. By the way, I'm the doctor here," Mason reminded them. "She needs mouth-to-mouth, I'm first in line. We got any Fritos or anything around here?"

"Got ten bucks says different." In an old habit, Austin boosted himself up to sit on the counter. "Maybe you could babysit so I can see if our resident babe would like a little stroll around the gardens. Seeing as I haven't heard you call dibs."

"She's not the damn last piece of pie." With some heat, Harper grabbed the beer from his brother, took a long swallow. "What the hell's wrong with you talking about her that way? You ought to have a little more respect, and if you can't come up with it on you're own, you and I can take a little stroll outside so I can help you find it."

With a grin, Austin jabbed a finger at Mason. "Told ya. Can I call 'em or can I call 'em?"

"Yeah, he's hooked on her. What kind of kitchen is it that doesn't have any Fritos?"

"In the pantry, top shelf," Roz said from the doorway. "I'm surprised you'd think I'd forget your childish addiction to corn chips. Austin, have you finished messing with your brother's head for now?"

"I was really just getting started."

"You'll have to postpone that portion of your holiday entertainment." She glanced over, had to smile when she heard Mason's cheer as he located the bag of chips. "We have company, and it might be nice if we present the illusion that I raised three respectable and mature young men."

"That's pretty well shattered since he's already juggled," Harper grumbled.

"There's a point." She moved over to touch Harper's cheek, then Austin's before she turned to Mason. "You may not be respectable and mature, but by God, the three of you sure are handsome. I could've done worse. Now get those drinks together, Harper, and take them out to our guests. Austin, get your butt off my counter. This is a house, not the neighborhood bar. Mason, put those chips into a bowl, and stop dropping crumbs all over the floor."

"Yes'm," they said in unison, and made her laugh.

CHRISTMAS DAY WENT BY IN A BLUR. SHE TRIED TO imprint specific moments on her mind—Mason's sheer delight in the antique medical bag she'd found him, Harper and Austin squaring off over a foosball table. There was Lily's predictable fascination with boxes and wrapping rather than toys, and Hayley's joy in showing off a new pair of earrings.

She loved seeing Logan sitting cross-legged on the floor, showing Stella's boys—his boys now—the child-sized tools inside the toolboxes he'd made them.

She wanted to slow the clock down—just for this day, just this one day—but it sped by, from dawn and the excitement of opening gifts, to the candlelight and the lavish meal David prepared and served on her best china.

Before she knew it, the house was quiet once more.

She wandered down to take a last look at the tree, to sit alone in the parlor with her coffee and her memories of the day, and all the Christmases before.

Surprised when she heard footsteps, she looked over and saw her sons.

"I thought you'd all gone over to Harper's."

"We were waiting for you to come down," Harper told her.

"Come down?"

"You always come down Christmas night, after everyone's gone to bed."

She lifted her eyebrows at Mason. "I have no secrets in this house."

"Plenty of them," he disagreed. "Just not this one."

Austin came over, took her coffee, and replaced it with a glass of champagne.

"What's all this?"

"Little family toast," he told her. "But that comes after this one last gift we've got for you."

"Another? I'm going to have to add a room on the house to hold everything I got this morning."

"This is special. You've already got a place for it. Or did at one time."

"Well, don't keep me in suspense. What have y'all cooked up?"

Harper stepped back into the hall and brought in a large box wrapped in gold foil. He set it at her feet. "Why don't you open it and see?"

Curious, she set her glass aside and began to work on the wrap. "Don't tell Stella I'm tearing this off, she'd be horrified. Myself, I'm amazed the three of you got together and agreed on something, much less kept it quiet until tonight. Mason always blabs."

"Hey, I can keep a secret when I have to. You don't know about the time Austin took your car and—"

"Shut up." Austin punched his brother's shoulder. "There's no statute of limitations on that sort of crime." He smiled sweetly at Roz's narrowed look. "What you don't know, Mama, can't hurt this idiot."

"I suppose." But she wondered on it as she dug through the packing. And her heart simply stuttered as she drew out the antique dressing mirror.

"It was the closest we could come to the one we broke. Pattern's nearly the same, and the shape," Harper said.

"Queen Anne," Austin added, "circa 1700, with that gold and green lacquer on the slanted drawer. At least, it's the best our combined memories could match the one Mason broke."

"Hey! It was Harper's idea to use it as a treasure chest. It's not my fault I dropped it out of the damn tree. I was the baby."

"Oh, God. Oh, God, I was so mad, so mad, I nearly skinned y'all alive."

"We have painful recollection of that," Austin assured her.

"It was from your daddy's family." Voice thick, throat aching, she traced her fingers over the lacquered wood. "He gave it to me on our wedding day."

"We should've been skinned." Harper sat down beside her, rubbed her arm. "We know it's not the same, but—"

"No, no, no." Swamped with emotion, she turned her face to press it against his arm for a moment. "It's better. That you'd remember this, think of this. Do this."

"It made you cry," Mason murmured, and bent to rub his cheek over her hair. "It's the first time I remember seeing you cry. None of us ever forgot it, Mama."

She was struggling not to cry now as she embraced each one of her sons. "It's the most beautiful gift I've ever been given, and I'll treasure it more than anything I have. Every time I look at it, I'll think of the way you were then, the way you are now. I'm so proud of my boys. I always have been. Even when I wanted to skin you."

Austin picked up her glass, handed it to her, then passed around the other three flutes. "Harper gets the honors, as he's the oldest. But I want it on record that I thought it up."

"We all thought it up," Mason objected.

"I thought most of it up. Go on, Harper."

"I will, if you'll shut up for five seconds." He lifted his glass. "To our mama, for everything she's been to us, everything she's done for us, every single day."

"Oh. That's done it." The tears welled into her throat, spilled out of her eyes. "That's done it for sure."

"Go ahead and cry." Mason leaned over to kiss her damp cheek. "Makes a nice circle."

* * *

GETTING BACK TO BUSINESS AS USUAL HELPED FILL THE little hole in her heart from kissing two of her sons goodbye.

It would be a slow week—the holiday week was, routinely—so she took a page out of Stella's book and shouldered in to organizing. She cleaned tools, scrubbed down worktables, helped with inventory, and finally settled on the style of potting-soil bag, and the design.

With some time to spare, she worked with Hayley to pour a fresh supply of concrete planters and troughs.

"I can't believe Christmas is over." Squatting, Hayley turned the mold as Roz poured. "All that anticipation and prep, and it's over in a snap. Last year, my first after my daddy died? Well, it was just awful, and the holidays dragged and dragged."

"Grief tends to spin time out, and joy contracts it. I don't know why that is."

"I remember just wanting it all to be over—so I wouldn't keep hearing "Jingle Bells" every time I went to work, you know? Being pregnant, and feeling alone, the house up for sale. I spent most of Christmas packing things up, figuring out what I was going to sell so I could leave Little Rock."

She sat back on her heels to sigh, happily. "And here, just one year later, and everything was so bright and happy. I know Lily didn't know what was going on, but it was so much fun to watch her play with her toys, or mostly the boxes."

"Nothing like a cardboard box to keep a baby entertained. It was special for me, for all of us, to have her, to be able to share that first Christmas with her."

With the mold full, Hayley tidied the edges with a trowel. "I know you love her, but, Roz, I just don't feel right about you staying home New Year's Eve to sit with her while I go out to a party."

"I prefer staying home New Year's Eve. Lily gives me the perfect excuse. And I'm looking forward to having her to myself."

"You must've been invited to half a dozen parties."

"More." Roz straightened, pressed the small of her back. "I'm not interested. You go on out with David and celebrate with other young people. Wear your new earrings and dance. Lily and I will be just fine seeing the new year in together."

"David said he never could talk you into going to this party, even though it's been a tradition for years now." She picked up a bottle of water, drank casually. "He said Harper would probably drop by."

"I imagine so. They have a number of mutual friends." Amused, she patted Hayley's shoulder. "Let's get this next one done, then call it a day."

She was tired when she got home, but in that satisfied way of knowing she'd crossed several chores off her list. When she noticed Mitch's car in her drive, she was surprised to find herself considering going up to change before seeking him out in the library.

Which was, she reminded herself, both a waste of time and hardly her style. So she was wearing her work clothes when she walked into the library.

"Have everything you need?"

He looked up from the piles of books and papers on the library table. Stared at her through the lenses of his horn-rim reading glasses. "Huh?"

"I just got in. I thought I'd see if there was anything else you need."

"A couple dozen years to organize all of this, a new pair of eyes . . ." He lifted the pot on the desk with him. "More coffee."

"I can help with the last at least." She crossed over, mounted the steps to the second level.

"No, that's all right. My blood level's probably ninety percent caffeine at this point. What time is it?"

She noted the watch on his wrist, then looked at her own. "Ten after five."

"A.M. or P.M.?"

"Been at it that long?"

"Long enough to lose track, as usual." He rubbed the back of one shoulder, circled his neck. "You have some fascinating relatives, Rosalind. I've gathered up enough newspaper clippings on the Harpers, going back to the mid-nineteenth century so far, to fill a banker's box. Did you know, for instance, you have an ancestor who rode for the Pony Express in 1860, and in the 1880s traveled with Buffalo Bill's Wild West Show?"

"My great-great-uncle Jeremiah, who'd run off as a boy, it seems, to ride for the Pony Express. Fought Indians, scouted for the Army, took both a Comanche wife and, apparently, another in Kansas City—at more or less the same time. He was a trick rider in the Wild West Show, and was considered a black sheep by the stuffier members of the clan in his day."

"How about Lucybelle?"

"Ah . . ."

"Gotcha. Married Daniel C. Harper, 1858, left him two years later." The chair creaked as he leaned back. "She pops up again in San Francisco, in 1862, where she opened her own saloon and bawdy house."

"That one slipped by me."

"Well, Daniel C. claimed that he sent her to a clinic in New York, for her health, and that she died there of a wasting disease. Wishful thinking on his part, I assume. But with a little work and magic, I found our Lucybelle entertaining the rough-and-ready crowd in California, where she lived in apparent good health for another twenty-three years."

"You really love this stuff."

"I really do. Imagine Jeremiah, age fifteen, galloping over the plains to deliver the mail. Young, gutsy, skinny. They advertised for skinny boys so they didn't weigh down the horses."

"Really." She eased a hip on the corner of his desk.

"Bent over his mount, riding hell-for-leather, outrunning war parties, covered with dirt and sweat, or half frozen from the cold."

"And from your tone, you'd say having the time of his life."

"Had to be something, didn't it? Then there's Lucy-belle, former Memphis society wife, in a red dress with a derringer in her garter—"

"Aren't you the romantic one."

"Had to have a derringer in her garter while she's manning the bar or bilking miners at cards night after night."

"I wonder if their paths ever crossed."

"There you go," he said, pleased. "That's how you get caught up in all this. It's possible, you know. Jeremiah might've swung through the doors of that saloon, had a whiskey at the bar."

"And enjoyed the other servings on the menu, all while the more staid of the family fanned themselves on the veranda and complained about the war."

"There's a lot of staid, a lot of black sheep here. There was money and there was prestige."

He pushed some papers around, came up with a copy of another clipping. "And considerable charm."

She studied the photo of herself, on her engagement, a fresh and vibrant seventeen.

"I wasn't yet out of high school. Green as grass and mule stubborn. Nobody could talk me out of marrying John

Ashby the June after this picture was taken. God, don't I look ready for anything?"

"I've got clippings of your parents in here. You don't look like either of them."

"No. I was always told I resembled my grandfather Harper. He died when I was a child, but from the pictures I've seen, I favor him."

"Yeah, I've come across a few, and you do. Reginald Edward Harper, Jr, born . . . 1892, youngest child and only son of Reginald and Beatrice Harper." He read his notes. "Married, ah . . ."

"Elizabeth McKinnon. I remember her very well. It was she who gave me her love of gardening, and taught me about plants. My father claimed I was her favorite because I looked like my grandfather. Why don't I get you some tea, something herbal, to offset the coffee?"

"No, that's okay. I can't stay. I've got a date."

"Then I'll let you go."

"With my son," he added. "Pizza and ESPN. We try to fit one in every week."

"That's nice. For both of you."

"It is. Listen, I've got some other things to deal with and some legwork I'd like to get in. But I'll be back on Thursday afternoon, work through the evening, if that's all right with you."

"Thursday's New Year's Eve."

"Is it?" As if baffled, he looked down at his watch. "My days get turned around on me during holidays. I suppose you're having people over."

"Actually, no."

"Then, if you're going out, maybe you wouldn't mind if I worked."

"I'm not going out. I'm going to take care of the baby, Hayley's Lily. I'm scooting her out to a party, and Stella and her boys are going to have a little family party of their own at Logan's house."

"If you weren't asked to a dozen parties, and didn't have twice that many men after you for a New Year's Eve date, I'll eat those newspaper clippings."

"Your numbers might be somewhat exaggerated, but the point is, I declined the parties, and the dates. I like staying home."

"Am I going to be in your way if I work in here?"

She angled her head. "I imagine you were asked to your share of parties, and that there were a number of women eager to have you for their date."

"I stay in on New Year's. A tradition of mine."

"Then you won't be in my way. If the baby's not restless, we can take part of the evening to start on that interview."

"Perfect."

"All right, then. I've been busy," she said after a moment. "The house full over Christmas, all my sons home. And those are only part of the reason I haven't brought this up before."

"Brought what up?"

"A couple of weeks ago, Amelia left me a message."

"A couple of *weeks* ago?"

"I said I'd been busy." Irritation edged into her voice. "And besides that, I didn't want to think about it through the holidays. I don't see my boys very often, and there were a lot of things I wanted to get done before they got here."

He said nothing, simply dug out his tape recorder, pushed it closer to her, switched it on. "Tell me."

Irritation deepened, digging a line between those dark, expressive eyebrows. "She said: *Men lie.*"

"That's it?"

"Yes, that's it. She wrote it on a mirror."

"What mirror? Did you take a picture of it?"

"No, I didn't take a picture." And she could, privately, kick herself for that later. "I don't know what difference it makes what mirror. The bathroom mirror. I'd just gotten out of the shower. A hot one. The mirror was steamy, and the message was written on it through the steam."

"Written or printed?"

"Ah, printed, with an exclamation point at the end. Like this." She picked up one of his pens, demonstrated. "Since it wasn't threatening or earth-shattering information, I figured it could wait."

"Next time don't—figure it can wait. What had you been doing before you . . ." Don't think about her naked in the shower, he ordered himself. "Before you went up to shower?"

"As a matter of fact, I'd been out in the garden talking to you."

"To me."

"Yes, that day you came by and I was mulching up branches."

"Right after your holiday party," he said, making notes. "I asked you out to dinner."

"You mentioned something about—"

"No, no, I asked you out socially." In his excitement, he came around the table, sat on it so they were closer to eye level. "Next thing you know, she's telling you men lie. Fascinating. She was warning you away from me."

"Since I'm not heading in your direction, there's hardly any reason to warn me away."

"It doesn't seem to bother her that I'm working here." He took off his glasses, tossed them on the table. "I've been waiting, actually hoping for some sort of sighting or confrontation, something. But she hasn't bothered about me, so far. Then I make a personal overture, and she leaves you a message. She ever leave you one before?"

"No."

"Hmm." But he caught something flicker over her face. "What? You thought of something."

"Just that it might be a little odd. I saw her recently right after I'd taken a long, hot bath. Shower, bath. Strange."

Don't think of her naked in the tub. "What had you been doing before the bath?"

"Nothing. Some work, that's all."

"All right. What were you thinking while you were in the tub?"

"I don't see what that has to do with anything. It was the night that I did that insane bout of Christmas shopping. I was relaxing."

"You'd been with me that day, too."

"Your ego looks a little heavy, Mitch. Need any help with it?"

"Facts are facts. Anyway, she might have been interested, or upset, by what you were thinking. If she could get into Stella's dreams," he said when she started to brush that aside, "why couldn't she get into your waking thoughts?"

"I don't like that idea. I don't like it at all."

"Neither would I, but it's something to consider. I'm looking at this project from two ends, Roz. From what's happening now, and why, to what happened then, and why. Who and why and what. It's all of a piece. And that's the job you hired me to do. You have to let me know when something happens. And not a couple weeks after the fact."

"All right. Next time she wakes me up at three in the morning, I'll give you a call."

He smiled. "Don't like taking orders, do you? Much too used to giving them. That's all right. I can't blame you, so why don't I just ask, politely, if I could take a look at your bathroom."

"Not only does that seem downright silly at this point, but aren't you supposed to be meeting your son?"

"Josh? Why? Oh, hell, I forgot. I've got to go." He

glanced back at the table. "I'm going to just leave this—do me a favor and don't tidy it up."

"I'm not obsessed with tidy."

"Thank God." He grabbed his jacket, remembered his reading glasses. "I'll be back Thursday. Let me know if anything happens before then."

He hurried toward the door, then stopped and turned. "Rosalind, I have to say, you were a lovely bud at seventeen, but the full bloom? It's spectacular."

She gave a half laugh and leaned back on the table herself when she was alone. Idly she studied her ancient boots, then her baggy work pants, currently smeared with dirt and streaks of drying concrete. She figured the flannel shirt she was wearing over a ragged tee was old enough to have a driver's license.

Men lie, she thought, but occasionally, it was nice to hear.

seven

WITH THE NURSERY CLOSING EARLY FOR THE HOLIDAY, Roz earmarked the time to deal with her own houseplants. She had several that needed repotting or dividing, and a few she wanted to propagate for gifts.

With the weather crisp and clear outside, she settled into the humid warmth of her personal greenhouse. She worked with one of her favorites, an enormous African violet that had come from a plantlet her grandmother had given her more than thirty years before. As Norah Jones's bluesy voice surrounded her, she carefully selected a half dozen new leaves, taking them with their stalks for cuttings. For now, she used a stockpot, sliding the stems in around the edges. In a month they would have roots, and other plantlets would form. Then she would plant them individually in the pale green pots she'd set aside.

They'd be a gift for Stella, for her new house, her new life.

It pleased her to be able to pass this sentimental piece of her heritage along to a woman who'd understand, to someone Roz had come to love.

One day she'd do the same for her sons when they married, and give to them this living piece of her heritage. She would love the women they chose because they did. If she was lucky, she'd like the women they married.

Daughters-in-law, she mused. And grandchildren. It didn't seem quite possible that those events weren't far around her next corner. Odder still that she was beginning to yearn for them. And that, she decided, had its roots in having Stella and Hayley and the children in the house.

Still, she could wait. She accepted change, but that didn't mean she was in a hurry for it.

Right now her life was in pretty good order. Her business was flourishing, and that was not only a personal triumph, it was an intense relief.

She'd risked a great deal by starting In the Garden. But it was a risk she'd had to take—for herself, and for her heritage.

Harper House, and she would never give it up, cost a great deal to maintain. She was well aware there were people who believed she had money to burn, but while she certainly wasn't at the point where she needed to pinch every penny, she was hardly rolling in it.

She'd raised three children, clothed and fed them, educated them. Her legacy had allowed her to stay home with them rather than seek outside employment, and her own canniness with investments had added a cushion.

But three college educations and medical school for Mason hadn't come cheap. And when the house demanded new plumbing, new paint, a new roof, she was obliged to see it got what it needed.

Enough so that she'd discreetly sold some things over the years. Admittedly, paintings or jewelry she hadn't cared for, but it had still given her a little twinge of guilt to sell what had been given to her.

Sacrificing pieces to preserve the whole.

There'd come a time when she'd been confident her sons' futures were seen to, as best she could, and the house was secure. But money was needed nonetheless. It wasn't as if she hadn't considered finding a job—considered very briefly.

Mitch was right, she didn't care to take orders. But she was, without question, very adept at giving them. Play to your strengths, after all, she thought with a glimmer of a smile. That's just what she'd done.

It had been a choice between gathering her courage to start her own business, or swallowing her pride to work for someone else.

For Roz, it was no contest.

She'd piled a great deal of her eggs into that single basket, and the first two years had been touch and go. But it had grown. She and Harper had made it grow.

She'd taken a hit with the divorce. Stupid, stupid mistake. While Bryce had gotten very little out of the deal—and only what she'd permitted him to get—it had cost her dearly in pride and in money to shed herself of him.

But they'd weathered it. Her sons, her home, her business were thriving. So she could think, a little, of changes. Of expansions on both her business and personal fronts. Just as she could enjoy the successful present.

She moved from the African violets to her bromeliads, and by the time she'd finished dividing, she decided Stella was going to get one of these, too. Pleased, she worked another hour, then shifted to check the spring bulbs she was forcing. She'd have narcissus blooming in another week.

When she was satisfied, she carted everything she wanted in the house inside, arranging, as she preferred them, a forest of plants in the solarium, then placing other pots throughout the house.

Last, she carried a trio of bulbs in forcing bottles to the kitchen.

"And what have you brought me?" David asked.

"David, I despair of teaching you anything about horticulture. They're very obviously tulips." She arranged them on the windowsill beside the banquette. "They'll bloom in a few weeks."

"I despair of teaching you anything about the choices of stylish gardening wear. How long have you owned that shirt?"

"I have no idea. What are you doing in here?" She pulled open the refrigerator, took out the pitcher of cold tea that was always there. "Shouldn't you be starting your primping marathon for tonight's party?"

"I'm making you up a nice platter of cold cuts and sides, as you refuse to come out and play with us tonight. And as I treated myself to a few hours at the day spa today while you were grubbing in dirt, my primping has already started."

"You don't have to go to any trouble with platters, David. I can find the makings for a sandwich myself."

"Nicer this way, especially when you have company." He chuckled. "The professor's in the library, and I put a couple of bottles of champagne in to chill so the two of you can—let's say—pop a cork."

"David." She gave him a light cuff on the side of the head before she poured the tea. "I'm not popping anything with anyone. I'm minding the baby."

"Babies sleep. Roz, my treasure, he's *gorgeous*, in that sexily rumpled academic sort of way. Jump him. But for God's sake, change your clothes first. I set out your white cashmere sweater, and those black pants I talked you into—the ones with lots of lycra, and those fabulous Jimmy Choo's."

"I'm certainly not wearing white cashmere, skintight pants—which I'd never have bought if you hadn't hypnotized me or something—or a pair of five-inch heels when

I'm babysitting for a seven-month-old. It's not even a date."

"Don't you just love those horn-rims? What is it about a man in horn-rim glasses?"

She took an olive out of the bowl he'd filled. "You're certainly wound up tonight."

He covered the bowls and the tray he'd prepared with plastic. "There now. You're going to have yourself a nice New Year's Eve picnic with the horn-rimmed hunk."

"David, why in the world do you think I need a man?"

"My darling Roz, we *all* need a man."

SHE DID CHANGE, BUT BRUTALLY REJECTED DAVID'S choices in favor of a simple cotton shirt and jeans, and her favored wool socks in lieu of shoes. Still, she had enough vanity to do her makeup.

In the nursery, she listened patiently to all of Hayley's nervous-mother instructions, assured, and reassured, swore an oath she would call if there was any sort of a problem. And finally nudged the girl out and on her way.

She waited, watching from the window until she saw the car drive away. Then, grinning, she turned to where Lily gurgled in her bouncy chair.

"I've got you all to myself now. Come on up here to Aunt Roz, 'cause I've just got to eat you right up like a bowl of sugar."

In the library, Mitch pretended to read, took sketchy notes, and listened to the baby monitor that stood on a table on the lower level.

Every room had one, at least every room he'd been in, he thought. Since the experiences last spring, he thought that was a wise and basic precaution.

But he wasn't thinking of safety or precautions now. He

was simply charmed and amused, listening first to Hayley's anxiety-filled departure, and now Roz's verbal love affair with the baby.

He'd never heard that tone in her voice before, hadn't known it could soften like that, like fragrant wax under low heat. Nor had he expected her to dote, as she so obviously doted, on a child.

She talked nonsense, cooed, laughed, made the silly noises adults habitually made around babies and, from the sounds of Lily's response, made the baby as happy as the sitter.

It was another angle to a woman he'd seen as formidable, confident, a little aloof, and oddly direct. All those facets had already combined into a woman he found smoothly sexy. Now this . . . softness, he supposed, was a surprising icing on an already desirable cake.

He heard her laugh, a long, lovely roll, and gave up even the pretense of working.

He heard the music and banging of toys, the child's burbling and giggles, and the undiluted pleasure in the woman's voice. Later, he heard her singing as she rocked the baby to sleep.

Soon after, he heard her murmured words, her quiet sigh, then the monitor was silent.

He sighed himself, sorry the interlude was over. Then reaching for his coffeepot, found it empty. Again.

He carried it into the kitchen to brew another pot, and was just measuring out the coffee when Roz came in.

"Hi," he said. "Be out of your way in a minute. David said I should just make myself coffee whenever."

"Of course. I was about to make use of the cold cuts he put together earlier, if you'd like something to eat."

"I would, thanks. He mentioned there'd be makings when he showed me where I could find what I needed for coffee. And . . ." He widened his eyes as Roz took out the tray, the bowls. "I see he meant it."

"He's constantly afraid I'll starve to death if he doesn't leave me enough food for six people." She glanced over. "And?"

"Sorry?"

"You started to say something else? Regarding David?"

"Oh well, just that I think he was hitting on me."

She got long, fresh rolls from the bread drawer. "Not very hard, I'm sure."

"No, not hard. Just . . . charmingly actually."

"I hope you weren't offended."

"No, I was, well, sort of flattered, really. Considering the age difference."

"He likes the way you look in your glasses."

"In my . . . what?"

"Horn-rims. They just turn him to mush, apparently. You want me to just pile everything on here, or would you rather pick and choose?"

"Just pile, thanks. I appreciate it."

"It's no trouble as I'm making some for myself as it is." She looked up sharply, as a voice, Amelia's voice, began to sing through the monitor.

"It's a jolt, isn't it?" Mitch said. "Every time."

"She doesn't go into Lily's room every night, not like she did with the boys. She favors boys. I suppose she knows Hayley's out, and wants to . . ."

She trailed off, her fingers fumbling, as they rarely did, with the sandwiches as she recalled the monitor in the library. And her own session with Lily.

"I hadn't thought about the monitor where you were working, disturbing you."

"It didn't—you didn't—in the least."

"In any case, feel free to switch it off in there when

you're working. God knows we have them everywhere. Hayley went out and bought one that has video, too, for her room. Amazing the sorts of things they have now, to make life a bit easier for new mothers."

"You must've been a good one. It came through," he added, "when you were up there with her."

"I was. Am. It's my most important job." But her interlude with Lily had been private—or so she'd thought. Just how many times had she sang the hokeypokey along with Elmo?

Best not to think about it.

"Would you like to take this back in, eat while you work, or take a break, and eat in here?"

"In here, if it's all right with you."

"That'll be fine." She hesitated, then opened the refrigerator again, took out the champagne. "Seeing as it's New Year's Eve, I'm going to open this. We can have something a little more festive than coffee with our poor boys."

"Thanks, but I don't drink. Can't."

"Oh." She felt abominably slow and stupid. Hadn't she noticed herself that he never took alcohol? Couldn't she have used her brain to put two and two together before embarrassing a guest? "Coffee it is, then."

"Please." He stepped over to lay a hand on her arm before she replaced the bottle. "Open it, enjoy it. It doesn't bother me when other people have a drink. In fact, it's important to me that they're comfortable. That you're comfortable. Here, let me do it."

He took the bottle. "Don't worry, opening a bottle of champagne isn't backsliding."

"I certainly didn't mean to make *you* uncomfortable. I should've realized."

"Why? I'm not still wearing that sign that says Recovering Alcoholic around my neck, am I?"

She smiled a little, walked to the display cabinet for a flute. "No."

He released the cork, a quick, celebrational pop. "I started drinking when I was about fifteen. Sneaking a beer now and then, the way boys often do. Nothing major. I did love an ice-cold beer."

He set both their plates on the table, then poured his coffee while she arranged the rest of the simple meal. "Went through the drinking insanity in college, but again, plenty do the same. Never missed a class because of it, never caused me any trouble, really. My grades stayed up—enough I graduated with honors, top five percent of my class. I loved college nearly as much as I did an ice-cold beer. Am I going to bore you with this?"

"No," she said, her eyes on his. "You're not."

"All right." He took his first bite of the sandwich, nodded. "Miz Harper, you make a hell of a po'boy."

"I do."

"So I went to grad school, got my master's. Taught, got married, worked on my doctorate. Had myself a gorgeous baby boy. And I drank. I was . . . an amiable drunk, if you know what I mean. I was never confrontational, never abusive—physically, I mean, never picked fights. But I can't say I was ever completely sober from the time Josh was born—a bit before that to be honest, until I set the bottle down the last time."

He sampled David's potato salad. "I worked—taught, wrote, provided my family with a good living. Drinking never cost me a day's work, any more than it had cost me class time. But it cost me my wife and my son."

"I'm sorry, Mitch."

"No need to be. Sara, my ex, did everything she could do. She loved me, and she wanted the life I'd promised her. She stuck with me longer than many would have. She begged me to quit, and I'd promise or reassure, or fluff her off. Bills were paid, weren't they? We had a nice house, and we never missed a mortgage payment. I wasn't some stumbling-down, sprawled-in-the-gutter drunk, was I, for God's sake? I just had a few drinks to take the edge off. Of course, I started taking the edge off at ten in the morning, but I was entitled."

He paused, shook his head. "It's easy to delude yourself that you're entitled, that you're just fine when you're in a haze most of the time. Easy to ignore the fact that you're letting your wife and child down in a dozen ways, every single day. Forgetting dinner parties or birthdays, slipping out of bed—where you are useless to her in any case—to have just one more drink, dozing off when you're supposed to be watching your own baby. Just not being there, not completely there. Ever."

"It's a hard thing to go through, I imagine. For everyone involved."

"Harder for the ones you shipwreck with you, believe me. I wouldn't go to counseling with her, refused to attend meetings, to talk to anyone about what she saw as my problem. Even when she told me she was leaving me, when she packed her things, and Josh's things, and walked out. I barely noticed they were gone."

"That was tremendously brave of her."

"Yes, it was." His gaze sharpened on Roz's face. "Yes, it was, and I suppose a woman like you would understand just how brave it was. It took me another full year to hit the bottom, to look around at my life and see nothing. To realize I'd lost what was most precious, and that it was too late to ever get it back. I went to meetings."

"That takes courage, too."

"My first meeting?" He took another bite of his sandwich. "Scared to death. I sat in the back of the room, in the basement of this tiny church, and shook like a child."

"A lot of courage."

"I was sober for three months, ten days, and five hours when I reached for a bottle again. Fought my way out of that, and sobriety lasted eleven months, two days, and fifteen hours. She wouldn't come back to me, you see. She'd met someone else and she couldn't trust me. I used that as an excuse to drink, and I drank the next few months away, until I crawled back out of the hole."

He lifted his coffee. "That was fourteen years ago next March. March fifth. Sara forgave me. In addition to being brave, she's a generous woman, one who deserved better than what she got from me. Josh forgave me, and in the past fourteen years, I've been a good father. The best I know how to be."

"I think it takes a brave man, and a strong one to face his demons, and beat them back, and keep facing them every single day. And a generous one, a smart one who shoulders the blame rather than passing it on, even partially, to others."

"Not drinking doesn't make me a hero, Roz. It just makes me sober. Now if I could just kick the coffee habit."

"That makes two of us."

"Now that I've talked your ear off, I'm going to ask you to return the favor, and give that first interview when we've finished eating."

"All right. Am I going to be talking for the recorder?"

"Primarily, yeah, though I'll take some notes."

"Then maybe we could do that in the parlor, where it's a little more comfortable."

"Sounds like a plan."

She checked on Lily first, and took the first phone call from Hayley. While Mitch gathered whatever he needed from the library, she pulled the tray of fresh fruit—David never missed a trick—and the brie and cheddar, the crackers, he'd stocked.

Even as she wheeled it toward the parlor, Mitch came up behind her. "Let me get that."

"No, I've got it. But you could light the fire. A fire'd be

nice. It's cold tonight, but thank God, clear. I'd hate to worry about my chicks navigating slick roads on their way home to roost later."

"I thought the same thing about my own earlier. Never ends, does it?"

"No." She set out the food, the coffee, then sat on the couch, instinctively propped her feet on the table. She stared at her own feet, surprised. It was a habit, she knew, but one she didn't indulge in when she had guests. She glanced at Mitch's back as he crouched to light kindling.

She supposed it meant she was comfortable with him, and that was fine. Better than labeling him a guest as she'd be trusting him with her family.

"You're right, it's nice to have a fire."

He came back, set up his recorder, his notebook, then settled on the other end of the couch, shifting his body toward hers. "I'd like to start off with you telling me about the first time you remember seeing Amelia."

Straight to business, she thought. "I don't know that I remember a first time, not specifically. I'd have been young. Very. I remember her voice, the singing, and a kind of comforting presence. I thought—to the best of my memory, that is—that it was my mother. But my mother wasn't one to look in at night, and I never remember her singing to me. It wasn't her way. I remember her—Amelia—being there a few times when I was sick. A cold, a fever. It's more that she was there, and expected to be in a way, than a jolting first time."

"Who told you about her?"

"My father, my grandmother. My grandmother more, I suppose. The family would talk about her casually, in vague terms. She was both a point of pride—we have a ghost—and a slight embarrassment—we have a ghost. Depending on who was talking. My father believed she was one of the Harper Brides, while my grandmother maintained she was a servant or guest, someone who'd been misused somehow. Someone who had died here, but wasn't blood kin."

"Did your father, your grandmother, your mother, ever tell you about their specific experiences with her?"

"My mother would get palpitations if the subject was brought up. My mother was very fond of her palpitations."

Mitch grinned at the dry tone, watched her spread some brie. "I had a great-aunt like that. She had spells. Her day wasn't complete without at least one spell."

"Why some people delight in having conditions is more than I can understand. My mother did speak to me of her once or twice, in a sort of gloom-and-doom manner—something else she was fond of. Warning me that one day I'd inherit this burden, and hoping for my sake it didn't shatter my health, as it had hers."

"She was afraid of Amelia, then."

"No, no." Roz waved that away, nibbled on a cracker. "She enjoyed being long-suffering, and a kind of trembling martyr. Which sounds very unkind coming from her only child."

"Let's call it honest instead."

"Comes to the same. In any case, other times, it was bearing and birthing me that had ruined her health. And others, she'd been delicate since a bout of pneumonia as a child. Hardly matters."

"Actually, it's helpful. Bits and pieces, personal observations and memories are helpful, a start toward the big picture. What about your father?"

"My father was generally amused by the idea of a ghost and had fond memories of her from his own childhood. But then he'd be annoyed or embarrassed if she made an appearance and frightened a guest. My father was fiercely hospitable, and mortified on a deep, personal level if a guest in his home was inconvenienced."

"What sort of memories did he have?"

"The same you've heard before. It hardly varies. Her singing to him, visiting him in his room, a maternal presence until he was about twelve."

"No disturbances?"

"Not that he told me, but my grandmother said he sometimes had nightmares as a boy. Just one or two a year, where he claimed to see a woman in white, with her eyes bulging, and he could hear her screaming in his head. Sometimes she was in his room, sometimes she was outside, and so was he—in the dream."

"Dreams would be another common thread, then. Have you had any?"

"No, not . . ."

"What?"

"I always thought it was nerves. In the weeks before John and I were married, I had dreams. Of storms. Black skies and thunder, cold winds. A hole in the garden, like a grave, with dead flowers inside it." She shivered once. "Horrible. But they stopped after I was married. I dismissed them."

"And since?"

"No. Never. My grandmother saw her more than anyone, at least more than anyone would admit to. In the house, in the garden, in my father's room when he was a boy. She never told me anything frightening. But maybe she wouldn't have. Of all my family, that I recall, she was the most sympathetic toward Amelia. But to be honest, it wasn't the primary topic of conversation in the house. It was simply accepted, or ignored."

"Let's talk about that blood kin, then." He pulled his glasses out of his shirt pocket to read his notes. "The furthest back you know, personally, of sightings starts with your grandmother Elizabeth McKinnon Harper."

"That's not completely accurate. She told me my grandfather, her husband, had seen the Bride when he was a child."

"That's her telling you what she'd been told, not what she claimed to have seen and experienced herself. But speaking to that, can you recall being told of any experiences that happened in the generation previous to your grandparents?"

"Ah . . . she said her mother-in-law, that would be my great-grandmother Harper, refused to go into certain rooms."

"Which rooms?"

"Ah . . . lord, let me think. The nursery, which was on the third floor in those days. The master bedroom. She moved herself out of it at some point, I'm assuming. The kitchen. And she wouldn't set foot in the carriage house. From my grandmother's description of her, she wasn't a fanciful woman. It was always thought she'd seen the Bride. If there was another prior to that, I don't know about it. But there shouldn't be. We've dated her to the 1890s."

"You've dated her based on a dress and a hairstyle," he said as he scribbled. "That's not quite enough."

"It certainly seems sensible, logical."

He looked up, smiling, his eyes distracted behind his glasses. "It may be. You may be right, but I like a little more data before I call something a fact. What about your great-aunts? Reginald Jr.'s older sisters?"

"I couldn't say. I didn't know any of them, or don't remember them. And they weren't close with my grandmother, or my father. There was some attempt, on my grandmother's part, to cement some familial relations between their children and my father, as cousins. I'm still in contact with some of their children."

"Will any of them talk to me?"

"Some will, some won't. Some are dead. I'll give you names and numbers."

"All," he said. "Except the dead ones. I can be persuasive.

Again," he murmured as the singing came from the monitor across the room.

"Again. I want to go check on Lily."

"Do you mind if I come with you?"

"No. Come ahead." They started upstairs together. "Most likely it'll stop before we get there. That's the pattern."

"There were two nursemaids, three governesses, a housekeeper, an under-housekeeper, a total of twelve housemaids, a personal maid, three female kitchen staff between 1890 and 1895. I've dug up some of the names, but as ages aren't listed, I'm having to wade through a lot of records to try to pinpoint the right people. If and when, I'll start on death records, and tracking down descendants."

"You'll be busy."

"Gotta love the work. You're right. It's stopped."

But they continued down the hall to the nursery. "Cold still," Roz commented. "It doesn't last long, though." She moved to the crib, slid the blanket more neatly around the sleeping baby.

"Such a good baby," she said quietly. "Sleeps right through the night most of the time. None of mine did at this age. She's fine. We should leave her be."

She stepped out, leaving the door open. They were at the top of the stairs when the clock began to bong.

"Midnight?" Roz looked at her watch to be certain. "I didn't realize it was so late. Well, Happy New Year."

"Happy New Year." He took her hand before she could continue down the steps and, laying the other on her cheek, said, "Do you mind?"

"No, I don't mind."

His lips brushed hers, very lightly, a kind of civilized and polite gesture to commemorate the changing year. And somewhere in the east wing, Roz's wing, a door slammed shut like a gunshot.

Though her heart jumped, she managed to speak evenly. “Obviously, she doesn’t approve.”

“More like she’s pissed off. And if she’s going to be pissed off, we might as well give her a good reason.”

He didn’t ask this time, just slid the hand that lay on her cheek around to cup the back of her neck. And this time his mouth wasn’t light, or polite, or civilized. There was a punch of heat, straight to her belly, as his mouth crushed down on hers, as his body pressed, hard against hers. She felt that sizzle zip through her blood, fast and reckless, and let herself ride on it for just one mad moment.

The door in the east wing slammed, again and again, and the clock continued to chime, madly now, well past the hour of twelve.

He’d known she’d taste like this, ripe and strong. More tang than sweetness. He’d wanted to feel those lips move against his as they were now, to discover just how that long, slender body fit to his. Now that he was, she settled inside him and made him want more.

But she eased back, her eyes open and direct. “Well. That ought to do it.”

“It’s a start.”

“I think it’d be best to keep everything . . . calm for tonight. I really should tidy up the parlor, and settle down up here, with Lily.”

“All right. I’ll get my notes and head home.”

In the parlor she loaded the cart while he gathered his things. “You’re a difficult woman to read, Rosalind.”

“I’m sure that’s true.”

“You know I want to stay, you know I want to take you to bed.”

“Yes, I know.” She looked over at him. “I don’t take lovers . . . I was going to say just that. That I don’t take lovers, but I’m going to say, instead, I don’t take them rashly, or lightly. So if I decide to take you as a lover, or let you take me, it will be serious business, Mitchell. Very serious business. That's something both of us need to consider."

"Ever just jump off the ledge, Roz?"

"I've been known to. But, except for the regrettable and rare occasion, I like to make certain I'm going to land on my feet. If I wasn't interested, I'd tell you, flat out. I don't play games in this arena. Instead, I'm telling you that I am interested, enough to think about it. Enough to regret, a little, that I'm no longer young and foolish enough to act without thinking."

The phone rang. "That'll be Hayley again. I need to get that or she'll panic. Drive carefully."

She walked out to get the phone, and heard, as she assured Hayley the baby was fine, was sleeping like an angel, had been no trouble at all, the front door close behind him.

eight

A LITTLE DISTANCE, MITCH DECIDED, WAS IN ORDER. The woman was a paradox, and since there was no finite solution to a paradox, it was best accepted for what it was—instead of puzzling over it until blood leaked out of your ears.

So he'd try a little distance where he could funnel his energies into puzzles other than the enigmatic Rosalind Harper.

He had plenty of legwork, or, more accurately, butt work. A few hours on his computer and he could verify the births and deaths and marriages listed in the Harper family Bible. He'd already generated a chart of the family ancestry, using his on-line and his courthouse information.

Clients liked charts. Beyond that, they were tools for him, as the copies of family pictures were, as letters were. He pinned everything onto a huge board. Two in this case. One for his office in his apartment, and one in the library at Harper House.

Pictures, old photos, old letters, diaries, scribbled family recipes, all of those things brought the people alive for him. When they were alive for him, when he began to envision their daily routines, their habits, their flaws and grievances, they mattered to him more than any job or project could matter.

He could lose hours paging through Elizabeth Harper's gardening notes, or the baby book she'd kept on Roz's father. How else would he know the man who'd sired Roz had suffered from celiac at three months, or had taken his first steps ten months later?

It was the details, the small bits, that made the past full, and immediate.

And in the wedding photo of Elizabeth and Reginald Junior, he could see Rosalind in her grandfather. The dark hair, the long eyes, the strong facial bones.

What else had he passed to her, and through her to her children, this man she barely remembered?

Business acumen for one, Mitch concluded. From other details, those small bits, found in clippings, in household records, he gained a picture of a man who'd had a sharp skill for making money, who'd avoided the fate of many of his contemporaries in the stock market crash. A careful man, and one who'd preserved the family home and holdings.

Yet wasn't there a coolness about him? Mitch thought as he studied the photographs on his board. A remoteness that showed in his eyes. More than just the photographic style of the day.

Perhaps it came from being born wealthy—the only son on whose shoulders the responsibilities fell.

"What," Mitch wondered aloud, "did you know about Amelia? Did you ever meet her, in the flesh? Or was she already dead, already just a spirit in this house when your time came around?"

Someone knew her, he thought. Someone spoke to her, touched her, knew her face, her voice.

And someone who did lived or worked in Harper House.

Mitch moved to a search of the servants he had by full names.

It took time, and didn't include the myriad other possibilities. Amelia had been a guest, a servant whose name was not included—or had been expunged from family records—a relative's relative, a friend of the family.

He could speculate, of course, that if a guest, a friend, a distant relation had died in the house, the information would have trickled down, and her identity would be known.

Then again, that was speculation, and didn't factor in the possibility of scandal, and the tendency to hush such matters up.

Or the fact that she'd been no one important to the Harpers, had died in her sleep, and no one considered it worth discussing.

And it was just another paradox, he supposed as he leaned back from his work, that he, a rational, fairly logical-thinking man, was spending considerable time and effort to research and identify a ghost.

The trick was not to think of her that way, but to think of her as a living, breathing woman, a woman who had been born, lived a life, dressed, ate, laughed, cried, walked, and talked.

She had existed. She had a name. It was his job to find *who*, *what*, *when*. *Why* was just the bonus question.

He dug the sketch out of his file, studied the image Roz had created of a young, thin woman with a mass of curly hair and eyes full of misery. And this is how they'd dated her, he thought with a shake of his head. By a dress and a hairstyle.

Not that it wasn't a good sketch. He'd only seen Amelia once, and she hadn't looked calm and sad like this, but wild and mad.

The dress could have been ten, even twenty years old. Or brand-new. The hairstyle a personal choice or a fashion statement. It was impossible to pinpoint age or era on such, well, sketchy information.

And yet, from his research so far, he tended to think they were close to the mark.

The talk of dreams, the bits of information, the lore itself appeared to have its roots during Reginald Harper's reign.

Reginald Harper, he thought, kicking back in his chair to stare at the ceiling. Reginald Edward Harper, born 1851, the youngest of four children born to Charles Daniel Harper and Christabel Westley Harper. Second and only surviving son. Older brother, Nathanial died July 1864, at age eighteen, during the Battle of Bloody Bridge in Charlestown.

"Married Beatrice . . ." He rummaged through his notes again. Yes, there it is, 1880. Five children. Charlotte, born 1881, Edith Anne, 1883, Katherine, 1885, Victoria, 1886, and Reginald Junior, 1892."

Big gap between the last two kids, considering the pattern beforehand, he thought, and noted down possibilities of miscarriages and/or stillbirths.

Strong possibilities with the factors of unreliable birth control, and the natural assumption that Reginald would have wanted a son to continue the family name.

He scanned the family chart he'd generated for Beatrice. A sister, one brother, one sister-in-law. But neither female relation had died until well after the first reports of sightings and dreams, making them unlikely candidates. And neither had been named Amelia.

Of course, he hadn't found a servant by that name, either. Not yet.

But for now he circled back to Reginald Harper, head of the house during the most likely era.

Just who were you, Harper? Prosperous, well-heeled. Inherited the house, and the holdings, because the older brother ran off to be a solider, and died fighting for the Cause. Baby of the family on top of it.

Married well, accumulating more holdings through that marriage. Expanded and modernized the house, according to Roz's notes. Married well, lived well, and you weren't afraid to spend the dough. Still, there'd been a consistent turnover of housemaids and other female staff during his years at the helm.

Maybe Reginald liked to play with the help. Or his wife had been a tyrant.

Was the long wait for a son frustrating and annoying, or was he happy with his girls? It would be interesting to know.

There was no one alive to say.

Mitch went back to his computer and contented himself, for the moment, with facts.

SINCE SHE HAD SO MANY HOUSEPLANTS FROM THE DIvision of her own, Roz rotated some into store stock, and at Stella's suggestion worked with her to use more in creating some dish gardens.

She enjoyed working with Stella, and that was rare. Primarily when she was potting or propagating, Roz preferred only the company of her plants and her music.

"Feels good to get my hands in the dirt," Stella commented as she selected a snake plant for her arrangement.

"I figure you'll be getting plenty of that soon enough dealing with your new gardens."

"Can't wait. I know I'm driving Logan crazy changing and redefining and tweaking the plan." She blew a stray curl out of her face and slid her gaze over to Roz. "Then again, *plan* isn't exactly the word for what he was doing with the landscape. It was more of a concept."

"Which you're refining."

"I think if I show him one more sketch he might make me eat it. This coleus is gorgeous."

"Focusing on the gardens helps keep down the nerves over the wedding."

Stella paused, hands in dirt. "Bull's-eye. Who'd think I'd be nervous? It's not the first time around for me, and we're keeping it small, simple. I've had months to plan, which hasn't made him all that happy, either. But we had to at least get the living room and the boys' rooms painted and furnished. You wouldn't believe some of the gorgeous pieces his mother gave him that he's had stuffed in a storage garage."

"This dracaena should work here. Nerves are expected, I'd think. A bride's still a bride, first time around or not."

"Were you nervous the second time? I know it turned out awful, but . . ."

"No, I wasn't." Her tone was flat. Not bitter, just empty. "Should've told me something. You're nervous because you're excited and you're happy, and because you're the type who'll worry over every detail. Worry especially when it's important."

"I just want everything to look special. Perfect. I must've been crazy, deciding to have the wedding outside in the backyard when the gardens weren't even finished. Now we only have until April to get it all done."

"And you will. You and Logan know what you're doing about the planting, about each other, about everything that matters."

"Remind me of that every now and again, would you?"

"Happy to. These look good." She stepped back, fisted her gloved hands on her hips. "You got prices worked up?"

"Thirty-four fifty. Forty-five ninety-five for the large size."

"Sounds good. Nice profit margin since the plants are mostly all divisions."

"And a good value for our customers since they're not going to see dish gardens this full or lush anywhere. I'll help you carry some in, then plug these into the inventory."

They loaded a flat cart, wheeled it into the main building. When Stella started to shift stock to rearrange, Roz nudged her aside.

"Go on, do the paperwork. If you start here fiddling with display, you'll be here an hour. You're just going to come back when I'm done and fool with it anyway."

"I was just thinking if we grouped some of the smaller ones over there, and used a couple of those tile-topped tables—"

"I'll figure it out, then you can come behind me and . . . refine it."

"If you put one of the larger ones on that wrought-iron patio table, and put one of the little brass lanterns with it, then set that sixteen-inch clay pot of bird of paradise beside it, it would be a strong display. And I'm going."

Amused, Roz shifted stock, arranged the new. And since she had to admit Stella was on target, as usual, set up the table as outlined.

"Why, Rosalind Harper, there you are!"

Because Roz's back was turned, she indulged herself in a single wince before schooling her face to more welcoming lines.

"Hey there, Cissy."

She allowed the standard greeting, a peck that stopped an inch from her cheek, then resigned herself to losing a quarter of an hour in chatter.

"Don't you look pretty," Roz said. "Is that a new suit?"

"This?" Cissy waved one of her French-manicured hands, dismissing the cherry-red suit. "Just yanked it out of my closet this morning. I swear, Roz, are you *ever* going to gain an ounce? Every time I see you, I feel obliged to sweat an extra twenty minutes on my exercise machine."

"You look wonderful, Cissy." Which was invariably true. One of the skills Cecilia Pratt had most honed was in turning herself out. Her hair was an attractive streaky blond worn in a ruler-straight swing that suited her round, youthful face with its winking dimples and walnut-brown eyes.

From the outfit, Roz assumed she'd just come from some lady lunch, or committee meeting, and had come by to sow and to harvest gossip.

Gossip was Cissy's other keen skill.

"I don't see how I could, I'm just worn *out*. The holidays just about did me in this year. Every time you turned around, there was another party. I don't think I've caught my breath since Thanksgiving. Now before you know it, it'll be the Spring Ball at the club. Tell me you're going this year, Roz. It's just not the same without you."

"Haven't thought about it."

"Well, do. Sit down here a minute and let's catch up. I swear I can't stay on my feet another *minute*." To prove it, she sat on the bench near the table display Roz had just completed. "Isn't this nice? It's just like sitting in a tropical garden somewhere. Hank and I are heading down to the Caymans next week for some sun. I need the break, let me tell you."

"Won't that be fun." Trapped by manners, Roz joined her on the bench.

"You ought to take yourself a nice tropical vacation, honey." Cissy patted Roz's hand. "Sun, blue water, handsome half-naked men. Just the ticket. You know I worry that you just chain yourself to this place. But you've got that girl from Up North managing things now. How's she working out for you, by the way?"

"Her name's Stella, Cissy, and she's worked for me for a year now. That should be a good indication it's working out just fine for both of us."

"That's good. You should take advantage of that and get away for a while."

"There's no place I want to go."

"Well, I'm going to bring you some brochures, that's

what I'm going to do. I don't know if I could get through the next day if I didn't know we'd be sitting on a beach sipping mai tais soon. You were smart to skip most of the parties, though I was sorry I didn't see you New Year's Eve at Jan and Quill's. Lovely gathering, really, though it didn't come *near* the one you put on. Flowers were on the skimpy side, and the food wasn't much more than mediocre. Not that I'd say so to Jan. Did you know she was going in for liposuction next week?"

"No, I didn't."

"Well, it's one of those ill-kept secrets." Cissy edged closer, her dimples doing a conspirator's wink. "Butt and thighs is what I hear. I just this minute came from lunch with her, and *she* says how she's going to be spending a week at a spa in Florida, when everybody knows she's going for the vacuum, then holing up in her house till she can get around again. And, bless her heart, since you could set a table for a family of four on the shelf of her ass, I'd say it'll be more than a week before she's walking straight again."

Despite herself, Roz laughed. "For God's sake, Cissy, her ass looks normal enough to me."

"Not compared to the new administrative assistant Quill's said to have his eye on. Twenty-eight years old, and you could set that table quite a bit higher on that one, as long as you don't mind eating off silicone."

"I hope that's not true, about Quill. I've always thought he and Jan were good together."

"Some men just lose all sense around a big pair of tits, no matter if God or man made them. Which brings me around to what I really came by to tell you. I'm just not quite sure how."

"I'm sure you'll find a way."

"It's just that I feel I must, I'm obliged . . . How long have we been friends, Rosalind?"

"I couldn't say." Since knowing someone since high school didn't make you friends, she thought.

"At our age, it's best not to count the years in any case. But since we've known each other longer than either of us cares to admit to, I feel like I have to let you know what's going around. But first I want to say, since I haven't had a minute to talk to you since . . . the *incident*, that I've never been so shocked or so *dumbfounded* as I was when that horrible Bryce Clerk walked into your house, just like he had a right to, the night of your party."

"It's all right, Cissy. He walked right back out again."

"And a good thing, too, as I don't know if I could've held myself back. I just don't know. I couldn't believe that Mandy. Of course, that girl hasn't got the sense God gave a retarded flea, but that's no excuse for not taking the time to find out who the man *was* before she came traipsing into your home on his arm."

She waved a hand. "I just can't speak of it."

"Then we won't. I really have to get back to work."

"But I haven't *told* you. My tongue just runs away from me when I'm upset. He was *there*, with that ridiculous, brainless girl again. He was there, Roz, at Jan and Quill's, big as life, like he didn't have a care in the world. Drinking champagne and dancing, smoking cigars out on the veranda. Talking about his *consulting* company. Just turned my stomach."

She held a hand to it, as if even now it threatened to revolt. "I know Jan said you'd sent your regrets, but I lived in horror that you'd change your mind and walk in any minute. I wasn't the only one, either."

"I'm sure." Very sure, Roz thought, that there'd been plenty of excited buzz, and half-hopeful glances toward the door. "Jan's entitled to have anyone she wants to in her own home."

"I certainly don't agree with that. It's a matter of loyalty, if not good taste. And I had lunch with her today to say just that."

As she spoke, she opened her purse and took out a compact to blot her nose. "Turns out Quill cleared the way for him. They're doing some business together, not that Jan seems to know a thing about that, the woman's just clueless when it comes to money matters. Not like you and me."

"Mmm" was the most polite response Roz could think of, as Cissy had never worked a day in her life.

"To her credit she was mortified while we talked about it over lunch. Mortified." Taking out a lipstick, she repainted her mouth to match her suit. "But there are some, and I admit I heard some of this at the party as well as here and there, there are some who feel some sympathy for the man. Who actually believed he was treated poorly, which just beats all, if you ask me. The worst of it is, the version that you physically assaulted him the night of the party, running him out when he attempted to make bygones, so to speak. That you threatened him and that silly girl even when they went out again. Of course, every time I hear it, I do what I can to straighten it out. I was there, after all."

Roz recognized the avid tone. Give me some fuel for this fire. And that she wouldn't do, no matter how angry, how vilified she felt. "People will say or think what they want to say or think. There's no point in me worrying about it."

"Well, some are saying and thinking that you didn't come to Jan's, or other get-togethers, because you knew *he* would be there, and sporting a woman nearly half your age."

"I'm surprised anyone would spend so much time concerned with speculating on how I might react to someone who is no longer a part of my reality. If you see Jan, be sure to tell her not to worry about it on my account."

Roz rose. "It was good to see you. I've just got to get back to work here."

"I want you to know I'll be thinking about you." Cissy got to her feet, gave Roz another air peck. "We've got to have lunch sometime soon, my treat."

"You and Hank have a good time in the Caymans."

"We will. I'm going to send you those brochures," she called over her shoulder as she walked out.

"You do that," Roz muttered.

She walked out the opposite way, furious with herself for being hurt and insulted. She knew better, knew it wasn't worth it, but still the score to her pride ached.

She started to turn into the propagation house, but veered off. In this mood she'd do more harm than good. Instead, she skirted around, headed into the woods that separated her private and personal domains, and took the long way home.

She didn't want to see anyone, speak to anyone, but there was David out in the yard, playing with Stella's boys and their dog.

The dog spotted her first, and with a few welcoming yips raced over to jump, and scrabble at her knees.

"Not now, Parker." She bent to scratch his ears. "Not a good time now."

"We're hunting buried treasure." Luke ran over. He wore a silly black beard hooked over his ears and hiding half his freckled face. "We have a map and everything."

"Treasure?"

"Uh-huh. I'm Blackbeard the pirate, and Gavin's Long John Silver. David's Captain Morgan. He says Captain Morgan can put a shine on a bad day. But I don't get it."

She smiled, ruffled the boy's hair as she had the dog's fur. She could use a belt of Captain Morgan herself, she decided. A double. "What's the treasure?"

"It's a surprise, but David—Captain Morgan says if we scallywags don't find it, we have to walk the plank."

She looked over at Gavin, who was hobbling around with a broomstick strapped to his leg. And David, sporting a black eyepatch and a big plumed hat he must have dug out of his costume party bag.

"Then you'd better go on back and find it."

"Don't you wanna play?"

"Not right now, sugar."

"Better find my pieces of eight," David said as he came over, "or I'll hang you from the highest yardarm."

With an un-piratelike squeal, Luke scrambled off to count off more paces from the map with his brother.

"What's wrong, honey?"

"Nothing." Roz shook her head. "Little headache, came home early. I hope to God you didn't actually bury something. I'd hate to fire you."

"New PlayStation game, up in the crook of the lowest branch of that sycamore."

"You're a treasure, Captain Morgan."

"One in a million. I know that face." He lifted a hand to it. "It'd pass most anybody, but not me. What's upset you, and what the hell are you doing walking all that way without a jacket?"

"I forgot it, and I do have a headache. Brought on by some foolishness Cissy Pratt was obliged to carry over to me."

"One of these days her flapping tongue's going to wrap around her own throat." He flipped up his eye patch. "And when she's in the funeral home, I'm going in and dressing her in an outdated, off-the-rack outfit from Wal-Mart. Polyester."

It brought on a half smile. "That's cruel."

"Come on inside. I'm going to fix us a batch of my infamous martinis. You can tell me all about it, then we'll trash the bitch."

"As entertaining as that sounds, I think what I need is a couple of aspirin and a twenty-minute nap. And we both know you can't disappoint those boys. Go on now, Captain." She kissed his cheek. "Shiver some timbers."

She went inside, directly upstairs. She took the self-prescribed aspirin, then stretched out on her bed.

How long, she wondered, how long was the albatross of

that joke of a marriage going to lay across her neck? How many times would it flap right up and slap her in the face?

So much for her superstitious hope that by letting the fifteen thousand dollars she'd discovered he'd nipped out of her account slide, she would have paid the debt, balanced the scales of the mistake.

Well, the money was gone, and no use regretting that foolish decision. The marriage had happened, and no point punishing herself for it.

Sooner or later he'd slip again, screw the wrong woman, bilk the wrong man, and he'd slither out of Memphis, out of her circle.

Eventually people would find something and someone else to talk about. They always did.

Imagine him being able to convince anyone that she'd attacked him—and in her own home. Then again, he did play the injured party well, and was the most accomplished liar she'd ever known.

She could not, and would not, defend herself on any level. Doing so would just feed the beast. She would do what she had always done. Remove herself, physically and emotionally, from the storm of talk.

She'd indulge in this brief sulk—she wasn't perfect, after all. Then she'd get back to her life, and live it as she'd always done.

Exactly as she chose.

She closed her eyes. She didn't expect to sleep, but she drifted a bit in that half-state she often found more soothing.

And while she drifted, she sat on the bench in her own shade garden, basking in the late-spring breeze, breathing in the perfumes it had floating on the air.

She could see the main house, and the colorful pots she'd planted and set herself on the terraces. And the carriage house, with its dance of lilies waiting to open wide.

She smelled the roses that climbed up the arbor in a

strong stream of golden sun. The white roses she'd planted herself, as a private tribute to John.

She rarely went to his grave, but often to the arbor.

She looked over beyond the rose garden, the cutting garden, the paths that gently wound through the flowers and shrubs and trees to the spot where Bryce had wanted to dig a swimming pool.

They'd argued over that, and had a blistering fight when she'd headed off the contractor he'd hired despite her.

The contractor had been told, she recalled, in no uncertain terms that if he so much as dipped a blade into her ground, she'd call the police to scrape up what she left of him.

With Bryce she'd been even less patient while reminding him the house and grounds were hers, the decisions made involving them hers.

He'd stormed out, hadn't he, after she'd scalded him. Only to slink back a few hours later, sheepish, apologetic, and with a tiny bouquet of wild violets.

Her mistake in accepting the apology, and the flowers.

Alone is better.

She shivered in the shade. "Maybe it is, maybe it isn't."

You did this alone. All of this. You made a mistake once, and look what it cost you. Still costs you. Don't make another.

"I won't make another. Whatever I do, it won't be a mistake."

Alone is better. The voice was more insistent now, and the cold deeper. *I'm alone.*

For an instant, only an instant, Roz thought she saw a woman in a muddy white dress, lying in an open grave. And for that instant, only that instant, she smelled the decay of death under the roses.

Then the woman's eyes opened, stared into hers, with a kind of mad hunger.

NINE

ROZ CAME INTO THE HOUSE OUT OF A NASTY, SLEETING rain. She peeled out of her jacket, then sat on the bench in the foyer to drag off her boots. David strolled out, sat beside her, and handed her the cup of coffee he'd brought out of the kitchen.

"Dr. Delish is in the library."

"Yes, I saw his car." She drank coffee, holding the cup in both hands to warm them.

"Harper's with him. He snagged our boy for an interview. We had ours over lattes and applesauce cake earlier."

"Applesauce cake."

"I saved you a big slice. I know your weaknesses. They're saying we might get some snow out of this."

"So I heard."

"Stella and the boys are at Logan's. She's going to fix dinner over there, and the boys are hoping the snow comes through and they can stay the night."

"That's nice. I need a shower. A hot one."

He took the cup she passed back to him. "I thought you

might want to ask our handsome professor to stay to dinner. I'm making some hearty chicken and dumplings to ward off the cold."

"Sounds good—the chicken—and Mitch is certainly welcome to stay if he likes, and doesn't have other plans."

"He doesn't," David said confidently. "I've already asked."

She chuckled at his broad grin. "Just who are you matching him up with, David? You or me?"

"Well, being the utterly unselfish person I am—and seeing as the doctor is unfortunately and absolutely straight—I'm going with you."

"Just a pitiful romantic, aren't you?"

She started up, and only rolled her eyes when he called out: "Put something sexy on."

In the library, Harper nursed his after-work beer. It didn't seem to him that he could tell Mitch much more than he already knew, but he'd answered the questions, filled in little gaps in the stories both his mother and David had already related.

"I've got David's rundown of the night you saw her outside, in the gardens, when you were boys."

"The night we were camping out, David, my brothers, and me." Harper nodded in acknowledgment. "Some night."

"According to David, you saw her first, woke him."

"Saw, heard, felt." Harper shrugged. "Hard to pin it down, but yeah, I woke him up. Couldn't say what time it was. Late. We'd stayed up eating ourselves half sick, and spooking ourselves out with scary stories. Then I heard her, I guess. Don't know how, exactly, I knew it was her. It wasn't like the other times."

"What was different?"

"She wasn't singing. She was more . . . moaning, I guess, or making these unintelligible sounds. More like what you'd expect from a ghost on a hot, moonlit night when you're a kid. So I looked out, and there she was. Only not like before, either."

Brave boy, Mitch thought, to look out instead of pulling the sleeping bag over his head. "What was it like?"

"She was in this white nightgown sort of thing. The way she was last spring when she was upstairs. Her hair was down, tangled and dirty. And I could see the moonlight going through her. Right through. Jesus." He took a deeper sip of beer.

"So I got David up, and Austin and Mason woke up, too. I wanted Austin to stay back with Mason, but there was no chance of that, so we all set out to follow her."

Mitch could imagine it very well. A pack of young boys, moonlight and lightning bugs and heavy summer heat. And a ghostly figure trailing through the gardens.

"She walked right over Mama's evening primrose, straight through the hollyhocks. Through them. I was too wound up to be scared. She kept making this noise, a kind of humming, or keening, I guess you could say. I think there were words mixed in there somewhere, but I couldn't make them out. She was going toward the carriage house. Seemed to me she was heading toward the carriage house anyway. And she turned, and she looked back. And her face . . ."

"What?"

"Like last spring again," he said, and let out a little breath. "She looked insane. Horror-movie insane. Wild and crazy. She was smiling, but it was horrible. And for a minute, when she looked at me and I looked back, it was so cold, I saw my own breath. Then she turned, kept walking, and I started after her."

"Started after her? An insane ghost? You had to be scared."

"Not so much, not that I realized anyway. I was caught up, I guess. Really fascinated. I had to *know*. But Mason started screaming. Then I was scared spitless. I thought somehow she'd gotten him, which was stupid since she was up ahead and he was behind me. Farther behind me, all of them, than I'd realized. So I went running back, and there was Mason on the ground with his foot bleeding. And Austin's running back to the tent for a T-shirt or something to wrap it 'cause we're not wearing anything but our jockeys. David and I were trying to carry him back when Mama came running out like the wrath of God."

He laughed then, eyes twinkling at Mitch. "You should've seen her. She's wearing these little cotton shorts and some skinny little T-shirt. Her hair was longer back then, and it's flying as she came hauling ass. And I see—the others didn't, but I see she's got my granddaddy's pistol. I tell you what, if it had been some ghost after us, or anything else, she'd have run it off. But when she saw what was what, more or less, she shoved the pistol in the waistband of those little shorts, around the back. She picked Mason up, told us all to get some clothes on. And we all piled into the car to take Mason into the ER for stitches."

"You never said you'd seen the gun." Roz stepped into the library.

"I didn't think you wanted the others to know."

She walked right to him, bent down, and kissed the top of his head. "Didn't want you to know, either. You always saw too much." She turned her cheek, left it on top of Harper's head as she looked at Mitch. "Am I interrupting?"

"No. You could sit down if you have a minute. I've gotten this story from two sources now, and wouldn't mind having your version."

"I can't add much. The boys wanted to sleep out. God knows why as it was hot as hell and buggy with it. But boys do like to pitch a tent. As I wanted to be able to keep an eye on things, and hear them, I closed off my room, and did without the air-conditioning so I could have my doors open to the outside."

"We were right in the yard," Harper objected. "How much trouble could we get in?"

"Plenty, and as events proved just that, it was wise of me to sweat through the night. Once they settled down, I drifted off to sleep myself. It was Mason screaming that woke me. I grabbed my daddy's pistol, which in those days I kept on the top shelf of my bedroom closet. Got the bullets out of my jewelry box and loaded it on the run. When I got there, Harper and David were carting Mason, and his little foot was bleeding. I had to tell them to hush, as they were all talking at once. Took the baby in, cleaned up his foot, and saw it was going to need stitches. I got the story on the way to the hospital."

Mitch nodded, then looked up from his notes. "When did you go to the carriage house?"

She smiled. "First light. It took me that long to get back, settle them all down."

"You take the gun?"

"I did, in case what they'd seen was more corporeal than they'd thought."

"I was old enough to go with you," Harper objected. "You shouldn't have gone out there alone."

She cocked her head at him. "I believe I was in charge. In any case, there was nothing to see, and I can't tell you if I felt anything, genuinely, or if I was still so worked up I thought I did."

"What did you think?"

"That it was cold, and it shouldn't have been. And I felt . . . it sounds melodramatic, but I felt death all around me. I went through the place top to bottom, and there was nothing there."

"When was the place converted?"

"Oh . . . hmm." She closed her eyes to think. "Around the turn of the twentieth century. Reginald Harper was known for wanting the latest things, and automobiles were one of them. He housed his car in the carriage house for a time, then he used the stables for them, and the carriage house became a kind of storage house, with the gardener living on the second floor. But it would've been later, more like the twenties, I think, before it was done up as a guest cottage by my grandfather."

"So it's unlikely she would have stayed there, or visited the gardener there, as those dates are after first sightings. What would've been kept in there while it was an actual carriage house?"

"Buggies, some tack, I suppose. Tools?"

"An odd place for her to go."

"I always wondered if she died there," Harper commented, "and figured she'd let me know once I moved in."

Mitch's attention sharpened on him. "Have you had any experiences there?"

"Nope. She doesn't have much to do with guys once they pass a certain age. Hey, it's snowing."

He popped up to go to the window. "Maybe it'll stick. You need me anymore?" he asked Mitch.

"Not right now, thanks for the time."

"No problem. Later."

Roz shook her head as he walked out. "He'll head right outside, try to scrape up enough for a snowball so he can throw it at David. Some things never change. Speaking of David, he's making chicken and dumplings if you'd like to stay, wait for this snow to peter out again."

"It's a foolish man who turns down chicken and dumplings. I've made some progress, if elimination is progress, the last week or so. I'm running out of candidates, those who're documented, in any case, for Amelia."

She wandered to his work board, studied the photos, the charts, the notes. "And when you run out of candidates who are documented?"

"I start looking outside the box. Off topic, how do you feel about basketball?"

"In what way?"

"In the going to a game sort of way. I scored an extra ticket to my son's game tomorrow night. They're playing Ole Miss. I was hoping I could talk you into going with me."

"To a basketball game?"

"Casual, lots of other people, a specific form of entertainment." He smiled at her easily, when she turned back. "Seemed like a good place to start. And you might be more inclined toward that sort of socializing than a quiet dinner for two. But if you prefer the latter, I find my calendar free the night after next."

"A basketball game might be interesting."

LILY SAT ON THE BOKHARA IN ROZ'S BEDROOM, BANGing the buttons of a toy phone with a plastic dog. Lily's mother had her head in the closet.

"Just try the eyeshadow, Roz." Hayley's voice was muffled as she pawed through clothing. "I knew it was the wrong color for me when I bought it, but I just couldn't stop myself. It'll look awesome on you, won't it, Stella?"

"It will."

"I've got enough makeup of my own for three women," Roz objected and tried to concentrate on using it. She wasn't entirely sure how her personal space had come to be invaded by females. She just wasn't used to females.

"Oh, my God! You *have* to wear these!"

Hayley pulled out the pants David had talked Roz into buying—and which, to date, had never been on her body again. "I certainly don't."

"Roz, are you kidding?" She waved them at Stella. "Look at these."

Stella did. "I couldn't get my hips in those with a crowbar."

"Sure you could, they stretch." Hayley demonstrated. "Besides, your hips are perfect, seeing as you have breasts. But these are too long for you. You know that sweater I got for Christmas, the red angora David gave me? It'd be fabulous with these pants."

"Then you take them," Roz suggested.

"No, you're wearing them. Watch the baby a minute, okay? I'll run and get the sweater."

"I'm not wearing your sweater. I have plenty of my own. And for heaven's sake, this is just a basketball game."

"No reason not to go looking like the complete babe you are."

"I'm wearing jeans."

Deflated, Hayley dropped onto the bed beside Stella. "She's a hardcase."

"Here, I'll use your eyeshadow. We'll consider it a compromise."

"Can I pick out your earrings?"

Roz shifted her gaze in the mirror until her eyes met Hayley's. "Will you stop nagging the skin off my back?"

"Deal." Hayley leaped up, and when Lily reached toward her, scooped the baby on the fly. Settling Lily on her hip, she began to go through Roz's everyday jewelry box one-handed. "What top are you wearing?"

"I don't know. Some sweater or other."

"The green cashmere," Stella told her. "The dark green mock turtle, and that great black leather coat? The knee-length."

Roz considered as she worked on her eyes. "Fine. That'll work."

"All right, then . . . these." Hayley held up silver spiral dangles. "Shoes?" she asked, turning to Stella.

"Those black leather half boots with the stubby heel."

"You get those, I'll get the sweater, and—"

"Girls," Roz interrupted. "Scoot. I can handle the rest of this myself." But she leaned over to kiss Lily's cheek. "Y'all go play somewhere else now."

"Come on, Hayley, before she decides to wear a sweatshirt and gardening shoes just to spite us. She was right about the eyeshadow," Stella added as she pulled Hayley out.

Maybe so, Roz decided. It was an interesting shade of brown, with a hint of gold to jazz it up. She knew how to use it to her advantage. God knew she had plenty of practice fixing herself up, and enough vanity to put effort into looking her best when looking her best was called for.

At the same time, there was a certain advantage to having other women, *younger* women in the household, she supposed, and she'd take their advice on the wardrobe.

Except for the pants.

She crossed to her dresser, opened the middle drawer where she kept her good sweaters. She did love those soft fabrics, she thought as she went through the folded garments. The cashmeres and brushed cottons, the silks.

She took out the dark green, unfolded it.

The chill hit with a shock, a punishing little slap, that had her taking a step back. Then freezing as the sweater was ripped out of her hands. She watched with disbelief as it hit the opposite wall, then fell to the floor.

Her knees wanted to buckle, but she kept her feet and walked slowly across the room to pick it up.

There were jagged tears across the front, as if angry nails had raked through the material. Her breath streamed out in visible vapors as she fought to stay calm.

"Well, that was nasty, and small of you. Petty and mean. I was fond of this sweater. Very fond. But it won't make a damn bit of difference."

Angry now, she whirled around, waiting, hoping to see something, someone, to battle. "I've got more, and if you're thinking to repeat this performance on the rest of my clothes, I'll tell you now I'll walk out of here bare-assed naked before I give in to this kind of blackmail. So you go have your temper fit somewhere else."

Roz tossed the sweater onto her bed, marched back to her dresser. She grabbed a sweater at random, dragged it over her head. Her fingers trembled as much with rage as distress as she pulled on jeans.

"I make my own decisions," she ranted, "and always have. Keep this up, you just keep this up, and I'll sleep with him just to piss you off."

She finished dressing, shoved her feet into her boots, grabbed the leather coat, then had to order herself not to slam the door.

On the other side, she leaned back against it, breathed in and out until she was calm again. One thing for certain, she decided, she and Mitch wouldn't lack for things to talk about en route to the game.

Still she waited until they were on their way, with the lights of Harper House behind them. "There are a couple of things I need to tell you, then I think it'd be nice if both of us put business aside for a few hours."

"Something happen?"

"Yes. First, I had an irritating encounter at work one day recently with an acquaintance who has gold-medaled in the gossip Olympics for more than twenty consecutive years."

"Hell of a record."

"And she's proud of it. It dealt with my ex-husband, and isn't important of itself, but it upset me a bit, gave me what I call a temper headache, so I went home, took some aspirin, and decided to lie down for a few minutes. I wasn't asleep, just sort of hovering in that nice, cozy in-between—and in my head I was out in the garden, sitting on the bench in the shade, and it was late spring."

"How did you know it was spring?"

"Late spring, early June. I could tell by the plants, the flowers that were blooming. Then it got cold."

She told him the rest, careful with every detail.

"This is the first dream you've mentioned."

"It wasn't a dream. I wasn't asleep." She gave an impatient wave of her hand. "I know people say that all the time, when they *thought* they were awake. I was awake."

"All right. You should know."

"She took me there in my mind. I felt the cold, I smelled the flowers—the white roses on the arbor—I felt the air on my skin. All the while I was aware, in another part of myself, that I was still in my room, on the bed, with the headache pounding."

"Disconcerting."

"You're subtle," she replied. "Yes, it was disconcerting. Disorienting and upsetting. I don't like having anyone direct my thoughts. And the way she looked at me, when she opened her eyes in that grave, it was with a terrible kind of . . . love. She's never hurt me, and I've never felt that she would. Until tonight."

He pulled off the side of the road, braked hard, then turned to her. The calm she most usually saw in him, felt from him, was replaced by a percolating anger. "What do you mean? Did she attack you? For God's sake—"

"Not me, but a very nice cashmere sweater. It was a birthday gift, so I've only had it since November, and I'm still mad she ruined it."

"Tell me exactly what happened."

When she had, he sat back, tapped his fingers on the wheel. "She didn't want you coming out with me tonight."

"Apparently not, but that's too bad. Here I am."

He looked at her again. "Why?"

"I said I would, and I do what I say I will. Then you can add that she made me mad, and I don't back down, either.

And lastly, I wanted to explore whether or not I'm going to like your company on a purely social level."

"You shoot very straight."

"I do. It irritates some people."

"I'm not one of them. Sorry about the sweater."

"So am I."

"We could speculate—"

"We could," Roz interrupted. "But I'd just as soon not, right now. She didn't stop the evening, so I don't see why she should drive it, either. Why don't we talk about something else until it's time to get down to business again?"

"Sure. What would you like to talk about?"

"I could start by wondering out loud how long you intend to sit here beside the road, and how late that's going to make us to your son's game."

"Oh. Right." He pulled onto the road again. "How about if I start this conversation off by telling you I've got a new cleaning lady."

"Is that so?"

"She's a friend of a friend of a friend. Sort of. She's into feng shui, so she's rearranging everything in the place—career areas, and health areas, I dunno. And making me lists for things I have to buy, like a money frog for my prosperity corner—or something. And these Chinese coins. And she says I have to have a green plant. I think it's for the health area, I'm not sure, and I'm too afraid of her to ask. So I was wondering if I could possibly have that plant back you took from my place last spring."

"The one you were murdering."

"I didn't know I was murdering it. I didn't even know it was there."

"Benign neglect is still neglect."

"Hardass. How about I sign an oath to take better care of it? The fact is, she'll be the one taking care of it, at least every other week. And you could have visitation rights."

"I'll think about it."

THE AUDITORIUM WAS ALREADY PACKED WHEN THEY arrived, and humming with pregame excitement. They moved through the noise and color and excitement, scooting down the row to their seats while both teams practiced layups on the court.

"That's Josh there, number eight."

She watched the tall boy in his trimmed-in-blue white jersey lope forward and tap the ball off the backboard and into the net. "Nice form."

"He was the NBA's number-ten draft pick. He'll play for the Celtics next year. It's hard for me to believe it. I'm not going to brag all night, but I had to get that one in."

"He's going pro? The Celtics? Brag all you want. I would."

"I'll keep it to a minimum. In any case, Josh is point guard, that's the position that directs the team's offense from the point."

She listened, sipping the soft drink he'd bought her, as he ran through a primer of basketball terms and explanations.

At tip-off she watched the action, enjoyed the lightning movements on court, the echoing voices, the thunder of the ball on wood.

Now and again through the first quarter, Mitch would lean closer to explain a call, a strategy, or a play.

Until she got to her feet with the rest of the Memphis crowd to boo a blown call. "What, do those refs need eye surgery? We had established position, didn't we—does he need *three* feet planted on the ground? That was charging, for God's sake. All he was missing was a Visa card!"

When she sat again, with a disgusted huff, Mitch scratched his chin. "Okay, either I'm an exceptional teacher or you know basketball."

"I have three sons. I know basketball. I know football and baseball, and at one time I knew entirely too much about professional wrestling. But they mostly outgrew that one." She took her eyes from the game long enough to smile at him. "But you were having such a nice time educating the little lady, I didn't want to break your stride."

"Thanks. Want some nachos?"

"I wouldn't mind."

She enjoyed herself, and was amused at halftime when Josh zeroed in on his father in the crowd and grinned. More amused when the boy's gaze drifted to her, then back to his father before Josh executed an enthusiastic thumbs-up.

And when at game's end, the Memphis Tigers clipped Ole Miss's Rebels by three points, she decided the experience had nearly been worth one cashmere sweater.

"You want to wait around, congratulate your boy?"

"Not tonight. It'll be better than an hour before he gets out of the locker room, and through the groupies. I'd like you to meet him sometime, though."

"I'd be glad to. He's a pleasure to watch on the court, not just his style and skill—though he has plenty of both—but his enthusiasm. You can tell he loves the game."

"Has since he was a baby." Mitch slipped an arm around Roz's waist to help maneuver them both through the departing crowd.

"It'll be tough on you, him moving to Boston."

"He's always wanted it. Part of me wants to move up there with him, but sooner or later, you've got to let go."

"Nearly killed me when my two youngest moved away. They were five years old yesterday."

He dropped his arm, then took her hand as they crossed the parking lot. "Can I interest you in a postgame meal?"

"Not tonight. I need to get an early start in the morning. But thanks."

"Dinner tomorrow."

She slid a look up at him. "I should tell you getting me out of the house two nights running generally takes a team of wild horses. And I've got a garden club meeting tomorrow, which for personal reasons, I can't miss."

"The night after."

"I sense a campaign."

"How's it going?"

"It's not bad." Not bad at all, she thought, enjoying the bracing air, and the warmth of his hand over hers. "I'll tell you what, you can come to dinner night after next, but I'll warn you, I'll be cooking. David's night off."

"You cook?"

"Of course I cook. Not that I'm allowed to when David's in the house, but it happens I'm a very good cook."

"What time's dinner?"

She laughed. "Let's make it seven."

"I'll be there." When they reached his car, he walked her to her side, then turned her around, slid his arms around her, and drew her toward him. Laid his mouth on hers in a long, lazy kiss.

She curled her hands around his arms, held on to them, to him, and let herself float on the sensation—the warmth of his body, the cool of the air, the simmering demand just under the lazy tone of the kiss.

Then he eased back, his eyes on hers, and reached around to open her door. "I did that now because I figured if I waited until I walked you to your door, you'd be expecting it. I'm hoping to surprise you, at least now and again. I don't think it's the easiest thing to do."

"You've managed it a few times so far."

When she slid into the car, he closed the door. And thought he might have a few more surprises up his sleeve before they were done.

ten

HARPER COULD AND DID SPEND HOURS A DAY IN THE grafting house without being bored or missing the company of others. The plants he worked with were an endless fascination and satisfaction to him. Whether he was creating another standard or experimenting with a hybrid, he was doing the work he loved.

He enjoyed the outdoor work as well, the grafting and propagation he performed with the field stock. He'd already selected the trees he intended to graft and would need to spend part of the week collecting his scions, and pruning the maiden trees he'd grafted the year before.

His mother left these sort of decisions up to him. The what, the how, the when. It was, he knew, a strong level of trust and confidence from her to step back and let him run that end of the show.

Then again, she'd taught him not only the basics of the work, but had instilled in him a love for what grew.

They'd spent countless hours together in the garden and greenhouse when he was growing up. She'd taught his brothers as well, but their interests had veered off where his had centered. In Harper House, in the gardens, in the work.

His college years, his studies there, had only cemented for him what would be his life's work.

His responsibility to them—the house, the gardens, the work, and the woman who'd taught him—was absolute.

He considered it a bonus round that love and obligation so neatly united for him.

Tchaikovsky played for the plants, while through his headset his choice of classic was Barenaked Ladies. He checked his pots, making notations on his various clipboards.

He was especially pleased with the dahlias he'd grafted the previous spring at Logan's request. In a couple of weeks, he'd bring the overwintered tubers into growth, and in spring take cuttings. In the Garden should be able to offer a nice supply of Stella's Dream, the bold, deeply blue dahlia he'd created.

Interesting the way things worked, he thought. Through Logan and tidy Stella falling in love—and Logan showing his sentimental side over the blue dahlia Stella had dreamed of. Dreamed of, Harper thought, because of the Harper Bride.

It sort of circled around, didn't it, back to the house, and what grew there.

There would be no Stella's Dream without the Bride. And no Bride without Harper House. None of it, he supposed, without his mother's steady determination to keep the house and build the business.

Since he was facing the door, he saw it open. And watched Hayley walk in.

She wouldn't be here, either, without his mother. There would have been no beautiful, pregnant woman knocking on the door of Harper House last winter looking for work and a place to live.

When she smiled, his heart did that quick, automatic stutter, then settled back to normal again. She tapped the side of her head, and he pulled off his headset.

"Sorry to interrupt. Roz said you had some pots mature enough for me to rotate into the houseplant stock. Stella's looking to do a winter sale."

"Sure. You want me to bring them out?"

"That's okay. I got boxes and a flat cart outside the door."

"Let me check the inventory, adjust it first." He walked down to his computer station. "Want a Coke?"

"Love one, but I'm still watching my caffeine."

"Oh right." She was nursing Lily, a concept that made him feel sort of warm and twisty inside. "Ah, got some water in the cooler, too."

"That'd be good. When you've got time, can you show me some grafting? Stella said how you do most of it, at least the field work, about this time of year. I'd really like to do something, then, you know, follow it on through."

"Sure, if you want." He handed her a bottle of water. "You can try your hand on a willow. It was the first graft my mother showed me how to do, and they're the best to practice on."

"That'd be great. I thought one day, when I get a place for me and Lily, I could plant something I'd made myself."

He sat, ordered himself to concentrate on his inventory program. The scent of her, somehow essential female, fit so perfectly with the smell of earth and growth. "You've got plenty of room at the house."

"More than." She laughed, tried to read over his shoulder. "Been there a year, and still can't get used to all the space. I love living there, I do, and it's wonderful for Lily to have so many people around, and nobody, nobody could be more amazing than your mama. She's the most awesome person I know. But sooner or later, I need to, well, plant Lily and me somewhere of our own."

"You know Mama loves having you there or she'd've nudged you along by now."

"Boy, that's the truth. She really knows how to structure things, doesn't she? Sets them up to suit her. I don't mean that exactly the way it sounds. It's just that she's strong and smart, and doesn't seem to be afraid of anything or anyone. I admire that so much."

"You seem to have plenty of guts and brains of your own."

"Guts maybe, but I've started to realize a lot of that came from not knowing any better." Idly, she picked up a scrap of raffia, twisted it around her finger. "When I look back, I don't know how I worked up to setting out six-months pregnant. Not now that I have Lily and realize, well, everything. I'm going to owe Roz for the rest of my life."

"She wouldn't want that."

"That's one thing she's not going to have any choice about. My baby's got a good, loving home. I've got a job that I swear I like more every day. We've got friends, and family. We'd've done all right, I'd've made sure of it. But we wouldn't be where we are now, Lily and I, without Roz."

"Funny, I was thinking how most everything—the house, this place, even Logan and Stella wind around to my mother. Maybe even the Bride."

"Why the Bride?"

"If Mama had sold the place—and there had to be times it would've been easier to do that—maybe the Bride wouldn't still be there. Maybe it takes a Harper being in the house. I don't know." He shrugged, got up to select the plants he'd checked off his inventory. "It was just something I wondered about."

"Could be right. You wouldn't sell it, would you, when it comes to you?"

"No. Fact is, every time I think, maybe I should move out of the carriage house, get some place, I just can't do it. It's where I want to be, that's one thing. And the other is no matter how smart or strong my mother is, I feel it's better that I'm around. I think she'd be sad, and a little lonely, if you and Lily went somewhere else, especially since Stella and the boys'll be moving into Logan's in a couple months."

"Maybe, and I'm not planning on anything right away. But with her and Mitch dating, it could be she'll have all the company she wants."

"What?" He stopped dead, with a young, healthy ficus in his arms. "Dating? What do you mean dating? They're not dating."

"When two people go out two or three times, to basketball games, to dinner and what not, when the *she* in the pair cooks the *he* dinner herself, I tend to call it dating."

"They're working on this project. It's like . . . meetings."

She gave him the female smile he recognized. The one that categorized him as a pitifully out-of-touch male. "You don't generally adjourn a meeting with a long, hot kiss—at least I haven't been lucky enough to have a meeting like that for some time."

"Kiss? What—"

"I wasn't spying or anything," she said quickly. "I happened to be up with Lily one night, looked out the window when Mitch brought Roz home. Okay, I sort of looked out on purpose when I heard the car, just to see what was what. And if the liplock I witnessed is anything to go by, that's some serious dating."

He set the plant down again, with a thump. "Well, for Christ's sake."

She blinked. "Harper, you don't have any problem with Roz seeing a man like that. That'd be just silly."

"Last time she was seeing a man like that, she ended up married to the son of a bitch."

"She made a mistake," Hayley said, heating up. "And Mitch is nothing like that bastard Bryce Clerk."

"And we know this because?"

"Because we do."

"Not good enough."

"He certainly is good enough for her."

"That's not what I said. I said—"

"Just because he isn't rich, or doesn't have that fancy Harper blood running through him doesn't mean you should build a case against him." She drilled a finger straight into Harper's chest. "You ought to be ashamed of yourself, talking like some snob."

"I'm not saying that, don't be stupid."

"Don't you call me stupid."

"I didn't call you stupid. Jesus Christ."

"I don't even want to talk to you right now." She turned on her heel, stomped out.

"Fine. I don't want to talk to you, either," he shot back.

He stewed about it, worked himself up about the entire situation while he loaded and transported the plants himself.

Ready for battle, he searched out his mother.

She was in the field, checking on the nursery beds, and the roses he'd t-budded earlier in the season.

She wore a stone-gray hoodie, fingerless gloves, and a pair of boots so old and scarred they were no discernable color. She looked, Harper realized, more like a contemporary than his mother.

"Hayley find you?" she called out.

"Yeah, it's done."

"You know, I'm thinking of adding a mist propagation tent, and doing more palms. Honey, I've got to tell you, I'm excited at how these multiple trees you did are coming along. Our customers are going to have fun with these. I'm thinking of taking one of the nectarine and peach myself."

She studied one of the young trees Harper had grafted, then fan-trained on stakes. "This is lovely work, Harper, and that weeping pear over there—"

"Mama, are you sleeping with Mitch Carnegie?"

"What?" She turned fully to face him, and the pleased smile, the glint of pride in her eyes both froze away. "What did you ask me?"

"You heard what I asked. I'd like an answer."

"And why would I answer a question that you have no business asking?"

"I want to know how seriously you're involved with him. I have a right to know."

"You certainly do not."

"I kept my mouth shut about Clerk. That was my mistake. I'm not making it again. I'm looking after you whether you like it or not. So if you don't tell me, I'll go ask him."

"You'll do no such thing, Harper." She paced away, stood with her back to him. He knew her well enough to be sure she was battling back a spew of temper. They both had a dangerous one, and were both very careful with it. "When's the last time I quizzed you about who you see socially, or who you're intimate with?"

"When's the last time I married a fortune hunter?"

She whirled back, and the temper was so close to the surface now, he saw it burning out of her eyes. "Don't you throw that in my face. I don't like it."

"I don't like doing it. I don't care how mad you get, nobody's going to hurt you like that again while I'm around. Just how much do we know about him? From where I'm standing he's already crossing a line hitting on someone he's working for."

"You're so damn proper about the oddest things. How did I ever manage that?" She let out a long breath. "Let me ask you this. Have you ever known me to make the same mistake twice?"

"Not so far."

"Your confidence in me is overwhelming." She took off one of the gloves she wore, slapped it against her thigh. "I'll tell you this. He's an interesting and attractive man who I've enjoyed seeing a couple of times on a social level. He has a strong and loving relationship with his son, and since I pride myself on the same, that goes a long way with me. He's divorced, and maintains a cordial relationship with the mother of his son and her second husband. This is not always an easy feat. He's done nothing improper, even by your lofty standards."

"They're lofty when it comes to you."

"Oh, Harper. I'm not a paragon."

"Who wants you to be? What I want you to be is safe and happy."

"Honey." She stepped to him then, laid her hands on his cheeks, shook his head gently from side-to-side. "That's supposed to be my line to you. If I promise you, take a solemn oath, that I learned my lesson with Bryce, will you relax?"

"Only if you promise to tell me if he pushes where you don't want to be pushed."

"Listen to you. All right, then, I'll promise. Come on, let's take a look at the rest of this before we go in."

IT CERTAINLY GAVE ROZ A LOT TO THINK ABOUT. How could she know her firstborn so well, yet have been completely surprised by the altercation that afternoon?

Then again, did any mother ever consider her children would worry about her? There just wasn't enough room in the brain or heart for that possibility, when they were both so full of worry and concern for the child.

Added to that, it had come home fully, for the first time, just how much she'd let him down with Bryce. She'd hurt Harper as much, and maybe more, than she herself had been hurt.

Was that something you could make up to those you loved, or was it something that just had to heal over, like a wound?

Because she wanted quiet, she went into her room from the outside entrance, peeled off her outer gear.

She wandered into her sitting room, intending to put on

music and spend some time sketching just to wind down from the day. But she saw the neat piles of mail on her desk. David, as was his habit, had separated the personal correspondence—not much these days as she and most everyone she knew had slid into e-mail posts—business, and bills.

Because she believed in handling the bad news first, she sat and began to open the bills. The utilities on the house made her wince a bit, but that was the price to be paid for having so much space, and so many people using it.

She got out her checkbook, promising herself that soon—before next month—she would master the bill-paying business on-line. Of course, she promised the same every month. But this time she meant it. She'd have Stella show her the ropes, first chance.

She paid the electric, the gas, the phone, a credit card bill. Then frowned at another envelope from another credit card company. She nearly tossed it, assuming it was a solicitation, then opened it, just to check.

Her eyes widened as she looked at the charges, the total. Over eight thousand dollars. Eight *thousand*? It was ridiculous, absurd.

She didn't have a card with this company, and certainly hadn't charged eight thousand dollars. Restaurants, electronics, the men's department at Dillard's.

Baffled, she picked up the phone to report the mistake, then spent the next half hour winding her way through tangled and sticky red tape.

The next call she made was to her lawyer.

Once the wheels were set in motion, she sat back, the sinking sensation in her stomach making her queasy. The card had been taken out in her name, with all her information—her address, her Social Security number, even her mother's maiden name. The other user on the card was listed as Ashby Harper.

Clever, she thought. Very clever.

He hadn't used his own name, and hadn't accumulated charges at his most usual haunts. By now, she had no doubt the card was destroyed. The last charge had been made three days before the end of the billing cycle.

Covered all the bases as usual—that bastard Bryce.

The money wouldn't have been the main thrust, she thought now. Not that he wouldn't enjoy the benefits of eight thousand and change. But the point would have been the trouble for her, the irritation, and most of all the *reminder* that he was still in her face. And there was little she could do about it.

It was doubtful the charges could be traced back to him, that it could be proved he'd defrauded the credit card company. It was she who would be forced to untangle the knots, spending the time, the effort, and paying any legal fees.

It was mean and small of him, and suited him perfectly.

And Harper, poor Harper, worried she'd make that kind of mistake again. Not in a million years.

To give herself more time to settle, she skipped dinner, then wrote long, detailed posts to her two younger sons before calling Harper.

Once she knew the children were in bed for the night, she asked Harper, David, along with Stella and Hayley to join her in the front parlor.

"I'm sorry," she began. "I know some of you might have plans for the night. I don't think this will take long."

"It's all right," Stella told her. "Something's the matter. Just tell us what it is."

"I've already taken steps to deal with it, but it's likely all of you will be asked, at least, to answer some questions. In going through my bills this evening, I came upon a credit card bill—a card I don't have, charges I didn't make. However, it was applied for and taken out with considerable personal information. The credit card company will, of course, follow this through. But as I was obliged to list all those who live in this house, I wanted you to be aware. I've no doubt the card was taken out by Bryce. He'd know the information, and it's just his style."

"You don't have to pay it," Hayley said quickly. "This kind of thing happened in the bookstore once where I used to work. You don't have to pay it."

"No, I won't pay it. It simply costs me time and energy, and upsets me—which would have been the motive. It also upsets the household, which he'd enjoy, I'm sure. I'm sorry for that." She looked at Harper. "I'm sorry."

"Don't say that again." He spoke very softly. "I don't want to hear you say you're sorry again, Mama. What about the police?"

"They may very well be involved. But I'm going to tell you what my lawyer told me. While the credit card company will follow through, it'll be very difficult to prove he's the one who used the card. He didn't use his name, and he didn't charge so much at any given time or place to raise an eyebrow. No one's going to remember he breezed into Dillard's and bought some shirts or a pair of shoes. This is the sort of thing he knows how to do quite well."

She had to get up, to move, so rose to add a log to the fire. "The best we can do is step back from it, as much as we can, and let it play out. Sooner or later, and I believe this, he'll do one of three things. He'll get bored with it, he'll find someone else to harass, or he'll go just a little too far and hang himself."

"I vote for Door Number Three," David put in.

"Your mouth, God's ear," Roz assured him, and made herself sit again. "I've written both Austin and Mason, because I want them, and all of you, to be on guard. He may very well choose to amuse himself by doing this same sort of thing to one or more of you."

At the thought of it, the tension in her shoulders increased until her muscles felt like iron rods under her skin. "And Stella, you and I should be particularly vigilant regarding any charges to the business."

"Don't worry. He won't get by us. Roz, I'm so sorry you have to deal with this. Anything I can do—anything any of us can do?"

"I'll let you know, I promise. All right." Roz got to her feet. "That's all, then. I'm going to go on up, get to some work I've put off."

"You haven't had any dinner," David reminded her. "Why don't I bring you something?"

"Not now. I'll get something later."

David stayed on his feet, watching her walk out. "Son of a bitch," he muttered when she was out of earshot. "Smarmy, sleazy, last-season Ferrogamo-wearing son of a bitch."

"Why don't you and I go pay him a visit?" Harper stayed in his chair. His voice was still soft, as it had been, but now it had an edge to it, a predatory edge.

"That's a damn good idea." Hayley sprang up, fists clenched at her sides. "Let's all go pay him a call. Right now."

"Stand down, Xena." David patted her shoulder. "While there's little more I can think of that would be more entertaining than breaking a few of his caps, it's not the answer."

"I hear four when you add two and two," Harper said. "I say it's the right answer."

"David's right," Stella pointed out. "It would upset and embarrass Roz, more than she's already upset and embarrassed."

"Then we won't tell her." Hayley threw out her arms. "We can't just *sit* here."

"I'm not," Harper said. "You are."

"Just a damn minute—"

"Hold on." Like a referee, David stepped between them. "Think, Harper, past your temper. We go take a few very deserved hits at Clerk, his bruises'll heal soon enough. And he'll have the satisfaction of knowing he got to her, that he upset her. That's the last thing she wants, and you and I know that. The most important weapon she has against him is indifference. She won't have that when she has to bail you out on assault charges."

"I'll tell you what else." Stella continued to sit, her hands gripped tight in her lap. "The more we make of it, the more upset she'll be. The best thing we can do for her is to take a page from her book. Treat it coolly, like business. And to remember, if it's hard for us to do that, how much harder it is for her."

"I hate it," Hayley raged. "I hate that you're right, and I wish you'd been right *after* we'd beat the hell out of him. It shows character, Harper, that you want to stand up for her. And it shows character, I guess, to know it's not the way."

MAYBE NOT, BUT HARPER COULDN'T QUITE ERASE THE picture of Bryce in a bloody pulp at his feet. It probably didn't hurt that he didn't know exactly where to find the man. Oh, he could find out, a few calls would do the trick. But those calls might trickle back to the source before he got there.

And in the end, he knew David was right.

But he couldn't just sit at home and stew. There was another matter he could deal with, and he didn't give a damn whether or not his mother liked it.

He was still spoiling for a fight when he knocked on Mitch's apartment door.

He half hoped he'd find Mitch with another woman. Then he could punch him in the mouth and defuse the sparking end of his temper.

But when Mitch answered, he appeared to be alone. Unless you counted the noise that Harper recognized as a televised basketball game.

"Hey. How's it going? Come on in."

"I want to talk to you."

"Sure. Wait." Mitch's attention had already swung back to the huge television screen that dominated one wall. "Less than a minute to halftime. We're down two. Damn it. Goddamn it, loose ball."

Despite himself, Harper found himself standing there, caught up in the action, calling out when number eight recovered the ball and, pivoting with a kind of magical grace, sent it sailing through the air.

"Three! That's three." Mitch punched Harper companionably in the arm. "And there's the buzzer. Want a drink?"

"Could use a beer."

"Don't have any, sorry. Coke?"

"Fine, thanks." He slipped his hands into his pockets as Mitch wandered off. Alone, he scanned the room, brow knitting over some coins dangling from red ribbons. "Hell of a TV," he said when Mitch came back with a can.

"Next to my son, my pride and joy. Have a seat."

"I'll get right to it. Where's this thing you've got going with my mother heading?"

Mitch sat, studied Harper as he lifted his own can. "I can't tell you, as a lot of it depends on her, and where she wants it to head. Obviously, since I'm not blind, deaf, or dead, I find her very attractive. I admire what she's done with her life, and enjoy her company."

"If any of that attraction has to do with her money or her position, you're going to want to step away, right now."

With apparent calm, Mitch picked up the remote, hit the mute button, then set it down again. "That's a very ugly thing to say."

"She had a very ugly time not that long ago."

"Which is why I'm not kicking you out of my home. Such as it is." He reached down below the insult and got a tenuous hold on patience. "Your mother doesn't need money or position to be attractive. She's one of the most beautiful and fascinating women I've ever known. I feel something for her, and I believe she feels something for me. I'm hoping we'll be able to explore those feelings."

"Your first marriage cracked up."

"It did. I cracked it." He turned the Coke can in his hand. "There's no beer in the fridge because I don't drink anymore, and haven't for fourteen years. I'm an alcoholic, and I destroyed my first marriage. All of which I've told your mother, in more detail than I'm willing to tell you. Because I thought she deserved to know before we took those initial steps into what I'm hoping is a relationship."

"I apologize for embarrassing you."

"You haven't. Pissed me off some."

"I'm not sorry about that. She's my mother, and you weren't there to see what she went through. What she's still dealing with."

"How do you mean, still?"

"She found out tonight he opened a credit card in her name—can't prove it, not yet anyway, but it was him. Charged on it, so she's got the hassle of closing it down, dealing with the legal end—and having to tell the rest of us about it."

Mitch set the drink aside, pushed out of the chair to pace a circle around the room. And it was the temper pumping off him that calmed Harper.

"I thought about hunting him down, beating the crap out of him."

"I'll hold your coat, then you can hold mine."

Another knot in Harper's belly loosened. It was exactly the sentiment he could respect. "David talked me out of it. David and Stella, actually. Mama would hate it. It's one of those things she'd find . . . unseemly—then there'd be the gossip that rolled out of it. So I came here to take a few punches at you instead. Work off some of the mad."

"Mission accomplished?"

"Seems like it."

"That's something." Mitch scooped both hands through his hair. "Is she okay? How's she handling it?"

"Like she handles everything. Straightforward, takes the steps. She deals. But she's churned up. More worried that he'll take the same sort of shot at me, or my brothers. Embarrassed, too," he added. "It's the kind of thing that embarrasses her."

Mitch's expression went grim. "He'd know that, wouldn't he? That'll be the perk, even more than whatever he charged on the bogus account."

"Yeah, you got that right. I want you to know, if you hurt her, any way, shape, or form, I'll make you pay for it. Seems fair to tell you up-front."

"Okay." Mitch came back to the chair, sat. "Let me lay this out so we understand each other. I'm forty-eight. I make a good living. Nothing spectacular, but I do fine. I like my work, I'm good at my work, and lucky for me it pays the bills and gives me enough to be comfortable."

As an afterthought, Mitch shoved the open bag of chips on the table in Harper's direction. "My ex-wife and her husband are good people, and between us—without much help from me for the first six years, we raised a hell of a young man. I'm proud of that. I've had two serious relationships since my divorce, and a few that weren't so serious. I care about your mother, I respect what she's accomplished, and I have no intention of causing her any sort of harm or unhappiness. If I do, I have a feeling she'll pay me back for it before you can get off the mark."

He paused, took a drink. "Is there anything else you want to know?"

"Just one thing right now." Harper picked up the bag, dug in. "Can I hang out and watch the rest of the game?"

eLeveN

WITH HER HANDS ON HER HIPS, ROZ STUDIED HER newly arranged In the Garden potting soil preparation area. It had taken two full days, eking out time between other chores and working with the precise-minded Stella to set it up.

In Roz's estimation it would have taken her half that time alone, but it wouldn't have been nearly as practical a work space. There were tubs of soil she'd already mixed herself, the worktables, the bag storage, the scale, scoops, bag sealer, stools.

Everything was arranged in assembly-line efficiency.

The outlay had been relatively little, which had pleased Stella, who had a head for profit as well as precision. With the simple design of the bags, some clever marketing, and what she knew to be an excellent product, Roz felt confident they'd do very well. Very well indeed.

Her mood was very bright when she turned to greet Harper as he came through the door of the work shed.

"What do you think of our new enterprise?" She held

out her arms. With a laugh, she picked up a five-pound bag she'd already filled and sealed and tossed it over to him.

"Good look," he said, turning the bag over. "No frills. It says this is serious dirt. Looks like something you'd see in a high-end garden boutique."

"Exactly, and we'll keep the price down initially, to get it moving. I'm having the bags overfilled by a couple ounces to give me a safety zone. I thought we'd put Ruby on the job, for a start anyway. Maybe see if Steve wants to take some part-time work. It won't be that labor intensive, or take that much time."

"It's smart business, Mama." He laid the bag down. "You've got a knack for it."

"I like to think so. We still mad at each other?"

"No, but we might be after I finish telling you I went into Memphis to see Mitch Carnegie."

Her face went blank; her voice turned cool. "Why would you do that, Harper?"

"One, I was pissed off. Two, David and Stella talked me out of hunting up Clerk and beating his face in. Third, I wanted to hear for myself what Mitch had to say about what's going on between you."

"I understand one perfectly. I appreciate two, on several levels. But I fail to comprehend why you would assume to interrogate a man I'm seeing. It's unpardonably rude and interfering. I don't run around snooping on the women you choose to see."

"It wasn't snooping, and I've never chosen to see a woman who stole from me or set out to interfere with my life or smear my reputation."

"You're young yet." Ice dripped from the words. "Do you think I'm the only woman foolish enough to get tangled up with an asshole?"

"No, I don't. But I don't much care about other women. You're my only mother."

"That doesn't give you the right to—"

"I love you."

"Don't use that weapon on me."

"I can't help it. It's all I've got."

She pressed her fingers to the center of her forehead, rubbed hard. "It would help if you added a little trust and respect to that love, Harper."

"I've got all the trust and respect in the world for you, Mama. It's the men I'm not so sure about. But if it helps any, I worked up plenty of trust and respect for Mitch last night. He might almost be worthy enough to court my mama."

"He's not courting me, for God's sake. Where do you get this sort of . . . We went to a college basketball game, we had dinner."

"I think he's stuck on you."

She stared, and this time lifted both hands to the sides of her head. "My head is reeling."

He walked to her, slid his arms around her, and drew her in. "I couldn't stand to see you get hurt again."

"Bryce only hurt my pride."

"That's a mortal wound for us Harpers. And he did more than that. I don't think Mitch will do the same, at least not deliberately."

"So, you approve."

He grinned when she tipped her head up to look at him. "That's a trick question, and my mama didn't raise any fools. I say yes, and you'll rip my butt reminding me you don't need my approval. So I'm just going to say I like him. I like him a lot."

"You're a slippery one, Harper Ashby. Tell you what." She patted his back, eased away. "You can give me a hand in here for a while. I want to do up twenty bags of each weight category."

"I thought you wanted Ruby to do that."

"Changed my mind. Doing some uncomplicated and

monotonous work ought to give you some time to reflect on the error of your ways."

"Talk about slippery."

"The day you can outwit me, my baby, is the day I see about moving myself into a home. Let's get started."

AFTER WORK SHE WENT STRAIGHT HOME, AND DIRECTLY upstairs to clean up. Wary now, she checked the mail on her desk, looked through the bills. She couldn't say she was relieved when she found nothing. It was like waiting for the other shoe to drop.

There had been a similar sort of harassment right after the divorce, then a nice period of peace. When, she assumed, he'd had some other woman on the string and was too involved to waste his time poking sticks at an ex-wife.

She'd handled it then; she'd handle it now.

As she was dressing the phone rang. When it hit the third ring, she assumed David was otherwise occupied and answered herself.

"Good evening. Is Rosalind Harper available?"

"This is she."

"Ms. Harper, this is Derek from the Carrington Gallery in New York. We're just following up to let you know the Vergano will be shipped to you tomorrow."

"I don't think that's a good idea, Derek, is it? I didn't order anything from your gallery."

"The Cristina Vergano, Ms. Harper. Your representative spoke with me personally only last week."

"I don't have a representative."

"Ms. Harper, I'm very confused. The charge has already been cleared to your account. Your representative indicated that you were very taken with the painting, and wished to have it shipped as soon as the showing was over. We've had considerable interest in this work, but as it was already sold—"

She rubbed hard at the back of her neck where the tension had settled. "It looks like we both have a problem, Derek. Let me give you some of the bad news." She explained briefly, caught herself pacing as she spoke, and as a fresh headache brewed. She noted down the credit card company and number.

"This is very upsetting."

"Yes," she agreed, "it certainly is. I'm sorry you and your gallery have been inconvenienced by this. Would you mind, just for curiosity's sake, telling me the name of the painting?"

"Vergano's a very powerful and dynamic artist. This oil on linen, custom framed by the artist, is from her Bitches collection. It's called *The Amazing Bitch*."

"Of course it is," Roz replied.

She went though the routine, calling the credit card company, and her lawyer, then writing to both to document the incident.

She took aspirin before going down to the kitchen and pouring herself a large glass of wine.

David's note sat propped on the counter.

Hot date. An exceptional lasagna's on warm in the oven. Hayley and the baby went over to Logan's with Stella and the boys. They're having a little painting party. More than enough lasagna for two. Dr. Studly's in the library. Just warm up the bread, toss the salad—in the fridge—and you're set. Buon appetito!

David

P.S. Appropriate CDs already loaded in the player. Now please *go up and put on those Jimmy Choo's.*

"Well." She noted David had set the kitchen nook with festive plates, fat candles, a bottle of San Pellegrino, pale green glasses. And it explained why a bottle of good Italian red was breathing on the counter.

"Lasagna's fine," she said aloud. "But I'm not putting on those shoes to eat it."

Content and comfortable in the thick gray socks she habitually wore around the house, she walked to the library.

He was sitting at the table, wearing his glasses and a Memphis Tigers sweatshirt. His fingers were moving quickly over the keyboard of his laptop. On the desk was a large bottle of water. David's doing, no doubt. He'd have nagged Mitch to rotate water with his habitual coffee.

He looked . . . studiously sexy, she decided, with his intellectual glasses and the mass of thick, disordered hair. That rich brown, with just a hint of chestnut.

There were good eyes behind those glasses, she thought. Not just the color, so deep, so unique, but good, direct eyes. A little intense, unnervingly intense, and she had to admit she found that exciting.

Even as she watched, he paused in his typing to scoop the fingers of one hand through his hair. And muttered to himself.

It was interesting to hear him mutter to himself, since she often caught herself doing the same.

It was interesting, too, to feel this long slow pull in her belly, and the little dance of lust up her spine. Wasn't it good to know those instinctive charges still had spark? And wasn't she curious to see what would happen if she took a chance, and lit the fuse?

Even as she thought it, books flew off the shelf, slammed into each other, then the walls, the floor. In the fireplace, flames leaped in hot reds, while the air shivered with cold.

"Jesus Christ."

Mitch shoved back from the table so fast his chair hit the floor. He managed to duck one book, then block another. As Roz rushed forward, everything stopped.

"You see that? Did you *see* that?" He bent, picked up a book, then dropped it on the table. It wasn't fear in that lovely, liquid drawl, she noted. It was fascination. "It's like ice."

"Temper tantrums." She picked up a book herself, and the cold nearly numbed her fingers.

"Impressive ones. I've been working in here since about three." Grinning like a boy, he checked his watch. "Nearly four hours. It's been quiet as, you'll excuse the expression, a tomb. Until now."

"I suppose I set her off, as I was about to ask if you'd like to have dinner. David left a meal."

Together they began to retrieve the rest of the books. "No question that she doesn't like the two of us together."

"Apparently not."

He set the last book on the shelf. "So . . . what's for dinner?"

She glanced over at him, smiled. And in that moment realized that beyond the lust, there wasn't anything about him she didn't like. "Lasagna, which David bills as exceptional. As I've sampled it in the past, I can vouch for his claim."

"Sounds great. God, you smell good. Sorry," he added when her eyebrows lifted. "Thinking out loud. Listen, I've been able to eliminate more names, and I've been transcribing the interviews we've done so far. I've got a file here for you."

"All right."

"I'm going to work on tracking down some of the descendants of staff, and what we'll call the outer branches of the family tree. But what I'm seeing as the oldest living relative is your cousin Clarise—and happily she's local. I'd like to talk to her."

"Good luck with that."

"She's still in the area, at the . . ."

"Riverbank Center. Yes, I know."

"She puts me a full generation closer to Amelia. It'd be simpler, I'd think, to approach her if you spoke to her first."

"I'm afraid Cousin Clarise and I aren't on speaking terms, or any sort of terms whatsoever."

"I know you said there was a rift, but wouldn't she be interested in what I'm doing with the family?"

"Possibly. But I can assure you, she wouldn't take my call if I made one."

"Look, I understand about family schisms, but in this case—"

"You don't understand Clarise Harper. She dropped her surname years ago, choosing to go legally by her first and middle names. That's how entrenched in the Harper name she is. She never married. My opinion being she never found anyone soft or stupid enough to take her on."

Frowning, he hitched a hip on the table. "Is this your way of telling me you don't want me contacting her, because—"

"I hired you to do a job, and don't intend to tell you how to go about it, so don't get your back up. I'm telling you she's chosen to banish me and mine from her plane of existence, which is just fine by me. The one good thing I can say about her is once she's made up her mind on something, she follows through."

"But you don't have any objection to me talking to her, involving her."

"None. Your best bet is to write her—very formally—and introduce yourself, being sure to use the doctor part, and any other impressive credentials you might have at hand. If you tell her you intend to do a family history on the Harpers, and play up how honored you would be to interview her, and so on, she might agree."

"This is the one you kicked out of the house, right?"

"In a manner of speaking. I don't recall telling you about that."

"I talk to people. She's not the one you chased off with a Weedwacker."

Amusement, very faint, ran over her face. "You are talking to people."

"Part of the job."

"I suppose. No, I didn't chase her with a Weedwacker. That was the gardeners. And it wasn't a Weedwacker, come to that. It was a fan rake, which was unlikely to do any serious damage. If I hadn't been so mad and thinking more clearly, I'd've grabbed the loppers those idiots had used on my mimosa trees. At least with those I could've given them a good jab in the ass as they skeddadled."

"Loppers. Would those be . . ." He made wide scissoring motions with both arms.

"Yes, that's right."

"Ouch. Back to your cousin. Why'd you give her the boot?"

"Because when I invited her, to my lasting regret, to a family barbecue here years ago, she called my sons disreputable brats and stated—she without chick or child—that if I were a proper mother I'd've taken a switch to them regularly. She then called Harper a born liar, as he was entertaining some of his young cousins with stories about the Bride, and told him to shut his mouth."

He angled his head. "And still she lives."

Temper had brought a flush to her cheeks, but his comment had a small smile curving her lips. "She was on shaky ground already as she constantly criticized my parenting, my housekeeping, my lifestyle, and occasionally my morals. But nobody stands on my ground and attacks my children. While I did consider murder, knowing my quarry, I was certain banishment from Harper House was a more painful punishment."

"As I believe I said before, you're a hardass. I like that."

"Good thing, 'cause that's not going to change at this

late date. In any case, on her way out the door, she cursed my name and said it was a black day when Harper House came into my grasping, incompetent hands."

"She sounds delightful. I'll write her tomorrow."

"Just don't mention you're working for me."

"It wouldn't be hard for her to find out."

"True enough, but the less you mention me the better. Anything else on your mind?"

"Other than wondering how you manage to work all day and still look amazing, no. Nothing that springs, anyway."

She waited another moment, nodded. "You're not going to mention it."

"What would it be?"

"The visit my son paid to you last night."

"Oh." Because she was watching his face, she caught the flicker of surprise that moved over it before he picked up the glasses he'd taken off and began to polish them with his sweatshirt. "He told you?"

"Yes. He was angry, so he acted rashly."

"Like grabbing a fan rake instead of loppers."

Her laugh snuck out. "Very like. We have, both of us, horrible tempers. Which is why we both make a concerted effort not to lose them. It doesn't always work. I'd like to apologize for his behavior."

"I can't accept."

There was distress, something he rarely saw from her, in her eyes. "Mitch, I know he overstepped, but he's young and—"

"You misunderstand. I can't accept an apology when there's no need for one. From either of you. He was looking out for you."

"I don't need, or want, looking out for."

"Maybe not, but that's not going to stop someone who loves you from trying. We discussed, came to understand each other, and that's all there was to it."

"And you're not going to elaborate on that."

"It was between him and me."

"You men do have your codes of honor."

"You weren't going to tell me about this latest harassment."

For an instant, she thought of the phone call from New York, then tucked it away again. "Nothing to tell. I'm dealing with it."

"What's happened since last night? You're good, so I must've caught you off guard. What else happened?"

"Just a minor irritation, one I've already handled. It's not important. More accurately, I won't let it be important. If I do, it makes me the victim, and he wins. I won't be his victim. That's one thing I never allowed myself to be, and I won't start now."

"Telling me, venting some of the stress, doesn't make you a victim, either."

"I'm not used to airing my problems. I'm not comfortable with it. But I appreciate the offer."

He took her hand, held it. "Consider it a standing one. For my next offer, *Chicago*'s coming to the Orpheum next week. Come with me, have a late supper with me after."

"I might. Are you courting me, Mitchell?"

His thumb grazed back and forth over her hand. "I like to think I'm romancing you, Rosalind."

"That's a pretty word, *romancing*. You've been careful not to pressure me into taking that romancing into intimacy."

"If I pressured you, it wouldn't be romance, or intimacy. Besides the fact, I imagine the door would hit me in the ass as you shoved me out of it."

Humor danced over her face. "That's astute. I think you're a clever man."

"I know I'm a besotted one."

"Another pretty word."

"I'll have to be careful with them. They're the sort of thing you'd distrust."

"Yes, a clever man. Well." She had a choice, and she made it. "Come upstairs."

For the second time that night, she watched surprise run over his face. Then he lifted her hand to his lips. "Would this be serious business?"

"It would. Very serious business."

"Then I'd love to."

She led him out of the room, and down the hall. "The house emptied out on me tonight. So it's just the two of us. Well, three." She looked up at him as they walked up the stairs. "Will that bother you?"

"The fact that she may be watching." He took a little breath. "I guess we'll find out. Did you—" He cut himself off, shook his head.

"What?"

"No, we'll save that."

"All right. I hope you don't mind putting off dinner a bit."

As an answer he turned to her, into her, backing her against a wall. Then laying his lips on hers.

It began warm and soft, then edged up to heat, and demand. She trembled, just once, a shiver of anticipation that spread through her system and reminded her what it was like to be poised on the brink.

He lifted his head, angled it. "You were saying?"

It made her laugh, and feel easy. Taking his hand, she drew him into her bedroom. Shut the door.

He took a moment, scanned the room with its lovely old four-poster and tall windows with the curtains drawn back to let in the night.

"It looks like you. The room," he explained, taking in the silvery green walls, the antiques, the clean lines and elegant details. "Beautiful and classy with a simple elegance that reflects an innate grace and sense of style."

"You make me wish I'd taken the time to fuss with myself a bit."

He looked at her then, the casual sweater, the comfortable trousers. "You are exactly right."

"Right or not, I'm what I am. I think a fire would be nice." She stepped toward it, but he laid a hand on her arm.

"I'll do it. You'd have a view of the back gardens from here," he began as he crouched in front of the fire.

And the terrace doors slashed open on a frigid gust of wind.

"Yes, I do." Calmly Roz crossed over, muscled the doors closed again. "Some mornings, when there's time, I like to take coffee out on the terrace."

He set the kindling to blaze, and his tone was as matter-of-fact as hers. "I can't think of many better ways to start the day."

She stepped to the bed to turn down the duvet. "Or end it. I often have a last glass of wine or cup of coffee out there before I go to bed. It helps smooth out any rough edges left over from the day." She reached over, turned out the lamp.

"Why not leave it on?"

She shook her head. "The firelight's enough, the first time. It's more flattering, and I'm vain enough to prefer that."

She stood where she was, waited for him to come to her. As he laid his hands on her shoulders, the bedroom door slammed open, and closed.

"I expect we might have more of that to contend with," she said.

"I don't care." His hands slid up to her face. "I don't care," he repeated and took her mouth with his.

She felt her pulse jump, what a glorious jolt. The sort that woke the whole system at once, brought it to quivering life. In answer, she lifted her arms to link them around his neck, changed the angle of the kiss to deepen it.

Clocks began to chime, insanely. In defiance as much as

need, she pressed her body to his. "I want you to touch me," she murmured against his mouth. "I want to be touched. By you. Your hands on me."

He eased her back on the bed, sank in with her. The weight of him made her sigh, the weight of a man, and what it meant. Then he touched, and she moaned.

He felt the heat from her. He'd known it was there, under that fascinating and cool veneer. Her skin was like velvet, warmed velvet, over her sides, her torso, the lovely curve of her breasts.

Slim, but not delicate, her body was tough and disciplined. Like her mind, he thought. And just as appealing.

She tasted of ripe, forbidden fruit and smelled of midnight gardens.

Her hands slid under his shirt, up his back. Hard, strong hands, an arousing contrast to the wand-slim body, the satiny skin.

She drew his shirt over his head, reared up enough to set her teeth on his bare shoulder. And the shock of it speared straight to his loins.

The terrace door flew open once more, and the wind burst through to slap over him. He simply reached down, hauled the duvet up. And burrowed under it with her.

She laughed, and found his mouth in the blanketing dark.

Tasting her, feasting on her, he tugged her sweater up and off. "Tell me if you're too cold."

"No. I couldn't be."

She was burning up from the inside out, and only wanted more. More of his hands, his mouth. She arched to him, demanding, exalting when those hands, that mouth claimed her breast. The thrill of it stabbed through her, the bliss of giving her body, of having it *used*.

They rolled together, tugging each other free of clothes, sliding together naked as flesh began to slick from heat and passion.

The blankets fell away, so firelight flickered over them. And if in some dim corner of her brain she heard someone weeping, she could feel only that steady rise of excitement. She could see only him, in the glow of the fire, rising over her.

She lifted to meet him, opened to take him. And sighed, sighed, when he slipped inside her.

He watched her now as she watched him, gazes and bodies locked. Then the movement, slow, intensely focused as her breath came short and ragged, as dark, deep pleasure flooded her, swept her away.

He watched her crest, the arch of her throat, the blur of her eyes, felt her fly over as she squeezed around him. He fought to hold on another moment, just another moment while she quaked under him, while her breath hitched, then released on a long, low moan. And her body went soft and limp in surrender.

He kissed her then, one last, desperate kiss before he plunged, and emptied.

THE DOORS WERE CLOSED AS THEY SHOULD BE. THE fire crackled and simmered. And the house was quiet, settled, and warm.

She was cocooned with him in the center of the bed, allowing herself to enjoy the bliss and the glow. With very little effort, she could have drifted straight off to sleep.

"Looks like she gave up," Mitch commented.

"Yes. For now, anyway."

"You were right about the fire. It's nice. Very nice."

Then he rolled so that she was under him again, and he could look down at her face. "Being with you," he began, then shook his head, touched his lips to hers. "Being with you."

"Yes." Smiling, she stroked her fingers through his hair. "That's very nice, too. I haven't wanted to be with anyone in a very long time. You know, you've got good arms, for a scholar." She gave his biceps a squeeze. "I like good arms. I don't like to think I'm shallow, but I have to say it's a pleasure being naked with a man who keeps in shape."

"I'll change that to a woman, then say the same. The first time I met you, I stood and watched you walk away. You've got one excellent ass, Ms. Harper."

"It happens I do." With a laugh, she gave his a light slap. "We'd better get dressed, go on down before everyone starts coming home."

"In a minute. It was your eyes that hooked me—hooked right through me."

"My eyes?"

"Oh yeah. I thought maybe it was because they're the color of good aged whiskey—and I did love a good whiskey. But that's not it. It's the way they look straight at me. Straight on. Fearless, and just a little regal."

"Please."

"Oh yeah, there's lady of the manor in there, and it beats the hell out of me why it's so sexy. Ought to be irritating, or intimidating at least. But for me, it's just . . . stimulating."

"If that's the case, I'm going to have to start wearing dark glasses so I don't get you heated up at inappropriate times."

"Won't matter a damn." He gave her a light kiss, then shifted. Took her hand. "This mattered. This was important. There isn't anyone else."

Her heart trembled a little, made her feel young and just a little foolish. "Yes, this mattered. This was important. There isn't anyone else."

"Serious business," he said, and drew her hand to his lips. "I'm going to start wanting you again, real soon."

She squeezed his hand. "We'll have to see what we can do about that."

twelve

ROZ FOLLOWED THE SCENT OF COFFEE, AND THE NOISE, into the kitchen. The dreary gray rain had canceled her morning run, so she'd channeled the energy into three miles on her treadmill. It was an alternative that usually bored her senseless, but today she'd found herself singing along with commercial jingles during the *Today* show breaks.

In the kitchen the baby was banging away on her high chair tray with the enthusiasm of a heavy metal drummer, and Stella's boys were whining over their cereal.

"Yes," Stella announced with the snap of motherly frustration in her voice, "you both have to wear your raincoats, because I'm mean and bossy and I want you to be miserable."

"We *hate* the raincoats," Gavin informed her.

"Really? That's not what you said when you begged me to buy them."

"That was before."

Perhaps in sympathy, perhaps for the fun of it, Lily stopped banging her teething rattle and threw it—along with her mangled Zwieback. The eagle-eyed Parker fielded the Zwieback before it hit the floor, and the rattle landed with a solid *plop* in Luke's bowl of Cap'n Crunch.

Milk fumed up and over the rim of the bowl, causing Lily to scream in delight. In a chain reaction, Parker let out a spate of ear-piercing barks and did canine flips while Gavin doubled over in hysterics.

Stella was quick, but for once Luke was quicker and had the rattle out of the bowl and tossed, dripping, into his brother's lap.

"Oh, for God's sake." Stella grabbed a napkin with one hand and held up the other to block Gavin's retaliation. "Don't even think about it."

"I'm sorry. I'm sorry." Hayley scooped up the bowl, more napkins as the boys shoved at each other.

A calm in the storm, David walked over with a damp rag. "We'll mop it up. Troublemaker," he said to Lily, who answered him with a huge, crumby grin.

Roz studied the chaos, and just beamed.

"Morning," she said and strolled in.

Heads turned.

"Roz?" Stella stared at her. "What are you doing here?"

"Since I live here, I thought I'd come in and get myself a cup of coffee." She bent down to brush a kiss over the top of Lily's head. "Hello, boys. That baby's got pretty good aim, doesn't she? Two-pointed it right in the goal."

The idea was so intriguing the boys stopped fighting. "Do it again, Lily!" Luke tugged on his mother's sleeve. "Give it back to her, Mom, so she can do it again."

"Not right now. You've got to finish up or you'll be late for school." She checked her watch and saw it was indeed just after eight, and a full hour after Roz was usually on her way out the door.

"My cereal's got baby spit in it now," Luke complained.

"You can have a muffin instead."

"Then I want a muffin." Gavin shoved his cereal aside. "If he can have a muffin, I can have a muffin, too."

"Fine, fine."

"I'll get them." Hayley gestured Stella back. "Least I can do."

"Mmm, don't they smell great?" Roz sniffed at the bowl filled with fresh apple muffins. She plucked one out for herself, then leaned back against the counter, her coffee in one hand, her muffin in the other. "Can't be a better way to start the day. And look at that rain. Nothing like a good all-day soaker."

After Hayley passed out muffins, she bent close to Stella's ear. "Somebody got her batteries charged."

Stella fought to swallow a snorting laugh. "We'll be out of your way in a minute."

"No rush." Roz bit into the muffin.

"You're usually gone, or finishing up before the invasion."

"Slept in a little today."

"That explains the bulletin I heard on the news this morning about hell freezing over." David didn't bother to hide the smirk as he brought the coffeepot over to top off Roz's mug.

"Aren't you full of sass this morning."

"I'm not the only one full of something. How'd the . . . lasagna go over?"

"Very well." She gave him a bland look over the rim of her cup, and wondered if she was wearing a sign: Recently Got Laid.

"You ought to have a nice big helping of it more often. Puts roses in your cheeks."

"I'll keep that in mind."

"I could use a nice hot dish of lasagna myself," Hayley commented. "Come on, baby doll, let's get you cleaned up." She took Lily out of the high chair.

"You guys go up and get your things—including raincoats," Stella ordered. "It's almost time to go."

But she loitered another minute. "You want to ride over with me?" she asked Roz.

"I guess I will."

STELLA WAITED UNTIL THEY WERE STARTING DOWN the drive. By her calculations, swinging just a half a mile out of the way to drop Lily off at the babysitter's should give them enough time.

"We made a lot of progress on the painting last night. It's going to be nice to have the dining room finished and put together by the wedding. I'd really like to have a dinner party once we're set. David and all of us, Harper, my parents. Oh and Mitch, of course."

"That'd be nice."

"He's around so much—Mitch, I mean—these days, he feels like part of the household." At Roz's noncommittal *hmmm*, Stella glanced in the rearview mirror to see Hayley rolling her eyes and giving get-to-it hand signals.

"So . . . ah, did you and Mitch work on the project last night, or take advantage of the quiet house and just relax?"

"Stella, why don't you just ask me if I had sex with him instead of beating around the bush? Nothing I hate more than seeing a bush beat half to death."

"I was being subtle," Stella replied.

"No, you weren't."

"I told her she didn't have to lead up to everything," Hayley said from the back. "Besides, we know you had sex. You've got that recently waxed and lubed look."

"God."

"Of course, it's none of our business," Stella put in, shooting Hayley a hot look in the mirror.

"Of course it's not," Roz agreed easily.

"But we just wanted to find a way to say that we're happy if you're happy. That we think Mitch is a terrific guy, and we're here to support—"

"Jeez." Hayley leaned forward as much as her seat belt would allow. "What she's trying to say in her Stella way is: Score!"

"I am not. Exactly. I'm trying to say, with some delicacy—"

"Screw delicacy. Hey, just because people are a little older and all doesn't mean they don't want and deserve some touch the same as the next guy."

"Oh," Roz declared. "I repeat, God."

"You're beautiful and sexy," Hayley continued. "He's great looking and sexy. So, it seems to me that sex is . . . She really can't understand all this, right?" Biting her lip, she glanced at Lily, who was busy playing with her own fingers. "I read this theory on how babies absorb all the stimuli around them, including voices and words, and kind of file them away, and shoot, here we are."

She gathered the diaper bag, then jumped out of the car in the rain. After jogging around, she opened the door to release Lily's harness and drape a blanket over her head. "Don't say anything interesting while I'm gone. I mean it."

When she dashed off, Roz let out a long, heartfelt sigh. "Half the time that girl makes me feel old and creaky, and the other half she makes me feel about eighteen and grass green."

"I know exactly what you mean. And I know it sounds like we're pushing and prying into your private life, but it's because, well, it's just because we love you, that's all. And added to it, we were wondering when you and Mitch might take things up a level."

"Wondering, were you?"

Stella winced. "The subject might have come up in casual conversation. Once or twice."

"Why don't I let you know when and if I'd like to have a casual conversation on the subject?"

"Sure. Absolutely."

When Hayley ran back out, jerked open the door, Stella cleared her throat—loudly—and gave a quick shake of her head. As Hayley let out a disgusted sigh, Stella pulled away from the side of the road and spoke brightly.

"So, I've been working on ideas for displaying the potting soil."

HER LIFE DIDN'T CHANGE, ROZ REMINDED HERSELF, just because she'd gone to bed with a man she found attractive and appealing. Life went on, with its duties and obligations, its irritations and its pleasures.

As she headed for her garden club's monthly meeting, she wasn't sure which category her current destination landed in.

A Harper had been a member of the garden club since her grandmother's day. In fact, her grandmother had helped form it in 1928, and Harper House had held many of its early meetings.

As the owner of a garden center, she felt a double obligation to support the group and remain an active member. And there were some pleasures attached to it. She enjoyed talking with like-minded people about gardening and felt the club had worked hard to implement fund-raisers for beautification projects.

But then, there were plenty who just wanted to dress up, have lunch, and gossip.

She walked into the meeting room at the country club into that beehive hum of female voices. Square enameled pots exploding with forced narcissus sat festively on tables draped with spring-green linen. A podium stood in front of the room for the various committee chairs who'd give their reports or pitches.

She could only thank God she wasn't chairing anything currently.

When she stepped farther into the room, glances shot her way, and the hum of voices trailed off. And died.

Almost immediately they started up again, just a bit too loud, just a bit too bright. She let the cold shield slide over her, and continued to walk straight to a table.

"Aren't these flowers sweet." She looked directly at Jan Forrester as if she couldn't hear the whispers under the forced chatter. "A nice reminder spring's just around the corner. How are you, Jan?"

"Oh, fine, Roz. I'm just fine, how about you?"

"Couldn't be better. How's Quill doing?"

She flushed, deep and rosy. "Oh, you know Quill."

"I certainly do. You just give him my best, won't you?"

It was pride that had her walking the gauntlet, mingling with the crowd, speaking with more than a dozen people before she moved to the pots of coffee and tea. She opted for tea, cold, rather than her habitual coffee.

Her throat felt scalded.

"Roz, honey, don't you look fabulous." Cissy sidled up, smelling of Obsession and smiling like a hungry cat. "I swear, nobody wears clothes like you do. What color would you call that suit?"

Roz glanced down at the trim jacket and pants. "I have no idea."

"Apricot. That's just what it looks like, a nice ripe apricot. That little turnip-head Mandy's been flapping her foolish tongue as fast as she can," she said under her breath. "You and me need to have ourselves a *tête-à-tête*."

"That's all right, I've got the picture. Excuse me." She walked deliberately to Mandy and had the small pleasure of watching the woman's cheeks go white even as she stopped speaking in mid-sentence.

"Mandy, how are you? I haven't seen you since before Christmas. You didn't make last month's meeting."

"I was busy."

Roz took a slow sip of tea. "Life is a circus, isn't it?"

"You've been busy yourself." Mandy jerked up her chin.

"If there's not one thing that needs doing, there's a half dozen."

"Maybe if you spent more time tending to your own business, you wouldn't have so much left over to make harassing phone calls or tell vicious lies."

All pretense of other conversation stopped, as if a switch had been thrown.

"You don't know me very well," Roz said in the same conversational tone, "or you'd know that I don't make any phone call that isn't necessary. I don't care to spend much time on the phone. And I don't lie. I just don't see the point in it when the truth usually serves best."

Mandy folded her arms, cocked a hip in an aggressive stance. "Everybody knows what you've been up to, but they're too afraid of you to say it to your face."

"But you're not—good for you—so you go right ahead and say what's on your mind. Or if you'd feel more comfortable, we can have this conversation in private."

"You'd like that, wouldn't you?"

"No, not any more than I like having it in public."

"Just because your family's gone back in Shelby County since God doesn't give you the right to lord it over everybody. My family's just as important as yours, and I've got as much money and prestige."

"Money and prestige don't buy good manners. You aren't showing any at the moment."

"You have nerve, talking to me about manners when you're doing everything you can to ruin Bryce's reputation, and mine."

"Bryce's reputation is of his own making. And as for

yours, honey, you haven't even been on my radar screen. You seem like a likable enough girl. I've got nothing against you."

"You've been telling people I was a cheap tramp, using my daddy's money to try to buy some class."

"And where'd you hear such a thing? Bryce, I imagine."

"Not only him." With her chin still lifted, red spots of color flagged in her cheeks, Mandy looked over at Jan.

"Jan?" Surprise softened Roz's voice, and regret flickered in her heart, just once as she saw the woman flush. "You know better. Shame on you."

"It was something I heard, from a reliable source," Jan said as she hunched her shoulders.

"A reliable source?" Roz didn't bother to temper the disgust in her voice. "And suddenly you're, what, an investigative reporter hunting up sources? You might've come and asked me. It would've been the simple and decent thing to do before spreading such nonsense any further."

"Everyone knows how mad you were when Bryce showed up at your house with Mandy. This isn't the place to discuss it."

"No, it isn't, but it's too late for that. At least this girl has the spine to say what she has to say straight to my face, which is more than you."

Dismissing Jan, Roz turned back to Mandy. "Mandy, did I seem mad when you arrived at my door with Bryce for my holiday party?"

"Of course you were mad. You turned us away, didn't you, when he was only trying to make peace with you."

"We can disagree on what he was trying to do. How did I seem mad? Did I shout and scream?"

"No, but—"

"Did I curse and push you physically out the door?"

"No, because you're cold-blooded, just like he says. Just like plenty others say when you're not around to hear. You waited until we were gone to go in and say awful things about us."

"Did I?" She turned, determined now to finish it out. "Most of you were there that night. Maybe someone here could refresh my memory, as I can't recall saying awful things."

"You did nothing of the sort." Mrs. Haggerty, one of Roz's oldest customers and a pillar in the gardening community, pushed her way through. "I'm as interested in juicy gossip as the next, and don't mind some enhancements to a story, but these are outright lies. Rosalind comported herself with absolute propriety under extremely difficult circumstances. And, young lady, she was kind to you, I saw that with my own eyes. When she came back inside, she said nothing whatsoever about you or that unfortunate bastard you've chosen to champion. If there's anyone here who can say different than that, let's hear it."

"She didn't say a word against you," Cissy put in, and gave a wicked smile. "Even when I did."

"He said you'd try to turn people against me."

"Why would I do that?" Roz said, wearily now. "But you'll have to believe what you have to believe. Personally, I'm not interested in speaking of this, or to you, any longer."

"I have as much right to be here as you."

"You certainly do." To end it, Roz turned away, walked to a table across the room, and sat down to finish her tea.

Ten humming seconds of silence followed, until Mandy burst into tears and ran from the room. A few women hustled after her after shooting glances at Roz.

"Lord," Roz said when Mrs. Haggerty sat down beside her, "she is young, isn't she?"

"Young's no excuse for being flat-out stupid. Rude, on top of it." She looked up with a nod as Cissy moved to join them. "Surprised at you."

"At me? Why?"

"For speaking straight for a refreshing change."

Cissy shrugged, sat. "I like ugly scenes, and I won't deny it. Sure does spice up a dull day. But I don't like Bryce Clerk. And sometimes speaking straight makes things more interesting anyway. Only thing better would've been seeing Roz give that bobble-headed fool Mandy a good smack. Not your style, though," she said to Roz.

Then she touched a hand to Roz, gently. "You want to leave, I'll go with you."

"No, but thanks. I'll stick it out."

SHE GOT THROUGH THE MEETING. IT WAS A MATTER of grit, and of duty. When she got home she changed, then slipped out the back to go in the gardens, to sit on her bench in the cool and study the little signs of coming spring.

Her bulbs were spearing up, the daffodils and hyacinths that would burst into bloom before too long. The crocus were already in flower. They came so soon, she thought, left so early.

She could see the tight buds on her azaleas, and the faint haze on the forsythia.

While she sat, the control she'd locked into place wavered, so she was allowed, finally, to shake inside. With rage, with insult, with temper, with hurt. She gave herself the gift of swimming in the sea of all those dark emotions while she sat, alone in the quiet.

While she sat, the fury peaked, then ebbed, until she could breathe clear again.

She'd done the right thing, she decided. Faced it down, though she'd hated doing so in public. Still it was always better to face a fight than it was to run from it.

Had he thought she would? she wondered. Had he

thought she'd break apart in public, run off in humiliation to lick her wounds?

She imagined he did. Bryce had never understood her.

John had, she thought, studying the arbor where his roses would ramble and bloom for her from spring into the summer, and well into fall. He had understood her, and he'd loved her. Or at least he'd understood and loved the girl she'd been.

Would he love the woman she'd become?

An odd thought, she decided, tipping her head back, closing her eyes. She might not be the woman she was if he'd lived.

He'd have left you. They all do. He'd have lied and cheated and broken you. Taken whores while you sat and waited. They all do.

I should know.

No, not John, she thought, squeezing her eyes tighter as that voice hissed in her head.

You're better off he died than if he'd lived long enough to ruin you. Like the other. Like the one you take to your bed now.

"How pitiful you are," Roz whispered, "to try to smear the memory, and the honor, of a good man."

"Roz." The hand on her shoulder made her jump. "Sorry," Mitch told her. "Talking in your sleep?"

"No." Didn't he feel the cold, or was it only inside her? Inside her along with the quivering belly. "I wasn't sleeping. Only thinking. How did you know I was out here?"

"David said he saw you through the window, heading out this way. Over an hour ago. It's a little chilly to sit out so long." He took her hand, rubbed it between his as he sat beside her. "Your hands are cold."

"They're all right."

"But you're not. You look sad."

She considered a moment, then reminded herself there

were things that couldn't be personal. He was working for her. "I am, I guess. I am a little sad. She was talking to me. In my head."

"Now?" His hands tightened on hers.

"Mmm. You interrupted our conversation, though it was the same old, same old 'men are deceivers' sort of thing on her side."

He scanned the gardens. "I doubt Shakespeare could have created a more determined ghost than your Amelia. I was hoping you'd come by the library, for several reasons. This is one."

He turned her face toward his, pressed his mouth to hers.

"Something's wrong," he stated. "Something more."

How could he see her so well? How could he see what she was able to hide from most? "No, just a mood." But she drew her hand from his. "Some female histrionics earlier. Men are so much less inclined to drama, aren't they?"

"Why don't you tell me about it?"

"It's not worth the breath."

He started to speak again, she could feel him check the instinct to press. Instead he tapped his shoulder. "Put your head here?"

"What?"

"Right here." To ensure she did, he wrapped an arm around her waist, drew her close to his side. "How about it?"

She left it there, smiled a little. "It's not bad."

"And the world didn't spin on its axis because you leaned on someone else for a minute."

"No, it didn't. Thanks."

"You're welcome. Anyway, other reasons I was hoping you'd come in while I was working. I wanted to tell you I've sent a letter to your cousin Clarise Harper. If I don't hear back from her in a week, I'll do a follow-up. And I have several detailed family trees for you, the Harpers, your mother's family, your first husband's. I actually found an Amelia Ashby. No, leave that head right where it is," he said, tightening his grip when she started to sit up straight.

"She's not connected, as far as I can see, as she lived and died in Louisiana, and is too contemporary. I spent some time tracking her back, to see if I could find a link to your Amelia—a namesake sort of thing—but it's not happening. I have some e-mail correspondence from the great-granddaughter of the housekeeper who worked in Harper House from 1887 to 1912. She's a lawyer in Chicago, and is finding the family history interesting enough to put out feelers of her own. She could be a good source, at least on that one branch."

His hand stroked gently up and down her arm, relaxing her. "You've been busy."

"Most of that's just standard. But I've been thinking about the less ordinary portions of our project. When we made love—"

"What portion of the project does that come under?"

He laughed at her dry tone, and rubbed his cheek over her hair. "I put that in the extremely personal column and am hoping to fill a lot of pages in that file. But I've got a point. She manifested—that would be the word, right?"

"Can't think of a better."

"She blew open doors, slammed them shut, set the clocks off, and so on. Without question showed her feelings about what was going on between us, and has since we started that personal file."

"And so?"

"I'm not the first man you've been personal with in that house."

"No, you're not."

"But you haven't mentioned her having similar tantrums over you and John Ashby or you and Bryce Clerk—or anyone you might have had a relationship with otherwise."

"Because it never happened before."

"Okay. Okay." He got up, walking back and forth as he talked. "You lived in the house when you and John Ashby were dating, when you became engaged."

"Yes, of course. It's my home."

"And you lived here, primarily, after you were married, exclusively after your parents died."

She could see him working something out in his head. No, she corrected. It's already worked out, he was just going through the steps of it for her benefit.

"We stayed here often—my mother wasn't well, and my father couldn't cope with her half the time. When he died, we lived here, in an informal sort of way. When she died, we moved permanently into the house."

"And during all that time, Amelia never objected to him? To John."

"No. I stopped seeing her when I turned, oh, eleven, I'd say, and didn't see her again until after I was married. We hadn't been married long, but were already trying to have children. I thought I might be pregnant, and I couldn't sleep. I went outside, sat in the garden, and I saw her. I saw her and I knew I was carrying a child. I saw her at the onset of every pregnancy. Saw or heard her, of course, when the boys were little."

"Did your husband ever see her?"

"No." She frowned. "No, he didn't. Heard her, but never saw her. I saw her the night he died."

"You never told me that."

"I haven't told you each and every time I . . ." She trailed off, shook her head. "No, I'm sorry, I didn't tell you. I've never discussed it with anyone. It's very personal, and it's painful still."

"I don't know what it's like to love and lose someone the way you loved and lost your John. I know it must seem like prying, and it is. But it's all of a piece, Roz. I have to know, to do the job, I have to know this sort of thing."

"I didn't think you would, when I hired you. That you'd have to know personal things. Wait." She lifted a hand before he could speak. "I understand better now. How you work, I think, how you try to see things. People. The board in the library, the pictures on it so you *can* see who they were. All the little details you accumulate. It's more than I bargained for. I think I mean that in a good way."

"I need to be immersed."

"Like you were with a brilliant and twisted poet," she said with a nod. "I also believe you have to know, and that I'm able to tell you these things, because of what we're becoming to each other. Conversely, that may be why it's hard for me to tell you. It's not easy for me to feel close to someone, to a man. To trust, and to want."

"Do you want it easy?"

She shook her head. "How do you know me so well already? No, I don't want it easy. I suspect easy. I'm having a time with you inside myself, Mitchell. That's a compliment."

"Same goes."

She studied him, standing there, vital and alive, with the arbor and its sleeping roses behind him. With warmth and sun, the roses would wake. But John, her John, was gone.

"John was coming home from his office in Memphis. Coming home late from a meeting. The roads were slick. It had been raining and the roads were slick, and there was fog."

Her heart gave a little hitch as it did, always, when she remembered.

"There was an accident. Someone driving too fast, crossed the center line. I was up, waiting up, and dealing with the boys. Harper had a nightmare, and both Mason d Austin had colds. I'd just settled them down, and was g to bed, irritated a little that John wasn't home yet. here she was, standing there in my room."

She gave a half laugh, brushed a hand over her face. "Gave me a hell of a jolt, thinking oh, hell, am I pregnant, because believe me, I wasn't in the mood for it right at the moment after dealing with three restless, unhappy children. But something in her eyes didn't look right. Too bright, and I want to say too mean. It scared me a little. Then the police came, and well, I wasn't thinking about her anymore."

Her voice had remained steady throughout. But her eyes, her long, lovely eyes, mirrored the grief.

"It's a hard, hard thing. I can't even imagine it."

"Your life stops right there. Just stops. And when it starts up again, it's different. It's never what it was before that moment. Never."

He didn't touch her, didn't comfort, didn't support. What was in her heart, for this moment, in this winter garden belonged to someone else.

"You had no one. No mother, no father, no sister, no brother."

"I had my sons. I had this house. I had myself." She looked away, and he could see her draw herself back, close that door to the past. "I understand where you're going with this, and I don't understand it. She never bothered to object before, not to John, or anyone I was with after, not to Bryce. She did, occasionally express some disapproval—I've told you that before. But nothing on the scale she has recently. Why would that be?"

"I've been trying to work that out. I have a couple of theories. Let's go inside first. The light's going and you're going to be chilled straight through. Not much meat on you. That wasn't a complaint," he added when she narrowed her eyes.

Deliberately she bumped up the southern in her voice. "I come from a line of women with delicate builds."

"Nothing delicate about you," he corrected and took her hand as they walked toward the house. "What you are is a long wild rose—a black rose with plenty of thorns."

"Black roses don't grow wild. They have to be cultivated. And no one's ever managed a true black."

"A black rose," he repeated and brought their joined hands to his lips. "Rare and exquisite."

"You keep talking like that, I'll have to invite you up to my private quarters."

"I thought you'd never ask."

thirteen

"I THOUGHT I SHOULD TELL YOU," ROZ BEGAN AS THEY walked toward the house, "that my . . . household is very interested in my more personal relationship with you."

"That's all right, so am I. Interested in my personal relationship with you."

She glanced down at their joined hands and thought what a lovely design it was that fingers could link so smoothly together. "Your hand's bigger than mine, considerably. Your palm's wider, your fingers longer. And see how your fingers are blunt at the tip where mine taper some?"

She lifted her arm so their hands were eye level. "But it makes such a nice fit."

With a soft laugh, he said her name. Said it tenderly. Rosalind. Then paused briefly to angle his head down and touch his lips to hers. "So does that."

"I was thinking the same. But I'd as soon keep those thoughts, and that personal interest, between you and me."

"Hard to do, since we have other people in our lives. My

son wanted to know where I came up with the brunette babe I was with at the Ole Miss game."

"And you told him?"

"That I'd finally managed to get Rosalind Harper to give me a second look."

"I gave you plenty of looks," she said, and sent him another as they started up the steps to her terrace. "But I've gotten into the habit of being selfish with my private life, and I don't see any reason we can't enjoy each other without filing regular bulletins on our sex life."

She reached for the terrace door. It blew open, barely missing striking her face. A blast of frigid wind gushed out of her room, knocking her back a full step before Mitch managed to grab her, then block her body with his.

"Good luck!" he shouted over the scream of air.

"I will not tolerate this." Furious, she shoved him aside and bulled her way through the door. "I will not tolerate this sort of thing in my house!"

Photographs flew off tables like missiles while lamps flashed on and off. A chair shot across the room, slamming into a chest of drawers with a force that had the vase of hothouse orchids spinning. When she saw the vanity mirror her sons had given her start to slide, she leaped forward to grab it.

"Stop this idiotic *bullshit* right now. I'm not going to put up with it."

There was pounding, monstrous fists of fury, on the walls, in the walls, and the floor trembled under her feet. A large Baccarat perfume bottle detonated, a crystal bomb that spewed jagged shards like shrapnel.

In the midst of the whirlwind, Roz stood, clutching the vanity mirror, and her shout over the explosions of shattering glass, the ferocious banging, was Arctic ice.

"I'll stop every attempt to find out who you are, to right whatever wrong was done to you. I'll do whatever it takes to remove you from this house. You won't be welcome here.

"This is *my* house," she called out as fire erupted in the hearth and the candlestick on the mantel spiraled up into the air. "And I will, by God, clear you out of it. I swear on my life, I will remove you."

The air died at once, and what had been spinning in it fell with thuds or crashes to the floor.

The door burst open instantly. David, Logan, and Stella pushed through it an instant before Harper barreled through the terrace doors.

"Mama." Harper lifted her right off her feet, his arms banded around her. "Are you all right?"

"I'm fine. I'm fine."

"We couldn't get in." Stella touched Roz's back with a trembling hand. "Couldn't get the doors open."

"It's all right now. Where are the children?"

"Hayley. Hayley's got them downstairs. When we heard—God, Roz, it sounded like a war."

"Go tell her everything's all right." She pressed her cheek to Harper's before she pulled back. "Go on now."

"What happened here?" David demanded. "Roz, what the hell happened?"

"We started to come in, and she objected . . . strongly."

"Your mother slapped her back for it," Mitch told Harper. "Let her know who runs this house."

"You're bleeding," Harper said dully.

"Oh, my God." Roz shoved the vanity mirror into Harper's hands and moved quickly to Mitch to touch the cut on his cheek.

"Some flying glass. Nothing major."

"Got some nicks on your hands, too." She lowered her own before they could shake. "Well, let's clean them up."

"I'll pick up in here," Stella offered.

"No, leave it be. Go down, make sure Hayley and the kids are okay. Logan, you ought to take them to your place."

"I'm not leaving you." Stella stood firm, shook her head. "That's not negotiable."

"I'll stay here." Logan draped an arm around Stella's shoulders. "If that's all right with you."

"That's fine." Letting out a breath, she took the mirror back from Harper. "She'd've gotten more than a tongue-lashing if she'd broken this." She set it back in place, then turned to give Harper's hand a squeeze. "It's all right, baby. I promise."

"She does anything to hurt you, I'm finding a way to get her out."

"Like mother, like son." She smiled at him. "I told her the same, and since she stopped when I did, she must know I mean what I say. Go down now. Hayley can't leave the children, and she must be frantic. Mitch, come on into the bathroom. I'll clean those cuts."

"I don't want her alone up here tonight," Harper said when his mother left the room.

"She won't be," Mitch assured him.

When he went into the bath, Roz was already damping a cloth with peroxide. "They're just scratches."

"Doesn't mean they shouldn't be seen to, and since I've never doctored cuts caused by some ghost's tantrum, I'm doing it my usual way. Sit down."

"Yes'm." He sat, studying her face. "Not a scratch on you."

"Hmm?" Distracted, she glanced at her own hands, then looked at her face in the mirror over the sink. "I guess you're right."

"I don't think she wanted to hurt you. Not that she won't, directly or inadvertently, being as she's more than a little crazy. But this was a warning. It's interesting."

"I admire a man who can get cut up by an angry bitch of a ghost and find it interesting."

"I admire a woman who goes toe-to-toe with an angry bitch of a ghost and wins."

"My house." Her voice gentled as she tipped up his chin. "Here now, this won't hurt."

"That's what they all say."

But she cleaned the cuts with a deft and easy hand while he continued to watch her face.

"Looking for something?" she asked him.

"I'm wondering if I found it."

"This one here barely missed your eye." Shaken more than she cared to admit, she bent down to brush her lips over the cut. "There." She stepped back. "You'll live."

"Thanks." He took both her hands, those sharp green eyes on hers. "I have some theories."

"And I'm anxious to hear them. But I want to clean up that mess in there first, then I want a glass of wine. A very big glass of wine."

"I'll give you a hand."

"No, I'd rather do it myself. In fact, I think I need to."

"You make it hard, always asking me to take a step back."

"I guess I do." She brushed a hand through his hair. "Maybe it'll help if I tell you it comforts me to know you're confident enough in yourself to take that step back when I need you to."

"Maybe that's something else that makes this a good fit."

"I think so. I'd appreciate it if you'd go down with the others, give me a half hour to put things back to rights. It'll settle me down a little."

"Okay." He got to his feet. "I'm staying the night. I'll take a page from Stella's book and tell you that part's not negotiable. But you can use the half hour to decide if I'm staying in there with you or in a guest room."

He left her frowning after him.

* * *

HE FOUND EVERYONE IN THE KITCHEN. LIKE FAMILY, he thought, gathered together in the hub of the house with something simmering on the stove, a baby crawling on the floor, and two young boys pulling on jackets while their little dog jumped with excitement.

Every eye shifted to him, and after a beat of silence, Stella began speaking brightly to her sons. "Go ahead and let him run, but stay out of the flower beds. We're going to eat soon."

There was a lot of scrambling, barking, a scream of laughter from Lily, then dog and boys were gone with a slam of the back door.

Stella's hand slipped into Logan's. "How is she?"

"Steady, as usual. She wanted half an hour." Mitch looked at Harper. "I'm staying tonight."

"Good. I think that's good," Hayley said. "The more the better. It gets so you're used to having a ghost in the house, but it's different when she starts throwing things at you."

"You, specifically, from the look of it," Logan put in.

"Noticed that?" Mitch rubbed absently at his cut cheek. "Interesting, isn't it? There was a lot of rage up in that room, but nothing—nothing tangible—was directed at Rosalind. I'd say there was deliberate care not to do her physical harm."

"If there hadn't been, she'd be out." Harper scooped up Lily when she tried to climb up his leg. "And I'm not talking about my mother."

"No." Mitch nodded. "And Roz expressed just about the same sentiment."

"And she's alone up there," David chimed in, then glanced up from his work at the stove. "Because she means it. Everyone in this house, dead or alive, knows she means it."

"And we're all down here, leaving her be because she runs this show." Logan leaned back against the counter.

"That may be, but after this, she'll have to get used to giving up the wheel from time to time. Is that coffee fresh?" Mitch asked with a nod toward the pot.

UPSTAIRS, ROZ PICKED UP THE PIECES OF THE PERSONAL treasures she'd kept in her bedroom. Little mementos, little memories, shattered now.

Willful destruction, she thought, that was the worst of it. The waste of the precious through selfish temper.

"Like some spoiled child," she mumbled as she worked to put order back to her space. "I didn't tolerate that behavior from my own children, and I won't tolerate it from you. Whoever the hell you are."

She straightened furniture, then moved to the bed to remake it. "You best just keep that in mind, Amelia. You best just remember who's mistress of Harper House."

She felt better, amazingly better, taking action, putting her room to rights, saying her piece, even if it was to an empty room.

Steadier, she stepped into the bathroom. Her hair, short as it was, stood up in spikes from the wind that had blown through her bedroom. Not, Roz decided, a good look for her. She brushed it into order, then idly freshened her makeup. And thought about Mitch.

Fascinating man. She couldn't remember the last man who'd fascinated her. It was interesting, and telling, that he'd stated he was staying the night—no polite request, just a flat statement. Then left it to her where he would sleep.

Yes, it was a fascinating man who could be both dominating and obliging in the same sentence.

And she wanted him. It felt wonderful to want, to need, to have this good, healthy lust bubbling inside her.

Certainly she was beyond the stage where she had to deny herself a lover, and smart enough now to recognize when that lover was a man she could respect. Maybe trust.

Trust was just a little tougher than respect, and a whole lot tougher than lust.

So they'd start with what they had, she decided, and see where it went.

When she came out, she heard music, Memphis blues played low, from her sitting room. Her frown was back as she stepped over to the doorway.

Dinner for two was set on her gateleg table—slices of David's roast chicken, snowy mashed potatoes, spears of asparagus, golden biscuits.

How the boy managed to put together her favorite comfort foods was beyond her, but that was her David.

And there was Mitch standing in the candlelight, pouring her a glass of wine.

She felt a lurch—heart and belly—like a blow. Sucker punch, she thought dully, that was both rude and shocking. More than lust, when lust was all she wanted. But more was standing there, with cuts on his hands and face, whether she wanted it or not.

Then he looked over, and smiled at her.

Well, damn it! was all she could think.

"We thought you'd like a quiet meal," he said. "A little calm in the storm. And since I wanted to talk to you, I didn't give your front-line soldiers any argument."

"Soldiers. That's an interesting term."

"Apt enough. Harper would pick up the sword in a heartbeat for you—and I imagine your other sons are the same."

"I like to think I can fight my own battles."

"Which is only more reason they'd stand for you. Then there's David." He stepped over, held out the wine. "Your fourth son, I'd say, in everything but blood. He adores you."

"It's mutual."

"Then there's Logan. Though I'm not sure he'd appreciate the imagery, I see him as a knight to your queen."

She took a sip of wine. "I'm not sure I like the imagery, either."

"But there it is."

He picked up his water glass, toasted her. "You're no more just his employer than you are to Stella or Hayley. And those kids? You're an intimate and vital part of their lives now. When I went downstairs, walked into the kitchen, what I saw was a family. You're the core of that family. You *made* that family."

She stared at him, then let out a huff of breath. "Well. I don't know just what to say to that."

"You should be proud. Those are good people in your kitchen. By the way, does Harper know he's in love with Hayley?"

This time when she stared, she lowered herself into a chair. "You're more intuitive and more observant than I gave you credit for, and I gave you credit for quite a bit. No, I don't think he knows—at least not completely. Which may explain why she's completely oblivious to what he feels for her. She knows he loves Lily. I suppose that's all she sees, at the moment."

"How do you feel about it?"

"I want Harper to be happy, and to have what he wants most in life. We should eat before this gets cold."

A polite way, Mitch surmised, of telling him she'd discussed the intimacies of her family enough with him. The woman had lines, he thought, very defined lines. It would be challenging, and interesting, to pick and choose which to cross, and the when and how of it.

"How are you feeling?"

"I'm fine. Really. Just needed to calm myself down a little."

"You look more than fine. How is it, Rosalind, you can look so beautiful?"

"Candlelight flatters a woman. If we had our way, Edison would never have invented that damn lightbulb."

"You don't need candlelight."

She lifted her brows. "If you're thinking you need to seduce me over roast chicken so I won't scoot you off to one of the guest rooms after dinner, you don't need to worry. I want you in my bed."

"Regardless, I'm going to seduce you. But at the moment, I was just stating the facts. Aside from that, this is some terrific roast chicken."

"I like you. Thought I'd say that straight-out. I like the way you are. I don't feel there are a lot of pretenses about you, not a lot of show. That's a nice change for me, in this area."

"I don't lie. Gave it up along with the bottle. That's the one thing I can promise you, Roz. I won't lie to you."

"As promises go, that's the one I'd value most."

"Then keeping with that theme, there's something I'd like to ask you. What happened earlier, that . . . upheaval, we'll call it. That was new."

"Yes, and I'm hoping it was a first and last sort of thing."

"She never objected in any way to your engagement or your marriage to John Ashby."

"No, as I told you before."

"Or to any relationship you had after, to Clerk."

She gave a little shrug. "Some irritation, we could say, off and on. Disapproval, annoyance, but no, not rage."

"Then I have a theory—one you may not like to hear. But in addition to not lying to you, I'm going to speak my mind, as I expect you'll speak yours."

"Should be interesting."

"She needs children in the house—that's what brings

her comfort, or gratification. You and John would bring children into the house, so she had no strong objection. He was a means to an end."

"That's a very cold theory."

"Yes, and it gets colder. Once there were children, there was no more need for him, so his death was, in my opinion, something she saw as right, even just."

Her color drained, leaving her face white and horrified. "If you're suggesting she somehow caused—"

"No." He reached out, laid his hand over hers. "No. Her limitations are this house, the grounds. I'm no expert in the paranormal, but that's what works. That's what makes sense. Whatever she is, or has, is centered here."

"Yes." Relaxing again, she nodded. "I've never experienced, or heard of anyone experiencing anything regarding her beyond the borders of my land. I would have. I'm certain I'd know, or have heard if there'd been anything."

"She's bound to this place, and maybe to this family. But I doubt the grief you and your sons felt when John died touched her. And she can be touched. We saw that with Stella last spring when she communicated with her as a mother. We saw it tonight, when you laid it on the line to her."

"All right." She nodded, reached for her wine. "All right, I'm following you, so far."

"When you began to socialize again, to see men, even to have lovers, she was only mildly annoyed. Disapproving, as you said. Because they didn't matter to you, not deeply. They weren't going to be a part of your life, of this house, not for the long run."

"You're saying she knew that?"

"She's connected to you, Roz. She knows what's inside you, at least enough to understand what you think and feel, things you might not say out loud."

"She gets inside my head," she said softly. "Yes, I've

felt that. I don't like it. But what happens to your theory when you add Bryce? I married him. He lived here. And though she acted up a few times, there was nothing extreme, nothing violent."

"You didn't love him."

"I married him."

"And divorced him. He wasn't a threat to her. It seems she knew that before you did. At least before you consciously knew it. He was . . . superfluous, let's say, to her. Maybe it was because he was weak, but for whatever reason, still, no threat to her. Not from her view."

"And you are."

"Clearly. We could suppose it has to do with my work, but that doesn't jibe. She wants us to find out who she was, what she was. She just wants us to work for it."

"You seem to know her very well, on short acquaintance."

"Short, but intense acquaintance," he pointed out. "And understanding the dead is part of my work. It's actually the part—the personalizing—that makes it the most compelling for me. She's angry that you've allowed me into your life, into your bed."

"Because you're not weak."

"I'm not," he agreed. "And also because I matter to you, or I will. I'm going to make sure of it. Because what we're moving toward, you and I, is important."

"Mitch, we're having an affair, and while I don't take that lightly, I—"

"Rosalind." He laid his hand over hers, kept his eyes on hers. "You know very well I'm falling in love with you. Have been since the minute I opened my apartment door and saw you standing there. Scares the hell out of me, but that doesn't change it."

"I didn't know." She drew back, and her hand pressed on her heart, ran up to her throat and back again. "I didn't, and that makes me as oblivious as Hayley. I thought we had a great deal of attraction for each other, and mutual respect along with . . . what are you grinning at?"

"You're nervous. I've never seen you nervous. How about that?"

"I'm not nervous." She stabbed at the last bite of her chicken. "I'm surprised, that's all."

"Scared's what you are."

"I'm certainly not." With some heat, she shoved back from the table. "I'm certainly not. All right, I am." She pushed to her feet when he laughed. "Yes, that should please you. Men love putting women into a state."

"Oh, bullshit."

There was a ring of steel, even through the humor. Intrigued by both, she turned back. "You're an awfully confident individual."

"You meant that as a compliment the first time you said it. This time you mean *arrogant*, and right back at you, honey."

With that, she laughed. Then pressed her fingers to her eyes. "Oh, God. God, Mitchell, I don't know if I've got it in me for another *important* relationship. They're so much damn work. Love can be, should be, so consuming, so demanding. I just don't know that I've got the stamina, or the heart, or the generosity."

"I have no doubt you've got plenty of all three, but we'll take it as it goes, and see."

He rose. "Can't say I mind making you a little nervous," he said as he walked to her. "Nothing much shakes you, at least not so it shows."

"You have no idea."

"Oh, I think I do." He slipped his arms around her, led her smoothly into a dance, swaying to the throb of the music. "One of the sexiest things about you is your unshakable capability."

"I'm capable." She tipped her head up. "I want my

accountant to be capable, but I sure as hell don't want to sleep with him."

"I find it devastatingly sexy."

"Is this the seduction part of the evening?"

"Just getting started. Do you mind?"

He thought her capable, she realized, and found that appealing. And he made her feel soft, and cherished. "You asked me that the first time you kissed me. I didn't mind then, either."

"I love that you're beautiful. Shallow of me, but there you go. A man's entitled to some flaws."

Amused, she trailed a finger up the back of his neck. "Perfection's boring—but, God, don't tell Stella I said so."

"Then I'll never bore you."

He touched his lips to hers lightly, once, twice, then slowly, slowly, sank into the kiss.

It spilled through her, the warmth, and the life, the thrill and the power. She moved with him, that sensuous dance, that sensuous kiss, and let herself glide. Like a woman glides over a path strewn with fragrant petals. Through moonbeams. And into love.

She heard a door shut quietly, and opened her eyes to see that he'd circled her into the bedroom.

"You're a clever dancer, Dr. Carnegie." Then laughed when he spun her out, and back. "Very clever."

He kissed her again, spinning until her back was pressed to the door, until the kiss took on a bite. Then he ran his hands down her arms, stepped back.

"Light the candles," he said. "I'll light the fire."

Shaken, right down to the soles of her feet, she leaned against the door. Her heart felt swollen and tender, and its beat was a throbbing ache in her breast. When she moved, she moved carefully, like a woman sliding through the fog of a dream. And she saw her own fingers tremble as she set flame to candlewick.

"I want you." Her voice was steady enough, and she was grateful. "And the want is stronger and different than any I've felt before. Maybe it's because I—"

"Don't question it. Not tonight anyway."

"All right." She turned, as he did, so they faced each other across the room. "We'll leave it that I want you, very much. That it presses on me, not entirely comfortably."

In the gilded light, he crossed to her, took both her hands. "Let me show you how I feel."

He lifted her hands, turning them palms up to press his lips to one, then the other. Then he cupped her face, stroking his thumbs over her cheeks as his fingers slid back into her hair.

"Let me take you," he said as his mouth cruised over hers. "Tonight, just let me take you."

He asked for surrender. And surrender was a great deal to ask. But she gave him her mouth, then her body as his hands stroked over her. And they were dancing again, circling and swaying as the dreamy pleasure he offered slipped into her like rich, red wine.

He slid her shirt aside, and was murmuring in her ear, about her skin, her scent. And the dance was like floating.

She was giving him what he'd asked. Surrender. Though it was slow, inch by inch, he could feel it, that gorgeous yielding of self. He undressed her as they danced, taking almost painful care, almost painful pleasure in removing each barrier that blocked his hands from her flesh.

It was incredibly erotic, dancing in the firelight, the candlelight, her naked body pressed to his while he was still fully clothed. To see that long, lean line of her in the mirror, the way the light played over her skin, to feel that skin shiver under his hands. To feel her pulses jump under his mouth.

When he slipped his hand between her thighs, he felt her body jerk, heard her breath catch.

She was hot, already hot and wet. And her nails dug into his shoulders as he began to play her, lazily. Little tortuous strokes that had her breath going short and harsh, and his own blood pumping.

Her body plunged, then melted against his when she came. Her head fell back even as he continued to arouse, and her eyes were glazed and stunned.

She was so pliant he could almost pour her onto the bed. They watched each other as he stood, undressed.

Then he skimmed his finger over her leg, lifted it, bent to it, and rubbed his lips along her calf. "So much more I want from you."

Yes, she thought. So much more. And surrendering to it, to him, gave him all he wanted.

His mouth found her, shot her up again, breathlessly, until she had to grip the spread or fly apart.

He exploited and explored, and took, took while the air went thick and sweet as syrup, and the deepest, darkest pleasures quivered inside her.

She could hear herself sobbing for him, even as he slid into her. His languorous pace never altered, only built arousal higher with a near brutal patience, a delicious, drugging friction. She had no choice, no control any longer, could only quiver, could only ache, could only enjoy as he nudged her closer and closer to the edge.

And when she fell that final time, it was like flying.

SHE WAS STILL TREMBLING. IT WAS RIDICULOUS, SHE told herself. It was foolish, but she couldn't seem to stop. She was warm, even overwarm, and only then realized both of them were slick with sweat.

She'd been thoroughly seduced, then thoroughly used. And she couldn't find a thing wrong with either.

"I'm trying to think of something appropriate to say."

His lips moved against her neck. "How about 'wow'?"

She managed to move her heavy arms enough to brush a hand through his hair. "That probably covers it. I came three times."

"Four."

"Four?" Her voice was as hazy as her vision. "I must've lost count."

"I didn't." And there was a wicked satisfaction in his tone, one that she saw reflected in his face as he rolled onto his back.

"Since I'm in such a blissful state, I'm going to admit that's the first time I've ever come four times."

He reached down, found her hand, linked fingers. "Stick with me, kid, and it won't be the last."

She laughed, a full-out bawdy roll of laughter, then shifted to prop herself up on his chest. "Pretty proud of yourself."

"Damn right."

"Me, too." She pillowed her head over his heart, shut her eyes. "I go running around six."

"Is that A.M.?"

"Yes, it is. Harper's got some spare clothes in the next bedroom, if you want to join me."

"'Kay."

She let herself drift, like a cat curled for a nap. "She left us alone."

"I know."

fourteen

Garbed in a suit and tie and armed with a dozen yellow roses and a box of Godiva chocolates, Mitch rode the elevator to Clarise Harper's third-floor apartment in the retirement complex. His letter from her was in his briefcase, and the formal, lady of the South tone had given him a broad clue that this was a woman who would expect a suit—and a floral tribute—just as Roz had instructed.

She wasn't agreeing to a meeting, he thought, but was, very definitely, granting him an audience.

No mention of Rosalind, or any of the occupants of Harper House, had been made in their correspondence.

He rang the bell and prepared to be charming and persuasive.

The woman who answered was young, hardly more than twenty, dressed in a simple and conservative black skirt, white blouse, and low-heeled practical shoes. Her brown hair was worn in what he supposed women still called a bun—a style that did nothing to flatter her young, thin face.

Mitch's first impression was of a quiet, well-behaved

puppy who would fetch the slippers without leaving a single tooth mark on the leather.

"Dr. Carnegie. Please come in, Miss Harper is expecting you."

Her voice suited the rest of her, quiet and well-bred.

"Thank you." He stepped inside, directly into the living room furnished with a hodgepodge of antiques. His collector's eye spotted a George III secretaire chest and a Louis XVI display cabinet among the various styles and eras.

The side chairs were probably Italian, the settee Victorian—and all looked miserably uncomfortable.

There was a great deal of statuary, heavy on the shepherdess and cat and swan themes, and vases decorated within an inch of their lives. All the china and porcelain and crystal sat on stiffly starched doilies or runners.

The walls were painted a candy pink, and the tweed beige wall-to-wall was buried under several floral area rugs.

The air smelled like the inside of a cedar chest that had been bathed in lavender water.

Everything gleamed. He imagined if an errant mote of dust dared invade such grandeur, the quiet puppy would chase it down and banish it instantly.

"Please, sit down. I'll inform Miss Harper that you're here."

"Thank you, Miss . . ."

"Paulson. Jane Paulson."

"Paulson?" He flipped through the family tree in his mental files. "A relative, then, on Miss Harper's father's side."

The faintest hint of color bloomed in her cheeks. "Yes. I'm Miss Harper's great-niece. Excuse me."

Poor baby, he thought when she slipped away. He maneuvered through the furniture and condemned himself to one of the side chairs.

Moments later he heard the click and step, and the woman herself appeared.

Though she was rail thin, he wouldn't have said frail, despite her age. More, he thought at first glance, a form that was tough and whittled down to the basics. She wore a dress of rich purple, and leaned on an ebony cane with an ivory handle.

Her hair was a pristine white helmet, and her face—as thin as her body—was a map of wrinkles under a dusting of powder and rouge. Her mouth, thin as a blade, was poppy red.

There were pearls at her ears and her throat, and her fingers were studded with rings, glinting as fiercely as brass knuckles.

The puppy trailed in her wake.

Knowing his role, Mitch got to his feet, even managed a slight bow. "Miss Harper, it's an honor to meet you."

He took the hand she extended, brought it to within an inch of his lips. "I'm very grateful you were able to find the time to see me." He offered the roses, the chocolates. "Small tokens of my appreciation."

She gave a nod, which might have been approval. "Thank you. Jane, put these lovely roses in the Minton. Please be seated, Dr. Carnegie. I was very intrigued by your letter," she continued as she took her seat on the settee and propped her cane on the arm. "You're not from the Memphis area originally."

"No, ma'am. Charlotte, where my parents and my sister still live. My son attends the university here, and I relocated in order to be close to him."

"Divorced from his mama, aren't you?"

She'd done her research, Mitch thought. Well, that was fine. So had he. "Yes, I am."

"I don't approve of divorce. Marriage isn't a flight of fancy."

"It certainly isn't. I confess my marital difficulties were primarily on my shoulders." He kept his eyes level with her piercing ones. "I'm an alcoholic, and though in recovery now for many years, I caused my former wife a great deal of distress and unhappiness during our marriage. I'm pleased to say she's remarried to a good man, and we have a cordial relationship."

Clarise pursed her bright red lips, nodded. "I respect a man who takes responsibility for his failings. If a man can't hold his drink, he shouldn't drink. That's all there is to it."

Old bat. "I'm proof of that."

She continued to sit, and despite nearly eight full decades of wear and tear, her back was straight as a spear. "You teach?"

"I have done. At the moment, I'm fully occupied with my research and writing of family histories and biographies. Our ancestry is our foundation."

"Certainly." Her gaze shifted when Jane came in with the flowers. "No, not there," she snapped. "There, and be careful. See to the refreshments now. Our guest can't be expected to sit here without being offered basic hospitality."

She turned her attention back to Mitch. "You're interested in the Harper family."

"Very much."

"Then you're aware that the Harpers are not only my foundation, but a vital part of the foundation of Shelby County, and indeed the state of Tennessee."

"I am, very keenly aware, and hope to do justice to their contributions. Which is why I've come to you, for your help, for your memories. And in the hope that you'll come to trust me with any letters or books, any written documentation that will help me to write a thorough and detailed account of the Harper family history."

He glanced up as Jane came out carrying a teapot and cups on a large tray. "Let me help you with that."

As he crossed to her, he saw the woman's eyes shoot over to her aunt. Obviously flustered, she allowed him to take the tray. "Thank you."

"Pour the tea, girl."

"Miss Paulson would be your great-niece on your father's side," Mitch began easily, and took his seat again. "It must be comforting to have some of your family so close."

Clarise angled her head, regally. "Duty to family is paramount. I would assume, then, you've done considerable research to date."

"I have. If you'll permit me." He opened his briefcase and took out the folder he'd prepared for her. "I thought you might enjoy having this. The genealogy—a family tree—I've done."

She accepted the folder, wagged her fingers in the air. On command, Jane produced a pair of reading glasses on a gold chain.

While she looked over the papers, Mitch did his best to swallow down the weak herbal tea.

"How much do you charge?"

"This is a gift, Miss Harper, as you've not requested my services. It's I who request your help in a project I'm very eager to explore."

"We'll be clear, Dr. Carnegie, that I won't tolerate being asked for funds down the road."

"Absolutely clear."

"I see you've gone back to the eighteenth century, when the first of my family immigrated from Ireland. Do you intend to go back further?"

"I do, though my plan is to focus more on the family here, in Tennessee, what they built after they came to America. The industry, the culture, their leading roles in both, as well as society. And most important, for my purposes, the family itself. The marriages, births, deaths."

Through the lenses of her reading glasses, her eyes were hawklike. Predatory. "Why are household staff and servants included here?"

He'd debated that one, but had gone with his instincts.

"Simply because they were part of the household, part of the texture. In fact, I'm in contact with a descendant of one of the housekeepers of Harper House—during your mother, Victoria Harper's, childhood. The day-to-day life, as well as the entertaining the Harpers have been known for are essential elements of my book."

"And the dirty linen?" She gave a regal sniff. "The sort servants are privy to?"

"I assure you, it's not my intention to write a roman à clef, but a detailed, factual, and thorough family history. A family such as yours, Miss Harper," he said, gesturing toward the file, "certainly has had its triumphs and tragedies, its virtues and its scandals. I can't and won't exclude any that my research uncovers. But I believe your family's history, and its legacy, certainly stands above any of its very human failings."

"And failings and scandal add spice—spice sells."

"I won't argue with that. But certainly, with your input, the book would have a stronger weight on the plus side, we could say."

"We could." She set the folder aside, sipped her tea. "By now you've certainly been in contact with Rosalind Harper."

"Yes."

"And . . . she's cooperating?"

"Ms. Harper has been very helpful. I've spent some time in Harper House. It's simply stunning. A tribute to what your family built since coming to Shelby County, and a tribute to charm and grace as well as continuity."

"It was my great-great-grandfather who built Harper House, and his son who preserved it during the War of Northern Aggression. My grandfather who expanded and modernized the house, while preserving its history and its traditions."

He waited a moment for her to continue, to speak of her

uncle's contribution to the estate. But when she stopped there, he only nodded. "Harper House is a testament to your family, and a treasure of Shelby County."

"It is the oldest home of its kind consistently lived in by one family in this country. The fact is, there is nothing to compare with it, to my mind, in Tennessee, or anywhere else. It is only a pity my cousin was unable to produce a son in order to carry the family name."

"Ms. Harper uses the family name."

"And runs a flower shop on the property." She dismissed this with another sniff and a flick of her ring-spangled fingers. "One hopes that her eldest son, when he inherits, will have more sense and dignity, though I see no indication of it."

"Your family has always been involved in commerce, in industry, in business."

"Not at home. I may decide to give you my cooperation, Dr. Carnegie, as my cousin Rosalind is hardly the best source for our family history. You may deduce we are not on terms."

"I'm sorry to hear that."

"It could hardly be otherwise. I'm told that even now she has outsiders, and one of them a Yankee, living in Harper House."

Mitch waited a beat, saw that he was expected to verify. "I believe there are houseguests, and one is also a distant relation, through Ms. Harper's first husband."

"With a baby out of wedlock." Those brightly painted lips folded thin. "Disgraceful."

"A . . . delicate situation, but one that happens, very often in any family history. As it happens, one of the legends I've heard regarding the house, the family, deals with a ghost, that of a young woman who may have found herself in this same delicate situation."

"Balderdash."

He nearly blinked. He didn't believe he'd ever heard anyone use that term in actual conversation.

"Ghosts. I would think a man with your education would be more sensible."

"Like scandal, Miss Harper, ghosts add spice. And the legend of the Harper Bride is common in the area. Certainly it has to be mentioned in any detailed family history. It would be more surprising if a house as old and rich in history as Harper House didn't have some whisper of hauntings. You must have grown up hearing the story."

"I know the story, and even as a child had more sense than to believe such nonsense. Some find such things romantic; I do not. If you're skilled or experienced at your work, you'll certainly find that there was no Harper bride who died in that house as a young woman—which this ghost is reputed to be. Not since the story began buzzing about."

"Which would have been?"

"In my grandfather's time, from all accounts. Your own papers here," she said as she tapped the folder, "debunk any such foolishness. My grandmother lived to a ripe age, as did my mother. My aunts were not young women when they passed. My great-grandmother, and all of her children who survived their first five years, lived well past their forties."

"I've heard theories that this ghost is a more distant relation, even a guest or a servant."

"Each nonsensical."

He fixed a pleasant smile on his face and nodded as if in agreement. "Still, it adds to the lore. So none of your family, to your knowledge, actually saw this legendary bride?"

"Certainly not."

"Pity, it would have made an interesting chapter in the history. I'd hoped to find someone who'd have a story to tell, or had written of it in a journal or diary. But as to journals or diaries, in a more earthbound sense. I'm hoping to add some to my research, to use them to personalize this family history. Do you have any that your mother or father, or other ancestors kept? Your grandmother's perhaps, your own mother's, aunts', cousins'?"

"No."

Out of the corner of his eye he saw Jane open her mouth as if to speak, then quickly close it again.

"I hope you'll allow me to interview you more in-depth, about specifics, and whatever anecdotes you'd care to share. And that you'd be willing to share any photographs, perhaps copy them at my expense for inclusion in the book."

"I'll consider it, very seriously, and contact you when I've made my decision."

"Thank you. I very much appreciate the time you've given me." He got to his feet, offered his hand. "Your family is of great interest to me, and it's been a pleasure to speak with you."

"Goodbye, Dr. Carnegie. Jane, show the man out."

At the door he offered his hand to Jane, smiled straight into her eyes. "It was nice to meet you, Miss Paulson."

He walked to the elevator, then rocked back and forth on his heels as he waited for the doors to open.

The old woman had something—something she didn't want to share. And the quiet little puppy knew it.

ROZ STROLLED HOME THROUGH HER WOODS IN THE best of all possible moods. It was nearly time for the major spring opening. Her season would begin with a bang, the work would be long, hard, and physical—and she'd love every minute.

The new potting soil was already beginning to move, and once the season got into swing, the twenty-five–pound bags were going to march out the door.

She just felt it.

The fact was, she admitted, she felt everything. The hum in the air that said spring, the streams of sunlight that spilled through the branches, the loose and limber swing of her own muscles.

Hardly a wonder they were loose and limber after last night, she thought. Four orgasms, for God's sake. And Mitch was a man of his word. Stick with me, he'd said, and it won't be the last time.

He'd proven just that in the middle of the night.

She'd had sex twice in one night, and that was certainly worth a red letter on her calendar.

With John . . . they'd been young and hadn't been able to get enough of each other. Even after the children had come, the sexual aspect of their marriage had been vital.

Then it had been a long, long time before she'd allowed another man to touch her. And to be honest, none ever had. Not really, not beyond the physical.

Bryce hadn't. But she'd thought, for a while at least, that it was her own fault, or her own nature. She hadn't loved him, not deep down. But she'd liked him, she'd enjoyed him, and had certainly been attracted to him.

Stupidly, but that wasn't the point now.

The sex had been adequate at best, and adequate had been enough for her. She'd wanted—needed—companionship, partnership.

Since the divorce, for a considerable time prior to it, if truth be told, she'd been celibate. Her own choice, and the right one for her.

Until Mitch.

Now he'd turned her inside out, and God, she was grateful. And relieved, if it came to that, to know her sex drive was in fine working condition.

He said he was falling in love with her, and that put a little knot in her belly. Love still meant specific things to her.

Marriage and family. And those were too enormous to take lightly.

She'd never take marriage lightly again, so she could hardly take love, what she considered its precursor, lightly.

But she could, and she would, enjoy him, and the way she felt on this spectacular evening.

She crossed her own lawn and saw that her earliest daffodils were blooming buttery yellow. Maybe she'd go in, get her shears, and cut some for her bedroom.

As she approached the house, she saw Stella and Hayley on the veranda, and raised her hand in a wave.

"I smell spring," she said. "We're going to want to start moving . . ." She trailed off as she saw their faces. "Well, don't you two look solemn. Trouble?"

"Not exactly. Mrs. Haggerty was in today," Stella said.

"Is something wrong with her?"

"Not with her. She wondered how you were doing, though, if you were all right."

"Why wouldn't I be?"

"She was concerned the scene at the garden club meeting had upset you."

"Oh." Roz shrugged. "She should know better."

"Why didn't you tell us?" Stella demanded.

"Excuse me?"

"She said that bitch, that walking Barbie, insulted you right there in front of everybody," Hayley cut in. "That she was spreading lies and rumors and accused you of harassing that asshole she's hooked herself up with."

"You seem to have most of the facts. She should have added, if she didn't, that Mandy came off looking foolish and shrill, and was certainly more embarrassed by the whole thing than I was."

"You didn't tell us," Stella repeated.

"Why would I have?" The tone was aloof.

"Because whether or not she was more embarrassed, it

had to upset you. And while you're the boss, and blah, blah, blah—"

"Blah, blah, blah?"

"And a little bit scary," Stella added.

"A little?"

"The fear factor has diminished considerably over the past year."

"I'm not afraid of you," Hayley said, then hunched her shoulders when Roz turned cool eyes to hers. "Very much."

"Despite us being your employees, we're friends. Or we thought we were."

"Oh, for God's sake. Girls are so much more complicated than boys." On a long sigh, Roz plopped down on the porch swing. "Of course we're friends."

"Well, if we're friends, especially *girl* friends," Hayley continued, and sat beside Roz on the swing, "you're supposed to tell us when some skinny-assed bitch rags on you. How else are we going to know we hate her guts? How else are we going to know to think up nasty things to say about her? Like, here's one. Did you know that seventy-three percent of women whose name ends with the *i* sound are bimbos?"

Roz sat a moment. "Is that one of your factoids or did you just make it up?"

"Okay, I made that one up, but I bet it's true if they dot the *i* with a little heart—after the age of twelve. And I bet, I just bet she does. So. Bimbo."

"She's just a foolish girl who believes a very smooth liar."

"I stand by bimbo."

"She had no right to say those things, to your face or behind your back." Stella sat on Roz's other side.

"No, she didn't, and she came out the worse for it. And all right, it did upset me at the time. I don't like my personal business aired in public forums."

"We're not a forum," Hayley stated firmly. "Or the public."

Saying nothing for a moment, Roz laid a hand on each of their thighs and gave them a little rub.

"As I said, females are more complicated than men, and even being female, I probably understand men better. I certainly didn't mean to hurt your feelings by keeping something like this to myself."

"We just want you to know we're here for you, for the good stuff, and the bad stuff."

Hayley's words touched her. "Then you should know I've long since put Mandy out of my mind, as I do with unimportant people. And I'm in much too good a mood to think about her now. When a woman, especially a woman within spitting distance of fifty, has herself a lover who performs excellently twice in one night, so well in fact that she needs the fingers on both hands to count the number of orgasms experienced, the last thing on her mind is some silly girl with no manners."

She gave each of their thighs another pat, then rose. "There, that's some good stuff," she said and strolled into the house.

"Wow," Hayley said after she managed to close the mouth that had fallen open. "I mean, mega-wow. How many times do you think he got her off? At least six, right?"

"You know what I thought the first time I saw Roz?"

"Uh-uh."

"That I wanted to be her when I grew up. And boy, do I."

ROZ WALKED STRAIGHT BACK TO THE KITCHEN, AND straight to the coffeepot. Once she had a cup, she sidled over and gave David's cheek a kiss as he stood at the stove making his famed hot chocolate.

"Boys outside?"

"Running off some energy with Parker, and working up anticipation for hot chocolate. My other guest, as you see, has conked on me."

Roz grinned toward the highchair, where Lily snoozed in the tipped-back seat. "Isn't she a doll baby, and aren't you a sweetheart for minding three children so those girls could waylay me."

"We do what we can. And you should've mentioned what that silly bitch pulled."

"You ever known me not to be able to handle a silly bitch?"

"I've never known you not to be able to handle anything, but you should've mentioned it. How else am I going to know what shape to make the voodoo doll?"

"Don't worry, Bryce'll stick plenty of pins in her before he's done."

"Don't expect me to feel sorry for her."

"It's her cross to bear."

"Dinner in about an hour," he called as she started out of the room. "And you've got some phone messages. They were on your line so I didn't screen them."

"I'll get them upstairs."

She took her coffee with her, and toed off her shoes after she crossed the threshold to her room. Then she pushed the button on the answering machine.

"Roz, I didn't want to bother you at work."

"What a nice voice you have, Dr. Carnegie," she mused aloud, and sat on the side of the bed to enjoy it.

"It's my pizza night with Josh. I forgot to mention it. I like to think you'll miss me, and that I can make up for it by taking you out tomorrow. Whatever, wherever you'd like, just let me know. In addition, I did some work today, and I'd like to talk to you about that tomorrow. I should be over there by noon. If I don't see you, you can reach me on my cell. I'll be thinking of you."

"That's nice to know. That's very nice to know."

She was still daydreaming a little when the next message began.

"Ms. Harper, this is William Rolls from the Riverbend Country Club. I received your letter this morning, and am very sorry to hear that you're dissatisfied with our services and have resigned as a member. I must admit to being surprised, even stunned, by your list of complaints, and only wish you had been able to speak with me about them personally. We have valued your association with Riverbend for many years, and regret your decision to end it. If you'd care to discuss this matter, please feel free to contact me at any time at any of the following numbers. Again, I sincerely regret the circumstances."

She sat very still until the entire message played through. Then she shut her eyes.

"Fuck you, Bryce."

WITHIN AN HOUR SHE'D NOT ONLY SPOKEN WITH William Rolls, had assured him she wasn't dissatisfied, had no complaints and had not written any letter, but she had a faxed copy of the letter in question in her hand.

And a head of steam that threatened to blow like a geyser.

She was dragging her shoes back on when Hayley popped in, the baby on her hips. "David says dinner's . . . whoa, what's wrong?"

"What's wrong? You want to know what's wrong? I'll tell you what's wrong." She snatched the letter up from where she'd tossed it on the bed. "Here's what's wrong. That miserable, snake-spined son of a bitch has tried my patience once too often."

" 'The admittance of individuals of lower-class backgrounds and mixed ethnicity,' " Hayley read, holding the paper out of Lily's reach. "'Staff members of dubious character. Demeaning intimacy between staff and members, substandard service.'" Her eyes were huge as she shifted them back up to Roz's face. "You didn't write this."

"Of course I didn't. And I'm going to take that letter, find Bryce Clark, and stuff it down his lying throat."

"No." Hayley jumped to block the door, her move so fast it had Lily laughing and bouncing in anticipation of another ride.

"No? What do you mean *no*? I'm done taking this. Finished. And he's going to know it when I'm done with him."

"You can't. You're too mad to go anywhere." The fact was, she'd never seen Roz this angry, and Stella's term of a little bit scary was currently bumped up too many levels to count. "And I don't know much about this sort of thing, but I'd bet a month's pay this is just what he's hoping for. You need to sit down."

"I need to kick his balls blue."

"Well, yeah, that'd be great. Except he's probably expecting it, and he's probably got something worked out so you'll get arrested or something for assault. He's playing you, Roz."

"You think I don't know that?" She threw her arms out as she spun around, looking for something to kick, to hurl, to punch. "You think I don't *know* what that bastard's doing? I'm not going to *stand* here and take it anymore."

The shout, the fury in it had Lily's face crumpling, her little mouth trembling an instant before the wail.

"God, now I'm scaring babies. I'm sorry. I'm sorry. Here, let me have her."

Lily continued to sob as Roz took her out of Hayley's arms and cuddled her in her own. "There, sweetheart, I'm not mad at you, I'm not mad at your mama. I'm so sorry, baby girl." She crooned, and nuzzled while Lily clung to her. "I'm mad at this no-account, slimy-assed, cocksucking son of a bitch who's doing whatever he can to complicate my life."

"You said *cocksucking*," Hayley whispered. Awed.

"Sorry. She doesn't know what I'm saying, so it won't hurt her." Lily's tears were down to sniffles as she began to pull at the ends of Roz's hair. "I shouldn't have yelled like that in front of her. It's the tone that scares her, not the words."

"But you said *cocksucking*."

This time Roz laughed. "I'm so mad," she said, walking the baby, and calming them both. "Just so mad. And you're right, and that's just annoying. I can't go tearing out of here and going after him. It's just what he's looking for. It's all right, it'll be all right. He can't do anything that can't be fixed."

"I'm sorry Roz. I wish I could go kick his balls blue for you."

"Thanks, honey, that's a sweet thing to say. We'll just go down to dinner." She held Lily up, blew on her belly to make her laugh. "We'll just go down to dinner and forget all about the asshole, won't we, baby girl?"

"You're sure?"

"Absolutely."

"Okay. You know, I don't know as snakes have spines."

Roz blinked at her. "What?"

"You said *snake-spined*—before, when you were raving about Bryce. I'm not sure they have actual spines. Maybe just some sort of skeletal cartilage. Could be wrong, though. I don't much like snakes, so I haven't paid a lot of attention."

"You never fail, Hayley, just never fail to baffle me."

fifteen

Roz put Mitch off for a day, then for two. She wanted her head clear, her temper calm, and it wasn't happening quickly. She needed a meeting with her lawyer, and felt obliged to schedule another with William Rolls at the club.

She hated, absolutely hated, being pulled away from her work, particularly at the very start of high season. She could thank God for Stella, as always for Harper, and for Hayley as well. She could be confident that her business was in the best of hands.

But those hands weren't hers, at least not while she was running around tidying up the mess Bryce had made for her.

With the hateful errands done, she trudged through a soaking rain toward the propagation house. For an hour or two, at least, she could dive into the final prep work for the spring season. And she could take her headache, and her sour mood, into a private spot and let the work do its magic.

When she was done for the day, she told herself, she was going to find Mitch. If he wasn't working in her library, she'd call him. She wanted his company—or hoped she would by that evening.

She wanted conversation, about something other than her problems. And wouldn't it be nice to relax with him, maybe up in her sitting room, by the fire—especially if the rain continued—and bask a little in the way he looked at her?

A woman could get very used to having a man look at her as if she were beautiful and desirable and the only one who mattered.

Get used enough to it, she might start to believe it. She'd like to believe it, Roz realized. What a difference it made, being drawn to a man you felt you could trust.

She opened the door to the propagation house.

And stepped into her own bedroom.

The fire was simmering low, the only light in the room. And it tossed flickers of gold, hints of red into the shadows. She heard them first, the quick breath, the low laughter, the rustle of clothing.

Then she saw them in the firelight, Bryce, her husband, and the woman who was a guest in her home. Embracing. No, more . . . grappling, hurrying to touch, to taste each other. She could feel the excitement from them, the snap of the illicit thrill. And knew, even in those few shocked seconds, this wasn't the first time. Hardly the first time.

She stood, with the sounds of the party dim behind her, and absorbed the betrayal, and the greasy slide of humiliation that was under it.

As she had before, she started to step back, to leave them there, but he turned his head, turned it toward her even as his hands cupped another woman's breasts.

And he smiled, bright and charming and sly. Laughed, low and pleased.

"Stupid bitch, I was never faithful. None of us are."

Even as he spoke, his face changed, light and shadow playing over it as it became Mitch's face.

"Why should we be? Women are meant to be used. Do you really think one of you matters more than another?" That lovely voice dripped derision as he fondled the woman in his arms. "We all lie, because we can."

Those shadows floated and the face became John's. Her husband, her love. The father of her sons. "Do you think I was true to you, you pathetic fool?"

"John." The pain nearly took her to her knees. So young, she thought. So alive. "Oh, God, John."

"Oh, God, John," he mimicked, as his hands made the woman he embraced moan. "Needed sons, didn't I? You were nothing more than a broodmare. If I'd been luckier, I'd have lived and left you. Taken what mattered, taken my sons, and left you."

"That's a lie."

"We all lie."

When he laughed, she had to press her hands over her ears. When he laughed, it was like fists pounding on her body, on her heart, until she did simply sink to her knees.

She heard herself weeping, raw, bitter sobs.

She didn't hear the door open behind her, or the startled exclamation. Arms came around her, hard and tight. And she smelled her son.

"Mama, what's wrong? Are you hurt? Mama."

"No. No." She clung to him, pressing her face into his shoulder and fighting to stop the tears. "I'm all right. Don't worry. I'm just—"

"You're not all right, and don't tell me not to worry. Tell me what it is. Tell me what happened."

"In a minute. Just a minute." She leaned against him, let him rock her there on the ground until his warmth seeped into her own icy bones. "Oh, Harper, when did you get to be so big and strong? My baby."

"You're shaking. You're not sick, you're scared."

"Not scared." She drew a deep breath. "A little traumatized, I guess."

"I'm taking you home. You can tell me about it there."

"I . . . yes, that's best." She drew back a little, wiped at her face. "I don't want to see anybody else just now. I sure as hell don't want anyone to see me. I'm a little bit of a wreck, Harper, and imagine I look like a major one."

"Don't worry. Want me to carry you?"

"Oh." Tears stung her eyes again, but warm ones. "My sweet boy. No, I can walk just fine. Tell me something first. Everything's the same in here, isn't it? Everything's as it should be in here?"

Because there was such tension in her voice, he looked around the greenhouse. "Everything's fine."

"Okay. Okay. Let's go home."

She let him lead her through the rain, around the buildings, and let out her first sigh of relief when she climbed into his car.

"Just relax," he ordered, and leaned over to fasten her seat belt himself. "We'll be home in a minute. You need to get warm."

"You'll make a good daddy."

"What?"

"You've got a nurturing bent—comes from being a gardener, maybe, but you don't just know how to take care, you take it. Christ, these have been a lousy couple of days."

"Did you have a fight with Mitch or something?"

"No." She kept her eyes closed as he drove, but her lips curved a little. "I don't get hysterical over a spat. I hope to God it takes more than that to bring me so low."

"I've never seen you cry like that, not since Daddy died."

"I don't guess I have." She felt the car turn, and opened her eyes so she could watch Harper House come into view. "Did you ever want me to give it up, this place?"

"No." His expression was utter shock as he looked over at her. "Of course not."

"Good. That's good to know for sure. I don't know if I could have, even for you."

"It's ours, and it's always going to be." He parked, and was out of the car and hurrying to her side before she could get out.

"I'm just a little shaky, Harper, not mortally wounded."

"You're going straight up, getting into some dry clothes. I'll bring you up some brandy."

"Harper, this is going to sound stupid, but I'm not quite ready to go upstairs."

"I'll get you some dry clothes. You can change in David's room."

"Thanks." He didn't even ask why, she thought. Didn't hesitate. What a man she'd raised.

"Go on back to David," he ordered. "Tell him I said you're to have some brandy, and some hot tea."

"Yes, sir."

Before she could move toward the stairs, Mitch came out of the library and started down the hall.

"I thought I heard the door—I've been keeping an ear . . ." He trailed off as he got closer, then lengthened his stride to reach her. "What is it? Are you sick, hurt?"

"No. Do I look sick?"

"You look pale as a sheet, and you've been crying. What is it?" He looked over her head into Harper's eyes. "What happened?"

"She doesn't really want to see anyone right now," Harper began.

"It's all right." She squeezed Harper's hand. "I did say that," she told Mitch, "but after I pull myself together a little more, I'd just as soon tell you both—all three of you, since I imagine David's in the kitchen—at once."

"She needs dry clothes," Harper stated. "If you'd take her back to David, get some brandy into her, I'll go fetch her some."

"For heaven's sake, this is what comes from being the little woman in a house full of big, strapping males. I don't have to be taken anywhere, and I can get brandy into myself."

"She's coming back." Harper nodded at Mitch. "You'll take care of her. I'll just be a minute."

"I've worried him now," Roz stated as Harper bounded up the steps. "I hate worrying him."

"Well, you're worrying me, too."

"I suppose it can't be helped. I wouldn't mind that brandy, though."

The minute they stepped into the kitchen, David rushed forward, concern tightening his face. Roz simply threw up a hand.

"I'm not hurt, I'm not sick, and there's no need to fuss. What I want is a shot of brandy, and the dry clothes Harper's bringing down. Mind if I change in your room?"

"No. Sit down." As he strode to a cabinet, he whipped the dishrag tucked into the waistband of his jeans, and used it to brush flour from his hands. "Who made her cry?"

Because the question was more of an accusation, tossed straight at Mitch, Mitch held up his hands for peace. "I've been here, remember? Harper just brought her in like this."

"I must point out, I'm sitting right here. And as I am, I can speak for myself. Thanks, baby." She lifted the snifter of brandy and took a quick, deep swallow. "Always hated this stuff, but it shoots straight to the spot."

She managed a smile as Harper came in with a sweatshirt, jeans, and thick socks. "My hero. Just give me a couple of minutes, and I'll try to explain what happened."

Harper waited until she'd gone into David's quarters, and the doors were closed.

"I found her sitting on the floor of the propagation house, crying. Just . . . sobbing. She hardly ever cries. Gets a little wet when something makes her really happy, or sentimental, but when she's sad or hurt—she doesn't let you see it."

"What's been going on the past few days?" Mitch demanded, and saw David and Harper exchange a look. "I knew there was something. She's been avoiding me."

"It's best if she tells you herself. David, she ought to have some tea, don't you think?"

"I'll put it on. Get that box of Nirvana caramels out of the fridge. Some chocolate will make her feel better. Mitch, why don't you light the fire there? I didn't bother with it today."

When Roz stepped back in, David was brewing tea, Harper was setting out fancy chocolates, and Mitch was babying a fire in the kitchen hearth.

"Makes me wonder why I haven't had some sort of jag long before this, if I get three good-looking men bustling around ready to wait on me. Before we sit down, Mitch, I should've told you before. I think you'll want your tape recorder."

"I'll get it."

It gave her a little more time, calming herself toward cool by the time they all sat together. She told them, was able to relay it matter-of-factly now. Though her hands went cold again, she simply warmed them on her teacup and finished describing her experience in the greenhouse.

"I always had a soft spot for the Bride," David began, "but now, I think she's just a stone bitch."

"Hard to argue." Roz picked up a piece of chocolate. "But it seems to me that she believes all this sincerely. Men are liars and cheats and no-good bastards. She wants me to believe it so I'm not used and hurt again."

"Mama." Harper stared hard into his own tea. "Do you believe Daddy wasn't faithful to you?"

"I don't believe anything of the kind. More than that, honey, I know he was faithful. Without a single doubt."

"She made you see him that way."

"She made me see him," Roz repeated. "And it broke my heart. To see him, just as he'd been. So young and vibrant and real. Just out of my reach. Out of my reach, when everything I felt for him came alive inside me again, just as vibrant and real. I knew it was a lie, even as it happened. And the cruel things she put into his mouth were never his. He was never cruel."

"She used your experience with Bryce, a painful incident," Mitch began. "And transferred that experience to the man who came before him. John. The man who came after him. Me. She'd rather hurt you, is compelled to hurt you, to save you from becoming involved with me."

"A bit late for that."

"Is it?"

"Do you think I'm so weak-minded, so spineless that I'd let her tricks influence me?"

"I think you're strong-minded, perilously close to a fault. I'm just not sure how much you disagree with her."

"I see. Well, well, well. I think I've told y'all what I can. I'm going to go on up, do some paperwork. Harper, it'd set my mind at ease if you'd go back to the nursery, just make sure everything's under control. David, the tea was just right, thanks."

She rose, strode out of the room without a second glance.

"Well, pissing her off brought the color back in her cheeks," David commented.

"Then she'll probably have a permanent healthy blush by the time I'm done. Excuse me."

"Brave, brave man," David stated as Mitch marched out.

"Or brick stupid," Harper said. "Either way, I think he's

in love with her. If he's stupid, she'll chew him up and spit him out, regardless. If he's brave, he might just make the cut. I hope he does."

ROZ HAD JUST REACHED HER BEDROOM WHEN MITCH caught up and walked right in behind her. She turned around, slow and deliberate.

"I don't believe I invited you in."

"I don't believe I asked for an invitation." Just as slow, just as deliberate, he closed the door. And to her shock, locked it.

"You're going to want to unlock that and step out again, or believe me, the wrath of this arguably psychotic ghost will be nothing compared to mine."

"You want a shot at me, take it. But I'll damn well know why first."

"I've just told you. I don't appreciate your invading my privacy this way, and presuming—"

"And that's bullshit. What led up to this? You've been brushing me off and evading me for days. The last time we were together, we were in that bed, and you were with me, Rosalind. I want to know what changed."

"Nothing. I've got my own life, just as you do." In a deliberate and, she could admit, petty move, she walked to the terrace doors, flung them open. "I had a lot to do."

He simply crossed over, slammed the doors shut. Locked them.

She wasn't sure she could get words past the fire of rage burning in her throat. "If you think for one minute I'll tolerate that—"

"Just be quiet." He snapped it out, and though blistering temper boiled inside her, she found herself measuring him in a new light.

"On second thought," he said before she could think of

a response, "answer one question. I told you I was falling in love with you. Was that a mistake?"

"Telling me? No. Falling, possibly. I'm a difficult woman."

"That's not a news flash."

"Mitchell, I'm tired, I'm angry, I'm emotionally . . . I don't know what the hell I am, but I don't want to fight with you now, because I'll fight dirty and regret it later. I don't want to talk to you. I don't want to be with you."

"I'm not leaving, because you're tired and you're angry, and in emotional turmoil. You don't want to talk or fight, fine. Lie down, take a nap. I'll wait until you're feeling stronger."

"God. God*damn* it." She whirled away, stormed toward the terrace doors, and unlocking them again, threw them open to the rain. "I need air. I just need some fucking air."

"Fine. Suck it in then, all you want. But this time, Rosalind, you're going to talk to me."

"What do you expect me to say? What do you want to hear?"

"The truth'll do."

"The truth, then. She *hurt* me." Emotion drenched her voice as she pressed a fisted hand to her heart. "She sliced me up and carved me out. Seeing John like that. I can't explain it, I don't have words for what it did to me."

She whirled back to him, and he saw her eyes were drenched, too. The tears didn't fall, and he could only imagine the vicious strength that held them back. But the golden brown swam with tears.

"She dropped me right down to the ground, and there was nothing I could do. How can I fight that? How can I fight something that doesn't really exist? Even knowing why she did it doesn't stop it from squeezing my heart into bloody pulp."

With an impatient gesture, she used the heels of her hands to swipe at any tear that escaped her control.

"He didn't deserve to be used that way. Do you see? He didn't deserve it. He was a good man, Mitchell. A good man, good husband, good father. I fell in love with him when I was fourteen. Fourteen years old, can you imagine? He made me a woman, and a mother, and God, a widow. I loved him, beyond measure."

"She can't touch what you feel for him. Nothing she can do can touch it. I didn't know him, but I'm looking at you, Rosalind, and I can see that. I can see him."

Her breath released on a shaky, painful sound. "You're right. You're right." She leaned against the doorjamb, stared out into the cool rain. "You didn't deserve to be used, either. You didn't—don't—deserve what she tried to make you in my mind. I didn't believe it of John, and I didn't believe it of you. But it hurt, nonetheless, it hurt."

She took another breath, a stronger one. "I don't equate you with Bryce. I hope you know that."

"I'd rather know what you feel instead of what you don't. Why haven't you wanted to see me, Roz?"

"Nothing to do with you, and everything to do with me. Don't you hate when people say that?"

"Enough that I'm having a hard time not grabbing you and shaking out the rest of it. You're not the only one with a healthy share of wrath."

"No, I believe I caught the leading edge of it just now. One of the things I like about you is you have a strong sense of control. I have such a vile temper, you've no idea. So I know all about control."

"Aren't we just two mature individuals."

"Oh, you're still mad at me." She let out a half laugh, then tried to give him what he'd asked for. The truth. "The last night I spent with you?"

She turned now, facing him fully with the open doors at her back. "It was beautiful, and meant so much in so many ways. The next day I thought of you, and when I came home from work, I was going to call you. There was a message from you on my machine."

"Roz, I have a standing date with Josh. My son—"

"I know. It wasn't that. God, don't start worrying I'm one of those needy females who craves a man's attention every minute of every day. It was the message after yours that set me off. It was about my membership at the country club, how I'd canceled it, and sent in some letter full of complaints and rude comments, and so on. Which, of course, I hadn't done."

"Clerk."

"Undoubtedly. Easy enough to straighten out, really— No." She shook her head. "Truth. It was irritating and embarrassing to straighten out. But either way it set me off. I was halfway out the bedroom door, blood in my eye, heading out to hunt him down like a sick dog when Hayley and the baby got in my way. She stopped me, for which I'm grateful. I don't know what I might've done with my temper up like that."

"I bet it would've been worth the price of a ticket."

"I'd probably have landed in jail for assault at the very least. I was raging so much I scared that baby, made her cry. And said a particularly foul word in front of her that dealt with Bryce's sexual activities should he have same with members of his own gender."

"Seeing Lily's not quite a year old, I don't imagine it made much of an impression."

"Regardless, I was nearly out of my mind with temper, and I got it under control, but it was simmering in there for a while. I wanted to cool down, all the way down. And I had to go meet with my lawyer, make a courtesy call at the club. Smooth everybody else's feathers."

"Next time it might occur to you that I'd like a chance to smooth yours."

"I'm mean when I'm mad."

"Bet you are."

She sank into a chair.

"Roz, you should go to the police with this."

"I did. One more embarrassment. And you don't need to tell me I've nothing to be embarrassed about. I feel it, so there it is. Nothing much they can do, of course, but I've documented all the things I know about. If and when it can be proved he's behind this, it's fraud, and it may be considered stalking. If I can burn his ass, Mitch, you can bet the bank I'll do just that."

He came over, crouched in front of her. "I'd like to help you light the match."

She laid a hand on his cheek. "I wasn't brushing you off. I was thinking of you, of finding you and seeing if you'd spend the evening with me. Right before I walked into that nasty little waking nightmare."

"Coincidentally, I've been thinking of you, and wondering if you'd spend the evening with me. Do you want to get out of the house for a few hours?"

"I don't. I really don't."

"Then we'll stay in."

"I'd like to ask you for something."

"Ask."

"There's a big, splashy affair coming up at the club. Formal dinner dance, the annual spring one. David was going to escort me. Even with what's happening with us, I'd planned to stick to that because I didn't like the idea of the talk and gossip that'll start if I was to show up with you. But screw that. I'd like you to go with me."

"Formal, as in tux?"

"I'm afraid so."

"I can manage it. We're all right, you and me?"

"We really seem to be, don't we?"

"You want to take a rest now?"

"No, I don't." Content, she leaned forward to kiss both

of his cheeks. "What I want is a long, hot bath. And I'd really like some company in the tub."

"That's a hell of an invitation." He got to his feet, drew her to hers. "Accepted. It may just be the perfect venue to tell you about my recent visit with Clarise Harper."

"Cousin Rissy? This I have to hear."

IT FELT LOVELY, IT FELT DECADENT, AND EXACTLY PERfect to soak in a bubble bath in the deep old tub, with her back resting against Mitch's chest.

Not even the end of the workday, and here she was having a sexy bath, with a man, music, and candles.

"Clarise gets meaner and leaner every blessed year," Roz commented. "I swear if she ever dies—because I'm not sure she'll agree to that eventuality—they won't even need a coffin. They'll just crack her in two like a twig and have done with it."

"I could tell she holds you in the same high regard."

"She despises me for many reasons, but the main is that I have this house, and she doesn't."

"I'd say that's high on the list."

"She's lying when she says she never saw or felt Amelia. I heard my grandmother talk about it. Clarise's memory is convenient and to suit herself. She doesn't tolerate any nonsense, you see, and ghosts fall into that category."

"She said 'balderdash.' "

Letting her head fall back, Roz laughed herself breathless. "Oh, she would. I can just hear it. Well, she can balderdash all she likes, but she's lying. And I know damn well she should have letters, maybe even journals, quite a number of photographs. There were things she took from the house when my father died. She'll deny it, but I know she helped herself here and there. We had one of our famous set-tos when I caught her taking a pair of candlesticks from the parlor, while my daddy was still being waked. Vicious old badger."

"I don't imagine she walked out with them."

"Not that time, anyway. I didn't care about the damn candlesticks—ugly things—but my daddy wasn't even in the *ground*. Still burns my ass. She claimed she'd given them to my father—which she certainly had not—and that she wanted them for sentimental reasons. Which was a load of stinking horseshit, as there isn't a sentimental cell in her dried-up body."

He rubbed his cheek over her hair as if to soothe, but she felt his body shaking with laughter.

"Oh, go ahead and let it out. I know how I sound."

"I love how you sound, but back to the subject. She might have taken other things, things you didn't see her with."

"I know she did, greedy vampire bat that she is. There was a picture of my grandfather as a boy, in a silver frame—Edwardian—a Waterford compote, two Dresden shepherdesses—oh, and other things that vanished after she paid calls."

"Hmm." He rested his chin on the top of her head, lazily soaped her arm. "What do you know about this Jane Paulson?"

"Not very much. I've met her at various weddings and funerals, that sort of thing, but I barely have a picture of her in my head. And when I do, I see this sweet-faced little girl. She's nearly twenty-five years younger than I am, if my math is right."

"Made me think of a puppy who's been kicked often enough to keep its tail between its legs."

"If she's living with Cousin Rissy, I can only imagine. Poor thing."

"She knows something, though."

Curious, Roz turned her head so she could see Mitch. "Why do you say?"

"Something went over her face when Clarise claimed not to have any journals, any diaries. As if she were going to be helpful and say: Oh, don't you remember the one . . . whatever. Then she caught herself, folded up. If I were a betting man, I'd wager heavy that Prissy Rissy has some information we could use."

"And if she doesn't want to share it, she'd burn it before she'd give it to you. She's that perverse."

"Can't if she doesn't know I know she's got it—and if we can persuade Jane to help us out."

"What are you going to do, seduce the poor girl?"

"Nope." He bent down to kiss Roz's wet shoulder. "You are. What I was thinking was that the girl could use a friend—maybe the prospect of another job. If you were able to contact her without Clarise knowing, give her some options . . ."

"And try to recruit her." Pursing her lips, Roz thought it through. "It's very sneaky, very deceptive. And I like it very much."

He slid his hands up, covered her breasts with them, and with frothy bubbles. "I was hoping you would."

"I don't mind playing dirty." With a wicked gleam in her eye, she squirmed around until she faced him. "Let's practice," she said, and dunked them both.

sixteen

UNDER THE HUMMING CHAOS OF SPRING SEASON WAS a kind of simmering stress for the grower, especially if she happened to be the owner as well. Had she prepared enough flats, was she offering the right types and numbers of perennials?

Would the blooms be big enough, showy enough to attract the customers? Were the plants strong enough, healthy enough to maintain the reputation she'd built for quality?

Had they created enough baskets, pots, planters—or too many?

What about the shrubs and trees? Would the sidelines compliment the plants or detract from those sales?

Were the mulch colorants she'd decided to carry a mistake, or would her customer base enjoy the variety?

She left a great deal of this in Stella's hands; that's why she'd hired a manager. Roz wanted to compartmentalize many of the details—in someone else's compartment. But In the Garden was still her baby, and she experienced all the pride and worry a mother might over any growing child.

She could enjoy the crowds and confusion, the customers wheeling their wagons or flatbeds around the tables, over gravel and concrete to select just the right plants for their gardens or patio pots. She could and did enjoy consulting and recommending, and used that to balance out the little pang she experienced at the start of high season when she watched the plants she'd nurtured ride off to new homes.

At this time of year she often lectured herself about being sentimental over what she'd grown. But they weren't, and never could be, merely products to her. The weeks, months, often years spent nurturing specimens formed a connection for her that was very personal.

For the first few days of every spring season, she mourned the parting. Then she got down to business.

She was in the propagation house, taking a break from those crowds and calculating which plants to move into the retail area next when Cissy burst in.

"Roz, I'm desperate."

Roz pursed her lips. The usually meticulously groomed Cissy had more than one highlighted hair out of place, and a panicked gleam in her eyes. "I can see that. Your hairdresser retire? Your masseuse run off with a musician?"

"Oh, don't joke. I'm serious." She hustled down the tables to where Roz worked. "My in-laws are coming to visit."

"Oh."

"Just dropped that bomb on me this morning. And they're coming in two days. I *hate* when people just assume they're welcome."

"They are family."

"Which only makes it worse, if you ask me. You know she picks on me. She's picked on me for twenty-six years. If they hadn't moved to Tampa, I'd be a crazy woman by now, or in jail for murder. I need your help, Roz."

"I'm not going to kill your mother-in-law for you, Cissy. There are limits to friendship."

"I bet you could." Eyes narrowed, she took a long and calculating look around. "I bet there are all sorts of interesting poisons around here I could slip into her martini, and end this personal hell. I'll just hold that one in reserve. You know what she said to me?"

"No, but I guess I'm going to hear it."

"She said she supposed I hadn't replaced the carpet in the dining room yet, and how she'd just love to go out while she's here and find just the right thing. Not to worry about the time it took her, she had plenty now that she and Don have retired. And how I'd find that out for myself soon, since I'm reaching that age. I'm reaching *that age*. Can you imagine?"

"Seeing as you and I are about the same age, I might find some poison around here."

"Oh, and that's not the half of it. I'd be here all day if I got started, and I can't because I'm under the gun. She started snooting at me about the gardens and the lawn, and how she wondered I didn't do more than I did with mine, why I didn't take more pride in the home *her son* has provided me with."

"You have a lovely yard." Not that it reached its potential, but it was, in Roz's opinion, well kept and pretty enough.

"She just pushed my buttons—like she always does—and I just blurted out how I'd been slaving away, and put in new beds and whatnot. I just blathered, Roz, and now, unless you help me out, she's going to see I was lying through my teeth."

"If you want Logan, we can ask Stella what his schedule's like, but—"

"I hit her on the way back. He's booked—solid, she says—for the next two weeks." She clasped her hands together, as if in prayer. "I'm begging you, Roz. Begging you. Pull him off something and give him to me. Just two days."

"I can't yank him off another job—but wait," she said

when tears gathered in Cissy's eyes. "We'll figure this out. Two days." Roz blew out a breath. "It's gonna cost you."

"I don't care. Money's the least of it. My life's at stake here. If you don't help me, I'll just have to fly down to Tampa on the sly and murder her in her sleep tonight."

"Then let's get started saving your life, and hers."

She had a vision in mind, and cut a swath through her own nursery as she built on it. Cissy didn't blink when Roz accumulated plants, shrubs, ornamental trees, pots, and planters.

"Harper, I need you to go to the house, bring my pickup on around. We're going to load this up, and I'm going to steal you for a few hours. Stella, you tell Logan to come on by here when he finishes for the day. He's going to be putting in some overtime. He can pick up what I've earmarked, and bring it to this address."

She scrawled Cissy's address on a scrap of paper. "You come with him. I can use your hands, and your eye."

"Do you really think you can get all this done in less than two days?" Stella asked.

"I will get it done in less than two days because that's what I've got."

SHE LOVED A CHALLENGE. AND THERE WAS NOTHING like digging in the dirt to take her mind off any worries.

She measured, marked, tilled, dumped peat moss, and raked.

"Normally I'd want to take more time to prep the soil. Starting a new bed's an important event."

Cissy chewed on her lip, twisted the string of pearls she wore around her fingers. "But you can do it."

"Not much I can't do with dirt and plants. It's my gift." She nodded to where Harper was already setting in a decorative metal trellis. "And his. And you're going to learn something today. Put those gloves on, Cissy. You're going to do some slaving away, then you won't have lied."

"I don't give a red damn about the lie." But she tugged on the gloves.

Roz explained, in basic terms, that they'd do a four-season perennial garden. One that would impress, whatever time of year the in-laws visited. Iris and dianthus, campanula. Bleeding heart and columbine for instant bloom. With spring bulbs, craftily placed annuals, and the foliage from later bloomers filling in now.

And once the massive planters she'd chosen were done and exploding with flowers, the bed would be a showpiece even a persnickety mother-in-law would love.

She left Cissy setting in crested cockscomb and dusty miller and moved off to reorganize and fluff up the already established beds.

At the end of another hour, she realized they would use everything she'd brought with her, and then some.

"Harper?" She swiped at her sweaty forehead with the back of her hand. "You got your cell phone?"

He stopped working the vines onto the trellis long enough to pat at his pockets. "Somewhere. Truck maybe?"

Like mother like son, she thought, sent him a wave, and went around front to find it. She called Stella, rattled off another list of needs—having no doubt her manager would record them all, invoice, inventory, and deliver.

She planted cannas at the back fence, along with blue salvia and African daisies. Then sat back on her heels when Cissy walked to her with a tall glass.

"I made lemonade, from scratch. For my sins. My manicure is wrecked," she said as she handed Roz the glass. "And I'm already aching in places I forgot I owned. I don't know how you do this."

"I don't know how you play bridge every week."

"Well, to each his own, I suppose. I owe you a lot more than the check I wrote."

"Oh, you're going to be writing a couple more before it's over."

Cissy just closed her eyes. "Hank's going to kill me. He's going to take his nine iron and beat me bloody and dead."

"I don't think he will." Roz got to her feet, handed the empty glass back, then stretched her back. "I think he's going to be pleased and proud—and touched that you'd go to all this trouble—ruining a manicure on top of it—to make your home more beautiful for his mother's visit. To show her, and him, how much you value the home he's provided you with."

"Oh." A slow smile spread. "That's damn clever of you, Rosalind."

"Just because I don't have a husband doesn't mean I don't know how they work. I'm going to warn you, you don't take proper care of all this, I'll come over here and beat you senseless with Hank's nine iron myself."

Cissy looked around at the dirt, the half-planted beds, the shovels and rakes and bags of soil and additives. "It's going to look really nice when it's finished. Right?"

"Trust me."

"I am. Completely. And this is probably not the best time to tell you that son of yours is one handsome devil. I swear, my heart nearly shut right down when I handed him that lemonade and he flashed that grin at me. God almighty, he must have the girls at his feet, four layers deep."

"Never known him to have trouble finding one. Doesn't seem to keep them long, though."

"He's young yet."

* * *

IT WAS DARK WHEN SHE GOT HOME. DIRTY, A LITTLE achy, she poked her head in the library before heading upstairs. She'd seen Mitch's car out front.

"Working late?" she asked.

"Yeah. You, too?"

"I had an amazing day. Time of my life. I'm going to go up and scrape several inches of that day off me, then eat like a pig."

"Want company? I've got a couple of things to run by you."

"Sure, come on up."

"Been playing in the dirt?"

"Most of the day. Gardening emergency." She shot a grin over her shoulder as she started up the stairs. "A friend, an unexpected visit by in-laws, passive-aggressive tendencies, and a desire for one-upmanship. This resulted in a hell of a profit for my business and a terrific day for me."

She walked straight into her bathroom, stripped off her shirt. "Been a long time since I got seriously involved in the design and landscaping end of things. I'd nearly forgotten how much I love to get my hands into somebody's dirt and create something."

She undressed while she talked, in a practical sort of way, dumping her clothes in the hamper, leaning in to start the shower and test the water temperature, while he stood in the doorway, listening.

"A lot of the place was virgin ground—unrealized potential. I should feel guilty for charging her when it was such a good time for me—but I don't. We earned it."

"We."

"Had to call in the troops." She stepped into the shower. "Took Harper with me, then had Logan and Stella swing by as reserves later in the day. I put in the nicest four-season perennial garden. Looks sweet now, and in a few weeks the early daylillies will pop, and the wild indigo, then it'll move right into the spirea and ladybells, the meadow sage and foxglove. Harper started this gorgeous purple clematis on a copper trellis and put in a trio of oakleaf hydrangeas. Then when Logan got there . . ."

She trailed off, stuck her head out, hair dripping. "I'm boring you senseless."

"Not at all. I may not know what you're talking about, but I'm not bored. You sound revved."

"I am. I'm going by tomorrow morning for some final touches and to present her with the final bill. She may faint, but she's going to wow her in-laws."

"You never did give me an answer about that plant for my apartment. You know, feng shui."

"No, I didn't."

He waited five seconds, heard nothing but water running. And laughed. "Guess that's answer enough. You know, I'm fairly intelligent and responsible. I could be taught how to care for a plant."

"Possibly, but your track record's ugly, Mitch. Just ugly. We may discuss a probationary period. I threatened to hurt Cissy if she didn't maintain what I did over there. I heard her talking to Logan about hiring him to come in twice a month to deal with it. And that's fine. We should all be self-aware enough to know our limitations."

"You water it. You put it in the sun. I can do that."

"As if that's all there is to it. You want to hand me a towel?"

She shut off the water, took the towel he handed her, and began to dry off. "We've been so busy at work I've barely been able to knock two thoughts together about anything else. Stella's wedding's right around the corner, too. And I know there are things that need my attention in this project."

He watched as she slathered on cream, as the scent of it mixed with the scent of her soap. "We'll manage it all."

"Winters fly by now that I've got the business. A lot more to do over the winter than people might think. And here we are, into another spring. I can hardly believe it's . . ."

Her eyebrows drew together, with that faint vertical line between them. Falling silent, she carefully replaced the top on her cream.

"Just hit you, didn't it?" he asked.

"What would that be?"

"The two of us, right now." He stayed where he was as she moved by him into the bedroom, as she opened a drawer for fresh clothes. "End of the workday, talking over the shower. It's all very married, isn't it?"

She slipped on cropped gray sweats, tugged a T-shirt over her head. "How do you feel about that?"

"Not entirely sure. A little nervous around the edges, I guess. Amazingly calm at the center. What about you?"

She rubbed the towel over her hair as she studied his face. "Getting married again wasn't just not on my radar, but top of my list of things to avoid. Such as poisonous snakes, frogs dropping out of the sky, ebola viruses, and such."

He smiled, leaned on the doorjamb. "I heard past tense."

"You have good ears. I fell in love once, very young. And when I fell in love, I married. It was very good, and I'll love John Ashby all of my life. I'll see him in the sons we made together, and know I wouldn't have them if we hadn't loved the way we did."

"People who can and have loved like that are fortunate."

"Yes, we are. At one time I was lonely. My boys were going their own way, and the house just seemed so empty, so quiet. I was sad, under the pride of seeing the young men I'd help create, I was so damn sad."

She walked back into the bathroom to hang the damp towel, then opened her daily moisturizer to smooth it over her face.

"I needed something to take that away, or thought I did. I wanted someone to share the rest of my life with. I picked someone who, on the surface, seemed right. That mistake cost me a great deal. Emotionally and financially."

"And because of that, you'll be very careful about another marriage."

"I will. But I'm in love with you, Mitchell." She saw the emotion rush into his eyes, and what a thrill it was to see it, to know it was there because of her.

She saw him start to step forward. And stop himself, because he knew she wanted him to wait. Another thrill, she thought, to be so well understood.

"I never expected to love again, not with the whole of my heart. That was the mistake I made with Bryce, you see. The basic mistake, in marrying someone I didn't love with the whole of my heart. Still, marriage is an enormous step. I hope you won't mind if I let you know when and if I'm ready to take it."

"I can work with that, because I love you, Rosalind. Mistakes I made before hurt people I loved. I won't make them again."

She walked to him. "We're bound to make new ones."

He leaned down, brushed his lips over hers. "That'll be all right."

"Yes, I think it might be all right. Why don't we go downstairs, see what David's got cooked up? Then you can tell me about your day instead of listening to me carry on about mine."

AS IT WAS LATE, THE CHILDREN HAD ALREADY EATEN and their parents were busy with bedtime rituals.

"Sometimes you can forget this house is full of people." Roz dug into spaghetti and meatballs. "Other times it's like being at the monkey house at the zoo."

"And you like it both ways."

"I do. I'm a contradictory soul. I need my solitude or I get mean. I get too much solitude, I get broody. I'm a pain in the ass to live with, you may want to factor that into the equation."

"I already have."

She paused, fork halfway to her mouth, then set it down as a long, rolling laugh spilled out of her. "Serves me right."

"I'm messy, often careless with details that don't interest me at that particular moment—and I don't have any intention of reforming. You can factor those in."

"Done. Now what did you want to talk over with me?"

"I never seem to run out of things I want to talk over with you."

"Men, in the first few weeks of love, talk more than they do or will for the following twenty years."

"See?" He gestured with his fork, then wound pasta around it. "Another advantage for finding each other a little later in life. We both know how it works. But what I wanted to discuss, primarily, was Clarise Harper."

"You're going to spoil my appetite, bringing her name up, and I do love meatballs and spaghetti."

"I paid another call on her this morning while, I assume, you were off digging gardens."

"Would you say you visited the third or fourth level of Hell?"

"Not that bad. She likes me, to a point. Finds me interesting, at least, and I'd say is amusing herself by feeding me what she likes and holding back what she doesn't want me to know."

He shoveled in spaghetti, then broke a hunk of garlic bread in half to split with her. "I have a tape, if you're interested. She told an entertaining story, she claimed her mother told her, about your grandfather when he was a boy—going off to sleep in a closet with a puppy he'd taken from a litter in the stables. He'd wanted it for a pet, and his mother had vetoed. No dogs in the house sort of thing. So he'd hidden it in his room for a week or so, keeping it in his closet, pilfering food out of the kitchen."

"How old was he?"

"About ten, she thinks. At least from what her mother told her. He was found out when he crawled into the closet with it, and fell asleep. Nobody could find him, turned the house upside down. Then one of the servants heard this whimpering and found the two of them in the back of his bedroom closet."

"Did he get to keep the dog?"

"He did. His father overruled his mother and let him keep it, though it was a mutt and apparently never learned any manners. He had it nearly eighteen years, so she remembers it herself, vaguely. He buried it behind the stables, put a little tree over the grave."

"Spot. My grandmother showed me the grave. There's even a little marker. She said he'd buried his beloved dog there, but must not have known the story about how he acquired it. She'd have told me."

"My impression is Clarise told me to illustrate that her mother's little brother was spoiled by his father."

"She would," Roz replied.

"I learned something else. Jane has every other Wednesday off. Or Wednesday afternoons. She likes to go to Davis-Kidd, have lunch in their café, then browse the stacks."

"Is that so?"

"Anyone who wanted to talk to her privately could run into her there. Tomorrow, in fact, as it's her Wednesday afternoon off."

"I haven't made time, recently, to go to the bookstore."

"Then I'd say you're due."

* * *

WITHOUT MITCH'S DESCRIPTION, ROZ DOUBTED SHE'D have recognized Jane Paulson. She saw the young woman—mouse-colored hair, drab clothes, solemn expression—come into the café and go straight to the counter.

She ordered quickly, like someone whose habits varied little, then took a table in a corner. She pulled a paperback book out of her purse.

Roz waited sixty seconds, then wandered over.

"Jane? Jane Paulson?" She said it brightly, with just a hint of puzzlement, and watched Jane jolt before her gaze flew up. "Well, isn't this something?"

Without waiting for an invitation, Roz took the second chair at the table. "It's been . . . well, I can't remember how long. It's Cousin Rosalind. Rosalind Harper."

"Yes, I . . . I know. Hello."

"Hello right back." Roz gave her hand a pat, then sat back to sip at her coffee. "How are you, how long are you in town? Just tell me every little thing."

"I . . . I'm fine. I live here now."

"No! Right here in Memphis? Isn't that something. Your family's well, I hope."

"Everyone's fine. Yes, everyone's just fine."

"That's good to hear. You give your mama and daddy my best when you talk to them next. What are you doing here in Memphis?"

"I, um . . ." She broke off as her cup of soup and half sandwich were served. "Thank you. Um, Cousin Rosalind, would you like something?"

"No, coffee's just fine." And she couldn't do it. She couldn't look at that miserable, distressed face any longer and lie.

"Jane, I'm going to be honest with you. I came here today to see you."

"I don't understand."

"I know you're living with Cousin Rissy, working for her."

"Yes. Yes, I . . . and I just remembered. I have errands to run for her. I don't know how I could've forgotten. I really should go and—"

"Honey." Roz laid a hand on hers, to hold her still, and hopefully to reassure. "I know just what she thinks of me, so you don't need to worry. I won't tell her we spoke. I don't want to do anything to get you in trouble with her. I promise you."

"What do you want?"

"First let me tell you that nothing you say will get back to her. You know how much she dislikes me, and the feeling couldn't be more mutual. We won't be talking about this, Clarise and I. So I'll ask you first, are you happy staying with her?"

"I needed a job. She gave me a job. I really should—"

"Mmm-hmm. And if you could get another job?"

"I . . . I can't afford a place of my own, right now." Jane stared into her soup as if it held the world, and the world wasn't a very friendly place. "And I don't have any skills. Any job skills."

"I find that hard to believe, but that can wait. If I could help you find a job you'd like, and an apartment you could afford, would you prefer that to working for and living with Clarise?"

Her face was very pale when she lifted her head. "Why would you do that?"

"Partially to spite her, and partially because I don't like to see family unhappy if the solution is a simple one. And one more partially. I'm hoping you can help me."

"What could I possibly do for you?"

"She has things from my home, from Harper House." Roz nodded as she saw the fear and knowledge flicker over Jane's face. "You know it, and I know it. I don't care—or have decided not to care—about the statuary, the things, we'll say. But I want the papers. The books, the letters, the journals. To be frank, Jane, I intended to bribe you to get them for me. I'd help you get yourself employed and established, give you a little seed money if you needed it, in exchange. But I'm going to do that for you anyway."

"Why?"

Roz leaned forward. "She would have beat me down, if she could. She'd have manipulated me, run my life, crushed my spirit. If she could. I didn't let her. I don't see why I should let her do the same to you."

"She didn't. I did it myself. I can't talk about it."

"Then we won't. I'm not going to browbeat you." She could, Roz knew, all too easily. And that's why she couldn't. "What I'm going to do is give you my numbers. Here's my home number, and my cell phone number, and my work number. You put these somewhere she won't find them. You must know she goes through your things when you're not there."

Jane nodded. "Doesn't matter. I don't have anything."

"Keep that attitude up, you'll never have anything. You think about what you want, and if you want me to help you get it. Then you call me."

"You'd help me even if I don't help you?"

"Yes. And I can help myself if and when I need to. She has what belongs to me, and I need it back. I'll get it. You want to get away from her, I'll help you. No strings."

Jane opened her mouth, closed it, then got quickly to her feet. "Cousin Rosalind. Could we . . . could we go somewhere else? She knows I come here, and she might . . ."

"Get reports? Yes, she might. All right, let's go somewhere else. My car's right out front."

SHE DROVE THEM TO A LITTLE DINER, OFF THE BEATEN path, where no one who knew them, or Clarise, was likely to dine. The place smelled of barbecue and good strong coffee.

She ordered both, for each of them, to give Jane time to settle her nerves.

"Did you have a job back home?"

"I, um, did some office work, at my father's company? You know he's got the flooring company."

"Do you like office work?"

"No. I don't like it, and I don't think I'm much good at it anyway."

"What do you like?"

"I thought I'd like to work in a bookstore, or a gallery? I like books and I like art. I even know a little about them."

"That's a good start." To encourage the girl to eat, instead of picking at the sesame seeds on her roll with restless fingers, Roz picked up half the enormous sandwich she'd already cut in two, and bit in. "Do you have any money of your own?"

"I've saved about two thousand."

"Another good start."

"I got pregnant," Jane blurted out.

"Oh, honey." Roz set the sandwich down, reached for Jane's hand. "You're pregnant."

"Not anymore." Tears began to slide down her cheeks. "Last year. It was last year. I . . . he was married. He said he loved me, and he was going to leave his wife. I'm such an idiot. I'm such a fool."

"Stop that." Voice brisk, Roz passed Jane a paper napkin. "You're no such thing."

"He was a married man, and I knew it. I just got swept away. It was so wonderful to have somebody want me, and it was so exciting to keep it all a secret. I believed everything he said, Cousin Rosalind."

"Just Roz. Of course you did. You were in love with him."

"But he didn't love me." Shaking her head, she began to tear the napkin into shreds. "I found out I was pregnant, and I told him. He was so cool, so, well not really angry, just annoyed. Like it was, I don't know, an inconvenience. He wanted me to have an abortion. I was so shocked. He'd said we were going to be married one day, and now he wanted me to have an abortion."

"That's very hard, Jane. I'm sorry."

"I said I would. I was awful sad about it, but I was going to. I didn't know what else I could do. But I kept putting it off, because I was afraid. Then one day I was with my mother, and I started bleeding, and cramping, right there in the restaurant where we were having dinner."

Tears spilled down her cheeks. Roz pulled a napkin from the metal dispenser and offered it.

"I had a miscarriage. I hadn't told her I was pregnant, and I had a miscarriage practically in front of her. She and Daddy were so upset. I was all dopey and feeling so strange, I told them who the father was. He was one of Daddy's golf partners."

This time she buried her face in the napkin and sobbed. When the waitress started over, Roz just shook her head, rose, and moved around the booth to slip in beside Jane, drape an arm over her shoulder.

"I'm sorry."

"Nothing of the kind. You go ahead and cry."

"It was an awful scene, an awful time. I embarrassed them, and disappointed them."

"I would think, under the circumstances, their minds and hearts should have been with you."

"I shamed them." She hiccupped, and mopped at her tears. "And all for a man who never loved me. I lost that baby, maybe because I wanted it not to be. I wished it would all just go away, and it did."

"You can't wish a baby away, honey. You can blame yourself some for conceiving it, 'cause that takes two. But you can't blame yourself for losing it."

"I never did anything in my life except what I've been told. But I did this, and that's what happened."

"I'm sorry it happened. We all make mistakes, Jane, and sometimes we pay a very stiff price for them. But you don't have to keep paying it."

She gave Jane's shoulders a last squeeze, then went back to her own side, so they'd be face-to-face. "Look at me now. Listen to me. The man who used you, he's out of your life?"

She nodded, dabbed at her eyes.

"Good. Now you can start deciding what you want to do. Build a life or keep sliding around on the wreck of the old one."

"You'd really help me get a job?"

"I'll help you get one. Keeping it would be up to you."

"She . . . she has a lot of old diaries. She keeps them in her room, locked in a drawer. But I know where the key is."

Roz smiled and sat back. "Aren't you something?"

seventeen

"SHE'S NOT EVIL, RIGHT?" HAYLEY SHIFTED LILY ON her hip and watched Harper plug some portulaca into the bed outside the back door of his cottage. "I mean she's nasty and mean, but she's not evil."

"Obviously, you haven't heard Mama describe Cousin Rissy as the Uber-Bitch Demon from Hell."

"If she really is, then maybe she had something to do with Amelia. Maybe she's the one who killed her."

"She wasn't born—or spawned, as Mama would say—when Amelia died."

"Oh, yeah." But she wrinkled her forehead. "But that's only if we're right on the dates. If we're wrong, she could've done it."

"Assuming Amelia was murdered."

"Well, okay, assuming that. She has to have some reason for taking the diaries, and for keeping them. Don't you think?"

"Other than being a selfish, tight-assed old biddy?"

"Other than. All right, honey." As Lily squirmed, Hayley

put her down and began to walk her, holding her hands, up and down Harper's patio. "There could be things in the diaries that implicate her."

"Then why didn't she burn them?"

"Oh, I don't know," she snapped. "It's a theory. We've got to have a theory and a hypothesis so we can work to the solution, don't we?"

"If you say so, but my solution is Cousin Rissy's just a sticky-fingered, black-hearted, selfish witch. Look here, sweetie-pie." He plucked one of his moss roses, held it out at Lily's level. "Isn't that pretty? Wouldn't you like to have it?"

Grinning, she released her mother's hands, reached out.

"Uh-uh, you come on and get it," he told her.

And when he held it just beyond her fingertips, she took three toddling steps.

"Oh, my God. Oh, my God! Did you see? She walked. Did you see that?"

"Sure did." Harper steadied Lily when she closed her fist around the flower. "Look at you. Aren't you the one?"

"She took her first steps." Hayley sniffled, knuckled a tear away. "She walked right to you."

Always uneasy with tears, Harper looked up. "Sorry. I should've had you hold out the flower."

"No, no, that's not it. She took her first steps, Harper. My little girl. I saw her take her first steps. Oh, we have to show everybody." She did a quick dance, then scooped Lily up, making the baby laugh as she turned circles. "We've got to show everybody how smart you are."

Then she stopped, sighed. Leaning down, she brushed her lips over Harper's cheek. "She walked right to you," she repeated, then hurried toward the main house with the baby on her hip.

* * *

ROZ LOVED HAVING COFFEE ON THE PATIO WITH THE awakening gardens spread out around her. She could hear Stella's boys playing with the dog, and the sounds turned back her memory clock to when those shouts would have been from her own sons.

It was pleasant to sit out like this in the early evening, with the light soft and blue and the smell of growing things quiet on the air. Pleasant, too, since she was in the mood to have company. She drank her coffee while Logan and Stella, David and Mitch talked around her.

She'd wanted Harper there, too, and Hayley. But Harper wasn't answering his phone—not a rare occurrence—and she hadn't been able to find Hayley or the baby.

"She said he was so happy with the way everything looked, he took her out so she could buy new patio furniture." Stella drained her glass of iced tea. "I've rarely seen a more satisfied customer—or a landscape design done and executed so quickly. Logan better keep his eye on you, Roz."

"Knew the yard, and the woman—and both well enough to be sure Cissy would love the changes. And hire Logan to keep it looking good."

"I'd hate to be that unhappy and intimidated by my mother-in-law." Stella smiled at Logan. "I'm getting a jewel."

"She feels the same, which is going to make my life a hell of a lot easier." He tipped his beer toward Stella. "Your days are numbered, Red."

"Two weeks, and counting. There's still so much to do. Every time I think I've got it all under control, something else pops into my head. Planning a small, simple wedding's full of complications."

"You say 'I do,' then you eat cake," Logan said, and earned a bland stare from his future bride.

"Jolene's been an enormous help," she went on. "So have Logan's mother and sister, by long-distance. And I just don't know what I'd do without you, David."

"Throw me the bouquet, and we're even."

"Speaking of your stepmama," Roz put in, "I spoke with Jolene today."

"You did?"

"If there's anyone who knows everybody in Shelby County, it's Jolene Dooley. And I recalled she had a friend who runs a nice little gallery and gift shop downtown. Jane's got a job interview next Wednesday afternoon."

"You work fast," Mitch said.

"That girl needed a break. Now we'll see what she does with it. Jolene also has a friend whose sister works at a rental management company. Turns out there's a one-bedroom apartment downtown, about six blocks from that gallery. Its current tenants are moving out in a couple weeks, and the lease fell through on the people who were going to move in."

"I should've said you work miracles."

"Oh, I just put in the request for them."

"Do you think she'll move on it?" Logan wondered. "Move out, and bring you the diaries? The way you described her, she didn't seem to have much spine."

"Some of us don't. And some of us find out we've got one, but misplaced it. She's young, and she doesn't have what you'd call a lot of spirit. And though I made it clear there were no strings, I'm fairly sure she'll feel obligated if she takes this job, and this apartment. Now whether she has the gumption to act on that obligation's another matter."

"If she doesn't?" Mitch asked.

"Then I expect Cousin Rissy and I are due for a come-to-Jesus talk. I have a few cards up my sleeve, and I'll play them if I have to."

David's eyes brightened as he leaned closer. "Dirt? Such as?"

"Family peccadilloes that she wouldn't care to have come to light, and that I'll assure her I will light up like Christmas unless she returns what belongs to Harper House." She tapped David on the chin. "But for now, they're my little secrets."

"Spoilsport."

She turned, as did everyone else, when Hayley shouted. Her face glowing, she rushed breathlessly to the table. "She walked. She walked right to Harper. Three steps!"

Nothing would do but that Lily demonstrate her new skill again. But she just buckled at the knees each time Hayley tried to nudge her into a step. And preferred crawling on the patio or trying to climb up Roz's chair.

"I swear she walked. You can ask Harper."

"I believe you." Roz hauled Lily up to nuzzle. "Teasing your mama, aren't you?" She pushed back, rose with Lily in her arms, then picked up a cracker, held it out to Hayley. "You might as well start early using one of the primary parenting tools. Bribery. Scoot down there, hold that cracker out."

As Hayley obeyed, Roz crouched, steadied Lily on her feet. "Harper held out a flower."

"That boy knows how to charm the girls. Go on, baby. Go get it."

To enthusiastic applause, Lily performed. Then she plopped down on her butt and ate the cracker.

When the others went inside, Roz sat with Mitch in thc twilight.

"Would you be insulted if I said you make a beautiful honorary grandmother."

"The term *grandmother* is a bit of a jolt yet, but since I couldn't love that baby more if she were my own blood, no. She took her first steps to my boy. To Harper. It's hard for me not to focus on that, on the significance of it."

"She's not seeing anyone? Hayley?"

"Her life's centered on Lily right now. But she's young and full of passion. There'll be someone sooner or later. As for Harper, I can't keep up with the females who come and go. Still, he doesn't bring them home to meet me. There's significance in that, too."

"Well, speaking of sons, mine's seeing a new young lady. A local girl. And it happens her parents are members of your club. He'll be at the dinner dance tomorrow night. I'm looking forward to introducing you."

"I'd love to meet him. Who's the girl?"

"Her name's Shelby—after the county, I'm guessing. Shelby Forrester."

"It's a small and crowded world. Yes, I know Jan and Quill, Shelby's parents. I know her, too—and she's a lovely girl. Her parents and I are currently on . . . tenuous terms. Quill is doing business of some sort with Bryce, and it makes things a bit sticky between us. But that won't touch on anyone else."

"No one does complex connections and tenuous terms like the South."

"I suppose not, and I only mention it so that if you sense any awkwardness, you'll know why. But I'm prepared to be excruciatingly polite, so you needn't worry."

"I'm not, whether you decide to be polite or otherwise. Why don't we take a walk? That way I can hold your hand and find some shadowy and fragrant corner of the garden where I can kiss you."

"Sounds like a fine idea."

"You're doing a fine thing for Jane Paulson."

"Maybe, but my motivations are murky."

He laughed and brought her hand to his lips. "If your motivations were always pure, I doubt I'd find you as fascinating as I do."

"I do love astute flattery. Let's walk around to the stables. I'll show you Spot's marker."

"I'd like to see it. It might be a good place for me to broach another theory. One I've been chewing on for a while now."

As they walked down the path, she gauged the progress of her flowers and kept out an eagle eye for weeds.

"I'd as soon you spit it out as chew on it."

"I'm not entirely sure how you're going to feel about this one. I'm looking at dates, at events, at key moments and people, attempting to draw lines from those dates, events, moments, and people to Amelia."

"Mmm-hmm. I've always enjoyed having these stables here, leaving them be. As a kind of ruin."

Head cocked, hands fisted on hips now, she studied the crumbling stones, the weather-scarred wood. "I suppose I could have them restored. Maybe I will if I get those grandchildren and they develop an interest in horses. None of my boys did, particularly. It's girls, I think, who go through that equine adoration period."

She studied the building in the half light, the sagging roof and faded trim—and the vines, the climbers, the ornamental grasses she'd planted around it to give it a wild look.

"It looks like something you'd see in a movie, or more likely, in a storybook."

"That's what I like about it. My daddy's the one who let it go, or never did anything to preserve the building. I remember him talking about having it razed, but my grandmother asked him not to. She said it was part of the place, and she liked the look of it. The grave's around the back," she said. "I'm sorry, Mitch, I interrupted. Mind's wandering. Tell me your theory."

"I don't know how you're going to feel about it."

"Poison sumac," she said, nudging him away before he brushed up against a vine. "I'll have to get out here and get rid of that. Here we are." She crouched down, and with her ungloved hands plucked at weeds, brushed at dirt until she revealed the marker with the hand-chipped name in the stone.

"Sweet, isn't it, that he'd have buried his old dog here,

carved that stone for him. I think he must've been a sweet man. My grandmother wouldn't have loved him as much as she did if he hadn't been."

"And she did," Mitch agreed. "You can see the way she loved him in the pictures of them together."

"He looks sort of cool in most of the photographs we have of him. But he wasn't cool. I asked my grandmother once, and she said he hated having his picture taken. He was shy. Odd thinking of that, of my grandfather as a shy man who loved his dog."

"She was more outgoing?" Mitch prompted.

"Oh, much. She liked to socialize, nearly as much as she liked to garden. She loved hosting fancy lunches and teas, especially. She dressed up for them—hat, gloves, floaty dresses."

"I've seen pictures. She was elegant."

"Yet she could hitch on old trousers and dig in the dirt for hours."

"Like someone else we know." He skimmed a hand over her hair. "Your grandfather was born several years after the youngest of his sisters."

"Hmm. There were other pregnancies, I think. My grandmother had two miscarriages herself, and I recall, vaguely, her mentioning that her mother-in-law had suffered the same thing. Maybe a stillbirth as well."

"And then a son, born at the same time we've theorized Amelia lived—and died. Amelia, who haunts the house, but who we can't verify lived there—certainly not as a relation. Who sings to children, gives every appearance of being devoted to children—and distrusting, even despising men."

She cocked her head. Twilight was moving very quickly to dark, and with dark came a chill. "Yes, and?"

"What if the child that was born in 1892 was her child. Her son, Roz. Amelia's son, not Beatrice Harper's."

"That's a very extreme theory, Mitchell."

"Is it? Maybe. It's only a theory, in any case, and partially based on somewhat wild speculation. But it wouldn't be unprecedented."

"I would have heard. Surely there would have been some mention of it, some whisper passed along."

"How? Why? If the original players were careful to keep it quiet. The wealthy, the influential man craving a son—and paying for one. Hell, it still happens."

"But . . ." She pushed to her feet. "How could they hide that kind of deception? You're not talking about some legal adoption."

"No, I'm not. Just run with me on this a minute. What if Reginald hired a young woman, likely one of some breeding, some intelligence, who'd found herself in trouble. He pays the bills, gives her a safe haven, takes the child off her hands if it's a boy."

"And if it's a girl, he's wasted his time and money?"

"A gamble. Another angle might be he impregnated her himself."

"And his wife just accepted his bastard as her own, as the heir?"

"He held the purse strings, didn't he?"

She stood very still, rubbing her arms. "That's a very cold theory."

"It is. Maybe he was in love with Amelia, planned to divorce his wife, marry her. She might have died in childbirth. Or it could've been a straight business deal—or something else. But if that child, if Reginald Harper Jr. was Amelia's son, it explains some things."

"Such as?"

"She's never hurt you or anyone of your blood. Couldn't that be because you're her blood? Her descendant? Her great-grandchild?"

She paced away from the little grave. "Then why is she

in the house, on the property? Are you theorizing she birthed that baby here? In Harper House?"

"Possibly. Or that she visited here, spent time here. Maybe as the child's nurse, that's not unprecedented, either. That she died here, one way or the other."

"One way or—"

The grave was not small, and it had no marker. It gaped open dark and deep.

She stood over it, stood over that wide mouth in the earth. She looked down at death. The body in the tattered and filthy gown, the flesh that was melting away from bone. The smell of decay swarmed over her like fat, humming bees, stinging her eyes, her throat, her belly.

The ground was damp and slippery where she stood. Over it a thin, fetid fog crawled, smearing the black dirt, the wet grass with dirty tongues of gray.

She plunged the shovel through that fog, into the earth and grass, filled the blade. Then threw the earth into the grave.

The eyes of the dead opened, gleaming with madness and malice. Lifting a hand, bones piercing horribly through rotted flesh, it began to climb out of the earth.

Roz jolted, and slapped at the hands holding her.

"Easy, easy. Just breathe. Nice and slow."

"What happened?" She pushed at Mitch's hand again when she realized she was on the ground, cradled in his lap.

"You fainted."

"I certainly did not. I've never fainted in my life."

"Consider this your first. You went sheet white, your eyes rolled straight back in your head. I grabbed you when you started to go down. You were only out about a minute." Trembling a bit himself, he lowered his brow to hers. "Longest minute of my life, so far."

He took a long breath, then another. "If you're okay, would you mind if I just sat here a minute until I settle down?"

"Well, that's the damnedest thing."

"I didn't mean to upset you. We'll just table the theories. Let's get you inside."

"You don't think I passed out because you had me thinking my grandfather might've been born on the wrong side of the blanket? Christ. What do you take me for? I'm not some silly, spineless woman who questions her own identity because of the actions of her ancestors. I know who the hell I am."

Her color was back now, and those long-lidded eyes were ripe with irritation.

"Then you want to tell me why . . ." Now he went pale as polished glass. "God, Roz, are you pregnant?"

"Get a hold of yourself. A few minutes ago you're calling me a grandmother, now you're going into shock thinking I could be pregnant. I'm not going to present either one of us with a midlife baby, so relax. I had some sort of spell, I suppose."

"Care to elaborate?"

"One second we were talking, and the next I was standing—I don't know where, but I was standing over an open grave. She was in it. Amelia, and she was not looking her best."

She couldn't stop the shudder, and let her head rest against him. That good, strong shoulder. "More than dead, decomposing. I could see it, smell it. I suppose that's what took me down. It was, to put it mildly, very unpleasant. I was burying her, I think. Then she opened her eyes, started to climb out."

"If it's any consolation, if that had happened to me, I'd have fainted, too."

"I don't know if it was here, I mean this particular spot. It didn't seem like it, but I can't be sure. I've walked by here countless times. I planted that pachysandra, those sweet olives, and I never felt anything strange before."

"To risk another theory, you were never this close to finding out who she was before."

"I guess not. We'll have to dig." She pushed to her feet. "We'll have to dig and see if she's here."

THEY SET UP LIGHTS AND DUG BEYOND MIDNIGHT. The men, and Roz, with Stella and Hayley taking turns between shovels and remaining inside to mind the sleeping children.

They found nothing but the bones of a beloved dog.

"COULD BE METAPHORICAL."

Roz looked up at Harper as they walked the woods toward home the next day. She knew very well why he was with her, his arm slung casually around her shoulder, because Mitch had told him she'd fainted.

She'd barely had five minutes to herself since it happened. That was going to change, she thought, but she'd give him and the rest of her honorary family a day before she shooed them back.

"What could be metaphorical?"

"That, you know, vision thing you had. Standing over her grave, shoveling dirt on her." He winced. "I don't mean to wig you out."

"You're not. Who used to have nightmares after watching that Saturday morning show? What was it, *Land of the Lost*?"

"Jeez. The Sleestak." He shuddered, and only part of the movement was mocking. "I still get nightmares. But anyway, what I'm saying is you never stood over her grave, never buried her. She died a long time ago. But if we do the metaphor thing, we could say how you're trying to open her grave—but by missing something, not finding something, whatever, you're burying her."

"So, it's all in my mind."

"Maybe she's planting it there. I don't know, Mama."

She considered a moment. "Mitch has a theory. We were discussing it before I keeled over."

She told him, sliding her arm around his waist as she did. Together, they stopped at the edge of the woods, studying the house.

"Doesn't seem so far-fetched, all things considered," Harper said. "It always seemed like she was one of us."

"Seems to me it only opens up another box of questions, and doesn't really get us any closer to finding out who she was. But I know one thing. I want those diaries more than ever. If Jane doesn't come through, I'm going to take on Clarise."

"Want me to play ref?"

"I might just. If Amelia is part of the family, she deserves her due. That said, I don't feel the same about Clarise. She's always wanted more than her due, in my opinion. I don't know what it makes me to feel more sympathy for a dead woman, who may or may not be some blood kin, than I do for a live one who unquestionably is blood kin."

"She smacked me once."

Instantly Roz stiffened. "She did what?"

"Gave me a good swat one day, when she was visiting, and she caught me climbing on the kitchen counter going after the cookie jar. I was about six, I think. Gave me a swat, pulled me off and told me I was a greedy, disrespectful little brat."

"Why didn't you tell me? She had no right to touch you. I'd've skinned her for it."

"Then skinned me," he pointed out. "As you'd told me never to climb on the counter, and not to take any cookies without asking first. So I took my lumps and slunk off."

"Anybody was going to give you lumps it was going to be me. Nobody lays hands on my children, and in my court there is no statute of limitations on the crime. That bitch."

"There now." He gave her shoulders a squeeze. "Don't you feel better?"

"I believe I'll make her very sorry before I'm done." She walked with him toward the house. "You knew better than to put your hand in that cookie jar, Harper Jonathan Ashby."

"Yes'm."

She gave him a light elbow jab. "And don't you smirk at me."

"I wasn't, I was just thinking there are probably cookies in it now."

"I imagine so."

"Cookies and milk sound pretty good."

"I guess they do. Let's go harass David until we get some. But we have to do it now. I've got a date to get ready for."

ROZ KNEW THE STYLES AND COLORS THAT NOT ONLY flattered her, but suited her. She'd chosen the vintage Dior for its clean, flowing lines, and its pretty spun-gold color. The straight bodice, thin straps and rear drape left her back and shoulders bare.

But that back and those arms and shoulders were toned. She saw to it. So she saw no reason not to show them off. She wore her grandmother's diamonds—the drop earrings and tiered necklace that had come to her.

And knowing she'd regret it, slipped on the high, thin-heeled sandals that showcased the toenails she'd painted the same delicate gold as the dress.

She turned, to check the rear view in the mirror, and called out an absent "come in" at the knock on her door.

"Roz, I just wanted to . . ." Stella stopped dead. "Holy Mother Mary. You look spectacular."

With a nod in the mirror, Roz turned again. "I really do.

Sometimes you just want to knock them on their asses, know what I mean? I got an urge to do that tonight."

"Just—just stay there." She rushed out again, and Roz heard her calling for Hayley.

Amused, she picked up her purse—what had possessed her to pay so much for such a silly little thing—and began to slip what she considered necessary for the evening out inside it.

"You've got to get a load of this," Stella was saying, then pulled Hayley into the room.

Hayley blinked, then narrowed her eyes. "You've got to do a spin. Give us a little twirl."

Willing to oblige, Roz turned a circle, and Hayley crossed her arms over her chest and bowed her head.

"We are not worthy. Are those real diamonds? I know it's tacky to ask, but I can't help it. They're so . . . sparkly."

"They were my grandmother's, and particularly special to me. Which reminds me. I have something I thought you might like to wear for your wedding, Stella. It would cover the bases of something old, borrowed, and blue."

She'd already taken the box out of her safe, and now handed it to Stella.

"Oh, God."

"John gave them to me for my twenty-first birthday." She smiled down at the sapphire earrings. "I thought they might suit the dress you'd picked out, but if they don't I won't be offended."

"There's nothing they wouldn't suit." Gently Stella lifted one of the heart-shaped sapphire drops from the box. "They're exquisite, and more, I'm so . . ."

She broke off, waving a hand in front of her face as she sat on the side of the bed. "Sorry. I'm just so . . . that you'd lend them to me."

"If I had a sister, I'd like to think she'd enjoy wearing something of mine on her wedding day."

"I'm so touched, so honored. So . . . I'm going to have to sit here and cry for a couple minutes."

"That's all right, you go ahead."

"You know, the something old in that tradition's a symbol of the bride's link to her family." Hayley sniffed.

Roz patted her cheek. "Trust you to know. Y'all can sit here and have a nice cry together."

"What? Where are you going?" Hayley demanded.

"Downstairs. Mitch should be here shortly."

"But you can't." Biting her lip, and obviously torn between sitting with Stella or preventing a catastrophe, she waved her arms like a woman trying to stop a train. "You have to wait till he gets here, then you have to glide down the steps. That staircase is made for a woman to glide down. You've gotta make an entrance."

"No, I don't—and you sound like my mother, who made me do just that for my escort—thank God it was John so we could laugh about it after—at the debut she forced me into. Believe me, the world will not end if I greet him at the door."

She snapped her purse closed, took one last glance in the mirror. "Plus, there's another tradition I have to follow. If I don't go down, get David's approval on my dress, I'll hurt his feelings. There are tissues in the drawer beside the bed," she called out.

She'd barely finished modeling for David and getting his approval when Mitch was at the door.

Opening it, she had the pleasure of seeing his eyes widen and hearing the low whistle of his breath. "Just how did I get this lucky?" he asked her.

She laughed, held out her wrap. "The way you look in that tux, Doctor, you may get considerably luckier before the night's over."

eighteen

"I WAS TRYING TO REMEMBER THE LAST TIME I WORE A tux." Mitch slid behind the wheel of the car, giving himself the pleasure of another long look at Roz as he hitched on his seat belt. "Pretty sure it was a friend's wedding. His oldest kid graduates high school this year."

"Now, that's a shame, since you wear one so well."

"Lean over here once." When she did, he brushed his lips over hers. "Yeah, tastes as good as it looks."

"It certainly does."

Starting the engine, he pulled away from the house. "We could skip this business tonight and run off and get married. We're dressed for it."

She sent him a sidelong glance as he turned onto the main road. "Be careful how you bat those marriage proposals around, Dr. Carnegie. I've already shagged two in my time."

"Let me know if you want to try for three."

It felt spectacular, she realized, to be all dressed up and flirting with a handsome man. "You getting serious on me?"

"It's looking that way. You need to consider I'm a rent-the-tux kind of guy, but I'd spring for one when you decide to take the jump. Least I can do."

"Of course, that is a deciding factor."

He laid his hand briefly over hers. "I make a good living, and your money isn't an issue one way or the other with me. What baggage I've got, I've pretty well packed up. For the past many years, my son's been the singular essential element in my life. He's a man now, and while he'll always be my great love, I'm ready for other loves, other essentials."

"And when he moves to Boston?"

"It's going to cut me off at the knees."

This time she laid her hand on his. "I know just how it feels."

"You can't follow them everywhere. And I've been thinking it's easy enough to visit Boston now and again, or take a trip here and there when he's got a game somewhere appealing."

"I'm looking forward to meeting him."

"I'm looking forward to that, too. I'm hoping you're not going to be too uncomfortable with whatever friction there is between you and his date's parents."

"I won't be. Jan will. Being a spineless sort of woman who's decided to be embarrassed by her friendship, such as it was, with me. It's foolishness, but she's a foolish sort. I, on the other hand, will enjoy making her feel awkward."

She stretched back and spoke with satisfaction. "But then, I have a mean streak."

"I always liked that about you."

"Good thing," she said as they turned toward the club. "Because it's likely to come out tonight."

IT WAS FASCINATING, TO MITCH'S MIND, TO SEE HOW this set worked. The fancy dress, the fancy manners were a kind of glossy coat over what he thought of as basic high school clique syndrome. People formed small packs, at tables, in corners, or at strategic points where they could watch other packs. There were a few butterflies who flitted from group to group, flashing their wings, dipping into some of the nectar of gossip, then fluttering off to the next.

Fashion was one of the hot topics. He lost count of the times he overheard a murmured variation of: Bless her heart, she must've been drinking when she bought that dress.

He'd had a taste of it at Roz's holiday party, but this time out he was her escort, and he noted that changed the dynamics considerably.

And he was the new kid in class.

He was given the once-over countless times, asked who he was, what he was, who his people were. Though the manner of interrogation was always charming, he began to feel as if he should have a résumé typed up and ready to hand out.

Ages ran from those who'd certainly danced to the swing music the band played when it was new, to those who'd consider the music retro and hip.

All in all, he decided as he discreetly avoided discussing the more salient details of his work on the Harper family with a curious couple named—he thought—Bing and Babs, it was an interesting change of pace for a guy in a rented tux.

Spotting Josh, he used his son as an excuse to cut the inquisition short. "Excuse me, my son's just come in. I need to speak with him."

Mitch made a beeline through the tuxedos and gowns. "Hey, you clean up good." He gave Josh a one-armed hug around the shoulders, then smiled at the little brunette. "You must be Shelby."

"Yes, sir. You have to be Josh's daddy. He looks just like you."

"That takes care of the intros. Wow." Josh scanned the room. "Some hot-dog stand."

The ballroom was draped with twinkling lights, festooned with spring flowers. Wait staff manned one of three bars or roamed the room with trays of drinks and canapés. Diamonds glittered, emeralds flashed as couples took the dance floor to a hot rendition of Goodman's "Sing, Sing, Sing."

"Yeah, a little *Philadelphia Story*."

"What?"

Mitch sent Josh a pitying glance. "There were movies made before *The Terminator*."

"So you say, Pops. Where's your date?" Josh asked.

"She got swept away. I've been . . . oh, here she comes."

"Sorry, got myself cornered. Hello, Shelby. Don't you look pretty."

"Thanks, Ms. Harper. That's an awesome dress. Josh said you were coming with his father."

"It's nice to meet you at last, Josh. Your father's full of talk about you."

"Same goes. We'll have to find a quiet corner and compare notes."

"I'd love to."

"I see my parents over there." Shelby nodded toward a table. "I'd like to introduce you, Josh, and your daddy. Then I'll have done my duty, and you can dance with me."

"Sounds like a plan. Dad says you're into plants, Ms. Harper."

"Roz, and yes, I am."

"He kills them, you know," he added as they worked their way around the room.

"So I've seen."

"Mostly when they see him they just commit suicide and get it over with."

"Shut up, Josh."

"Just don't want you to pull a fast one on her." He gave his father a lightning grin. "Shelby says you live in that amazing house we passed on the way here."

"Yes, it's been in my family a long time."

"It's totally huge, and great looking." He angled his head enough to send his father a quick, and not-so-private, leer. "Dad's been spending a lot of time there."

"Working." Mitch managed, through years of practice, to give his son a light elbow jab in the ribs.

"I hope you'll come spend some time there yourself, very soon."

Roz paused by the table where Jan and Quill sat talking to other friends. "Hello, everyone." As Roz had expected, Jan stiffened, went a little pale. Deliberately, Roz leaned down, air-kissed Jan's cheek. "Don't y'all look wonderful."

"Mama, Daddy." Shelby angled herself around to make introductions. "This is Joshua Carnegie, and his father Dr. Mitchell Carnegie. My parents, Jan and Quill Forrester, and Mr. and Mrs. Renthow."

Quill, a solidly built man with a glad hand and subtle comb-over, pushed himself to his feet to pump Mitch's, then Josh's hand, then inclined his head to Roz. "Rosalind, how are you doing?"

"I'm doing just fine, Quill. How's business?"

He pokered up, but nodded. "Bumping right along."

"That's good to hear. Jan, I swear, Shelby's grown up to be an absolute beauty. You must be so proud."

"Of course. I don't think I understood you were acquainted with Shelby's escort."

"His father and I are great friends." Beaming, she slid her arm through Mitch's. "In fact, Mitch is researching the Harper family history. He's finding all sorts of secrets and scandals." Playing it up, she gave a little head toss, a little laugh. "We just love our scandals here in Shelby County, don't we?"

"That's where I've heard the name," Renthow spoke up. "I've read one of your books. I'm a bit of an amateur genealogist myself. Fascinating business."

"I think so. In any case, the Harper ancestors led me to Roz." In a smooth move, Mitch lifted her hand, kissed it. "I'll always be grateful."

"You know," Renthow put in, "I've traced my ancestry back to the Fifes in Scotland."

"Really?" Mitch perked up. "A connection to Duncan Phyfe, before he changed the spelling?"

"Yes, exactly." Obviously pleased, Renthow shifted in his chair to angle toward Mitch. "I'd like to put something more detailed together. Maybe you can give me some tips."

"Happy to."

"Why don't we all sit down for a few minutes?" Shelby began. "Then y'all can get acquainted while—"

"We're expecting friends," Jan interrupted. "Our table's full. I'm sure Rosalind and Dr. Carnegie can find another table. And we'll all be more comfortable."

"Mama," the word was a shocked whisper that Roz overrode with an easy smile. "We already have one, thanks. In fact, we're going to steal this handsome young couple here. Shelby, why don't I show you where we're sitting, and Josh and Mitch can get us both a drink?"

Hooking her arm through the girl's, Roz led her away.

"Ms. Harper, I . . . I'm sorry, Ms. Harper, I don't know what's the matter."

"Don't you worry about it. Here we are right here. Let's sit down, and you can tell me how you met that gorgeous young man before they get back. And you call me Roz, now. Why, we're practically on a double date here."

She put the girl at ease, chattering away until their dates returned with drinks and canapés. Only when Josh took Shelby to the dance floor did Roz show any fire.

"She didn't have to embarrass that child the way she

did. If she had a brain in that spiteful head of hers, she'd have known I wouldn't have sat with them. That's a sweet girl. I can only conclude she does not come by it naturally."

"You smoothed it over. One of the reasons I eased out of academia was to rid my life of these little snarling matches and petty grudges. But wherever you go, life's just pocked with them, isn't it?"

"I suppose. I mostly stay out of this arena, too. I have no patience for it. But I feel obliged to make an appearance now and then."

"You're not the only one," he said, and linked his fingers with hers on the table. "How much is it going to upset you to know Bryce Clerk just came in, with that same blonde he was with when he tried to crash your party?"

Her hand stiffened in his, then slowly relaxed. "I had a feeling he'd show. Well, that's all right. I'm just going to slip off to the rest room for a minute, give myself a little talking to, and freshen up. I don't intend to have another public scene, I promise you."

"Wouldn't bother me."

"That's nice to know, in case the talking to doesn't work."

She rose, walked out of the room, and turned down the corridor toward the lounges.

Inside, she freshened her lipstick and began to lecture herself on proper decorum.

You will not lower yourself to his level, no matter what the provocation.

You will not allow that silly girl to draw you into a catfight, even though you'd leave her bleeding on the floor without chipping a nail.

You will not—

Roz broke off the self-lecture when Cissy slipped in.

"I had to use a chainsaw to sever myself from Justine Lukes. Bless her heart, that woman can talk you deaf, dumb, and blind without having a single interesting thing come out of her mouth. I wanted to get over to your table. I swear, Roz, could you look any more glamorous?"

"I think I've reached the top of my game. How'd the visit with the in-laws go?"

"If I'd've cold-cocked her with a cast-iron skillet, she wouldn't have been any more stunned. I tell you, honey, even she couldn't find anything to pick at, though I did have to spill wine on my new shirt as a distraction when she asked me about one of the shrubs. The one with the arching branches and all those white flowers? Smells delicious."

"The drooping leucothoe."

"I suppose. Anyway, I owe you my very life on this one. Isn't that Jan's girl you're with?" Cissy sidled up to the mirror to fuss with her hair.

"Yes, she's with my date's son, as it happens."

"Both of whom I'm just dying to meet. I do love adding to my quota of handsome men. I suppose you saw Bryce slither in."

She shifted her gaze from her own face in the mirror to Roz's. "I broke away from Justine so I wouldn't have to pretend to be civil to him. I don't know if you've heard the latest, but—"

She broke off, zipping her lip when Jan came in with Mandy.

Both women stopped, but while Jan looked ready to move by quickly, Mandy marched forward and jabbed a finger at Roz.

"If you don't stop your harassment, I'm going to get a court order and have you arrested."

Entertained, Roz pulled out her compact. "I don't believe attending a country club event could be considered harassment, but I'll have my lawyer look into it in the morning."

"You know damn well what I mean. You called my spa

pretending to be me and canceled all my treatments. You're calling me day and night and hanging up when I answer."

Casually Roz dusted her nose. "Now why would I do any of those things?"

"You can't stand the fact that I'm going to marry Bryce."

"Has it come to that?" Roz closed her compact again. Part of her—that mean streak—did a little dance of joy. If Bryce had a rich one hooked, he was bound to leave her, and her family, alone. "Well, despite your rude behavior, you have all my sympathy."

"I know what you've been doing to Bryce, too, and to Jan because she's standing as my friend."

"I haven't done anything to any of you." She looked over at Jan. "And couldn't be less interested."

"Someone called one of Quill's top clients, pretending to be me," Jan said stiffly. "A drunken, vicious phone call that cost Quill an important account."

"I'm sorry to hear that, Jan. If you honestly believe I'd do something like that, I won't waste my time, or yours, telling you different. Excuse me."

She heard Cissy's exasperated, "Jan, how can you be so slow-witted" as the door shut behind her.

She started down the corridor only to come up short when she saw Bryce leaning against the wall. In hopes of avoiding a scene, she turned and started in the opposite direction.

"Retreating?" There was a laugh in his voice as he caught up with her. "You surprise me."

She stopped. She hadn't finished that talking to, she thought. In her current mood, it would've been a waste of time. "You never surprise me."

"Oh, I think I do and will again. I wasn't sure you'd be here tonight." His expression turned sly, and smug. "I heard somewhere that you'd dropped your membership."

"That's the thing about rumors, they're so often lies. Tell me, Bryce, what are you getting out of all this effort? Writing letters, making phone calls, risking criminal charges by falsifying credit cards."

"I don't know what you're talking about."

"Nobody here for the moment but you and me." She gestured up and down the empty corridor. "So let's move straight to the bottom line. What do you want?"

"Everything I can get. You'll never prove I made any calls, wrote any letters, used any credit cards. I'm very careful, and very smart."

"Just how long do you think you can keep it up?"

"Until I'm bored. I had a lot of time and effort invested in you, Roz, and you flicked me off. I don't like being flicked off. Now I'm back, and you won't get through a day without remembering that. Of course, if you were to make me a private, monetary offer—"

"That's never going to happen."

"Your choice." He gave a shrug. "There are things I can do to keep chipping away at you. I think you'll come around. I know just how important your reputation, your standing in Shelby County is to you."

"I don't think you do." She kept her eyes on his even when the lounge door opened several feet behind them. "You can't touch me, either, where it counts, no matter how many lies you spread, how many people you convince to believe them. Quill isn't a complete fool, and it won't take long for him to realize you're taking him for a ride. A costly one."

"You give him too much credit. What he is, is greedy. I know how to play on greed."

"You would, having so much of it yourself. Tell me, how much have you taken poor Mandy for so far?"

"Nothing she can't afford to lose. I never took what you couldn't afford, Roz." He skimmed his fingers over her cheek, and she let him. "And I gave you good value for your money. If you hadn't been so narrow-minded, we'd still be together."

"If you hadn't stolen from me, cheated on me with another woman in my own home, we might be—so I'll have to thank you for that. Tell me, Bryce, what is it about Mandy that appeals to you?"

"She's rich, but then so were you. After that, she's young and you weren't, and she's remarkably stupid. You weren't that, either. A little slow, but never stupid."

"Are you really going to marry her?"

"She thinks so." He took out a gold lighter, idly flicking the lid open and closed. "And who knows? Money, youth, malleability. She may just be the perfect wife for me."

"It does seem small of you to be going around, making prank calls, complicating her life—oh, and screwing with Quill and Jan, losing Quill clients. I think you need more constructive work."

"Two birds, one stone. It keeps them sympathetic to me and chips away at you."

"And what do you think will happen when they find out the truth?"

"They won't. As I said before, I'm careful. You'll never prove it."

"I don't think I'll have to. You always did like to boast and brag, Bryce." This time she patted him on the cheek, and thought of it as her kill shot. "Only one of your many failings." She gestured behind him to where Jan and Mandy stood, faces shocked, bodies still as statues.

Beside them, Cissy began to applaud lightly. Roz took a small bow, then walked away.

It was her turn to be surprised when she saw Mitch at the end of the corridor.

"Caught the show," he said casually, and slipped his hand over hers. "I thought the female lead was exceptional."

"Thank you."

"You okay?"

"Probably, but I wouldn't mind some air."

He led her out on the terrace. "Very slick," he said.

"Very impromptu," she corrected, and now, after it was done, her stomach began to jump. "But there he was, just dying to nip at me and posture around, and there they were, those pitiful, annoying women. The bonus being Cissy's presence, too. That little play will be making the rounds, word-for-word, in a New-York minute."

On cue, there was the sound of raised female voices from inside the ballroom, an abrupt crash, hysterical sobbing.

"Want to go in for the second act?"

"No, I don't. I think you should ask me to dance, right here."

"Then I will." He slipped his arms around her. "Beautiful night," he said while the scene played out through the open doors behind them.

"It really is." With a long sigh, she laid her head on his shoulder and felt all those sharp edges smooth out. "Just smell that wisteria. I want to thank you for not riding to my rescue back there."

"I nearly did." He brushed his lips over her hair. "But then, I thought you had it so completely under control, and I was enjoying my front-row seat."

"Lord, listen to that woman wail. Doesn't she have any pride? I'm afraid Bryce had one thing right. She is stupid, bless her heart. Dim as an underground cave on a moonless night."

"Dad!" Josh charged through the doorway. "You've *got* to come see this."

Mitch just continued to circle Roz on the terrace, though the music had long stopped, giving way to shouts and scuffling feet.

"Busy here," he replied.

"But Shelby's dad just clocked this guy. Punched him *out*. And this woman ripped into him—the other guy, not Shelby's dad. It's all about teeth and nails. You're missing it."

"Go on back, you can give us the play-by-play later. I'm going to be busy kissing Roz for a while."

"Man. I've got to come to country clubs more often." With that, Josh rushed back inside.

And Mitch lowered his mouth to Roz's.

SHE NEEDED TO RELAX. SHE'D HANDLED HERSELF, ROZ thought as she replaced her jewelry in its case, and she believed that what she'd been able to do had finally pried the monkey of a vindictive ex-husband off her back.

But the cost had been yet another public scene.

She was tired of them, tired of having her dirty linen flapped around for avid eyes to see. And she'd have to get over it.

She undressed, slipped into her warm flannel robe.

She was glad they'd been able to leave the club early. Hardly any reason to stay, she thought with a sharp smile. The place had been a glorious mess of overturned tables, spilled food and drink, horrified guests, and scrambling security.

And would be the talk of the gossip circuit for weeks, as she would be.

That was fine, that was expected, she told herself as she ran a warm bath. She'd ride it out, then things would get back to as close to normal as they ever did.

She poured in an extra dose of bubble bath, a lovely indulgence for a midnight soak. When she was done, all relaxed and pink and fragrant, she might just wander down to the library and crook a finger at Mitch.

Bless him for understanding she needed a little alone time. With a sigh, she slid into the tub, right down to the tips of her ears. A man who recognized a woman's moods, and accepted them, was a rare find.

John had, she remembered. Most of the time. They'd been so beautifully in tune, moving in tandem to build a family, enjoying their present and planning their future. Losing him had been like losing an arm.

Still, she'd coped, and damn well if she said so herself. She'd raised sons she, and John, could be proud of, kept a secure home, honored her traditions, built her own business. Not bad for a widow woman.

She could laugh at that, but the tension gathered at the base of her neck as she moved to the next phase. Bryce. A foolish, impulsive mistake. And that was all right, everyone was entitled to a few. But this one had done such damage, caused such upheaval. And public speculation and gossip, which in some ways was a bigger score to her pride.

He'd made her doubt herself so often during their marriage, where she'd always been so confident, so sure. But he had an eroding way about him, slick and sly with all those insistent little rubs under the charm.

It was a lowering thing to admit she'd been stupid—and over a man.

But she'd cooked him good and proper tonight, and that made up for a lot of irritation, embarrassment, and pain. He'd served himself up on a goddamn platter, she thought, and she'd stuck the fork in. He was done.

So good for her. Woo-hoo.

Now maybe it was time for yet another phase in the Life of Rosalind. Was she ready for that? Ready to take that big, scary step toward a man who loved her just as she was? Nearly fifty, and thinking about love and marriage—for the *third* time. Was that just insane?

Idly she played her toes through the trickle of hot water she'd left running to keep the bath warm.

Or was it a gift, already wrapped in pretty paper, tied with a big fat bow, and tossed in her lap?

She was in love, she thought, her lips curving as she let the tension drain away, closed her eyes. In love with an interesting, attractive, considerate man. A good man. With enough flaws and quirks to keep him from being boring.

She sighed, as contentment began to settle over her. And a thin gray mist crawled along the tiles.

And the sex? Oh, thank God for the sex, she thought with a lithe stretch and a purr in her throat. Hot and sweet, tender and exciting. Stimulating. Lord, that man was stimulating. Her body felt *juiced* again.

Maybe, just maybe they could have a life together. Maybe love didn't have to come at convenient and sensible times. And maybe the third time was the charm. It was something worth considering, very, very seriously.

Marriage. She drifted, drowsy now, trailing her fingers through the frothy water while the mist thickened, rising off the floor like a flood.

It came down to making an intimate promise to someone you not only loved, but trusted. She could trust Mitch. She could believe in him.

Would her sons think she'd lost her mind? They might, but it was her life, after all.

She'd enjoy being married—probably. Having someone else's clothes in the closet, someone else's books on the shelf. The man wasn't what you'd call tidy, but she could deal with that if . . .

The foamy water went ice cold. On a gasp, Roz shoved up from her lounging position, instinctively clutching her arms. Her eyes popped wide when she saw the room was full of fog, so dense she couldn't see the walls, the door.

Not steam, she realized, but a kind of ugly gray mist, as cold as the water and thick as iced soup.

Even as she started to stand, to climb out, she was dragged under.

With a leap in the belly, shock came first, before the fear. The utter shock of the frigid water, the sensation of being yanked down, held under, froze her before she began to fight. Choking, kicking, she strained to surface as the cold stiffened her limbs. She could *feel* hands clamped on her head, then nails digging into her shoulders, but through the film of the water, she saw nothing but floating bubbles and swirling mists.

Stop! Her mind screamed it. Using all her strength, she braced hands and feet and pushed up in one desperate lunge. Her head came up, broke through into the icy fog. She took one frantic gulp of air before the steely pressure on her shoulders shoved her under again.

Water sloshed over the rim of the tub as she struggled, burned her eyes and throat. She could hear her own muffled screams, as she flailed against what she couldn't see. Her elbow slammed against the side of the tub, shooting pain through terror.

For your own good. For your own good. You have to learn!

The voice was a hiss in her ear, a hiss that cut through the frantic beat of blood. Now she saw it, the face swimming above her, over the churning water, its lips peeled back on a grimace of fury. She saw the madness in Amelia's eyes.

He's no different. They all lie! Didn't I tell you? Why don't you listen? Make you listen, make you stop. Tainted blood. His blood's in you. Ruined you after all.

She was dying. Her lungs were screaming, her heart galloping as she fought wildly to find purchase, to find *air*. Something was going to burst inside her, and she'd die in the cold, scented water. But not willingly, not easily. She pounded out, with her hands, her feet. And with her mind.

Let go of me. Let go! I can't listen if I'm dead. You're killing me. If I die, you'll stay lost. If I die, you'll stay trapped. Murderer. Trapped in Hell.

She gathered herself again, fueled her straining muscles with the strength of survival, and rocketed up.

Water fumed, sliced through the mists to splash walls and floor in a small, violent tidal wave. Gripping the edge of the tub, she leaned over, choking, coughing out what she'd swallowed. Her stomach heaved, but she locked her arms around the rim. She wouldn't be pulled under again.

"Keep your hands off me, you bitch."

Wheezing, she crawled out of the tub and dropped weakly onto the soaked mat. As shudders racked her, she curled into a ball until she could find her breath. Her ears rang, and her heart thudded so brutally she wondered if she'd have bruised ribs to add to the rest.

She heard weeping.

"Your tears don't mean a lot to me at the moment." Not trusting herself to stand, she scooted over the floor until she could reach for a towel with a shaking hand, and pull it around her for warmth.

"I've lived with you all my life. I've tried to help you. And you try to drown me? In my own tub? I warned you I'd find a way to remove you from this house."

The words didn't come out nearly as strong or angry as she wanted. It was hard to sound in charge when her teeth were chattering, as much with fear as cold.

She jolted when the robe she'd hung on the back of the door drifted down and settled over her shoulders. "Why, thank you," Roz said, and did manage sarcasm well enough. "How considerate of you, after trying to kill me, to see that I don't catch cold. I've had about enough."

She shoved her arms in the robe and drew it close as she got shakily to her feet.

Then she saw Amelia, through the thinning mists. Not

the madwoman with crazed eyes and wild hair who'd loomed over her while she'd fought for her life, but a shattered woman with tears on her cheeks, and her hands clasped as if in prayer.

As she faded away, as the mists melted, another message appeared on the mirror. It said simply:

Forgive me.

"YOU COULD'VE BEEN KILLED."

Mitch paced the bedroom, anger all but sparking off his fingertips.

She'd gone down to make a pot of hot coffee, and to ask him to come upstairs. She'd wanted to be assured they weren't overheard when she told him.

"I wasn't. Happily." The coffee was helping, but she was still chilled, and willing to bundle under a thick cashmere throw.

"You might've died, while I was downstairs putzing around with books and files. You were up here, fighting for your life, and I—"

"Stop." But she said it gently. A woman who'd lived with men, raised sons, understood ego. "What happened, could have happened, didn't happen—none of it was your fault. Or mine, for that matter. The fault lies in what is no doubt an emotionally disturbed ghost. And I don't care how ridiculous that sounds."

"Rosalind." He stopped in front of her, knelt down, rubbed his hands over hers. They felt strong on hers, and warm. They felt solid. "I know how you feel about this house, but—"

"You're going to say I should move out, temporarily. And there's some good, solid sense in that, Mitch. But I won't. You can say it's because I'm stubborn, because I'm too damn hardheaded."

"And I will."

"But," she said, "besides that, and the fact I won't be chased away from what's mine, the problem won't be solved by moving out. My son lives on this property, as do others I care about very much. My business is on this property. Do I tell everyone to find other accommodations? Do I shut down my business, risk losing everything? Or do I stick it out, and work to find the answers?"

"She's escalating. Roz, for years she did little more than sing to children, an odd but relatively charming addition to the household. A little mischief now and then, but nothing dangerous. In the past year she's become increasingly unstable, increasingly violent."

"Yes, she has." Her fingers linked with his, held firm. "And you know what that tells me? It tells me we must be getting close to something. That maybe because we are, she's more impatient, more erratic. Less controlled. What we're doing matters to her. Just as what I think and feel matters, whether she approves or not."

"Meaning?"

He probably wouldn't take it well, she considered. But it had to be said. She'd promised him honesty, and took promises seriously. "I was thinking of you. Of us. When I finished sulking about tonight, and started to relax, I was thinking of the way I feel about you, and the way you feel about me."

"She tried to kill you because we love each other." His face stone hard when he pushed to his feet. "I'm the one who needs to leave, to stay away from here, and you, until we finish this."

"Is that how you deal with bullies? You give them their way?"

He'd started to pace again, but whipped around now, fury ripe in his eyes. "We're not talking about some asshole trying to steal lunch money on the playground. We're talking about your safety. Your goddamn life!"

"I won't give in to her. That's how I stay alive. That's how I stay in charge. You think I'm not furious, not frightened? You're wrong."

"I notice fury comes first."

"Because it's positive—at least I've always felt a good, healthy mad's more constructive than fear. That's what I saw in her, Mitch, at the end."

Roz tossed the throw aside and rose to go to him. "She was afraid, shocked and afraid and sorry—pitifully. You said once she didn't want to hurt me, and I think it's true."

"I also said she could, and I've been proven right." He took her face in his hands, then slid them down to her shoulders. "I don't know how to protect you. But I know I can't lose you."

"I'll be less afraid if you're with me."

He cocked his head, very nearly smiled. "That's very tricky."

"It is, isn't it?" She wrapped her arms around him, settled in when his came around her. "It also happens to be true. She asked me to forgive her. I don't know that I can, or will, but I need the answers. I need you to help me find them. And damn it, Mitch, I just need you—and that's hard for me to say."

"I hope it gets easier, because I like hearing it. We'll keep things as they are for now."

"Thank you. When I got out of there." She shifted her gaze toward the bathroom. "When I got out and pulled it together enough to think, I was so relieved you were downstairs. That I could tell you. That I wouldn't be alone tonight."

"Alone isn't even an option. Now." He scooped her off her feet. "You're getting into bed, bundling up."

"And you'll be . . ."

"Taking a closer look at the scene of the crime before I mop it up."

"I can take care of that, the mopping up."

"No." He tucked her in, firmly. "Give a little, get a little, Roz. Do what you're told, and stay in bed like a good girl. You've had a long and interesting day."

"Haven't I just?" And it felt wonderful to snuggle in the bed, knowing there was someone to look after some of the details. "I'm not sure what I'll have to give, but I'm going to ask you for a little something more."

"You want some soup? Something hot? Tea? Tea'd be better than coffee."

Look at you, she thought, Dr. Studly, with your black tie loose, and your tux shirt rolled up to the elbows, offering to make me soup. She reached for his hand as he sat on the side of the bed.

"No, but thanks. I'm going to ask you to keep what happened here between us for now."

"Roz, how does your mind work?" Frustration was so clear in his voice, on his face, she nearly smiled. "You were almost drowned in the tub by our resident ghost, and you don't want to mention it?"

"It's not that. We'll mention it, document it, go into great detail and discussion if need be. I just want to wait until after Stella's wedding. I just want a little calm. When Harper hears about this . . . Well, he's not going to take it well."

"Let me just say a big fat: Duh."

She laughed. "Everyone'll be upset, distracted, worried. And what good will it do? It happened, it's over. There are so many other things to deal with right now. I'm already going to be dealing with the fallout from what happened at the club. I can promise you word will be out, and it'll be a topic at my breakfast table tomorrow."

"And that bothers you."

"Actually, I think I'll enjoy it. I'm just small enough to bask in it. So let's leave this between us, until Stella's had her wedding. After that, we'll tell everyone, and deal with the fallout. But for the time being, we could use some undiluted happiness around here."

"Okay. I don't see that it'll matter."

"I appreciate it. I'm not so mad and scared now," she added, and slid down on the pillow. "I stopped her. I fought her off. I could do it again. That has to count for something."

Mitch leaned over to press his lips to her cheek. "Counts for a hell of a lot with me."

NINETEEN

WITH THE BABY ON HER HIP, HAYLEY BOLTED INTO THE kitchen the next morning. Her hair was bunched in a short tail at the back of her head, her eyes were huge, and she'd misbuttoned her pajama top.

"I just talked to Lily's sitter," she announced to the room at large, "and her aunt belongs to the country club. She says Roz was in a fight last night."

"I certainly was not." Life could be heartwarmingly predictable, Roz thought and continued to spread jam thinly on a triangle of toast.

"What kinda fight?" Gavin wanted to know. "A punching fight?"

"I was not in a punching fight." Roz handed him the toast. "People exaggerate things, little man. It's the way of the world."

"Did you kick somebody in the face?"

Roz raised her eyebrows at Luke. "Of course not. You might say, metaphorically, I kicked somebody in the ass."

"What's met . . ."

"A metaphor's a fancy way of saying something's like something else. I could say I'm a cat full of canary this morning." She winked at Luke. "And that would mean I'm feeling very satisfied and smug. But I never laid a hand on him."

"Who?" Stella demanded.

"Bryce Clerk." The answer came from David as he poured more coffee. "My intelligence network is far-flung and faster than the speed of light. I heard about it last night, before eleven o'clock, Central Standard Time."

"And didn't tell anybody?" Hayley glowered at him as she strapped Lily in her high chair.

"Actually, I was waiting for all to be present and accounted for before I brought it up. Ah, here comes Harper now. I told him his presence was required at breakfast this morning."

"Really, David, it's no big deal, and I need to get ready for work."

"On the contrary." Shaking his head over his coffee, Mitch looked around the table. "It was extraordinary. The woman," he said with a long look at Roz, "is extraordinary."

Under the table she took his hand, gave it a warm squeeze. A silent thanks for letting this play out without any of last night's horror marring the mood.

"What's up?" Harper demanded. "We're having omelettes? How come we're having omelettes?"

"Because your mama likes them, and she needs to recharge her energies after hauling out her can of Whoop Ass last night."

"Don't be ridiculous," Roz replied, even as a chuckle tickled the back of her throat.

"What about last night? What Whoop Ass?"

"See what you miss when you don't go to the club?" David told Harper.

"If somebody doesn't fill in the blanks soon, I'm going

to go crazy." Hayley gave Lily a sip-cup of juice and plopped down. "Spill, every deet."

"There's not that much to tell," Roz began.

"I'll tell it." Mitch returned Roz's bland look equably. "She'll leave stuff out. Now, some of this I pried out of her, because I wasn't there at the time, and some of the other I got from my son. But I'll tell it all in one piece—more impact."

He started with the brief stop by the Forresters' table, then moved to the bathroom scene, then dramatized the altercation between Roz and Bryce outside the lounge area.

"Oh, my God, they walked out while you were talking to that . . ." Hayley cleared her throat, amended her first thought as she remembered the children. "Man."

"His back was to them," Mitch filled in. "It was perfectly staged."

Hayley fed Lily bits of egg and gaped at Roz. "It's so cool. Like, I don't know, a sting."

"The timing was exquisite," Mitch agreed. "You should've seen your mother, Harper, cool and slick as an iceberg, and just as dangerous."

"This kitchen is full of metaphors this morning," Roz commented. "Isn't anyone going to work?"

"Seen her like that." Harper scooped up some omelette. "Scary."

"It happened I was in a position to see the reaction of the ladies behind them," Mitch said, "and it was beautiful. He's mouthing off, bragging about how he can keep screwing around, the phone calls, the credit cards, and so on, and nobody'll pin him. He's insulting Quill, calling Mandy stupid. Utterly full of himself, and Roz just stands there—he doesn't even know she's just brought the ax down on his neck. She doesn't flick an eyelash, just keeps prompting him to say more and more until the son of a . . ." He remembered the kids. ". . . gun is buried in his own words.

Then, then, when it's done, she just waves a hand, so he turns and sees they're behind him. And she strolls away. It was beautiful."

"I hope they fell on him like dogs," Stella said under her breath.

"Close enough. Apparently, he tried to talk his way out of it, convince them that it was all a mistake, but the blonde, she's hysterical. Screaming, crying, slapping at him. The other goes straight to her husband, fills him in, so he knows it was Bryce's vindictiveness that lost him one of his top clients. He loses it—according to my son—and bulls his way to Bryce and punches him. People are jumping up, glasses are crashing, the blonde jumps on Clerk and starts biting and scratching."

"Holy cow," Gavin whispered, awed.

"They had to drag her off, and while they were, Quill took another shot, and they had to drag *him* off."

"I wish I'd seen that." Harper rose to get his choice of morning caffeine and came back to the table with a can of Coke. "I really do."

"People were running for cover, or pushing to get closer to the action," Mitch continued. "Slipping on olives from martinis, sliding around in salmon mousse or whatever, knocking over tables. They were at the point of calling the cops when in-house security broke it up."

"Where were you?" Hayley wondered.

"I was on the terrace making out with Roz. Dancing with Roz," he corrected with a wink. "We had a decent view through the doors and windows."

"It'll be the talk of the town for some time," Roz concluded. "As far as I'm concerned, all of them got just what they deserved. A bellyful of embarrassment. Now, I don't know about the rest of you, but I've got to get to work."

"Wait, wait, what about Bryce?" Hayley forked up some eggs for herself. "You can't leave us hanging."

"I couldn't say, but I suspect he'll scamper out of Shelby County with his tail between his legs. I don't think he'll be around anymore."

"That's it?" Hayley wondered. "You're not going to—" She broke off, wiped Lily's face. "That's good. It's good he's gone."

Roz ruffled both boys' hair, then got up to lay a kiss on the top of Lily's head. "I'll be giving the police my statement regarding possible charges for fraud this afternoon, as will Mitch, who heard everything Bryce said. I imagine they'll speak with the others who heard him flapping. Then we'll see what happens next."

"Even better," Hayley said with a smile. "Even much better."

"I don't punch or kick people in the face, at least not to date. But I don't get pushed around for long, either."

She walked out, pleased, even comforted, that the day had begun with laughter instead of worry.

ROZ STOOD ON THE LITTLE SLOPE AT THE EDGE OF HER woods and studied the spread and form of In the Garden. There were wonderful blocks of color, tender spring green, bold pinks, exotic blues, cheery yellows, and hot, hot reds.

The old, time-faded brown tables were full of those colors, displaying bedding plants in flats and pots. The ground itself erupted with it, blooming in an enthusiastic celebration of the season. The buildings looked fresh and welcoming, the greenhouses industrious. There were planters exploding with color and shape, hanging baskets dripping with them.

From this vantage she could see slices of the shrub area, and the ornamental trees, and all the way back to the field-grown, with its ruler-straight rows and muscular machines.

Everywhere she looked there were people, customers

and staff, bustling or browsing. Red wagons chugged along like little trains carrying their hopeful cargo. Flatbeds bumped over the gravel paths, and out to the parking area where their loads could be transferred into cars and trucks.

She could see the mountains of mulch, loose and bagged, the towers of pavers, the rails of landscape timbers.

Busy, busy, she thought, but with the charm she'd always envisioned in homey touches. The arbor already twined with morning glory vines, the curved bench strategically placed by a bubbling garden fountain, the flashy red of a hummingbird feeder dangling from a branch, the music of a wind chime circling gently in the breeze.

She should be down there, of course, doing some bustling herself, babying her stock, calculating inventory. Having a manager—even an exceptional one like Stella—didn't mean she shouldn't have her finger on every pulse.

But she'd wanted the air, the movement of it around her after hours in the denseness of the propagation house. And she wanted this view of what she'd built. What she'd worked for, gambled on.

Today, under a sky so freshly blue it might have been painted on glass, it was beautiful. And every hour she'd spent over all these years sweating, worrying, calculating, struggling was worth it.

It was solid and successful, and very much the sprawling garden she'd wanted to create. A business, yes, a business first and foremost, but a lovely one. One that reflected her style, her vision, her legacy.

If some insisted on seeing it as her hobby, let them. If some, even most, thought of her as the woman who'd glided around the country club in a gold gown and diamonds, that was fine. She didn't mind slipping on the glamour now and again. In fact, she could enjoy it.

But the truth of her, the core of her, was standing here,

wearing ancient jeans and a faded sweatshirt, a ballcap over her hair and scarred boots on her feet.

The truth of her was a working woman with bills to pay, a business to run, and a home to maintain. It was that woman she was proud of when she took the time to be proud. The Rosalind Harper of the country club and society set was a duty to her name. This, all the rest, was life.

She took a breath, braced herself, and deliberately pushed her mind in a specific direction. She would see what happened, and how both she and Amelia would deal with it.

So she thought: If this was life, hers to live, why couldn't she gamble yet again? Expand that life by taking into it, fully, the man who excited and comforted her, who intrigued and amused her?

The man who had somehow strolled through the maze that grief and work and duty and pride had built around her heart.

The man she loved.

She could live her life alone if need be, but what did it prove? That she was self-sufficient, independent, strong, and able. She knew those things, had been those things—and would always be those things.

And she could be courageous, too.

Didn't it take courage, wasn't it harder to blend one life with another, to share and to cope, to compromise than to live that life alone? It was work to live with a man, to wake up every day prepared to deal with routine, and to be open to surprises.

She'd never shied away from work.

Marriage was a different kettle at this stage of life. There would be no babies made between them. But they could share grandchildren one day. They wouldn't grow up together, but could grow old together.

They could be happy.

They always lie. They're never true.

Roz stood in the same spot, on a gentle rise at the edge of the woods. But In the Garden was gone. There were fields, stark with winter, barren trees, and the feel of ice on the air.

"Not all men," Roz said quietly. "Not always."

I've known more than you.

She walked across the fields, insubstantial as the mist that began to spread, a shallow sea, over the bare, black ground. Her white gown was filthy, as were her naked feet. Her hair was a tangle of oily gold around a face bright with madness.

Fear blew through Roz like a sudden, vicious storm. But she planted her feet. She'd ride it out.

The light had gone out of the day. Heavy clouds rolled over the sky, smothering the blue with black, a black tinged with violent green.

"I've lived longer than you," Roz said, and though she couldn't stop the shudder as Amelia approached, she stood her ground.

And learned so little. You have all you need. A home, children, work that satisfies you. What do you need with a man?

"Love matters."

There was a laugh, a wet chortle that screamed across Roz's nerves. *Love is the biggest lie. He will fuck you, and use you, and cheat and lie. He will give you pain until you are hollow and empty, until you are dried up and ugly. And dead.*

Pity stirred under the fear. "Who betrayed you? Who brought you to this?"

All. They're all the same. They're the whores, though they label us so. Didn't they come to me, ram their cocks into me, while their wives slept alone in their saintly beds?

"Did they force you? Did—"

Then they take what's yours. What was mine!

She slammed both fists into her belly, and the force of the rage, the grief, and the fury knocked Roz back two full steps.

Here was the storm, spewing out of the sky, bursting out of the ground, swirling though the fog and into the filthy air. It clogged Roz's lungs as if she were breathing mud.

She heard the crazed screams through it.

Kill them all! Kill them all in their sleep. Hack them to bits, bathe in their blood. Take back what's mine. Damn them, damn them all to hell!

"They're gone. They're dust." Roz tried to shout, but could barely choke out the words. "Am I what's left?"

The storm stopped as abruptly as it began, and the Amelia who stood in the calm was one who sang lullabies to children. Sad and pale in her gray dress.

You're mine. My blood. She held out a hand, and red welled in the palm. *My bone. Out of my womb, out of my heart. Stolen, ripped away. Find me. I'm so lost.*

Then Roz was alone, standing on the springy grass at the edge of the woods with what she'd built spread out below her.

SHE WENT BACK TO WORK BECAUSE WORK STEADIED her. The only way she could wrap her mind around what happened at the edge of the woods was to do something familiar, something that kept her hands occupied while her brain sorted through the wonder of it.

She kept to herself because solitude soothed her.

Through the afternoon she divided more stock plants, rooted cuttings. Watered, fed, labeled.

When she was done, she walked home through the woods and raided her personal greenhouse. She planted cannas in a spot she wanted to dramatize, larkspur and primroses where she wanted more charm. In the shade, she added some ladybells and cranesbill for serenity.

Her serenity, she thought, could always be found here, in the gardens, in the soil, in the shadow of Harper House. Under that fresh blue sky she knelt on the ground, and studied what was hers.

So lovely with its soft yellow stone, its sparkling glass, its bridal white trim.

What secrets were trapped in those rooms, in those walls? What was buried in this soil she worked, season after season, with her own hands?

She had grown up here, as her father had, and his father, and those who'd come before. Generation after generation of shared blood and history. She had raised her children here, and had worked to preserve this legacy so that the children of her children would call this home.

Whatever had been done to pass all of this to her, she would have to know. And then accept.

Settled again, she replaced her tools, then went into the house to shower off the day.

She found Mitch working in the library.

"Sorry to interrupt. There's something I need to talk to you about."

"Good, I need to talk to you, too." He swiveled away from his laptop, found a file in the piles on the desk.

"You go first," she told him.

"Hmm? Oh, fine." He scooped a hand through his hair, took off his glasses. Gestures she knew now meant he was organizing his thoughts.

"I've done just about all I can do here," he began. "I could spend months more on your family history, filling in details, moving back generations. In fact, I plan to do just that. But regarding the purpose for which you hired me, I'm at an impasse. She wasn't family, Roz. Not a Harper," he amended. "Not by birth, not through marriage. Absolutely none of the data—names, dates, births, marriages, deaths—nothing I have places a woman named Amelia in this house, or in the Harper family. No woman of her approximate age died in this house during the time period we've pinpointed."

"I see." She sat, wishing vaguely she'd thought to get coffee.

"Now, if Stella is mistaken regarding the name—"

"She isn't." Roz shook her head. "It's Amelia."

"I agree. But there's no Amelia Harper, by birth, by marriage, in any record. Oddly enough, considering the length of time this house has stood here, there's no record of any female in her twenties or thirties who died here. In the house. Older or younger, yes, a few."

He set the file on top of a pile. "Ah, one of the most entertaining deaths to occur here was back in 1859, one of your male ancestors, a Beauregard Harper, who broke his neck, and several other bones, falling off the second floor terrace. From the letters I've read describing the event, Beau was up there with a woman not his wife engaged in a sexual romp that got a little overenthusiastic. He went over the rail, taking his date with him. He was dead when members of the household reached him, but being a portly fellow, he broke the fall of the female houseguest, who landed on top of him and only suffered a broken leg."

"And terminal embarrassment, I imagine."

"Must have. I have the names of the women, the Harper women, who died here listed for you. I have some records on female servants who died here, but none fit the parameters. I got some information from the Chicago lawyer I told you about."

He began to dig for another file. "The descendant of the housekeeper during Reginald Harper's time. She actually discovered she had three ancestors who worked here—the housekeeper, the housekeeper's uncle who was a groundsman, and a young cousin who served as a kitchen maid. From this, I've been able to get you a detailed history of that family as well. While none of it applies, I thought you'd like to have it."

"Yes, I would."

"The lawyer's still looking for data when she has time, she's entrenched now. We could get lucky."

"You've done considerable work."

"You'll be able to look at the charts and locate your great-great-uncle's second cousin on his mother's side, and get a good sense of his life. But that doesn't help you."

"You're wrong." She studied the mountain of files, and the board, crowded with papers and photos and handwritten charts behind Mitch. "It does help me. It's something I should have seen to a long time ago. I should have known about the unfortunate and adulterous Beau, and the saloon-owning Lucybelle, and all the others you've brought to life for me."

She rose to go to the board and study the faces, the names. Some were as familiar as her own, and others had been virtual strangers to her.

"My father, I see now, was more interested in the present than the past. And my grandfather died while I was so young, I don't remember having him tell me family stories. Most of what I got was from my grandmother, who wasn't a Harper by birth, or from older cousins. I'd go through the old papers now and again, always meaning to make time to do more, read more. But I didn't."

She stepped back from the board. "Family history, everyone who came before matters, and until recently I haven't given them enough respect."

"I agree with the first part, but not the second. This house shows the great respect you have for your family. Essentially, what I'm telling you is I can't find her for you. I believe, from what I've observed, what I feel, Amelia is your ancestor. But she's not your family. I won't find her name in family documents. And I don't believe she was a servant here."

"You don't."

"Consider the time, the era, the societal mores. As a servant, it's certainly possible that she was impregnated by a member of the family, but it's doubtful she would have been permitted to remain on staff, to remain in the house during her pregnancy. She would've been sent away, given monetary compensation—maybe. But it doesn't hold for me."

After one last glance at the board, she walked back to her chair and sat. "Why not?"

"Reginald was head of the house. All the information I have on him indicates he was excessively proud, very aware of what we could say was his lofty standing in this area. Politics, business, society. To be frank, Roz, I don't see him banging the parlor maid. He'd have been more selective. Certainly, said banging could have been done by a relative, an uncle, a brother-in-law, a cousin. But my gut tells me the connection with Amelia's tighter than that."

"Which leaves?"

"A lover. A woman not his wife, but who suited his needs. A mistress."

She was silent for a long moment. "You know what I find interesting, Mitchell? That we've come, from different directions, to the same point. You've gone through so many reams of documents that it gives me a headache just to think of them. Phone calls, computer searches, courthouse searches. Graphs and charts and Christ only knows. And by doing all that you've not only given me a picture of my family I've never looked at, people whose names I didn't know, but who are, in a very real sense, responsible for my life. But you've eliminated dozens of possibilities, dozens of perhapses as to who this poor woman was, so that we can whittle it down to the right answer. Do you think, when we do, she'll have peace?"

"I don't know the answer to that. Why are you so sad? It rips me to see you so sad."

"I'm not entirely sure. This is what happened today," she said, and told him.

"I was so afraid." She took a long breath. "I was afraid the night she locked us out of the children's room, and when you and I came in from the terrace and she had that fit of temper, tossing things around. I was afraid that night in the tub, when she held me under. I thought I wouldn't be that afraid again. But today, today when I stood there watching her walk toward me over the field, through thc fog, I was petrified. I saw her face, the madness in it, a kind of insane purpose. The sort, I think now, that overcomes even death."

She gave herself a little shake. "I know how that sounds, but I think that's what she's done, somehow. She's overcome death with madness, and she can't break free."

"She didn't touch you this time. She didn't hurt you?"

Roz shook her head. "Not even at the peak of her rage. I couldn't breathe—felt like I was drawing in dirt, but part of that might've been sheer panic on my part. She spoke of killing, bathing in blood. There's never been any talk of murder in this house, but I wonder—oh, God, could they have killed her? One of my family?"

"She was the one talking of doing murder," he reminded her, "not of being murdered."

"True, but you can't trust a crazy woman to have all the facts straight. She said I was her blood. Whether it's true or not, she believes it." She took a deep breath. "So do you."

He got up from the desk to come around to her. Taking her hands, he drew her out of the chair and into his arms. "What do you believe?"

Comfort, she thought as she rested her head on his shoulder. There could be such comfort in a man if you allowed yourself to take it. "She has my father's eyes. I saw it at the end today. I've never seen it before, maybe never let myself. Did he take her child, Mitch, my great-grandfather? Could he have been so cold?"

"If all this is fact, she could have given the baby up. They might have had an arrangement, and she came to regret it. There are still a lot of possibilities."

"I want to know the truth now. Have to know it, whatever it takes."

She drew back, managed a smile. "Just how the hell do we go about finding a woman who may have been my great-grandfather's lover?"

"We have a first name, an approximate age, and we assume she lived in the Memphis area. We start with that."

"Is that natural optimism, or are you trying to smooth my feathers?"

"Some of both."

"All right, then. I'm going to go pour myself a glass of wine. Do you want anything?"

"I could use about a gallon of water to offset the five gallons of coffee I'd downed today. I'll come with you." He draped an arm around her shoulders as they walked to the kitchen.

"I might have to put this aside until after Stella and Logan's wedding. It's snuck right up on me. Seems to me, however demanding the dead may be, the living ought to have priority." She got out a bottle of water and a fresh lemon. "I can't believe those boys aren't going to be part of the household in a few more days."

She poured and sliced, then offered him the glass.

"Thanks. I think they'll be around enough you'll feel like they are."

"I like to think." She poured her wine, but the phone rang before she took the first sip. "Where is David anyway?" she asked, and answered herself.

She listened for a moment, then smiled slowly at Mitch. "Hello, Jane," she said and lifted her wine in a toast.

"THIS IS SO EXCITING. IT'S LIKE A SPY THRILLER OR something." Hayley bounced on her toes as she, Roz, and Stella rode the elevator up to Clarise Harper's apartment. "I mean, we spend the morning getting manicures and pedicures, and the afternoon sneaking around to hunt up secret documents. It's totally glamorous."

"Say that later if we're arrested and spending the night in jail with Big Bertha," Stella suggested. "If Logan has to marry me through jailhouse bars tomorrow, I'm going to be royally pissed."

"I told you not to come," Roz reminded her.

"And miss this?" After a bracing breath, Stella stepped off the elevator. "I may be fussy, but I'm no coward. Besides, Hayley has a point. It is exciting."

"Going into a crabby old woman's overfurnished apartment and taking away what's rightfully mine—along with a scared little rabbit—doesn't strike me as exciting. Jane could have gotten them out herself, saved us the trip. There's enough to do with the wedding tomorrow."

"I know, and I appreciate, so much, you giving us the day off so we could primp." On impulse, Stella kissed Roz's cheek. "We'll work twice as hard after the wedding to make up for it."

"You might just have to. Now just pray the old ghoul is out getting her hair permed, as advertised, or this will be ugly."

"Don't you sort of hope it is?" Hayley began, but the door creaked open. Jane peeked out through the crack.

"I . . . I didn't expect anyone but you, Cousin Rosalind. I don't know if we should—"

"They work for me. They're friends." With no patience

for dithering or ado, Roz nudged the door open, stepped inside. "Jane, this is Stella and Hayley. Jane, did you pack all your things?"

"Yes, there isn't much. But I've been thinking, she's going to be so upset when she gets home and finds me gone. I don't know if I should—"

"This place is as horrible as ever," Roz observed. "Positively reeks of lavender. How do you stand it? That's one of our Dresden shepherdesses there, and that Meissan cat, and . . . screw it. Where are the diaries?"

"I didn't get them out. I didn't feel right—"

"Fine. Give me the key, show me where, and I'll get them. Let's not waste time, Jane," Roz added when the girl simply stood biting her bottom lip. "You have a new apartment waiting, a new job starting bright and early Monday morning. You can take them or leave them, your choice. But I'm not leaving this lavender-stinking apartment without what's mine by right. So you can give me the key, or I'll just start tossing things around until I find what I'm after."

"Oh, God. I feel sick." Jane dug into her pocket, pulled out an ornate brass key. "The desk in her room, top drawer." Pale as glass, she gestured vaguely. "I'm dizzy."

"Snap out of it," Roz suggested. "Stella, why don't you help Jane get her things?"

"Sure. Come on, Jane."

Trusting Stella to deal with the situation, Roz turned to Hayley. "Watch the door," she ordered.

"Oh, boy, hot damn. Lookout man."

Despite herself, Roz chuckled all the way into Clarise's bedroom. There was more lavender here, with an undertone of violets. The bed had a padded headboard of gold tufted silk, with an antique quilt Roz knew damn well had come out of Harper House. As had the occasional table by the window, and the art nouveau lamp.

"Pilfering old bitch," Roz grumbled and went directly to the desk. She turned the key, and couldn't quite hold back the gasp when she saw the stacks of old leather-bound journals.

"This is going to be a kick right in your bony ass," she decided and, opening the satchel she carried over her shoulder, carefully slid the books inside.

To make certain she had them all, she opened the rest of the drawers, riffled without qualm through the nightstands, the bureau, the chest of drawers.

Though she felt silly, she wiped off everything she'd touched. She wouldn't put it past Clarise to call the cops and claim burglary. Then she left the key, plainly in sight, on top of the desk.

"Stella took her down," Hayley announced when Roz stepped out. "She was shaking so hard we thought she might have like a seizure unless she got out of here. Roz, the poor thing only had one suitcase. She got everything she owned into one suitcase."

"She's young. She'll have plenty of time to get more. Did you touch anything in here?"

"No. I thought, you know, fingerprints."

"Smart girl. Let's go."

"You got them?"

Roz patted the satchel. "Easy as taking candy from a baby, which Clarise has been known to do."

It wasn't until they'd settled Jane into her apartment and were well on the way home that Roz noticed Hayley was uncharacteristically silent.

"Don't tell me you're having second thoughts, guilty qualms, whatever."

"What? Oh, no. No. Those journals are yours. If it'd been me, I'd have taken the other things that belonged to Harper House, too. I was thinking about Jane. I know she's younger than me, but not all that much. And she seems so,

I don't know, fragile and scared about everything. Still, she did a brave thing, I guess."

"She didn't have what you had," Roz said. "Your gumption, for one, and a lot of that's just the luck of the draw. But she didn't have a father like yours. One who loved her and taught her, and gave her a secure and happy home. She doesn't feel strong and attractive, and you know you are."

"She needs a good haircut, and better clothes. Hey, Stella, wouldn't it be fun to make her over?"

"Down, girl."

"No, really. Later when we've got the time. But I was thinking, too, how she looked when she walked into that little apartment. How grateful and surprised she was that you'd sent some things over, Roz. Just basic things like a couch and bed, and food for the kitchen. I don't guess anyone's ever done anything for her, just to be decent. I felt so sorry for her, and happy for her at the same time, the way she looked around, all dazzled and weepy."

"Let's see what she does with it."

"You gave her the chance to do something. Just like you did with me, and Stella, too."

"Oh, don't start."

"I will. We all came to this corner, and you're the one who gave us a hand to get around it and start down the road. Now Jane's got a place of her own, and a new job. I've got a beautiful baby and a wonderful home for her. And Stella's getting married tomorrow."

She began to sniffle, and Roz rolled her eyes toward the rearview mirror. "I *really* mean don't start."

"I can't help it. I'm so happy. Stella's getting married tomorrow. And y'all are my best friends in the whole, wide world."

Stella passed tissues over the seat, and kept one out for herself.

* * *

THERE WERE SIXTEEN JOURNALS IN ALL, FIVE OF HER grandmother Elizabeth Harper's, and nine written by her great-grandmother Beatrice. And each was filled, first page to last.

There were some sketches as well, Roz noted on a quick flip-through—her grandmother's work. It made her feel warm to look at them.

But she didn't need Mitch to tell her that even though they had the books, the job of reading them and finding anything pertaining to Amelia was daunting.

"They're not dated." Rubbing her eyes, Stella leaned back on the sofa in the parlor. "From what I can tell at a quick glance, Beatrice Harper didn't use a journal per year, but simply filled each, however much time that involved, and moved to the next."

"So we'll sort them as best we can," Mitch said, "divide them up, and read each through."

"I hope I get a juicy one." Due to the circumstances, David had put together an elaborate high tea, and now helped himself to a scone.

"I'll want them all accounted for, at all times. But we have a wedding tomorrow. Stella, I don't want you to overdo it. I'm not going to be responsible for you getting married with circles under your eyes. Who could that be?" Roz said when the doorbell rang. "Everyone's here. No, sit, David. I'll get it."

She walked out with Parker prancing at her heels, barking as if to let her know he was on the job. When she opened the door, Roz's eyebrows winged up. And her smile was sharp as a blade.

"Why, Cousin Rissy, what an unpleasant surprise."

"Where is that useless girl, and my property?"

"I haven't the vaguest idea what you're talking about, and

care even less." She noted her aunt had hired a sedan, and driver, for the trip from the city. "I suppose good manners dictate I ask you in, but I warn you, I'm not above arranging a strip search before you go—which would be traumatic for all parties—so don't even think about taking anything."

"You are, and always have been, a rude and dislikable creature."

"Isn't that funny?" Roz stepped back so Clarise could march into the foyer with her cane. "I was thinking the same thing about you. We're in the parlor, having tea." Roz stepped to the doorway. "Cousin Rissy is paying a call. Isn't that unfortunate? You may remember my son, Harper. You always enjoyed complaining about him incessantly on your other visits. And David, Harper's childhood friend who tends Harper House, and would have counted the silverware."

"I'm not interested in your sass."

"I have so little else to offer you. I believe you've also made the acquaintance of Dr. Carnegie."

"I have, and will be speaking to my lawyer about him."

He smiled broadly. "It's Mitchell Carnegie. Two els."

"This is Logan Kitridge, friend, neighbor, and employee, who is the fiancé of Ms. Stella Rothchild, who manages my garden center."

"I have no interest in your motley arrangement of employees, or your questionable habit of crowding them into Harper House."

"These are her children, Gavin and Luke, and their dog, Parker," Roz continued as if Clarise hadn't spoken. "And a young cousin of mine, on the Ashby side, also an employee, Hayley Phillips, and her beautiful daughter, Lily. I believe that covers everyone. David, I suppose you'd better pour Clarise a cup of tea."

"I don't want tea, particularly any prepared and poured by a homosexual."

"It's not catching," David offered, unfazed.

"Why, David, you're a homosexual?" Roz feigned surprise. "How amazing."

"I try to be subtle about it."

"Where is Jane?" Clarise demanded. "I insist on speaking to her this instant."

Roz picked up a tiny cookie and gave it to a delighted Lily. "And Jane would be?"

"You know very well. Jane Paulson."

"Oh, of course, Cousin Jane. I'm afraid she's not here."

"I won't tolerate your lies." At her tone, Parker sent up a warning growl. "And keep that horrible little dog away from me."

"He's *not* horrible." Gavin sprang up, and was immediately grabbed by his mother. "You're horrible."

"And if you're mean," Luke piped up, "he'll bite you, because he's a good dog."

"Gavin, you and Luke take Parker outside. Go on, now." Stella gave Gavin a little squeeze.

"Get the Frisbee," Logan suggested, with a wink for the boys. "I'll come out in a few minutes."

Gavin picked up the dog, scowling on the way out, and Luke stopped at the door. "We don't like you," he said and strode on his sturdy little legs behind his brother.

"I see your employees are no better equipped to raise well-mannered children than you, Rosalind."

"Apparently not. I'm so proud. Well, since you won't have tea, and I can't help you regarding Jane, you must want to be on your way."

"Where are the journals?"

"Journals? Do you mean the journals written by my grandmother and my great-grandmother that were taken out of this house without my permission?"

"Your permission was not required. I'm the oldest living Harper, and those journals are mine by right."

"We certainly disagree on that, but I can help you as to their location. They're back where they belong—morally, legally, and ethically."

"I'll have you arrested."

"Oh, please, try. Won't that be fun?" The dangerous iceberg was back as she sat on the arm of a chair, crossed her legs casually. "Won't you just relish having your name, the Harper family name, smeared all over the press, talked about all over the county?" Her eyes went hot, in direct contrast to the chill of her voice. "Because I'll see that it is. I'll grant every interview and discuss the whole unseemly mess over cocktails at every opportunity. Such things don't concern me."

She paused, leaning down to take the cookie Lily was holding up to her. "Why, thank you, sugar-pie. But you?" she said to Clarise. "I don't think you'll enjoy being the butt of gossip and innuendo and jokes. Particularly when it'll come to nothing. I have possession of what is my legal property."

She picked Lily up, set her on her knee, and gave the cookie back while the room remained silent but for Clarise's outraged breaths. Roz decided it was one of the rare times she could actually, and accurately, describe a scene with the phrase *her bosom heaved.*

It was glorious.

"If you want to have the police question how I came to regain possession, I'll be happy to tell them. And I hope you enjoy explaining to them how you had what belongs to Harper House, and therefore me, locked away in your desk. Along with several other expensive pieces that are catalogued as Harper House property."

"You'll dirty the family name!" Her face dark with rage, Clarise stepped forward. "You have no right. You have no business digging into what is best left buried."

Calmly Roz passed the baby to Mitch, where Lily

babbled and generously offered to share her mangled cookie. She heard Mitch's murmured "Take her down, honey" as she got to her feet. "What are you afraid of? What did they do to her? Who was Amelia?"

"Nothing but a tramp, a low-class whore who got no more than she deserved. I knew, the minute you were born, that blood would tell in you. I see it has."

"So I am from her," Roz said quietly.

"I'll speak no more about it. It's a crime and a sin that a woman like you is mistress of this house. You have no right here, and never did. You're no-account, grasping, nothing but a blight on the family name. My grandmother would've set the dogs on you before she let your kind cross the threshold of Harper House."

"Okay, that's about enough." Before Roz could speak—and she had plenty to say—Harper was up and across the room. "You're leaving, and you're never coming through that door again."

"Don't you back-talk me, boy."

"I'm not eight anymore, and you're not welcome here. You think you can stand here and insult my mother? A woman with more class in one eyelash than you could cobble together out of every dried-up bone in your body? Now, I can show you the way out, or I can kick you out. Your choice."

"You're just like her."

"That's the first genuine thing you've said since you came in. This way, *Cousin* Rissy."

He took her arm and, though she tried to swat him away, led her out of the room.

There was a beat of silence, then Hayley's low whistle. "Go, Harper."

twenty

Upstairs in the sitting room, Mitch lifted Roz's feet into his lap, and began to rub. "Long day for you."

"Wasn't it just."

"You got in some mighty swings, Slugger."

"I did, but Harper sure did bat clean-up and knock it out of the park."

"I know I'm in love when my girl can talk in baseball analogies." He lifted her foot higher to kiss her ankle. "I'll take my share of the journals with me. I should be able to get a start on them tonight."

"You've had a long day yourself. After the wedding's soon enough." She tipped her head back, closed her eyes as his thumb pressed into her arch. "Besides, if you go, you'll stop rubbing my feet."

"I was hoping this would be a suitable bribe."

"You don't need a bribe. I was hoping you'd stay."

"It so happens I have my suit for the wedding out in the car."

Her eyes stayed closed; her lips curved. "I like a man who thinks ahead."

"I wasn't sure there'd be a place for a man in the house tonight. Wedding eve, female rituals."

"We started our rituals at the salon this morning, and we'll pick them up tomorrow. They're going to make a lovely family, aren't they?"

"They already do. I enjoyed watching those boys stand up to the old woman, and your elegantly executed shots. Followed by Harper's base-clearing run."

"We were all wonderfully rude, weren't we? Of course, she won't speak to you again. Won't help you with your book."

"I'm not worried about it. And—we'll call it postseason play—she's unlikely to be entertained by what I write about her."

"I will be. She knows. She knows who Amelia is, what happened to her. I suppose she always has. There's a possibility she destroyed any journals with a mention of her—a small one, as anything pertaining to Harper House is sacrosanct to her. But it's something we should be prepared for."

"We just need a few seeds. I can propagate from there."

She opened her eyes. "Aren't you clever? I know I'm in love when my guy can talk in gardening terms."

"You haven't seen anything yet. Rosalind, I'm seduced by your feet."

"My feet?"

"Crazy about them. I just never know . . ." Slowly he drew off one of her thick socks. "What I'll find. Ah." He brushed a finger over her toenails, painted pale shell pink, with just a hint of glitter. "Surprise, surprise."

"They're often one of my little secrets."

He lifted her feet, traced his lips down her arch. "I love secrets."

There was something powerful about pleasuring a strong woman, watching her, feeling her surrender to sensation. A tiny quiver, a quiet sigh was unspeakably erotic when you knew the woman yeilded to no one.

From attraction to passion, from passion to love. It was a journey he'd never planned to make again. Yet here he was. When he touched her, he knew she was the woman, the only woman he wanted to spend his life with. He wondered how he'd reached this point in his life without knowing, and needing, her scent, the sound of her voice, the fascinating textures of her skin.

When she rose up, locking her arms around him, fixing her mouth warmly on his, his heart nearly burst.

"I can see you in the dark," he told her. "I can hear you when you're miles away."

The small sound she made was pure emotion as she sank into him.

She held tight, tight a moment with her head on his shoulder, her heart knocking against his. How love could be so many different things at so many different times, she'd never understand. She could only be grateful for it, grateful to have found this love at this time.

She would cherish it. Cherish him.

She eased back to take his face in her hands, so their eyes met. "It's harder when you come into something like this, knowing more, having more behind you. But at the same time, it's more itself. Fuller, richer. I want you to know that's how I feel with you. Full and rich."

"I don't think I can do without you, Rosalind."

"Good." She touched her lips to his. "Good," she repeated and slid slow and deep into the kiss.

She curled around him, breathing him in. His hair, his skin. Here, unbearable tenderness, and there, a simmering excitement. While her mouth clung to his, her fingers flipped open the buttons of his shirt, lifted her arms so he could draw her away and they could press together, warm flesh to warm flesh.

He pressed her back onto the couch, let his hands and lips roam over her. Breasts and shoulders and throat, down to that impossibly narrow torso.

There were signs of the children she'd borne, the men she'd made. For a moment he lay his cheek on her belly, amazed he'd been given the gift of a woman so vital, so potent.

She stroked his back, gliding on the shimmer that coated her senses, lazily working her hands between them to unbutton his jeans. She found him hard and hot, and felt her own muscles bunch and quiver in anticipation.

Now they tugged at clothes, and once again she rose up. This time she straddled him, staring into those bottle-green eyes as she slowly, slowly took him inside her.

"Ah. God." She gripped the back of the couch, her fingers digging in.

With a brutal hold on control, she rode, hips moving in a tortuously gentle rhythm, strong thighs caging him as she set the pace.

She could feel his hands on her, a desperate grip on her hips as he struggled to let her lead. Then a smooth caress up her back, a slick stroke to cup her breasts.

She tightened around him, pressing her mouth to his when she came so he could taste her moan. He was buried in her, their arms locked around each other, when she threw her head back. When her eyes, glassy with arousal, finally closed.

And she whipped him, joyfully, to the finish.

ROZ WOKE AT FOUR, TOO EARLY TO JOG, TOO LATE TO talk herself back to sleep. She lay awhile, in the quiet dark. It amazed her how quickly she'd gotten used to having

Mitch in her bed. She didn't feel crowded, or even surprised to have him sleeping beside her.

It felt more natural than she'd expected—not something she had to adjust to, but something she'd discovered she no longer wanted to do without.

She wondered why it didn't feel odd to wake with him, to start the daily routine with another person in her space. The bathroom shuffle, the conversation—or the silence—while they dressed.

Not odd or strange, she decided, maybe because some part of her had been waiting to make this unit again. She hadn't looked for it, or sought it, hadn't pined without it. In some ways, the years alone had helped make her the woman she was. And that woman was ready to share the rest of her life, her home, her family, with this man.

She slipped out of bed, moving quietly. Another change, she realized. It had been a long time since she'd had to worry about disturbing a sleeping mate.

She moved to her sitting room to choose one of the journals. She ran her hand gently over one of her grandmother's. Those she would save for later, those she would read for pleasure and for sentiment.

What she did now, she did for duty.

It took her less than fifteen minutes to conclude she and her great-grandmother wouldn't have understood each other.

> *Weather remains fine. Reginald's business keeps him in New Orleans. I was unable to find the shade of blue silk I'm seeking. The shops here are simply not* au courant. *I believe we must arrange a trip to Paris. Though it's imperative we engage another governess for the girls before we do. This current woman is entirely too independent. When I think of the money spent on her salary, her room and board, I find myself most dissatisfied by her service. Recently*

I gave her a very nice day dress, which didn't suit me, and which she accepted without a qualm. However, when I ask for some small favor, she behaves very grudgingly. Surely she has time to run a few simple errands when there's nothing else on her plate but minding the girls and teaching a few lessons.

I have the impression she considers herself above her station.

Roz stretched out her legs, flipped through pages. Most of the entries were more of the same. Complaints, tidbits about shopping, plans for parties, rehashes of parties attended. There was very little dealing with the children.

She set that one aside for later, picked up another. Skimming, she found an entry on dismissing a maid for giggling in the hallway, another on a lavish ball. Then stopped, and read more carefully when an entry caught her eye.

I've miscarried again. Why is it as painful to lose a child as to birth one? I'm exhausted. I wonder how I can suffer through this process yet again in the attempt to give Reginald the heir he so desperately wants. He will want to lie with me again as soon as I am able, and that ordeal will continue, I suspect, until I conceive once more.

I can find no pleasure in it, nor in the girls who are a daily reminder of what I have yet to accomplish.

At least, once I conceive yet again, I will be left to myself for the months of waiting. It is my duty to bear sons. I will not shirk my duty, and yet it seems I am unable to bring forth anything but chattering girls.

I want only to sleep and forget that I have failed, once again, to provide my husband and this house with the heir they both demand.

Children as duty only, Roz thought. How sad. How must those little girls have felt, being failures because of their sex? Had there been any joy in this house during Beatrice's reign as its mistress, or had it all been duty and show?

Depressed, she considered switching to one of her grandmother's journals, but ordered herself to glance through one more.

I'm sick to death of that busybody Mary Louise Berker. You would think because she's managed to birth four sons, and is once again fat as a cow with yet another child, she knows all there is to know about conception and child-rearing. This is hardly the case. Her sons run around like wild Indians, and think nothing of putting their grubby little hands on the furniture in her parlor. And she just laughs and says boys will be boys *when they and their scruffy dogs—three of them!—come romping in.*

She had the nerve to suggest I might see her doctor, and some voodoo *woman. She swears she'll have the girl she pines for this time because she went to this hideous person and bought a charm to hang over her bed.*

It's bad enough she dotes on those ruffians in a most unseemly way, and often in public, but it's beyond belief that she would speak to me about such matters, all under the guise of friendship and concern.

I could not take my leave soon enough.

Roz decided she'd have liked Mary Louise. And wondered if the Bobby Lee Berker she'd gone to high school with was a descendant.

Then she saw it, and her heart took a hard jump into her throat.

I have locked myself in my room. I will speak to no one. The humiliation I have been dealt is beyond bearing. For all these years I have been a dutiful wife, an exceptional hostess, I have overseen the staff of this house without complaint, and worked tirelessly to present the proper image for our societal equals and Reginald's business associates.

I have, as wives must, overlooked his private affairs, satisfied that he was always discreet.

Now this.

He arrived home this evening and requested that I come to the library so he could speak to me privately. He told me he had impregnated one of his mistresses. This is not a conversation that should take place between husband and wife, and when this was my response, he brushed it aside as if it was no matter.

As if I am no matter.

I am told that I will be required to create the illusion that I am expecting. I am told that if this creature delivers a son, it will be brought into our home, it will be given the Harper name and raised here. As his son. As my son.

If it is a girl, it will be of no matter. I will have another "miscarriage" and that will be that.

I refused. Of course I refused. To take a whore's child into my home.

Then he gave me this choice. Accept his decision, or he would divorce me. One way or the other, he will have a son. He prefers that I remain his wife, that neither of us are exposed to the scandal of divorce, and he will compensate me well for this one thing. If I refuse, it will be divorce and shame, and I will be sent away from the home I have cared for, the life I have made.

So there is no choice.

I pray that this slatern delivers a girl child. I pray it dies. That she dies. That they all burn in Hell.

Roz's hands shook. Though she wanted to read on, she stood first, walked to the terrace doors. She needed air. With the book in her hand, she stood outside, breathing in the early morning.

What kind of man had this been? To have forced his illegitimate son on his wife. Even if he hadn't loved her, he should have respected her.

And what love could he have had for the child, to have subjected him to a woman who would never, could never, care for him as a mother? Who would always resent him? Even despise him?

And all to carry on the Harper name.

"Roz?"

She didn't turn when she heard Mitch's voice behind her. "I woke you. I thought I was quiet."

"You were. You just weren't there."

"I found something. I started reading through some of the journals. I found something."

"Whatever it is, it's upset you."

"I'm sad, and I'm angry. And I'm surprised that I'm not surprised. I found an entry . . . No, you should read it for yourself." She turned now, held the book out, open to where she'd stopped. "Take it into the sitting room. I just need another minute here."

"All right." He took the book, then, because there was something in her eyes that pulled at his heart, he cupped her chin in his free hand and kissed her softly.

She turned back to the view, to the grounds and the gardens going silver with oncoming dawn. The home that had been her family's for generations. Had it been worth it? she wondered. Had the pain and humiliation one man had caused been worth holding this ground under one name?

She walked back in, sat across from Mitch. "Is this where you stopped?" he asked her.

"I needed to absorb it, I guess. How cruel he was to her. She wasn't an admirable woman, not from what I've read in her own diaries. Selfish, self-absorbed, petty. But she deserved better than this. You haven't given me a son, so I'll get one elsewhere. Accept it, or leave. She accepted."

"You don't know that yet."

"We know." She shook her head. "We'll read the rest, but we know."

"I can go through this, and the others, later. Myself."

"No, let's do it now. It's my legacy, after all. See what you can find, will you? I'm going down to make coffee."

When she came back, she noted he'd gotten his reading glasses. He looked like a rumpled scholar, she thought, pulling an all-nighter. Shirtless, jeans unbuttoned, hair mussed.

That same tenderness floated over her, like a balm over the ache in her heart.

"I'm glad you were here when I found this." She set the tray down, then leaned over, kissed the top of his head. "I'm glad you're here."

"There's more." He reached up for her hands. "Do you want me to summarize?"

"No, read her words. I want to hear her words."

"There's snippets here and there, her thoughts on this worked into daily entries. Her humiliation and the rage under it. She made him pay in the only way she knew, by spending his money lavishly, by shutting him out of her bed, taking trips."

"A stronger woman would have thumbed her nose," she said, pouring coffee, "taken her children and left him. But she didn't."

"No, she didn't. Times were different for women then."

"The times may have been different, but right's still right."

She set down his coffee, and this time sat beside him. "Read it, Mitch. I want to know."

"He brought the bastard home, with some trollop of a wet nurse he brought in from one of his country holdings. Not the mother, he says, who remains in the house in town where he keeps her. He has his son at last, a squalling thing wrapped in a blanket. I did not look at it, and will not. I know only that he has paid the doctor to keep him quiet, and that I am required to continue to remain in the house, receiving no callers for another few days.

"He has brought this thing home in the dead of night, so the servants will believe I delivered it. Or will pretend to believe it. He has named it. Reginald Edward Harper, Jr."

"My grandfather," Roz murmured. "Poor little boy. He grew to be a fine man. A kind of miracle, I suppose, given his beginnings. Is there anything on his mother?"

"Not in this book, though I'll go through it more carefully."

"There will be more, in one of the other journals. She died here, Amelia did. At some point Beatrice must have seen or spoken with her, or dealt with her in some way."

"I'll start looking now."

"No." Tired, she rubbed at her eyes. "No, there's a wedding today. Today is for joy and fresh starts, not for grief and old secrets. We know enough for today."

"Rosalind, this in no way changes who you are."

"No, it doesn't. Of course it doesn't. But it makes me think, that for people like this . . . for people like Reginald and Beatrice, marriage was a practicality. Social standing, breeding, family backgrounds. Maybe there was some affection, or some attraction, but at its core, it was business. The business of maintaining families at a certain level. And children were just tools to accomplish that. How sad for them, and how tragic for the children. But today . . ."

She drew a deep breath. "Today we're seeing it shouldn't be that way. We're going to watch two people who love each other make promises, make a marriage, cement a family. I'm glad you're here, Mitch, and I'm glad we found this today. Because this wedding is just what I need now."

IT WAS THE PERFECT DAY FOR IT, TAILOR-MADE WITH candy-blue skies and balmy air scented with flowers. The gardens Logan and Stella had made bloomed in a lovely array of color and shape.

There were chairs set up on the lawn, covered with pale peach drapes and forming an aisle where Stella would walk on her father's arm, toward Logan and her sons.

Roz turned from the window to watch Jolene fuss with the flowers in Stella's hair.

"You make a picture," she said. "Both of you."

"I'm going to start crying again." Jolene waved a hand in front of her face. "I can't count how many times I've repaired my makeup. I'm going to run out just for a minute, honey, check on your daddy."

"Okay." Stella waited until Jolene scurried out. "I was going to be mad and upset that my mother refused to come. Too much trouble to make the trip—not like it's my first time—and she wasn't going to sit around in the same space as *that* woman, which she continues to call Jolene even after all these years."

"Her loss, isn't it?"

"It is—and my gain, really. It's Jolene I want today

anyway. And you, and Hayley." Stella lifted her hand to touch the sapphires in her ears. "They're so perfect."

"They do the trick. Look at you." Feeling a little misty herself, Roz stepped closer to study her friend.

The dress was simple, a pale, pale blue with narrow straps, a straight bodice and a long skirt with a slight bell. There were two dahlias pinned in her curling red hair. One white, one blue. And her face was luminous, as a bride's was meant to be.

"I feel absolutely beautiful."

"You should. You are. I'm so happy for you."

"I'm not nervous anymore, not even a little jump in the belly." Stella pressed a hand to it as she blinked tears back. "I think about Kevin, my first wedding, the years we had together, the children we made together. And I know, in my heart, I know he's okay with this. Logan's a good man."

"A very good man."

"I made him wait almost a year." She let out a laughing breath. "Time's up. Roz, thank you for all you've done."

"You're welcome. Ready to get married?"

"I'm absolutely ready."

It was sweet, Roz thought, and it was lovely. The man and woman, the young boys, coming together in the gardens of the home they'd share. Logan, big and strong and handsome in his suit, Stella, bright and beautiful in her bride dress, and the children grinning even when Logan kissed the bride.

The guests broke into spontaneous applause as Logan swept Stella off her feet and spun her in a circle. And Harper topped off the moment by popping the first bottle of champagne.

"I don't know when I've seen a happier couple," Mitch commented, and tapped his glass to Roz's. "Or a prettier family. You do good work."

"I didn't do anything."

"It's like a family tree. These two come from one of

your branches. May not be blood, but it comes to the same. It's their connection to you that brought them together. They did the rest, but the connection started it."

"That's a nice thought. I'll take it." She lifted her glass, sipped. "There's something I want to talk to you about a little later. I wanted to wait to bring it up until after Stella had her day. A wedding day, by rights, belongs to the bride."

"What's it about?"

"I guess you could say it's about connections." She rose on her toes to kiss him. "We'll talk about it after we go home. Fact is, I've got to run back real quick. With all this commotion I forgot the special bottle of champagne I have back home for the bride and groom and their wedding night."

"I can run get it."

"No, it'll be quicker if I do. I'll be back in fifteen minutes."

As she got to the car, she stopped as Hayley called her.

"Roz! Hold up. Is it okay if we ride with you?" A little breathless, she stopped at the car with a crying Lily in her arms. "I've got a cranky girl here, needs a little nap. But she won't go down. Car ride'll do the trick. We can take mine, it has the car seat."

"Sure. It's going to be a quick run, though."

"That's all right." She walked to her own car, battled an objecting Lily into the seat. "Rides always calm her down, and if she goes to sleep, I can just sit out here with her until she wakes up. Then we'll both have a better time at the party."

As advertised, the crying stopped, and Lily's head began to droop before they were down the lane to the main road.

"Works like a charm," Hayley said.

"Always did with mine, too. She looks so sweet in her pink party dress."

"Everything looked so beautiful. If I ever get married,

I want it to be just like that. Springtime, flowers, friends, shiny faces. I always thought I wanted a big church extravaganza, but this was so romantic."

"Just right for them. It's nice to— Slow down. Stop the car!"

"What? What's the . . . oh, my God."

They looked over at In the Garden. Roz had closed for the day so everyone could enjoy the wedding. But someone, she could see, had been there. Someone, she thought, still was.

Several of her outdoor displays were overturned, and a car was parked sideways, crushing one of her beds.

"Call the police," Roz snapped and was already out of the car. "You and the baby get out of here now. Go back to Logan's right now."

"Don't. Don't go in there now."

"This is my place." And she was already running.

Her flowers, she thought. Plants she'd started from seed or cutting, babied along, nurtured and loved. Destroyed, beaten down, ripped to pieces.

Innocent, she thought as she took only a moment to grieve for the loss and waste. Innocent beauty crushed to nothing.

There would be payment made.

She heard glass shatter, and charged around the back of the main building. She saw Bryce, swinging a baseball bat at another window.

"You son of a bitch."

He whirled. She saw the shock first, then the rage. "Thought you were busy today. Figured I'd be done before you came by."

"You figured wrong."

"Doesn't matter a damn." He slammed the bat into the next window. "Time you learned a lesson. You think you can humiliate me in public? Set the cops on me?"

"You humiliated yourself, and if you don't put that down and get the hell off my property, I'm going to do more than set the cops on you."

"Such as? Just you and me now, isn't it?" He slapped the bat against his palm, took a step toward her. "Do you know what you cost me?"

"I've got a general idea, and it's going to be more. Trespassing, destruction of property."

He didn't use the bat, though she saw in his eyes, just for an instant, that he considered it. But he swung out with his hand, cracking her across the cheekbone and sending her sprawling.

That was all it took. She was up like a flash and launching herself at him. She didn't use nails and teeth as Mandy had. She used her fists, and took him so by surprise, he fell to his knees before he managed to block her, and strike out at her again.

But the blow didn't land.

The wind came up so fast, so cold, so furious, that it flung Roz back against the building. Her head rapped sharply against wood so she had to shake it clear.

When she did, she saw Amelia sweeping across the ground, dirty white gown flying, hands curled like lethal claws. Murder in her eye.

And so did Bryce.

He screamed, a single high-pitched shriek of terror before he began to claw at his throat and gasp for air.

"Don't. For God's sake." Roz tried to push forward, but was slapped back by the pressure of the wind. "Don't kill him. It's enough, it's enough! He can't hurt me. He won't hurt me."

Gravel spat and spun, and the figure in white circled, vulturelike, over the man collapsed on the ground raking his own throat bloody.

"Stop. Amelia, stop. Great-grandmama."

Amelia's head lifted, turned, and her eyes met Roz's.

"I know. I know I come from you. I know you're trying to protect me. It's all right. He won't hurt me now. Please." She pushed forward again, managed two steps with an effort that sucked her breath out of her lungs. "He's nothing!" she shouted. "A bug. But he taught me some important lessons. And I'm going to teach him some hard ones. I want him to live so he pays."

She fought forward another step, holding her hands out, palms up. "There will be payment, I swear to you. For me, and on the blood we share, I swear there'll be payment for you."

He was breathing again, Roz noted, short, harsh breaths, but air was wheezing in and out of Bryce's white, white lips. She crouched down, spoke calmly. "Looks like it wasn't just you and me after all."

The wind began to die, and through it she heard shouts and running feet. When she straightened, Amelia was gone.

She staggered back on rubbery legs as Harper flew around the side of the building two strides ahead of Mitch.

"I'm all right. I'm fine." Though she felt her head circle like a carousel. "But this one might need a little medical attention."

"Fuck him. Mama." Harper grabbed her, feathered his hands over her face. "Jesus Christ. Jesus, he hit you?"

"Sucker punched me, but I got him back, believe me. Got him worse. And Amelia finished him off. I'm all right, baby, I promise you."

"Cops are on their way." She looked over at the tremble in Mitch's voice, and saw from his face it was partly from fear, partly from rage. "Hayley called them on her cell on the way back to get us."

"Good. Good." She was *not* going to faint again. No matter what. "Well, we're just going to press all sorts of charges." She brushed at her hair, then her dress, and noticed a tear on the skirt. "Goddamn it, I bought this especially for today. All *sorts* of charges."

She drew in a breath, struggling with temper and giddiness. "Harper, honey, will you do me a favor and take this worthless piece of trash around front, you and Mitch wait for the police. I don't want to see him for a minute or two. I might finish what Amelia started."

"Let me haul him up first." Mitch bent down, yanked Bryce up on his buckling legs. Then with eyes burning green, he glanced toward Roz.

"Sorry," he said before he plowed his fist into Bryce's face and sent him sprawling again. "Hope you don't mind."

"Not a bit," Roz told him, and despite the churning in her belly found her lips spreading into a wide, wide grin. "Not a damn bit. Harper, you mind taking it from here? I'd like a word with Mitch."

"Happy to." He dragged Bryce off, and shot a look over his shoulder. "Mama, you sure can kick ass."

"Yeah." She drew in a breath, let it out. "If it's all the same to you," she said to Mitch, "I'm just going to sit down right here until I get my feet back under me. That ass-kicking took something out of me."

"Wait." He peeled off his jacket, spread it on the ground. "No point in messing up that dress any more than it is."

She sat down, then tipped her head onto his shoulder when he joined her. "My hero," she declared.

epilogue

SHE SAT QUIETLY UNTIL HER HEART RATE SLOWED TO normal, until the tangle of nerves, of rage, of reaction in her belly eased a little.

Broken glass glittered in the sunlight. Glass could be replaced, she reminded herself. She'd mourn her flowers, but she'd save some of the wounded, and she'd grow more.

She'd grow an abundance of more.

"How's your hand?" she asked Mitch.

"Fine. Good." He all but spat it out. "He's got a chin like a marshmallow."

"Big strong man." She turned to wrap her arms around him, and didn't mention Mitch's raw, scraped knuckles.

"He must've gone crazy to think he could get away with this."

"A little, I guess. I imagine he planned to be done wrecking my place before the reception was over. He'd figure we'd blame it on kids—or the police would. And all I'd have was a mess on my hands. A man like that doesn't have any respect for women, doesn't believe one can best him."

"One did."

"Well, two. One live one, one dead one."

Since the faintness had passed, she got to her feet, held out a hand for his. "She was like fury, Mitch. Flying over the ground, through tables, and so fast. Wicked, wicked fast," she stated. "He saw her, Bryce saw her coming at him, and he screamed. Then she was choking him. Or, I think, making him believe he was choking. Her hands weren't on him, but she was strangling him."

She rubbed her arms, then clutched gratefully at the lapels of his jacket, drawing them tight when he draped it over her shoulders. She didn't know if her bones would ever be warm again.

"I can't describe it. I can hardly believe it happened. Everything so fast and wild."

"We could hear you shouting," he explained. "You cost both me and your son several years of our lives. I'm going to say this once."

He turned, took the lapels himself to hold her still and facing him. "And you're going to hear it. I respect and admire your steely will, Rosalind, and appreciate your temper and your capability. But the next time you so much as think about taking on some lunatic with a bat on your own, *I'm* doing some ass-kicking. And it's going to be your ass with the bull's-eye painted on it."

She angled her head, studied his face, and saw he meant exactly what he said. Son of a gun.

"You know, if I hadn't already decided on this thing I'm about to ask you, that would've done it. How could I resist a man who lets me fight my own battles, then when the moment's right, steps in and cleans house? After the dust is clear he gives me a good piece of his mind for being an idiot. Which I was, no question, no argument."

"Glad we agree on that."

She took the last step toward him, lifted her arms, and hooked them around his neck. "I really love you."

"I really love you back."

"Then you won't have a problem marrying me."

She felt his body jerk, just a little, just once, then it settled in against her, warm and true. "I don't see a problem with that. You're sure?"

"Couldn't be more sure. I want to go to bed with you at night, wake up with you in the morning. I want to sit and have coffee with you whenever I please. Know you're there for me, and I'm there for you. I want you, Mitch, for the rest of my life."

"I'm ready to get started on that." He kissed her bruised cheek, her uninjured one, her brow, her lips. "I'm going to learn how to tend at least one flower. A rose. My black rose."

She leaned on him. She could lean on him—and trust him to step back when she needed to stand on her own.

Everything inside her calmed, even when she looked at the destruction of what was hers. She would fix it, save what could be saved, accept what couldn't.

She would live her life, and plant her gardens—and walking hand-in-hand with the man she loved, watch both bloom.

And in the gardens of Harper House, someone walked, and raged, and grieved. With mad eyes burning into the candy-blue sky.

Can't get enough of Nora Roberts?
Try the #1 *New York Times* bestselling
In Death series, by Nora Roberts
writing as J. D. Robb.

Turn the page to see where it began . . .

NAKED IN DEATH

She woke in the dark. Through the slats on the window shades, the first murky hint of dawn slipped, slanting shadowy bars over the bed. It was like waking in a cell.

For a moment she simply lay there, shuddering, imprisoned, while the dream faded. After ten years on the force, Eve still had dreams.

Six hours before, she'd killed a man, had watched death creep into his eyes. It wasn't the first time she'd exercised maximum force, or dreamed. She'd learned to accept the action and the consequences.

But it was the child that haunted her. The child she hadn't been in time to save. The child whose screams had echoed in the dreams with her own.

All the blood, Eve thought, scrubbing sweat from her face with her hands. Such a small little girl to have had so much blood in her. And she knew it was vital that she push it aside.

Standard departmental procedure meant that she would spend the morning in Testing. Any officer whose discharge of weapon resulted in termination of life was required to undergo emotional and psychiatric clearance before resuming duty. Eve considered the tests a mild pain in the ass.

She would beat them, as she'd beaten them before.

When she rose, the overheads went automatically to low setting, lighting her way into the bath. She winced once at her reflection. Her eyes were swollen from lack of sleep, her skin nearly as pale as the corpses she'd delegated to the ME.

Rather than dwell on it, she stepped into the shower, yawning.

"Give me one oh one degrees, full force," she said and shifted so that the shower spray hit her straight in the face.

She let it steam, lathered listlessly while she played through the events of the night before. She wasn't due in Testing until nine, and would use the next three hours to settle and let the dream fade away completely.

Small doubts and little regrets were often detected and could mean a second and more intense round with the machines and the owl-eyed technicians who ran them.

Eve didn't intend to be off the streets longer than twenty-four hours.

After pulling on a robe, she walked into the kitchen and programmed her AutoChef for coffee, black; toast, light. Through her window she could hear the heavy hum of air traffic carrying early commuters to offices, late ones home. She'd chosen the apartment years before because it was in a heavy ground and air pattern, and she liked the noise and crowds. On another yawn, she glanced out the window, followed the rattling journey of an aging airbus hauling laborers not fortunate enough to work in the city or by home 'links.

She brought the *New York Times* up on her monitor and scanned the headlines while the faux caffeine bolstered her system. The AutoChef had burned her toast again, but she ate it anyway, with a vague thought of springing for a replacement unit.

She was frowning over an article on a mass recall of droid cocker spaniels when her telelink blipped. Eve shifted to communications and watched her commanding officer flash onto the screen.

"Commander."

"Lieutenant." He gave her a brisk nod, noted the still-wet hair and sleepy eyes. "Incident at Twenty-seven West Broadway, eighteenth floor. You're primary."

Eve lifted a brow. "I'm on Testing. Subject terminated at twenty-two thirty-five."

"We have override," he said, without inflection. "Pick up your shield and weapon on the way to the incident. Code Five, Lieutenant."

"Yes, sir." His face flashed off even as she pushed back from the screen. Code Five meant she would report directly to her commander, and there would be no unsealed interdepartmental reports and no cooperation with the press.

In essence, it meant she was on her own.

BROADWAY WAS NOISY AND CROWDED, A PARTY THAT ROWDY guests never left. Street, pedestrian, and sky traffic were miserable, choking the air with bodies and vehicles. In her old days in uniform she remembered it as a hot spot for wrecks and crushed tourists who were too busy gaping at the show to get out of the way.

Even at this hour steam was rising from the stationary and portable food stands that offered everything from rice noodles to soy dogs for the teeming crowds. She had to swerve to avoid an eager merchant on his smoking Glida-Grill, and took his flipped middle finger as a matter of course.

Eve double-parked and, skirting a man who smelled

worse than his bottle of brew, stepped onto the sidewalk. She scanned the building first, fifty floors of gleaming metal that knifed into the sky from a hilt of concrete. She was propositioned twice before she reached the door.

Since this five-block area of West Broadway was affectionately termed Prostitute's Walk, she wasn't surprised. She flashed her badge for the uniform guarding the entrance.

"Lieutenant Dallas."

"Yes, sir." He skimmed his official CompuSeal over the door to keep out the curious, then led the way to the bank of elevators. "Eighteenth floor," he said when the doors swished shut behind them.

"Fill me in, Officer." Eve switched on her recorder and waited.

"I wasn't first on the scene, Lieutenant. Whatever happened upstairs is being kept upstairs. There's a badge inside waiting for you. We have a homicide, and a Code Five in number eighteen-oh-three."

"Who called it in?"

"I don't have that information."

He stayed where he was when the elevator opened. Eve stepped out and was alone in a narrow hallway. Security cameras tilted down at her, and her feet were almost soundless on the worn nap of the carpet as she approached 1803. Ignoring the hand plate, she announced herself, holding her badge up to eye level for the peep cam until the door opened.

"Dallas."

"Feeney." She smiled, pleased to see a familiar face. Ryan Feeney was an old friend and former partner who'd traded the street for a desk and a top-level position in the Electronics Detection Division. "So, they're sending computer pluckers these days."

"They wanted brass, and the best." His lips curved in his

wide, rumpled face, but his eyes remained sober. He was a small, stubby man with small, stubby hands and rust-colored hair. "You look beat."

"Rough night."

"So I heard." He offered her one of the sugared nuts from the bag he habitually carried, studying her, and measuring if she was up to what was waiting in the bedroom beyond.

She was young for her rank, barely thirty, with wide brown eyes that had never had a chance to be naive. Her doe-brown hair was cropped short, for convenience rather than style, but suited her triangular face with its razor-edge cheekbones and slight dent in the chin.

She was tall, rangy, with a tendency to look thin, but Feeney knew there were solid muscles beneath the leather jacket. But Eve had more—there was also a brain, and a heart.

"This one's going to be touchy, Dallas."

"I picked that up already. Who's the victim?"

"Sharon DeBlass, granddaughter of Senator DeBlass."

Neither meant anything to her. "Politics isn't my forte, Feeney."

"The gentleman from Virginia, extreme right, old money. The granddaughter took a sharp left a few years back, moved to New York and became a licensed companion."

"She was a hooker." Dallas glanced around the apartment. It was furnished in obsessive modern—glass and thin chrome, signed holograms on the walls, recessed bar in bold red. The wide mood screen behind the bar bled with mixing and merging shapes and colors in cool pastels.

Neat as a virgin, Eve mused, and cold as a whore. "No surprise, given her choice of real estate."

"Politics makes it delicate. Victim was twenty-four, Caucasian female. She bought it in bed."

Eve only lifted a brow. "Seems poetic, since she'd been bought there. How'd she die?"

"That's the next problem. I want you to see for yourself."

As they crossed the room, each took out a slim container, sprayed their hands front and back to seal in oils and fingerprints. At the doorway, Eve sprayed the bottom of her boots to slicken them so that she would pick up no fibers, stray hairs, or skin.

Eve was already wary. Under normal circumstances there would have been two other investigators on a homicide scene, with recorders for sound and pictures. Forensics would have been waiting with their usual snarly impatience to sweep the scene.

The fact that only Feeney had been assigned with her meant that there were a lot of eggshells to be walked over.

"Security cameras in the lobby, elevator, and hallways," Eve commented.

"I've already tagged the discs." Feeney opened the bedroom door and let her enter first.

It wasn't pretty. Death rarely was a peaceful, religious experience to Eve's mind. It was the nasty end, indifferent to saint and sinner. But this was shocking, like a stage deliberately set to offend.

The bed was huge, slicked with what appeared to be genuine satin sheets the color of ripe peaches. Small, soft-focused spotlights were trained on its center where the naked woman was cupped in the gentle dip of the floating mattress.

The mattress moved with obscenely graceful undulations to the rhythm of programmed music slipping through the headboard.

She was beautiful still, a cameo face with a tumbling waterfall of flaming red hair, emerald eyes that stared glassily at the mirrored ceiling, long, milk-white limbs that called to mind visions of *Swan Lake* as the motion of the bed gently rocked them.

They weren't artistically arranged now, but spread lewdly so that the dead woman formed a final X dead-center of the bed.

There was a hole in her forehead, one in her chest, another horribly gaping between the open thighs. Blood had splattered on the glossy sheets, pooled, dripped, and stained.

There were splashes of it on the lacquered walls, like lethal paintings scrawled by an evil child.

So much blood was a rare thing, and she had seen much too much of it the night before to take the scene as calmly as she would have preferred.

She had to swallow once, hard, and force herself to block out the image of a small child.

"You got the scene on record?"

"Yep."

"Then turn that damn thing off." She let out a breath after Feeney located the controls that silenced the music. The bed flowed to stillness. "The wounds," Eve murmured, stepping closer to examine them. "Too neat for a knife. Too messy for a laser." A flash came to her—old training films, old videos, old viciousness.

"Christ, Feeney, these look like bullet wounds."

Feeney reached into his pocket and drew out a sealed bag. "Whoever did it left a souvenir." He passed the bag to Eve. "An antique like this has to go for eight, ten thousand for a legal collection, twice that on the black market."

Fascinated, Eve turned the sealed revolver over in her hand. "It's heavy," she said half to herself. "Bulky."

"Thirty-eight caliber," he told her. "First one I've seen outside of a museum. This one's a Smith and Wesson, Model Ten, blue steel." He looked at it with some affection. "Real classic piece, used to be standard police issue up until the latter part of the twentieth. They stopped making them in about twenty-two, twenty-three, when the gun ban was passed."

"You're the history buff." Which explained why he was with her. "Looks new." She sniffed through the bag, caught the scent of oil and burning. "Somebody took good care of this. Steel fired into flesh," she mused as she passed the bag back to Feeney. "Ugly way to die, and the first I've seen it in my ten years with the department."

"Second for me. About fifteen years ago, Lower East Side, party got out of hand. Guy shot five people with a twenty-two before he realized it wasn't a toy. Hell of a mess."

"Fun and games," Eve murmured. "We'll scan the collectors, see how many we can locate who own one like this. Somebody might have reported a robbery."

"Might have."

"It's more likely it came through the black market." Eve glanced back at the body. "If she's been in the business for a few years, she'd have discs, records of her clients, her trick books." She frowned. "With Code Five, I'll have to do the door-to-door myself. Not a simple sex crime," she said with a sigh. "Whoever did it set it up. The antique weapon, the wounds themselves, almost ruler-straight down the body, the lights, the pose. Who called it in, Feeney?"

"The killer." He waited until her eyes came back to him. "From right here. Called the station. See how the bedside unit's aimed at her face? That's what came in. Video, no audio."

"He's into showmanship." Eve let out a breath. "Clever bastard, arrogant, cocky. He had sex with her first. I'd bet my badge on it. Then he gets up and does it." She lifted her arm, aiming, lowering it as she counted off, "One, two, three."

"That's cold," murmured Feeney.

"He's cold. He smooths down the sheets after. See how neat they are? He arranges her, spreads her open so nobody can have any doubts as to how she made her living. He does it carefully, practically measuring, so that she's perfectly aligned. Center of the bed, arms and legs equally apart. Doesn't turn off the bed 'cause it's part of the show. He leaves the gun because he wants us to know right away he's no ordinary man. He's got an ego. He doesn't want to waste time letting the body be discovered eventually. He wants it now. That instant gratification."

"She was licensed for men and women," Feeney pointed out, but Eve shook her head.

"It's not a woman. A woman wouldn't have left her looking both beautiful and obscene. No, I don't think it's a woman. Let's see what we can find. Have you gone into her computer yet?"

"No. It's your case, Dallas. I'm only authorized to assist."

"See if you can access her client files." Eve went to the dresser and began to carefully search drawers.

Expensive taste, Eve reflected. There were several items of real silk, the kind no simulation could match. The bottle of scent on the dresser was exclusive, and smelled, after a quick sniff, like expensive sex.

The contents of the drawers were meticulously ordered, lingerie folded precisely, sweaters arranged according to color and material. The closet was the same.

Obviously the victim had a love affair with clothes and a taste for the best and took scrupulous care of what she owned.

And she'd died naked.

"Kept good records," Feeney called out. "It's all here. Her client list, appointments—including her required monthly health exam and her weekly trip to the beauty salon. She used the Trident Clinic for the first and Paradise for the second."

"Both top-of-the-line. I've got a friend who saved for a year so she could have one day for the works at Paradise. Takes all kinds."

"My wife's sister went for it for her twenty-fifth anniversary. Cost damn near as much as my kid's wedding. Hello, we've got her personal address book."

"Good. Copy all of it, will you, Feeney?" At his low whistle, she looked over her shoulder, glimpsed the small gold-edged palm computer in his hand. "What?"

"We've got a lot of high-powered names in here. Politics, entertainment, money, money, money. Interesting, our girl has Roarke's private number."

"Roarke who?"

"Just Roarke, as far as I know. Big money there. Kind of guy that touches shit and turns it into gold bricks. You've got to start reading more than the sports page, Dallas."

"Hey, I read the headlines. Did you hear about the cocker spaniel recall?"

"Roarke's always big news," Feeney said patiently. "He's got one of the finest art collections in the world. Arts and antiques," he continued, noting when Eve clicked in and turned to him. "He's a licensed gun collector. Rumor is he knows how to use them."

"I'll pay him a visit."

"You'll be lucky to get within a mile of him."

"I'm feeling lucky." Eve crossed over to the body to slip her hands under the sheets.

"The man's got powerful friends, Dallas. You can't afford to so much as whisper he's linked to this until you've got something solid."

"Feeney, you know it's a mistake to tell me that." But even as she started to smile, her fingers brushed something between cold flesh and bloody sheets. "There's something under her." Carefully, Eve lifted the shoulder, eased her fingers over.

"Paper," she murmured. "Sealed." With her protected thumb, she wiped at a smear of blood until she could read the protected sheet.

ONE OF SIX

"It looks hand printed," she said to Feeney and held it out. "Our boy's more than clever, more than arrogant. And he isn't finished."